GAUNTLET

GAUNTLET

A NOVEL OF INTERNATIONAL INTRIGUE

RICHARD AARON

SAN DIEGO, CA

sales@glasshousepress.com

www.glasshousepress.com

www.richardaaron.com

Gauntlet is a work of fiction. Apart from well-known actual people, events, and locales that figure in the narrative, all names, characters, places, and incidents are the products of the author's imagination or are used fictitiously. Any resemblances to current events or locales, or to living persons, is entirely coincidental.

Published in the United States by Glass House Press, 2009

GLASS HOUSE PRESS and colophon are trademarks of Glass House Press

Aaron, Richard

Gauntlet / Richard Aaron

ISBN: 978-0-9816768-8-3

LCCN: 2008925619

Printed in Canada on acid-free paper

14 13 12 11 10 09   1 2 3 4 5

Book Design by Mike Lee

Cover Design by Chris Decatur

THIS BOOK IS DEDICATED TO...

Ping, Doon, Bubbles, Foxy Lady, and my very own "Turbee." I love you all.

1

SO JUST HOW BIG A CRATER *will* it make if we blow up 660 tons of Semtex?" Richard Lawrence asked Sergeant Jason McMurray.

"No clue," replied the taciturn McMurray, scratching his chin. "There's no precedent for something like this. It's an unconfined explosion, and it's gonna be a damned dangerous one. But if I can't handle it, no one can." McMurray was from the Army's 184th Ordnance Battalion, stationed in Fort Gilles, Georgia. He'd had more than 15 years of training in the disposal of conventional, chemical/biological, and nuclear weapons. He had defused or disposed of bombs, warheads, mortar shells, and land mines, and had a pronounced scar on his left cheek as a daily reminder of the danger of his vocation. He was the best of the best. And he was already planning a 30-day leave after he'd wrapped up this particular circus. Cold beer, family, and golf.

Now he looked around the place once again, this time with annoyance. What had started as a solid, common sense idea had turned into a carnival. The Islamic Republic of Libya had finally come around to the idea of repudiating its position of the '70s and '80s. Libya, with its ample reservoir of oil, had announced that it wished to join the community of nations. The western world, led by the United States and the United Kingdom, had announced in turn that they were prepared to accept the olive branch. And the oil. But first, reparations needed to be made, especially to the families of the Pan-Am flight that had been destroyed in mid-air over Lockerbie, Scotland. Among other things, the desert nation was required to dismantle its nuclear, chemical, and biological weapons programs. More importantly, it had to give up its enormous stockpile of the Czechoslovakian plastic explosive known as Semtex. The question had quickly become how the United States would dispose of the explosive once it was surrendered. Then some bright executive in the Pentagon had come up with the perfect solution. Cart the explosive to the middle of the Sahara Desert and blow it up, where it wouldn't hurt anyone.

Sergeant McMurray was in charge of a crew of 20 soldiers from the 184th — men who had been hand picked to take care of the mess. At the moment they were busy receiving, counting, packaging, and then transporting the packets of Semtex from an abandoned landing strip near Bazemah, which was nothing more than a tiny town adjacent to an oasis in the eastern Libyan Sahara. A strange base for such a large operation, but it had been the best they could do. Most of the Semtex had been delivered by air, in a variety of planes. Some had also come by Jeep, and, amazingly, some by camel. Most came in the cellophane-wrapped "bricks" that had been sold by Czechoslovakia in the '70s; each ten inches in length, four inches in width, and two inches in depth. There was 660 tons of the stuff — approximately 600,000 kilos. Each brick was measured for size, weight, and contribution to total, and turned over to the Army for transport to the detonation site.

Richard Lawrence was the CIA's contribution to the field trip. He was a trained pilot who had flown for the Navy, then retired his wings to become a Federal field agent. He didn't know anything about explosions, and was demonstrating his ignorance at every turn.

"And we're looking at what, about 120,000 bricks?" he asked.

"Yup," came the terse reply.

Richard performed a few calculations. "Have I got it right, McMurray?" he asked. "The pile's going to be 20 feet wide, 25 feet long, and 11 feet high, more or less?"

"Well more or less," replied McMurray. "The thing you have to realize, though, is that you can't blow it up cartoon style, with one fuse running to the pile. If you did that, a fair amount of the material would be blown free through the kinetic forces. Not all of the Semtex would be destroyed."

"So what are we doing instead?" pressed Richard.

"Multiple blasting caps and fuses, together with Amtec timers, so that separate electrical signals are transmitted to the pile at precisely the same instant," said McMurray. "And by 'precisely,' I mean within a nanosecond. It's actually not that different from detonating a whopping big pile of C4. These bricks are a little larger, but the characteristics are similar."

"Oh obviously," said Richard, flicking a fly off his clipboard. "How big will the blast be?"

"We're looking at two-thirds of a kiloton, but this is Semtex, not TNT. I'd say we're looking at the equivalent of a kiloton of TNT. That will make the explosion, if things are fused properly, the equivalent of a small nuclear blast."

Richard reflected on that for a minute. "How far back should they be?" he asked, referring to the pack of reporters that appeared to be growing by the hour.

"I would say at least two miles," responded McMurray. "Maybe more."

Richard hadn't counted on the growing crowd of reporters, journalists, and gawkers that had started to assemble around them. But August was a slow news month, and the destruction of Libya's Semtex stash was starting to make the front pages.

He'd also overlooked the political wile of Libya's leader, General Minyar, who had assembled a large tent near the center of operations. He wasn't there yet, but would be when the demolition began. His communications department had gone out of their way to make his presence known. "Minyar the good," the headlines would say. "Libya now open for business."

This had further motivated the news stations, which were there in force. News Corp was setting up a camp, and CNN, BBC, and Al Jazeera were also there to record the fireworks. The official moment of detonation was still two days away, but Bazemah had already seen a substantial increase in tourists, all waiting to see the "big bang." Several movie studios had sent crews and cameras, for the sole purpose of shooting footage of such a large explosion, to be used in some future high-budget action film. A festive atmosphere prevailed. The overriding concern shared by the news crews was that they would run out of cold beer before the explosion occurred. A fitting worry, since the explosion was taking place in the heart of the great Sahara; it was, by early afternoon, 120 degrees in the shade.

The question about the size of the explosion, and specifically the size of the crater it would create, was starting to tease the airwaves. There were many predictions, and there was even a Las Vegas betting agency setting odds on calling the crater size. What would it be… 500 feet across? Maybe 600?

Richard already had a throbbing headache from the pressure. He tried to ignore it, continuing to review the inventory counts that arrived with each new shipment, counting again and again the number of bricks, and entering them into a spreadsheet on his laptop. "God-damned bean counter now," he muttered aloud, the corners of his mouth drawing down in a grimace. He longed for a return to his Navy days, when he was landing Tomcats on what, from a short distance out, appeared to be postage stamp-sized aircraft carriers. He had taken pride in his skills, and was devastated when, in his early 30's, his vision started to deteriorate, and he could no longer meet the Navy's requirements. Of course he hadn't told anyone what was going on at the time, and had continued to do his job as best he could. Everything had been fine until one night, when he splashed a Tomcat in the course of a difficult nighttime carrier landing. It hadn't been a mistake the Navy was willing to forgive. After that he had taken a lateral transfer to the SEAL program and had served in the second Gulf War as a special operations officer.

He had grown up in Islamabad, Pakistan, where his parents had worked at the US Embassy. When he was 16, both his mother and father had died in a car crash, and he'd moved to California to live with the Goldbergs, a family that had also been stationed at the Islamabad Embassy, and who had known Richard's parents well. On his nineteenth birthday, he signed with the Navy. When he'd been forced to leave after the carrier crash, his background and his skill with languages, especially Arabic, Farsi, and Urdu, had made him a natural choice for the CIA's very busy Middle East operation. His dark complexion didn't hurt either.

So here he was, 45 years of age, turning gray, counting bricks of Semtex like they were loaves of bread in an American supermarket, in this stinking, ungodly heat. Some promotion. He was well on the way to "Greeter" status at the local Wal-Mart. He popped a couple of Vicodin and continued the seemingly endless count. Since getting kicked out of the Navy, nothing had gone the way he'd planned, and his problems seemed to be growing. If his life was a river, he thought, it had definitely changed from a bright sparkling mountain stream to a mass of sludge and mud blockaded by a dam.

THE ONE AGENCY MISSING on the Semtex scene was the relatively new Terrorist Threat Integration Center. TTIC (pronounced "tea tick") had been established on May 1, 2003, partially in response to devastating terrorist attacks on American soil. The concept behind the new agency was simple enough. Analysts from every agency in the US Intelligence Community received a steady stream of information to be developed by their agents and sources. Intelligence officers from every department continuously fit those pieces into the ongoing and ever-changing factual mosaic. Information was probed, developed, questioned, validated, and analyzed. Further information might come to the surface at any time and require immediate attention. The stream of "Intel" was continually sent "up the chain" from these Intelligence Agencies, and now also went laterally to TTIC. That agency received reports from the National Security Agency, the CIA, FBI, BATF, Secret Service, and all military Intelligence Agencies. It also received reports from security agencies from other countries; MI-5 and MI-6 reports were received daily from the United Kingdom, and Israel's Mossad and Canada's security organization, CSIS, reported daily. All told, 27 countries sent information on a regular basis. The people working with TTIC had distinguished themselves in their own Intelligence Agencies prior to their TTIC assignment. Generally, they were also individuals with highly developed computer skills. All in all, it was a brainy crowd, with an incredible amount of information at their fingertips.

The true power of TTIC was in its ability to access hundreds of thousands of databases in countries all over the world. Cellular phone, driving, and criminal records, and records from all the large retail chains, were at their beck and call; dozens of new databases were added to their vast addressing system each day. TTIC had access to trillions of bits of information — pieces that it could splice, dice, and parse in many ways, and at very high speeds. If someone bought a prescription, TTIC could find it. If they applied for a fishing license, TTIC would hunt it down. With debit and credit cards, commerce was becoming "cashless," and slowly turning toward being completely "digital." TTIC was designed to take advantage of this digital age.

The agency was powered by an experimental IBM computer known as Blue Gene/L. The computer was originally built for the Livermore National Laboratory in California, installed in 2004 with much fanfare. It contained 16 towers, each approximately six feet in height, and came with an elaborate Freon cooling system. The system had stolen the supercomputer crown from Japan, which had built the exotic Earth-Simulator supercomputer a few years earlier. Blue Gene/L had staggering amounts of RAM, and could perform more than 300 trillion calculations per second, far outweighing anything else that had ever been built.

What was not made public was that IBM had actually manufactured several such systems — one for Livermore Labs, and a second for TTIC, in Washington, DC. The TTIC model had roughly 25% more processing power than the Livermore model, and several times more disc space. Sixteen systems were also given to the National Security Agency. The existence of these systems was kept secret, even from most of the Intelligence Community. They were networked in a 16-system cluster, and together they performed at more than 1 quadrillion calculations per second. The NSA had operated the fastest computers on the planet since the beginning of the computing era, although few outside the walls of Crypto City, their home base, knew that. They saw this new system as nothing more than their God-given right.

At TTIC, the processing modules, power supplies, and disc drives took up an entire floor of their own, below the floor that housed the control room. Unlike the supercomputers of the past, which required armies of staff to keep the hardware operational, Blue Gene required only 20 people; essentially four shifts of five employees, working to ensure that the infrastructure remained intact. Given the computer's sophistication and self-reliance, it was a fairly simple job. Their main responsibilities were virus patrol and making pots of coffee.

The second floor of the building contained some administrative offices, boardrooms, and secretarial stations. The main floor had reception, storage rooms, and little else. Not seen, but omnipresent, were many armed security personnel. The front of the building was marked by a small sign that said "Donovan and Sons Information Processing Corporation." It was an inside joke.

The building had a large number of dedicated and highly secure fiber optic telephone and data connections. Should some enterprising soul have found a way to compromise those links, they would have run into an extremely high level of encryption — the cutting edge of what hundreds of mathematicians working at the NSA had developed. The lines were linked to the CIA offices, the Pentagon, the White House, and the 15 other agencies that made up the American Intelligence Community.

The most important floor in the building was the fourth floor, which housed the huge TTIC control room — this was where the eyes, ears, and hands of the organism lived. The room was built on a circular plan. The curved front wall contained nine large flat panel displays, specially built by IBM, each with a diagonal measurement of approximately 101 inches. Currently, one was tuned in to CNN, another to BBC, and a third to Al Jazeera. There were three satellite images — two from KH-11's focused on Iraq, and the third a feed from one of three spectacular new ORION satellites, currently focused on a North Korean factory site. Two more screens displayed video feeds from Predator Drones, and the ninth displayed Google's homepage. Twenty 48-inch screens were vertically stacked on the extreme left and right sides of the wall.

The rest of the room consisted of two raised circular terraces with built-in desks, each with inlaid computers and display panels. Some of the stations had five or six additional independent display screens of various configurations and sizes. In all, there were 40 such stations. The center of the room contained a large, recessed, illuminated world map, some 35 feet across. The map was in fact a specially manufactured, interactive LCD display; if any portion of the map were activated, detailed information appeared in a separate window, which could in turn be enlarged for even greater detail. Using technology similar to the LCD mapping programs found in high-end cars, information could be drilled down to street level. Data about who lived, worked, or had significant connections in the area could also be brought up, or displayed on any of the larger monitors on the front wall. The staff had started to call it the "Atlas Screen."

Hamilton Turbee was one of those fortunate enough to be working with these elite systems at TTIC. He had been personally invited by the Senate subcommittee in charge of TTIC to join. "Turbee" didn't need the money. He didn't need the job. He was by nature resistive of authority, and didn't fit into an orderly bureaucracy. He was also affected with a social disorder, though he had medication to control it. He had known from the start that the atmosphere wouldn't be easy for him. But the thought of playing with the most powerful computer on the planet was too seductive for him to pass up. When invited, he agreed to become one of the first employees of the new agency. He was distressed when he discovered, several months later, that the NSA actually had more computing horsepower than TTIC.

Daniel Alexander, the TTIC director, had immediately regretted the decision made by the subcommittee to employ Turbee. A number of Dan's closest advisors had told him that the new employee would be an excellent addition to the exclusive TTIC employee list. The youth possessed great skill in mathematics, and particularly in the development of complex search algorithms. But once inside the department, Turbee had fared poorly. Most of his coworkers were analysts from the Intelligence Community, or leading academics, or both. Most were workaholics. Most fit naturally into the TTIC culture. They were fastidious in habit and buttoned down in dress and attitude. Turbee shared none of these characteristics. He was 5′6″ and only 26 years old. He had never worked for the CIA, FBI, or any branch of the Armed Forces. He slouched. He dressed poorly. He came and went as he pleased and was as pale as a ghost. These eccentricities, along with a number of others, placed him immediately on Dan's blacklist, though the youth didn't realize it. Turbee knew nothing about reading nuances and tonality of voice, and did not understand what people thought of him. Dan, on the other hand, knew everything about these things. It was second nature to him.

Daniel Jonathon Alexander, IV was born April 4, 1952 to a high-class family in Hartford, Connecticut, a child of war and fortune. Rumor had it that the family was worth several billion dollars, although the exact sum was a closely guarded family secret. Dan's various ancestors had fought in the First and Second World Wars, the Korean War, the Vietnam War, and in the first Gulf War. The family had distinguished itself not only on the battlefield, and in the worlds of commerce and industry, but also in service to country in high-level administrative positions. Various members had served as Under Secretary of State, Deputy Director of the CIA, and, for a brief period, Deputy Chairman of the Joint Chiefs of Staff. Honesty, forthrightness, hard work, and intelligence characterized the various chieftains of the Connecticut Alexanders. Unfortunately, none of these qualities had been passed down to Daniel IV.

This particular Alexander simply gloried in the family wealth; he'd spent more than $20 million on a mansion on 600 acres in Connecticut, and a further $5 million on a condo in Washington, DC. He had an undergraduate degree in history from Yale, and a law degree from that same institution. But while most students worked diligently and, in the case of law school, extremely diligently, Dan had never exhibited the ability to work hard. He threw money around liberally, having other students do his term papers and take notes for him in class. He spent many of his school hours on the golf course and in the bars, either practicing his chip shot or bedding women.

He did enjoy the sense of connection and power brought by his name. The family pull had gained him an invitation to join the Skull and Bones Society, and he instinctively knew which additional strings to pull in order to gain entry into the halls of power. He'd thought briefly about joining the military in family tradition, but abandoned that idea when he realized the amount of work involved, and that route's attenuated opportunities for shortcuts.

Instead, he developed his high-level associations by using his wealth to gain entry to the Republican Party's inner circle. It was rumored that he had given more than $10 million to Republican presidential campaigns, through various funding vehicles. As a direct result of these connections, he held a number of high-ranking posts within the Intelligence Community. He hadn't come by them honestly, but he knew how to use them to his benefit. And what he lacked in candor was more than made up for by his shrewdness and ruthless craft. He had developed the habit, early in his career, of "building files" on perceived adversaries. Individuals standing between him and a particular objective would soon be mired in scandal, usually involving some youthful indiscretion or sexual misadventure. Dan took steps to ensure that the same fate did not befall his own reputation; he had a PR firm on full-time retainer, building his resume and polishing his image. And there was no arguing that he looked the part — his handsome aristocratic features seemed to portray infinite strength and intelligence. To those who didn't know him.

Dan was a gifted speaker, and quick with a witty retort. He did well speaking on TV news shows like CNBC and MSNBC. He had coauthored a book on terrorist threats inside American borders (the truth was that he paid the author $1 million to be noted as coauthor). These activities were all well-represented on his resume. His staff of PR people had spent years weaving an image of Daniel Alexander IV, dean of homeland security issues, expert on terrorism. Underneath it all, however, his character had not changed. He was lazy, arrogant, ruthless, and not overly bright.

Like so many modern playmakers, Dan eventually found that wealth, pleasure, and luxuries were not enough for him. Power was the ultimate aphrodisiac, and once he had tasted it, in his undergraduate years at Yale, he became obsessed with its pull. He had obvious designs on the presidency, and was looking for a post that would vault him to national prominence.

Hamilton Turbee, on the other hand, was a (comparatively speaking) simple mathematician and programmer. He and Dan were destined for conflict from the start. He had no Intelligence background, didn't have secret wishes to climb to high governmental positions, and was clueless about the internal workings of the CIA (most people thought this was a positive attribute). He was totally lacking in social graces and skills. He had been categorized by the pediatric psychiatrists at Georgetown University Hospital many years earlier as a "highly functioning autistic." He was born with repetitive motion problems in his right arm, couldn't tolerate loud or obtrusive noises, and hated being "outside." He avoided all eye contact, needed a maid to keep him and his small apartment clean, and was able to make himself tolerable to others only through a rich cocktail of antidepressants, mood stabilizers, and stimulants. Without the medicinal support, his mother claimed, he would have spent his time "bouncing off the walls."

In university, his social issues had been eclipsed by the achievements brought on by his nearly photographic memory and dazzling skills in mathematics. He wrote a number of "fuzzy" search algorithms that were picked up by Lexis and Google. He was also the author of unique search programs that matched similarities across multiple databases. Turbee's father, James Turbee, was the managing partner of an international law firm headquartered in Washington, DC, and had been able to utilize his firm's intellectual property lawyers to negotiate reasonable compensation for these efforts. James Turbee also managed his son's funds, which had become quite extensive; his net worth was well into the range of eight figures. Not that Turbee cared. As long as he had more computing power and larger screens than anyone else, he was content. So he came to be TTIC's wunderkind, to play with one of the most powerful supercomputers on the planet. And with any luck, to find and stop terrorists in his free time.

Turbee's first months in the new workplace had been rocky. He had not fit in very well; the majority of the staff avoided him. More than once he had been told by Dan, in aristocratic tones, to "take a shower and behave." He was introduced daily to new and increasingly severe individuals from different components of the Intelligence Community. He hated dealing with strangers, and knew many of his colleagues more by footwear than facial characteristics. His deathly pale complexion and darkly circled eyes became a source of comment. Was he sick? Was he on drugs? People who tried to ask received either a silent shrug or no answer at all.

He became ostracized and quickly withdrew into his own world, allowing himself to take the role of outcast. TTIC was a miracle agency, but even among people who should have been smart enough to understand him, Turbee had become the misfit. His depression increased, and he looked for a way to silently disappear. Soon after he started working there, Turbee began retreating from the TTIC community on a regular basis by playing Internet video games instead of working. He'd almost immediately stopped participating in any of the agency's social activities. Though possibly the smartest person on the entire team, Turbee was not a functioning member.

ON ONE OF THOSE EARLY DAYS, before all the equipment was fully operational, when there were still technicians crawling under worktables and cables littering the stepped floors, there was a commotion, and a collective muttering of "oh shit." A small detail of Marines entered through the rear doors, and one announced, "Ladies and gentlemen, the President of the United States." Through the doors stepped the man himself. He was wearing his usual awkward grin, and dressed casually, without a suit jacket or tie.

"Sit down, everyone," said the President. "Get comfortable. I won't take up too much of your valuable time." Turbee noticed Dan's purple features out of the corner of his eye. Clearly Dan had not been expecting this. No one had.

The crowd of engineers, technicians, scientists, and Intelligence personnel sat down as one, shocked. The techs without desks simply sat on the floor.

"I know that this is a little bit unusual," said the President. "But I think it's important for you to hear directly from me why you are here, and why this is going to be an agency of critical importance to my presidency, and those that will follow.

"You probably know that this country is still reeling from the terrorist attack we recently experienced," he continued. "While it was not the first terrorist attack weathered by this country, it was the attack that woke us up. The entire nation could see that there was, for whatever reason, a frightful collection of terrorists aligned against us, with means of great destruction at their disposal. They declared war on the free and democratic nations of this world, and especially against our own country.

"There were, unfortunately, a great many Intelligence failures that led to these tragic events, and many committees, investigations, and inquiries have been created to find how this could have happened, and to make sure that it never happens again."

There was a general nodding of agreement in the audience. The mood was electric. It wasn't every day that the President dropped by to say good morning and welcome the team.

"One of the findings of all of those investigations," the President continued, "was that there was not adequate coordination and communication between the various agencies charged with keeping the security of this nation. Too often, our Intelligence Agencies were passing one another like ships in the night, not being receptive to the information that other agencies had developed, or duplicating information unnecessarily. Sometimes the left hand did not know what the right hand was doing. And too often, patterns that could have been gleaned from streams of information developed by different agencies were not discerned, primarily because information was not being shared. That's where you guys come in."

Suddenly the President gave one of the disarming "awe shucks" grins for which he was so famous. "We have in this room," he continued, "some of the most respected analysts, gathered from all of the agencies that form our Intelligence Community. In addition, we have highly educated people hailing from our great universities: Harvard, Princeton, UCLA, Yale… maybe I should reverse the order," he chuckled, and the room chuckled with him. "We have individuals in this room who have been station chiefs in Riyadh, in Islamabad, in Khartoum, and elsewhere. We also have people who excel in finding patterns in oceans of data where others see nothing but chaos."

At that point Turbee saw those powerful eyes fall directly on him, and immediately looked down at his feet. The speech continued for a little longer, and he was impressed in spite of himself. Having only recently graduated from the university life, Turbee, like most university students, felt that the man was a twit and had come to power only because of his last name. But there was nothing stupid about this speech, and nothing weak about the man. Turbee felt a grudging respect begin to grow, and found that he was actually looking forward to working for and with this man. As the President finished his speech and was ushered out, Turbee wished he could go out and shake his hand, but found himself instead rooted to the floor.

AT TTIC, the day began with a discussion of the President's Daily Brief, or PDB, and the issues that it raised. The PDB was a briefing prepared every day for the President by the Office of Current Production and Analytic Support, a division of the CIA. Over the years, the PDB had been expanded, until the people handling it renamed it the National Intelligence Daily. During the Kennedy administration, it was reformatted and rearranged, and took on the appearance of a small newspaper. One President had even joked that it should contain a few ads and a sports section. It reflected the Intelligence Community's perspective on the affairs of the present day, and was the most important newspaper in the country, possibly in the world. The PDB came into play when TTIC was charged with specific tasks by the Director of Central Intelligence or the Deputy Director of Central Intelligence. On a number of occasions, the orders came directly from the President. Through hard work and the enormity of their responsibility, especially in regard to issues that made the front page of the PDB, the members of the team soon began to respect one another and to resemble the team that their President had directed them to be.

Many of them continued to wonder about Turbee, though. His messiness, his proclivity to bring food into his workspace without eating it, his pale features, and his unusual repetitive motor mannerisms all puzzled them. One day, however, Turbee showed the team why he was there. On that day, at 7:34AM, Madrid time, unknown terrorists detonated explosives on four trains in that city, using cell phone transmissions. More than 200 people were killed, and 1,500 were injured. It was the worst terrorist action that Spain had ever experienced. The bombings occurred during a national election, so the Spanish government immediately blamed the ETA, a Basque separatist organization. The matter was front and center in the PDB the next morning in Washington, and was vigorously discussed during the TTIC morning meeting.

The man leading the discussion was Liam Rhodes. Rhodes, age 45, came from a family that had a history with the CIA — his sure ticket into the Intelligence world, if he wanted to take it. He was a West Point graduate, a former Marine, a Desert Storm vet, and a scholar. After leaving the Marines, he had been admitted to Harvard, where he had obtained a Ph.D. in Middle East Studies in a record three years. After taking time off to handle some family issues, he had re-entered the Intelligence arena as an analyst in the CIA's Middle East Department. Within ten years, as his skills, intelligence, and education showed through, he was promoted to Director of that department. From there he had been appointed to TTIC.

"No way," he was saying. "It's al-Qaeda. The organization of it. The audaciousness. No way the ETA could pull something like this off. One bomb, maybe, but not all of this, and certainly not simultaneously."

Rather than paying attention to the discussion, Turbee was noodling his way along the Internet, not really following the thread of the conversation. An article had just appeared in one of the Spanish newspapers, stating that an unexploded bomb had been found, and that it had an unusual detonator — a Goma-2 ECO.

Turbee smiled; this was way more interesting than what was going on in the office. He immediately started looking into which corporation produced these detonators. Having determined the culprit, he took a few minutes to hack into its corporate database, and discovered that 20 such detonators had recently been purchased by a numbered company registered in the Cayman Islands. That got his attention. People using numbered companies in the Caymans were generally doing something that they wanted to keep hidden. Like purchasing detonators for bombs they meant to use. Using the power of Blue Gene, he was able to hack into the corporate registry of the Grand Cayman records system, and found the only listed director of that numbered company to be a person from Morocco, by the name of Abu Dujan al-Afghani. Running this man's name through a Madrid street address database, and further databases for power and telephone service, Turbee found that al-Afghani and one James Zoughan lived across the hall from one another in an apartment building in Madrid. Further searches on the supercomputer revealed that these two individuals had been living side by side in various other buildings in Madrid for the past two years.

Turbee sat back in his chair and considered. If you live beside a terrorist once, that's a coincidence. If you live beside him three times, in the same city, over a space of two years, that smacks of conspiracy. These two were connected. Using his personal web-bots, which could hack into a server, scour its contents, and send back anything they found, Turbee teased the names of 12 likely conspirators from the various databases to which he had access. Then he stepped it up — he got their current addresses as well. Just as the group meeting was about to finish up, Turbee gingerly raised his hand.

"This ain't school, Turbee. You can say what you want," Dan snapped.

In a quiet and somewhat shaky voice, Turbee answered, "It is al-Qaeda. In fact, al-Afghani, the mastermind, claims elsewhere that he is al-Qaeda's military chief in Europe. His coworkers in this bombing were James Zoughan and 12 others." Then he gave their names.

The rest of the TTIC team looked at him in astonishment. "How the hell did you get that so fast?" one man asked slowly.

Turbee slowly explained his process, looking down at his shoes to keep from meeting anyone's eye.

"Get it down on paper," said Dan. "We need to get that to the President right now."

"I don't do paper," replied Turbee. "Someone else can write it down. Oh, and I've got their addresses too."

With one phone call, Dan was connected to the President's Chief of Staff, and, after a few tense seconds, he found himself talking to the President of the United States. He gave him the names and addresses of the conspirators.

"How sure are you of this information, Danny?" asked the President.

"It's this odd whiz kid I've got, named Turbee. He used his search algorithms to work the information out of literally hundreds of databases. He explained it to the team. Rhodes is convinced Turbee's got it. I would say it's pretty reliable, sir," Dan answered.

"OK, Dan. I'm going to run with it. If we miss it's going to be embarrassing, but if you've nailed it, Spain will owe us."

The President put down his phone and asked for his Chief of Staff. "Get me Acedo on the line as well," he ordered. Acedo was the prime minister of Spain, and currently in the midst of an election battle. Within five minutes the call was put through, and the President delivered to Acedo the names and addresses of his terrorists.

It took Acedo and his government several hours to retract their Basque terrorist theory, but in due course they acted on the tip, and arrested the terrorists who hadn't yet committed suicide. For the subsequent press release, the Spanish security service indicated that a telephone belonging to Zoughan had been found, and that a quick search of the recent phone calls had revealed the names of the other terrorists. That was easier and less embarrassing than saying that some kid with a foreign supercomputer had tweaked out the names in 20 minutes just to pass the time. Even though TTIC was never acknowledged, and Acedo never publicly thanked the US government, word of the coup spread rapidly through the normally tight-lipped Intelligence Community.

On that day, Turbee made his bones with the TTIC team. Despite his many eccentricities and blemishes, he was adopted and accepted. For the first time, he learned what it was to be at home in an organization and with other people.

JOHNSON, turn up the sound on the CNN feed for a second," barked Dan. Ted Johnson was the custodian of the master controls, in charge of deciding what image or feed went to which of the big 101 screens. He also managed the conference room's phone lines. The TTIC staff had nicknamed him "the yellee," due to the fact that he was almost always addressed by Dan in a somewhat elevated tone of voice.

"OK," Johnson answered.

It took only seconds for everyone in the room to tune in to the events taking place in Libya. On the central 101, a CNN reporter was in the middle of an interview with a demolitions expert on the US mainland. "How big will the explosion be?" asked the announcer. "How big a crater?"

"I can't say for sure," said the expert. "But I agree with the Army representative — this explosion could be the equivalent of firing a kiloton of TNT. It could level any block in New York City. It could create a crater, in my opinion, of more than 500 meters across, and deeper than 20 meters."

The reporter moved on to talk about the odds makers in Vegas, and the rapidly growing pool of cash to be paid to the participant who most accurately called the depth and diameter of the crater. A sly grin slid across Turbee's usually serious face. He turned to his computer and went to work.

INSPECTOR INDERJIT SINGH, of the Royal Canadian Mounted Police, was watching the same CNN feed on a small, 20-year-old television set. He sat alone in his cramped office at the RCMP provincial headquarters on Heather Street in Vancouver, British Columbia, shaking his head in disbelief. "Tons," he muttered to himself. "Almost 660 *tons* of Semtex. And now they're betting on the size of the crater. Nuts. Totally nuts." Indy, as he was affectionately nicknamed by the other denizens of the cramped complex, went back to the problem at hand.

British Columbian marijuana, known on the streets of California as "BC Bud," was pouring across the border separating Canada and her southern neighbor in record quantities. There seemed to be no stopping it. The border was evidently full of holes. Millions of dollars were being spent by four different levels of government, namely British Columbia, the state of Washington, and the two Federal governments, to stop the flow. With no success on either side. A tidal wave of pot, thought Indy. A veritable tsunami.

The source of the drugs was, to the dismay of Indy and many of his colleagues, transparently obvious. After four decades of lax marijuana laws, minor or nonexistent sentences, budget cuts, and a local government that did not seem to care, BC had developed a fruitful and potent marijuana crop. A local economist had suggested, on the basis of fairly reliable evidence, that the marijuana industry had replaced the forest industry as BC's number one exporter. Marijuana was freely smoked on the streets of downtown Vancouver every day. A number of restaurants and "hemp shops" were openly selling it. To Indy's utter amazement, a local TV broadcaster had aired interviews with the proprietors of those establishments, even giving their street addresses. Still nothing had been done.

Many of Indy's colleagues knew judges, prosecutors, and high government officials who made no secret about the fact that they smoked weed. The drug children of the '60s and '70s were now holding the levers of power, and they saw nothing wrong with smoking marijuana. Not surprisingly, organized crime had become involved, and BC Bud was now being transported and warehoused by local motorcycle gangs. But how was it getting across the border? Indy leaned over his desk, running his hands through his hair. No matter how many times he asked himself this question, there was never an answer. Every inch of the border was monitored. The American Coast Guard had extra vessels plying the waters between Vancouver Island and the American mainland. Remote aerial craft with TV cameras were being employed. Monitoring rooms with hundreds of video feeds existed in BC and Washington, and yet the border leaks continued, unimpeded. There was obviously a hole, but where the hell was it?

The issue before him, however, was even more serious. High-grade heroin was now showing up in California, Oregon, Washington, and other neighboring states. It was a new and very serious aspect to the problem. Agent Stanley Hagen, of the Seattle FBI field office, had been particularly aggressive about the issue during their telephone call earlier that day.

"And now heroin is coming into the US through BC," Hagen had literally shouted into the phone. "Load after load after damn dump truck load of high-grade marijuana, and now, and now HEROIN!" He had seen many good kids go sideways because of marijuana; he didn't want to think about the added criminality that came with the more serious use of heroin yet. He was going to take it up with the State department, he said. He was going to DC with this. It had to stop.

Indy knew Hagen was right. Indy also had a reasonably good idea about what would happen next. The FBI would lean on State. State would lean on its Canadian Embassy, who would start a chain of events that would end with the Inspector General of the RCMP proceeding to shit on Indy and his colleagues. Indy's protestations about low budgets, lax laws, and easy courts with dope-smoking judges would simply fall on deaf ears.

The evidence Hagen presented to Indy seemed clear enough. The heroin coming into the United States was from the Middle East or the golden triangle of Southeast Asia. And it was repeatedly showing up in raids of marijuana wholesalers in the state of Washington. That meant that the same hands were involved. It was coming over the BC/Washington border somehow. Somewhere. But where? And how?

THE CONVOY CAME at the expected time. An old Humvee. An even older Volvo N86. And another Humvee. The vehicles came rumbling down the Al Jawf Highway in Libya, surreal in the shimmering bands of heat. "Highway" was a bit of a misnomer, since the road was only a rutted single-lane trail, often disappearing completely beneath the shifting sands of the Sahara. The heat and the late afternoon sun were unrelenting. Without water, no human could last more than two days in this environment. Abu bin Mustafa was born in Egypt, but on the Nile delta. He had spent years in the deserts of Yemen and Afghanistan, but still found the endless sandy solitude of the southern Sahara to be unnerving.

He shifted from one foot to the other, pulling his attention off his thirst. "This should be easy," he told himself, speaking aloud simply to break the heavy silence. Just get the job done and he could get on a plane and have all the water and air conditioning he wanted. The location was perfect for an ambush — the roadway descended slightly, and rounded a sharp curve. Mustafa had his men park their Toyotas across the road, where they would be least visible. Then he and the three others assumed positions behind the rock formations that rose up on both sides of the highway. The sun's position was in their favor. There would be ten, he'd been told. Four in the lead vehicle, two in the Volvo, and four more in the third vehicle. Three American soldiers. Seven Libyan soldiers. Mustafa and his men communicated through collar microphones, and each carried a Heckler and Koch PSG-1, equipped with a 6x Hensoldt scope. The rifles were extremely accurate, auto-loading, and equipped with 20-round magazines. The ammunition used had also been modified to maximize the weapons' killing power. The modifications were not popular, because of the expense, but that had never deterred Mustafa's employer, who was the mastermind behind the attack. Mustafa drew a breath and gave the count as the vehicles drew to within firing range.

At Mustafa's signal, four rifles cracked as one. Four soldiers keeled over, dead. Two soldiers in the last Humvee and the two soldiers in the Volvo were hit. Within a split second, four rifles fired again. The two soldiers left in the trailing Humvee slumped over. Two soldiers in the lead Humvee were hit. One more split second reload. As the two remaining soldiers in the lead Humvee rolled out of their vehicle, attempting to gain some cover, they were also killed. Mustafa was astounded at the ease of it. It was just as Yousseff, his boss, had said to him more than once. Preparation was everything.

The men rose as one and headed down to the vehicles. Barking a quick command at the others to check the bodies, Mustafa pulled back the tarp slung over the Volvo's deck and smiled as he saw row upon row of what appeared to be reddish cellophane-wrapped bricks. Again, it was as Yousseff had told him. The two old Humvees were driven off the road and parked behind the same rock formations that had hidden Mustafa and his men. The bodies were pulled out of the Volvo and placed in the Humvees, and the Volvo, with its valuable cargo, was turned around. A new convoy formed, this time heading north — a Toyota in front, a Toyota in the rear, and the Volvo with the Semtex in the middle. Mustafa rode shotgun in the Volvo.

The three vehicles raced northward as quickly as the tattered roadway allowed, and within an hour turned right, heading east on a barely visible goat-path of a road that serviced, occasionally, the desert village of Zighan. Another five miles, and a decrepit, weatherworn building came into view. Behind it sat a few single-engine craft and a reconditioned DC-3. It had taken Mustafa and his colleagues several days to find this isolated and rarely used airport, and a goodly sum of money to cover the bribe that would permit them to take off without a flight plan. When they arrived, the Volvo was backed up to the DC-3, and the four men worked quickly to transfer the bricks, row by row, to the cargo compartment of the plane. This would be the first of many transfers. Mustafa saw the airport manager watching the process with interest. Not a good sign.

The sun had set by the time the task was finished. Mustafa ordered his sweating men to board their plane. He went back into the tiny terminal, and smiled at the master. He didn't like this part of the job, and wished one of Yousseff's paid assassins had been sent along to take care of it. The station-master appeared friendly, with lines of laughter circling his eyes. But he had seen too much, hadn't he? Yousseff hated loose ends, and would commend his judgment. When he was four feet from the man, Mustafa pulled out his 9 mm Glock and shot him once in the head. One more bullet in the heart for good measure, and that was that.

One of the other men had already started the engines of the DC-3 when Mustafa reached it, and within minutes the plane, loaded down with 4,300 kilos of Semtex, was on a southeastern course, headed toward the Sudan. Mustafa reached for the Thuraya Sat-phone.

THREE THOUSAND MILES and several time zones to the east, in a large hangar in Jalalabad, a phone was ringing. Three times, then a pause, then twice more. Then silence. It was the signal. Yousseff smiled to himself, setting down what he had been reading and leaning back in his chair. The plan was in motion, and there would be no turning back now.

A MILE OR SO DOWNRIVER from the hangar, Zak Goldberg was making his first transmission in a week, using the tiny transmitter engineered by the propeller heads at Langley. Smaller than a matchbox, it contained only two buttons — an on/off switch and a Morse code communication button for sending out an encrypted Morse code signal. More than 90 percent of the device was battery. When turned on, it transmitted its position to one of the several unmanned Global Hawks cruising 60,000 feet above him; they in turn transmitted the position, and the Morse code message, to the US Embassy in Islamabad. The Morse code was translated to alphanumeric characters, and printed out on a high-speed printer located in the communications room in the Embassy's basement. When this newest message came in, the clerk on duty glanced at it, yawning. Then he snapped to attention and read it quickly, and wide-eyed, a second time. It was no fine judgment call in this case to ring Michael Buckingham, the CIA station chief. This information needed to be passed along immediately. He picked up the telephone and quickly dialed Buckingham's local number.

2

AUGUST 10 CAME TOO EARLY for Richard. The last of the convoys had arrived near midnight the night before. It was well past 2AM by the time the bricks had been fully unloaded at Ground Zero, under the watchful eyes of Jason McMurray and his men. McMurray himself worked through the rest of the night, threading the fuses through the mass of Semtex. The pile had been laid out in concentric circles, and stacked pyramid style. Each segment was separately threaded with fuses designed for shaped charge explosives, and hooked up to a series of Amptec Research timers. The timers were hooked up in parallel and linked to a complicated switching device, which was in turn connected to McMurray's laptop. At zero hour, which had now been set for 3PM, the laptop would electronically signal the timers, which would simultaneously send powerful currents through the mass of fusing cables to each layer of the Semtex pyramid. McMurray was so obsessed with the simultaneous ignition of the entire mass that he had cut the fusing cable himself and then calculated the exact volume that each layer would take. He had spent days reviewing his calculations over and over again to ensure that the ignition would be simultaneous and complete. Richard had thought it might be as simple as shoveling it all in a heap and firing an RPG into it, but McMurray was horrified at the suggestion.

Other military units had now become involved. The Air Force Materiel Command out of Wright-Patterson had sent a detachment of six people, who had, to McMurray's frustration, peppered the growing Semtex pile with sensors of various sorts. They'd also laid out further concentric circles of thermo graphic, electromagnetic, and percussion sensors at various distances from Ground Zero. The Air Force Research Laboratory Munitions Directorate, stationed at Eglin Air Force Base in Florida, had seen the coverage on CNN, and had sent its own team of experts to monitor the blast. Richard and McMurray both found it highly amusing that these groups had found out about the blast from news reports, and not from the Air Force internal command structure. "Would never happen in the Navy," Richard muttered to himself.

"They're Air Force weenies," said McMurray, trying to lighten the mood. "Any explosion bigger than a fart and they need to study it. You know how it goes."

To round it out, four Navy Night Hawk Helicopters, with support and ground crew, had been sent from the *Theodore Roosevelt* Battle Group, stationed in the Mediterranean, along with a small Marine Expeditionary Unit to supplement the Libyan security forces.

"There are too many guys in uniforms running around here," said Richard. "That's how things go wrong." A familiar pain was invading his temples, and he dug into his pockets for some of his medication. He popped a couple of Oxycontins — not ideal, but it was the first thing he found.

"Know the feeling well," said McMurray, watching Richard throw back what he assumed to be aspirin or ibuprofen. "When I'm done with this job I'm off with my kids and wife. She inherited this gorgeous place on a lake in southern Arizona. I negotiated 30 days."

"Kids?" asked Richard.

"Yup, three girls. Two, four, and six. They're the reason I put up with a lot of this bull. You?"

"Two. Out of the house. Gone. My wife took them when she left. Sometimes wish they were two and four again. I'd do anything to go back." McMurray shuddered a bit when he heard the hollow tone in Richard's voice. It was well known that Richard's first wife had left him, and taken the kids, shortly after he was asked to leave the Navy.

McMurray turned back to his counts, anxious for a way to end what had suddenly become an awkward conversation.

AS ZERO HOUR APPROACHED, the anticipation became palpable. CNN tried to bring a helicopter into the area, but the Libyans wouldn't approve the use of the airspace. "Bloody good thing, too," Richard said when he heard. He didn't want to have to deal with the fallout if a news chopper and crew were destroyed by their little explosion. McMurray had been on the Sat-phone with some of the propeller heads at Fort Gilles, and he told Richard that the observation post should be pushed back to five miles from Ground Zero. Minyar himself was present, in his tent, and his camp needed to be moved as well.

With two hours left to go before the moment of truth, a team of frantic scientists from the Livermore National Laboratory arrived, begging for a 24-hour postponement. They had spent a billion dollars in the past decade to study non-nuclear high explosives, and just a minor repositioning of the pile, and the insertion of a few hundred more sensors (which were on their way) would provide an extraordinary research opportunity. Richard told them to get stuffed.

"It's going to be one hell of a blast, Richard," McMurray said, watching the offended scientists drive away in a huff. "I'm not really sure what will happen. None of these scientists even know. Nothing of this magnitude has ever been done before in a controlled environment. The pressure wave will be immense, and it's going to throw up one monster of a dust cloud. That's why everyone wants to be here to see it."

"Pretty screwball idea to invite the media, if you ask me," Richard replied. "But I suppose Minyar wants to score some brownie points on the international stage."

"Actually, I agree with what we're doing here," said McMurray. "Semtex is like play dough. You can stick it anywhere. Took less than a pound to do the Lockerbie thing. It's too versatile a weapon. It's good for the world to see this big a pile of it destroyed. Makes everyone safer."

"Well, I'll tell the crowd to move back. We can't take the chance of fucking this up in front of the world media." Richard had the Libyan soldiers demobilize the media camp and move it back a few more miles. Then he went over the inventory sheets one last time, checking off the volumes of Semtex delivered to Ground Zero with the inventories that had been counted by the joint Libyan and CIA teams when they first started loading it up. Everything was looking on track, with 20 minutes left to run.

Then he noticed a problem. Something that didn't quite match up.

"Wait a second, what's this?" he muttered to himself. He was looking at the Benghazi Marine Base tallies. More than 200 tons of the Semtex had been stored there, and some 35 truckloads were required to bring it to Bazemah. "Let's see," he continued. "Exactly 192,800 kilos in Benghazi. Thirty-five loads. Thirty-four tallies. Total, total... 188,500 kilos from Benghazi in Bazemah... wait a minute..." The numbers were dancing off the pages in front of his eyes.

McMurray interrupted his thoughts. "Fifteen minutes to lift-off, Richard. We're wired up and ready to go."

"That's good, Sergeant," murmured Richard, a trickle of sweat running down his forehead. "That's good." He was starting to fret. His blurring vision was causing the fine print on the tallies and inventory sheets to drift in and out of focus. The eleventh-hour move from two miles back to five miles back had been irritating. The haste of the operation, and the deadline created by Minyar for the benefit of the press, had made for less-than-optimal planning. The magnitude of the task had been underestimated, and the delivery schedule over the past week had turned out haphazard at best. The presence of the research teams and the growing satellite uplink camp being assembled by various news services was too distracting. Richard had never received training for this sort of thing. He looked again at the delivery tallies and inventories. He was missing a sheet. He went back to the Humvee that had served as his base of operations, knowing that his movements were becoming frantic. Surely the sheet was there. Surely.

"Ten minutes," called McMurray, oblivious to Richard's panic. This was going to be the biggest bang of his career. After spending more than a decade and a half with explosives, this was his Nirvana.

WHILE MCMURRAY AND RICHARD were waiting for that colossal explosion, the Intelligence Community experienced a seismic blast that was significantly larger on the Richter scale of importance. Zak Goldberg's Morse code message had been sent from Michael Buckingham to Robert Baxter, head of the CIA Office of Middle East and African Intelligence. Buckingham trusted Baxter to get the message immediately, regardless of the time zone change. Baxter never seemed to sleep. Come to it, he never seemed to leave his office. There would be no problem with getting his immediate attention.

Baxter did indeed receive the message the moment it came in, and sent the report on to Jeremy Kendall, who was the Director of Intelligence of the CIA. From there it landed at the White House, and, recently added to the list of recipients, the TTIC control center, where Dan had Johnson display it on all nine of the 101's. The theory was that images repeated multiple times had greater impact. Dan did not announce anything. He simply displayed the message and waited for the busy background noise of beepers, telephones, pagers, and conversations to subside. The silence that spread through the room was similar to the sudden hush caused when a maestro walked onstage unannounced. Dan was about to raise his conductor's wand and start the show when a distressingly familiar noise broke the silence.

"I've got it!" yelled Turbee, in obvious triumph. "It'll be 258 meters across, 27 meters at its deepest point, providing the Semtex is properly detonated." He had just finished a burrito, and was jumping around in the mess he always left after food.

"Turbee, what the hell are you ranting about now?" asked the irritated maestro.

"The crater, sir. The size of the crater. You know, the hole in the desert in Libya. There's this big betting pool in Las Vegas on how big the crater will be, and I've been able to apply some discrete fluid mechanics equations to the vectors–"

"Stuff it, kid. We've got serious shit happening and we don't care about the size of some crater or betting pool. Stick with the program," interrupted Dan.

"E-mail it in, anyway," whispered Khasha, who worked at the station next to Turbee's. "Make some money. Buy me dinner. Ignore the pompous ass."

"Well, why not?" he whispered back. The pool had been growing rapidly, and the winner would stand to make a tidy sum. Within seconds, Turbee had sent in his estimate on the crater size, and put the $1,000 bet on his American Express.

Now that he'd dealt with the interesting stuff, he turned his focus to the screens behind his boss.

"This came in less than an hour ago," Dan was saying. "The transmission is from the Jalalabad area of Afghanistan. The source is Zak Goldberg, who is the CIA's top asset in Afghanistan. He's been operating undercover there for close to four years. Buckingham, the Embassy Chief in Islamabad, is of the opinion that this message should be considered solid and accurate information, with a high degree of reliability. Most of the Langley people involved seem to agree. As you can see from this communication, it is an indication of a serious, severe, and imminent threat to the country. Please take your time to read this. Let it sink in for a bit."

He stepped to the side, gesturing dramatically at the image displayed behind him. All eyes turned to the screens at the front of the room, and read the message Zak had sent.

> HAVE RECEIVED CREDIBLE, VERIFIABLE INFORMATION THAT A MAJOR TERRORIST STRIKE AGAINST THE USA IS IN ADVANCED PLANNING STAGES AND WILL BE PUT INTO EXECUTION WITHIN DAYS. LIKELY DATE OF ATTACK WILL BE EARLY SEPTEMBER THIS YEAR. POSSIBILITY THAT ATTACK WILL BE BY WATER. ATTACK DESIGNED TO CAUSE 100 TIMES THE DAMAGE TO AMERICAN LIVES AS PAST ATTACKS. EMIR GLOATS THAT THIS COULD DESTABILIZE AMERICA ENTIRELY. REPEAT — THIS INFORMATION IS HIGHLY CREDIBLE. PASHTUN DRUG LORDS ARE WORKING WITH EMIR. WILL TRAVEL WITH THEM TOMORROW TO FIND OUT MORE. MISSION HAS BECOME EXTREMELY DANGEROUS BUT THE MAGNITUDE OF THE THREAT REQUIRES THAT I CONTINUE. WILL ATTEMPT TO COMMUNICATE AGAIN TOMORROW.

For a few moments silence reigned in the control room. At length Dan himself broke the tense calm.

"Does anyone here know Zak Goldberg? Do we have an assessment of the quality of his information?"

"I never knew him personally, Dan," Rhodes spoke up. "But I was head of the Middle East Intelligence Directorate for a long time. I know his reputation. He's as close to platinum plated as an agent can get. He has intimate knowledge of the lay of the land there. He grew up hanging around places like Rawalpindi, Khandahar, Jalalabad, and Kabul. He knows the customs and speaks the native dialects perfectly. He had a very impressive career with the Marines, and an even more impressive run with the Firm before he went underground in Kabul four years ago. If Zak says it's a credible threat, and about to be put into execution, then it's a credible threat and about to be put into execution. Zak is the best there is." His brow knit together, transmitting his growing worry. Zak's position at the moment didn't sound like a good one.

"Johnson, get the station chief at Islamabad on the line, would you? He can give us the goods," commanded Dan.

After 15 minutes, Johnson gave up. Apparently the President, the Secretary of Defense, the heads of the CIA, FBI, and NSA, and just about everyone else, ranked ahead of Dan's agency. All those who could do so had pulled rank to get to the station chief in Islamabad. As Dan fumed about life's slights and inequities, Rhodes came up with a suggestion.

"Dan, Goldberg has a very close friend. Since childhood, same background — they grew up together in Islamabad. They did the armed forces together, then the CIA. That person happens to be the agent looking after the Libyan Semtex project."

At the mention of the Semtex, Turbee, who had lost interest, was suddenly paying attention again. Rhodes smiled when he saw the attentive gaze snap back onto the *enfant terrible's* face.

"You mean Richard Lawrence?" asked Dan.

"The very same. Get Johnson to dial him up. He'll probably give you the straight story."

"Over to you, Johnson," Dan ordered.

Five minutes later, Richard answered his phone. The call was routed through TTIC's state-of-the-art control room speaker system, so that everyone could hear the call.

"Richard, this is Dan Alexander of TTIC. Could I ask you–"

"T-who?" came the impatient voice.

"TTIC," repeated Dan. "The Terrorist–"

"Sorry. Don't want any. I'm in the middle of important stuff here." There was a sharp click as Richard hung up.

There were eye rolls from almost everyone except Turbee. This was humor he could recognize; this was Homer Simpson. His shrieking laughter cut through the silence in the room.

"Turbee, shut the fuck up. Johnson, get that asshole back on the line." Dan rubbed his temples, trying desperately to think around Turbee's laughter.

In due course Johnson did get Richard back on the line. This time Rhodes led the charge, and the interview went a bit more successfully.

"Richard, you know Zak Goldberg better than anyone. He's given us some disconcerting information about a possible terrorist strike. I can't go into details with you here and now, but can you tell me your view as to the reliability, the quality of Intel passed along by him?"

"Sure, that I can answer. I've been in this business for years. I've known Zak all my life. There is no one finer, none more careful. He's doing what he's doing right now because he is the best. If he says there's going to be a terrorist attack, and gives you chapter and verse, then it's going to happen, unless you stop it. Period."

Similar validation and corroboration was being received up and down the command chain. If Goldberg said it, you could take it to the bank. This was the real deal.

3

THEY HAD BEEN CLIMBING since dawn. They were a small party of four on horseback, in the Sefid Koh range just northeast of Mount Sikarim. The Daka Plain lay more than 2,000 feet below them. The roofs and minarets of Jalalabad reflected the light of the rising sun, now that the early morning fog had started to burn away. The Kabul River could be seen weaving its serpentine course through the ancient city, and the view of the Hindu Kush was breathtaking. The Khyber Pass lay northeast, and the tiny village of Haft Chah, which clung to the western slopes leading to the pass itself, was just visible. The party had stopped for a few minutes to give the horses time to rest and graze on the mountain bluegrass.

Zachariah Goldberg was one of the horsemen. Zak's father, Joe Goldberg, had been one of the CIA officers in charge of advising and assisting Afghani resistance groups in their insurgency against the Soviet invasion. It was rumored that Joe had met Osama bin Laden himself, when the villain had still been favored by the Intelligence Community. Once upon a time, bin Laden had been the enemy of the enemy, and the closest thing the US had to a friend in the area.

In the course of his journeys through the Middle East, Joe had met Zak's mother, a stunning Pashtun woman from Kabul. Zak was a product of that union. When Afghanistan began to destabilize, Joe moved his family to Islamabad, and ultimately settled there. With Zak's parents being stationed in Islamabad alongside Richard's, it was natural that Zak and Richard, being of the same age and inclination, had become good friends. Their relationship had remained close, and always affectionately competitive. It was a competition in which Zak usually came out ahead. If Richard ran a seven-minute mile, Zak did it in 6.45. If Richard benched 100 pounds, Zak did 125. If Richard scored 92 percent on a physics exam, Zak scored 95 percent. Zak was slightly taller than Richard, and had the broad shoulders, clean-cut good looks, and dark blue eyes of a born leader. Richard was younger by a couple of months, and naturally fell into a secondary role in their friendship. He never took their competitions seriously, choosing instead to look up to Zak for his talents, and enjoying the fact that they could push each other to greater and greater heights. Over time he'd come to view Zak as the older brother he'd never had, turning to him for guidance and support in times of trouble.

They'd both ended up in California in their late teens. Zak went because his parents wanted a safer and more secure environment for their son. Richard had gone to California to live with the Goldbergs when his parents were killed in a car accident. If he thought of Zak as his brother, he considered Joe and his wife to be stepparents. When they became older, there were periods when the two men saw little of each other, as Zak went to the Marines and Richard went to the Navy, but they had stayed in touch. They had always been able to count on each other, regardless of their situations or locale.

Both eventually went to the CIA, and, in one of those strange coincidences of life, both returned to the Islamabad Embassy in response to acts of terrorism against the USA. They both had the language skills and knowledge of that country that the Intelligence Community so desperately needed. Zak, who had the greater ability and promise, went undercover, first in Kabul and then in Jalalabad. He proved to be a brilliant and courageous operative who, over the years, gravitated closer and closer to important inner circles in Afghanistan and Pakistan. Richard would have followed suit, but there were growing concerns about his ability to remain cool under fire, and there were whispers about a substance abuse problem of some kind. Now Zak hadn't seen or heard from Richard in almost four years; his status as an undercover agent kept him from contacting anyone from home. He'd heard the rumors, before he went under. But he still considered Richard to be his brother and closest friend. He missed the man.

Since leaving traditional service and going undercover, Zak's path had twisted and turned, leading him to now find himself with three other horsemen, standing at the fork of a rocky trail, enjoying the majestic view and sipping water from their canteens. With Zak were Yousseff, his lieutenant Marak, and Ghullam, Marak's right hand and protégé. The other men were speaking about the *Haramosh Star,* a ship that was currently concluding a refit at Karachi Drydock and Engineering, Yousseff's private Skunk Works. There were great plans in store for the ship. Yousseff himself was the mind behind a vast drug-fueled business enterprise and, had statistics of such things been kept, was the single largest employer in northern Afghanistan and Pakistan. The US government had been interested in his drug smuggling activities for some time, although there was no concrete information on him. Zak's mission in this circle was to get close enough to Yousseff to bring him down.

Zak looked up, trying to figure out which way they were heading. Ahead of them, a massive cliff of granite rose vertically for almost 5,000 feet, forming a wall between Afghanistan and Pakistan. A slender crack split the granite, and through that crack wound an extremely narrow and dangerous trail — the continuation of the path they were currently on. It was a famous smuggler's route, on which Yousseff was rumored to have grown up. The local people called this thin and treacherous cliff trail the Path of Allah. Horses had to be led through it on foot, and even then only horses that knew the route and traversed the path often made the trip safely. The path was completely invisible from the air, and did not appear on any map. Once the trail passed over the cliff, there was a climb of another 1,000 feet, over the course of half a mile, before the route's completion. The average slope was 45 degrees. It was high mountain country, subject to extreme changes in weather. Even in August, a snowstorm could dump several feet of snow on the pass, rendering it unusable. Travel from mid-October to mid-February was impossible.

To the south, across a flinty bank of shale, the Path of Allah's sister trail led to Mount Sikarim. There too the horses had to be led, the men going on foot; it was too dangerous to ride across the treacherous slope. After half a mile of shale, that path found solid land again. Twelve miles further, after a myriad of false trails, forks, and high mountain passes, lay the Sikarim caves. This was the path they would be taking today.

The others knew Zak as Shayam. He had spent quite a bit of time in the al-Qaeda training camps farther to the south, and had been involved in terrorist raids against Americans. He had distinguished himself in battle, and earned loyalty and trust, by sending his fair share of RPG's into American camps and supply columns. He'd made a career of trying desperately for the near miss, deviating his aim just a fraction to the right or left to minimize damage. Without getting caught. But he had dealt with this eventuality with his commanding officers when he went into the field. He had to maintain his cover, no matter what the circumstances. He had even been on several missions with al-Qaeda into Iran, and was amused at the ease with which the Iranian border opened up for his grim crew. They were even supplied with weapons, apparently by the Iranian army. If he ever returned to Langley, his debriefing would take many months. When he had gone undercover, his orders had been clear, and had come from the highest levels — do what needed to be done to connect with the inner circle of the enemy. This he had done, and over the years he had drawn ever closer to the prize. More than four years undercover. More than four years away from home. Zak sighed deeply. It had been a long road. He hoped to reach the end of it soon, and go home.

Pulling his focus back to the current situation, he let go of the reins and allowed his hand to creep toward his robes. He had with him the GPS Morse code transmitter, hidden deep inside one of his pockets, and started to type out a new message, his hand hidden. He kept his face passive. He knew that those with him were warriors who lived and died by spotting enemy action, even that done in a surreptitious manner, immediately. The risk was huge, but so was the impending threat.

AM HEADING TOWARD EMIR HIDEOUT. EARLIER COMMUNICATION CONFIRMED. TARGET PROBAB–

That was as far as he got. In his effort to conceal what he was doing, he'd been holding his hand at an unnatural angle on the small transmitter. It slipped and flew out of his hand, and through a hole in his cloak, landing on the hard shale and clattering as it bounced off the rocks. Marak looked up instantly, his hard and ruthless eyes scanning the slope to find the cause of the noise. With a quickness that belied his size, he dismounted and threaded his way between the shale and rock to retrieve the small device.

"Yousseff, look at this." Marak held up the small silver device, no larger than a watch, with its two small buttons and softly pulsing red light. Yousseff immediately identified it.

"It is a GPS locator." Yousseff had used similar devices many times in his own business. He motioned to the two other riders. "Who?" he asked.

"Him." Marak pointed to Zak. "It fell out of his *chapan*."

"You, Shayam? You would betray us?" Yousseff shook his head. "Marak, take him," he ordered.

ZAK KNEW the game was up. He would be Shayam no longer. So close, he thought. More than four years getting here. Now here he was, almost on top of the lair, and the mission was disintegrating, thwarted by a hole in a damn cloak. Zak had seen other men caught betraying Yousseff, and knew that the next few hours would not be pleasant. He made the quick decision that he would rather die fighting, and reached for his revolver, a copy of a 9 mm Beretta. He pulled it out and fired a round, but Marak had reached for his own weapon at the same instant, pushing his master to the ground.

"Down Youssi!" he yelled, firing simultaneously.

Zak's bullet only grazed Yousseff's right shoulder. When he fired, his horse bolted at the abrupt noise, and caught Marak's bullet in the neck. It reared in shock and pain, throwing Zak into the hard shale rock, almost at

Marak's feet. The sharp rock he landed on sliced open his thigh.

Pain flooded through him. He saw Marak's massive arms reaching down for him, to yank him up off the stony ground. He could feel blood running down his leg from the wound, and wondered vaguely if the bleeding was serious. Then he forgot about his leg. Marak was a large and powerful man, standing over six feet tall, with the body of a weightlifter and the fists of a boxer. He grabbed Zak by the neck and rammed his enormous fist into his nose, smashing it. A second blow and Zak felt his jaw crack. His nervous system was flooded with piercing waves of pain, then mercifully shut down as he plunged into unconsciousness.

Yousseff reached for the device and examined it. He found the on/off switch and turned it off. "Here is what we need to do," he said, wiping a bead of sweat from his forehead and speaking quickly. "Take this man, Shayam, or whoever he is, along the Path of Allah, and to the dungeon below Inzar Ghar. Extract from him whatever information you can, and drop his body into some remote canyon in the Hindu Kush. Vince will be waiting for me at the shipyard in Karachi, as we've already planned. I need to be there in three days. Marak, Ghullam, be at the Islamabad hangar early tomorrow morning. There will be much to arrange."

"What about you?" asked Ghullam. "Surely you're not going the rest of the way alone?"

"There is no choice, Ghullam. It will be fine. I grew up in these mountains. They are home to me." Yousseff turned again to Marak. "Marak, old friend, you saved my life. Thank you."

"Yousseff, you have saved mine many times. And in any event, you are the boss," replied Marak. "You do recall that, don't you?" he added with a grin, rather sheepishly rubbing the back of his head with his hand.

"Yes I do remember," said Yousseff, looking down on Jalalabad. For a few moments he grew quiet as his mind wandered back. "Yes I do." He had never forgotten it. He allowed his mind to return to the childhood fight that had shaped his life. The day he had learned never to be where his adversaries assumed he would be. Now he based his life on that principle, and his vast smuggling operations incorporated the theme over and over again.

YOUSSEFF SAID AL-SABBHAN was 12, and weighed in at 87 pounds. Marak el Ghazi was 14, and weighed over 110. Yousseff, while physically quick, was no match for Marak's snake-like reflexes, or his much greater physical strength. Marak had already earned the nickname *Rasta*, which meant "snake." If the match had been taking place in Las Vegas, the odds would have been 50:1, or worse, against Youssef. The younger boy knew this, but had no choice. Marak had cast dishonor on Youssef's family by calling one of his sisters a whore. When Youssef had demanded an apology, Marak had responded by calling all of his sisters, and his mother, whores. He had then continued the taunting, saying that he would only apologize if he was forced to. Marak had challenged Youssef to fight, and the small boy had accepted. He now regretted having acted so impulsively. He knew he had no chance of winning, much less coming out undamaged. But the duel had been set. The Four Cedars. Noon. Tomorrow.

"Youssi," said Izzy, the little friend who had been faithful since his earliest memories. "What are you going to do? He's twice your size, and mean as a cornered dog. He'll kill you!"

"Don't know, Iz. But I can't back down."

"Youssi, please don't," sobbed Rika, the bright-eyed ten-year-old girl who thought she was in love with him. "He's too big, he's too mean. Don't."

"Rika, he has called my sisters whores. He can't get away with that."

The Four Cedars was in fact a small cedar grove just south of Jalalabad. The space marked by the four trees formed a large arena, about 20 feet square in dimension. Schoolboys often settled disputes there; the statement "I'll see you at the Four Cedars" was clearly understood as a call to battle. Youssef knew the area well — not from fighting, which he was not interested in or good at, but from the climbing that he loved. He had spent many delicious afternoons perched in the tops of these cedar trees. There was a special group of branches near the crown of one of the trees that permitted him to lie securely, flat on his back, more than 60 feet above the ground. He loved to gaze upwards at the clouds and feel the gentle rocking motion of the tree in the wind, drifting, free from gravity. He had made a bet with one of his friends earlier that year that he could scoot to the top of one of the trees and make it back down in less than 20 seconds, and won. When Marak had said to name the place, he, for reasons he did not understand, had named the Four Cedars. Maybe instinctively he had felt that battles are more easily fought on home turf. The Four Cedars were more a home to him than to Marak, albeit from a different vantage point.

On the day before the fight, as the shadows were lengthening, Youssef went to the Four Cedars. He walked around the area once, slowly. He kicked the turf and mentally measured distances. He knew that he needed an edge, any possible advantage. He measured the area again and again, looking for an equalizer. He climbed up one of the trees and looked down on the arena, then went down and looked skyward at the tree branches. At midnight he was still there, walking, measuring, and thinking. He was going to have only one chance. One shot. One move. He would have to focus all his power and concentration on that one move, and make it count. It would be a gamble, but there was only one way forward. If he miscalculated, it would be over, and he would find himself paying a severe price. Once he had his plan, he practiced it over and over again. One shot. He made a few minor alterations to the scene, and went through it again. More alterations, more practice. Eventually he walked home, head down, deep in thought. It was well past 2AM.

It was still morning when the first spectators started showing up for the battle. Word had spread through the entire school community — this was going to be a "biggie." Yousseff was going to be utterly destroyed by Marak. It was going to be great sport, royal entertainment. Secretly, everyone wanted Marak to be soundly thrashed. Realistically, they knew that it was simply not going to happen. No one wanted Yousseff to be seriously hurt, either, as he was well liked. But, at the end of the day, they all believed that Yousseff would take some shots to the head, cry "uncle," and that Marak would continue to make lewd remarks about and to his sisters. After a week or two, he would get bored with the sport and switch to terrorizing someone else. Life for children in a small town on the border of Afghanistan was not that different from life in any country's small town.

The gathering crowd was met by an odd sight. A large, round stone, some four feet in height, had been rolled into the arena, and Yousseff was perched upon it, silent and unmoving. A number of the children laughed and poked fun at him. "Praying to the gods before your demise?" they asked. There were questions about where the stone had come from, and what on earth he thought he was doing, but Yousseff sat, unmoving and unresponsive.

Eventually even Izzy prompted him, trying to get some reaction from the silent boy. "Youss, he's coming. Do something," he whispered. But still Yousseff did not move.

Izzy turned to Rika, whose eyes were red from crying. "He's gone crazy, Rik. He is so fearful that he is now mad."

Rika called to Yousseff. "Youssi. Youss. Do something! This is crazy." She came to the base of the rock. "Youssi, he will kill you." But Yousseff remained impassive. Or did he? Rika stared closely at her friend. She could have sworn that he'd winked at her.

At length, amidst a crowd of friends, well-wishers, and a few of the older girls from the community school, Marak arrived. He snorted with laughter when he saw the immobile Yousseff, sitting quietly on a large rock in the center of the arena. The crowd moved back to the perimeter of the circle, and the noise diminished until there was a tense silence. The only sound was the wind in the trees, and the distant waters of the Kabul River. After a minute of uncomfortable silence, Marak spoke.

"Hey, look. A little Buddha, sitting on a rock. Does little Buddha want to play?" He gave Yousseff a rough shove, but Yousseff said and did nothing. A harder shove almost knocked Yousseff off the rock. Still Yousseff neither moved nor spoke.

"Okay then, soft little boy with no penis, I must go and give that little dock whore sister of yours some pleasure. Then maybe satisfy your ugly mother too, since your father can't."

Yousseff remained mute and motionless.

"Fine then, soft little girl. I am going." Marak turned to leave.

As Marak began to walk away, Yousseff finally stood up. The rock itself was very large, and it had taken Yousseff several hours of hard work to roll it into the center of the arena. But now he had the advantage of looking down on his opponent.

"Ahh," said Marak. "The little boy wants to play after all. Well, we'll play. Then I shall go please your sister."

Yousseff looked directly at Marak, but still said nothing. Marak took a fighter's stance, curled his hands into fists, and shifted his weight rapidly from foot to foot.

"Let's go, little lamb. Time to play," he mocked.

Yousseff continued to look at him, but remained in the same position, relaxed and with his hands at his sides. Marak feigned one or two imaginary punches in Yousseff's direction, then a few more.

"Come on, little boy," he said more aggressively. Still Yousseff remained unmoving, his feet resting on the rock, four feet above the ground upon which the ever more agitated Marak danced. The punches hit the air in flurries, with no reaction from Yousseff. Eventually a few punches landed on Yousseff's shins, first lightly, then with increasing intensity. Still there was no reaction from Yousseff. Finally Marak turned and walked away from the stone, his hands in the air.

"I guess the little piece of worm vomit wants me to pleasure his sister and mother after all," he said. There was general laughter and some booing from the crowd. Then, as Marak was about to leave the perimeter of the Four

Cedars, Yousseff spoke.

"Marak, we are having a fight. It is not over. Are you walking away from me? Are you unwilling to fight me? Are you acknowledging defeat?"

Marak stopped in his tracks, the blood rushing to his face. "What?" he thundered.

"We're having a fight. Are you walking off the battlefield? Only a sick little coward with a dog for a mother and a pig for a father does that."

"That's it. Now you die." Marak came rushing at Yousseff, and launched himself directly at the smaller boy, aiming for his knees, to bring him off his perch American-football style. Marak felt a glorious surge of power and adrenalin as he rocketed toward Yousseff. But when he got there, Yousseff had disappeared. As he sailed forward over the rock, Marak felt blinding pain in his lower back, in both kidneys. There was a shattering blow on the back of his head, then a second, and a third. He quickly started to pray for unconsciousness.

The battle was recalled by many people over many years, and was embellished some in each retelling. Yousseff himself recalled the truth of it for the rest of his life. When Marak came charging, Yousseff had emptied his mind. His field of vision had narrowed, and his focus came to include only the image of Marak hurtling toward him. "One shot, one shot," was his mantra.

At the last possible instant before contact, Yousseff jumped straight up and threw his arms skyward, with open hands. Maybe it was luck, or maybe it was the practicing that he had done. His outstretched hands grabbed a lower bough of one of the large cedars, a branch whose position he had memorized, and in one move he pulled himself another foot upwards. As he had anticipated, Marak's momentum caused him to fall on the large rock. Looking down, Yousseff let his body drop downward, using the large branch as leverage. He rammed the heels of his boots into Marak's kidneys as hard as he could. Yousseff was a voracious reader; he'd read every book in the small school library, and in the small public library in Jalalabad. He knew some anatomy, and knew what a hard blow to the kidneys could do, especially if it was unexpected. In the moment of pain and disorientation that followed, Yousseff dropped out of the tree to the ground, where he had left a few strategically placed rocks around the base of the larger stone. He grabbed one and smashed it with all his might across the back of Marak's head, once, twice, three times. Then, for good measure, he gave the larger boy a tremendous whack across the forehead. As Marak fell off the large central rock, screaming and clutching his head, Yousseff kicked him as hard as he could in his exposed groin, and then delivered a final vicious kick to Marak's head.

Youssef stood over the incapacitated, grievously wounded and bleeding Marak. Copious amounts of blood flowed from his head wounds. Youssef held the stone above Marak's head.

"Apologize to my sisters. Apologize now or you will die."

Between moans and sobs, Marak did indeed apologize. Not only to Youssef's sisters, but to his mother, to his father, and to him.

"You are my servant, Marak. Say it."

Marak said this too, and in saying it Marak obeyed the Pashtun tradition of *nanwatal*. Absolute submission of the vanquished to the victor; the loser goes to the winner in utter humility and begs for forgiveness, after which his dignity is considered restored. The winner must accept this, and put aside the differences that had divided them. This was known more specifically in the tribal lands as the way of *badal*. Youssef knew the politics of *badal* and *nanwatal* very well, and would use them effectively throughout his life. It was *badal* and *nanwatal* that made Marak his servant at a very early age.

Youssef extended a hand to him, squeezed his shoulder, and said to some of the others, "Clean him up."

The speed and ferocity of Youssef's attack astounded everyone present, and Marak most of all. Youssef had never fought before, and had no history of violence that anyone could recall. Marak was vastly superior to Youssef physically, and fought constantly, deriving great pleasure from it. Yet, in the space of five seconds, Marak lay on the ground between the Four Cedars, a moaning, weeping mess. On that day, Youssef gained the respect of the children around him and became Marak's master. It was a relationship from which they would both profit for years to come.

4

THE COUNTDOWN had been initiated. The audience was diverse and colorful, consisting of the locals from Bazemah (most of the town had turned out), military people from both Libya and the United States, munitions experts, and Richard and his small crew of CIA personnel. A small village of reporters from around the world was also assembled and, of course, Minyar himself, for the benefit of the media and his image. With him, Minyar had a large entourage of security people, counselors, military representatives, and various assistants. A festive atmosphere prevailed.

McMurray had set up monitors to project the countdown that was taking place on a Dell laptop, now ten miles away at Ground Zero. The final countdown had begun. Ten. Nine. Eight…

IT WAS STILL PRE-DAWN at the RCMP complex in Vancouver. Indy smiled as he hung up his telephone. At present he was appreciating that, as so often happens in police work, an amazing lead had just fallen into his lap. He had been speaking with Catherine Gray. She was 30 years old and already a Corporal, running the drug section in the Kootenays, headquartered in Cranbrook, BC. She was at work at 6AM, and was as obsessed with finding "the hole" in the border as Indy was. Now maybe, just maybe, she had found something.

"We had a strange situation out of Fernie last week," Catherine told him. Fernie was a small but scenic mountain town located in the BC Rockies, near the Alberta and Montana borders.

"A man named Benny Hallett showed up at the local clinic with a grossly infected knee. Osteomyelitis, that's what the doctors said. A dangerous bone infection. He'd been involved in some kind of accident. Somehow he shot himself, or someone shot him in the knee. He was moved to Vancouver General. He's there right now." She was speaking in rushed and excited tones.

Vancouver General Hospital happened to be a ten-minute walk from Indy's Heather Street complex. A short morning stroll. "Well, what's so strange about that?" Indy asked. "Gunshot accidents are not all that unusual. Accidents happen all the time."

When she told him what she meant, and who Benny Hallett was, Indy was definitely curious. "I'll check him out," he said. He was in such a rush to grab his coat and get out the door that he forgot to turn off the small television sitting in the corner of his cubicle-sized office. "Seven, six, five..." chanted the CBC reporter, live from the Libyan desert.

IT WAS 9AM IN WASHINGTON, DC. Turbee had stumbled in to work ten minutes earlier. He was paler than usual, and there were deep black circles under his eyes. He hadn't gone out, partied, or done whatever it was his age group did. He just hadn't slept. Sleep had never come easy for him, and sometimes it was downright impossible. His mind would become obsessed with a mathematical problem and refuse to let go, for days on end. He would pace, talk to himself, and fret at a computer screen all night in his small apartment. In one of these sleepless episodes a few years earlier, he had worked for seven days straight, cobbling together a series of fuzzy search algorithms that had made him millions of dollars. This tendency didn't bother him as much as it would have bothered someone else — the lack of sleep was bearable. It was the autism and fear of social situations that actually kept him from leading a normal life. The Paxil and Ritalin derivatives he took for his autism didn't help much with the sleeping, but without them life would have been unbearable, for both him and those around him. He would never have been able to function, even minimally, in the loud TTIC control room.

Dan and the rest of his crew had been at their stations since 6:30 or 7AM. The director glanced up coldly as Turbee entered, one shoelace untied, and unshaven. Was he wearing the same clothes as yesterday? Did he sleep in those jeans? Did he ever even comb his hair? Dan's disapproving observations were short-lived, as the countdown on the other side of the planet reached its final stages. The large central screens all showed the unfolding drama in Bazemah. One screen was tuned to CNN, two others to BBC and Libya's own national television network. The countdown was in full swing.

"Four, three, two..." muttered Turbee, sitting down and looking up for long enough to notice what was going on in the world.

THE LOWER SIKARIM CAVES were well lit. They had been created millions of years earlier by mountain run-off penetrating the softer limestone, carving out a cave system that reached for endless miles and to unknown depths. The supply of water was endless and pure, and the power generated by the waterfalls was plentiful. The complex that had been built there had its own hydroelectric generators, utilizing one of the many waterfalls that cascaded from Mount Sikarim. Miles of electrical cable ran through the tunnels, distributing the power rendered by that generator. The cave system's lower entrance was only 12 miles south of the ancient smuggler's trail, but was impossible to find without one of the local peasant guides. The main cave opening was hidden beneath cliff formations and foliage, and was used sparingly. Still, its occupants were constantly surveying the skies for the Predator Drones of the enemy. They knew that the Great Satan was corrupt and morally bankrupt, but devilishly clever. And they did not want this hideout discovered.

The people who tended the Emir lived in these caves. There was a large kitchen, stocked with many provisions. This was where the bread was baked, and the vegetables and meats stored. There were sleeping quarters for a number of servants in the various smaller caves. Passageways connecting the rooms to different areas and other passageways made a maze of the endless cave system.

Food and servants were not the only things housed here. Enough ammunition and material to wage a devastating terrorist attack had been built up over the years. The caves had also given the local peasants shelter from many an invading army, and were set up to take in a large number of people with little or no advance notice. Any invader gained control only of the plains and river valleys. The Pashtun people, Yousseff's people, had never been controlled or ruled by anyone. They had not been conquered or dominated by Alexander the Great, the Mongols, the English, the powerful and mechanized Soviet Army, the Taliban, or the Americans, with all their fabulous war technology. The caves were vast and complex, and unarguably under the sole dominion of the Pashtun mountain people. Many countries had conquered Afghanistan; none had conquered these mountains, the caves within them, or the people who took shelter there.

The upper caves were more than a mile removed from the lower entrance, and over 1,000 feet higher. The routes were complex; there were many paths and tunnel openings along the climb. Only the experienced guides knew the route from the lower caves to the upper. The Emir made this walk daily, for exercise and discipline. The upper cave opened onto the northeastern wall of the mountain, and provided a breathtaking view of the Kabul River Valley, with Kabul in the distance, and the soaring Hindu Kush beyond. It broke into a cliff wall that was more than 3,000 feet in height and was so sheer that no man had yet climbed it. The opening was more than 20 feet wide, and 12 feet high, and the cliff wall angled out over it, making the cave invisible from the sky. Only a low flight pass through the valley, with dangerous and unpredictable crosswinds and along precisely the correct angle, would reveal it. Even then it appeared to be only an innocent recession in the cliff wall. The Emir had spent many hours on this very cliff edge, in solitary study and silent meditation, without fear of discovery. There was seldom any activity in this highest reach. It was here that the meeting was going to take place.

When Yousseff entered the chamber, he found the Emir sitting robed and cross-legged on the floor, his beard long, his one living eye a deep black orb, recessed in a crevassed face. The other eye was white and dead, burned and destroyed by torturers many years earlier. He sat with his Egyptian and Pakistani engineers. At the outer perimeter of the large cave stood the Emir's armed guards.

The Emir saw Yousseff appear in the doorway, and motioned for him to sit down. The cave floor was richly carpeted, and tapestries hung on the walls. It was lit with soft lights, creating fleeting reflections on weathered tribal faces. One set of electrical cables ran along the wall, leading to the other caves. Yousseff observed all of this silently, making himself familiar with his surroundings, and then sat down across from the Emir.

The Emir had been born Gul Zhar Samaradan. As a child he studied in the Madrasas in Pakistan, but in the early '80s he had joined with many of his colleagues and taken up arms against the invading Soviets. He fought courageously and well and was held in high regard by his clan when the Soviets left. He had been an important part of the Taliban takeover in Afghanistan. Then, in the wake of the terrorist attacks on America, he'd been captured by the Americans. It was thought at the time that he knew the whereabouts of the terrorists responsible for the attacks. The Americans sought to extract this information from him, but to no avail. The CIA had eventually decided to send him to a military base in Uzbekistan. The secret police of that nation were advanced and very effective in the art of questioning their prisoners.

The Emir had ultimately escaped, but not before losing, in a most painful way, toes from both feet, a number of fingers, and the sight in one eye. His back was a mass of scars, and his genitalia were covered with the scars of third-degree electrical burns. He returned to the mountains of the Sefid Koh a changed man, harder, more determined, and consumed with rage against, above all, the Americans.

This was the man with whom Yousseff was now doing business. For several minutes after his entrance, no one spoke. Yousseff was intently studying the plans and diagrams he had been handed, and hadn't yet greeted the others.

At length the Emir broke the silence.

"Can you do it?" he asked Youssef.

"Yes, I think I can. We already have the Semtex. But this plot will take much planning, and many people will have to be involved," Youssef replied. His face remained passive, but his brain had kicked into overdrive. The possibilities. The magnificent possibilities. When he had first received the messages from the Emir, inviting him to take control of this mission, he had been doubtful. He had put some of his people to work on it, and had quickly uncovered the Emir's plans. With the pieces the Emir already had in place, and the connections and funding Youssef himself possessed, he had quickly realized that the plan would work. And that he would make a fortune in the execution of the mission. It had all started with the simple theft of the Semtex. This hadn't been difficult. The Emir's tendrils ran far afield, and were powerful enough to find supporters within Libya's Benghazi Marine Base, in the warehouse where a substantial portion of the Semtex had been stored. From the point of the theft it would be a race against time; his people would be running a gauntlet, focused on a destination that would take them through dangers too numerous to mention. But it could be done. And the Emir would make it worthwhile.

Youssef was here to finalize the arrangements, and to start negotiations regarding control of the mission and payment for his time and efforts. He didn't tell the Emir that he had already set his own pieces in motion.

"We have six people undercover in California," the Emir said, interrupting Youssef's thoughts. "Four of them have been in place for many years. Here is the name of the leader, and his telephone number, and the code sequence. Two of them are licensed and have experience driving large trucks." The Emir handed Youssef a sheet of paper with the information. "The other two live at the Grand Mosque of south Los Angeles. Here is the number of their caretaker. You should use them for any delivery needs."

"Thank you, this will help." Youssef tucked the folded sheet of paper into a pocket. He looked at the blueprints and then at the engineers. "Are you certain that a bomb of this design can destroy the structure?" he asked the engineers.

"Yes," replied one. "But the tolerances must be exact. There can be no deviation. Even a change by as little as one millimeter would alter the focus of the blast, and the structure would withstand the attack. And more importantly, the weapon must be placed at precisely the right spot. Again, small deviations will cause the mission to fail." He pointed to a number of the plans scattered around the floor of the cave.

Youssef looked at the Emir. "I can have the weapon built. I will use your people to deliver the explosives. If your engineers are correct, I can do the rest."

"I can assure you, sir, that if you build the weapon according to these specifications, and place it where we say it should be placed, the structure will fail catastrophically. We have obtained the weapon design directly from Livermore Laboratories in the United States. We have independently reached the same result. This weapon will destroy that structure," one of the engineers said, with some vigor. "That is a certainty."

"Once the structure is destroyed, a large part of America will fall into chaos, and the loss of life and property will be significant. It will far surpass what our warriors have already done," said the Emir. He gazed directly at Youssef with a smoldering look. "Far surpass."

Youssef shook his head at the madness that burned in the man's eye. He was not doing this for religious or political reasons, and could not understand those who did. "I will have great expenses, and will incur grave risk. Any of my men may be injured, incarcerated, or killed," he replied in soft and even tones. "My ships might be seized, my airplanes shot down. Men have already died. I require funds for this operation."

The Emir grimaced as though he had just swallowed something bitter. It is always about the money, he thought to himself. Always money. He looked at Youssef, his one good eye blazing. "How much?"

"Twenty-five million American dollars," Youssef answered, his face showing no emotion whatsoever. "To be transferred to this account as soon as your messengers can do it." He handed the Emir a sheet of paper with banking particulars.

"Do it," the Emir snapped to one of his hirelings. "Get someone to Jalalabad and see that it is done."

One of the engineers picked up a laptop and sent an email to the lower caves, where a servant received it and scrambled onto a horse for the ride to Jalalabad. As soon as the servant reached the city, he would make the appropriate transfers, through a discrete Caribbean bank. It was as good as done. Youssef knew that the Emir didn't care for money. A mistake, he thought. The Emir wanted power. Yet power was money, and money was power.

"It will be done before the sun sets today," the Emir confirmed.

Youssef considered for a moment. "I will require details of the engineering plans and of the structure itself," he said at length.

One of the engineers handed Youssef a DVD. "Everything is on this," he said.

Youssef reached for it and smiled. "Thank you." He waited silently for a few moments. Then he spoke again. "There is something else I need."

"What is it?" asked the Emir.

"It is a simple matter, especially for these people and their computers. I need information to start floating about on the Internet. I need the Great Satan to be looking for us elsewhere. I need the Americans looking to the East, when I will be traveling in the West."

One of the engineers nodded. "We can do this," he said.

"And can you convince the faithful from other countries to collaborate?" asked Youssef.

The reply was quick in coming. "Yes, we can."

"I will need someone with great computer skills. I need to plant false trails when the Americans come. I need the best you have," added Youssef, softly stroking his forehead. He had a headache. He needed to relax.

Two of the engineers looked at each other, nodded, and said as one, "Vijay Mahendra. In Rawalpindi."

"Have him contact me," replied Youssef. "He can reach me through Rasta, at the number you already have. There must be no delay. We are already in motion. He must meet me at my Islamabad hangar tomorrow at sunrise." He intentionally used Marak's nickname — the only name the Emir and his people had been given. In situations like this it was important for Youssef and his associates to keep their true identities hidden.

The Emir motioned to one of the young guards who stood on the outside of the chamber. "Go to Jalalabad," he barked in sharp tones. "Immediately. Go to our people there and contact Vijay by telephone to give him the directions. Tell him it is my command."

"Yes, Emir," came the sharp retort, and the young man was gone.

Youssef was already bidding farewell and readying himself for the long trek back to the Islamabad hangar. He wanted to travel alone and work everything out — it was the only way he would be able to organize his thoughts and go over his plans. A golden opportunity had presented itself. The Emir wanted to destroy, to create chaos for the Great Satan, to wage a *jihad*. He could give the Emir what he desired, and in the process, he could vastly increase his own wealth and empire. He needed to think, to chase the dragon, to plot things out in the fluidity of opium dreams as he always did when he was faced with a big decision.

"Let the prophet's words be wings to your feet. And may Allah be with you on this, the most noble of tasks," the Emir blessed him, smiling in his condescending way.

Yousseff smiled back. He didn't care for this half-mad old man and his barren religion. Yousseff cared only about one thing — money. It bought power and safety. This particular plan would bring him an avalanche of money. The $25 million was just a small down payment. Maybe the crazy old man knew this. Maybe they were just using each other. Then again, that was how the game was played, wasn't it?

"And may He also be with you," he replied.

Yousseff bowed and left the room, the DVD tucked away in an inner pocket of his coat. He thought again of his great battle with Marak so many years ago, and the lesson he had learned. Impossible odds, yes, but with clarity of mind and precise planning he could do this. One shot, and he would be one of the wealthiest and most powerful men on the planet. One shot, one move. And it would not be the move the world was expecting.

The Emir returned to his upper chamber and sat in meditation, his gaze drifting over the unending peaks of the Hindu Kush. He felt a stirring in his soul. Truly, one day of *jihad* was better than a thousand years of prayer in the mosque. Much better.

THOUSANDS OF MILES to the east, a string of zeroes flashed across the screen of McMurray's computer.

5

AT ZERO HOUR the Dell sent an electronic signal to a series port replicator, which forwarded simultaneous signals to the bank of Amptec timers, which in turn sent instantaneous, but much more powerful, signals to the fusing cables. From there the line went to the archipelago of more or less equidistant blasting caps embedded within the monstrous pile of Semtex, and a chemical reaction took place that, notwithstanding its robust disposition, the Dell would not survive.

The Semtex was an amalgam of two different explosive compounds, PETN and RDX, held together by an oil-based bonding agent. The two chemicals were relatively stable, even combined, and were therefore reasonably safe to handle. The bonding agent gave the material its elasticity, and hence its utility. But when an initial shock such as that provided by the ignition of a blasting cap occurred, the compound became far from stable. The shock would compress the highly explosive material, heating it, and causing dangerous chemical changes. These changes would then release an enormous amount of energy; a process that would sustain and build a shock wave, which would travel at a supersonic velocity, producing rapidly expanding hot gasses in its wake. In that brief instant of detonation, the shock wave would turn out pressures of up to half a million atmospheres, traveling at ten kilometers per second. Temperatures would reach 5,000 degrees Celsius, with power approaching 20 billion watts per square centimeter. Modern science still did not understand all that happened on the edge of such a chemical reaction, which was why a team from Livermore Laboratories was hoping to be present in the desert for the Semtex detonation.

It wasn't anyone's fault when the explosion didn't go as expected. No one could have taken into account McMurray's positioning of the blasting caps, or the lens-like effect they would have, especially within a pyramid-shaped mass. This was just one of the reasons that Turbee's calculations on the crater size turned out to be a little off. No one fully appreciated how much explosive 660 tons of Semtex really was. Until now.

The pressure wave, traveling at a little less than six miles per second, arrived at the control area in less than a second. Richard, McMurray, and their men were sheltered behind a small convoy of Humvees. The shock almost lifted the heavy vehicles off the ground, and they were all shoved back a few inches. Cameramen foolhardy enough to be standing in unprotected areas were knocked off their feet. General Minyar's tent almost became unattached, and received an unwelcome storm of sand in its interior.

It took 15 seconds more for the sound to reach the encampment. It came as a sharp crash, followed by a low rumbling that sounded like thunder. The initial pressure wave had created a dust storm, and it took several minutes for the cloud to subside. Looking toward Ground Zero, McMurray could see a well-defined mushroom cloud, reaching to a height of more than a mile above the blast site. Seismographs as far away as Tel Aviv and Ankara picked up the blast. The only feature distinguishing the detonation from a nuclear warhead was the lack of radiation. They hoped.

"Holy shit, Richard," McMurray breathed.

Richard was likewise impressed. The Livermore Labs and the Army and Air Force high explosive research facilities were going to have a lot to analyze. And beyond that, the planning gnomes in the Pentagon would be looking at this. It wouldn't cost a lot of money (in Pentagon terms) to detonate a few thousand kilos of high explosives. The military could have bombs as powerful as small nuclear devices, without all the unpleasant publicity that using that kind of weapon created. As Richard watched the aftermath, he realized what else this explosion might mean. He quailed at the thought of anyone other than the American government ever getting their hands on that much explosive, or even a fraction of it. If he was right, and there was Semtex missing… who had it, and what terrible things might they be planning to do with it? If someone had taken the time to steal Semtex, they probably already had a move in mind. It was bad enough that this particular explosion had taken place in Libya, one of the most aggressive terrorist nations in the world.

Richard retrieved his tallies, which he'd dropped during the chaos of the explosion. What White House idiot had decided to keep this much explosive sitting around in the Middle East, anyhow? He grunted to himself, pressing his fingers against his eyes and trying to think. Those assholes had been asking for trouble from the start.

Minyar himself, as he was picking himself up off his tent floor and shaking the sand out of his hair, felt a twinge of regret. What if he had packed the stuff on a barge and sent it up the Thames to the British Parliament buildings? Or across the Atlantic, to be detonated underneath the Brooklyn Bridge? Had he passed up the opportunity to become the Twenty-First Century's Saladin, the new sword of Islam? Had he lost the courage and the vision he'd had when he, still in his 20s, seized control of Libya from a crumbling and ineffective monarchy? Had he blown it? This is what he was truly thinking when the microphones and cameras were thrust into his face. What he said was something entirely different.

"This is a great moment for peace. Libya has now joined the community of nations, and is open for trade, oil exploration, and business. A new economic power is being created on the shores of the Mediterranean. A nation that wants to trade and work with the European Economic Community, and with the Americans. A new day is…"

THE DC-3 had just reached Yousseff's island retreat. Mustafa was watching CNN, and General Minyar, from the hangar workshop. "Horse shit for brains," he muttered to himself. Across the world of radical Islam, the reaction was much the same. Another self-proclaimed avenger of Allah selling out, turned to camel dung. Mustafa shook his head and looked around. He had a few hours of work ahead of him, using a helicopter to transfer the Semtex from the DC-3 to the *Mankial Star,* anchored some five miles offshore. Even with the marvelous devices created by Karachi Drydock and Engineering, the work would be heavy. Turning off the TV, he and his men began their labors.

RICHARD WAS ON A SECURE LINE to Jon Duncan, the station chief in Cairo, since Libya didn't yet have an Embassy. Jon had traveled a path parallel to Richard. He was an ex-Marine, and had fought and been wounded in the first Gulf War. Since then he'd moved to the Intelligence Community, and had served in many different offices and departments. The two had met many times, over the course of years, and respected one another. Jon, like so many others, had heard the stories and worried about Richard. They were stories about needing 1,093 feet of runway on a *USS Theodore Roosevelt* runway that was only 1,092 feet long. Stories about too much drinking, and lately, stories about drugs. Stories about a brilliant pilot and a passionate and dedicated soldier who had somehow, for some reason, taken a hard left turn at what should have been the peak of his career. He seemed to dwell too much in the past, still thinking about flying sorties off the flight decks of the Nimitz class carriers, when his life had moved beyond that. Jon had seen it before with other soldiers. Perhaps it was too much war, too much violence.

The truth was that it had all started with Richard's imperfect vision. It was a problem that had presented, for the Navy brass, an easy way to terminate the services of one of its pilots without venturing into more personal and difficult territory. Richard had been a problem for some time; a man who had always had trouble following orders, he had long since developed a problem with drugs and alcohol. It started simply, with a back injury during basic training. It was a minor wedge compression fracture of the thoracic spine, and most of the time he functioned well in spite of it. But occasionally it would flare up and create severe back problems and headaches, and he had found that ever more powerful medication was required to curb the pain. Aspirin led to ibuprofen, then to Codeine, and ultimately to Percocet, Oxycontin, and more powerful synthetic morphine substances. He had quickly discovered that dowsing such chemical concoctions with alcohol made their pain relief capabilities even stronger. The situation could have led to an embarrassing discharge for Richard, and public complications for the Navy. Luckily, his vision problem had provided a convenient cover story for a more honorable end. Jon had been well on his way to a leadership position in Cairo at the time, and a personal friend of Richard's. He'd been called in as a character witness on many of the conversations that led to the man's eventual discharge. He liked to think that he'd helped Richard, in a way, by taking his side during those conversations. Now it looked like he'd be coming to Richard's aid once again.

"How much did you say is unaccounted for, Richard?"

"According to my calculations, it's 4,303 kilos. About 4.5 tons," Richard answered, frowning.

"Jesus," said Jon. "That's a big pile of play dough. Any idea where it went?"

"Jon, at this point it could be as simple as a clerical error. We're going over the inventory sheets again, and double-checking against the delivery slips. But I've got a bad feeling about this. Too much of this stuff was moved too quickly. I think you should let Langley know, just to put them on notice. If that much Semtex went wandering off into the wilderness, there's no telling what might happen. And believe me, I just saw an explosion of this stuff that would blow your mind. We don't want it in the wrong hands." Richard was speaking too fast, and Jon could hear the stress in his voice.

"I know," said Jon. "Lord knows there's enough nasty stuff floating around below the radar screens these days. I'll inform HQ. Let me know if something pops up."

Richard hung up the phone, immensely relieved that Jon would make the call to Baxter.

After that it didn't take long for matters to progress. An hour after the blast, a pilot from the nearby airport barracks of Zighan left his home to take his wife up to see the still-smoking crater. On the way, he came upon the body of the avuncular airport master. A call went to the police constabulary in Zighan, who, suspecting foul play, called the constable in Bazemah. Word filtered up and across the various chains of command, and ultimately Richard heard the news.

A drive along the ancient highway toward Zighan uncovered two Humvees and ten bodies. Soon afterward, they found the Zighan landing strip, and the deserted vehicles there. Ten murders, thought Richard. Eleven if you included the guy at the airport. Someone was serious about this. Someone already knew what the Semtex could do, and they'd gone out of their way to get their hands on some. He'd bet his life that they already had a plan in place for it.

He was back on the phone to Jon later the same day. "Here's what I think happened. We found the two Humvees hidden halfway between Zighan and Bazemah. We found the empty Volvo flat-deck at the Zighan landing strip. That Volvo was used by the Libyan army to transport the Semtex. We also found two Toyota pickups at Zighan, and the airport attendant was murdered."

"I think I can figure it out from there," said Jon.

"Yeah, it ain't rocket science," replied Richard. "They had a plane standing by. The authorities are checking for a flight plan, but nothing so far. I'm going to guess they used an old DC-3. They, whoever they are, loaded the stuff onto the plane, and flew off into the wild blue yonder."

"Think you're right. Time for some police work, Richard. Do you have any idea what time the plane might have taken off?"

"Just a range. There were several loads moved from Benghazi in the past three days. Most of the Semtex was stored up there. The initial indication from the bodies is that the murders probably happened sometime yesterday. We don't have much in the way of forensics here, Jon. We're in the middle of the fucking wilderness."

"Look, given the seriousness of this, I think we'll probably get some cooperation from the Libyans. This doesn't look too good for them, and they'll want it resolved. Maybe they'll allow some of our people over to look at the crime scene. It might give us a better indication of what we're dealing with here. I'll call Bob directly. This is going to move pretty quickly." Jon hung up the phone and dialed Robert Baxter.

Jon knew it would be early morning when the call reached Baxter. He also knew that Baxter would be there. He always was. He worked 70, 80, and 90 hours a week. He had worked through three marriages before he quit trying. He was married to his job, and his greatest fear was his retirement, scheduled to happen in about five years. Baxter was the head of the Middle East and Africa Office, within the CIA. In fact, he had been awarded the position when the brilliant Liam Rhodes had moved over to TTIC. His reaction to the news was the same as Jon's had been.

"How the hell much, Jon?"

"Lawrence says 4,303 kilos."

That was the extent of the conversation. Baxter took a moment to think it over, and fired off an email on the encrypted line.

Jon Duncan of the Cairo bureau advises that Richard Lawrence, who was in charge of the Libyan Semtex destruction operation, advises that 4,303 kilos (aprx. 4.5 tons) has been stolen, likely by a highly organized terrorist operation. We believe that the material, once stolen, was transported by air, likely to Sudanese airspace. We will need NRO and other agencies to assist in search. Three American soldiers were killed. All overseas embassies should be cautioned that a very large amount of plastic high explosive has now entered the terrorist marketplace.

It never occurred to Jon to mention the seven Libyan soldiers who had also been killed, or that one Libyan civilian had died. The email was sent to the CIA executive director, the DDCI, the DCI, the Office of Information Resources and, as an afterthought, to Rhodes at TTIC.

JOHNSON," said Rhodes. "Can you put the email on my screen up on the central 101? We're going to need to talk about this." He was also motioning to Dan.

"You'd better have a look at this, Dan," he said, when the commander finally walked over. "This one looks ugly."

Dan nodded in agreement as he read the email from the large central screen. He motioned to his staff. It was still early in the workday. The latest PDB had been dissected, but nothing else of importance appeared to be happening.

"Could I have everyone's attention please?" Dan asked, rapping his pen on the desk surface. "Let's all have a look at the email on the central 101."

"Here we go," muttered Rhodes to himself.

"Maybe I should start it this way. Rahlson, how much trouble could you cause with 4,303 kilos of Semtex?"

"Well, Dan, I could probably knock the planet off its axis with that much play dough," Rahlson quipped.

Some nervous laughter threaded through the group. "No, Rahlson, not you personally. The garden-variety terrorist. The plane crasher. The train exploder. You know, your basic al-Qaeda death-wish *jihaddist*," Dan clarified.

"Oh, right," retorted Rahlson. "Well let me tell you what you can do with that much of that particular explosive." Derek Rahlson proceeded to give them his Plastic Explosives 101 lecture. He was the closest thing the agency (as he called TTIC) had to James Bond. He was retired from operations now, and had been for a number of years, but in his day he had been involved in many a melee, on both sides of the Iron Curtain. When, to his great disappointment, the curtain fell, he became involved in operations in the Middle East. He had gone behind the lines in the first Gulf War. He knew almost everything that anyone could want to know about firearms, explosives, and barehanded combat. He apparently knew no fear, and had a restlessness about him that was somewhat unsettling. As the only "operations" person at TTIC, he was there because someone in the President's inner circle felt that TTIC needed a "real spook." He reviewed and assessed the operations reports as they came in. Like Turbee, he had initially felt like a fish out of water with the more highbrow TTIC crowd. But he was as bright as any of them, and had a gallows sense of humor that made up for any other perceived inadequacies.

"Let's start with Lockerbie," he began. "Flight 103 was brought down by approximately 11 ounces of Semtex. So 4,303 kilos could theoretically knock down, umm..." He paused for a second, looking for a calculator.

"About 13,769 jumbo jets," Turbee piped up.

"Yeah OK, kid. Something like that. Now, take the Madrid train disaster," he continued. "Each packsack contained, we think, about 50 pounds of plastique. The quantity of Semtex you're talking about would yield about... Turbee, how many 50-pound packets?"

"By my count, 189," replied Turbee.

"That would be enough packsacks to totally destroy the subways of New York, London, Paris, and Tokyo, all at once. London, for one, would be paralyzed for months, because of how many people use the Underground there. New York and Paris would be hit almost as badly. Not to mention the civilians killed in the explosions. It would be a devastating terrorist strike."

"Now hold up a second, Rahlson," said Dan. "I don't believe that theory for a second. Before, when al-Qaeda was at its height, it could pull off multiple strikes simultaneously from different launch points. But not today. We've been kicking the crap out of them for more than five years now. They're pretty much done in Afghanistan, and their leaders, if they're still alive, are hiding in a cave somewhere for fear of detection by the Predator Drones or satellite systems. Their communications are totally compromised. Cell or Sat-cell calls would inevitably be picked up by the NSA, especially with the resources we've devoted to the Middle East in the past years. Internet connectivity is out of the question. Regular telephone communication, or Internet communication, stands in high jeopardy of detection, and everyone knows it. Communication, if it's done at all, has to be done the old-fashioned way, by camel, horseback, and written note. Anything high tech would be intercepted. There is no way that al-Qaeda could possibly take out an entire city, or hit several targets at once."

"Or else that's just what they want us to think," interrupted Rhodes. "Maybe that's precisely where we're weak."

"Well I'm not impressed by the 13,000 jumbo jets thing. There was no airport security to speak of when Lockerbie happened," said Dan. "But it would be impossible to smuggle plastique onto a plane today. Since that idiot shoe bomb affair we have sniffer devices, and dogs for that matter, at most airports. Carry-on baggage is x-rayed and spot searched. Cargo is x-rayed and spot searched. Good luck trying anything like that today. For the past five years it's been next to impossible. The big problems now are runaway nukes and underground anthrax labs. That's what we should be looking for. Not airplane and train bombings. Not a few tons of explosives. That's just plain stupid." Dan waved his hand, brushing off Rahlson's suggestion and the thought of anyone attacking a railway system.

Rhodes thought for a moment. "Suppose, Rahlson… suppose our terrorists were to use all, or substantially all, of the explosive in one strike, rather than spreading it around to several targets. What kind of damage would they do?"

"I'm not completely sure, Liam," shrugged the Cold War warrior. "They could destroy a high-profile target, like the Hancock Center in Chicago, the Transamerica Pyramid in San Francisco, the Brooklyn Bridge, the Golden Gate Bridge, the Statue of Liberty, you name it. The problem they would have is that all of those targets have been designated as high security. It would take a lot of resources on their part to get access to them at all."

"What about non-high-profile, but still very damaging, targets like the

Indian Point Nuclear Power Plant in New York, the LAX or O'Hare airports, or, say, a major dam, pipeline, or chemical processing facility?" Rhodes continued.

"Well, sure," continued Rahlson. "But all of those types of targets also have a high degree of security around them. The Indian Point facility is guarded like Fort Knox, although the general population doesn't know that. And you can forget about anything in DC, given the closed airspace and the fuss about security."

"What about malls, shopping centers, water towers, or just dense downtown cores, like football stadiums, basketball courts…" Rhodes continued, thinking aloud. "Those are all places they could use anthrax as well."

"You can't protect everything all the time," replied Rahlson. "That's what makes terrorism terrorism. As the threat level goes up to Orange, and to Red, the level of protection increases, but you just can't protect it all. That's why we're here, isn't it, Dan? To figure out what they're going to hit before they hit it?"

"That's a nice, succinct way of stating our mandate," replied TTIC's commander. "I guess that's why we're here." Dan picked up the phone and asked for the office of the President's Chief of Staff. "Turbee, as long as we're on this wild goose chase, why don't you see what you can hunt down on Blue Gene," he added, as he was waiting for the call to go through.

6

INDY REACHED THE ORTHOPEDIC WARD of Vancouver General Hospital within 15 minutes, and spoke briefly with the ward's head nurse.

"The amputation was performed last night. The osteomyelitis had become too severe and entrenched, and was threatening to spread. It was an above-the-knee amputation. He's pretty depressed, so go easy on him."

"Thanks, ma'am," replied Indy. "I'll be cool." He went to room 412, where he found Benny Hallett dozing.

"Benny," he said softly, shaking Benny's shoulder. "Benny, we need to talk."

"Screw off," croaked Benny, in a voice laced with resignation and pain. "I don't want to talk to no cops. Not now. Not ever."

Indy was struck by the fact that Benny had immediately recognized his profession, though he was not in uniform and had not introduced himself. The underworld was sensitive to such things. It had always been easy for them to tell, somehow, which side of the law someone came down on. This made it easy, in turn, for the cops to tell whether they were talking to a good citizen or a criminal.

"Benny," he repeated. "I'm Inspector Inderjit Singh, with the RCMP. You need to talk to me more than I need to talk to you. You need to tell me what happened. You need us."

"Oh fuck, a Hindu cop," came the reply. "Double trouble."

Indy didn't react to the slur. He had spent most of his life dealing with racism. He was small of stature, only 5′7″, and had weighed in at 150 pounds when he applied to the Force, just squeaking by the entrance requirements. His background had also been a little sketchy for law enforcement. Growing up as a minority teenager in Toronto had not been easy, and he had gravitated to the East Indian gangs, for protection more than anything else. Bright, eager, and clever, he had been bored with what school had to offer and had quickly fallen into a life of petty crime and drugs. But for the intervention of an experienced social worker, Indy might have lived a short, fast, and high life, ending in deadly addiction, murder, or jail. But, with the assistance of some state-provided mentors from the Force, he had applied, and after much internal debate, been accepted to the academy in Regina, Saskatchewan.

When he finished his basic training, his facility in Punjabi and his knowledge of the gang and drug trade had made him a natural to go undercover. It was a move he'd made with great skill. His work led to the near total destruction of the Vancouver Punjabi trade in narcotics in the '80s. It struck him as ironic that, with his success in eliminating the East Indian drug trade, the Triads from Hong Kong and mainland China had simply taken over. Something was definitely wrong with the nation's drug enforcement agenda. But he shrugged it off and kept going, continuing to serve with distinction, and making the coveted inspector badge by his early 40s.

Indy already knew a great deal about the Halletts, and their cousins the Lestages, two ne'er-do-well families living mostly south of Fernie, on the Corbie-Flathead Forest service road. No one really knew how many Halletts and Lestages there actually were, but the local law enforcement thought that there were perhaps 30 all told. Members of the families kept drifting in and out of Fernie. A fair amount of crossbreeding took place. Petty crime was their stock in trade and they lived on Social Assistance most of the time. Many of the family members had racked up convictions for theft, marijuana possession, assault, and public drunkenness. During the summer months the families jointly operated a bike tour in the fabulous Akamina-Kishinina Provincial Park, located in the extreme southeastern corner of the province, abutting both Alberta and Montana. While it was surrounded by other great parks, such as Banff and Kootenay National Parks, Glacier National Park, and Waterton Provincial Park, the Akamina-Kishinina was remote and seldom talked about, primarily because of its isolation. The only road approaching the park was the Corbie-Flathead, and it did not enter the park itself, but stopped just to the west of it.

The park's very isolation and sparse population made it a prime spot for underworld activity, if you asked Indy.

The Hallett/Lestage operation was grandiosely called the Akamina-Kishinina Bicycle Tour Co. Ltd., and for a small, family-run business it caused the local RCMP detachment in Fernie no end of grief. Tourists were constantly complaining about paying for the tour in advance, then having no tour guide show up at the appointed place and time. Worse yet were the bicyclists that left the Akamina and found no bus waiting to pick them up and take them home. Reports came in that the tour guides were usually smoking marijuana while driving the bus to or from the park, along a roadway that crossed precipitous canyons via perilous and steep switchbacks. Usually the bus developed incapacitating engine problems and the tour would be canceled before reaching its destination, or returned back home to Fernie. There were even complaints of the Hallett/Lestage group stealing bicycles from a business competitor. What troubled Indy, though, was that the operation of the company actually required the application of effort and organization, attributes for which the Hallett/Lestage gang was not well known. He wondered what was going on behind the scenes that would make such an elaborate façade necessary. It was particularly curious that this company charged less than half the cost of any competition, easily driving everyone else out of business.

Catherine Gray had told him that earlier that month Benny Hallett, age 23, had been seen driving around the streets of Fernie in a brand new, cherry red Dodge pick-up, complete with four doors, hemi, long box, and dualies on the back. The truck was tricked out with chrome roll bars, running boards, and driving lights. A stereo to die for, built-in telephone, and computer mapping system rounded out the extras. All told, a vehicle of that sort, a king amongst trucks, would cost at least $60,000 (Canadian).

One of the local constables had become suspicious. He noted a small moniker across the rear license plate advertising the dealership that had sold the vehicle to Benny. A quick telephone call and the officer learned that the new truck had been paid for by way of a draft issued by the Scotia Bank. "Bank draft!" exclaimed the constable. "No way." It was well known that Benny had never had a job in his life. He spent most of his days living off the public purse. And now he'd managed to find some $60,000 to pay for this shiny new toy? Highly unlikely.

The constable pulled Benny over the next time he saw him, and asked where he got the money for the truck. Benny simply said that he had earned it, and told the constable to get lost. The officer had responded by calling Corporal Catherine Gray, the local drug expert, and divulging the story to her. Both agreed that based on facts and the family's shady history, drugs were likely to be involved. But the where and how was a mystery, and there certainly wasn't enough evidence to procure a search warrant. So the matter died, for a while.

Then the burned-out shell of the Dodge was found at the bottom of a mountainous ravine on Highway 43, north of Fernie. About a week later, Benny showed up in the emergency ward of Cranbrook General Hospital, west of Fernie. According to the admitting nurse, Benny had been in bad shape. He'd had a fever of 104. His skin was flushed and dry and he was very, very sick. His knee was a higher order of hell altogether. It appeared that Benny had taken a shot to the knee from a Colt .45 about a week before being admitted. It had been wrapped in what appeared to be a portion of a bedsheet and held together by duct tape. With no medical care or dressing. Once the homemade bandages had been removed, and the knee exposed, it was readily apparent that the wound had become a stinking, festering mass of infection. The kneecap had shattered into multiple fragments. The ligaments were totally disrupted. The head of the tibia was destroyed, as was the medial aspect of the fibula. After careful cleansing and irrigation with saline and various antibiotics, it was obvious that the bone itself was seriously infected, and that Benny was in fact suffering from what was now a life-threatening osteomyelitis infection. Not being qualified to handle anything so complex, Cranbrook General transported Benny to Vancouver by air ambulance. The surgeons there, after a few minutes of consultation, told Benny that it was the leg or his life. The amputation took place half an hour later. That was where things stood when Inspector Inderjit Singh came into the picture.

To Indy it was all transparently obvious. The expensive truck. The destruction of said truck. The "kneecapping," compliments of Mr. 45. Benny had taken money that he shouldn't have, from dangerous people, and had been reprimanded for his mistake. It was a pattern Indy had become familiar with during his many years working the Vancouver and Toronto drug scenes. The question was who got to Benny. And why.

"Benny, you're a mess and I can help you," said Indy softly.

"Yeah. And help me lose the other leg too?" Benny replied. His cousin Leon had visited him only the night before, threatening a slow and painful death if he uttered one syllable to the cops. Talk? He'd rather eat snails, thanks.

"Look, let's just talk for a bit," said Indy quietly. "I don't even want to know who did it. Let's talk about what got you here."

"Whatever, rag head. Whatever." Even in his humbled state, Benny maintained his brittle edge.

"You know, I ran with the gangs when I was a kid. In Toronto. We moved loads of stuff. And some good people were able to set me on a straighter course," said Indy. Slowly, he told Benny bits and pieces of his personal history. It was a wonderful interrogation technique, one that Indy had used in the past. Gradually, Benny started to open up. Maybe it was the Demerol coursing through his system. Maybe it was the need to talk, or the comfort and genuine concern in Indy's soft voice. Or the fact that the inspector was talking about non-taboo subjects, or his great skill at the art of non-violent interrogation. Maybe it was just that Benny actually was a dolt. But ever so slowly, his tongue began to loosen.

"Heroin?" he answered the suggestion Indy had just made. "Maybe. Maybe not. But I'm not going there. I'm not gonna tell you who or how. And I'm sure as hell not gonna tell you why my truck got whacked, or about the bullet in my leg. It was all an accident, that's all. An accident."

Indy smiled to himself. The fact that Benny was using so many words to deny something made it obvious exactly what was going on. The interrogation was going very well.

"It's OK," said Indy. "You don't need to tell me anything about the truck. I'm not going to push you." Instead they continued to talk about the possibility that there had been serious drugs involved. And how it probably wasn't Benny's fault.

"Look, Benny, I'll come back in a few days. And here's my card. Headquarters are only a ten-minute walk from here, and if you need anything, call me. I may be able to help you. It seems to me that you could use a friend, so far from home and with a major injury."

Indy shook Benny's hand, and wished him well. Benny, in his simple mind, was warmed by Indy's concern; while Indy was a cop, and a Hindu cop at that, he was one of the few nice people that Benny had ever encountered.

Indy left the orthopedic ward edgy and excited. Could he do it? Did he have enough for the affidavit? In Canada, a search warrant could be issued only by a judge, and only if the informant had reasonable and probable grounds that a crime had taken place. It was a bit of a stretch, but with the destruction of the fancy truck, the bullet in the knee, and the bank draft that paid for the truck, along with the "maybe there were drugs involved" statement from Benny, Indy knew he could get the order. It might not withstand cross-examination, but the object of the exercise wasn't Benny's prosecution. All he wanted was an order compelling the Scotia Bank to disclose all records in its possession with respect to the account number that had appeared on Benny's bank draft. In this business, the trick was to follow the money trail, not the drugs. If his hunch was right, he'd just found a major drug ring. In a place right on the American border. If this was big enough, maybe he could plug a hole, get Ottawa, Hagen, and the FBI off his back. That's what he wanted. He really didn't care whether Benny was convicted, or even charged. Benny was obviously a very small piece of the puzzle.

LEON LESTAGE was speeding toward the Kootenays, his long, graying hair streaming in the wind. It was a warm summer night, with no rain. He was cursing Benny Hallett with every ounce of his will, barely paying attention to the road as he navigated his stunning Harley Davidson Road King through the Highway 401 traffic. He rode past the farming communities of Abbotsford and Chilliwack, past Hope and onto the Coquihalla, a mountaintop freeway that was a marvel of engineering. He had made a mistake, he thought. He should have put the bullet through Benny's moronic forehead. Now Benny was in Vancouver General. Too close to a major police station by half. And with Benny's soft, malleable mind anything could happen. Twenty million dollars, Joseph had told him. Twenty million. And real dollars. American dollars. Big dollars. The best part was that it wasn't cash. It would be sitting in a jungle of offshore accounts somewhere. That meant no laundering problems, no taxes to worry about. Just to let the guy use his mine and have a truck waiting. He could buy a bigger jet, a place in Whistler, and a beach house spread on Maui, with a couple of Harleys at each house. With the funds that he had already squirreled away, another $20 million would pave the way to retirement. He could travel the world as he pleased, riding through the night on any continent. But now that addled half cousin of his was in Vancouver General, threatening the whole plan with his big mouth. His visit had been short, and the message terse. You talk, you die. Low-level bikers in some wannabe gang would see to that. Benny would die slowly, and painfully; that much had been emphasized. Now Leon was kicking himself. He had gone soft. He should have put the bullet in Benny's brain, if there even was one, the first time, and torched him along with the Dodge. Then there'd have been no worries, no mess.

Leon came back to the real world just as the speedometer crept over 90. He quickly applied his brakes. The last thing he needed right now was to get pulled over by some dumbass cop. Thinking about cops reminded him of something he'd heard that day, on some fragment of a newscast, about an enormous amount of plastic explosives that had been blown up somewhere in the Libyan Sahara. Big bang; big deal. He didn't care all that much. At heart Leon was a straightforward man, not given to flights of fancy or emotion. And he didn't care for those who put stock in such things. An explosion in the desert didn't affect his life in any way, regardless of what it meant to Western civilization.

All he knew was that an extremely valuable cargo would arrive in the very near future. He had received the signal — Devil's Anvil needed to be ready, and soon. Now he was on his way home; for that much money, he wanted to be personally involved. There could be no screw-ups. No more of that bullshit that Benny always brought with him. This transaction had to be smooth and seamless. The call had come in, cryptic and short, but the directions were very clear. So, first to Missoula, Montana, to arrange for an appropriate truck to be waiting, and then to Devil's Anvil, to prepare for the cargo that was, apparently, incredibly valuable.

He rode on through the warm August night, wrapped up in his own greed and arrogance.

7

RICHARD SWITCHED OFF the Thuraya Satellite telephone. He smiled wryly as he realized that he could use the system, here, deep in the desert, without fear of detection. Only the satellites of the National Reconnaissance Office could detect and track Sat-phone transmissions, and since the CIA and the NRO had the same boss, and that's who he wanted to speak with, he didn't care if the call was detected.

"You need Kingston from the NGA," Baxter had told him. "He's been reading Keyhole images for the past ten years. If anyone can help you, he can. No one does IMINT like he does." IMINT was short for Image Intelligence.

Richard shook his head. "Has it ever occurred to you, Baxter, how weird you guys sound? Keyholes. NSA. NRO. IMINT. Perhaps we should add that I'm LOL and you're FUBAR?"

Baxter snorted. It was well known that Richard's sense of humor tended toward the dark side, and was drier than the sands of the Sahara. Personally Baxter had always found him quite funny, but this wasn't the time for jokes. "The Prez says this one has priority. Everyone in the community has been advised. Washington is getting a little concerned about this," he said. "Langley is definitely on edge, and in the last day or two we've had increased chatter about WMD. Goldberg's message suggests a pretty big attack, possibly on one of the ports. Even compared to that, this Semtex thing is gaining ground on the radar screen."

"OK," Richard replied. "Well tell the Prez to take a Valium or something. We're on it."

"You'll get all the help you need, on the ground and at Langley, and pretty much anywhere else you want to turn. It's going to share the front page of the PDB with that Goldberg message, especially with American servicemen being killed." With that, Baxter hung up.

Richard was in the process of reciting the conversation back to McMurray when the Thuraya rang again. "Under 60 seconds," muttered the Sergeant. "They must be worried."

Richard picked it up after the first ring. "Lawrence," he barked.

"This is Captain Martin Kingston, from NGA. Just got a personal call from the Deputy Director of Central Intelligence telling me to drop everything I'm doing and talk to you. Seeing as how you're Navy, I figured that probably means you're out of toilet paper, but an order is an order. What do you need?"

The NGA was the latest alphabet soup concoction served up by DC bureaucrats, and stood for the National Geospatial Intelligence Agency. It had been known as the National Imagery and Mapping Agency, an amalgamation of various other mapping and imaging organizations within the Intelligence Community. The NGA was closely affiliated with the NSA, and was connected, via dedicated fiber optic lines, to the supercomputers used in Crypto City. Kingston was in daily communication with his counterparts at the NSA, and had in fact trained many of that department's image readers. These days, he had workspaces in both agencies.

Kingston usually worked on the top floor of what was now the NGA headquarters building in Bethesda, Maryland. Like so many others in his profession, it was rumored that he slept and lived in his office, which covered almost a quarter of the floor. His name was legendary in the small but somewhat eccentric school of image analysts. He was responsible for creating the term "blobologist" — a person who specialized in identifying fuzzy images on a computer screen. He had an identical office in the basement of the NSA OPS1 building at Fort Mead, where he was equally famous for his work. He was well into his 70s, but his skills were so valuable that both the NGA and NSA had done considerable lobbying to keep him on after his official retirement age. Not that he had complained. They would have had to drag him, kicking and screaming, from his office.

"Not funny, Captain," replied Richard. "This is actually pretty serious. We've got a bit of a problem here."

"OK, how can I help?"

Richard resisted the impulse to suggest that he could help by sending over 400 Percodans, stat. The pain in his back and head was becoming unbearable. "Well, sir, I think 4.5 tons of Minyar's Semtex just disappeared," he stated bluntly. He gave Kingston a basic outline of what had occurred.

"So when do you think the DC-3 took off?" asked Kingston.

"That's the question at hand. We think it left a little strip just south of Zighan, in the middle of the Libyan desert, sometime in the 12 hours preceding the blast," said Richard, ducking away from the wasp that was buzzing around his forehead. "It probably vectored south, then entered northwest Darfur for refueling."

"OK," said Kingston. "I'll have a look. But most of the NRO-deployed assets are focused on Iran, Iraq, Afghanistan, and Korea. You know, the problem areas. We don't have any of the new ORION's covering your area. We may have something from one of the older Keyholes… maybe a KH-12 would have picked it up. I'll put a team of people on this immediately, and get the guys at the NSA to help out. I'll get right back to you."

The KH-12 had been the designated workhorse for the Intelligence Community in the '90s. When launched, it weighed more than seven tons. Most of that was an excess of fuel, which allowed the satellite to maneuver extensively while in orbit, to reach areas of greater interest. It could be serviced and refueled by the space shuttle. This particular satellite had sophisticated optics that digitally enhanced any images before relaying them to Earth, to provide full-spectrum image Intelligence data virtually instantaneously. It had high-res infrared imaging technology, capable of detecting camouflage and buried structures, with an image resolution of less than ten centimeters. An astounding feat, really, but nothing in comparison to what the KH-14's and the new ORION's could do. Richard would still be glad to have anything a KH-12 might have picked up.

"Well, now what?" asked McMurray when he hung up. Richard shrugged. He was about to suggest that a cold beer would be nice when he was hailed by one of the Night Hawk captains.

"We've been ordered to hang around," Second Lieutenant George Clinton of the US Navy told them. "Two of the choppers are staying on the ground, and when we get the order we're supposed to take you to an undisclosed location. Weird fucking orders, but apparently Langley's involved, so that would explain it. Don't go far," he warned, smiling.

"Yeah, right," laughed Richard. "I'm heading for the nearest sports bar to have a cold beer with the good Sergeant here." He pounded McMurray on the back.

"Nah, I'll be in southern Arizona," replied McMurray. "Golf. Beaches. Wife and kids. The works." They all laughed and hunkered down in the shade of the Night Hawk, trying to pretend they were anywhere other than the middle of the Sahara Desert.

SO YOU KNOW this Goldberg?" asked McMurray. Richard had just finished filling him in on his telephone conversation with the new Washington Intelligence Agency.

"Yeah. He's kind of like a brother," said Richard. "We grew up together. His family took me in when my parents died in an accident in Pakistan. Then we served together. Crossed paths often. We both ended up in Islamabad, which is home for me, really. Haven't seen Zak in years. He's in deep cover somewhere in the Middle East. Went under about four years ago. Can't really say more about it than that."

McMurray could see that Richard was concerned. There were deep grooves carved into his brow, and he was speaking too quickly. His hand was automatically reaching for some sort of pain medication in his pocket. Not that he blamed the man. News of the Goldberg memo had spread far and wide within the Intelligence and military communities. There were no illusions about what it might mean… or the obvious danger Zak was facing.

GLEANING MEANINGFUL INFORMATION from satellite imaging systems was a black art, studied by many and mastered by only a few. Martin Kingston had a knack for it. He loved it. What to the untrained eye was just a blur inside a shadow, a dark spot inside a smudge, was to Kingston a vehicle. Beyond that, it was a Ford or a Chevy, a model, and sometimes even a color. He boasted that someday he would even be able to read the serial numbers of cars found in this way. On the ORION's, the image resolution was less than three centimeters. Now the scientists at the NRO and NASA were working on resolutions of one centimeter. Before long they would have Hubble-type telescope satellites, pointed back at Earth. Kingston joked that soon they'd be reading briefing notes from space, and that using infrared, the government could have a detailed account of who was having sex with whom, at any given moment. A brave new world indeed.

Kingston quickly determined, through the Master Progressive Scan Imaging Database (MP-Sid to those who knew it personally), which satellites had been scanning the area and time frame Richard needed. Three satellites — KH-11/02B, KH-12/021B, and KH-13/002 — would have taken, in rapid succession, digital images of the desert sands of Zighan, at the very edge of their focusing area. He divided each satellite's footage into four three-hour segments, and collared 12 of his coworkers to analyze, frame by frame if necessary, the appropriate area.

It was like looking for a needle in a haystack, but IMINT personnel had received assignments like this many times before. "Find out where Yeltsin's plane was yesterday afternoon," they had been told. "Find out if there was an explosion at such-and-such a place three days ago," or "Find out how many tanks were at this location in North Korea at this time." Many years earlier, when the art was still in its infancy, and the equipment was of stone-age caliber, one President had tested a boast from a four-star General of the Joint Chiefs of Staff.

"OK," the President had joked. "A couple of my cows found a break in a fence, and disappeared into the Texas Mesa. Find them."

And IMINT had. Finding a DC-3 would not be that big a problem for them. Once the workload had been appropriately segmented, the assignment wouldn't take long at all.

AS EXPECTED, Richard's Thuraya rang within an hour.

"Lawrence," he answered sharply, holding his head. Standing in the 120-degree heat of one of the largest deserts in the world, dealing with this situation, was doing nothing for the pounding taking place inside his skull.

"Richard, this is Captain Kingston from the NGA," Kingston said. "I think we've got it. We've compared and isolated more than 500 frames from the area in question. A DC-3 did arrive at the Zighan airstrip sometime between 7 and 9PM, local time. It left around midnight. We have a couple of thermal scans that show maybe four or five individuals in the area just before then. They may have been loading or unloading cargo. We're not sure."

"Can you tell where the plane came from?" asked Richard.

"We can't. But there are a couple of frames that tell us which direction it went."

"Where?"

"It headed south by southeast." Kingston gave Richard the exact coordinates.

"Any idea where it landed, or where it was heading?"

"No, sorry. It headed toward the Sudan, but we didn't have any satellites scanning northwest Darfur during the time frame when it would have landed. You're on your own on that one," said Kingston.

"OK," said Richard. "But maybe you could help me with one more thing. Your computers have access to a lot of image and mapping data. Given the vector of the DC-3, is it possible to draw up a list of places they might have been heading? Are there any landing strips in Darfur along the path they were taking? Options for us to check out?"

"Well, we could check that," replied Kingston. "But it would take us awhile. The boys at TTIC could get it to you faster. They have access to an incredible pile of information, way more than us. And they have this monster interactive map, all done digitally. I haven't seen it, but I've heard what it can do."

“TTIC? I think I talked to them earlier. Aren’t they the ones who figured out the Madrid thing before Madrid figured it out?”

“Yeah, that’s them. Kind of an odd group of people, but they have access to pretty much everything. Their supercomputer is as powerful as the ones at the NSA. I’m going to see if I can put you through directly. Need to get authority. Hang on.”

Kingston called the head of IMINT, who called the DDCI’s office. Admiral Jackson called TTIC immediately.

Johnson answered. “TTIC control.”

The Admiral identified himself. Johnson nearly dropped his coffee in his lap when he heard the name. Big Jack. He straightened up instantly. “How can we be of assistance, sir?” he asked.

Big Jack, aka Admiral Jackson, aka the DDCI, explained the problem to him. “Look, we’re going to conference in Richard Lawrence, who’s in Bazemah at the moment, and Kingston from the NGA.”

There was a pause, and the sound of a line connecting. “Mr. Lawrence, are you there?” Big Jack continued, officially starting the call. “This is Admiral Jackson. We’ve got IMINT and TTIC on the line. Can you explain your problem?”

“One moment, sir,” Johnson interrupted. “I’m going to put you on our speaker system here in the control room, so that everyone here can hear this. Everyone has clearance.” He flipped a switch. The whole room was now in on the conversation. The advanced microphones, speakers, and feedback suppression electronics brought the conversation into the control room with virtually no distortion, hissing, or feedback.

“Turbee,” Johnson said. “Flip the map to Libya and Sudan.”

“One second, please,” mumbled Turbee, as he kept the DDCI, Richard, and his entire agency waiting while he saved his latest Grand Theft Auto chase sequence. “There.” He jumped up from his work area and went to the Atlas Screen control station. Dan, who’d been missing all morning, finally entered the room. Something important was officially up. Everyone sat up and started paying attention.

Meanwhile, Turbee was fumbling haplessly with the controls to the map. He was not as familiar with the system as some of the other members of the team. He had only played with it once before. He was desperately trying to put Libya and Sudan on the Atlas Screen, and having little success. Bolivia was displayed in great detail. Then Antarctica, followed by Mongolia. Then he managed to turn off the massive computer subsystem that served mapping images to the Atlas Screen. It would take a full five minutes to reboot.

"Are you guys there?" Admiral Jackson's voice boomed out over the speakers.

"Yes we are," replied Dan as he shoved Turbee off the map control station. "Can you hold for a minute? We have some technical issues."

The five-minute reboot was like dead air at a rock concert. Each second seemed to last an hour. "You know, at a hundred trillion calculations per second, I think you guys have already done more calculations than God did when he created the universe," Jackson commented impatiently as minute three ticked by.

"No, no," said Richard. "It took at least that many calculations to create a woman. The rest of the universe, just a little more." Chuckles erupted up and down the conference call.

"OK, we're live," breathed Dan, as he watched the Atlas Screen come back online. "What do you need to know?"

"We're at the explosion site, near Bazemah," said Richard. "We're trying to determine where the DC-3 went with the stolen Semtex. Kingston came up with a vector of the DC-3's direction when it left Zighan, a little airport to the north of us. Kingston, are you still there?" asked Richard.

"Yeah, I'm still online here. You want to know the vector?"

"Yeah, let's hear it," said Richard. "What I need to know is if there are any landing strips along that path, assuming it maintained its direction. Landing strips in northern Sudan. TTIC, can you guys give me that?"

Dan looked perplexed. His knowledge of the mapping system was rudimentary, and he had no clue how to find what Richard was asking for. The day was rapidly sliding into a tar pit. Another minute ticked by as Dan slipped deeper into the quagmire.

"Sheesh," said Kingston, after a few moments. "I could have figured it out with a protractor and a ruler by now."

Fortunately, George Lexia had entered the room just after Dan did. George was a Silicon Valley engineer and programmer. He had written large chunks of the GPS-mapping programs that were becoming popular in vehicles and pleasure craft. George, like Turbee, had become very wealthy before joining TTIC. In his case it was from his roles and stock in several successful companies. He did not need the work but, like Turbee, loved playing with the largest computer, and the most complex mapping system, that had ever been devised. Like so many others in the Intelligence Community, he was married to his job and took it very seriously. George was also the leading architect of the program that controlled TTIC's massive interactive map.

"A vector, you say," said George as he gently nudged Dan out of his workstation. "Not a problem." His fingers raced over the console, and a red line magically appeared on the interactive map, moving southerly along the direction that Kingston had given him.

He touched his keyboard a few more times, and northern Sudan appeared, highly magnified. Even the villages, streets, and alleys of the tiny desert towns were illustrated. "Ahh, here we are," he said. "Yarim-Dhar. The vector goes directly over an airstrip about ten miles north of Yarim-Dhar, a tiny village that's 400 miles south by southeast of Zighan. I'll give you the vector and distance from where you are."

After hearing this, Jackson barked some orders at his secretary, who immediately repeated them to the Commander of the *Theodore Roosevelt* Battle Group. From there, the orders were relayed to Major Lewis Payton, commander of the small Night Hawk force that had transported Richard, the Marines, McMurray, and the other men providing American support for the Semtex demolition job.

As a result of the lessons learned in two Gulf wars, and in the war in Afghanistan, American communications had become so efficient that Payton and Richard received their orders almost simultaneously. Richard turned off the Sat-phone and walked toward the helicopters. At the same instant, Major Payton hailed Richard. They looked at each other and said "Yarim-Dhar," together.

Richard motioned to McMurray. "He's Army," he said to Payton, "but he knows about this play dough stuff. He needs to come along."

"OK, Richard. We normally don't let Army on Night Hawks, but we'll make an exception here. Let's head out. How far away is Yarim-Dhar?"

"About 400 miles, give or take."

Payton frowned. "There had better be a gas station there. We'll be running on empty by the time we get there."

"I'm certain there is. Might be self serve, though," Richard quipped. Then he, Payton, and McMurray headed toward the Night Hawks, where George Clinton still sat, awaiting orders.

8

YOUSSEFF'S MIND was racing. There were a thousand facets to the enterprise that the Emir had entrusted to him. Delivery of the Semtex. The construction of the various devices they'd be needing. The creation of false trails, to divert the investigation that was sure to follow the attack. But the possibilities and the potential gain were breathtakingly large. This was another turning point, another Four Cedars. Youssef had already set his people in motion, and the plans were already drawn up. But did he dare bet everything on one shot?

Dusk turned to nightfall as Yousseff's horse gingerly picked its way through the difficult mountain terrain on its own. He barely considered the dangers of the path. He had been crisscrossing these mountain ranges since he was a child, and to him the trail was as familiar as the main street in any town. He was alone, lost in his thoughts, pondering both the task that lay ahead of him and the journey that had brought him to where he was.

YOUSSEFF HAD BEEN 13. His mother and younger sister were both ill, and his father did not want to leave either one. Twenty kilos of opium had been gathered. The family needed the $60 or $70 that this sale would bring in the markets of Peshawar.

"Go," Yousseff's father had said to him, over the objections of his mother. "Go. We need money for supplies. For food. Go, and may Allah be with you."

Without further word, Yousseff had saddled one horse, placed the saddlebags across a second, and rode toward the mountains that rose impenetrably behind the home of his uncle. Izzy al Din, still his faithful sidekick, had wanted to come with him.

"Not this trip, Iz. Too dangerous. Maybe next time. But come with me, ride to my uncle's place, then you can go back from there."

Izzy was content with this, and they had a pleasant, easy ride to the edge of Jalalabad, and up the trail that ultimately led to that treacherous mountain pass, the Path of Allah.

After Yousseff sent Izzy home, he had stopped at the home of his uncle, and told him of the trip. He had asked if there was any opium there, and learned that his uncle had about ten kilos, and was planning to make the trip himself in a week or two. Yousseff volunteered to take it; he had already become familiar with the many smuggling paths and uncharted horse trails through the Hindu Kush and the Sefid Koh. His uncle had seen for himself the sureness of the boy's steps in traversing the perilous higher passes with him in earlier years. He had seen the bright spark of intelligence in Yousseff's eyes, and had nodded approvingly as the boy became acquainted with the Pashtun smuggling ways. Yousseff never needed to be told anything more than once; a trait almost unheard of in young boys.

"Yes," he had said. "Take these ten kilos. Bring me the money in American dollars when you return."

Yousseff asked if he could use a third horse, and his uncle gave him the pick of his mounts. The boy had been gone for hours before it occurred to his uncle that this seemed a strange request, given Yousseff's meager 30 kilos of opium, which could be packed onto one horse. There was certainly no need for three.

The Path of Allah was aptly named, earning its moniker because it had sent so many of the faithful to Paradise before their time. The Path had its origin on a trail a short distance from where, more than three decades later, Zak would be found out. From there the trail switched back and forth along increasingly steep terrain, until it reached a point more than 8,000 feet above the Kabul Gorge. At that point the trail leveled out and traversed rolling slopes, until it reached a precipice that plunged nearly 3,000 feet, straight down. Here the Path of Allah became a narrow trail that was in some places only three feet wide, and never grew to be more than five or six feet in width. This cliff was the border between Pakistan and Afghanistan, but no army had ever enforced it, and no monarch or government exercised sovereignty here.

Storms could come on unexpectedly at this elevation, and even in the hot summer months a foot or two of snow could fall within a few hours. Ice was common, and the Path was often wet and slippery. Even experienced horses sometimes needed to be blindfolded or blinkered, and it was still possible that they would panic, rear up, and lose their footing, plummeting to their deaths more than half a mile below. Each year saw several horses and men fall to their deaths along the dangerous and precipitous route. For a boy to travel it alone, with three horses, was an act of madness. But then so was challenging Marak to a duel at the Four Cedars.

For almost a mile, the treacherous Path rose and fell, until it reached the ancient fortress of Inzar Ghar. Built on a foundation that was more than 1,000 years old, this fortress served as a storage area for opium, an armory, and, courtesy of a number of sub-levels beneath it, a dungeon. In order to enter Pakistan via the Path of Allah, one had to pass through the gates of Inzar Ghar. From there it was another day's journey, down much gentler terrain, to Peshawar.

The weather had been with Yousseff on the journey. His trip, with three horses in tow, had been uneventful. In nearly record time, he found himself in the bustling and historic city of Peshawar, Pakistan. Here the young Yousseff elected to depart somewhat from the usual script. He sold the ten kilos for his uncle to their usual dealer in the Peshawar market, for $2.50 per kilo. Twenty-five dollars. With that money he went down the crowded streets with his three horses, bumping into the horse-drawn carts, rickshaws, bicycles, and motorcycles, following the Cantonment along Railway Road, and entering the Khyber Bazaar. Here, moving along a series of crooked back roads and alleys, he reached a business that to the untrained eye appeared to sell carpets. The initiated knew that this particular shop sold much more. He had learned much from his many visits to the Peshawar marketplace with his father and uncle. Too much, his mother had told him. Specifically, he had learned the art of reducing opium to its essentials, cooking it, transforming it, converting it to a morphine base, and ultimately refining it to pure heroin. He knew exactly what was required: calcium hydroxide, liquid ether, ammonium chloride, acetic anhydride, and a few other sundries. These were the things he purchased at the "carpet" shop.

He loaded the chemicals onto his second and third horses, and went a short distance into the mountains of the Sefid Koh. He had made a friend there, Ba'al Baki, who was also about 13 years of age. On their many trips through this area, he, his father, and his uncle had often stopped at the small homestead owned by Ba'al's parents. They were loquacious people, friendly and giving. The travelers would often eat dinner there and pay the Baki family a few rupees for their trouble. This always became a friendly argument, since *melmastia*, the Pashtun code of hospitality, required people to accommodate all travelers, without any expectation of reward. The casual acquaintance had soon grown into a firm friendship between the two families, and Yousseff was happy to make his way back to the homestead.

It was a hot summer afternoon when he arrived. He left his three horses tethered a short distance away, and went ahead to meet Ba'al. He told the other boy about his plan in hushed and hurried tones, and invited him along. He would cut Ba'al in, of course. Ba'al begged his parents for permission to accompany Yousseff to Peshawar for a few days, and they agreed. Because of their experience with his father and uncle, Mr. and Mrs. Baki had a great amount of trust in Yousseff. They had few concerns about Ba'al spending time with him.

The two friends had gone to an abandoned home about ten miles from the homestead, and had given themselves three days to attempt to convert the remaining opium to heroin. Together, they placed an empty 55-gallon oil drum on bricks about a foot above the ground and built a fire under the drum. They added 30 gallons of water to the drum and brought it to a boil. After a leisurely cup of afternoon tea, they added the 20 kilograms of raw opium that Yousseff had not sold at the marketplace.

Over the course of the next 24 hours, Yousseff and Ba'al went through more than 30 steps, including filtering, adding chemicals like ammonium chloride and sodium carbonate to the mixture, then purifying and purifying again to produce heroin. It was a very complex process, which Yousseff had learned only through watching the elders and listening to their stories.

After they were done, Yousseff had taken their product of 15 kilos of heroin and gone directly to the docks, where the Kabul River carved its way through Peshawar. He knew precisely where to go, having listened to the many conversations between his father and uncle, not to mention the endless banter of the Peshawar marketplace. Without much ado, he sold the heroin to a riverboat captain for $1,500, which made his profit more than $1,400. He paid Ba'al $50, and bid his friend goodbye. But not before he had loaded all three horses with the rest of the precursor chemicals.

He returned home via the Path of Allah. It was the first of many trips. In later years, every Afghani and Pakistani patrolling the Pass would be in Yousseff's pay, helping him with his smuggling operations. In the early days, though, he took the Path of Allah many times on his own, with an ever-increasing number of horses and employees. On some trips he would lose a horse or two, but no man ever fell to his death while in Yousseff's charge. Over the years he had committed to memory every twist and turn, every boulder and shrub of the precipitous pass. The talk amongst his workers was that Yousseff could navigate the pass as blindfolded as his horses. In due course, Yousseff even acquired the fortress of Inzar Ghar, although he disliked the dark, foreboding structure.

Upon his return from that first trip, he had paid his uncle the $25 and his father $50. With the $1,275 left over, he purchased a small 12-acre spread of fertile opium-producing land. He had agreed to pay the owner a further $500 within four months. Over the next two months he worked night and day in the fields, personally scoring the opium buds and collecting the resin.

He enlisted the aid of some of his relatives, paying them more than the going rate for a day's labor in the fields, but mostly he performed the work by himself. Izzy pitched in for free, incredibly pleased to be helping Youssef. At the conclusion of the harvest, they had 50 kilos of cooked opium, which Youssef turned into 40 kilos of heroin. This time he took a team of ten horses, and a number of his cousins and friends, and made the trip back to Peshawar. After expenses, he netted $4,000, $500 of which he used to pay off his debt on the property, and $3,000 of which was used for purchase of another 50 acres of farmland. His only expenses were in the purchase of the chemicals required for reducing the opium to heroin, and for further cooking, purifying, and screening equipment.

By the time Youssef reached his fourteenth birthday, he owned more than 400 acres of land. Ba'al, following Youssef's lead and at his friend's suggestion, had purchased an additional ten-acre spread near his parents' home. This land was also used for opium production. At this point, one trip to Peshawar netted more than $15,000 American. Before long Youssef was starting to experience a problem that would dog him for the rest of his life — what to do with all the money.

THE SOFT NEIGHING of his horse pulled Youssef out of his reverie. He was near the place where his uncle's farm had once been. Years ago, the Taliban, bent on some holy mission or other, had burned it to the ground. Youssef had purchased it and converted it into poppy fields. The entire valley was his, and he had for years been employing means of modern farming and mass production to increase the crop volume and decrease costs. Instead of using old oil drums and rice bags, he had built a state-of-the-art underground laboratory, with spotless floors and proper ventilation. He had horticulturists, engineers, and chemists on his payroll. No one important had noticed the change. During the Soviet war, no one had cared about what was going on in this little corner of Afghanistan. The Taliban was easily bought off. The Americans seemed to have too much else on their minds. His business had flourished for many years, uninterrupted.

INDY COULDN'T BELIEVE his eyes. He'd never seen account activity like this. In the end it hadn't taken much time or effort to gather the information. He'd gone back to the Heather Street complex and put his affidavit and application materials together. The Dodge dealership faxed him a copy of the bill of sale and bank draft for Benny's truck. He had one of the staff lawyers review the materials, and had the affidavit sworn. He was so eager to get to the courthouse that he took a marked police cruiser and flipped on the lights and sirens. He quickly found his way into a judge's chamber and gained the order he wanted. He bribed the secretaries with coffee and donuts, to have the order typed and signed. By 11AM he had the account records from Scotia Bank, dating back two years. At 11:15, still standing in front of the bank, he woke Catherine Gray at her home. She had just finished a busy night shift. Indy would normally have been apologetic, but right now he was thinking of other things.

"Oh man, Indy," came the sleepy reply from Cranbrook, BC. "This had better be good." She knew it would be — even half asleep, Catherine could recognize the excitement in his voice.

"It is, Cath. I've never seen an account history like this. We have deposit after deposit after deposit."

"Big deal. If you were to pull my account, you'd see withdrawal after withdrawal after withdrawal," she sighed, trying to smile past a yawn.

"Not this way. We've got cash deposits, all through automatic cash machines, throughout the province, and in Alberta. Sometimes as many as 30 or 40 a day."

"Oh yeah?" Catherine responded. "For how much?"

"It varies, but it seems to be around $1,000 a pop. Sometimes as much as $2,000. Sometimes as little as $500. It's averaging out to about $20,000 or $30,000 a day, if you add up all the separate deposits."

"A day?"

"Yes. A day. Every day. Maybe $150 to $200 grand a week. Every week. Every month. From all over. Calgary. Edmonton. Vancouver. Kelowna. Kamloops. I've got one document showing more than 30 deposits at various Vancouver ATM's in one day," said Indy, excitedly. "In fact, if they're doing this with five or six different banks, pretty soon you're looking at real money."

Suddenly Catherine's brain woke up. "You know, I've heard of people doing this," she replied. "We've got these automatic tellers everywhere now. In grocery stores, drug stores, 7/11's, even Starbucks coffee shops have them. You put your cash in a little envelope and press a few buttons and you're done."

"Yup. It's called 'smurfing.' The easiest and oldest way to launder money.

Little bit here, little bit there, no one's ever the wiser. Even a clan of morons could legitimately put a lot of cash into the financial system this way. Just give each one of them $10 grand a day, and if you have 15 of them, you could quite easily put away half a million in a week. All expenses are paid for in cash. All it takes is 20 or 30 people, and none of them need to be overloaded with brains. It pretty much describes the Hallett/Lestage group." Indy was almost jumping up and down in his excitement.

"Smurfing?" asked Catherine, thinking of little blue creatures in furry hats. "Did you say smurfing?"

"Smurfing. The Lestages and Halletts might be big-time smurfs. And with these numbers, in just this one account, we might be looking at a major operation. This could be indicative of a major league drug conspiracy. These characters may be able to lead us to the hole in the border. They may be involved in getting drugs into the States." Indy was practically babbling now, jumping from one thought to the next without bothering to connect them.

"Oh, and here's something else," he added, reviewing the stack of printouts more closely. "Every couple of months we have close to half a million dollars withdrawn, electronically, and going to some other bank or institution."

"Which banks?"

"Not sure. There are number and letter codes beside the transactions, but I don't know what they mean."

"I think they're probably bank identifier codes. We ran into that in a commercial crime case that we dealt with couple of years ago. The banking people will be able to tell you."

"OK Cath," replied Indy. "I'll call you back. Get some ideas down on paper about the manpower required to send people around western Canada for these deposits. And what it might mean for someone to be using that kind of manpower." With that, he hung up, whirled around, and headed back into the bank.

9

YARIM-DHAR was even more desolate than Zighan. It was located in the northern part of the vast Darfur wilderness, where the waves of desert sand met thousands of square miles of grassland. Sharp-edged sandstone pinnacles in shades of ochre and vermilion, some rising more than 1,000 feet above the plain, punctuated the limitless sand. Here the Sahel, desolate and remote, was separated from southern and eastern Sudan by the ancient basalt of the 10,000-foot Jebel Marra massif. This was an area ruled by tribes of nomadic Bedouin warlords with ever-changing loyalties. Each sought ultimate dominion over the surreal landscape, cut off from the rest of the world. Some of these ruthless groups were at the heart of the ethnic cleansing of non-Arabic peoples in northwest Darfur. The terrain, the climate, and the desolation were all similar to Saudi Arabia, Afghanistan, and the lawless Northern Frontier areas of Pakistan itself.

Richard viewed the lands below him with growing anxiety as the Night Hawk traveled ever further from its Mediterranean carrier base. It was no longer pure desert, but bleakness and oppressive heat still radiated from the rocky grassland below him. When they found the airport, it was really nothing more than a dirt strip adjacent to a rundown terminal no larger than a couple of Atco trailers put side by side, and a small fuel depot. One ancient Jeep was parked beside the terminal. Waves of heat were rippling from the small structures.

"OK, Clinton," said Payton over the Com-Link. "Let's set them down near the fuel depot." There was an edge to his voice. Sudan north of Khartoum was lawless, in a continual state of anarchy, and subject to brutal, pitiless civil war. It wasn't the kind of place he wanted to hang out.

"You betcha, Major," responded Clinton. Both Night Hawks landed simultaneously, coming down in swishing vortices of sand. "Heads up, people. Safeties off and weapons ready. We have no idea what's here," he ordered his crew. "We don't want another Somalia."

"There's only one Jeep," observed one of the other men. "I don't think it'll be too bad. Can't be more than one or two people here."

"It only takes one to kill you," said McMurray. "Least that's what they teach you in the Army."

"I'm going inside the terminal to see if a DC-3 came through here in the last few hours," said Richard, opening the door of the helicopter and climbing out.

"Don't think you're leaving me here," McMurray snapped. Stressful situations tended to make him even sharper than usual. "Someone has to make sure this damn thing goes right." He jumped out of the chopper and followed Richard toward the terminal.

"Clinton, gather a couple of the guys, we're going with them," ordered Payton. "See what we can do about getting fuel. We're on empty here. Thompson, get on the radio and let home base know we're here and that we're looking for fuel. Tell them it's quiet, so far."

Unbeknownst to Payton, a swarthy man inside the terminal had just made a short call of his own on his Sat-phone. "Two helicopters," he said. "Maybe ten soldiers. Americans. Send the trucks."

What that man didn't know, in turn, was that the NSA had received a directive from the DDCI, just hours before, ordering them to monitor everything monitorable in southern Libya and northwestern Darfur. The NSA most definitely had that capability. Headquartered in Fort Mead, Maryland, the several thousand employees of the NSA worked within the second-largest building in the world (the Pentagon being the largest). If the NSA was ordered to monitor a specific region, it was all but done.

The problem with using a Thuraya Satellite telephone in the middle of a wasteland is that there are only a few such telephones within a thousand square-mile area. For this reason, the NSA's mission was a very different proposition than monitoring the Islands of Indonesia, where there were almost 200,000 such devices, and millions of cell phones. With the warning that the agency had received, they had no problem picking up the call from the airstrip to the little village of Yarim-Dhar, about ten miles distant. One of the translators yelled at his supervisor the moment it happened. "It's a set-up! They're going to be attacked!"

The supervisor immediately relayed that to the executive director of his section, who relayed it to the DDCI's office. The message went across to the Pentagon, and to the *Theodore Roosevelt* Battle Group in the Mediterranean. From there it was linked to the AWAC-2 aircraft circling high above the Mediterranean, and to Thompson, who was still on the Com-Link in the second Night Hawk.

The end result was that four FA-18/E Super Hornets were immediately scrambled from the deck of the *Theodore Roosevelt,* while, miles away, two dozen Darfur warriors were racing toward seven trucks in the village of Yarim-Dhar, with heavy machine guns in tow. The trucks were about ten miles from the airport and were moving at 50 miles per hour, the maximum speed permitted by the rough terrain. The Hornets maxed out at Mach 1.7, but had some 700 miles to go. Clearance across Libya was approved almost immediately, once General Minyar was briefed on the situation. No one really cared about clearance in northwest Darfur.

At that moment, Thompson was yelling to the Major and his small group, who were halfway to the main terminal. Richard and McMurray had already entered the building. "Major, take cover! It's an ambush!"

Two heads appeared on the roof of the terminal building. The so-called warriors had taken an inside ladder to the roof of the terminal after the choppers landed. Each had an RPG launcher. They fired simultaneously, each aiming for a helicopter.

YOUSSEFF COMPLETED his long, lonely journey to Jalalabad, slept for a few hours, and had his pilots fly him over the mountains into Pakistan, to an almost identical hangar, with identical offices and suites, at Islamabad International. It was there that he reconnected with Marak, just after dark. He did not ask Marak what had become of the unfortunate Zak, nor did he care to know. It was, thankfully, an operational detail that he, as CEO, did not need to trouble himself with. Yousseff had never had the stomach for death or torture, and was glad to leave that aspect of the business to Marak. His role was master and planner. Now he made a number of telephone calls, all on a pre-paid cell phone that Marak had brought with him. Various aspects of the mission were discussed and revised.

As he hung up, he turned to Marak. "Can you have Vijay and Mahari here tomorrow morning?" he asked.

"That will not be a problem," Marak replied. "First light."

"Then I should call Omar in Karachi, and Kumar in Los Angeles," said Yousseff. "We can't give them all of the information, but they need to know some aspects of the plan. Especially Kumar."

IT WAS LATE in the evening, Pacific Standard Time, when Kumar's personal cell phone rang. He flipped it open. "Hanaman here," he answered. Kumar had been born in Pakistan, where he'd first met Yousseff. With some passport trickery, he had moved to Long Beach, California, where he'd been living for more than a decade now. There he had built a thriving company that manufactured and sold small commercial submarines to the military and private enterprises.

"It's Yousseff. How are you Kumar?"

A broad smile crept over Kumar's face. "It is good to hear your voice, Yousseff. It's been too long. All is fine here. What do you need?"

Yousseff never wasted much time on pleasantries. Over the years he had found that it was best to deal with the details first, and take time for pleasure second. "I need you to build something for me, Kumar. Something very unique, very unusual. It will take all of your immense talent."

Kumar's eyebrows rose, nearing his curly black hairline in surprise. "Oh?"

"But," continued Yousseff, "I know that you, in that plant of yours, can build anything. It will be difficult, but not impossible. We will email the plans to you shortly. Encrypted, of course, but you know the code. I will call you again in a day or two."

"Sure, Youss," came Kumar's voice, with an edge of uncertainty. "Email what you have. I'll look at it. Then I can let you know if it's possible or not."

"One more thing, Kumar. I have a telephone number for you. Do you still have the simulator for the PWS-14 in the plant?"

"Yes, I do. I've actually spent some time in it myself. It can be quite entertaining."

"There are two young men at this telephone number. Their names are Javeed and Massoud. They are staying at the south LA Mosque. Take them in. Put them up in the suite you have behind your office. And get them to log hours on the simulator."

"Sure, Yousseff. Are you going to tell me what any of this is about?" asked Kumar.

"I do not want to lay out all the details here and now. Once you start building the device, and training Massoud and Javeed, I will call again. I will be in Los Angeles in about two weeks, and we can connect then. I look forward to seeing you."

"Likewise," said Kumar, puzzled. He hung up the phone.

YOUSSEFF TURNED OFF his phone and stared at it for a moment. Kumar was a good friend, and he didn't like keeping him the dark. Neither did he enjoy getting the younger man involved in something that would be dangerous and perhaps fatal. But he had no choice. This was a gamble he had made on the behalf of all his employees and friends. As long as everything went well, they would have no reason to second-guess him for his decision.

As long as everything went well. He sighed and shook his head. He wasn't used to that stipulation. But he'd been put in a position he wasn't used to, and was taking part in something he'd never before considered. It was bringing on questions that made him nervous. Questions that might cost him his life, and many important friendships.

Trying not to consider that, he picked up his phone again and punched a second series of numbers. A warm female voice answered. "Executive offices of Karachi Star Line. How may I help you?"

"Please advise Omar that the first mate of the *Janeeta* is on the line," said Youssef.

"Mr. Jhananda is meeting with the Executive Planning Committee, and is not available at the moment," the secretary replied somewhat sharply.

"Just interrupt him for a moment," said Youssef, persuasively. "He will want to take this call."

The wait was less than 30 seconds. "Youss," said Omar. "Good to hear your voice. I just heard from Vince, and he told me you might call."

"Yes. How soon can the *Haramosh Star* be ready for travel?"

"She is ready now, Youssef," answered Omar. "We put extra crews on overnight and she was put into the water earlier today."

"Wonderful. And is the submersible with her, in the pod?"

"Yes, Youssef, we did that too. Everything is ready to go."

"Go back to your meeting, old friend," said Youssef. "I will be in Karachi tonight. I'll call you from the plane. Perhaps we can have dinner together before I move on."

"It will be a pleasure. Goodbye." Omar's phone clicked and the line went dead.

Youssef leaned back and closed his eyes. With only two telephone calls and those bare directions, a lot of iron had been put in motion. They were growing closer and closer to the point of no return.

AT TTIC, Dan was feeling rather less successful. In fact, he was in a black mood. He was furious over the mapping calamity. "Do something useful for a change," he had snapped at a hapless Hamilton Turbee after the boondoggle, forgetting for a moment who had solved the Madrid terrorist attacks. "See if you can turn some of that dazzling intellect of yours into something other than video games and Simpson re-reruns. Get into that pile of information about the Semtex robbery, and see if you can figure out who did it. The rest of us are going to look at this nuclear threat to our harbors. Now get cracking, Turb, or you're out of here."

Turbee turned a bright crimson. "Yes sir," he said softly. Turbee was not accustomed to TTIC's military psyche, or its "law and order" and "chain of command" biases. He could barely handle the loose structure of a university post-grad department. Once again he thought about walking out, but then he thought of big Blue Gene, and realized that leaving was unthinkable. He also had some friends here, and for Turbee, with his social handicaps, friends were few and far between. So he straightened up, and initiated a series of database correlation and search routines. "OK, let's make it a little treasure hunt," he murmured. While Blue Gene was running the routines, he scanned through the initial Intelligence reports about the heist.

"Heckler and Koch PSG-1's? What are those?" he asked Rahlson. A search team from the 184th Ordnance had recovered a number of bullets from the assault scene, and had used their expertise to establish the type of weapons used in the attack.

"A rapid-fire, highly accurate sniper rifle," Rahlson said. "Very rare. Expensive."

"Who makes them?" asked Turbee.

Rahlson turned his head to one side and was about to tell Turbee how monumentally stupid he thought the kid was when he remembered their differing backgrounds, and Turbee's utter lack of experience with anything even remotely associated with firearms. "Why, Heckler and Koch, of course."

"How do you spell that, sir?"

This time Rahlson actually bit his tongue. But then he thought he saw Turbee's lower lip trembling, and thought about the effort it must be taking for the youngster to control himself in this situation. Oh Jesus Christ, he swore silently. He spelled it out. Turbee dutifully entered the letters into a little batch file he had created, and dispatched an armada of web-bots onto the Internet.

RICHARD WAS INSIDE the tiny terminal, one step ahead of McMurray, when he heard one and then the other helicopter explode. He felt the pressure and heat from each shock wave. Focusing his attention inside the terminal, he saw the Bedouin behind the small counter reach into his desert robes and bring up an AK-47. Richard was not famous for his marksmanship, but he did practice from time to time. His 9 mm Glock had been in his hands as he entered the terminal, and now he fired twice before the clerk could pull the trigger. Both bullets found their mark, and the man went down. A third shot finished it.

Richard bolted outside just in time to hear the sharp cracks of three rifle shots, and, almost simultaneously, another massive thud as a third RPG hit the fuel dump, causing further explosions in the area where Payton and his men had taken cover. It was a horrific scene. Thompson had been inside the second chopper when it was hit, and was killed instantly. Three of the men had been grievously wounded by the force of the explosion, and two more had died immediately in the fuel dump explosion. There seemed to be bodies everywhere, and they were all American. All men that Richard had talked to only moments before.

The two attackers on the terminal roof had been killed by return fire, but that was small consolation. The Americans were without helicopters, without communication, without medicine, and probably without water, in the burning heat of the northern Sahel.

Clinton and Payton were looking after two of the soldiers who had been burned in the explosion. The third wounded man had already succumbed to his injuries. That meant that a total of four were already dead. Two were wounded and possibly dying. There were only four of them left to fight. Two Navy. One Army. One CIA. Things were not looking good.

"Payton, I'm going to see if there's any water or first aid inside the terminal. Why don't you move these two fellows inside." Richard had seen his share of battle, but mostly from the sky. He knew about battlefield injuries, and had trained for this, but close up, the carnage and the moans of the two wounded men were horrific. He was fighting the impulse to vomit.

Payton yelled for Clinton to assist him, and they carried the two burned soldiers toward the terminal. As he was about to cross the doorstep, Payton saw dust clouds along the southern horizon.

"We're not done with these guys yet, Richard!" he yelled.

Richard followed his gaze and saw the growing dust trails. He knew what they meant. "How long do you think?" he asked.

"Ten minutes. Fifteen tops."

"Any place here where we can mount any kind of defense?" asked Richard.

"Doubt it," Payton replied. He had just lost four of his men, and two more were badly injured. Although he was highly trained, he felt himself to be on the verge of shock. Reinforcements were coming, but for the wrong side. "If we stay in the terminal, they'll just lob another dozen RPG's in there until we're Kentucky Fried Chicken. Or pick us off when we come running out. I think we're done."

At that point Richard realized that he still had his Sat-phone. "Maybe we can buy some time," he suggested. "Let's see if I can get through to the *Theodore Roosevelt* on this." He dialed Baxter, and got through on the first ring.

"Robert, we've been attacked. Four of our guys are dead, two wounded. And the locals have reinforcements coming," he said. "Can you put me through to the Teddy Roosevelt?"

"Jesus," replied Baxter. "I can switch the call. But I'm going to stay on the line." He immediately connected the call to the bridge of the huge carrier, and from there to Captain Dick Sebatier, commander of the four Super Hornets already screaming toward Yarim-Dhar at 1,300 miles per hour. "Richard, you're on," he shouted, to start the call.

Richard took a deep breath. "This is Richard Lawrence, CIA. We've been attacked at the Yarim-Dhar airstrip. We have four dead and two wounded. There are four of us left to fight. The bad guys are sending reinforcements in trucks. It looks like they're about 15 minutes away."

"We're stepping on the gas, up here, Richard. We have four Super Hornets, but we're 20 minutes out. Maybe a titch more. We're maxed out at Mach 1.7. You guys have got to hang on." This came from the commander of the planes.

Richard turned to his colleagues. "The Super Hornets are on their way. Twenty minutes, they said. Maybe a bit more."

"Dammit, Richard," said Payton. "Those trucks are only 15 minutes away. We're deep in the glue here. I don't think we're going to make it that long."

Richard wasn't so ready to throw in the towel. He didn't know if they were going to be able to get out of this, but giving up and accepting a fiery death in the middle of the desert wasn't high on his list of life priorities. "Maybe we can buy another five minutes or so. I have a plan," he said slowly, still thinking. He laid it out, and it was quickly critiqued and improved by the others. Then they set about putting it into motion.

While the situation was unfolding in Darfur, Baxter patched the DDCI into the telephone link. With the clicking of a few more keys on Admiral Jackson's phone, the President's office was connected as well. One ring and the call was picked up; within a matter of seconds, the President himself was given the telephone. It was still early morning in Washington, and he was reviewing the PDB with his senior staff. Thanks to the switching capabilities of the military, Richard's Sat-phone call now had the attention of the President, his Chief of Staff, the DDCI, Baxter, the bridge of the *Theodore Roosevelt,* and Captain Sebatier. All were listening with growing trepidation, powerless to do anything but wait.

As the seconds ticked on, Admiral Jackson outlined the situation for the President. "We've already encroached on Sudan's airspace with the two Night Hawks, sir. And we are now moments away from doing the same with the Super Hornets. We should call the Sudanese ambassador and brief him on this."

"Fuck Sudan," answered the President. "Those guys have been sending terrorists our way for more than a decade now. This was al-Qaeda's home turf for years. If they want to take on our F-18's, they're welcome to. It's about time it was a fair fight, I'd say."

"What should the press release say, sir?" asked Jane van Buren, his principal press secretary. "The world doesn't know about the missing Semtex yet. They'll wonder what a bunch of Navy boys are doing in the middle of the Sahara. There are no ships out there."

"Let's think about that later. In the meantime, I'm not going to deprive any of our boys of the protection they deserve. Have the Super Hornets go full tilt. Hang in there, Lawrence, my boy," said the President. "Hang in there."

THE SEVEN VEHICLES slid to a stop in front of the terminal. To one side, the wreckage of the two helicopters still burned. The fuel dump had been completely obliterated. The dust clouds kicked up by the trucks mingled with the smoke of the dying fires in and around the helicopters. The only sound was that of the desert wind, and the crackling of a few flames from one of the destroyed Night Hawks. Nothing moved for a full 30 seconds. Then the leader barked a sharp command, and crews from four of the vehicles disembarked and entered the terminal.

Richard, McMurray, Clinton, and Payton lay buried under the sand in a small dip approximately 100 feet in front of the terminal. Their four dead comrades were prominently displayed in the vicinity of the ruined helicopters; it was a chore they had all had found repugnant, but necessary. The two wounded men were even further behind them, also hidden by sand, a chore that had been even more disturbing.

Richard had clambered up the little ladder inside the terminal and found that, as he had suspected, there was one RPG left — the accurate return fire provided by Payton and Clinton had prevented its launching. There was also one barrel of fuel that had not exploded, having been knocked away from the conflagration by the force of the explosion. McMurray, with his vast experience in explosives, had instructed the men on just how it was to be positioned. And then they had waited.

Now Payton initiated the silent count. Richard held his breath. This would be the moment of truth. On cue, the four rose as one. McMurray fired the RPG through an open window in the terminal. At the same instant, three rifles cracked. All three of the terrorist gunners fell, their bodies sprawling across the large-caliber machine guns mounted on the truck decks. Richard, whose bullet was meant for the driver, noticed sourly that he was the only one who had missed and hit the wrong man.

The terminal exploded when the RPG hit, propelling a number of bodies outward, one going spectacularly through the terminal wall. The quiet scene turned instantly into pandemonium. All the available AK-47's started firing in their direction. Richard knew that they had to capitalize on the element of surprise, or all would be lost. Three more of the Bedouin warriors were quickly taken down, but McMurray was nicked by return fire. That left three of them still able to fight. Three against a good seven or eight, with no cover, and no room to maneuver.

The leader barked a series of orders.

"What's he saying?" asked Payton.

"He told them to get behind the trucks! He says there's only a couple of us and they can pick us off easy! Wish I could tell you that he was saying 'run,' but that'd be a lie!" yelled Richard. He had to shout to be heard above the noise of the burning wreckage, gunfire, and explosions, adding stress to an already bad situation. He turned to McMurray. "How're you doing, Sergeant?" he asked the wounded man.

"Took a shot in my right arm. Just a flesh wound, but it's my shooting arm. I can't help you guys right now," answered McMurray.

"Great. Three of us, and Richard, dammit kid, you need more training," groaned Payton. All of them were envisioning scenes of American soldiers being dragged through East African village streets.

Richard saw that the leader was loading another RPG into his launcher. The Thuraya telephone was still with him, and still on.

"What the hell is going on?" asked Big Jack.

"We surprised them. We fired an RPG into a gas drum in the terminal just as the bastards were entering it. We've killed or disabled about half of them. The rest are regrouping. They're getting behind their trucks. I can see at least one RPG launcher from here. They've got the high ground now. Where the fuck are those planes?" snapped Richard.

"We're two minutes away," said Sebatier over the communications link. "Look, we've got all kinds of armaments here. We've got Sidewinders. We've got AMRAAM's, we've got Vulcan Canon. But how far are you from the enemy?"

"About 70 or 80 feet," said Richard, quickly realizing the problem Sebatier and the other pilots were facing.

"This is not going to work. If we fire anything, you guys are at risk. We're a minute away, but if we let go with missiles, if we fire anything, we'll take you out with the bad guys," said Sebatier. "You'll be nailed by friendly fire."

"Here's what we do," said Richard, "and we've got to do it fast. You're coming up behind the terminal. The bandits are in front of the terminal and we're on the other side of them. The four of you will make one hell of a racket if you go over the terminal at Mach 1.7. How low can you fly?"

"Well, it ain't responsible flying, but the landscape is pretty flat. We can get down to 50 feet or so," Sebatier answered.

"Do it," said Richard, as he watched the leader of the Bedouin group casually attach a grenade to the end of his RPG launcher. "For God's sake, do it now! Go max speed! Do it now!"

Richard quickly explained what was going on to Payton, Clinton, and McMurray. "Cover your ears, boys. In less than 20 seconds we're getting four Super Hornets low and at Mach 1.7. The bandits here will tip over with the sound and surprise of it, and then we go for them. The trick will be to cover your ears, and then pick up your rifles the instant the sonic boom passes over us. They'll be temporarily deafened and confused. They won't hear our rifle shots."

Major Payton saw them first. Four dots on the horizon, coming up behind the smoldering terminal. The terrorist leader was still smirking, slowly bringing his RPG launcher level with the ground. He obviously thought he had the Americans where he wanted them, and was looking forward to the imminent carnage.

"About ten seconds, guys," Payton said, watching the robed warrior casually poke around the corner of one of the Jeeps with his fully loaded RPG launcher. "Nine, eight…"

At that instant, Richard, even with his less-than-perfect vision, saw them. The four Super Hornets were growing shapes low on the horizon, behind the terminal, moving at an incredible rate of speed. On the ground, the Arab leader of the group was serenely taking aim, smiling. He was the picture of arrogance, smirking with perceived victory, and utterly oblivious to the four F-18's bearing down in the sky behind him.

Suddenly an ear-splitting roar shattered the still desert air. Payton, McMurray, Clinton, and Richard had their guns down and fingers tightly stuck in their ears when the Super Hornets screamed by. They were less than 50 feet above the desert sands — a high-risk maneuver allowed only because of the desperate situation. They were so low that a long wake of sand kicked up from the desert floor as they flew over. The sonic boom that followed was so powerful that what was left of the burning terminal shuddered and collapsed. The Darfur warriors were completely unprepared for the incredible scream of eight General Electric F414 engines, each one generating more than 40,000 pounds of thrust. They dropped their weapons. One panicked and ran. The leader looked instantly upward, which exposed his face to the full force of the sonic blast. Payton and his men were ready. All took aim and fired, and then fired again. The ear-shattering force of the sonic boom had temporarily robbed the desert bandits of their hearing, as planned, and they did not hear the rifle shots. They saw their friends falling dead, struck by unheard and unknown weapons, and were frozen in place. Within ten seconds it was over. All the enemy warriors were dead.

"Did you get that, Mr. President?" asked Richard. "That's what our flyboys sound like at Mach 1.7." He relayed what had occurred to those listening to the call, holding the phone so that the rest of his crew could listen in.

Captain Sebatier came back on the line. "Two more Night Hawks are on their way. They should be at the airstrip to pick you up in 15 minutes."

"Thanks, guys. We've got wounded to look after," said Payton. "By the way, Captain, that was one hell of a fly move. You should try that over the Potomac sometime."

"Hell, let's do it over the Hudson or LA. That was a blast," replied Sebatier.

With that, the battle of Yarim-Dhar was over. The rush of victory abated as Richard saw the four dead, and the two wounded. They won, all right. Some victory, though. He could already feel the omnipresent headache increasing.

10

A RUSTING DOOR deep beneath the Inzar Ghar fortress opened, and the dead-eyed Hamani Lowki, accompanied by a small phalanx of guards, strode into the damp, dark cell area. There was no natural light here; the only illumination came from one small, low-wattage ceiling bulb. Two of the guards had brought powerful flashlights with them, which they now used to illuminate the prison dungeon. There were a total of four cells, with two or three prisoners in each. A total of 11 prisoners, in various stages of mutilation.

Hamani looked around in expectation, feeling himself to be in a particularly good mood. Today he would be finishing off an old patient, and then commencing work on a new one. As is the case with all individuals who enjoy their work, Hamani would have performed these chores for nothing. The handsome paycheck he earned, in American dollars, was just the icing on the cake.

"Those two," he told his men, pointing to two of the prisoners. "Bring those two wretched bastards along to the Operating Theater. We have a special assignment for the day."

He whistled a happy tune to himself as the guards opened the cell where two prisoners, Darius Petroni and Zak Goldberg, were kept imprisoned. Petroni had been an occupant of the dungeon for almost two months, and the experience had nudged him, day after day, off the coil of sanity. He was, at this point, also unable to walk.

Petroni screamed when he saw the door swing open. The guards merely smirked at him. He was handless, and had only one foot, in which every individual bone had been crushed by a collection of small hammers. He had been pierced, flogged, flayed, and desecrated in a hundred different vicious and callous ways. He was now nothing more than a ghost of a human being, his body mutilated and his face unrecognizable. It was a wonder that he had any sanity left. No one had ever lifted a finger to help him, or to alleviate any of the pain. The guards had minds similar to Hamani's, and enjoyed watching the master at work. Some even considered themselves his students.

As he watched them walk in and grab the subject of their current attentions, Zak's adrenaline spiked. He had been told by the other prisoners what it was that lay beyond the door. He had heard the screams, and listened in shock and fury to the horrifying tales of the others. He could hardly believe that such things were still done. But he himself had seen such torture performed in many training camps and prisons over the past four years. He'd attempted to harden himself against the sights, knowing that if he failed to live up to his cover story, he would be discovered. That task had been far easier when he wasn't the next one in line for the torture chamber.

Since he'd regained consciousness to find himself locked in this dank cell and awaiting Hamani's attention, he'd tried to come to grips with what was to come, and to build some sort of protection for himself. He'd had training as an undercover agent, and had been taught how to build a wall in his mind, to separate his mental self from his physical self, to take his consciousness out of his body to protect himself and the information he carried during possible torture. But every time he came close to achieving this separation, he would look up and see another prisoner, another example of what was in store for him.

This was part of Hamani's process, for he was also a master of psychological torment. He carried on the punishment of his prisoners, making sure they lasted weeks, and sometimes months. He did this to maximize his power, to increase the terror of those held captive in the prison. Even if a prisoner was still whole, he was presented every day with the gruesome vision of what would happen to him when his time came. He would wake up every morning wondering what this day would hold. Perhaps he would just be made to watch the torture of another prisoner today, or perhaps he was about to experience some unimaginable violation of his person. The fear and anticipation alone were enough to break many of the prisoners.

At this point, Zak had been aware of his environment for only a couple hours. But he'd already had enough of the tension and fear. In the last hour, he'd changed his philosophy. This wasn't the way he wanted to die. This wasn't the way he *planned* to die. He'd stopped trying to ready himself for torture and had now turned to plotting his escape. As the guards grabbed him and dragged him out of the cell, he wondered if he'd get the chance.

The Operating Theater, as Hamani preferred to call it, was well lit. It was an ample room, some 30 feet by 30 feet, and very clean. There was a drain in the floor, in the center of the room. The only prominent features were two large tilting wooden tables. Each table had six darkly stained leather restraints — four at the corners of the table and two on the face of the table itself. Zak knew from experience that they were restraints to fix the arms, legs, midriff, and head tightly to the table. Along one wall of the room was a large work bench, with various tools — hammers, drills, pliers, alligator clips, a stack of batteries, and a host of other devices for bending, piercing, burning, and cutting. Zak swallowed heavily, and for a moment his vision blurred. There were definitely some disadvantages to knowing exactly what was going on, he thought wryly.

Petroni screamed and jerked violently as he was led to the table, but, being already savagely mutilated, he had little power or mobility left for resistance. Taking advantage of the commotion, Zak glanced furtively around the room again, looking for something, anything, that might be of use in an escape attempt. The tools on the table? Impossible, how would he ever get to them? And what of the guards? At seven to one, and all seven of them bearing arms, the odds were certainly not in his favor. He only had the full use of one leg. And he was bound, another complication.

As he was contemplating the chances of slipping the ropes from his wrists, he noticed that the action at the table had changed. Petroni had been bound to the table, naked and spread out, immobilized by the leather thongs. The other table was being turned toward Petroni, to stand about 15 feet away from it. The guards began dragging Zak toward this second table.

"Ah, Darius Petroni," said Hamani, walking toward the bound man. "You have given me and my students much from which to learn. We are grateful, and sad to see you go, after… what is it now?" he asked, flipping through a notebook with his pen. "Ah yes, we've had the pleasure of knowing you for nine weeks."

Jesus Christ, thought Zak to himself. This little fucker actually takes notes. Thinks he's running an experiment for Anatomy 101. This had all the makings of becoming truly ugly.

Hamani walked back and forth between the two tilting tables, setting them so that they were positioned vertically. He looked thoughtfully at Zak, who was now standing next to the second table. "What to do, what to do," he muttered as he paced. "You see, my friend," he said, addressing Zak directly, "usually I would have you strapped to this second table, so that you could witness firsthand the torture and death of this man. But I have my orders…" he tapped his pen to his lips, thinking.

Zak stood absolutely still, trying to focus on his plans rather than what the man might say next.

Finally Hamani continued. "Yes, I have my orders, and I am not certain that you should watch, just yet. We need your mind intact, for the time being."

He turned to the guards holding Zak. "Take him outside. He may hear the screams. He may hear the blows, and the sound of saw on bone. But he is not to watch yet. That will come later."

Zak sagged with relief. It was little consolation, in the long run, but for now it was some reprieve. At this point the present seemed to be the only thing that mattered.

As the guards dragged him from the room, Hamani added one last command. "Stay by the door. Tell him everything that happens." Then Zak saw him turn back to Petroni.

Before they were out the door, Petroni began to scream.

"Ah, my friend," smirked one of the guards, "it is too bad you do not get to see. Our good doctor has just plunged his pen into Petroni's eye. As I'm sure you can imagine, it is quite a painful action, from the patient's point of view."

He led Zak to a chair, allowing him to collapse into it, and quickly securing his hands behind his back. Zak listened to the screams of the man in the torture room and groaned to himself. He thanked God that he wasn't being forced to watch the actions, but hearing them described, in concert with Petroni's screams, wasn't going to be easy on his mind.

Suddenly the screams reached another level entirely, and the guard watching through the door grinned in delight.

"Oh, well done, well done." He turned slightly to address Zak, his eyes still focused on what was going on inside the room. "The master has taken one of our sharpest swords and severed the man's other foot."

There was another scream from the room, accompanied by the sound of the sword hitting the wood of the table.

"And his right arm."

The sound of another blow.

"And now his left."

Zak's stomach seemed to shrink, and then expand very quickly. There had never been any training for this. Dealing with his own pain was one thing… being forced to listen to another man dying in this way was something for which his government had never prepared him. He felt his entire body tighten, as though his extremities were attempting to retract into his body. His legs grew tense, as his natural instinct to draw himself into the fetal position tried to take over.

It took all of Zak's strength and will to remain sitting in the chair. He gasped, trying to recall his self-discipline. He remembered that he had been chosen by his government, one of the few men in the world who was strong enough to be put undercover in such a dangerous situation, and sat up a bit straighter. He had no choice but to find a way out of this situation. Biting his cheek to draw blood and focus his attention, he pulled his consciousness inward and thought only of escape, and how he would do it.

Eventually he became conscious of Hamani standing next to him. The man was staring at him oddly, evidently waiting for his attention. He still carried the bloodied machete in his hand.

"Ah, there we are," he said, as he saw Zak's eyes turn to him. He shrugged. "You will be glad to know that I've put him out of his misery. I think you missed many delightful things while you were… unconscious. We've had him for nine weeks now. I'm sure we could have used him for another month, but orders are orders. And these came from the top." He pointed at Petroni's body, still strapped to the table. "What's left of this man is to be put into bags and deposited in front of the American Embassy in Islamabad." He glanced at the guards. "See that it is done."

Then he turned to Zak again. "You," he said. "You, I think, will give me better, more pleasurable days."

"Weren't we supposed to put this man," said one of the guards, pointing at Zak, "in bits and pieces in front of the Embassy?"

Hamani glared at the man who had questioned him. "No. I am certain it was Petroni that was to be dumped. We are to interrogate this one," he said, pointing at Zak. "And that will take a month or two. He is not to be killed immediately." He brandished the machete, looking around to see if anyone else was going to contradict his orders.

"Yes, of course sir," was the immediate response.

Hamani walked too and fro, hand rubbing his chin, reflecting, then turned to one of the guards. "I think I know how we will start with this man. Heat up the cauterizer, please."

Zak felt a cold chill flow through him. He was about to lose a part of his body, and it would not be pleasant. As he was pulled back into the room, he glanced at Petroni's body. Hamani had said a month or two. That meant that tonight would not be his night to die. It was something, at least. In theory. He watched as Hamani went to his tool bench and examined several instruments, finally settling on an old carpenter's saw. He took it from the counter and checked its sharpness with a flicking thumb.

"Dull, gentlemen," he said to the guards. "It is difficult to do one's work when instruments are not up to scratch." He laughed a strange, high-pitched laugh of excitement. "Let's see now. Where to begin?" He circled Zak, looking for all the world like Michelangelo surveying a block of marble. "Let's see."

Zak took a deep breath, trying to maintain his composure. As Hamani approached him, he stared the man in the eye, refusing to show any fear. Instead of thinking about what was going to happen, he tried to think about what he'd do to put the torturer in his place, were he free of the bonds and guards. He pulled against the leather thongs with all his might, praying that they would break, and give him the chance to do just that. The muscles in his well-defined arms and torso strained until he thought his tendons and ligaments might burst, but there was no give in the restraints.

Hamani simply looked on in approval. "Lots of fight in this one," he said, nodding. He brought the saw to Zak's left wrist, touching blade to skin, slowly increasing the pressure. Unwilling to take this lying down, Zak bucked with his torso and used what limited movement he had from shoulder to hand. "We'll need some assistance here," murmured Hamani, and again laughed his freakish, high-pitched cackle.

Zak realized that he had never hated anyone with such intensity. His plans for escape quickly began to include a slow and painful death for this man who thought to play God with the lives of others. He renewed his struggles, wishing with every ounce of his will that it would happen now. He had been trained in self-defense for years, by both the Marines and the CIA, and then for his undercover role. He was incredibly strong, and equally determined, fueled by both hatred and the strong disinclination to lose his hand. In the end, two of the guards were required to immobilize his wrist.

"You know, whoever you are, we are certainly going to enjoy your time with us," Hamani smiled. Then, in light, slow motions, he began to move the saw across Zak's wrist joint.

The pain was searing, blinding. Zak remained silent for the first three or four saw strokes, certain that his discipline would see him through. Then, in spite of himself, he began to moan aloud, eventually finding temporary mercy in unconsciousness.

YOU DID WELL, sir," Hamani told him when he came to. "I am impressed with a man who does not scream, but merely moans, as his hand is severed. And here it is. Your very own left hand."

Hamani brought it closer to Zak's eyes, until it was only an inch away, and then even closer, touching his prisoner's face with the fingers that were no longer his. Zak passed out again, from shock, blood loss, and the conscious decision to leave the situation. Hamani quickly motioned to one of his men, commanding that the cauterizer be brought to him. The device, resembling an oversized branding iron, had been electrically heated, and was, at this point, white hot.

The shock of the burning heat on his arm brought Zak back to consciousness with a scream of pain. The cauterizer was hissing against his wrist joint, and the smell of charred flesh nearly choked him. He struggled in pain and anger, straining once again at his bonds.

Hamani smiled at Zak. "You see, I will become your benefactor. I will stop the bleeding. I will lengthen your life, a life that you will pray ends quickly. A life where your last words will be to thank me for letting you go. You will go mad, as the other prisoners do. But we have many weeks before that happens."

He turned to the guards. "Take him back to his cell," he said. "Take him, but with care. He is powerful and there is much fight in him. Use the restraints whenever you escort him to and from the cells."

Hamani tossed Zak's left hand onto the small pile of body parts that had once been Petroni. "Take that shit and drop it in front of the Embassy," he said, motioning to the carnage. "Be certain that you don't lose any of it."

AS TWO OF THE MEN lugged Petroni's remains up the steep staircase that led to the outside world, his head tumbled from a poorly closed burlap sack. The second guard bent to retrieve it, and threw it up to his coworker, who threw it back down. The second guard threw the head up again, this time deliberately throwing it behind the first. This action led to an impromptu game of soccer. When the game ended another guard took what was left of Petroni's head and threw it into a deep ravine behind the fortress.

"No need to worry about it now. The animals will get it. No one will ever find it," he said, scuffing dirt at the disappearing head.

LATER, ZAK AWOKE to find himself in his cell once again. With Petroni gone, he had the place to himself. For a moment he forgot where he was, but then glanced down at where his hand should have been and nearly screamed as his memories came crashing back. Along with the memories of pain and frustration, though, came another realization.

Hamani had spoken of keeping him for a month or two. For interrogation. At the time he'd been able to think only of seven or eight weeks of torture, if he didn't get out. But now Zak remembered something else. And it was a far cry from what Hamani had said. Engulfed in waves of pain and partial unconsciousness after being attacked by Marak, Zak had still distinctly heard Yousseff say, "Extract from him whatever information you can, and dump his body in some remote canyon in the Hindu Kush."

That seemed clear enough; Yousseff had wanted him killed. But the orders had evidently been lost. Hamani had confused the instructions. Instead, he was to be kept alive and questioned. Zak's mind grabbed the idea and focused on it with a fierce intensity. He had prayed to God for a reprieve. It had been handed to him, through the death of the wrong man. Instead of being killed immediately, as he should have been, he had time… time to be tortured, from Hamani's standpoint. Time to plan an escape, from Zak's.

11

IT WAS CLOSE TO MIDNIGHT when Turbee slouched back to his apartment. Most of his colleagues left by five, and a few hung around till six, but even George was normally gone by nine. Turbee loved challenges, though, and didn't rest until he had them figured out. He had stayed in the office until he had the Heckler and Koch issue sorted out, and thought now that Dan would certainly be pleased tomorrow. Another major victory, yet elation eluded him. The embarrassment of the day still stung. He wasn't working on the possible WMD strike on one of the nation's ports. Dan had deliberately excluded him from that and relegated him to the lower-priority problem of finding some stolen Semtex.

The mapping subsystem that Turbee had screwed up was accessible by Blue Gene, but it was in fact powered by a different network of computers, which stored and served the maps to the IBM-designed Atlas Screen. He simply had not known where the switches were, and had never bothered to learn the re-booting sequence, until this day. He could have learned it in a matter of minutes, but not under pressure.

In a situation like today's, when the anxiety was notched up a tick or two and all eyes were on him, Turbee tended to stop functioning. Now, because he'd panicked at using a system with which he wasn't familiar, he had been rebuked before his colleagues and in the presence of what was apparently a large and distinguished audience on the conference call. Dan's sarcasm had stung. The laughter of the TTIC group, and the condescending attitudes of those on the conference call, bit like acid rain. Once again he was back in the Third Grade, with the laughter of his classmates ringing in his ears, when he had been unable, try as he might, to stop the repetitive movements of his right forearm. He heard his instructors mutter derisively about failures and disasters. He felt the isolation, the exclusion, and the cutting pain of not belonging. Before the medications, he had been unable to control and focus his thoughts, no matter how much he struggled. Socially, he had been almost totally dysfunctional. He recalled the tears at age 11, as he cried in his tutor's arms. "I have no friends. None. I can't think. I can't do anything. I can't even ride a bike," he had sobbed in despair. Things didn't seem to have changed much with time.

He crossed 19th Street and walked the one block homeward, his right forearm moving back and forth to his head. He was agonizingly alone. He had 'colleagues.' He had a 'supervisor.' He had fans and detractors. He had money. He thought he had some friends at TTIC, but didn't think he had anyone who would truly stand by him. He didn't have a girl. He walked, because he didn't have a driver's license. He knew he would never be able to drive. The whizzing of traffic overwhelmed his brain to the point of utter confusion. He had never learned to ride a bike, although he understood the mathematics of centripetal and carioles forces better than most. His father had purchased the small condominium he lived in because he had no sense of money or commercial transactions. He owned a basic four-room basement apartment in the middle of Washington, DC, although he could have purchased a palace by the nearby ocean. He could have bought a Leer jet, or an armada of Harleys, or a Ferrari or two, but he walked.

Nothing had really changed at TTIC. He'd thought it had, but he'd been wrong. He was still the stranger. He was the outsider. He knew that he'd live that way for the rest of his days. Blue Gene had become his only real friend. "I'll always be alone, always, and no hope for it," he muttered to himself as he unlocked his apartment door, oblivious to the curious stare of his neighbor, who was entering from across the hall.

Over the years, Turbee had built a substantial set of armor for himself; protection for when his self-deprecating humor didn't work as a defense against the rest of the world. As part of that armor, and as a refuge from inferiority, he had created Lord Shatterer of Deathrot. When the games turned serious, and when the stakes were high, in the international multi-player Doom-type games that he played, he rolled out Lord Shatterer. Lord Shatterer was a master web-bot, capable of making his own decisions and instigating his own actions, as well as following Turbee's orders in intricate detail. An incredibly high level of programming and design had gone into his creation. No one had ever associated this legendary cyberspace slaughterer with Turbee, but whenever he entered the arena, those acquainted with him took note, and either fled or prepared to die. He had rarely been vanquished, and then only when a conspiracy rose against him on the Internet. Further, Turbee's programming skills were such that, in the middle of a Doom game, he could send a smaller web-bot to invade the computer of an enemy and reprogram it, mid-battle. There were many tales of Lord Shatterer's opponents being reprogrammed during a fight and turning their blasters or cannons on themselves. In this digital world, he was the antithesis of slight and small. There were no physical incapacities, no mental or emotional handicaps. Heaven help those who dared laugh at *this* version of his personality.

He entered his apartment and walked directly to his main computer, shedding his coat and shoes carelessly on the floor. After the day he'd had, it was definitely time to play.

INDY SLAMMED the telephone down. Two weeks? Probably longer? A cabinet decision? He was living in an idiotic country tied up by bureaucracy. He was a cop. But he had risen quickly through the Force, and he had gained the coveted inspector status, complete with his own office at the Heather Street complex, before he had turned 50. Fast work for his field. But he had worked his entire professional life fighting a losing battle against an ever-growing influx of drugs into his country. And the laws were now so screwed up in Canada, and particularly in British Columbia, that he, the king of the undercover drug sting, did not know whether the possession of marijuana was legal or not within his province.

Marijuana was legal for "medicinal" purposes. So now, tens of thousands of people were using the drug for anxiety, depression, chronic headaches, back pain, arthritis, irritable bowel syndrome, restless leg syndrome, and a host of other real, imagined, and sometimes contrived afflictions. He snorted. Everybody had a headache every now and then. Everyone had to deal with anxiety and depression at times. The identities of doctors willing to write prescriptions for marijuana were well known. Now people had a perfectly legitimate medical reason to possess and grow the drug. And who couldn't fake up a constellation of subjective maladies to qualify for marijuana use? To add insult to injury, the courts were now throwing out simple possession charges. Possession of a large amount of marijuana for the obvious purpose of trafficking was dealt with, in the Canadian courts, by a few months of probation. The unfortunate truth was that the students and drug experimenters of the '60s and '70s were now the ones in control. They were the judges, prosecutors, and politicians, and to them the possession of a joint or two was not a big deal. Edgy after a difficult day at the office? Have a toke. Got a migraine? Role a fattie. Wife bitchy? Reach for the weed and rolling papers. It was completely out of control. No wonder Washington was putting pressure on Ottawa to do something about it.

Indy slammed his fist down on his desk, causing pens and paper to go flying. It was because of this lax stand on drugs, and marijuana in particular, that Indy was being stopped in his investigation. He slammed his fist down on the desk again. Here he was, in possession of documentation that demonstrated an obvious money laundering scheme, and he couldn't get his country's cooperation. All he wanted to do was pressure a financial institution in the Grand Caymans to release account information. But no. The Federal cabinet would have to "consider" the rules of international law. It had to be "placed on the agenda." It required "briefing notes" from the solicitor general's office. And besides, it was August. Didn't he know that all important people went on holiday in August? Come back in September, they said. Ease up a little.

He dialed Corporal Catherine Gray, more for commiseration than anything else.

"Can you believe those assholes in Ottawa?" he moaned. "Here we have the clearest evidence you could have of a large money laundering operation, leading directly to a Cayman account, and we can't get at it."

"Yes you can, Indy," replied Catherine, trying to be soothing. "You just need to be patient. You know what they're like east of the Rockies. They want to look at it. They want to work behind the scenes. They want to exert diplomatic pressure. You'll get what you want, Indy. It's obvious what we're dealing with here. Even the government will be able to see it, eventually. Just give it some time."

"And in the meantime, the evidence is going to disappear. Going, going, gone," Indy muttered.

"No it's not, Indy," she said. "No it's not. We need to apply more manpower to this. We need to get undercover people into Fernie. We need to get close to the Hallett and Lestage operation. We can build our evidence and do the same thing you've done so many times in the past. We can find out how these guys are getting their marijuana and heroin across the border. We might even find out how it's getting into BC in the first place. It would all help the case, in the end. Let's just do the normal, steady, slogging police work we always do. We'll get into the heart of what's going on and then we'll throw the lot of them in jail."

Indy knew she made sense, but it didn't ease the sting. "Throw the lot of them in jail? Well, that's another problem, isn't it?" he retorted. "Someone is found with a couple hundred kilos of heroin, and some two-bit doper judge in Vancouver is going to give him two months of probation and ten hours of community service."

"Indy, Indy, Indy. You can't change the world. You just have to do your job," replied Catherine. "Just do the job."

She was right, of course. Still, the frustration of it was getting to him.

With some political will and focus, this problem could be eradicated completely, but the will was absent and the smugglers knew it. BC was becoming an easier point of entry into the American drug market than Mexico. What a revolting thought. But do the job. OK, he thought. Time for a ten-page memo to the head of the Ottawa drug section, setting out why he needed to pressure the Caymans. Time to get onto the computer. Again. He sighed heavily.

"You're right, Catherine. We'll throw some manpower at this. I'm going to deal with Ottawa. Stay in touch." Indy hung up the phone, then groaned as his computer, a ten-year-old Dell, flickered and crashed.

12

IT WAS FIVE IN THE MORNING in Islamabad. Youssef was now in the small personal apartment that he kept in one corner of his large hangar. He was exhausted and sleeping like the dead. Marak woke him with a sharp knock on his door.

"I'm coming, Rasta," he called in an irritated tone. When they were together, he often used Marak's tribal nickname. It was also useful for times when their real names were dangerous or inconvenient. Or when they were dealing with strangers, as they would be today. And the man did indeed have the eyes of a snake — slate gray, almost black, and unblinking. And he had a demonic-looking cobra tattooed across his left upper arm and shoulder. Despite his size, he also had the lightening-quick speed and instinct of his namesake. "Get Badr up."

He was referring to his pilot, Badr al-Sobeii, who had been with the ragtag Afghanistan Air Force during the Taliban's rule. He flew all manner of craft — fixed wing, fighter jet, helicopter, whatever. If it could gain elevation, Badr could fly it. In all, Youssef had eight pilots on his staff. Besides Badr, there were two here in Islamabad. A third pilot, Abu bin Mustafa, was as skilled as Badr, and was currently overseeing the last step of the Libyan operation. Two more lived and worked out of the Karachi hangar, and two others were in Long Beach. They were all essential to his organization.

Youssef rose and began to prepare for his day. He did not bother with breakfast, but quickly showered, shaved, and met Marak and Badr outside his door. As he walked out of the apartment, he glanced around the Islamabad hangar. He had similar apartments in the Jalalabad, Karachi, and Long Beach hangars, where he often did business. Each was absolutely identical in size, furnishings, and personal effects. Even the colors of the toothbrushes were the same. He spent more time in these hangar apartments than he did anywhere else, and needed them to be as much like home as possible. In the opposite corner of each hangar were small offices, each with a few chairs and a desk. Marak and Youssef turned in that direction, while Badr went to check the plane.

As the industrial lights in the hangar were turned on, Youssef could see, in addition to the Gulfstream, three helicopters, two Jet Rangers, and an upgraded Westland EH-101, with modified GE TH-700 engines. Theoretically, it could fly at elevations of up to 22,000 feet. So far it had negotiated mountain passes at 18,000 feet, which was nerve-racking even for Marak, though Yousseff, with his love of the sky, had found it exhilarating. The hangar also housed a large single-engine King Air, and a smaller Cessna. A large and well-equipped machine and maintenance shop was located along one wall, manned by two full-time mechanics. Everything was always in perfect running order. This part of Yousseff's enterprise was essentially a large transportation company; it couldn't be run on equipment held together with duct tape.

"Are we organized, Rasta?" Yousseff asked.

"Yes, we are. The scheme is nicely planned."

"All the details? Everything?"

"Yes, of course. Everything," Marak replied.

"Who do we meet with first?"

"Vijay Mahendra. The computer whiz. He will be working with Ghullam on putting the cover-up in place."

"Excellent," said Yousseff. This was part of his standard fare — creating diversions and cover-ups parallel to the main plan. He knew that the Western powers would leave no stone unturned in tracking down the culprits behind the plan he had set in motion. The cover-up and the plan had to proceed in lockstep if they were to work, and if he was going to be safe afterwards. A plan was not a plan until it had a backup, and then a backup to the backup.

Also in accordance with Yousseff's usual MO, Marak would do the talking. Yousseff always took great pains to keep himself in the background, while someone else did the dirty work for him. He let Marak take the lead as they walked toward the opposite corner of the hangar, where the office was already lit up and waiting for them. He opened the door himself, ushering Marak inside.

A slender, clean-shaven, and restless young Indian man, in his early 20s, was sitting in one of the bamboo chairs. He was wearing rimless glasses, and could do with a haircut. Vijay Mahendra, the Emir's computer expert. He stood up to greet them as they came in. As agreed, Marak carried the conversation. Yousseff, dressed in simple peasant clothes, remained mute.

Marak laid the scheme out slowly for Vijay. Or at least he outlined the aspects for which they would need Vijay's formidable talents. It involved half a dozen break-ins, and a lot of computer manipulation. There were clarifications, and details, and then more discussion. At length Vijay agreed, which was fortunate for him. Had he, after the information that had been discussed, told them sorry, no deal, Marak would have snapped his neck like a twig, and dropped him into some appropriately deserted riverbed.

"Yes, I can do the computer stuff. It is not too difficult. But break-ins? Police? I am not sure I can deal with that," said the young man.

"No need," said Marak. "No need at all. You will have all the assistance and support you require. All you need to do is access the computers. Everything else will be done for you."

"Fine. Good," said Vijay. "We need to talk money."

"No problem," Marak answered. "But you will be paid in cash. In American dollars. Will that be a difficulty for you?"

"No. It would be nicer. No taxes." This response made it immediately obvious to Yousseff that Vijay did not have an inkling about the true nature of Yousseff's enterprise. There was no hesitation whatsoever, no momentary struggle with principles or conscience. He smiled to himself at this show of youth.

After half an hour of haggling over details and payment, they had the deal sorted out. As Vijay was leaving, he finally nodded to Yousseff, who had not been introduced, but had not spoken a single word.

"Who is this man?" he asked, pointing to Yousseff.

"Ah, he's a Pashtun peasant. The gardener. Does the landscaping around here. A friendly bastard — loyal but stupid," said Marak, with an immense grin. "Dumb as a post."

Yousseff held his tongue. Over the years he had become more and more obsessed with protecting his identity. Most days, in Pakistan or Afghanistan, he dressed as he had this particular day. Sometimes he would elevate himself to wearing jeans with an old sweater or perhaps an aging shirt. When the situation demanded it, he could easily pass for an aristocrat, but generally he avoided the Gucci outfits. He was the same way about the other aspects of his life. He was constantly hiding his identity, or changing it. He had Canadian, American, Mexican, Pakistani, and Afghani passports, all in different names. He disguised or hid his presence everywhere he went. This was also true of all his possessions. The legal ownership of the hangars, the properties, and the aircraft was characteristic of how Yousseff owned and operated any asset. His name was not associated in any way. There was a Byzantine system of trusts and numbered companies, with one owning the other, and controlling yet a third or even a fourth. If someone had the time, effort, and resources to apply, and had the political power or the skill to breach the seemingly impervious walls of security and nondisclosure found in places like Liechtenstein, Switzerland, and the Caymans, their search would still come to a dead end. Even if the thread of ownership could be untangled and divined from all of these legal devices, the ultimate owner of a company would be listed as Badr, Mustafa, Izzy, Ba'al, Marak, Rika, or any one of a dozen other individuals. The deeds and title documents of the vast poppy fields in Afghanistan held names other than Yousseff's. "There is no such thing as ownership," Yousseff would say from time to time. "There is only control."

It seemed to Yousseff that he had always known that business had to be done in this obscure manner. That way there would be no paper trail, and less danger. By the time he reached his early 20s, he had taken care to become all but invisible, with business always being done through surrogates.

At the sound of Marak saying goodbye, Yousseff pulled his attention back into the office. The meeting was ending, and Marak was escorting Vijay to the door. Once he'd seen the young man out, Marak picked up the telephone and dialed a number. "Please come now," was all he said. Ten minutes passed in silence, then there was a knock on the front door of the office. Yousseff directed Marak to open it and saw Mahari Dosanj, a rising star reporter with Al Jazeera. The young Mahari had one major shortcoming — he was married to a woman who spent money endlessly, no matter how he reprimanded her. He loved her deeply, but could not support her spending on the salary of a reporter. Far from it. He had descended precipitously into a death spiral of debt and was now flirting with bankruptcy. Most men would probably have left such a woman, but he could not imagine life without her. Yousseff had learned about these circumstances, and had decided that the time had come to exploit them.

An intense discussion soon started between Mahari and Marak. Mahari was not interested in what Marak had to say, and did not want to hear about the deal he was being offered by people he saw as lawless hooligans. Yousseff shrank noiselessly against a corner, allowing Marak to sort things out. After some threats and posturing on Marak's part, Mahari finally realized that he was in tough with some scary people, and that there was no easy way out of the situation.

"Here is the first DVD," said Marak in even tones. "It contains the first message. There will be a number of others. If you betray me, if you break your word on this, I will feed your body to the dogs, little bits at a time. While you watch. Do you understand what I'm telling you?"

"Yes, yes sir. Yes I do," Mahari stuttered.

"I, or one of my men, will notify you of further messages," continued Marak. "And with each, we will provide you with one of these briefcases, filled with American dollars. Each contains a quarter of a million, more or less. All that is required is that you take the message that we give you and get it on Al Jazeera airwaves immediately."

Marak flipped the Samsonite briefcase open, and Mahari gazed hungrily at its contents. In the corner, a small smile curled around Yousseff's lips. It was always the same, he thought. The hunger for mountains of money. This was $250,000 in cash, which Yousseff considered more of a millstone than anything else. He had, in his various houses and fortresses around the globe, rooms and barns full of the stuff. He couldn't buy or expand businesses quickly enough to absorb it. And this man, this reporter, was willing to put his life and career in danger just to get his hands on it.

"Do we understand each other?" Marak repeated.

Mahari shifted uncomfortably in his chair. "Yes, we do. I will not betray you. But I do have a concern."

"And that is…" said Marak softly.

"The Americans will come looking for me. They may find me. They may find this DVD and that will end all of this. I would be looking at a lifetime in some miserable Karachi jail cell."

"I will protect you. If necessary, the police forces of both Islamabad and Rawalpindi will protect you. No harm will befall you. You have my word on this," said Marak.

Mahari smiled weakly. He found little comfort in Marak's disturbing eyes, and had been around long enough to know that he couldn't trust people like this. Had he known what was happening to Zak Goldberg at that moment, he would have run screaming for the door.

"And what of this DVD here?" he asked, pointing to the silvery disc lying on the desktop. "When do I do the story for Al Jazeera?"

"Why, now of course. You have been paid. Deliver it to your employer. Do the story," commanded Marak.

"And if I am pushed by anyone to reveal your name or identity?"

"It is journalist confidentiality. The Americans understand the concept very well. You protect your sources. And, as a further inducement, if you do not protect your sources, you will die. Slowly." Marak hissed his last words.

"Yes. Thank you. I understand. I will be on my way, then," said a shrinking Mahari. The young reporter was obviously aching to be out of the room.

"Oh, one more thing, Mahari," said Marak. Mahari halted halfway out the door.

"Yes?"

"Do not throw that money around. Do not tell your woman. Stuff it away in a corner someplace. You can go wild with it once this project is done."

Marak glanced at Yousseff at that point, and the two understood one another perfectly. Marak knew what his own task would be once the project was done. Mahari would never have the chance to spend any of the money.

"I will be careful, sir," Mahari said, opening the outside door of the hangar and stepping out into the blazing August sun.

WHEN THE DAY finally grew dark, the meetings were concluded, and the last of the loose ends put together, Yousseff bid Marak farewell and boarded the sleek Gulfstream. "Let's get to Karachi, Badr," he said, settling into a soft leather reclining seat.

They taxied to the main runway and, after a short wait, roared down the strip and rocketed skyward. The familiar rush of power was as intoxicating as it had always been for Yousseff. But he wondered if the dual engines could be tweaked a bit more, to extract even more horsepower. He should broach the topic with Kumar.

As they flew, the winding Indus River appeared 40,000 feet below them, and Yousseff turned his thoughts again to his younger self. He had begun to think more and more about his formative teenage years as the pieces of this new plan started to come together. Perhaps it was another way to escape the stress of what he was now setting out to do. He had no experience with the kind of destruction he was planning, and he wasn't entirely comfortable with it. But he had decided to use the Emir to gamble everything he had on this one mission. If things went well, he would be able to take a break from everything else, and relax for a while. It was a breathtaking chance, but these kinds of moves had characterized Yousseff's path from his earliest years. How old had he been when he took his father and uncle's horses through the Path of Allah? Twelve? Thirteen? How old had he been when he became Marak's master at Four Cedars? This plan, this high-stakes chess match, was no different. He wondered why he was suddenly filled with trepidation and uncertainty. Why was he so afraid of failure now, when he had created the Karachi Drydock and Engineering Company, Pacific Western Submersibles, the chains of stores on the West Coast in America and Canada, and the Karachi Star Line, all without any fear or uncertainty? Was this the creeping insidiousness of the years? Was he getting too old for this job? He let his mind drift as he considered. He longed for his opium pipe, but his pilots had made it clear to him that it would not be tolerated on the planes, regardless of whether he owned them or if Mohammed himself had ordered it. Yousseff closed his eyes instead, and thought back to the beginning.

IN YOUSSEFF'S EARLY DAYS of drug running, when he was still a teenager, and small in stature, one or two stubborn peasants in the frontier highlands had challenged him. One peasant in particular stood out in his memory. Yousseff had purchased, for a fair price, the lands of one Besham al Gulapur — 30 hectares of fine farmland. The usual arrangements had been made; the lands would be held in trust. Izzy al Din was Yousseff's eyes and ears in the poppy fields; he managed and oversaw every aspect of the operations there. Yousseff had the power to buy, mortgage, sell, or cultivate the land, and to reap the profits. Izzy managed the land itself. And peasants like Besham kept the legal titles. It was Yousseff's protection.

One year after the purchase, Besham fraudulently sold the land to one of his cousins. A few days later, Yousseff, Marak, and half a dozen of his men arrived at Besham's door, heavily armed. He was in the process of moving out, to retire to a nice home by the Indus River in lower Pakistan. At least that was the plan.

"Take him, Rasta," Yousseff commanded Marak, who, now in his early 20s, had become a muscular and powerful man who struck like a panther, and whose eyes were flat. Gone was the high-tempered youth. He had become Yousseff's emotionless killing machine. The muscle of the operation, totally dedicated to his master. Now he smashed Besham's head against a low dining table and ordered his men to pin him there, holding the man's right arm out along the length of the table. Marak raised his sword, ready to strike.

"You know what the Koran teaches us to do with a thief, do you not?" demanded the young Yousseff.

"Yes, yes, yes," groaned the hapless and bruised Besham. "Please, not in front of my wife. Not in front of my children. I know your mother. You are a kind man. Please." Besham had two daughters, not much younger than Yousseff, and both sat shaking, with his wife and cousin, in a corner of the small home. "Please, Yousseff, not in front of them."

Yousseff ignored the whimpering. "You know it is the Pashtun way. It is the code of the smuggler. I treated you well. Yet you betrayed me. Why should I show you any mercy?"

He motioned to Marak. "Do it, Rasta," he said in the sharp voice that he used when giving an order. "Now."

Marak lifted the sword high. He had taken his shirt off to ease his movement, and now the muscles in his forearms rippled. His bulging shoulders caused the newly tattooed snake to twist and coil. The blade came down with great ferocity and speed, accompanied by the screams of the two daughters. It was the way of *badal.* It was revenge, and the law of the land in the Northwest Frontier Province.

"No. No!" screamed Besham's wife.

The blade stopped, as though held back by an invisible wire, hovering mere millimeters above the wrist that Marak's men had stretched across the table. Besham, whose eyes were tightly closed, opened one with trepidation. The daughters' eyes opened behind their Burkas. There was dead silence for almost 30 seconds… a disturbingly long time to have a razor-sharp blade suspended above an outstretched arm, waiting for the blow to fall. Then Yousseff spoke, so quietly that even in the small room, Besham strained to hear him.

"I have shown you mercy, Besham al Gulapur. By right I could have fed your right hand to the dogs outside. You have deceived me, and I could kill you, and your wife and daughters as well. But I value loyalty above anything. Now you will give your cousin his money back. You will continue to work on my land and do my bidding. And if you take from me again, be it so much as a single poppy seed, I will cut off both your hands and send you to beg in Kabul or Rawalpindi. Do you hear me well?"

"Yes, master, yes I do. I will be your loyal servant until I die, and my family after me. I will never take from you. I will always do your bidding." The act of *badal* and *nunwatel* now ruled Besham's relationship with Yousseff, as it did the friendship between Yousseff and Marak. Besham was now one among the many who called Yousseff master and served him faithfully.

"Good. I think we have an understanding. Now go and do your work."

Besham's story spread like wildfire through the mountain passes, as Yousseff had known it would. His reputation as a natural leader — and a man to be respected and feared — grew with each telling of the story. The only truly disappointed party was Marak. But even he feared Yousseff, and would be loyal to him until death. So he said nothing.

Over the years, of course, there were farmers, and horsemen, and holders of property, ships, and aircraft, who tested Yousseff again. And yes, there were a number of beggars in Rawalpindi or Kabul who were missing both hands, and whose digits had been devoured by pigs or dogs, much to Marak's glee. It was this road that led to Yousseff's great wealth, and these techniques that allowed him to hold such power without resorting to that wealth. To legal authorities in Pakistan, Afghanistan, and the other local jurisdictions, it posed a conundrum that they were unable to unravel. On paper, it appeared that Yousseff did not exist at all. And yet it was common knowledge that he controlled everything that took place in those areas.

IT WAS AFTER the confrontation with Besham that Yousseff rediscovered Rika. She was no longer the teary-eyed little girl at the Four Cedars, begging Yousseff to abandon his dispute with Marak. She had grown up to be slender and stunning, even in the tribal costumes that she wore when in the village. Her full name was Amrika Mahafika, and she let people know it. Only Yousseff got away with calling her Rika. In the mountains, on horseback, she discarded the Burka and dressed as the men did. If anyone made a comment about it, they risked Yousseff's anger. They quickly became the closest of friends.

As things turned out, Rika had a dazzling mind for numbers. She could calculate the exchange rates between currencies in Peshawar or Rawalpindi faster than anyone, even Yousseff. She gradually became the keeper of currencies in Yousseff's operation, and was often with him when he bought and sold property and goods.

One day she approached Yousseff with a proposition. "Youssi," she said. "I want to go to school. I want to have a trade. I want to study accounting and banking. I could become very useful to you. Will you help me with that?"

After much discussion, Yousseff agreed, but stipulated that at the conclusion of her education she would have only one employer, and that would be him. Her job would be to help him with the rapidly growing stash of money, in various currencies, that he kept in several safe houses.

For the next six or seven years, while Rika went to school, Yousseff saw little of her, to his regret. When she graduated and started to work for a large accounting firm in Karachi, he felt slighted. He sought her out and reminded her of their agreement.

"You broke your word," he chided, his voice heavy with regret. "You said that after you finished your education you would come and work for me. I need you."

"What, are you going to cut off my hands now? Is that what I get when I share a bed with you every now and then? You misunderstood what I said, Youss," she told him. "My education is not yet finished. I need to work in a large firm, and be exposed to the practical aspects of the business. I am working in a division of a firm that specializes in foreign accounts. You need to learn this, and I will teach you. I will organize all these things for you. Be patient." Her voice was gentle but firm, and Yousseff agreed.

When Rika married someone else, Yousseff felt doubly hurt, and assumed that their relationship was at an end. He had been deceived by a beautiful woman, and one he had thought was his friend. But it wasn't the first time that had happened, and he shrugged and moved on. He decided that he would not send Marak and his sword to her house.

Then one afternoon she walked into the office of Karachi Drydock and Engineering, one of Yousseff's newest ventures.

"Hello, Youssi," she had said, with a thoroughly modern smile. "I am ready."

Another man, who she would later learn was Kumar, said, "Yousseff, you are a lucky man tonight."

"For what?" asked Yousseff, ignoring Kumar's comment.

"To work for you, Youssi. You paid for my education. I am now educated. Let's talk about my job description," Rika answered.

So they talked. And Kumar had been right.

YOUSSEFF REMEMBERED THESE THINGS as the Gulfstream flew toward Karachi. He saw the valley floor recede, and was moved by the first rays of the sunrise over the towering peaks of the distant Himalayas. He missed those early days, before his affairs had become so complex, before the arrival of the dark and brooding Emir, and the dangerous political and international turbulence that he had introduced into Yousseff's homeland.

This great plan of his would make him one of the wealthiest men in the world. But why did he run the risk? With his palace in Socotra, his yacht, and the Gulfstream already at his beck and call, he wondered why he was doing it. His wealth and skill had enabled him to obtain, among others, Canadian and American passports, and he had palatial homes in both Vancouver and Los Angeles. Not to mention his own private island in the Mediterranean. He was over 50 now, and growing tired. Why this great, grand, complex scheme? Why the restlessness? Perhaps it was the roving, nomadic life that was in his Pashtun genes. The constant traveling from valley to valley that had been going on since the time of his forefathers. Except that now he used ships and aircraft instead of horses and camels.

THE GULFSTREAM made the 700-mile trip from Islamabad to Karachi in just over an hour. After a flawless landing, it rolled into Yousseff's hangar and coasted to a gentle stop. The pilot opened the hatchway and Yousseff descended the stairs, to be greeted by Vince Ramballa and Omar Jhananda.

"Good to see you again, Youss," said Vince. "You must be tired."

"A little, Vince, but I slept on the plane. Is the *Haramosh Star* ready?"

"Yes she is," Vince replied. "It really did not take much in the way of modification. We used the systems we had in place. Just refined them a bit."

"Good to see you again," Omar broke in, shouldering Vince aside in his rush to speak to Yousseff. "It's been a few months. You are well?"

"Of course," said Yousseff. "Let's head out to the docks straightaway. The hours are precious."

The trip from the airport to the docks took longer than the flight from Islamabad to Karachi had, but the three eventually found themselves standing on the bridge of the *Haramosh Star*. It was just before noon.

"Like old times, isn't it?" said Vince, with a smile. Vince and Yousseff had become acquainted long ago, when Yousseff signed on to learn the shipping business on a ship Vince was captaining. At that time, Vince had been the master and Yousseff the supplicant. Their roles were now reversed, but Yousseff had never forgotten Vince's teachings, or that Vince had saved him from a watery grave one night in the middle of the Atlantic.

"Yes. Get me a mop and a bucket," replied Yousseff, also smiling, thinking of his initiation into the sailor's way of life. "But enough of that. Take me to the lowest level. I want to see the modifications myself. This is as important a trip as we've ever been on, Vince."

The three descended into the bowels of the ship, through claustrophobic passageways and down steep, narrow ladders, until they reached the enlarged engine room, which had been modified years earlier, when Yousseff first acquired the ship. Yousseff felt a twinge of nostalgia as he surveyed the familiar sight.

"The trapdoor lies directly underneath the first engine," said Vince. "The switch to unlock it is hidden in the ceiling, right here. Impossible to find if you don't know it's there." He motioned to one of the plates bolted into the ceiling. "Even if you do find the switch, you have to get right underneath that engine to slide the trapdoor back. And to do that, you have to activate a second switch in the floor."

Omar was nodding his approval. He too recognized how far the company had come since the early days of drug smuggling along the Indus. No one could possibly find this unless they knew to look for it.

"Let's do it, Vince. I want to get down there and see for myself."

"Are you sure, Youss?" asked Vince.

"Yes," Youssef said with emphasis, already on his knees beside the large MAN B&W engine, and reaching toward where Vince told him the trapdoor was. He fumbled around for the second switch and, after a minute of Vince's instructions, found it. The little door slid open, and a narrow stairway led downward into inky blackness.

"Can you get some light in here?" asked Youssef as he descended. Vince told him where the master switch for the electrical power was, and after further fumbling Youssef found it. Vince and Omar saw him step down into the small stairway and orient himself in the tiny compartment below.

"How can anyone possibly be in this for six or seven hours?" Youssef's voice drifted out of the shaft.

"Not sure, but Jimmy can do it. We'll have to pay him a bundle," said Vince. "But he'll do it. We needed extra storage space to fit the Semtex, and in doing that, we had to reduce the size of the cockpit. As it stands, we will have just enough room, providing our calculations are correct."

Youssef stayed in the lower chamber for a few more minutes, inspecting the technological marvel that was hidden there. Eventually he came back up the ladder and had to half slide, half roll from beneath the B&W to get back to Vince and Omar.

"Slide more grease and dirt underneath there once the Semtex is secured. Throw some old pipes and whatever else over the door. It must be absolutely and totally invisible. The mission rides on this, Vince," said Youssef, as he brushed the dirt and grease from his clothes. "Now let's get back to the bridge. It's time to pull anchor. We will have a day and half to travel, at full speed. We rendezvous with the *Mankial Star* just northeast of the Maldives."

When they reached the main level, Youssef and Vince bid goodbye to Omar and walked up to the bridge.

"Are you ready for this, Youssef?" Vince asked as they watched the other man walk away.

"Yes, I am," Youssef responded. He noticed the other crewmembers eyeing him suspiciously, and quickly retreated to his normal silence. It wouldn't serve the plan to have outside interference, and the crew was already wondering why a greasy, dirty 50-year-old should be standing on the bridge of the *Haramosh Star,* let alone touring the ship with Omar Jhananda, who some of them recognized as the owner of the very successful, rapidly expanding

Karachi Star Line.

"He's a relative," said Vince, responding to the looks of his men. "He's a bit, you know," he added, tapping his forehead demonstratively. "He needs a job, and he's pretty much unemployable. I thought I could have him along for the trip to clean floors and decks. Give him something to do."

For his part, Youssef had already found a mop and bucket, and commenced working. Over the next 32 hours, he hardly said a word to anyone.

13

THE NATIONAL SECURITY AGENCY held the dubious honor of being the largest and most secretive organization in the Intelligence Community. More than 35,000 people worked there, and every one of them was sworn to absolute secrecy. Because the principal occupation of the NSA was to solve intercepted but encrypted electronic signals ("Sigint"), and because cryptologists, computer scientists, and mathematicians were the main inhabitants of its corridors and buildings, the agency's headquarters and the surrounding community came to be known as Crypto City. It was, in fact, a city unto itself — 5,415 acres, with 65.5 miles of paved roads, 3.3 miles of secondary roads, and about 60 buildings. Within its fences were a modern mall, banks, credit union, post office, chapels, a police station, and many other facilities. There were a number of restaurants and, inside its main building, a 45,000-square-foot cafeteria. Also present were numerous recreational spots, including eight gyms, a number of theaters, and many large childcare facilities. The area even contained its own institute of higher learning — the National Cryptological Center.

The recent terrorist attacks on American soil, and the destruction and tragedy they had brought about, had served as a wake-up call. The sudden need for the ability to access and process communications, especially in the Middle East, became painfully apparent, and the NSA budget was increased dramatically. The organization was once again busy interpreting the billions of snippets of information vacuumed up by its many satellites and listening stations around the world. The need for translators was now great, and American citizens with proficiencies in Arabic, Urdu, Punjabi, and other Middle Eastern languages became acute.

The NSA used many different methods to gather information. Microwave towers were monitored, and the delicate art of splicing into fiber optic cables was now one of the skills taught in NSA classrooms at Fort Meade. Priority was given to monitoring Internet traffic, and many of the NSA programmers learned the stealthy skill of depositing bits of monitoring code onto the hard drives of suspicious servers or websites. Many a terrorist ploy had been foiled in its infancy by the developing stealth and skill of Crypto City's investigative capabilities. These programmers were so skilled that they could, if so inclined, crash the Internet, possibly permanently.

Information poured into Crypto City in vast torrents; trillions of megabytes of information cascaded through its electronic portals. If human hands were being used to parse and analyze all of it, a workforce of one million people still could not have handled the flood. Hence, the initial stage of processing the information was always handled by computers. And such computers they were.

Only a small percentage of all information intercepted by the NSA was passed up the chain for a higher level of analysis. The first level of filtering was performed exclusively by computer, and specifically by the squadron of Blue Gene/M's at the Bunker, through a program called ECHELON. These first-level searches hunted for a predefined set of "keywords," which were either verbal or written. They could be in the form of faxes, images, or even collections of pixels. With the newest modifications, they could even be found in faces or sequences of sounds. The streams of data being searched were microwave, cellular, fax, TV or closed circuit camera, Internet email, and even data on private intranets. The immeasurably vast fields of data, and the complexity of the keywords, created the need for huge amounts of processing power.

The keywords were collated and kept on a series of smaller computers tied into the Blue Genes at Crypto City. These computers were collectively named the "Dictionary," and hundreds of employees at Crypto City were charged with the task of keeping them current. The smaller computers tied into the Dictionary were each home to a different language or function. For instance, there was an "English Dictionary" cluster of computers, a "French Dictionary" cluster of computers, and so on. The Dictionary computers were continuously updated. If a certain telephone number was fed into the Dictionary, or the name of an individual, or a face, or a grouping of pixels of any sort, the specific Dictionary computer for the particular language affected was immediately updated.

Khasha Jamila's job at the NSA had been to ensure that the Urdu Dictionary remained updated. She had, in the space of three short years, become the head of the Urdu Dictionary group, which included some 15 or 16 employees. Khasha had been born in Pakistan to an American father and an American-born Pakistani mother. She had moved to America at age 17, when her parents got tired of working abroad and started to long for the comforts of home. Like most of the TTIC employees, she was very bright, and had attended UCLA, majoring in Middle East Studies. She graduated with honors, and had applied to the CIA and been accepted into the Middle East Bureau. There she distinguished herself in analysis of news and events in Pakistan. She had an uncanny ability for picking up languages and was well acquainted with many Pakistani dialects — Urdu, Pashto, and Wahki, among others. She was an omnivorous reader of all things Pakistani and visited many chat rooms and websites daily. Because of her familiarity with Pakistan, she had ended up working with the Intelligence Directorate, and the American Embassy in Islamabad. While she had no formal training in computer science, she intuitively understood how to use the ECHELON program. She was in constant communication with crews at the satellite download stations in Waihopia, New Zealand, Diego Garcia, Morwenstow, and England. She had an always-open line to the Misawaw Cryptologic Operations Center in Misawaw, Japan. She became a key player in uncovering the various terrorist plots that originated in Pakistan and Iran, and played a roll in identifying the location of the terrorists responsible for the attacks on the USA, by picking up significant keywords within Urdu chatter emanating from Jalalabad.

Khasha also had excellent personal communication skills, and it was difficult for anyone to dislike her. When she was seconded to TTIC, she maintained almost constant communication with her work group in Crypto City, and even telephoned or emailed crews at the various download stations she'd worked with from around the globe. Even when she moved to TTIC, she maintained more familiarity with the Urdu Dictionary than most of her former work group.

At the moment, she was watching the three large digital displays in front of her with rapt attention. Eventually, she circled around the various workstations, and pulled up a chair next to Dan.

"Dan," she said, "we're getting a high level of Internet traffic in Egypt, Pakistan, and Saudi Arabia referring to a nuclear attack."

"How much weight do you put on it, Khasha?" asked Dan.

"We always get a bit of chatter like that, but in the last few days it's escalated by quite a bit. It is a little worrisome." What Khasha did not realize was that the "increased chatter" about nuclear weapons was just one of the many diversionary tactics that Vijay Mahendra had utilized to keep the Great Satan confused and floundering. What she was looking at was a complex ruse, set in place as one of Youssef's backups.

"Do you have any idea what the potential target could be?" asked Dan.

"No, not a clue," replied Khasha. "The NSA has decreased the filtering somewhat, and put extra manpower to work on all Mid-East intercepts.

The level of surveillance is increasing, but at this point we have nothing concrete."

"Let's get Rhodes in on this," said Dan. He turned toward Rhodes' desk, on the other side of the room, and raised his voice to be heard over the noise of the rest of the TTIC group. "Liam!" he shouted. When he got no response, he elevated his voice another notch. "Yo, Liam, are you with us?"

Rhodes abruptly swivelled toward Dan, his face blackening at the tone Dan was using. "Relax, Dan, for God's sake," he snapped. "I'm here. What is it?"

Dan smirked at Rhodes' obvious frustration and gave Khasha a knowing look. It had become all too obvious to the rest of the crew that he reveled in having high-level people like Rahlson and Rhodes answering to him. Khasha narrowed her eyes and bit her tongue, waiting for her question to be addressed. She was looking forward to the day when someone stood up to Dan and told him a thing or two about leadership. But now wasn't the time.

Finally Dan turned back to the business at hand. "Liam, we're getting an elevation in chatter about a nuclear strike in the offing. Put that together with what Goldberg said — that it's likely to be an attack against one of our ports. How many nukes have gone astray since the dissolution of the Soviet Empire?"

"Not as many as the conspiracy wackos talk about on the net," responded Rhodes. "But there are concerns. General Leben of the Soviet Union stated on the record a couple of years ago that not all of their small nuclear weapons could be accounted for. Caspian Sea countries, like Georgia and Kazakhstan, were the homes of large military bases that we believe contained nukes of some description. The unraveling of the Soviet Union could potentially have put nukes in the hands of at least five or six countries. Some of those countries, like Georgia, are seriously unstable. Places like Pakistan have nukes, and there's a powerful Islamic extremist contingent there. Iran definitely has a couple. The list really goes on and on."

"What do you make of the higher level of chatter that we seem to be getting in a few Mid-East countries about nuclear weapons being used against the West?" asked Dan.

"I'd be worried. Definitely, when viewed in the context of Goldberg's message."

"Perhaps we should recommend to the President that we go to Threat Level Yellow around all American ports," suggested Dan. He was fishing for advice, while trying to look as though he didn't need to ask. It was a pretty common move from the TTIC director, who had never done anything to prepare for this type of position.

"It might be too early for that, but we should definitely be considering it at some point. If we get further clues and talk about this, then I think we should," said Rhodes. "Definitely."

TURBEE ARRIVED at work at eleven. Not eight, thought Dan. Not nine. Not even ten. But eleven. It was outrageous. The PDB had been dissected and discussed. The battle of Yarim-Dhar had been reviewed in detail. Big Jack was on edge. Three American soldiers dead at Zighan. Four American soldiers dead in Yarim-Dhar. Two severely wounded. Thousands of kilos of Semtex gone AWOL, and a growing concern about a possible nuclear strike by terrorists. And this propeller-head sleeps in. Sleeps in. Unbelievable, thought Dan. Fucking sleeps in.

"You missed all the briefings, Turbee," he snapped. "This is a team. Your skills are needed here. If you don't want to be a part of us, just let me know."

"Oh, Dan, leave it alone," came a slow, soft voice from the other side of the control room. It was Khasha.

An ally? thought Turbee. No way. That never happened. Not to Hamilton Turbee.

"Shush," came Dan's retort. "We're all getting paid good money to be here. We have a developing crisis, and Mr. Turbee drags himself in here at eleven. That's a little over the top, isn't it?"

Khasha had never backed down from anyone. With her rapier-sharp intellect, she had never needed to. She didn't even feel the need to raise her voice. "He works on his own clock, Dan. And he works hard. Maybe he's actually on Pakistan time right now."

"Look, sir, I was up most of the night concentrating on the Heckler and Koch thing," added Turbee. He didn't think this was a wise time to enlighten Dan about Lord Shatterer of Deathrot, who had been slaying people left and right while Turbee worked.

"Turbee, I know who's here and who's not. You left here last night before midnight. Blue Gene tells me when people come and go. You weren't doing any such thing," Dan responded, condescension dripping from his voice.

Turbee wanted to tell the man that he had hacked a little back door into the operating system and that he could access Blue Gene from pretty much anywhere on the planet if he wanted to. He could have been working all night from his apartment, and had actually done just that. But it was probably best that Dan not know about that either. So he demurred.

"What about the Heckler and Koch thing?" Dan finally asked, after an uncomfortable pause.

"OK. OK. It's like this. OK. We start with the PSG-1's. Definitely a rare gun. Less than 1,000 sold. Germany has several dozen, Israel has more than 100. We have…" He looked up to see Dan's fingers drumming on his crescent-shaped desk. "OK. Ten were sold in the Sudan in the past year."

"OK, now I'm interested," said Dan. Turbee noticed some other heads perking up and starting to pay attention.

Proudly, he started to explain how the guns were initially sold by their German manufacturer to someone named "Mohammed," which was pretty much like selling them to "John Smith" in the US. He described how he had hacked into the H&K servers to find out where the guns had gone. He related how he had reasoned that Mohammed wasn't the real name he was looking for, so had started combing through the databases of hotels, property owners, aliases, and known associates — anyone who might have had an interest in obtaining such guns. He had ultimately discovered that the guns were acquired by one Musa Hilal, the leader of a terrorist group in northwest Darfur known as the "Janjawiid," or "devils on horseback." He had also discovered that this was a group that was, through Musa Hilal and its other leaders, affiliated with al-Qaeda.

That'll show them, thought Turbee, drawing a deep breath. Another Madrid. Turbee, the weird little pale kid, solves another international crisis. He saw the entire group, thirty-some people, eyeing him closely. All that was missing was a drum roll and a "tah-daa."

"That's it?" asked an incredulous Dan.

"That's it," said Hamilton Turbee, tapping his pencil on this desk for greater emphasis. "That is it." Tap tap tap. He couldn't understand why Khasha's head clunked down on her desktop.

"That's real good, Hamilton, but everybody already knew that," said Rahlson from across the room. "The Janjawiid are a well-known terrorist group in Darfur. They make the *Washington Post* and the *London Times* on a regular basis. They're a surrogate for Khartoum, and are at the center of the ethnic cleansing campaign that's being claimed by the Arabian factions there. Christ, Turbee, just read the newspapers," he added. "There is no doubt, there never *was* any doubt, that the Janjawiid were involved. We all knew that. It was the Janjawiid that attacked the Americans in Yarim-Dhar two days ago. There was never any question."

This was, of course, the problem. Turbee did not read the newspapers. He didn't watch CNN. He rarely communicated with anyone outside his small group of acquaintances. He very rarely knew what was going on in the world outside of his small circle. Now he looked around the large central control room. He heard the snorts of laughter.

Rhodes saw their wunderkind ready to dissolve into tears, and came to the rescue. "OK, people, we need to get on track here. What did you expect? You put him on a project by himself, totally unassociated with what the rest of the team is doing. And you ask him to answer a question most of us could have answered already, based on everyday knowledge. Why're we doubling up on things like this? We're not working together. Yes, Turbee used a few quadrillion computing cycles to figure out that the world is not flat, but look how he did it," he pointed out. "He used Blue Gene to find out who is staying in which hotel rooms, who traveled where, on what airplane, bought which weapons, and used them in whatever location. He got from there to the information he just shared, by himself. It shows the power of our computing resources.

"You asked him yesterday to find out what he could about the PSG-1's," he continued. "And from that and that alone, he gave us the correct answer. He told us which terrorist group pulled off this heist, and that they were affiliated with al-Qaeda. Just imagine what he could do if you put him on something important."

"You're not getting paid to make speeches, Rhodes," snapped Dan. "The kid was late. He ignores the rules. And on top of that, he's giving us information we already fucking *had*."

"What do you know about rules anyway, Danny?" Rhodes retorted sharply. He'd done his research before coming to TTIC, and knew a thing or two about Dan's privileged but shortcut-filled life. There were already a few employees in the room who thought that Dan should be replaced by someone who knew something — anything — about the Intelligence Community. So far their opinions had come to nothing. But the knowledge of Dan's background gave Rhodes, and a few others, what they considered to be a responsibility to argue with their commander when it came to issues of importance.

Dan hadn't yet realized that his team knew anything about his past indiscretions. "What's that supposed to mean?" he asked slowly, his tone low and dangerously quiet.

"Just forget it," said Rhodes, quickly deciding that now wasn't the time to take a stand against their commander.

"Why don't you just remember your place, Rhodes," Dan snapped. "Let me handle Turbee how I choose to. He's not your son. If you want to stand up for a kid, why don't you go home and practice on your own? You have a couple, don't you?"

Rhodes' face grew dark at the underhanded reference to his family. "Excuse me?" he thundered, rising to his feet.

Rahlson stood and interrupted before it got out of hand, stepping in front of Rhodes, who showed every intention of going after Dan. "He's not worth it, Liam," he murmured quietly, taking the other man's arm. "Let it go."

Rhodes gave Rahlson a long, level stare, then nodded slowly. He turned and strode out of the room, taking care to give Dan a large berth, and closing the main door quietly behind him. Dan turned back to his work, shrugging to himself and gloating at what he saw as Rhodes' disgrace in front of the team.

Back at the cluster of desks that housed Turbee, Rhodes, Rahlson, Khasha, and himself, George watched his friend's exit in amazement. "Jeez, what's eating him?" he asked in shock. "I thought I was the only person here with an anger management problem."

"He's carrying some personal crap around," Rahlson told him. "Evidently Dan knows about it. Or he just has the worst timing in the world."

Khasha looked up at the older man. She was equally concerned about what had just happened. "What kind of personal crap?" she asked.

"It happened about a year and a half ago," Rahlson explained. "Car accident. He and his wife lost a couple of kids. He went a bit mental for a while, went to an institution of some kind. Saw piles of psychiatrists, got prescriptions for every kind of antidepressant out there. He got straightened out, eventually. For the most part."

"You mean the shrinks actually helped him?" George asked slowly.

"Apparently so."

"Well I suppose there's a first time for everything," George said dryly. "Let's just hope it doesn't keep him from concentrating on important stuff."

14

THOUSANDS OF MILES to the southwest, across the Arabian Sea, Mustafa was giving staccato orders to the deck hands of the *Mankial Star,* Yousseff's private yacht. A portion of the aft deck of the yacht, between the helicopter pad and the rear cabin, was opened to reveal a small cargo hold. An ingenious scissors lift system could be raised, so that cargo transported by helicopter onto the ship could be unloaded onto the lift deck and then lowered. The recessed decking then slid back into place to hide the hold. Special fittings attached to both the helicopter and the lift system made transferring cargo simple and quick. Mustafa's DC-3 had traveled from Bazemah to Yarim-Dhar, and, after being refueled by the Janjawiid, on to Socotra, a small island just south of Yemen. There the Semtex had been unloaded and repackaged into 23 pallets containing around 200 kilos of Semtex each. The chopper they were using had a carrying capacity of only 1,500 pounds, and it had taken six trips to deliver all of the explosive to the yacht. Transferring loads from the helicopter to the scissors lift had been the phase that Yousseff was particularly concerned about. "There are satellites," he had said. "If one passes overhead at the time of the reload, they might see." Mustafa had thought the chances were remote, but Yousseff was not one to be second-guessed. Hence, the reloading was undertaken with great speed and efficiency, planned down to the smallest move. For added safety, a tarp was stretched from the aft cabin to the rotor blades of the chopper to cover the path. The transfer ended up taking ten minutes per load.

The *Mankial Star* had already been fully fueled and stocked. As soon as the scissors lift receded for the last time, the captain pointed her on a southeastern course. They had a day to get to their rendezvous, and there was little time to waste. In a different part of the ocean, Captain Vince Ramballa was standing on the bridge of the *Haramosh Star,* shouting directions out for her speedy southern voyage. The two ships had an appointment to meet at the southern edge of the Malabar Coast of India for the next step of the plan.

AT THAT MOMENT, in the TTIC control room, Turbee was striving to gain a better understanding of the drug and terrorist connection. Khasha, the only member of the team who took him seriously, was leaning over his desk helping him.

"OK," he said in a tremulous voice, speaking for the first time since the argument with Dan. "I have a question. The gun order from H&K. It included a lot more than the PSG-1's. In fact, it was a truly massive order, for many, many different types of weapons and ammunition. Here's the invoice." He motioned to one of the large 101's at the front of the control room. "As you can see, it's for more than 400,000 Euros. The question is, where did they get that kind of money? And I think it may have been in cash, because I can't find a check for that amount anywhere. Blue Gene could have found it if it existed, but after hours of searching thousands of databases and financial institution records, I still drew a blank. If Blue Gene can't find it, it's not there. So where do you get that kind of money in cash?"

"Well, that one's easy," drawled a voice from another desk. "A no-brainer, actually. It's drug money. That's how most of these bandits finance their operations." The voice came from Lance Winters. Lance, formerly one of the top guns at the DEA, was in his early 40s, and had worked on the China White cases — heroin imported from Laos, Burma, and Vietnam. He was well aware that when the American police forces put their sizeable dent in the cultivation, manufacture, and transport of China White, an Afghani pipeline had quickly replaced it. He had also dealt with Columbian and Mexican marijuana, heroin, and cocaine operations. Immediately prior to his transfer to TTIC, he had been dealing with the growing problem posed by BC Bud.

"You guys are talking about al-Qaeda and its surrogates," he continued. "That means opium cultivated in Afghanistan, and heroin processed there, or in the Northwest Frontier Province, in Pakistan. That's where the drugs came from. In some way, that's where the money came from too. That's where you should be looking."

"I think he's right," said Rhodes, having just returned to the room. "If we're talking cash provided to a quasi-terrorist group like the Janjawiid, we're talking drugs. And if we're talking drugs, we're talking Afghanistan. Al-Qaeda has for years been funding its operations through the use of drug money. We have a lot of documentation on it."

"I agree," said Khasha. She was the other resident expert, having spent years pouring over Pakistani websites and newspapers, and connecting daily with her many friends in Pakistan. "I'd say that it's definitely drugs. Probably heroin. The opium is grown by the Pashtun farmers in the mountain valleys of northeastern Afghanistan. It comes into Pakistan via hundreds of uncharted mountain passes, known only by the locals. It's refined in portable labs in the

Northwest Frontier Province, and gets shipped to America and Europe from there. The heist we're looking at cost a lot of money, and shows a lot of organization. And it's probably part of a much larger operation. Assuming all this stuff is related, it means that someone got their hands on a DC-3, and had a pilot to fly it. They acquired weapons from Germany. They bribed air terminal supervisors, so that no flight plans were filed. They had someone who knew the route the Semtex was going to take from Benghazi to Bazemah. They probably had a smart place to stash it once they got it. There's a lot of sophistication behind this, and to me, that means they had a lot of money to spend. The answer to this riddle lies in Pakistan or Afghanistan. Once we know who provided the money, we may know where the explosives went after we lost track of them."

"I think we need to focus more manpower on this Semtex thing," added Rhodes, raising his voice to draw attention to what he was saying. "All this stuff we're picking up on the Internet about a nuclear attack could be just a ruse. The only solid evidence we have of things going amiss is the stolen Semtex." He turned to Dan, who had just walked up to the group. "Maybe we need more people than just Turbee looking at this issue."

"Why?" argued Dan. "And what's the hurry?"

"As a group, we're certain that this heist is being financed and operated by drug lords in Afghanistan," Rhodes answered, annoyed at having to answer to someone who understood so little about the international stage. "Some of those characters possess the means to transport that Semtex a long distance in a hurry, by ship or by air. Europe and America are the prime drug destinations. It stands to reason that they'd be the prime Semtex destinations, too. The people who are now transporting the Semtex have the means to slip through borders easily. It's what they do for a living. We'd never see it coming, Dan. That's why."

"Maybe we need someone in the field in Peshawar or Jalalabad," said Lance. "Who have we got?"

"No one good," said Rhodes. "With Zak Goldberg already undercover, I think all we have left in that area is Richard Lawrence." He winced as he said this, knowing full well the minimal number of human agents America had in the region.

Dan stood quietly for a moment, considering. "Let me call the commander of the *Theodore Roosevelt,"* he said finally. "We should be able to get Richard to Islamabad in less than two hours in one of the Super Hornets. Johnson, get me the *TR* on the line. Now."

YOUSSEFF WATCHED the cranes and gantries of Karachi Drydock and Engineering recede into the distance. As the *Haramosh Star* proceeded southward, the smog and crowded streets of Karachi were replaced by the endless mud swamps and wetlands that formed at the delta of the Indus River. These were the places that he and his inner circle had used so effectively in the early years of his enterprise. Again he was flooded with memories, sharpened with nostalgia. He drifted back into his dreams.

HE WAS 16 AGAIN. He already had substantial land holdings in both Pakistan and Afghanistan. Izzy and Ba'al were becoming wealthy, just through their association with him. Marak was piling up stacks of money in his safe house in Pakistan. Yousseff's success was spectacular for his age. Yet his restlessness only seemed to increase. He had gone with the drug traders from time to time, as far as Islamabad. His parents had forbidden him to travel further, and out of respect for them he didn't. But the ever-greater desire to see what lay beyond the next horizon finally overcame him.

He had come to know, over the years, a pleasant and rotund man by the name of Mohammed Jhananda, who was the owner and captain of a small 30-foot riverboat. He ferried goods up and down the Indus and its tributaries, from Islamabad to the mud flats and islands that dotted the enormous river delta just south of Karachi. His boat, if it could be called that, was a dilapidated, ancient vessel named the *Indus Janeeta.* Its single diesel motor spewed dark black smoke and made hideous clanking and rattling noises. Mohammed liked Yousseff, and admired his hard-working ways and sensible head. Transporters were always looking for another swamper, especially one who was young, strong, and eager to work. Eventually Yousseff started working for Mohammed on his occasional trips to the coast. Although he had spent most of his life on high desert plains and mountain passes, he took to the ways of the river, and loved the easy travel and customs of the great inland waterway.

Mohammed had a son, Omar, who was a few years older than Yousseff. It hadn't taken long for Omar and Yousseff to become firm friends. They enjoyed fishing off the end of the boat when she was anchored, and worked like dogs together moving goods of one sort or another from ship to dockside, or vice versa. Once they reached their teens, they moved on to chasing women together. Occasionally they would share hashish or opium, and dream about future conquests.

Sometimes Mohammed purchased half a kilo of heroin in Peshawar and transported it from there to Islamabad, and ultimately to the vast Indus Delta. But he was terrified of being caught by the authorities, and didn't push his luck with drugs very often. For the most part, Mohammed was a cautious and wily man, not given to ostentatious or wild behavior. He knew how to operate below the radar of the river police, and how to stay out of trouble. From him Youssef learned the ways of the river, where to deliver drugs, who to trust, who to avoid, and how to survive and prosper. He paid attention to the many river tales of drug transporting and pirating. When he felt he was ready, Youssef decided to transport a kilo of his own product to the coast. For a cut of the price, Mohammed gave his approval, and Youssef conducted the transportation and sale with his usual skill.

He was amazed by the fact that the very act of moving heroin from an inland city to saltwater increased its value from $1,500 to $10,000 per kilo; he'd never realized that transporting a substance could so increase the price. He then considered the larger question. If that kilo were moved to Los Angeles, or New York, or Vancouver, what would its value become? And why shouldn't he reap the advantages of that? Why shouldn't Youssef Said al-Sabhan be entitled to that greater increase? If all it took was a boat — albeit, a boat somewhat larger than Mohammed's — why not?

Already Youssef's wealth was skyrocketing, just from his land holdings and current drug operations. He now took pains to ensure that, with every trip he took, Mohammed had at least five kilos of heroin with him. It was so easy. Roll it in a robe or coat, and add it to the deliveries Mohammed was already making. He gave Mohammed 10 percent of every sale, and Mohammed realized that Youssef, with his clever tongue and agile mind, could make him wealthy with little effort on his own part. The old man could see that Youssef possessed a great talent for this, and felt much more comfortable with Youssef in command than he was on his own.

Omar, on the other hand, began to develop an impressive talent for mechanics and working with metals. He became skilled at monkey wrenching and making do with what he had. He spent most of his time repairing portions of the *Janeeta* as they broke or wore out. He could make any motor work, and coaxed many extra hours out of the old diesel that powered the riverboat. He was clever with a welding torch and was always visiting machine shops to find new parts for the aging craft. Youssef suspected that Mohammed could easily have bought a larger vessel, but was too attached to the *Janeeta* to scuttle her.

Youssef would join the father and son on river trips three or four times a year, generally avoiding the rainy season. One day, however, as he drove his old Jeep to the Soan River docks just south of Rawalpindi, he found the boat still docked, its engines quiet. Instead of readying the vessel for the trip they had planned, Omar was sitting, glum, head down, legs dangling off the end of the dock, staring unblinking into the dirty brown river water.

"What is it, Omar?" Yousseff had asked his older friend, pulling up behind him. "What is troubling you?"

"It is my father. He has been arrested. They found two kilos of drugs on the *Janeeta.* The boat is going to be impounded. He will probably be executed." The law in Pakistan was harsh, and drug runners were normally put to death publicly. Omar continued to stare down at the brown river water below him. "Tortured and executed."

Yousseff was shocked, and concerned for the older man. "This is not good news. Which police detachment was it?" he asked. "Maybe I can do something."

But Omar was inconsolable, and not interested in discussing possible escape for his father. "There is nothing you can do. He was caught red handed. Someone must have tipped off the police. It is over for him. Maybe for me too," he groaned. Yousseff was only 17, but Omar was now 18, a man by Middle Eastern standards, and punishable on adult terms.

"No, no. You give up hope too easily. Maybe I can help. Which detachment?" Yousseff pressed.

"It was the southern precinct at Rawalpindi. The river patrol wing."

Yousseff knew this particular constabulary. A group of lazy do-nothings, surviving mostly on bribes and payments from business owners for "security." Everyone knew how they worked. Mohammed simply had not wanted to bother with this little detail. Yousseff shook his head and sighed at the man's shortsightedness. Omar was right. His father would be dragged in front of the magistrates, and would very likely receive the death penalty. An example would be made of him, and the officers would be commended for their outstanding police skills. This was not good at all. But Mohammed was at fault as well — he had not done what was necessary for the orderly conduct of business. People needed to be paid, and paid well, for their services. Whether the individuals involved were mountain valley farmers, sure-footed Pashtuns taking horses across perilous mountain passes, or providers of security, they needed to be compensated. Old Mohammed, for all his fox-like ways, had never completely respected it. Yousseff, on the other hand, knew it to be the most basic fact of business; he had been born with the knowledge in his blood. With a clever tongue, and some courage, he knew that he might be able to repair this.

So it was, with resolve, that Yousseff found himself in the office of the arresting constable.

"And so, what can I do for you, young man?" asked Constable Noor Udeen. "How can I help you?"

"It is my uncle," Yousseff lied. "Mohammed Jhananda. You have him in custody."

"Yes, yes we do. A serious matter. Very grave. Very grave indeed. Drugs." The constable looked serious and authoritarian.

"My uncle is a simple man, officer. He just doesn't understand good business," said Yousseff, deciding to be honest and direct.

"Oh?" inquired Noor, eyeing the boy before him. "And what do you know about business?"

"Very little, sir," responded Yousseff. "I do not have many years. I know little, but I know that for business, you need security. You need protection. That is what the police are for. My uncle maybe did not realize that."

It was a typical high-wire performance from the young man. Had he been a few years older, the play would not have worked. Had the constable been of stronger character, it would undoubtedly have failed. Just being there to defend a drug runner and law breaker would have been enough to send Yousseff himself to the gallows, regardless of his age. But the winds of fortune blew favorably for the boy, as they so often had.

"And you say you know that?"

"Yes, sir, I do. My uncle erred. He did not have security for his business."

"And what do you have in mind?" asked Noor.

"Well, I know the rate. I think I could probably pay double," said Yousseff, trying to calm his racing heart and keep his gaze steady on the eyes of the constable. This was the most important moment of the deal. He would live or die with this. It was the moment of truth.

"Double?"

Yousseff nodded. "Double. And if you never bother him or me again, I will make you wealthy. Just give us peace. Do we have an arrangement?"

The seconds passed. Each one felt like an hour. Yousseff listened to his heartbeat, and the swishing of the overhead fan. He did not breathe. He did not move a muscle. Not a twitch.

"Meet me tomorrow by the Soan River docks. Nine in the morning." Constable Noor stood up, and showed Yousseff the door.

Youssef fought hard to stifle the smile that had sprung to his lips.

THE FOLLOWING MORNING came bright and early. Constable Noor had thought about the money the boy had offered him. It amounted to $20,000 American. A fortune. He could purchase a large farm with that much money. Or a large boat. A car. Maybe two. A car and a boat. An ongoing relationship, the boy had suggested. A car, a boat, and a farm. The closer he came to the docks, the grander his visions became.

He met Youssef at the appointed hour. The sun was already high in the sky, and it was a beautiful cloudless day. Youssef and Omar had been there for some time, surveying the area. They had escape routes. They had exit strategies. They had backup plans and backup plans for those. They were both ready to bolt, charged with adrenalin and fear. Marak was hidden in the background, equipped with an old but very functional army rifle, in case of disaster.

Noor was straightforward. "Do you have the money?" he asked as he walked up to Youssef.

"Well, yes I do. Where is my uncle?" retorted Youssef.

Ka-ching, thought Noor. This was too good to be true. "He is in the police van."

Youssef gave Noor the money. Tens and twenties, mostly, in a cardboard box. Noor did not count it. He rushed back to the police van, and released a fatigued and somewhat beat-up Mohammed. He didn't bother to say good-bye, either. Farms. Cars. Boats. Ka-ching, ka-ching. He literally danced into the van and peeled out of sight. Youssef watched him go.

"Idiot," he said to himself. Noor would be behind bars within months. He would spend his money like a drunken sailor. Others would notice. Notice and talk. He recalled discussing this very thing many times with Marak. "We can do better, Rasta. We can do better. I have a new occupation in mind for you." Marak was about to join the police force. He would start in the anti-drug section in Rawalpindi, to their mutual profit. Thanks to Youssef's dealings, Noor's position would soon be opening up. He thought that Marak would probably be the perfect fit.

Released from his imprisonment, Mohammed stumbled toward them and fell into his son's arms. He looked at Youssef with tears in his eyes.

"The *Janeeta* is yours. You are now a son of mine. I do not know how to thank you."

"It is fine," said Youssef, wondering what he was going to do with a dilapidated boat and an equally dilapidated Mohammed. "Just let Omar and me use the boat. We will look after you."

"You have, my son, you have," replied the wet-eyed man. "You have."

With that, Yousseff acquired not only a boat, but customers as well. He became the master of the old man's trading business, and gained the protection of the Rawalpindi police force. There was one difference, however. Instead of a kilo, or perhaps two, being delivered to the deep-sea captain at the appointed time, Yousseff came on his first trip with ten kilos. After a hasty conversation with the ship's captain, he returned, 30 days later, with 30 kilos. And 30 days after that, with an astounding 100 kilos of heroin.

By the time he reached his 18th birthday, he had a problem that few 18-year-olds had. He was sitting on a mountain of cash. By his estimate, he had at least $2 million, locked away and heavily guarded in Inzar Ghar, on the eastern edge of the Path of Allah. Now he needed a plan. That money needed to be put to work.

At that point, he bought a new 40-foot riverboat, and Omar replaced the engines with powerful B&W's. Ba'al and Izzy were continuing with their land and property businesses. Yousseff bought a river warehouse in Rawalpindi, and began looking at property in Karachi. But he was still sitting on a warehouse full of cash from his smuggling activities. You could buy a small farm for cash, but to buy a commercial complex in a major city with suitcases full of American dollars was a different proposition. Something needed to be done.

MAX HER OUT, Johnny!" yelled Richard as a blast of adrenaline rocketed through his system. It had been more than ten years since he'd flown, which was like saying that it had been more than ten years since he'd had sex. Unbearable, really. More than ten years had passed since the specialists at the National Navy Medical Center in Bethesda, Maryland had told him that his vision had dropped below the levels required for a Navy pilot. It had been a time when the Super Hornet was only whispered about, since its existence was still classified. Now here he was, in the secondary seat of a Super Hornet F-18, tearing up the atmosphere at Mach 1.7. He felt the rush of power from the twin General Electric power plants, and the ecstasy of unbridled flight. This was beyond the experiences he'd had in the plain old non-super Hornet days. The original Hornet had been a fine plane, and had served the Navy well, but this thing — this plane — was orgasmic. It was the only metaphor that Richard could think of.

Halfway through the flight he'd convinced Major John Trufit to turn the controls over to him. Just for a few minutes, he had said. In the end, Trufit had to override the rear control and forcibly reassert his dominance over the plane. He'd smiled wryly to himself as he did it. Everyone knew the stories of Richard Lawrence, hotshot pilot. In his prime he'd been one of the star pilots of the Navy. It was no surprise that he wanted to fly again. And it was no surprise when he didn't want to return the controls once he had them.

"And what's with that HUD?" Richard was asking. He was used to the black and white Heads Up Displays in the old Hornets. He'd never seen anything like the modern displays before. Multi-colored, three-dimensional, forward views, rear views, even simultaneous views if you could handle them. The days were long gone when a first-year college student had more computing power than a Navy warplane. Raytheon had made the HUD touch sensitive, and the Hughes Corporation had created some truly exotic advance targeting and forward-looking infrared radar systems. Richard's heart had jumped when he'd seen it. This plane was to die for.

He'd been incredibly pleased when the commander of the *Theodore Roosevelt* Battle Group had called him directly, while he was flying back to the carrier group in the Night Hawk helicopter.

"Get ready to put a flight suit on, and I hope you packed a toothbrush. You're turning around and going back to Islamabad," the commander had told him.

Richard grinned. "Islamabad? You bet. It's home."

"Good. You're needed back there. This is straight from Washington. You're going to be working for the anti-terrorist work group. US Embassy personnel will be at the airport in Islamabad to pick you up."

"You've already got clearance to go through the airspaces of I don't know how many Middle Eastern countries?" asked an incredulous Richard. "That's amazing." The State Department was in high gear on this. It obviously came from the top.

"Yup. The weenies at State said rush rush."

The Super Hornet transporting Richard back to Islamabad had cruised at 1,200 miles per hour across the Mediterranean, then southeast, flying over Israel, Jordan, and Saudi Arabia, with a quick southern detour to skirt along the Gulf to avoid Iranian airspace (not even the State Department had that much power). Then they'd headed into the Gulf of Oman, where the plane refueled in flight. Finally there was a gentle turn to the northeast and into Pakistani air space. Now here he was in a top US military plane, heading home to Islamabad. Had Richard had the eyes to see, he would have noted the *Haramosh Star* heading southward along the Indian coastline as they passed over. He might also have seen the *Mankial Star* proceeding southeast from Socotra toward its rendezvous with the larger ship.

THE ONLY INDIVIDUAL who was not in motion at this point in time was Inspector Inderjit Singh, in Vancouver. The only distance Indy could cover was from one corner of his small apartment to the other. He was going absolutely nowhere, and felt it acutely. Yes, Catherine was right. He had to do the basic slogging police stuff. Let the process work. But when he needed undercover operators, they were all busy on various other operations in and about western Canada. When he needed access to bank records, the people who could give him access were away on holiday or on Very Important Trade Missions. The damn process wasn't working, not when he needed it to! He should've just gone to law school, like his older brother. Been retired by now. Sitting on a pile of cash. Spent his time fishing. But not Indy, he'd never taken the easy route. He'd been too stubborn.

He growled to himself and turned back to retrace his steps, waiting in vain for a return call from his superiors.

THAT DAY, Mahari aired the first message on Al Jazeera. Within minutes it was picked up by Reuters, CNN, and the other world media giants. The communiqué was immediately analyzed in great detail, again and again, by the reporters of these news agencies. But that analysis was nothing compared to what the US Intelligence Community did with it. The mathematicians and engineers of the NSA examined every pixel of the video. Psychologists and doctors considered every nuance of expression. An army of translators and linguists replayed every tone and syllable. Backgrounds, shadows, eye reflections, and the warp and weave of fabrics were dissected to molecular levels. Hundreds of memoranda, reports, and opinions blossomed in the Intelligence Community almost immediately. All were, in due course, directed to and digested by Blue Gene/L. While there was extensive debate about some aspects of the recording, there was certainty about one thing. The man in the footage was the Emir. The Intelligence Community had seen him before, and wasn't surprised. Thanks to the message, it was now a face known by billions.

The footage contained the usual salutations to the holiness and glory of the *jihad*. It consisted of all the usual praises for the martyrs — the young men who had gladly given their lives for the prophet, Allah, and Islam, all for the standard promises of Paradise and an unending supply of virgins. And, of course, it contained the usual fulminations against the Great Satan and the Lesser Satan.

But this message differed from earlier missives in two respects. The first was that it was video — high-quality, high-definition video, shot with a digital video recorder. This gave the message considerable impact. While analysts had verified that prior audio recordings were those of the Emir, to see the man himself, with his coal-black eye and the shadows of a deeply crevassed face, was disconcerting. It was apparent to anyone who paid attention to a TV set for longer than 30 seconds that the face radiated power, strength, and, to Westerners, absolute evil. This was no feeble or dying revolutionary living in a culvert somewhere.

The second frightening aspect was the promise made during the message. Not a possibility, or even a probability, but a certainty. The words were delivered in an emphasized, sharp, staccato style. There was no ambivalence. There was no room for confusion. That was what was so disquieting about the whole thing. Why would a high priest of terrorism make a promise, a guarantee, of a massive strike, if he could not in fact deliver? If he failed, the loss of face would be irreparable. But if he succeeded, his stature would be elevated to God-like among his own people. The comparison to other major terrorist attacks was especially unnerving. The bureau offices of the CIA, FBI, and NSA, the offices of the major military Intelligence Agencies, the Department of Homeland Security, the boards of the DDCI, the DI, and the Cabinet, and the office of the President all played the same extract of the message over and over.

...the soldiers of Allah are in place. The weapons of Allah are positioned. The means of delivery has been secured. Within 30 days the great terror will strike, somewhere on this globe, in a manner that will make prior attacks on the Western powers seem insignificant. The holy jihad will make a mighty strike upon the Great Satan and her allies throughout the world. Praise be to Allah, and to His prophet. Within 30 days, the terror will come...

IS THIS the real McCoy?" the President asked his security advisors in the White House Situation Room. "Do we take it seriously? Is it a threat to use a nuclear weapon?"

The response around the room was unanimous. This was the real thing.

A long debate ensued as to whether or not to raise the threat level status from its present "Green" (careful monitoring) to "Yellow" (some concern). Because of the great cost to local economies, airports, police payrolls, and a host of other security-conscious industries, the President decided to keep the threat level at Green. The message, after all, suggested that the attack would take place somewhere on the planet. Not necessarily in the United States. However, bulletins went out to all embassies, and travel advisories were issued for some areas.

15

IT WAS 4AM when Ghullam climbed the steep and narrow stone steps that led up from the dungeons of Inzar Ghar. He walked slowly toward the row of Jeeps parked in the lower courtyard. There he found two burlap rice bags, each containing approximately 90 pounds of grisly cargo. He threw the bags into the back of one of the waiting Jeeps, then paused to light a cigarette and survey the moonlit, rocky slopes of the Sefid Koh, stretching into the distance. Behind him loomed the stone walls of Inzar Ghar, with its huge stores of heroin, weapons, and cash. Below him were the dungeons and cells reserved for those who had come down on the wrong side of one of Yousseff's operations.

When his cigarette burned out, he started the Jeep and drove down the steep canyon road. He was humming a nameless tune, smiling as he thought of the devilish little stunt that he was about to perform. These orders came from Marak rather than Yousseff — a consideration that made them more pleasing to Ghullam. Yousseff didn't have the stomach for this kind of work, so his orders, in Ghullam's opinion, lacked the creativity of Marak's. Today's plan was a welcome diversion from the norm. When he reached the main highway west of Peshawar, he headed toward Islamabad. It was still dark when he reached the city, threading his way through the empty streets of Pakistan's capital and coming to a halt in front of the American Embassy, at Ramma 5 of the Diplomatic Enclave. He deposited the two burlap sacks in the middle of the driveway, and searched his pockets for the GPS transmitter that had dropped from the spy's *chapan* two days earlier. He turned it on, deposited the device on top of one of the sacks, and sped off into the night, still happily humming to himself.

THE SIGNAL was quickly picked up by a Global Hawk drone and relayed to a Milstar satellite. The Milstar system circled the globe, and the electronic signature of the GPS was bounced from satellite to satellite until it reached the Air Force Space Command headquarters at Peterson Air Force Base in Colorado. From there it was relayed via ground signal to the large monitoring center beneath the Pentagon. The junior officer in charge of a section of screens immediately reached for the phone and called his superior.

"We've found him," he said. "Zak Goldberg has re-established contact. Looks like he's back in business."

"Where is he? What are the coordinates?" asked his supervisor. He was vastly relieved, as he knew others would be. Zak's long silence, in such a dangerous situation, had been nerve-wracking.

The junior officer read out the numbers. There was a perplexed silence. "Are you certain? That's the location of the Embassy in Islamabad. He must be standing just in front of it. I'll make the call."

TWELVE TIME ZONES AWAY, the world was just beginning to stir at Ramma 5, Diplomatic Enclave, Islamabad. Morning dew was weighing down the grass, and the eastern sky was crimson. Corporal Tucker of the Marine Corp was on guard duty, along with his friend of many years, Corporal St. James.

"Yo, Tucker," said St. James. "What the hell's that out there?" Beyond the second perimeter, past the concrete antitank obstacles and the tire shredders, and outside the main gate, just becoming visible in the gathering light, were what appeared to be two large cloth rice bags. Just sitting there.

"I think they're bags of some kind, Ronnie," said Tucker. "They're rice sacks or something."

"Bags don't just appear in front of American embassies, Tucker. Especially not in this Islamic hell-pit," replied St. James nervously.

Tucker could tell that St. James had been away from South Carolina too long. He had been edgy for the past three weeks. He'd had a "premonition," he said. A "premonition of doom." And maybe this was it. There had been rumors yesterday about stolen Semtex being taken from that crazy situation in Libya. Maybe a couple hundred kilos were now sitting here, less than 100 feet away, with some crazy Paradise-obsessed Mohammed ready to push the button. "Maybe we should use the Rover," he suggested.

"Yo. Good idea. I'll radio it in," said St. James.

A few minutes later, two Marines showed up with a contraption that looked like a cross between a miniature excavator and R2D2. It was the Rover 3, the latest robotics toy from Raytheon. It came with a sophisticated remote control panel, and had two video eyes at the end of cantilevered, multi-jointed arms. It had two other arms with rotating pincers that could pick up, lift, and turn objects. It came on a set of crawler tracks. High tech all the way. Langley was in the process of equipping every embassy with one of these devices.

"I want one of those for my house," said St. James. "You could get a beer while watching the Super Bowl. Never have to get up again."

"That's what wives are for," joked Tucker.

"Yeah, dream on, I guess. This puppy cost half a mil. We're po' boys," St. James said.

"No way. It'll be $49.95 at Future Shop within three years. Now, let's see what we have," said Tucker, as the Rover 3 approached the gray, shapeless bags.

"It is a bag… I mean a couple of bags," said St. James. "Tucker, see if you can pull it back a bit. Use one of the pincers, like this…" St. James grabbed the controller from Tucker. "Here, let me do it. I have more experience with it than you do."

"What the hell?" asked Tucker, giving up the controls and moving over to fiddle with the focus on the screen. "That looks like… Jesus, it is. Ronnie. It's part of a body. It's an arm. It's a body. It's… oh Jesus Christ," he exclaimed, showing St. James the small video screen.

"Shit," said St. James. "Damn good thing we're Marines. A Navy guy would be puking by now."

"Yeah, never mind some tech at Langley."

As if on cue, another Marine yelled at them from the front doorway of the compound. "Hey Tucker. Some big shot asshole's on the line from the Pentagon. He's saying something about some guy standing right outside the front gate. Needs to talk to you."

"Well," said Tucker, "we've got news for him. Nice to know it's a guy, but the poor bastard sure as hell ain't standing. He's not going to be standing ever again."

16

INDY'S FACE GRIMACED in a silent scream. He had just come from the office of the Deputy Commissioner of "E" division, British Columbia. It was the highest RCMP command in the province. He had hoped that the Deputy Commissioner would go to the Commissioner and take steps to pry open the Cayman account. But no such luck. "Procedures are procedures, Indy. They're there for a reason. You need them in any organization. This is bigger than you. You can't get at it right now."

So Indy did the next best thing. He took a week of vacation. He threw some things in a battered suitcase and tossed it in the back of his old Chevy pickup truck. He pointed the truck eastward, along Highway 1, and took the highway toward the southeastern portion of the province, referred to by the locals as "the Kootenays." After eight hours of driving through what he thought was some of the most beautiful scenery on the planet, he found himself sitting at Tim Horton's donut shop with Corporal Catherine Gray. It was early evening, and she was off shift, but did not complain.

Indy was flipping through the criminal records of the Hallett/Lestage clan. "How many of them are there, anyway?" he asked.

"Thirty maybe. Forty. Not sure. Most of them are into petty mayhem. Small-time drugs. Assault, wife beatings, shoplifting… you know, the basic stuff. Most of them aren't around most of the time, which might support the smurfing theory."

"Sure it would," replied Indy. "They would be going from city to city, like a roving band of gypsies. All expenses would be paid for in cash. If there are enough of them, and they travel enough, say throughout all of western Canada, you could place an awful lot of cash into the system. It doesn't take a lot of intelligence to do that."

"For the record," replied Catherine, "none of them are overloaded with brains, except maybe Leon."

Indy arched an eyebrow. "Leon?"

"Yeah, Leon," said Catherine, taking a sip of coffee. "There are rumors going around that he's a bona fide Hell's Angel with one of the Vancouver clubs. We've never been able to verify that. We have confirmed that he has a residence in Vancouver. He's lived there for awhile; worked on the docks as a longshoreman. He quit that a few years ago and now just seems to travel a lot. He's also got a run-down place just north of the Flathead-Boundary Range, near Akamina Park. In fact, his property is the closest there is to the park, and to the Montana border. He owns a gorgeous Harley. Out of the whole clan he's the cleanest. No record at all, other than a few marijuana convictions 20 years ago."

"What about Benny Hallett?" inquired Indy, recalling his visit with the pathetic kid two days earlier.

"Well, he might just be the dumbest of the clan, which is really saying something. IQ of three above a head of lettuce, I'd say."

"Who do you think torched his truck and put him in the hospital minus a leg?" asked Indy, working on his second donut.

Catherine paused a moment to sip her coffee before answering. "We have no evidence at all on that. Zilch. But my gut says it was Leon. I've thought about what you said yesterday. About the Scotia Bank account. I have absolutely no doubt that we're talking about drugs. Large quantities, with a basic brute force laundering scheme, the oldest in the book. Just send people smurfing away from town to town making small deposits. I've had a look at the printouts you faxed me. I absolutely believe that temptation did it for our friend Benny. All that money. He just had to spend some of it. The leader of the clan reprimanded him. And I'm pretty sure the leader is Leon."

"You know, Catherine, if we're right about this, there could be dozens of accounts just like this one. All the other Halletts and Lestages could be cruising around western Canada, making these deposits. If you multiply this account by 15 or even 20, we've got a big-time operation going. What frustrates me is that the Force doesn't have the manpower to deal with this." Indy sighed in exasperation. "The Force" was how insiders referred to the RCMP, and had nothing to do with Star Wars. "I'm going to end up getting ulcers."

Catherine looked out the large window at one of the many stunning mountain ranges in the vicinity. "What do you want to do, Indy? I'll help in whatever way I can. I might be able to squeeze some manpower out of Nelson and Castelgar."

"Not yet," responded Indy. "You said they have some kind of tourist business going in the summertime. Tell me about that."

Catherine snorted. "Yeah that. Kind of a joke. The fabulous Akamina-Kishinina Bicycle Tour Company, Ltd."

"Joke?"

"Yeah. Joke. They own one run-down, beat-up tour bus. They never show up on time. They never come back on time. The Fernie Town Counsel wants them out of business. Not good to have a group of Japanese tourists with big bucks stood up. Not good to have a bus break down 20 miles out of town." She continued looking out the window. "I can't figure out why they do it. If they have this much cash floating around, why run this idiotic tourist service? Makes no sense, unless…"

"Unless it ties into the scheme somehow. Maybe they don't want anyone else going out that way," said Indy.

"That's where they all live, you know. Up and down that road," she said.

"How close to the border is the Aka- whatever?" asked Indy.

"Akamina-Kishinina. The park is right on the border with Montana. Maybe that explains the bus service. Maybe," said Catherine, a trace of excitement in her voice, "maybe that's how they're getting drugs across the line, somehow. Maybe through the park…"

"That looks to be pretty rugged country," said Indy. "Don't think you'd be able to drive a broken-down bus through those mountain ranges, no matter how desperate you were to smuggle drugs. Maybe…"

"What are you thinking?" she asked.

"It's the middle of August, Catherine. The height of the tourist season. They've got to be running right now."

"Yeah, they are. Thinking of going on a trip?"

"Yes, as a matter of fact. Where do they muster?"

"In front of city hall. Any morning. Nine sharp."

Indy thought he might be less conspicuous if she came along. Tourist couples were more common. But Catherine thought not. "This is a small place, Indy, and we've busted these ne'er do wells for plenty of infractions. They'd probably make me."

"Yeah, I guess you're right. But I doubt they'll make me. The only one that's ever met me is Benny, and he ain't going anywhere right now."

Catherine nodded, rising and donning her sweater. "Let me know if I can help you with anything. I'm going for a run. Don't suppose you'd care to join me?"

Indy smiled to himself. In Catherine's case, "a run" was usually five or ten miles, 15 if the weather was nice. One of her main bragging rights was that she could outrun anyone on the Force, and probably most of the guys in the military as well. Indy had personally seen her make grown men cry. "No thanks Cath, I'm no masochist. I'm hunkering down in a hotel for the night."

Catherine laughed and strolled out of the donut shop. Indy headed to the hotel, already planning his outing for the next day.

FIVE AM hit Indy like a hammer. "This is way too early for us old guys," he mumbled to himself as he nearly fell into the shower. It was a good three-hour drive to Fernie, and while the Halletts and Lestages might be late, he could not afford to be. He showered and dressed tourist style, in shorts, a T-shirt with a Bugs Bunny cartoon drawn on the front, and an old pair of sneakers. He got from the first alarm ring to being checked out and behind the steering wheel of the old Chevy in a record 12 minutes. Again he headed eastward. Again the picturesque towns with quaint names went racing by. Salmo. Yahk. Elko. His watch was edging toward 9AM when he pulled into the parking lot of the small one-story building that apparently served as the Fernie Town Hall. There were a few people milling about and waiting in front of the building. Indy parked his truck and strolled over to join them.

Nine AM came and went. Then 9:15, then 9:25. At around 9:30, as the grumbling was escalating, a pale blue bus finally came clattering to a halt in front of them. Its engine was not silenced by functioning mufflers, and a cloud of blue-black exhaust engulfed the waiting crowd. The vehicle was a converted Bluebird School Bus, and had the words "Akamina-Kishinina Bicycle Tour Co. Ltd." stenciled in faded black letters across the sides. Twenty mountain bikes, in various stages of disrepair, were fastened along the back and sides of the bus. The driver rolled to a stop directly in front of the City Hall and opened the passenger door.

"AK Bike Tour folks. Tickets please. Get ready for the adventure of your lives." His voice was flat and unexcited.

Indy was staring in amazement at the bus and bicycles. It looked like something out of a comedy skit. When the driver stepped out, Indy shut his mouth with an audible snap and put on his best tourist act.

"Whazit cost?" he drawled, trying to look as stupid and innocuous as possible.

"Fifty bucks. Big money I know, but it is the adventure of a lifetime, partner."

Indy fished through his wallet. All he had was two twenties. "That'll do partner. That'll do." The driver was sloppy, overweight, and thirty-something, with dark sunglasses that hid his eyes. He had on a name tag that advertised his name: Dennis Lestage. He carelessly motioned for Indy to enter the bus and have a seat, then moved on.

Indy sat, and the journey began. He watched the scenery go by, seeing mostly rain forests of hemlock and spruce. Occasionally the trees parted to allow views of snow-clad mountains and deep gorges. The bus was climbing at over 80 miles an hour, hugging cliffs and slamming over potholes, on a road barely wide enough to accommodate it. As they neared Akamina-Kishinina, Indy noticed a familiar, acrid odor. Could it be? He saw other tourists looking around as well. The Japanese couples were wide eyed in horror. Dennis had pulled out a joint, almost as fat as a cigar, lit it, and was happily smoking away.

"Hey, buddy, put that thing out," Indy said, unconsciously switching back to his RCMP authority voice. "Right now,"

"Relax, partner. Just relax," said Dennis. "I've got a medical license to smoke this puppy."

Indy's shoulders slumped in defeat. The same old thing, he thought. No point in trying to argue over the legality of the joint. Not even the judges and prosecutors knew for sure where the lines were anymore.

"Got glaucoma," continued Dennis. "People with glaucoma can smoke this legally. It's medicine partner. Medicine. Like Lipitor."

"Isn't glaucoma an eye disease?" asked Indy. "Doesn't it make you go blind?"

"Yeah, I guess so," said Dennis, taking another toke as he downshifted, grinding the gears of the old Bluebird.

"Great. Just friggin' great," mumbled Indy, as he watched the valley floor recede into the distance. "Perfect. A stoned and blind doper taking an old, broken bus up a winding mountain road. Wonderful." Whatever he found, it had better be worth the risk he was taking with his life.

THE SUN HAD SET, and it was approaching midnight when the *Haramosh Star* neared the rendezvous point. They were just west of the Indian island of Cherlyam, at the northern tip of the geological formation that included the Maldives.

The *Mankial Star* was already at anchor, waiting for them. She was some 80 feet in length — far too small, by Yousseff's estimation. He was in the transportation business, after all. A length of 80 feet meant that there was barely enough room on the rear deck for the helicopter. His one consolation was the ship's power. Every piece of equipment that Yousseff owned had been modified in one way or another to increase its horsepower, from his new Gulfstream to the ancient *Haramosh Star*. He was obsessed with pulling as much power out of each piece of machinery as he could. His personal yacht was no different. The *Mankial Star* had four MTU Friedrichshafen Diesel Turbos, producing 2,400 horsepower each, which meant she had close to 10,000 horsepower, all told. She could carve up the Arabian Sea at an amazing 50 knots.

Yousseff gazed at the jewel in his crown with affection. He would have liked to be on his yacht, but had decided to watch the next step of the process from the darkened rear deck of the *Haramosh Star.* Now that they were involved in such an international scheme, his anonymity was more important than ever before. There was no telling who he could trust and who was a spy. For this reason, he saw no reason to let the men on the *Haramosh Star* see him directing the operation, when others could do it equally well. It went against his nature, but in this case he chose to sit back and watch.

The most difficult part of the operation would be connecting the two ships. While both ships were small, they were not insignificant in proportion. The *Haramosh Star* was 300 feet in length, and her main deck was a good 20 feet above the water. But the system designed so many years ago by Kumar, and subsequently modified by the engineers of Karachi Drydock and Engineering, worked with a simple and polished elegance. Two parallel metal arms slid out of two small hatches on the *Haramosh Star,* seated about ten feet above the water line. The hatches were so carefully integrated into the ship's hull that only the most scrutinizing of investigations would have uncovered them. They were approximately 60 feet apart, with the metal arms beautifully balanced on a hydraulic suspension system, also of Kumar's design. Two rubber-coated metal clamps were fixed to the distal ends of the arms. With a little careful maneuvering, these connected to two indented rectangular sockets on the starboard sides of the front and rear decks of the *Mankial Star.* Thus secured, the two ships rode the sea together, with only 15 feet of water separating them.

Yousseff smiled as he watched the process. The seas were calm, with a slightly warm late night breeze. From start to finish, the connecting maneuver took only five minutes. Once they were connected, the *Mankial Star* would appear from the air to be a catamaran extension of the much larger *Haramosh Star.* Now the rear deck hatch doors on the *Mankial Star* slid open, and the scissors lift elevated the pallets of wrapped Semtex to approximately four feet above the deck. A third, larger hatch opened in the port side of the hull of the *Haramosh Star,* and two more rails slowly extended toward the *Mankial Star.* The additional rails extended the full distance toward the yacht, and slid along her deck to attach to the lift mechanism. The railing that lined the *Mankial Star's* deck was folded back, opening a path that led from the lift to the *Haramosh Star,* complete with rails for easy transportation. There was none of the usual yelling of crewmembers while the procedure was coordinated. The crews on both ships were wired with microphones and spoke on the same radio frequency.

The lift platform on the *Mankial Star* rested on four small wheels, not dissimilar to miniature locomotive wheels (which is where Kumar had obtained his inspiration for it). The four wheels were locked by an ingenious locking mechanism, which, with the flip of a switch, retracted into the lift platform itself. Three men, pushing in unison, were able to push the platform with its first 1,500 kilos of Semtex off the lift, through the now-open gate on the *Mankial Star's* deck, and across the twenty-some feet of rail. Two men on the *Haramosh Star* stopped the small railcar as it drifted, casually, into the aperture in the ship's hull. The only noise that accompanied this exercise was the lapping of small waves against the hulls of the two ships, and the occasional forlorn cries of seagulls. The load of Semtex was detached from the transport system and disappeared into an internal compartment on the cargo ship. The other loads followed, all noiselessly and easily.

Yousseff and Vince walked together to the lower deck level, where the pallets of Semtex now sat. Yousseff looked at the volume of material that had arrived. "Are you sure it will fit in the PWS-12?" asked Yousseff.

"Well, I'm not," replied Vince. "But some of those clever characters back in Karachi did the volume calculations, and they tell me that there is enough room. In fact, we could probably have handled another 500 kilos of it, according to their estimations. It should not be a problem."

"Good," said Yousseff. "I want you to personally supervise the transfer. When it is done, make sure the trapdoor is completely covered with junk. Hose down the deck, and the lower deck. In fact, hose it down several times. The Americans may come. They may already be on your tail. So long as they don't find that," he said, pointing to the pallets, "things will be fine."

They hugged each other, feeling a pang of nostalgia at another parting. They both recalled too well Yousseff's earlier trips on this very ship — the start of their long and very close history. Yousseff drew away and stepped out onto the rails that joined the two ships. "Oh, one last thing," he said, reaching into his shirt pocket. "Here's a digital camera. If the Americans do come, take many pictures. We could have some fun with that." He tossed the camera toward Vince, who pocketed it. "Goodbye, old friend," he said, walking over the water to the *Mankial Star*.

"Goodbye Youss," said Vince, a lump in his throat. He didn't know the full extent of the plan, but he knew full well that he might never see his friend again.

The sailors of the *Haramosh Star* returned to their positions as soon as Yousseff stepped onto the *Mankial Star*. They wondered who this so-called idiot relative of Vince's was, who walked so boldly across the waters of the Indian Ocean, toward a stunningly beautiful yacht, complete with a helicopter attached to its rear deck. Most of them turned away, shaking their heads. They were paid extremely well not to ask questions of their captain, or the men with whom he saw fit to consort.

The process then reversed itself, as silently as it had been executed. The empty platform was pushed back to the *Mankial Star*. It locked in place on the scissors lift. The rails were detached from the lift, and the lift retracted into its lower storage berth. The two rails retracted into the hull of the cargo ship, and the large hatch closed. Crewmembers on the front and rear decks of Yousseff's yacht unhooked the connecting arms, which also retracted into the hull of the larger ship. The two small hull hatches closed. The captain of the *Mankial Star* reversed his engines, while the *Haramosh Star* went forward. As soon as there was a safe distance between the two vessels, both proceeded at full speed. The *Haramosh Star* continued on a southerly route along the Malabar Coast, while the *Mankial Star* turned west, toward Yousseff's retreat on the island of Socotra, just south of Yemen. The entire operation had taken less than 20 minutes. Silently, elegantly, and efficiently, thought Yousseff. It was the only way to do these things. He heaved a great sigh. Now he had a chance to rest in his own home before he was needed again. Thank Allah.

THE METALWORKERS at Karachi Drydock and Engineering had built two inner frames in the hull of the *Haramosh Star*, below the engine compartment. The first was for the storage of contraband — usually drugs, but in this case, explosives. The second acted as ventilation, to direct the fumes through the engine exhaust system. After this construction, Kumar's sophisticated measurements had shown that, in spite of the precise manufacture and assembly of these inner floors, several parts per billion of chemical traces still leaked into the engine compartment itself. These traces could give them away, and destroy the mission. Yousseff had instructed Kumar to build a third compartment, on top of the other two, for further insulation and venting of fumes. A few parts per trillion of the fumes still escaped, but not enough to trigger detection equipment that might be brought onboard. The likelihood of detection was almost nil. The metalwork was so precise that there was no indication whatsoever that there were three layers of compartments beneath the engine room.

It was the recently added lower layer that was the most interesting. Nestled in this large bay was a PWS-12 submarine, built in Kumar's Long Beach manufacturing facility and modified at Karachi Drydock and Engineering. A crew from the *Haramosh Star* immediately set to work, reloading the Semtex into the hold of the submersible.

THE AKAMINA-KISHININA, with Waterton Lakes Park to the immediate east, in Alberta, and Glacier National Park to the immediate south, in Montana, formed the crown of the continent. Here one could find a combination of biological, geological, and climatic factors that occurred nowhere else in North America. The three parks were home to the densest grizzly bear population on the continent. Together they formed a UNESCO World Heritage site, at the narrowest point of the Rocky Mountains. High and spacious alpine ridges, deep secluded valleys, and windswept passes provided terrain for the large grizzly population, as well as an abundance of goats, caribou, and big horn sheep. The trails and passes of the Akamina-Kishinina were used for millennia by aboriginal tribes to travel from the Flathead Basin to the Great Plains. The area was so isolated that fewer than 100 individuals made the Flathead-to-Waterton trek each year, and only a few hundred people braved the one-day bike tours. Because of the fragile ecosystem and international importance of the area, no motorized transportation of any sort was permitted in the park.

The mountains here were as unique as the wildlife, and the park featured the highest peaks in the Clark Range of the Rockies. Mount Starvation and Mount King Edward measured at 9,301 feet and 9,186 feet, respectively. The Akamina-Kishinina also protected some of the oldest mineral formations in the Canadian Rockies. Most of the rocks were varieties of limestone, deposited on the shallow floor and tidal flats of an ancient ocean that had existed there 1.5 billion years earlier. Nunatuk, an ancient rock formation in the center of the park, thrust its peaks sharply upward, soaring in jagged cliffs straight up for more than 2,000 feet.

In the early Twentieth Century, the area was explored by geologists, and a number of mines were started and then abandoned. A number of test oil drilling sites had also been created and deserted. There were numerous coal deposits in the area, and several attempts had been made to commercially extract coal, but these attempts were discontinued when larger, more commercially viable coal deposits were found to the west, in the Kootenay Valley — an area more accessible to railways.

Indy knew the history of the area, and now took note of the terrain and the homes as the Bluebird cruised southeast, approaching the park. Ramshackle trailers, mostly run-down and in various states of disrepair, were the predominant architecture. Most of these places were owned, he knew, by various constituents of the Hallett/Lestage clan. Behind the southernmost trailers rose a high granite flat-topped ridge that the locals referred to as Boundary Peak. A few miles before they hit the park border itself, Indy noticed an overgrown driveway that had seen recent traffic, given the tire marks through the grass. He wondered if that was Leon's place.

The Bluebird Bus, engulfed in a cloud of diesel smoke, finally shuddered to a halt at a turnabout in front of the park gateway itself.

"The bus stops here, everybody," said Dennis, who appeared to be in a relaxed and jovial frame of mind. "No motorized traffic permitted in the park. We have some maps here about trails you can take. Suggest you go uphill till about 2:30 or so, and then turn around. The bus leaves at 4:30." He led the tourists out of the bus and started to undo the bungee cords that held the mountain bikes to the sides of the vehicle. Indy smiled to himself as he watched Dennis struggling to do the job one-handed, the other hand busy scratching various parts of his anatomy.

When he thought that Dennis was fully preoccupied with other matters, which seemed to be the case most of the time, he scooted behind the bus and took one of the bicycles. He headed down the road, back toward the Flathead Valley, instead of going up into the Akamina-Kishinina. The sky was overcast, but it was warm and pleasant. Indy caught himself relishing the spectacular scenery. Not a bad way to spend a day, he thought.

It didn't take him long to arrive at the overgrown trail that led to what he suspected was Leon's home. He had with him one of the high-resolution 11.2 megapixel Sony Cybershot cameras that were kept at the Heather Street complex. He already had pictures of the side of the bus, featuring the lengthy name of the corporation, which he would use to conduct other searches when he got back to his Dell. He had a picture of its license plate. He had a few pictures of Dennis, one of which showed him smoking his extra large fattie.

Now he took a few shots of the driveway, with the granite walls of Boundary Peak rising less than half a mile beyond. Inhaling deeply, he started to walk down the narrow lane. He had done undercover work for more than a decade, and had 25 years of service with the Force. Walking into a potential criminal's driveway was really nothing new. He looked around, clearing his mind and concentrating on finding anything that might strengthen his case. There were fresh tire marks, probably from a pickup truck. He took a few photographs of them, then kept walking. He had walked close to two miles, and was almost at the vertical walls of Boundary Peak, when the trail opened into a small grassy area, with an older mobile home standing forlornly in the center. There were no signs of habitation; no smoke from the chimney, no barking dog, and no vehicle in the driveway, although he could see a couple up on blocks behind the small home. His heart rate sped up, and his blood pressure increased. Was this the place where it all happened? Slowly he walked right up to the mobile home, snapping a few more pictures on his approach. There appeared to be a large blue Harley parked in the living room. He saw now that there was an old Ford pickup parked behind the trailer. The road continued on past the trailer, heading, judging from the bearing of the sun, due south. He snapped some pictures of the rear of the home, and then a few more of the trail leading past it. There were further fresh tire marks in the grass, indicating the passage of a vehicle, probably in the past 24 hours. He was about to move forward when he heard a chilling "click" behind him.

"Right there, bastard. Hold it right there. Turn slowly or you're toast," came a voice from behind him.

17

THE TTIC CONTROL ROOM had an eerie glow about it after hours. George had created a screen saver for the Atlas Screen that randomly illuminated different countries, with light fading in and out, cycling through a random pattern. The large 101's at the front of the room were displaying current network news feeds. The 101 closest to Turbee was playing an Elmer Fudd cartoon. The large workstations surrounding the Atlas Screen were empty. Here and there a screen or an on/off switch on a computer glowed. It was 1:30AM. Turbee was the only inhabitant in the large room. He was hunched over, mumbling to himself. He had adopted a few of the digital screens from surrounding workstations and now had, in total, seven flat panel displays in front of him — one 30 inch, three at 21 inches, and three 19 inchers. All showed windows of scrolling numbers. Complex formulae were splashed across the largest screen. He was attempting to find correlations in dozens of databases, mostly databases that contained electronic information relating to the residents of Pakistan.

THE "WEST" was often guilty of smugness, and an arrogant certainty that their system functioned better than any other, and that their way of life was better and more sophisticated than anyone else's. The popularly held misconception in the Western world was that Pakistan was a desert-bound Third World country, with more camels than people. Nothing could have been further from the truth. Other than some lawless areas to the northwest and adjacent to the Karakorum Highway, Pakistan could actually be classified as a country with considerable sophistication. While there were poverty-ridden areas and shantytowns, there were also numerous universities within its borders and a high literacy rate. Pakistan had shared in its neighbor India's recent computer hardware and software revolution. America's Silicon Valley jobs were not only exported to Mumbai, but also to Karachi. Most citizens had debit cards. Electronic banking was comfortably entrenched in the country. There was a well-developed cellular network, and in the larger cities everyone seemed to possess a cell phone. Water and power were commodities parceled out by computer. Foreign exchange was reconciled electronically. Wages were automatically deposited into bank accounts by all but the smallest of companies. Pakistan even possessed nuclear weaponry.

All this technology meant that there existed, within the borders of Pakistan, a rich broth of electronic information for Turbee and Blue Gene to sample and tease. As was often the case with Turbee, once he was able to focus his formidable intellectual resources, he lost track of time and place. It had taken only a brief, highly productive tutorial session with Rhodes, Lance, and Khasha to get him on the right track. Even Rahlson had chipped in once he saw where it was going. Turbee had needed to learn about the chemistry and economics of the drug trade.

"OK. OK. Where is this stuff grown?" Turbee had asked Lance and Khasha. "Where are these poppy fields?"

"Mostly in the high desert of Afghanistan. Some in Pakistan, but the local police seem to have done a good job of controlling it on that side of the border," said Khasha.

"How do you make opium from poppy plants?" he continued.

Lance explained to him the process of scoring the bulbs of the plants during the harvest season, and the collection of the brown resin a few days later. He described the cooking and refining process in more detail.

"Fine, OK. But no one talks about smuggling opium. Everyone talks about smuggling heroin. How much more valuable is heroin than opium?"

Lance saw this as an open invitation. He had a captive audience, even if it was only Turbee, Rhodes, and Khasha. "Depends on where it is, Turbee," he said. "Heroin is one of those commodities whose price varies profoundly depending on its location. A kilogram of heroin in Peshawar can be purchased for under $2,000. By the time it reaches Karachi, its value has quintupled to $10,000. Once it reaches a major marketplace, like Los Angeles, London, or New York, its wholesale value is over $100,000 a kilo, with a retail value three or four times that. It's a remarkable industry, really. The value is added, once it's refined, simply by transporting it."

"You guys said to me yesterday," responded Turbee, "that this is a cash business. No visa. No debit cards. No checks. All cash. So what happens to all that cash?"

"That," said Rhodes, "is the central, number one problem the drug industry faces. What to do with all that cash. The Colombian drug lords, in the '90s, made regular visits to the Caribbean banks with planeloads of cash. Huge suitcases and duffle bags full of cash. The USA has put a lot of pressure on the offshore banking community to halt that practice. But it's still going on."

"How much money are we looking at?" asked Turbee.

"No one is really sure, but the order of magnitude, worldwide, is in the hundreds of billions of dollars," answered Rhodes.

"Are you telling me that every year hundreds of billions of dollars of cash circulates through the world's financial systems illegally?"

"Yup," said Lance and Rhodes as one.

"So if someone in Pakistan is involved in the heroin trade in a large way, he has a problem dealing with large amounts of illegal cash, right?"

"Yes," said Rhodes. "Especially in Pakistan. We believe that most of the heroin shipped out through Pakistan eventually ends up in the United States. Hence, most of the money would be in American dollars, rather than something like Euros or pounds."

"How do you hide large amounts of cash?" Turbee mused aloud.

"Well," said Rhodes, "there are a lot of ways to do it. You can hide it in the balance sheets of companies. Take a simple example. You own a little taxi company. It takes in $300 in a night. But you're selling some dope on the side. Making the odd trip to the odd client. You just add it to the take. You're now making $600 a night. All you say, if anyone asks, is that you believe in work ethic. You work twice as hard as anyone else, or much more efficiently, or something. Or you can send out armies of smurfs…"

Lance and Rhodes spent an hour educating Turbee on the various ways to hide, place, layer, and reintegrate illegal cash. By the end of the discussion, he had a good idea which digital seas he and Blue Gene would be sailing.

"What about the chemicals that are used to turn opium into heroin?" he asked, seeking to explore another vein.

"We call those precursor chemicals," explained Lance. "Ammonium chloride, Lysol, calcium hydroxide, hydrochloric acid, and acetic anhydride, plus a few others. Some of these precursor chemicals are quite valuable, and there's an underground trade of sorts for them too."

"Hold on a bit," said Turbee, struggling to keep up with Lance's rapid speech. "Have to get all this straight in my head." He was furiously clicking away on his keyboard.

By the time they were through, Turbee had the ABC's of the drug trade down pat, and had a plan set out for where to go with his research. That had been almost 12 hours ago. Now his mind was working at a fever pitch. Precursor chemicals. Foreign exchange accounts. Balance sheets of import/export firms. Police records. Felons. Neighbors of felons. Smurfs. Precursor smurfs. Foreign exchange accounts of precursor smurfs…

Khasha had been tapping on his shoulder for a good 30 seconds by the time he finally noticed. He gave her a long, uncomprehending stare. Consecutively opened accounts at successive banks of…

"Turbee. You get that crazy look in your eye, don't you know?" she said. "It's me. Khasha."

"What are you doing here?" he asked, eventually.

"I live ten blocks away. I couldn't sleep. I saw the fourth-floor lights on in the building, so I walked over. Crazy thing to do in DC at this time of night. But here you are. What on earth are you doing here?"

"I'm working, Khasha. I'm trying to help Lance and Rhodes. I think I'm onto something. A few more hours, and I may have it."

"Turbee, in a few more hours it'll be dawn."

"So?" he responded. Khasha didn't know his habits. She didn't understand how his condition, and the many drugs he was taking for it, played havoc with his behavior. His mind would race and focus, and then fragment and turn sluggish. When he was racing, as he was now, it was almost impossible for him to stop. In elementary school, before he had been properly diagnosed, he would literally bounce off the walls of the classroom in the morning and, in the afternoon, stick his head inside his oversized sweater and fall asleep. There was one famous story of him falling asleep inside the large lower drawer of his Second Grade teacher's desk.

He explained a bit of it to her. "Khasha, I'm not completely comfortable talking about it, but I'm autistic. I can't control these things sometimes. You are very pretty and I want to talk, but I can't right now. I have to do this. I have to do it now, or it will escape. I would be very poor company — I can't sit still and I would end up embarrassing myself. I need to finish this."

"That's OK, Turbee. I understand. I have a cousin who has Asperger syndrome. It's pretty much the same. I brought you some coffee, although in hindsight, maybe water would have been better."

"I'll take the coffee, thanks. Thanks for dropping by. Really. Thanks." He dropped his eyes and went back to his small armada of screens. He felt himself flushing; he wanted badly to talk to her, but he knew he couldn't. Instead, he concentrated on the foreign exchange account of a particular shipping company that he'd hacked into. He didn't hear her leave.

FOR ONCE Turbee was at work before anyone else, but the circumstances greatly displeased Dan. The youth had found his answer by 6AM, and once he had accomplished his task, he was overwhelmed by fatigue. He had a larger workstation than anyone else, and thought he could probably just fit on the working surface of his desk. He pushed aside the many empty Styrofoam coffee cups, the candy wrappers, and the half-empty containers of Chinese food, lay down, and closed his eyes. Just for a few minutes, he thought. Just a short nap.

Eight AM came quickly. This was the hour Dan had scheduled to collectively review the PDB, an exercise that Turbee almost never attended. It was the official start of the workday, although most of the TTIC staff were "keeners," and it was a badge of honor to be early; the earlier, the better. No one woke Turbee when they came in. The scene was too comical. There were a few sniggers. Someone had a digital camera, and most had camera phones, so a few photographs were taken. The cartons, cups, and wrappers were brought in a little closer to the sleeping Turbee to add to the effect.

"Aww Jesus Christ," cursed Dan when he arrived. "Will someone please whack the poor bastard a few times and clean up that sorry mess? Why we keep him I don't know."

One of the Army captains on staff, never known for subtlety, walked to within a foot of Turbee, and yelled directly into his ear. "It's ROLL CALL, Turbee!" he howled. "Wakee WAKEE!"

Turbee stirred. The man had no sense whatsoever of Turbee's condition, or even that he had a condition. It was a simple matter of discipline, he thought. Hell, nothing Army Basic Training wouldn't fix. "YO, BOY! Up and at 'em! NOW!"

"Go away," was all Turbee could manage. A wake-up call of this sort would leave most people disoriented, but it made Turbee physically ill. Abrupt, loud noises never went well with his particular brand of autism. He fought the urge to vomit and covered his ears with his hands. The captain persisted, much to Dan's glee, and Turbee slumped down from his desk and looked around, perplexed and confused, from the floor.

"Oh God, Turbee. Major-league raccoon eyes," Dan exclaimed sarcastically. "You'd better have been doing some productive work to justify this."

"Umm. Yeah. Sort of. If you give me a sec, I'll tell you. I know who organized the Semtex heist, and how to find it," Turbee responded through his teeth.

"What was that?" exclaimed Dan. "What did he say?"

"Look, I'm sorry for the mess and all, and I'm sorry I fell asleep on my desk, but Blue Gene and I worked all night on this. I think I've got it figured out."

"OK, Turbee," Dan said in a softer tone. "That might make this worthwhile. What've you got?"

Turbee took a deep breath, pressed his thumbs to his eyelids, and gathered himself. "It's a company called the Karachi Star Line. They started with an inland ferry service, shipping people and cargo up and down the Indus. About 15 years ago they bought a few tramp ships, and converted them into small container ships. They expanded rapidly, and now own about 30 ocean-going ships, some container, some dry cargo, and 50 large ferries, running between Islamabad and Hyderabad, and up the Indus River, mostly."

"How do you get from there to terrorist drug smuggler?" prompted Dan.

"OK. OK. They started as a cash business. They paid all their employees in cash, usually American dollars, for the first few years of their existence."

"How do you know that?"

"There were a few newspaper articles about it 12 or 15 years ago. Also, payment for cargos went through unusual offshore banks, first in the Caymans, and more recently, St. Vincent, in the Caribbean. The transactions are very complex — unnecessarily so, if you ask me. In the last couple of years, they used obscure banks in Russia, and a couple of financial institutions in, of all places, Nigeria."

"And?"

"Those precursor chemicals that we've talked about. This company buys a significant quantity of them. Those transactions are also cloaked, but some of the same financial institutions are involved. And they're in the transportation business."

"Why would that be important?" asked Dan.

"Well, I don't know much about the heroin business," said Turbee, somewhat tentatively. "But Lance explained some of it to me yesterday. He said that in the heroin trade, and the illicit drug trade generally, the unique thing is that you add all the value to it by transporting it from one point to another around the globe. So I ranked transportation companies higher than non-transportation companies in my search parameters."

"That's it?"

"No, that's not it," Turbee responded. "Their rate of growth is absolutely astounding."

"So?"

"They've grown from nothing to become a very large shipping firm. In record time," said Turbee.

Now Rhodes broke in. "He's got a point there, Dan." He turned back to

Turbee. "How certain are you that they're the ones we're looking for?"

"Positive. I have some really strong evidence."

"Do you know which ships may be involved in the smuggling?"

"Yes," said Turbee. "The private yacht of the owner of the company, some guy by the name of Jhananda. It's a yacht called the *Mankial Star.* She's large — 80 feet, perhaps a bit more. She was anchored off the eastern coast of a small island called Socotra, where Yemen has jurisdiction. There are several pictures; here, I'll flip them on the 101's for you. There they are. Note the times. There were repeat helicopter visits to the yacht. These are from one day after the Semtex was stolen. There's a small runway on the island, just to the west of what appears to be a huge estate overlooking the Gulf of Arabia."

Everyone was paying attention now. The pictures on the 101's showed exactly what Turbee said they would. He had the floor. "I am positive that the Semtex is on that ship, Dan. It's headed east, toward us."

"How did it get from Darfur to a ship off the coast of Socotra, of all places?" asked Rhodes. "That's a long distance to travel."

"Well," said Turbee, "look at the runway. There's a plane there, and I'm told by Kingston at the NSA that it's a DC-3. Look at the next set of pictures. You can clearly see the helicopter that's landed beside the DC-3. You can also see it, an hour later, sitting on the rear deck of the *Mankial Star.* That helicopter was ferrying cargo of some sort from the DC-3 on the runway to the ship."

"It's all kind of circumstantial, isn't it?" asked Dan. "In any event, how do you know that ship is the *Mankial Star?"*

"Simple," responded Turbee. "The Office of Naval Intelligence has a database for every ship larger than 70 feet in length. The database has measurements for the length, width, and shape of any hull, along with other distinguishing features. I ran that particular photograph through the database, and it spit out the name of the ship, its owners, its beam size, and so on. It's the *Mankial Star."*

"Dan, I'm not sure what you mean by circumstantial, but it gives us enough reason to have a closer look at least," said Rahlson. "We should check it out."

"I think I'll call the DDCI," said Dan, motioning to Johnson to get the Deputy Director on the line. "He should hear this, although I'm sure the heavies are more concerned about nuclear weapons gone astray than a few tons of high explosive. I mean any large construction company in the States could probably acquire this if they wanted to."

After a moment, Johnson motioned that he had the connection. Dan asked for him to put the conversation on the large control room speakers.

"What do you have?" came the booming voice of Admiral Jackson. "We're in the briefing room right now."

Dan outlined Turbee's theory, and the evidence supporting it. "Give us a few minutes, would you," came Big Jack's reply.

Dan muted the speaker and told his crew that Jackson was probably briefing the President, the Joint Chiefs of Staff, and other military or Intelligence leaders at that very moment.

The reply was not long in coming. "Dan, Richard Lawrence is apparently at the Islamabad Embassy right now. Call over there, and check with him and the station chief on what our next move should be. The station chief is Michael Buckingham, and Jennifer Coe is one of his main researchers. They know more about the drug trade in Afghanistan and Pakistan than anyone else. If the Karachi Star Line is owned by heroin dealers, we have it nailed. Get back to us." The line went dead.

Dan motioned to Johnson. "Islamabad, now," he snapped. Within seconds, Michael Buckingham's voice crackled across the conference room speakers. He was a career civil servant, having spent a lifetime in the Middle East Intelligence business. He was 55 years old, and had been part of the 1980 operation that armed the Afghani rebels against the Soviets. Buckingham was very familiar with the geography, tribal politics, and languages of Afghanistan, and knew more about that country than most of its citizens. The stress of his job had led him into chain smoking and heavy drinking at an early age, and he was trying to quit both. Aside from those bad habits, he had a sterling reputation as a man who could get the job done in the Middle East.

"Let me get Jennifer and see what I can do about Richard," he said, once they had him on the phone. "Is Khasha around?" he added as an afterthought.

"I'm right here, big boy," said Khasha. She had worked for a few years with the Islamabad desk, and knew Buckingham well. Jennifer Coe had taken over her duties when she moved to TTIC.

"Is Richard around?" asked Dan.

"He's around, Dan, but not exactly available," replied Buckingham.

"Meaning?" asked Dan.

Buckingham sighed. When a body had shown up in front of the Embassy, he'd been the one in charge of inspecting it. He had known Zak Goldberg and his parents personally, so it had been extremely upsetting when he'd recognized Zak's ring on the hand they'd received. Declaring the body parts to be those of Zak Goldberg had been one of the hardest things he'd ever had to do. Talking about it wasn't getting any easier.

"Well it's a bad situation," he began. "And it starts with an unpleasant coincidence."

"Go on," urged Dan.

"The CIA wanted Richard back in Islamabad, because they thought he would be of value to them, given his involvement in the Semtex case. And you know how Langley is. When they finally decide to do something, they want it done yesterday."

"Yeah, we know," came the refrain from several workstations at TTIC.

"So they put him on a Super Hornet with a Captain Trufit, to get him back here in record time. At about the same time, a bag of body parts was found in front of the Embassy. I looked them over, and I believed that they belonged to Zak Goldberg. But Langley wanted a top notch forensic analysis done, and the closest decent and friendly lab is in Tel Aviv. Since he was going to be in the area, Langley assigned Trufit to the mission. Let me tell you, he was not happy about it."

"Can you blame him?" asked George, disgusted.

"Not really," said Buckingham. "Anyway, Trufit bitched at the only person he could when he found out. That person happened to be Richard, sitting in the copilot's seat. Trufit didn't know that the remains were Zak's, but he did know that they came from an undercover agent, and evidently he said so. Richard got curious, and when he deplaned, he met the ground crew, who had these plastic bags. They didn't even put them in freezers. Just here you go my good man, here's your body parts. Richard got suspicious of all the weird treatment, and opened one of the bags. Out drops this severed hand, with a ring on it. He ID's the ring — it's very rare, and you can only buy it in the Peshawar marketplace. He knew Zak was undercover here. And he knew the ring. Zak had it on most of the time, and it's actually how I made my initial ID of the body. It didn't take long for Richard to make the same connection."

"Okay, so?" asked Dan.

A few of the TTIC employees stared at him, shocked. For anyone who knew Richard and Zak's history, the conclusion of this scene was obvious.

"Jesus, Dan, what do you think?" Buckingham snapped. "He started rooting around in the bags, looking at the various body parts, most of which showed signs of the most brutal torture. Then he sat down on the tarmac and started to just blubber. It was pretty bad. He seems to be in some kind of shock. The medics here are with him now. They've shot him up with a bunch of tranquillizers."

"Oh my God," breathed Lance. "He's going to need to decompress. He needs a whole staff of doctors looking after him, Michael."

There was some murmuring around the TTIC control room. Many of the people there knew Richard, and were concerned over his physical and mental well-being. At length, Dan pulled them back together, asking several people to help outline what they knew so far for Buckingham and Jennifer Coe.

"The Karachi Star Line is an interesting creature alright," said Buckingham. "It seemed to come out of nowhere. We're not even sure who owns it, but we think it's probably a gentleman by the name of Omar Jhananda. His father was an old Indus River ferryman, who probably smuggled more than his fair share of heroin from Rawalpindi to the saltwater, though no one's really sure. We've always thought that the company was involved in drugs in some way, but no one has been able to prove it for sure. If you're asking for my gut feeling on it, yeah, I'd say that they're in the trade."

Buckingham's gut was seldom wrong on these things.

"What about you, Khasha? You grew up there. What's your take on it?" asked Dan.

She shrugged. "I think they're in the business. When I was going to school there, they were called the Indus Star Cargo Company. They ran goods up and down the river. They paid their employees in cash. They grew really fast. Everyone knew about it. The people who run it are from the border areas of the Northwest Frontier Province. I agree with Michael, but it's only an educated guess."

"Jennifer, what about you?" asked Dan.

"I'm too damn tired to think," came the reply. "I knew Zak personally, and let me tell you, it's harsh to see his body so beat up and ruined. All I can say is the timing works out. But it's all circumstantial. It's intelligent speculation."

"What do the locals think about this, Michael?" asked Rahlson.

"I'm not sure. This is unraveling pretty quickly," Buckingham replied slowly. "We haven't really had a chance to do any research on it yet."

"Let's find out, people," said Dan.

"Can you hold off a minute?" responded Buckingham. "I want to get the Deputy Commander of the Pakistani Interior Police on the line. His office is here, in Islamabad, and I know him well. His office has been spectacularly successful in drug arrests in the past ten years or so. They've almost single-handedly destroyed the Peshawar-to-Karachi drug pipeline. He knows more about this than anyone else I know. Give me a few minutes, and I'll get in touch with him. His name is Marak el Ghazi. If I can I'll get him to call you personally."

18

IN A DARK CELL buried under the mountains in the Sefid Koh, Zak lay very still on a pile of straw. He thought he'd been there almost 24 hours. It had been hours now since the guards had brought him back to his cell, minus one hand. He was trying hard not to think about his left hand, or what had happened in the room down the hall. Instead he was focusing on his chances of escape, and formulating several different plans.

He knew that by this time his government probably thought he was dead. He'd never gone more than 30 hours without establishing contact in one way or another. But there hadn't been any way to let them know exactly where he was, and it had been years since he'd had any contact with anyone who could actually track him using anything other than his GPS broadcasts. He was well and truly on his own, with no one coming to his rescue. His only hope was to find a way out.

He took a deep breath and started going over his options once again, trying to ignore the throbbing in his wrist.

AT THE SAME TIME, three time zones west of Washington, DC, Indy was turning around very slowly. His blood had turned to ice water in his veins. The sight that met his eyes as he turned made it run even colder. This must be Leon. Up close. All 6′2″ of him. Leather vest, faded jeans. His chest and arms were enormous, built up from years of pumping iron. Both of his arms were covered in tattoos. He sported a gold earring in one ear and had long, graying hair pulled back in a ponytail. He was shouldering an old US Army M-14, pointed directly at Indy. But the most frightening aspect of the situation was Leon's eyes. They were a pale, expressionless blue, and were unblinking. Indy had seen eyes like that on men before. They always meant trouble. In that instant Indy realized that Leon was cut from vastly different cloth than Dennis or Benny. The first two had been biting and sarcastic, but stupid and harmless for the most part. Eyes like Leon's belonged only to a man capable of murder. Leon could and would kill, as easily as he might flick away an irritating mosquito. Indy was in a dangerous spot, and he definitely knew it.

But Indy had survived more than a decade of undercover work, using his quick wits to stave off misadventure. He hadn't risen to the coveted rank of inspector by blowing cases, or by needlessly endangering the lives of himself or others. He possessed a lively intelligence, and knew how to operate smoothly, even in situations like this.

"No shoot sir. No speak English. No shoot. See bear. Beeg bear." He pointed to his camera, and then behind the house. He let loose with a sting of Punjabi, which, loosely translated, meant, "Dear God, please get me the hell out of this mess." Then again. "Beeg, beeg bear. On tour with bike company." He pointed to his bicycle, left standing just a few feet away. And then more Punjabi, even faster. "Lord, get me the hell out of this mess now and I will be your humble servant forever."

Leon started to snigger. "What are you jabbering about, you little brown fucker? No bears here. But you better haul your little rag head ass the fuck off my property or I'll fucking feed you to the fucking bears. This here is no trespassing country. Dig it?" He pointed to a faded no trespassing sign affixed to a nearby tree.

"No read English. So sorry. So very very sorry." And then more Punjabi. "Yes Lord, I am praying very hard now. Hear my prayer…"

Leon gave Indy a shove, and Indy bowed deeply, several times.

"Fuck off. Now," said Leon again, motioning with the gun. He'd have to talk to Dennis about this. He shouldn't be letting his tourists come up this road.

A bowing Indy backed out of the driveway. Leon snorted with laughter. Maybe he should have shot him after all, he thought. Just for the fun of it.

Indy turned around on his bike and headed back toward the Akamina. He would need to study the photos. He thought he had seen something, but that was only a moment before Leon had intercepted him. He knew Leon's type. He had been in precisely this situation earlier in his career, and had rescued himself in precisely the same way. Guys like Leon wore their prejudices rather loudly. He was almost back at the bus before it occurred to him that Leon, if he were smart, would have taken the camera from him. In his self-righteous mirth, he had completely ignored it. A rather large error, that.

THE BOARDROOM at Ramma 5, Diplomatic Enclave, Islamabad was once again connected to the TTIC control room. Once again, Buckingham's voice boomed through the large room. Once again, all eyes turned to Turbee.

"How sure are you guys of the information you developed? The police boss I just talked to laughed when you mentioned Karachi Star Line as a prime suspect."

"Look," said Dan. "We have access to unlimited information here. We know more about what's going on in Islamabad than the cops in Islamabad do."

"Yeah," blurted Turbee, seeing the opportunity to be funny. "We know more about you than you do."

"Who was THAT?" asked Buckingham, somewhat shocked.

"Nevermind. One of our technicians," said Dan. "Now what did the cop say?"

"He used the word *borange*. The cop who's been putting drug runners behind bars for the past two decades thinks you and your supercomputers are full of, well, *borange.*"

"What? Bo-what?"

"Merde. Crap. Shit. You know," said Buckingham. "*Borange*. That was Marak's word. He says that they've checked into that company and found nothing. Thinks the cash is a way to evade taxes, more than anything else."

"Fine," Dan muttered. "Turbee, you explain it."

Turbee steeled himself, and went into a detailed explanation of the comparative database searching technology that he had used to discover the Pakistani shipping company. Halfway through his dissertation on the correlations between the trafficking of precursor chemicals and the unusual financial transactions that had characterized the company, Dan interrupted him.

"Are you getting the picture, Buckingham?" he asked.

"Sort of. But isn't it just as plausible that the Semtex headed south toward the Sudan proper? In fact, once it was loaded onto the DC-3, we basically lost track of it. How confident are you about this, Turbee?"

"Extremely. We're continually measuring confidence factors on things like this. This whole process is probabilistic. And this one is up there at like 99 percent. I have a higher confidence rating in this than we had in the Madrid bombing case. While nothing is certain, this one is close."

It was as bold a speech as Turbee had ever given. No one could see his knees shaking, although he knew some of the old-timers in the room could probably hear the anxiety in his voice, and see the whiteness in his knuckles as he clasped his hands together. But he knew. He was certain. These guys were running drugs in a big way. And he stood by it. It was important that everyone else see the certainty of it.

"What about the rest of you guys?" asked Dan, addressing the control room as though there were no women in it. There were a few voices here and there, in general consensus. "OK Michael, we have your view, or rather, the view of the police in Islamabad. We're going to pass it along. But we've got a billion-dollar computer here, and a brain trust to match it. We're going to talk to the White House."

It was with some nervousness that Dan called Admiral Jackson back. He was still in his meeting with the President, most of his Cabinet, and the Joint Chiefs of Staff. They were waiting for TTIC's call.

"Dan," said Jackson, "you're on the speaker phone here. We have the President, the Vice President, the Secretary of Defense, the Secretary of State, the Head of the National Security Council, and the Chairman of the Joint Chiefs of Staff. You have the floor."

The usually unflappable Dan Alexander gulped. If this telephone call went badly, it could end his career. And his main support came from a raccoon-eyed kid who had fallen asleep on a workstation, amongst a sea of coffee cups and food and candy wrappers. A kid who, for God's sake, was on a cornucopia of medications and had never learned to ride a bicycle. He'd better be right, Dan thought. Dammit, here it went…

"We believe that the stolen Semtex is on a large yacht called the *Mankial Star*. At this moment she is in the Arabian Sea, heading east toward India."

"How do you know this, Dan?" This came from the President. Dan was desperately in need of a glass of water. His lips were as dry as sandpaper. His throat was parched. He looked to Turbee for assistance, but none was forthcoming. Turbee's face was pointed directly downward, and he showed no signs of changing his posture.

Dan folded under the pressure. "Actually, sir," he stuttered, "we're not sure. This is just a theory cooked up by Turbee, and who knows–"

"Mr. President, if you'll allow me," interrupted Rhodes, standing and shooting Dan a black glare. "Obviously I have a better understanding of the situation than our *director*." There was an obvious emphasis on the word "director." It wasn't hard to notice Rhodes' feelings on the matter. Most of the team agreed; Dan was demonstrating his incompetence at every possible opportunity.

Turbee chuckled, then breathed a sigh of relief as he realized that Rhodes was going to be the one supporting his research. The second in command quickly outlined the correlations that Turbee had uncovered. He went into the history and significance of the unusual banking mechanisms, the rapid growth, and the trade in precursor chemicals.

"J-2 has developed similar information," drawled General Pershing, the Chairman of the Joint Chiefs. J-2 was a little-known Intelligence Agency that provided all source Intelligence to the Joint Chiefs themselves. This agency was in charge of keeping the Chairman informed about foreign situations and Intelligence issues that might affect national security policies, objectives, and strategy. It was an overlap in military and Intelligence Agencies, yes, but the men in charge all agreed that it served American security. It was also a prime example of the type of redundancies that drove the congressional overseeing committees crazy. Rhodes, however, was pleased at the mention of the smaller agency. J-2 was on board with TTIC. He knew exactly who they were; it was good to have them on TTIC's side.

"I'm happy to hear that different Intelligence Agencies are reaching similar conclusions," he said. "However, we've run it past Michael Buckingham, the CIA station chief in Islamabad. He's run it by a local high-ranking law enforcement official, who scoffed at it. He said that they knew about the company's unusual financial transactions but that it was more an endeavor to dodge taxes than anything else. Evidently Karachi Star is highly regarded in Pakistan as a model corporate citizen, at least by the police, and is definitely not thought to be involved in the drug trade."

"Well, there's a major problem with what anyone in northern Pakistan says, isn't there?" Admiral Jackson responded. "I mean, half the bastards support al-Qaeda anyway, and who knows how many high-ranking al-Qaeda guys are actually hiding on the Pakistan side of the border. Hell, by the time you get into the Northwest Frontier areas, there really isn't any government at all, is there? I mean, Pakistan says it runs the area, but we all know that a bunch of Pashtun warlords are the only real authority there. We've got these guys practically running the Karzai regime, using drug money as grease."

There was a nodding of agreement in the TTIC control room. Then the voice of the President came over the speakers. "I think I've seen this one before, gentlemen." The President also forgot that there were women in the TTIC room. "You think the stolen Semtex is on the *Mankial Star.* That's great. We interdict it. We search it from top to bottom. And if we don't find Semtex? That's kind of like saying there are weapons of mass destruction in Iraq. We had to go in. We took a crap kicking when it turned out there weren't any. But if we hadn't gone in, and it turned out there *had* been WMD, we'd have taken a beating because we did nothing. Damned if you do and damned if you don't. General Pershing, what assets do we have in that area of the Indian Ocean that we can use to get to the *Mankial Star?"*

"We have a couple of fast destroyers sitting in the Gulf of Oman at present. The *USS Cushing* is closest, I think. We would need some updated imaging to draw a bead on the *Mankial Star,* but she's probably our best bet. She tops out at well over 30 knots, and we have a couple of Sea Hawks on board, I think. We should be able to nail this. I'll give the orders on your say so, Mr. President."

The orders were given, and the *USS Cushing* headed southeast, toward the eastern shores of the Arabian Sea. At the same time, the NRO was tasked with finding the *Mankial Star.*

THE NAVY found the *Mankial Star* in record time, but she was moving at a gentle speed of ten knots, and heading west, not east. She made no effort to get away, and the boarding party was made to feel most welcome.

"Have some tea with us," Yousseff said. He was dressed in the clothes of a deck hand — a pair of faded denim cut-offs, and an even more faded T-shirt. And giving his best impression of a strong accent. "We will of course let you search this ship, but you must sit and have tea with us. We are honored that the commander of so mighty a vessel," he added, motioning to the vast hull of the *USS Cushing,* looming above them, "would pay us a visit. You are most welcome here. You want to search the boat, go ahead, but don't wake up the captain. He is having his afternoon nap."

The other deck hands nodded. Another showed up with a tea tray, half a dozen cups, and some baked goods. "Please, please make yourself at home, gentlemen. Have some tea, kind sirs," said Yousseff, thoroughly enjoying himself. "Please feel at home. Search the ship from stem to stern. Go ahead."

The boarding party from the *USS Cushing* felt obliged to have some tea and sit and chat for a few moments. Then they went through the ship from stem to stern, checking every nook and cranny they came across. They marveled at the scissors lift assembly and the small helicopter on the aft deck. They wondered about some of the mechanical structures within her hull, and about the enormous size of her engines, but they were not there on an engineering expedition. They were there to find the Semtex. Of course, none was found.

What the boarding party did not realize was that most of the visit was recorded by hidden DVD recorders. Yousseff made sure that he was never in the camera field.

19

DAN LEVELED A BRUTAL GAZE at Turbee as the gangly young mathematician wandered into the TTIC control room. Late, as usual. The story of the *USS Cushing* interdicting the *Mankial Star* had spread like a tumor through the Intelligence Community. A mighty American warship, more than 500 feet in length, had, on direct orders from the President, intercepted a private yacht in the Arabian Sea, and sent a boarding party onto the smaller vessel. A boarding party that had been invited to tea, and had then found no weapons — not so much as a slingshot. They had been shown by some deck hands where all the storage areas were. Yes, the yacht did have a cavernous hull, but nothing was found there. There appeared to be some false positives, but 4.5 tons of Semtex, well… where could you hide that?

"You know, Mr. Turbee, that was a huge embarrassment for TTIC," Dan began. "The President himself gave the order, on information you provided. We came up empty-handed. There was zero. Nothing."

Turbee responded quietly, staring at his feet. "I'm pretty sure, Dan, that the Semtex was there. They off-loaded it someplace. They must have."

"That doesn't help things, Turb," groused Dan. "The US Navy intercepted a private vessel in international waters, for no good reason. If the press were to get wind of this story, there would be hell to pay."

"Dan, it was there. I can feel it."

"Well feel with more intelligence, kid! You let me down. You let us all down. Now hunt down the crap. The rest of us are going to work on this nuclear thing. And clean up your goddamn workstation! It looks like a barrel of monkeys have been partying over there. You're a disgrace." Dan turned away from the youth to deal with other, more important issues.

"Hey Dan, lay off the kid, would you?' Lance said. "Maybe it was there. After all, the *Mankial Star* was going west, not east, when she was intercepted. In the satellite photographs, she was definitely heading east. Now–"

Dan interrupted him. "Lance, the goddamn Joint Chiefs, with the DDCI and the goddamn President, were on the goddamn line. You've got a death wish if you fuck up in front of them. A death wish. Don't you dare defend him, not right now."

Turbee began moving some of his cups and wrappers around, dismally looking for a garbage can. Third Grade Science had been like this. Physical Ed in Eighth Grade had carried a similar sting. Girls in his senior year of high school — pretty much the same. Khasha came over to help.

"He's a blowhard, Turb," she said. "Just ignore him. I think it was the right call, and I think you're right. The *Mankial Star* unloaded someplace. We just need to figure out where."

"Khash, he's the boss. And he's right. I did mess it up in front of the President, and apparently a bunch of really important military people."

"Turbee, find out where she unloaded. Get the Keyhole and ORION feeds from the NSA, and go through them. Kingston will help. Maybe they unloaded somewhere off the coast of India. Maybe, somehow, they transferred it to another ship. Figure it out. I think we have some data about how fast that ship can go. You can plot the vectors as well as anyone else. Find it."

After several minutes of cleaning and talking, Turbee finally gave a slight nod. "I'll give it a whirl, Khasha. Thanks for helping," he said, turning back to his computer.

THE UNITED STATES had developed, as part of its defense and Intelligence-gathering activities, 12 sets of satellites, designated by the letters "KH." They became known as the "Keyhole" satellites. The KH-1 through KH-11 series were all widely publicized. A KH-12 series existed, but its particulars were tightly classified. There were rumors about a KH-13 series as well, but knowledge of its existence was available only to a very small group of individuals, which included the President, the Secretary of Defense, the Director of Intelligence, and the people at Edwards Air Force Base, who controlled the satellites.

What was even more classified was that a further iteration had been created, the KH-14, which was known only by the code name "ORION."

The ORION weighed 32 tons, almost half of which was fuel, and had been assembled by the crews of many highly classified Space Shuttle missions. Only three existed — two above the Middle East, and a third above North Korea. The ORION's were, in effect, giant telescopes similar to the Hubble, focused back on the earth's surface instead of out toward space. They were able to focus down to a resolution of approximately half an inch. The information obtained by these three monsters was forwarded through the Milstar network of satellites, and relayed from Edwards Air Force Base through dedicated fiber optic lines to, amongst other places, the NSA, where it was kept in the MP-Sid database.

The problem with the ORION's, of course, was that while they were the most advanced spy satellite ever created, there were still only three of them, and the Middle East was a very large place. Turbee reflected on the problem. The MP-Sid database of Keyhole satellite imagery was the largest database in existence on the planet. It put the databases of Amex, Wal-Mart, and the other giants of Twenty-First Century commerce to shame. Even Blue Gene would spend decades of computing power searching for a needle in a universe of haystacks. Limiting parameters would be needed for this kind of search.

He had an approximate timeline for when the *Mankial Star* had left Socotra. He knew when and where the *USS Cushing* had intercepted the yacht. He knew the distance between Socotra and India. He toyed with this for awhile. Then he recalled what one of the Navy people had said about the *Mankial Star*. "The biggest engines I have ever seen on a ship that small," he'd said. Turbee frowned to himself. Why would the yacht need such big engines? What would incredibly fast speed mean for a pleasure yacht? With a bit of noodling on the net he came up with a speed of 45 knots, maybe a bit more, based on the engines. If she was carrying Semtex, she would have wanted to unload as quickly as possible. She would have been going as fast as she could. With this information, Turbee developed a time/distance probability cone as to where the ship could have been at different times and coordinates. He fed the dimensions of the ship, as per the Naval Intelligence data, into his model. Then he programmed, from scratch, a web-bot that could sort through the pixel maze and, hopefully, with only a few hours worth of tera flops, locate the *Mankial Star* at various coordinates in the southern Arabian Sea. He sent the web-bot on its mission and sat back. Time to order some Chinese food and see what was on the cartoon channel.

GENERALLY, there were three things that could cause Turbee to lose track of time. The first was computer or mathematical problem solving, the second was watching cartoons, and the third was playing video games. As the clock reached and then passed midnight, Turbee was doing all three. Waiting for a web-bot to return data was a lot like putting a loaf of bread in the oven and waiting for it to rise. There was a delicious anticipation to the process, but it took time, and to pass the time, he played his own recoded version of Quake-4 against the endlessly multiprocessing Blue Gene. Lord Shatterer of Deathrot was constantly being decimated by Blue Gene, which was why Turbee preferred that sport to playing with the mostly moronic Internet crowd. In a way he felt that it helped both him and Blue Gene fret away the hours.

Turbee had a delightfully quirky sense of humor, although few ever saw it. Rather than a boring computer message flashing across the screen, saying something dull like "search results ready," he had programmed a host of cartoon characters — Daffy Duck, Elmer Fudd, Homer Simpson, of course, and many others — to take part. They came dancing across all the 101 screens simultaneously, singing, in Mormon Tabernacle Choir fashion, that his webbot search had yielded results. He had thought of playing this little ditty during the day, perhaps when some very important person or other was touring the facility. Dan would probably have an aneurysm, or break out in hives, but it would be fun.

Now he looked at the results, reorganized the data somewhat, and smiled when he realized that he would be able to show everyone, later that day, where the missing Semtex was. It was 3AM when he finally stole the three blocks homeward, to his small basement suite.

IT WAS EARLY AFTERNOON before Turbee was able to shake the cobwebs, re-emerge from his cave, and head back to the office. He always wore a pair of dark sunglasses, since bright sunlight brought on migraines. As he stumbled into the control room, he forgot to remove said glasses. To the buttoned-down crowd in the TTIC control room, it looked as though a Goth-band groupie had just come lurching in. Almost everyone there wore a suit and tie. A fair number wore military uniforms. Many would give a salute before a handshake, and none would dream of showing up to work any later than 7AM. All washed, and shaved, and ironed their clothes before they allowed themselves to be seen in public. Yet here was this peculiar creature, white as a ghost, painfully thin, dirty blond hair too long, unshaven, unwashed, un-ironed, generally unclean, and now sporting dark sunglasses, somehow sitting in their control room. It just was not done.

Dan was about to make an acerbic remark, but before he could say anything, Turbee took off his glasses. That made things even worse, since it showed the dark circles beneath his eyes. Dan muttered to the man next to him that this had to be what drugs looked like.

"Dan, I've found the Semtex. I know exactly where it is."

"Yes, well, let's see where it is this time," Dan muttered sarcastically.

"OK. It was on the *Mankial Star.* I am positive. It got transferred."

"Aw for Chrissakes–" began Dan.

"No, Dan. He's a bit of a wunderkind," said Rahlson. "He hears a different drummer. Maybe he's figured something out. Let's hear what he's got."

There was a short argument about that, involving several different members of the team. At the conclusion, Turbee was given the floor.

"OK. OK. Well it's like this. OK." It had been a hard few days, and he'd taken a lot of bad publicity within the agency. With all the attention suddenly focused on him again, Turbee's thoughts started to spin out of control, becoming circular and repetitive, in the same way that his right forearm sometimes flexed uncontrollably. He panicked, and his mouth became dry. His lips turned to cardboard, and his tongue felt glued to the top of his mouth. Desperately looking around for something to help, he grabbed a cup of coffee from Rahlson's desk and drank half of it in a single swig. Rahlson knew that particular cup to be at least four hours old. He raised one eyebrow in amazement.

"OK. It's like this. OK. You see, I took the… uhh… the Office of Intelligence of Navy stuff and I fed it to the web-bot and then–"

"Jesus, Turbee. Most of us are looking for lost nukes, and you're over there blathering away about God knows what," said Dan. "Get to the fucking point."

"Dan," said Rahlson sharply. "Hear him out." He turned back to Turbee. "Go on, boy. Let's hear what you've got."

Turbee's nerves settled somewhat. The panic subsided. "OK. I know the dimensions of the *Mankial Star*. I created a web-bot to go through the millions of pages of data left by the Keyhole satellites, and by the ORION's–"

"How the hell did you know about ORION? No one knows about that," shouted an Air Force Intelligence wonk from the other side of the room. "You got clearance for that, kid?"

"Don't know what you mean about clearance, but when I was looking through the NRO image database, one of the streams of data was 128 bit and couldn't be parsed by the standard decryption algorithms that are commonly used at Fort Mead, so I hacked into a–"

"Nevermind, Turbee. Just go on," Rahlson urged.

"OK. OK. So I found all of the images that we had of the *Mankial Star* from the various satellites, and I was able to put them together. When I had the first few positions of the *Mankial Star* and by the way, holy cow, you have no idea how fast that boat was going, but anyway, I was able to get to within a few miles of the spot where she turned around. Then I got lucky." He paused for a few seconds and grabbed another slurp of cold coffee, this time from Khasha's desk, to his left. "Real lucky. At the perimeter of one of the ORION shots we got the following three pictures. Have a look," he said, motioning to the 101's.

The first photograph showed the *Mankial Star* and a second, much larger ship, in close proximity; they were parallel to one another, but unconnected. The second photograph showed the same two ships connected by two fuzzy, but discernable, rails. The third photograph showed the two ships connected by the initial two rails and by what appeared to be third and fourth connecting devices of some sort.

Turbee continued. "The second, larger ship is the *Haramosh Star* — one of the older, smaller ships in the Karachi Star Line. She came from Karachi earlier that day. I ran her dimensions through the ONI database to find her name. I ran it through the Keyhole and ORION image database to determine that she had come from Karachi that day. I also did something else."

Turbee had an irritating habit. Someone had to ask, or he wouldn't, or maybe couldn't, go on, given his peculiar brain wiring. It had become a sly insider's joke at TTIC. Everyone waited for Dan to say it, just because his reaction was the most entertaining. The seconds ticked by.

"Oh fuck it, Hamilton. WHAT?" Dan finally snapped.

"Yes. OK. I took the time/space coordinates and fed them into the subsystem that powers the Atlas Screen. George showed me how to use it a week ago."

George cast his eyes skyward. Now they were all going to blame him for giving Turbee another huge computer and the largest screen on the planet to play with.

"Look at the Atlas Screen people." Turbee fiddled with a few commands on the keyboard before him. "You should see two red lines. The first starts from Socotra and heads east, toward the rendezvous point you're seeing on the 101's. It begins when the *Mankial Star* started to head in that direction. You'll see a second red line heading south from Karachi to the rendezvous point. That line traces the *Haramosh Star's* route. Watch what happens."

Turbee had found a way to control the house lights from his workstation, and now he brought them down a little, while increasing the luminescence of the Atlas Screen.

"The kid may be weird, but he does have a sense of theater, doesn't he?" Lance whispered to Rahlson.

The overall impact of the presentation was powerful. The two red lines slowly approached the rendezvous point, with the *Mankial Star* line moving at about twice the speed of the *Haramosh Star* line. When the ships reached their destination, a melodic "ping" was emitted by the system. After the meeting, the *Mankial Star* reversed its direction, while the *Haramosh Star* continued southward along the Malahat Coast. Turbee allowed the simulation to cycle continuously as he raised the house lights.

"Dan, there is no doubt whatsoever that the *Mankial Star* was on a return voyage from the rendezvous when she was intercepted. You have photographic evidence of that rendezvous on the screens behind you. You have the routes of the ships on the screen before you. When the *USS Cushing* intercepted her, the Semtex had already been transferred to the *Haramosh Star.* In fact, there were some indications that trace amounts of Semtex were found in the hull of the *Mankial Star,* but they were attributed to false positives. The Semtex is on the *Haramosh Star,* right now."

"Where is this ship heading?" asked Rahlson.

"I've checked that on the Net. Shipping schedules are pretty much public information these days. She's heading to Vancouver, Canada," replied Turbee.

It didn't take long for this particular piece of information to be passed up the chain. There were the usual phone calls, emails, and electronic messages of various sorts sent to various important people. After 15 minutes Dan had an announcement to make.

"The DDCI, the Deputy Director, and the Secretary of Defense are all in Washington, and are all on their way over here. They want to see the demonstration that you just gave us, Turbee. This is a moment of critical… Turbee?"

There was a bit of chuckling. Turbee was gone, like the ghost he sometimes appeared to be.

20

IT WAS JUST BEFORE SUNRISE, and a thin red line was creeping along the eastern horizon. The seas were calm, and the *Haramosh Star* was heading due east, at an exhilarating 45 knots. Captain Vince Ramballa himself was on the bridge, rolling a cigarette. He had a cup of steaming hot, freshly ground Java sitting on the console before him. The gauges and computer screens showed that the powerful new engines were functioning perfectly, and that there were no obstructions or ships ahead.

Vince was thinking vaguely about some dockside chatter he'd heard in Karachi, about an American Carrier Group that was conducting naval exercises northeast of Diego Garcia, when an ear-splitting scream shattered the serene predawn air. He instinctively brought his hands to his ears, and in the process of doing so, knocked the coffee into the tobacco can and the rolling papers to the floor.

"Holy–" was all he managed to spit out, as six F-14 Tomcats in tight formation roared overhead, only a few hundred feet above the water. "What the hell was that?" he exclaimed.

His chief navigator was likewise shocked, and the two of them peered at the still-dark overhead skies. Metal doors slammed, as other crewmembers rushed to the bridge. Alarm clocks were unnecessary when there were Tomcats roaring by at supersonic speeds. Sailors were shouting, asking what was going on. They knew that it couldn't be good. Every man on the ship knew that, less than 12 hours earlier, they had made an unusual rendezvous with a large private yacht. Most had witnessed the slick engineering and mechanics that had been employed to move cargo of some description onboard. A number had worked on the further reload, moving the red brick-like packages received from the *Mankial Star* to the cargo hold of the PWS-12, stored in a secret pod in the belly of the *Haramosh Star*. Now they began to wonder exactly what they had on board.

Ten minutes passed, and the distinctive sound of helicopter engines became audible. There was a sharp gust of wind, and two US Navy HH-60H Seahawk helicopters appeared from the aft, matching the ship's speed.

"This is the US Navy. Cut your engines. Cut your engines now and prepare to be boarded."

Vince shook his head; he was known by his friends for his tendency to be bullheaded in situations like this. "Fuck them. Who are they anyway? These are international waters." He told the engineer to keep the course and speed steady. The others looked at him fearfully. The Seahawks had a profoundly menacing appearance. "Keep going," he said to the crew in his native Urdu. "Those Yankee bastards don't own this part of the planet."

"Cut your throttle NOW or we will blow your little tin can boat out of the water," came the command from the helicopters. "Prepare to be boarded."

The chief engineer reached for the throttle, but Vince put out his hand to stop him. "No," he said. "We are in international shipping lanes. We ignore them."

The engineer looked at Vince as though he was out of his mind. "It's the US Navy. Are you nuts? These guys are from some carrier battle group south of here, and they could blow up all of India if they wanted to."

"No," said Vince. "Let's see what they do."

The engineer, navigator, and crewmen now assembled on the bridge were starting to look truly pained. A couple were looking toward the lifeboat stations.

"We repeat. This is the US Navy. Cut your throttle or we'll blow your asses to Ceylon." The Navy SEALs aboard the helicopters didn't have orders to do that, but they figured they might as well have a little fun.

"No," said Vince, keeping his hand on the throttle.

Another 30 seconds passed. There was enough light now to see the helicopters clearly. A large machine gun was hanging from the base of one of the Seahawks. Abruptly, a spray of 20-mm bullets walked along the starboard side of the *Haramosh Star.* The engineer reached once again for the throttle. Vince once again stayed his hand.

"No. We keep our speed and course."

He was now facing a near mutiny from his men. But Vince was wily. He knew what the Americans were looking for, but he didn't think they'd actually board his ship, or do any major damage. Yousseff had told him that the Americans, if they accosted him at sea, for all their military might and technological wizardry, did not have the political will to sink this little container ship. It would be international suicide. It just wouldn't happen.

"Easy, comrades. Easy. They are not going to sink us. They are Americans. No balls at all."

There was uneasy laughter from the crew. Vince reached underneath the command console and grabbed the small digital camera that Yousseff had given him. He set the focus and snapped a couple of shots of the helicopters, hoping there would be enough light to pick them up.

"Last warning, ladies. This ship stops or we will do things to it that are going to make you feel uncomfortable. Cut the throttle. Now."

Vince stared dead ahead. The crew braced itself. Now what?

They did not have long to wait. On one of the choppers, the pilot turned to his Chief Gunnery Officer. "Let's give 'em a little fireworks, Sam," he said. "A mild shot. Stick an RPG into that front container there."

"OK, boss," said Sam, smiling. "It'll be a pleasure." He attached the RPG to the launcher, and took aim. This shot would have been impossible to miss.

Back on the ship, the front container shuddered and danced. Then there was a great roar, and a flash of fire and smoke. "Holy shit!" exclaimed more than one crewmember. Vince snapped a few more pictures and sighed. It looked like the Americans were serious about searching the small ship.

"OK, cut the throttle," ordered Vince. "Let's be gracious hosts and let these people on board. Put this on the International Emergency Frequency," he told the radio operator. He picked up the microphone and began to speak quickly, in English. "This is the *Haramosh Star,* a container ship flying the flag of Pakistan. We are being attacked in international waters by the United States Navy. This is the *Haramosh Star...*"

As the ship drifted to a halt, a series of ropes were dropped from the two helicopters. Eight SEALs descended from each helicopter, and the small team assembled on the still-smoking front deck. They marched, in full battle gear, toward the bridge house, ascended the stairs, and gathered on the bridge itself. Vince was still giving his emergency signal when the soldiers entered the small bridge, but he slid the digital camera into his pocket. With most of the crew there, and 16 armed Americans, it was getting crowded.

"We know that you're sailing a ship full of explosives, for terrorist purposes," said the leader of the small SEAL command. "Where are they?"

"No, sir, you are mistaken. We have no explosives aboard this ship. These containers are full of mostly mechanical parts, for automobiles, headed for Vancouver. No explosives here. None."

"Don't give us that bullshit, sir," said the SEAL. "We know that there are explosives aboard this ship. Either you show us where they are or we will rip this ship apart to find them."

"Sir, please. There are no explosives. Please do not rip apart my ship. We are carrying automobile parts. No explosives."

"Last warning, buddy. The easy way or the hard way. Where are the explosives?"

Vince merely shrugged.

The SEAL commander smiled grimly. "OK boys, we have work to do. Let's start with the containers."

The team broke into four groups of four. Each had the latest high-tech version of an ion mobility spectrometer. The devices were designed to detect the presence of explosives, particularly plastique, C4, and Semtex. Developed in the wake of terrorist attacks on American soil, the technology had come far in five short years. The devices could pick up Semtex if there were even a few parts per million present. If there was any on this ship, or in its containers, the SEALs were certain that they would find it.

The Americans spent most of the day crawling over, under, and through the ship and its cargo. Fortunately it was a small ship. Its load was only 100 containers, and the soldiers went through each one. They worked hard, sweating profusely in the rising tropical sun. They were not particular in how they opened the containers, or how they sorted through the contents. They left chaos and disarray behind them, but they hadn't received orders to be neat about the job. Their orders were to find the Semtex. Vince got plenty of excellent photographs.

The sun was directly overhead when the *USS Curtis Wilbur,* a new Arleighe-Burke class destroyer, pulled alongside the *Haramosh Star.* "Reinforcements and lunch," joked one of the soldiers. The hot, thankless job continued, taken on by the new boarding party. Down into the cargo holds, into the engine room, behind the hydraulics, underneath the diesels, into the stern; they went into, under, over, and behind pretty much everything on the ship. There was some brief excitement when one of the teams thought they had picked up traces of something near the port hull, beside the engine room, but it was transitory, and was chalked up to another faulty reading.

Things became more interesting when, at three, the *Rajput,* a Ranvir class destroyer from the Indian Navy, sailed into view. Vince saw her coming, and knew that she was responding to his earlier distress call. He also knew that the modifications made to the *Haramosh Star* at the Karachi Drydock and Engineering yard had served their purpose. No crew of American soldiers, or any soldiers for that matter, would find the cargo that had been placed aboard his ship scant hours ago. And now the Indian Navy was getting involved. This was going to be delightful. Vince picked up the microphone and hailed them on the international frequency.

"I have visual contact with you. We have been illegally boarded in international waters by the American Navy for God knows what reason. We request assistance."

This kind of situation simply didn't occur very often on the international stage. An Indian warship was about to court danger to assist a Pakistani vessel. For whatever reason, an American warship from the mighty John C. Stennis Carrier Group was harassing a pitiful little civilian container ship. Few countries in the world could resist an opportunity to show up the Americans when given the chance.

Things escalated rapidly. The commander of the Rajput got into a shouting match with the commander of the Curtis Wilbur. The Curtis Wilbur called for backup, and the *John C. Stennis* scrambled another squadron of Tomcats. The testosterone was starting to fly.

The United States was by far the largest military power in the world, and had, without question, the largest air force. India, by comparison, had only the fourth largest air force on the planet. The problem for the Americans that day was that most of her mighty military force was elsewhere. There were but four squadrons of aircraft on the *John C. Stennis*. India, on the other hand, was local, and had thousands of planes in the area. It put the Americans in a difficult position.

The dispute continued to escalate. Ten Tomcats flew by the *Haramosh Star*. A few minutes later, 20 Mig-21's with Indian markings appeared in the sky. Fortunately, the parading and chest thumping stopped before it got completely out of hand. High-order American officials talked to high-order Indian officials, and a conflagration was averted, but not before Vince had a wealth of photographs. More than 100, all told — the final shots being composed of American and Indian warplanes roaring low overhead. Then the SEALs left, the Curtis Wilbur left, and the Rajput left. In the almost deafening silence that followed, Vince's men surveyed the mess on their ship. The disrupted containers, the torn wall and floor panels, and the general mayhem left behind by the SEALs painted a far-from-pretty picture.

"I guess we start cleaning it up?" one of them asked.

"No," said Vince. "We wait."

Then the reporters came. First, a crew by helicopter from the *Sri Lanka Times*, whose reporters had monitored most of the exchange on short-wave radios. Then reporters from the *Mumbai Herald* arrived, then Reuters, CNN, News Corp, the *London Times*, the *Washington Post*, and all the rest. Vince let them all download the contents of his camera. He gave all of them the run of his ship. He said to all of them, in broken English, somewhat faked, "No explosives here. None. But still they destroy this little ship."

Back in Langley, the Pentagon, and the White House, the wise men and spin doctors knew that they had a complete disaster on their hands. The word "clusterfuck" was used liberally and with intensity when no explosives showed up. The frequency of its use notched upward when the *Rajput* came on the scene. When the Indian Air Force made its appearance, "goatfuck" replaced "clusterfuck." The media feeding frenzy was beginning. Then came the icing on the cake.

Somehow CNN, with its immense resources, was able to score an interview with His Excellency, the president of Pakistan. "I have no idea what the Americans were thinking," he said, smiling sagaciously into the camera. "We told them that there was no Semtex on that ship. We told them that the Karachi Star Line is a model corporate citizen and represents one of the finest examples of Pakistan's new and growing economy. We told them that we sympathized, and that we would do everything to assist them. But they insisted on looking in the wrong direction."

The reporter was no fool. "Semtex you say, Your Excellency. What Semtex?" Up until that point, every official account had used the word "explosives."

"Why, sir, that plastic explosive, that Semtex, that came from Libya. That is what the Americans say was on board the *Haramosh Star.*"

"But, Mr. President, the Semtex was all destroyed a few days ago. We all saw the footage of that dramatic blast at Bazemah."

"Well, young man, according to the Americans, not all of it. Obviously, not all of it."

It went downhill from there. In the course of explaining the theft of the explosives en route from Benghazi to Bazemah, the President's press advisor was forced to disclose that there were American casualties during that theft. The Presidential cover-up was uncovered, and it was admitted that various soldiers from the *Theodore Roosevelt* Group had died, not on further covert missions in Iraq, but on covert missions in Libya.

Further questioning and probing by reporters during the press conference revealed that there had been more troop deaths in the Sudan, in the raid at Yarim-Dhar. This in turn led to a Sudanese complaint to the United Nations about the USA unlawfully invading its airspace, and a demand for sanctions.

When things could not possibly have gone any worse, they did. Al Jazeera received a copy of a DVD showing the interdiction of the *Mankial Star* by the *USS Cushing*. The camerawork had been skillfully done, and made good use of the image of the *USS Cushing* looming high over Yousseff's yacht. It picked up the politeness of the banter coming from the *Mankial Star* crew, and the invitation to sit down and have tea on board the yacht. It prompted a further complaint by Pakistan, protesting the fact that the US government seemed to be waging a vendetta against one of the country's corporations, for no apparent reason. There were protests and parades, and the usual burning of American flags in Karachi, Islamabad, and elsewhere.

Within three days of the aborted SEAL search, Congress was crying for the President's impeachment. The President had fired the Secretary of Defense, but not before the Secretary of Defense had removed General Pershing as Chairman of the Joint Chiefs. General Pershing had just finished demoting the Chief Admiral of the Navy. The Navy looked like fools, as did both the Pentagon and Langley. Word got out that a new super Intelligence Agency called TTIC had created the false lead in the first place. The newspapers and TV talk shows had a field day, and the late night comedians were outdoing themselves with wheelbarrows full of jokes. It was a complete and utter military, political, and Intelligence Community disaster. Had the PDB supported fonts for three-inch headlines, they would have been used over and over again.

A PALL HAD FALLEN over the TTIC control room. At 10:30AM, three days after the *Haramosh Star* disaster, Turbee entered a room that was filled with depression, defeat, and the knowledge of their impending closure.

Dan was under pressure. There was already talk in the Congressional subcommittees that oversaw the Intelligence Community that TTIC had turned into an expensive boondoggle. Dan was getting the emails, hearing the whispers, and feeling the weight. It wasn't good for him to be at the head of the agency that had screwed up.

"Turbee, goddamn you, you're late," he snarled as Turbee stumbled in the door.

Turbee ignored him and sat down, flipping on his various screens. One of his systems had the volume turned up a bit, and the boardroom could clearly hear the voice of Homer Simpson.

"Turbee, turn that shit off, and tell me why I shouldn't shitcan you here and now!" Dan shouted.

"I'm sorry, sir," he mumbled. "I really am."

"Look at the bullshit you've caused. You tell us the Semtex is on one ship. It's not there. Then you point us all in another wrong direction. The President took it in the teeth. TTIC is near death. Because you fucked up on your research, and led us all astray." A fulminating Dan was watching his carefully crafted career, his rise to power, become thoroughly derailed by a wacko who was in love with Homer Simpson. The platinum-plated resume that his PR firm had built for him was spiraling down the toilet.

"Well, just a minute there, Dan–" Rahlson began.

"No, Rahlson. He screwed up. There was no Semtex on that ship."

"Actually, Dan, there was," said Turbee. "The SEAL guys just didn't find it."

"Excuse me?!" Dan practically screamed, now gathering a full head of steam.

"It was there, sir. It's probably still there. The SEALs didn't find it. The probability that it's NOT on that ship is astronomically low. It's got to be there. Uhh… somewhere on that ship."

Dan drew a deep breath. He'd obviously heard enough. "That's it Turbee, you're done here. The Intelligence Community can do without you. You're history. Fuck off. Pack your bags. Get out."

"What?" asked a white-faced Turbee. "I'm sorry, Dan, you want me to go?" TTIC had been starting to look like a home to Turbee, in spite of the culture clash. Now this?

"Yes, I do. There's the door. You're out."

A stunned Turbee rose slowly to his feet. He slouched toward the door, paler and thinner than he had ever been, his raccoon eyes filled with tears. Khasha noticed, as he limped out the door, that one sock was blue, the other green. She fought back a tear of her own.

"Jesus, Dan, you shouldn't have done that," said Rahlson. "The kid was doing his job. He's smart. He's just weird. You shouldn't have done that."

Dan made a chopping motion with his hand, cutting Rahlson off. He didn't care what anyone else had to say about it. "This is my agency, isn't it? It's my decision who stays and who goes. I don't want to hear another word."

An angry and depressed gloom drifted through the room like dust in a desert wind. No one said much after that.

ON THE OTHER SIDE of the world, Yousseff was relaxing on one of the upper balconies of his Socotra home. The house was immense, covering more than 20,000 square feet, surrounded by pools and small waterfalls, with many verandas and balconies that all presented spectacular views of the surrounding Arabian Sea. His yacht, back from its rendezvous with the *Haramosh Star,* was anchored in the harbor just below his home. He was smoking a pipe of deliciously cooked opium, and watching the satellite feeds from the American media giants. He smiled. The *USS Cushing* crew had definitely been amusing. He could speak English as though he had been educated at Oxford, but had thought it would add to the fun to speak in the manner of a recent immigrant. "Oh no, sir. No sirree. Semtex, what is that? Oh no, not here kind sir…" Their reactions had been priceless.

Mustafa and his crew had performed brilliantly in Libya. But the Americans were clever, and seemed to have discovered the Semtex heist as soon as it happened. Youssef had anticipated a chase to northern Darfur, and had a defense scheme in place. He hadn't expected the Americans to be so quick, which had led to a malfunction in that defense plan. The Janjawiid had come on the scene a bit late, and the resulting affair showed just how dangerous the Americans were. What should have been a turkey shoot ended up with two dozen Janjawiid dead. Who knew Yankees could be so clever with puzzle pieces?

They had tracked down, and presumably captured via satellite, the reload to the *Haramosh Star.* But they had stumbled badly when they interdicted the small container ship. They had not counted on the magical technology of Karachi Drydock and Engineering and Pacific Western Submersibles. Youssef smiled to himself and inhaled deeply. For a moment, he let himself feel safe.

21

MAHARI COULD NOT BELIEVE his good fortune. A message, delivered tersely by telephone, directed him to get himself to a location in the busy market area of Peshawar. Before he knew it, he was in possession of a second DVD and, of course, a second Samsonite case. As soon as he had driven what he felt to be a safe distance back toward Rawalpindi, he pulled over and, with trembling fingers, flipped the locks and opened the case. Sure enough, it was crammed full of American dollars. All he had to do was go to the Al Jazeera station and create a news clip featuring excerpts from the DVD. Things were finally starting to go his way, he thought; he would make his career, and become fabulously wealthy in the process. He was living a dream — a fabulous, multicolored dream.

Within minutes of his entry into the Al Jazeera station, the message was being played around the world, with Mahari's name and face attached. Most major news services interrupted regular programming to broadcast the clip.

WE SHOULD COLLAR that son of a bitch," snorted Admiral Jackson. "Cut off his appendages one by one until he talks." That became a serious point of discussion in the meetings with the President, the new SECDEF, and the others entrusted with the nation's security. But, given the recent public relations disaster of the *Haramosh Star,* it was decided that the prudent course was to keep on the safe side of the law, whether it be international, Pakistani, or American.

Once again, every pixel and nuance of the new message from the Emir was analyzed by all the constituents of the US Intelligence Community. Reports were generated, and then further reports. Reports analyzing other reports, and reports synthesizing reports, spread like rabbits throughout the numerous agencies. The talking heads, the gurus of American cable television, debated it endlessly.

The Emir's dress and appearance were identical to that in the first message. The consensus was that both messages had been recorded at the same time. An analysis of the background lighting, and the nature and quality of shifting light and shadow, appeared to confirm this. The message contained the same salutations to the young martyrs for the *jihad*. It contained the same condemnations of the Great Satan, and, of course, the Lesser Satan. It contained the same exhortation to faithful Muslims, asking them to strike at America and Israel anywhere and everywhere in the world. Then came the part that made the President and his war council nervous.

> *...the soldiers of Allah, peace be upon them, are in place. The weapons of Allah are positioned. The means of delivering those weapons has been secured. Within 21 days the great terror will strike, somewhere in North America, in a manner that will make all previous attacks seem insignificant in comparison. The holy jihad will make a mighty strike upon the Great Satan. Praise be to Allah, and to Mohammed, His prophet. Within 21 days this great day of terror will come. It will come. It cannot be stopped.*

Discussion raged throughout the Intelligence Community. Was the Emir threatening a nuclear attack? Had he somehow acquired a nuclear weapon? Could four or five tons of Semtex level a city? Was it a radiologically dirty bomb? There were more questions than answers. The prevailing wisdom was that it probably was not the Semtex. Most thought that it would be nuclear. It had to be. It was the consensus at Langley, Fort Meade, the White House, and within most of the Intelligence Community. Four or five tons of high explosives was a lot, but it could not possibly do the damage the Emir was promising.

The anxiety was generated chiefly, once again, by that very promise that a strike would take place. If such a promise were made, and then there was no such strike, the Emir would lose face and power. But if he promised it, if he gave America ample warning, and still pulled it off, his stature would become mythic. He would accomplish what all the terrorist leaders had attempted, but failed to do. He would become the new Sword of Islam. He would be unstoppable.

THE PRESIDENT had received the report from Tel Aviv a few hours earlier. He had met with his press secretary and his Chief of Staff about how to use this information to its maximum advantage. The report was lurid and clinically detailed. It had incredible shock value. He thought that he could use it politically. It would take the focus off his country's blunder. Maybe cool some of the heat that had been generated by the *Haramosh Star* incident. And why not? The information contained in the report was shocking. A gang of thugs had tortured an American agent to death, and then mocked America by placing his dismembered remains in front of the American Embassy in Islamabad. This was a true atrocity. It was an outrage. This was not the sort of sophomoric behavior that had come out of Abu Ghraib — flushing the Koran down the toilet, or letting a dog into an interrogation room. This was vicious, calculated torture that ended in a terrible death… something of a different class altogether.

"I'm going public with it," he said to his inner circle. "I'll call a press conference. We are going to deal with this issue, and this issue alone. I will answer questions about Zak Goldberg, and how he died, and who we think killed him, and what we're going to do about it. It will draw the media's attention away from the *Haramosh Star* business. We are going to expose these people for the monsters they are. No one does this to one of our guys and gets away with it."

He had spoken to Zak's parents a few hours earlier, and had extended to them his personal condolences. He had asked their permission to make a public statement as to the manner of their son's death. It was a measure of the complexity of the President, a matter often overlooked by the media. He could have bombed the entire Middle East back into the Stone Age were he so inclined, and yet he felt compelled to ask the permission of two ordinary retired folk before announcing to the world what had happened to their son.

"How sure are we that this was actually Zak Goldberg?" asked the Chief of Staff. "After all, it was, grisly as it may sound, a collection of body parts. And there was no head, so facial recognition is out of the question."

"We've got a perfect match on the fingerprints," said the President. "I don't know what better proof you can have."

"Well, DNA maybe?" replied the Chief of Staff doubtfully.

"Takes too long," replied the President. "The guys who prepared the report said it would take at least two days to get a reliable DNA fingerprint. I want to air this immediately. I want to take a bit of the steam out of this rotten *Haramosh* Star thing. We need this now. Plus we have the ID of the ring by that other character… his brother?"

"Richard Lawrence. His best friend."

"Right. As far as I'm concerned, we don't need anything more than what we have. A terrible crime has been committed against an American, and the world needs to know about it. We do this now." The President was resolute, and his position reasonable. Fingerprints were conclusive ID in any courtroom.

THE FOLLOWING MORNING, his press secretary also tried to talk him out of it, for more public reasons. While the President had considerable intelligence and skill, he could appear wooden before the media. He could, and had on many previous occasions, forgotten or mispronounced words, much to the glee of the media and detractors. But the President would not be dissuaded, and he started the day by appearing in person before the media of the world.

"Good morning everyone," he began. "This morning I am going to tell you how a courageous and highly skilled American CIA agent was murdered. The name of this individual was Zachariah Goldberg, one of our own — a man who had served his country with dedication in many positions for nearly three decades. You might even say that this man was born into the position."

A murmur drifted through the crowd. This was unusual. They had expected to see the press secretary, or, these days, even the assistant press secretary. Yet here was the man himself, making a death announcement. It had never been done before, by any president. With thousands of American soldiers having been killed in Afghanistan and Iraq, and with the tidal waves generated by the *Haramosh Star* incident not yet subsided, this had to be special.

"Agent Goldberg was working undercover, in an area of Afghanistan near Kabul and Jalalabad. He had been working undercover there for almost four years, seeking to penetrate the al-Qaeda organization. Our Intelligence Community believes that the senior leaders of this terrorist group are holed up somewhere in the mountains in that region.

"We believe that Zak Goldberg found out precisely where those leaders were located, and that he was attempting to provide us with that information when he was apprehended. Yes, he was an agent in the field, in the midst of a dangerous mission. But when the United States of America finds an enemy agent in its midst, say for instance an agent who wants to smash mighty buildings into powder and murder thousands of civilians, we incarcerate him. We give him rights, lawyers, and courtrooms. And if we convict him, we put him in jail, where we give him three square meals a day, medical assistance, exercise facilities, and television. Sometimes we even let him have a pet.

"I want you to keep that in mind when I tell you what these people did to Zak Goldberg when they discovered him. I am going to read to you the conclusions of some of the top forensic pathologists on the planet, in both Tel Aviv and Washington."

The media scrum was becoming uneasy. The President himself reading a coroner's report? What was up with that? The President sensed the growing discomfort in the room, but continued. He read slowly and deliberately, pausing a second or two between phrases or sentences, to let the awful magnitude of what had happened to Zak truly sink in.

"They smashed his right leg to pieces. They tore the tibia completely from its surrounding flesh and tissue, and discarded it. It was not with the rest of the body. They smashed most of the bones in his feet to pieces with some kind of blunt instrument, probably a hammer. They ruptured both testicles, through blunt force trauma. The forensic scientists who examined him think this was done through repeated, incredibly vicious blows to the groin. He had many internal injuries, some occasioned by blunt force, others by surgical instruments."

The President was speaking with a slow and measured deliberation. He wanted to make sure that everyone understood what had happened. The fidgeting in the room increased.

"Worse yet, they proceeded to flay the skin from his body. The skin was removed from his entire left arm, and most of his right arm received the same treatment. There was similar abuse to the skin on his back. Some of these injuries were old when he died, which means he was tortured again and again, over many weeks."

The President stopped reading for a moment. It was not for dramatic effect. He too was feeling the pain and outrage of what had happened, and his voice was going to fail him if he continued. He took a long sip of water, looking out over his audience. The press began shifting nervously in their seats. They did not want to hear anything else. But there was more, and the President wasn't going to let them off the hook.

"At some point in this hideous crime, Zak's captors proceeded, while he was still alive, to dismember him. Both feet were chopped from his body. We received only one hand, which seems to have been cut off using a dull carpenter's saw. We can only hope that he was unconscious for much of this abuse. Both his arms and both his legs were also cut off before he was killed.

"His remains were placed in rice bags and deposited in front of the American Embassy in Islamabad. That is where he was found. Only one hand and one foot were included, and his head was missing. We do not know why this was done, but it makes it extremely difficult to say exactly how our man finally died."

For a full 30 seconds there was dead silence from the usually raucous press corp. No one dared speak. There was no coughing, no shuffling of feet, no raising of a hand. Any remaining questions about the *Haramosh Star* were forgotten. The President slowly leaned forward, pinning the reporters with his gaze, and spoke into the bundle of microphones. "We will find his killers. We know exactly where they are located. And we will bring them to justice. That is a promise. Thank you."

He turned and left, leaving his press secretary to answer the questions, which began slowly, but continued for a full 30 minutes.

THE CENTRAL BALLROOM at Ramma 5, Diplomatic Enclave was crowded, with all eyes focused on the wide screen TV. Almost everyone in the Islamabad Embassy had known Zak. None had heard the coroner's report yet. As the President's speech went on, some started to sob, while others curled their fists in anger. How could they? How could the cold-hearted, murderous bastards do this to any person, and how could it have happened to someone who had been their colleague and friend?

None took the briefing harder than Richard. He had considered Zak a brother. He had grown up with him, and lived with Zak and his family in California when his own mother and father were lost in the car crash. Zak had been his family; his best friend and brother. When he first found out about the man's death, he had gone on a binge of alcohol and painkillers. He had let the fog of drugs and alcohol numb his system, and transport him back to an earlier time. A time when he had thought life was over, and when Zak had been there to pick him up and carry him on.

IT HAD BEEN A WARM September evening in 1970 when a young Richard heard a sharp knock on the door of his stately family home on Ramma 5, Islamabad, just a few steps over from the American Embassy. He had been deeply immersed in an introductory calculus text, attempting to solve derivative equations. Because of his nationality and his parents' positions at the Embassy, his schoolwork was done partially through correspondence and partially through the local high school. Exams were approaching, and he had been deeply engrossed in his work. When he didn't respond to the knock, it was repeated, more insistently. Richard put his pen down, and walked toward the front door. As he reached the central foyer the knock was repeated a third time.

"I'm coming, I'm coming," he said in Urdu, hastening to open the door. There stood a 20-year-old Michael Buckingham, red faced and out of breath. Michael had held a junior CIA position at the time. He would soon leave the Embassy for field work, to return more than 20 years later as the station head.

"Michael, what's up?" Richard had asked, watching a small rivulet of sweat crawl down Michael's forehead.

"It's bad, Richard. It's… it's very bad. Richard…"

"What Michael? You're scaring me. What?" A small core of anxiety had formed in the pit of Richard's stomach.

"There's really no easy way to say this. It's your folks. Your parents. Both dead. Both. Richard I'm so so sorry."

The words had pounded into him like a sledgehammer on an anvil. "Michael. Both? You're serious? How?"

"Car accident. Toward Peshawar. A huge transport truck drove right over their car. Driver was drunk." The words tumbled out of Michael in a rush of sorrow. "Or stoned. They never had a chance. They died instantly. Richard, I am so sorry."

"Where are they? Where are their bodies? Michael, take me to them. Now." By this time the adrenalin had been pumping into Richard's system, and his mouth was as dry as sandpaper. He'd thought that it had to be a mistake.

"Richard, you need to come with me to the Embassy. The station chief will handle it from there. Come on, please." Michael had gently reached out to take Richard's arm.

Senses numbed, Richard had followed the older man. They had reached the Embassy gates before he realized that he'd forgotten his shoes. Richard had been an only child. Now he was an orphan. The shock had pushed everything else from his mind.

Richard had continued to insist on seeing the bodies after he got to the Embassy. "Take me to them. I want to see them," he said. "Show me the bodies." Over the protestations of the station chief, he was taken to the basement morgue of Islamabad General Hospital.

"Look, Richard, you don't have to do this," the station chief had told him.

"I need to know that they're dead, that there is no hope or possibility of them living. I need to know it. Let me see them," Richard had told the older man. He was still in shock, and spoke with no emotion whatsoever.

The stainless steel drawers were pulled back, and Richard had come face to face with his parents — two wonderful, kind, and generous people, with whom he had eaten breakfast no more than four hours earlier.

The accident had been horrific. The truck had driven through the small Volvo his parents had been driving. Both his mother and father had sustained massive long bone fractures and internal injuries. Their heads had been crushed between thousands of pounds of tire and steel. Death had been instantaneous, but the results were ugly and disturbing. Try as he might, Richard had never been able to purge the image of his parents in death from his brain, even after almost 20 years had passed.

The days that followed the accident, the memorial services, the funeral, the interment, the wake, and everything else became a mind-numbing series of rituals, through which Richard had stumbled like a zombie.

It was at the wake that he met Zak Goldberg again. Zak, who was his age, had left the Islamabad station two years earlier when his parents were transferred stateside. Before that, Zak and Richard had been close friends, growing up together in a foreign country. They'd been close enough that Richard had treated Zak as a brother, and vice versa. When Zak left, Richard felt as though he'd lost his best friend and idol, and had been incredibly unhappy. They'd remained in close contact by telephone and letter, and Zak and his parents had returned to Islamabad as soon as they heard news of the crash.

"Come back with us to California," Zak had said after the funeral. "You can move in with us. Mom and Dad said it would be fine."

Richard had checked with Zak's parents directly.

"Yes, of course you can move in with us. Your parents were our closest friends. We were shocked when we heard what happened. We'd love to have you," they had responded.

It hadn't taken Richard very long to weigh the pros and cons of the Goldberg's offer. With his parents gone he was absolutely alone in the world. The prospect of having a family again, of being surrounded by people who cared for him, had seemed like a dream come true for the young man.

THAT WAS HOW Richard and Zak had moved from being good friends to actually being brothers. As he sat in the central ballroom of the American Embassy, those memories played painfully in Richard's head. He was sitting on the edge of a couch, his hands covering his face, rocking slowly back and forth. Most people didn't notice, given the impact of the statement the President was reading. Michael Buckingham did.

MARAK'S PRIVATE LINE RANG. He looked up and frowned. Almost no one had this number — not even his closest subordinates. It was a line that rang only in moments of great urgency. He cautiously picked it up. "Yes?"

"Marak, you fool, you crazy dumb camel-shit-for-brains fool! What in God's name were you thinking?"

Marak recognized Yousseff's voice. He couldn't recall the last time that he'd heard his friend so upset.

"Yousseff, what is it?"

"You goddamn moron! Do you have any idea what you did with that body-in-front-of-the-Embassy stunt?" The anger was definitely there, and it was riding the edge of a knife.

Marak thought fast. "It was Ghullam who put it there, actually. But I thought it was a poetic touch, Yousseff. A nice way to let those Yankee bastards know not to mess around in our territory."

"Nice way my ass," retorted Yousseff. "I told you to extract whatever information you could, and dump the body in some canyon. Instead you drop it in front of the American Embassy?"

"Yeah. What's the big concern? The Pashtun will love it."

"She is a sleeping tiger, America is!" snapped Yousseff. "And you have just awakened her. Do not ever underestimate the power of the enemy, you dumb ox. And do not ever disobey an order from me again. Not ever! I am repeating what I said 35 years ago. Do not forget that day, Marak."

"I am sorry, Yousseff. I over reached."

"Yes you did, Marak. Yes you did. And in doing so, you may have jeopardized the whole mission."

"Yes, Yousseff. I am sorry. But in my defense, I did direct the attention of the Americans away from Karachi Star Line."

"Just for awhile, Marak. Just for awhile. They'll be back."

Yousseff hung up the phone and gazed long and hard at the blue of the Arabian Sea, thinking furiously.

22

INDY HAD CHEATED DEATH, yet again. Leon had let him live. He had biked furiously back to the gates of the park and climbed back into the bus, with a stoned Dennis Lestage none the wiser about his tourist's extra-curricular activities. On the way back to the bus, Indy had phoned Catherine and arranged to meet with her before making the long trip back to Vancouver. Now he was relating his experiences to her over yet another cup of coffee.

"It was his eyes, Cath. Utterly cold. Deadly eyes. Lizard eyes. I've seen that before. He'd have pulled the trigger if I hadn't done the moron-tourist thing," he told her.

"What are you going to do with this?" asked Catherine, nudging the camera. "How far ahead are you, anyway?"

"In my mind, he's clearly within the reasonable doubt test," responded Indy, referring to the Canadian standard required for proving a criminal charge before a jury. "In fact, I am absolutely, drop-dead sure about this," he continued. "Before I came here I had our commercial crime people attempt to trace the ownership of a number of these smurfing accounts. While it wasn't easy to do, because they were owned by other numbered companies, Leon's name did appear here and there. I think that there's a strong possibility that these boys are running drugs across the border into Montana in a big way. There's just too much money in that account. Especially for losers like these. I've now had the opportunity to meet three members of the Lestage/Hallett gang. Two are dumb as a bag full of hammers. The third, Leon, is a cold-blooded killer, who I'll wager has murdered more than a couple of people over the years."

"Fine, Indy. You've shown that they're not Boy Scouts. We kind of knew that already. But how does it play out in court? You're sure. But now you need to prove it. You need to establish the method. You need to show the mechanism of the crime. So far, we've got a lot of petty crimes, and maybe even money laundering. But you need to show that a massive drug importing/exporting operation is actually taking place. How do you do that?" Catherine asked.

"Look," he said, watching the sun slip behind the mountains. "Leon is sitting right on the border of Montana. He's found a way to get large quantities of drugs over it, somehow. I know it. He's found a way past the satellites and the video cameras and the sensors and whatever else the Americans have on the border." He was shoving his coffee mug back and forth, sloshing coffee over the rim in his excitement.

Catherine watched him with a smile on her face. She could practically see the wheels turning. "So what's the next move, Indy?"

"I'm not sure. I'm going to think about it. I'm going to talk to Hagen. I'm also going to analyze the photographs I took, pixel by pixel. There may be something there that I'm missing. We've got a pretty decent digital lab back at headquarters. I'm sure we'll be able to get something. Anything."

EVENTUALLY, Indy bade Catherine goodbye, and headed west on the long trip back to Vancouver. En route, with more than eight hours to do nothing but think and drive, he worked himself into a fine lather. He began to ruminate about the idiocy of it all. He was fed up. Fed up with Ottawa bureaucrats. Fed up with cabinet subcommittees. Fed up with dopers pointing guns in his face. Fed up with judges releasing hardened criminals back onto the streets, instead of putting them in prison where they belonged. "It's only marijuana, my boy. What's the big deal? This is British Columbia in the Twenty-First Century. Wake up. Get a life." That's what they told him. And he should have done just that, he thought sometimes. With his knowledge, built up over decades of police work, decades of breaking rings of smugglers, cultivators, importers, exporters, retailers, and manufacturers, he'd be able to make a fortune overnight. And instead here he was, with a cramped little bullshit office on Heather Street in Vancouver, driving an aging Chevy pickup truck, with most of his meager salary going to his living expenses. What the hell was the point, anyway? One awesome play, and he would have it all. He had the means and the knowledge. It wouldn't even have to be a Hail Mary.

But no, he argued against himself. He couldn't abandon everything he'd worked for all his life, just because he knew how to use a back door or two. He spent hours going back and forth on the issue, weighing the pros and cons of everything in his life. By the time he got back to town, he was so frustrated that, even after an all-night drive, he drove right past his tiny apartment and went straight to his office. He walked in, dropped his bag on the floor, and called Hagen.

"Can you help me, Stan?" he asked. "We've got a laundering account for sure. The Halletts and Lestages are smurfing one hell of a lot of cash. It's got to be coming from cross-border sales of BC Bud, and maybe even heroin.

Probably cocaine coming back the other way."

Indy spent some time laying out the background for the FBI agent. He told him about Benny Hallett's tale of woe, the new Dodge, the destruction of the same, the bullet to his knee, and the visit to the hospital. He described the trip to the Akamina-Kishinina, the location of Dennis or Leon Lestage's home, and Leon's likely connection to the Vancouver chapter of the Hell's Angels. He explained how he'd obtained the subpoena, issued on the strength of an affidavit that was sitting on the outside edge of legality, the bank account that had come to light, and the large transfers to an offshore bank, identity unknown.

"You've got something there, alright," said Hagen. "This may not be small-time stuff after all. How can I help?"

"You guys should be able to get the details of that offshore account for me. It may be an accumulation account. The transactions there could be very revealing."

"Sure, we can do that, Indy. With the new Patriot Act, and a few other things, I should be able to get the information for you."

"Let's do it. What do you need from me?"

"Are you able to swear an affidavit that it's your honestly held belief that the account is being used to launder drug revenues?" asked Hagen.

"You bet I can, Stan," Indy answered. "I can get that sworn, if I can find a lawyer around here, and send it to you within an hour. I'll get right on it."

Indy quickly set out to repeat his labors of a few days before. He laid out in neat numbered paragraphs the extent of his knowledge relating to the apparent drug activities of the Halletts and Lestages. He attached the Scotia Bank ledger as an exhibit, collared a lawyer, had the affidavit sworn, and immediately faxed it to Hagen.

That accomplished, Indy headed to the video lab with his digital camera. He downloaded the contents and started flipping through the images, magnifying here, adding light or contrast there, looking for anything. He hardly noticed the small TV in a corner of the lab, tuned in to CNN, where a reporter was discussing the growing Semtex scandal in the context of the hideous murder of one Zak Goldberg.

INDY SAT BACK, thinking. He had all 37 photos displayed as thumbnails on the large screen where he was working. He'd reviewed each image a dozen times, magnifying them again and again, changing the contrasts, and using software developed by the FBI, and licensed to the RCMP, to increase the resolution of obscure details. A number of them showed a trail and tire marks heading further south, to some destination behind the mobile home. On one he could see an old sign, tilted, sitting in the underbrush beside the trail. There were words on it, but they were partially obscured by weeds, willows, and shadows.

Indy didn't have the computer expertise required to manipulate the images as much as he needed. But the Heather Street compound also served as a resource center for organizing evidence and documents in major crime cases. Video analysis had become a staple for police work. There were a number of technicians working at the complex, and it didn't take Indy long to bring one in. He was somewhat frustrated about asking for help from someone who looked to be half his age, but shrugged it off. Computers and digital evidence were a young man's game, and he was willing to do whatever it took to nail this case.

Indy had the young tech isolate the sign on the photograph, rotate it, enlarge it, and add some highlighting… then tweak it some more. "e…A…vil" was all they could make out.

"Let's get rid of the shadows from the underbrush and interpolate the pixels," suggested the technician. "That might help some."

"Whatever you suggest," said Indy, unsure of what that even meant.

The youth's fingers raced over the keyboard, the mouse traced the shadows on the screen, and, like magic, the underbrush shadows disappeared. They both sat back and observed the result.

"Not much difference," said Indy.

"We need more contrast. There is a phrase there, I can see it. We just need to sharpen the edges. We can change the fractal coefficient. I'm sure we can bring out whatever's there." A few more keystrokes and mouse clicks. More of the sign became apparent. "..ev..l's..A.vil" was the message.

"We can get more. The image on the sign clearly contains letters. Everything's linear. We can do a bicubic linear interpolation based on the differential color components of the missing letters. I'm positive we can get it, Indy."

"Yes. Bicubics. Of course. Should have thought of it myself," Indy mumbled in response.

More keystrokes. More mouse clicks. "There," said the tech finally.

"You're a magician," breathed Indy. He leaned forward, getting closer to the screen for a better view. "Save that image. We need to figure out what it means," he said, gazing at the words "Devil's Anvil" on the screen.

"Let's Google it," suggested the tech.

"Sure," said Indy, happy to be letting the young man do so much of his work for him.

Nothing much came of that. "Devil's Anvil" was apparently a psychedelic hard rock New York garage band of the '60s. Well, Leon could conceivably be a fan, thought Indy. There were also "anvil devils," something used by boot companies. Other than that, there were no hits of significance. Perhaps a motorcycle gang? A warning? A joke?

"Y'know what it sounds like, Indy?" the tech finally asked.

"What?"

"It sounds like an old mine. If I were a geologist, and I had developed a mining property somewhere, a name like 'Devil's Anvil' would be pretty cool. You know, deep in the earth and all that."

"You know, that twigs a chord," said Indy. "I did some reading on the Akamina before heading out there. Got some stuff off the net. The region is pretty rich in coal deposits. That whole area is littered with abandoned mines. The only reason they didn't become commercially viable was that rail transportation was never implemented in the area. Large coal deposits were subsequently discovered in the Kootenay Valley, and that's where the spur lines stopped. The area south of Fernie never became a possibility because of it. But in the 1920s no one knew that's how it would turn out. Think I'll look into it a little more."

Indy rose from his chair, grabbing the pad on which he'd been taking notes.

"Where are you going?" asked the tech.

"Off to Victoria. The BC Ministry of Mines is headquartered there. They'll have maps, plans, memos, and what have you. If anyone has information about a mine on the border south of Fernie, it'll be that office."

With that, Indy turned and was gone.

AT THAT MOMENT, a couple time zones to the east, Turbee was fleeing from the TTIC control room, rushing past the heavy security on the main floor, pushing his way out onto the street. Dan's words stung his face like wasps, attacking his body with the poison of adders. "You're history. There's the door. Fuck off. Pack your bags. Get out. Get out. Fuck off. There's the door, pack your bags, get out, get out, fuck off…" The venomous phrases circled around his autistic brain in infinite echoing loops, the volume ever increasing. "Fuck off. Pack. History. Out. Out. OUT!"

Turbee raced down the street, heading east along Pennsylvania Avenue. He ran for several blocks, until his underused lungs started to ache. His eyes lost their focus, and cars and buildings swirled around him. “Out, out, out. Fuck off. Pack. History. Out!” The comments of his First Grade class joined the chorus chiming in his brain. “Loon. Moron. Idiot. Retard.” He couldn’t control the sound in his head, which was starting to disintegrate like a Hendrix guitar note. “Stupid, stupid, STUPID!” His heart was racing and sweat was pouring out of his pores. His anxiety reached a fevered pitch, and the feeling was becoming as audible as a highly pitched warbling electronic yowl.

The voice of Kathy, his tutor from Fourth to Tenth Grade, gradually emerged from the confusion of images, sounds, and memories. Kathy, who had replaced the mother that he had lost to parties, alcohol, and strange men. “Don’t ever forget this, Hamilton,” Kathy had told him once. “If this ever happens again, breathe slowly and deeply. Stop moving. Close your eyes. Think back to this moment and remember my voice. Slow your breathing. Shut out the noise and the lights, and stay calm. Breathe, Hambee. Breathe slowly… breathe… breathe…”

He opened his eyes, and felt the howling concerto of Dan Alexanders begin to fade out. His panic dropped somewhat, and he started walking again. His brain switched to autopilot, and for awhile he distracted himself by mentally solving five-dimensional Fourier transform equations.

He wandered about in this fugue state for most of the day, stopping at the occasional corner store to purchase chocolate and root beer, two of his comfort foods. He was now completely lost, but didn’t care. When he became weary he simply sat down on a curb or nearby bench. The entire day slid past while Turbee wandered the city aimlessly.

THE *HARAMOSH STAR* rounded the northern tip of Sumatra silently, with Lhok Alurayeun to the north, and Banda Aceh to the south. It was three in the afternoon, and a hot tropical sun was beating down on the ship. The waters were calm. Vince had slowed the ship to a pace of ten knots, and was alertly watching both the radar and sonar screens. The Straight of Malacca was one of the most crowded marine traffic lanes on the planet. Any eastbound vessel from Africa, the Suez Canal, the Middle East, Pakistan, or India went through these waters. Furthermore, the great earthquake of 2004, and the tsunami that followed, had been severe enough to alter the course of the shallow channel. The old channel maps were no longer accurate, and in the year following the great earthquake many vessels had run aground in places where the maps showed that there should have been sufficient depth. Vince was determined to avoid this fate.

He watched as the reconstruction sites of Banda Aceh crawled by. With billions of dollars of aid from many governments, agencies, and organizations, the area was now witnessing one of the greatest building booms in history. Vince shuddered at the reason behind the rebuilding. Oceanographers and mathematicians had calculated that the tsunami that had swept over this peninsula and resulted in the need for rebuilding had been a towering, unbelievable 80 feet in height. The height of a six or seven-floor building. The poor bastards never had a chance, he thought, as his eyes followed the coastline, simultaneously tracking the screens in front of him. Not a prayer of a chance. He continued to look at the shoreline, and was deeply, deeply troubled. The explosives he had stowed away on his ship would be capable of much greater damage than what he was looking at. His sailor's heart thanked God that he wouldn't be there to see it.

GOVERNMENTS being what they are, notorious entanglements of inefficiency and tepid bureaucracy, it took Indy the better part of a day in downtown Victoria, BC to find the proper building. He was sent first to the Ministry of Mines executive offices, and from there to the MOM Operations Building, and from there to the MOM Annex, then to the MOM New Building, and finally to the BC Mining Archives building. Once in the building, it had still taken him an hour of deferential waiting to be shown, by a relatively young man who moved at a glacial pace, to the sub-basement stacks. It was another hour before he found the shelving units that contained the precious nuggets of information he was seeking.

The office closed for business by 4:30PM, which of course meant that almost everyone was gone by four. The lights dimmed, and Indy listened to the scurrying of feet and the locking of doors somewhere above him. Good. They had forgotten he was there, which meant he had the place to himself. He renewed his search, relieved that he wouldn't be interrupted.

Eventually he found what he was looking for, and it turned out to be a priceless morsel of information. Lying on a bottom shelf, covered with dust and hoary with age, was a file folder bearing the name "Devil's Anvil." His hands trembling in anticipation, Indy found the application, the permit, the development plan, and the subsequent modifications and alterations of the disused mine. There were also some interesting old memos. Everything was there. There was even a series of maps enclosed with the application.

Indy compared the 1920 surveying maps to the modern map he'd brought with him. A grin started to play across his face. Sure enough, the Leon Lestage property was located precisely at the entrance to the Devil's Anvil mine. Some of the shafts and tunnels appeared to be very close, if not touching, the 49th parallel (otherwise known as the US/Canada border in Montana). He looked more closely at one of the development plans on file. At the bottom of a large map of the mine itself was a signature. It was unmistakable — James Leon Hallett. No doubt one of the progenitors of what was to become the Hallett/Lestage gang 60 or 70 years later.

Is this how they're doing it? he wondered. Is this the route? Was this the border hole? More work was required. Dangerous work. He'd have to get into that mine. He needed to know what modifications the Lestages and Halletts had made. How they were doing this. It would be critical, and perilous, and would have to be done when Leon was away. He would definitely need Catherine's help.

THE PHONE at the Cranbrook detachment rang a few times. A receptionist picked it up and promptly put Corporal Catherine Gray on the line.

"Ready to do some spelunking, Cath?" Indy asked.

"Sure, but it had better not be dirty," she answered.

"Spelunking. Exploring underground cave systems. In this case, underground mine systems. That's what spelunking is. And sorry, but it can be dirty — especially if it's a coal mine we're exploring."

"Where?"

"Leon's trailer is positioned right at the entrance of an abandoned coal mine called Devil's Anvil. Carved out of the stone in the 1920s by a mule-stubborn Scottish miner by the name of James Leon Hallett. The mine was pretty rich too, according to the assay reports." Indy was talking so quickly that his Punjabi accent was starting to come through.

"Slow down, Indy. Where are you?" asked Catherine. "What have you found? And what's with the Devil's Anvil nonsense?"

"I'm at the BC Mining Archives, in Victoria, in the basement."

"Where?"

Indy explained to her how an RCMP computer analyst had teased the name Devil's Anvil out of one of the digital photographs he had taken on his recent trip to the Akamina-Kishinina. He told her that it had been a lucky guess that it was the name of an old mine. "At the time it must have looked like it would be a good commercial proposition, but the railway never extended that far south, and the American railways never went that far north," he told her. "So James Hallett was stuck. He ranted and raved in Victoria, and apparently did the same in Ottawa. According to this file he was arrested for waving a gun around in the Nelson District Mining Office. Ultimately, it seems that he drank himself to death, probably unable to come to terms with the fact that he was sitting on one of the richest coal deposits in the Rockies, with no one who wanted to put in a railway. It's kind of a sad story, actually."

"But how does all of this help you?" asked Catherine.

"Looking at the maps, I think James Hallett may have either deliberately or accidentally dug underneath the border. There are a couple of deep, long, southbound tunnels. We need to follow them and see what we get. We need to get some GPS equipment, so that when we surface we know where we are."

"That's pretty wild, Indy. You'll need a warrant, I think."

"No problem. I can get one, with the material I have. It'll be a legal seizure, if we find anything. Is Leon there, now?"

"Actually he isn't. He left the same day you did. Hasn't been back. We have some of our boys looking out for him."

"In that case, what are you doing tomorrow?"

"Tomorrow was supposed to be a paper day. Reports to Crown Counsel, letters to lawyers, that kind of thing," she answered.

"Well, let me brighten it up for you. Come with me. Get some powerful flashlights. I'll bring the GPS transmitters. We can go spelunking in Devil's Anvil."

"Indy," giggled Catherine, "that sounds almost sexual. 'Spelunking in Devil's Anvil.' Shame on you!"

"I'm too old for that, kiddo. This is just plain old police work. See you tomorrow at 7AM."

Another day wasted, thought Indy. Might as well pack. He arranged to take the heli-service back to Vancouver. En route, his cell phone rang. It was Hagen.

"Indy, that stuff you faxed me was pure gold. You're dealing with a major league drug operation. You have no idea how much money passes through the Cayman banks. I faxed most of what I got directly to you. Call me once you've seen it."

Indy thanked Hagen, and, when the helicopter landed at the Vancouver Harborside Heli-Port, proceeded directly back to the Heather Street complex. When he reached his office in the late afternoon, the fax and a number of enclosures were sitting on his office desk. Hagen was right — millions of dollars flowed in and out of the account. The money came in primarily from the five large Schedule "A" Canadian Banks — the Scotia Bank, the Royal Bank, the Toronto-Dominion Bank, the Canadian Imperial Bank of Commerce, and the Bank of Montreal. The deposits averaged out to $500,000 per week. That meant $2 to $3 million a month, and, if they worked seven days a week, running what was probably the world's largest smurfing exercise, maybe $25 to $30 million per year. And that was just from the Canadian side of the operation. The American side was probably pulling in a lot more. Indy shook his head in wonder. James Hallett's lame duck mine had turned out to be profoundly productive after all. Just not in the fashion that he had envisioned. And probably long after he was dead and gone.

After he'd read the fax, Indy had another affidavit sworn, using the information he had uncovered at the archives. As before, he found a lawyer at the Heather Street complex who was prepared to take his affidavit. He raced to the courthouse, sweet-talked the court registry staff, and found himself, once again, in front of a judge in almost record time. He explained the situation to the judge, who stamped the appropriate warrants. By five that evening he had what he needed.

Indy arrived back at his home at 6PM. Not having slept in almost 48 hours, he set two alarms for midnight. Leaving at 12:30 would give him enough time to drive back to the Kootenays and meet up with Catherine. In spite of his physical fatigue, his mind was now racing so quickly that he had difficulty getting to sleep at all. The biggest case of his career had just landed in his lap. At this point, he couldn't begin to imagine how big it might actually be. He finally drifted off, just as he was imagining further promotions, and hopefully a big raise.

When the alarms went off at midnight, he rolled over with a moan and turned them both off. He made the same mistake that so many overtaxed individuals make, thinking that he would snooze for another 15 minutes, and then get up. As it was, the body demanded more sleep, and Indy didn't come back to consciousness until the up-tick in traffic noise woke him at 6:30 in the morning. He called Catherine.

"Indy, I'm sorry, but I'm going to be stuck in court tomorrow. If you arrive here tonight, I'll be busy reviewing transcripts and preparing for it. I won't be able to leave until four or five tomorrow afternoon. And I don't want to start out at five in the evening, especially after a day in court. You know how exhausting that can be, don't you?" she asked.

"Yeah, I know," sighed Indy. "I know too well. So we'll start up in the early morning the day after tomorrow?"

"Yeah, I can do that," she answered, understanding his frustration. "Go and do your paperwork. Every cop I know is backed up on that sort of thing. And rest. Use today and tomorrow to catch up, so you'll be well rested when we start out. That's reasonable, isn't it?"

"Suppose it is," he grumbled. "Day after tomorrow it is. I'll meet you at that same coffee shop at 7AM?"

"Yup. Seven it is."

So much for that, thought Indy. Here he was, with the biggest lead of his career, and he was off to do paperwork at Heather Street. That was police work for you.

TURBEE crossed the Anacostia River at around midnight, stopping for a few minutes at the bridge's crest to gaze down at the black river waters below. He knew that his meds had long since worn off but didn't care. He had failed. That was all he could think about. He had let down TTIC, Big Jack, the Secretary of Defense, the President, and the nation. Dan Alexander had been right. Pack your bags. Out. It was what he deserved.

He continued walking, more slowly, past the aging Anacostia Naval Station and the once-important Bolling Air Force Base. At 1AM he was walking through the large jumble of streets that constituted the District of Columbia's eighth ward. He didn't realize that he had now wandered into the most dangerous area of a crime-ridden city. At 3AM, he stumbled across the empty parking lot of the infamous Ballou High School. That was where he was spotted by Ziggy, the kingpin of a collection of teenage skinheads who called themselves the Aryan Knights.

The situation was just too good to be true for the bored, intoxicated thugs, who were looking for an easy thrill — cheap and easy sex, perhaps, or a car to steal, or a bum to roll.

"Hey, Ziggy, look at the skinny little Goth fuck coming down the road. He looks lost. Let's give him directions," one of the boys muttered.

"Yo," replied Ziggy. "Let's be neighborly."

They watched Turbee come slouching across the parking lot, moving his right forearm rhythmically back and forth, and making peculiar spitting noises with his lips. He walked by the three Aryan Knights as though they didn't exist.

"Little Goth fuck ain't being neighborly, is he?" said Ziggy. "We really need to give him a little Ballou welcome."

"Hold up there, little miss Goth. We want to talk to you," said one of the henchmen.

Turbee kept walking, as though the three didn't exist. He didn't even realize that anyone was talking to him.

Two of the gang members stepped in front of Turbee, blocking his path. Turbee walked right up to them, and was forehead to nose with them before he stopped, realizing that he was looking down at large black-laced boots that weren't his. His right forearm continued its rhythmic motion, and he kept making the spitting noises, unable to control them.

"Hey little piece of Goth shit. No one walks past Ziggy without saying hello. No one," said the first henchman.

Ziggy caught up with them and peered at Turbee. "Good drugs, guys," he said. "The Goths have always had better stuff than us." He grabbed Turbee's right hand. "Hold still you little bastard."

It was at that moment that a drop of spittle from Turbee's mouth landed on Ziggy's naked forearm.

"Whoa. Dude. Nobody spits on the Zigster. Especially not some fucked up little fucking Goth fuck. No-fucking-body."

The so-called Zigster was already developing a gut at 19, was 6′2″, and weighed in at 220. He towered over the slight, pale Turbee. He also had the size and reflexes of a boxer, two attributes that had helped him gain leadership of the Aryan Knights. Within a split second, a powerful left to Turbee's nose was followed by an even more powerful right to his temple. Turbee went down like a stone, his broken nose gushing blood. He cried out in pain, and was instantly transported back to his childhood, when he had constantly been teased, beaten, and bullied for his as-yet undiagnosed condition.

"Ready to show some respect to the Aryans, you piece of shit Goth fuck?" Ziggy demanded.

Turbee could only moan. He felt the razor edge of pain, and had no idea what had caused it. The coppery taste of blood flowed into his mouth and he slowly drew himself into a fetal position.

"Get up! Get the fuck up you fucking skinny little puke," ordered Ziggy. When nothing happened, he gave the command to his two henchmen. "OK boys, boot fuck the little bastard."

23

A NEW DAY WAS DAWNING on Socotra. Youssef was enjoying the beauty of the sunrise. Two of his pilots, Abu Yusuf and Mustafa, had breakfasted with him. Now the three drove together toward the airstrip that ran along the south coast of the island. The Gulfstream was fully fueled and outfitted, and had been rolled out of its hangar to wait for him. Nobody said much. Mustafa knew aspects of the plan, but certainly not all of it. He knew that this trip was yet another step in the journey that had started with the theft of the Semtex more than ten days earlier at Bazemah. Had he known what the final steps of the plan were, he might not have been as eager as he was. But it wasn't his place to ask questions.

When they took off in the Gulfstream, Youssef found himself reveling in the power of the craft as it roared heavenward in a steep trajectory. They went northward toward Yemen; they were scheduled for a brief stopover in Reykjavik for fuel, after which they would head over the polar ice and south toward Los Angeles. He smiled as he saw the blue waters of the Arabian Sea fall away. He thought of his early days on the water, as a deck hand on the *Indus Janeeta,* where he had learned the ways of the water, and had his initiation into smuggling. They had been dangerous and intoxicating times.

When he'd taken over, Youssef had quickly purchased a replacement for the *Indus Janeeta,* which he named the *Janeeta II.* She was a full 15 feet longer and had powerful, newly rebuilt diesel engines. She had a greater capacity for carrying legitimate cargo, but carried the obscure industrial chemicals used in his heroin refinement business more often than she carried commercial cargo. It was just another step in Youssef's rapidly growing empire.

The brief captivity of Mohammed Jhananda had done more than put Youssef into the river ferrying business. It taught him the power of police, and the value of their corruption. It had reinforced his plans for Marak. "You will become a police constable. You will excel in it. You will follow the law. You will root out these evil drug smugglers… always excepting ourselves, of course. And you will watch my back and share in my wealth, just so long as you don't act like that idiot, Noor."

They had agreed on it, and Marak had gone to the police academy in Islamabad. There he had indeed excelled, especially in martial arts and the handling of weapons, as he'd already had unparalleled skills in those areas. He passed the courses and the initial training with flying colors. He asked for, and was assigned to, the drug enforcement unit. With Youssef's assistance he was able to make a number of high-profile arrests, and rooted out numerous conspiracies in Peshawar and Karachi. With each new arrest, his power and prestige grew within the Pakistani Police Force. He used his new power to help Youssef, going after his competitors in the drug business, and making sure they were safely behind bars. Gradually Youssef's competitors were diminished, arrested, or killed. He was able to leverage this advantage to consolidate his holdings on both sides of the border.

His two property landlords, Ba'al in Pakistan and Izzy in Afghanistan, had prospered mightily, and both had to hire many bodyguards, rent collectors, and people to count and track the river of money. Youssef stayed true to his word with his friends, and Marak, Izzy, and Ba'al each had many millions of American dollars deposited in accounts around the world. Youssef seldom saw his comrades, but he always stayed true to them, and they to him.

FOR MAHARI, this was the gift that kept on giving. A third DVD. A third Samsonite case stuffed with American money. He thought he had died and gone to Paradise. As ordered, he did not share the money with his free-spending wife, choosing instead to hide it away and wait for the project to finish. He had settled on a second apartment, in a more upscale and secure building, as his hiding place. He had extra locks installed. The only things he kept in the apartment were the Samsonite cases, stacked in a closet.

The messages themselves were powerful and ominous. The cameraman had chosen to begin this third message with an extreme close-up of the Emir's face. The contrast between his one cloudy, dead eye and the black, living eye was striking. The media labeled it as malevolent, vengeful, and ominous. FOX, as always, sought to one up its competitors, and enlarged the two eyes to use them as a backdrop when its pro-American commentators discussed it.

The image of the man was overpowering and hypnotic. Perhaps it was the power and hatred that showed in the living eye, or the deeply furrowed brow, or the sharp hooked nose. This was not a man you would discount or ignore, whether he be warrior, judge, or religious leader. He was, in fact, all three. With this third message, it was a face the American public was learning to hate and fear.

Many of the American commentators noted that all three of the messages appeared to have been made at the same time, given the similarities of lighting, dress, and colors. A few said that because of that, the third message could be ignored. A few noted, though, with mild anxiety, that the time frame of the messages was accelerating. The first message said that the attack would come within 30 days, the second said within 21 days, and this, the third, promised an attack within ten days. They also noted that the target area was shrinking geographically. The first message noted that the attack would take place "somewhere on this globe," whereas the second said "in North America." This new message seemed to be referring to the United States directly. This particular portion of the third message, in its English translation, was played over and over again on every channel.

> *Praise be to Allah and His foot soldiers. Give thanks to His prophet, Mohammed, and His soldiers of the jihad. Mighty are His works, and blessed be His name. After a perilous but courageous voyage, the soldiers are in place, even in the lair of the Great Satan, within the very walls of her house. The weapons of Allah are positioned, and the means of delivery has been secured, praise be His name. Within ten days the great terror will strike within the serpent's house. One of her great cities, a city of vile iniquity, will be destroyed. The strike will make every other strike insignificant. The holy jihad will come. The day of Allah is at hand. All you warriors in the path of Mohammed, reach for the sword, and strike down the Great Satan in her moment of peril...*

There was also much commentary and speculation as to the identity of the "city of vile iniquity." America being what it was, there was no short list, but rather a long list of "sinful" cities. New York, Washington, DC, and Los Angeles were referred to most frequently, but, of course, San Francisco, New Orleans, Nashville, and Las Vegas were all possibilities as well. One pundit listed the safest cities, which allegedly included Omaha, Salt Lake City, and Topeka. The city council of Topeka then threatened MSNBC with a libel suit for slighting the city; an action that only increased that network's ratings.

ZAK WAS SITTING at the back of his cell. He'd just been strapped to the second table for an hour while another man was "questioned" by Hamani and his assistants. When the man had passed out, and they'd released Zak, he'd almost run back to his solitary prison. There had been guards there to guide him, but he knew the way, and hadn't given them any trouble. After listening to another man's screams for an hour, he was desperate for the deathly quiet of his lonely cell. Desperate for another stretch of time to think of some way — any way — to get out of this hell.

The escape had become more important than ever, because the night before, while he was praying for sleep to come, he'd remembered something. In the pain and stress and fear of the last weeks, it was something he'd forgotten. Now that it had come back to him, he couldn't stop thinking about it.

Before his capture, when he'd still been traveling with Yousseff and his men, when he'd still been Shayam, he'd been privy to the same information as every other man in the group. He'd known where they were going, although he didn't know the exact location. And he'd known what they were going to do there. He wasn't supposed to know, but he'd learned over the years how to read between the lines, how to hear things that weren't meant for his ears. He'd never had a chance to pass the information on to his superiors, because he'd been found out by Yousseff and Marak. But he knew what was going to happen within the next month. He was probably the only Westerner who knew.

If he could get out in time, if he could get in contact with someone from headquarters, he might be able to stop it.

24

TURBEE FELT A SHARP, stabbing pain in his left side. The first kick from one of the Aryan Knights broke two ribs. The second broke two more.

"C'mon, boys, I said boot fuck the bastard. I didn't mean soft little pussy kicks. I mean boot fuck him good," raged Ziggy, feeling a rush of power.

It was a command the other thugs had eagerly awaited. They took turns kicking Turbee about the head and chest. They broke two more ribs, and would have caused brain injury had Turbee not used his forearms to shield his head. Ziggy was about to insist on his turn, growing weary of the somewhat lame efforts of the henchmen, when familiar red and blue flashing lights appeared at the far end of the lot. He paused in the middle of a mighty kick aimed at Turbee's head, and stood up in the glare of a hand-held spotlight.

"Time to high tail it boys. The fuckin' heat's arrived."

One policeman raced after the Aryans, while the second stood over Turbee. The youth was utterly dazed and disoriented, and covered in blood. He knew only that he was being attacked, and that he might die. They were big and mean, whoever they were, and at that instant Turbee wanted more than anything to live. He felt powerful hands close in around his wrists again. He tried to pull away and struck out with a fist, hitting the constable weakly on the shoulder.

The constable, not one of DC's finest or brightest, immediately slapped the cuffs on Turbee. The youth had just assaulted a police officer. When he continued to struggle, that charge was bumped up to include resisting arrest. After a long ride and some processing, he ended up lying, bloodied, bruised, and broken, on the floor of the calamitous holding cell at PSA 706. Turbee had committed assault, and of a police officer no less.

Turbee had not been aware of it at the time, but Ballou High stood in the center of the toughest area in Washington, DC; an area festering with violence, drugs, crime, and general mayhem. The local police were accustomed to seeing the Aryan Knights, or the African Brotherhood, or a host of other gangs, terrorizing the streets after dark. The scene they had just encountered was not unusual. Turbee did not appear to be bleeding too severely. The constable, not being trained in medicine, or particularly bright, did not notice the dried blood caked around his smashed nose, or the evidence of six broken ribs. Turbee had technically struck a police officer in the course of his duty. That was a felony. The courts would take care of it from there.

THE PRE-TRIAL CENTER was bright and loud — two environmental stressors that were beyond Turbee's capacity to tolerate. It stank, and was full of belligerent louts of all creeds and colors, in various stages of intoxication, withdrawal, and madness. For all these reasons, Hamilton Turbee was in one corner, curled up into a ball, attempting to make himself disappear entirely.

The clerks and other officers on duty attempted to drag a name from him, but Turbee had been off his meds for hours, had just been violently assaulted, and had a badly damaged chest. He simply sank deeper into his depression and isolation. He was still carrying the thought that he had single-handedly created so much damage to TTIC that Congress would probably shut it down. He was also shouldering the burden of having handed the President and his cabinet a devastating blow. In regard to real life, Turbee had almost totally shut down, and was in a borderline psychotic state. Even sitting on a cold bench before the admitting clerk, he had held his knees tightly up to his chest, clasping them together with his arms, and rocking slowly back and forth. "Hambee" was all he could say when pressed again and again for his name. "Hambee." The name his mother and father had used when they were still together, in a house flooded with warmth. His name before he had realized that his mother was spending hundreds of thousands of dollars a year on trinkets, trips, affairs, and alcohol. "Hambee"... his name when the world had been as it should be, when he had spent his time wandering with delight around the vast family mansion at Brambleton Narrows.

The officers recognized the signs. "This guy is off his rocker. Too many drugs, probably. Crystal meth. He needs a psychiatric assessment."

They all agreed. This Hambee character, whoever he was, needed to be sorted out a little more. There was no way he had the mental capacity to understand or plead to the charge he was facing.

It was obvious to everyone that this individual needed to be assessed at St. Liz's before any further steps could be taken. Saint Elizabeth's, or St. Liz's, as the locals called it, was a medical facility in Washington, DC that dealt with the criminally insane. They'd be able to figure out "Hambee," whatever his real name, soon enough. He was kept handcuffed. Had to be, said the arresting officer. He called the kid unpredictable and violent. He was placed in a police van, and taken to an imposing brownstone building on Martin Luther

King Jr. Avenue. Once there, his instinctive fetal position tightened to the point that it took four officers working together to get him into a wheelchair. He was rolled down a series of long hallways that smelled of antiseptic and piss, and deposited in a small cell. The officers simply tipped the wheelchair over onto its small front wheels, dumping him on the floor of the cell in much the same manner as a dump truck might deposit a load of dirt. His head smashed onto the cold stone floor, and his body drew up into a fetal position once again. The last sound he heard was the clanging of a metal door, and the sounds of heavy locks clicking into place. The echoes continued in Turbee's troubled brain long after the hallway became still.

CASE OF JOHN DOE #17, Your Honor," announced the clerk.

"Who?" asked the vexed judge. "What did you say?"

"John Doe #17, your Honor," chimed the clerk and prosecutor as one.

"We don't know who he is, your Honor," explained the public defender.

Proceedings in Courtroom 107, in the Washington, DC Moultrie Building, ground to an irritated halt.

"What do you mean you don't know who he is?" snapped Judge MacDonnell. "How can a person not know who he is? Are you really telling me that no one knows who John Doe #17 is?" The owly, graying judge stared penetratingly at Hamilton Turbee, who was sitting in the prisoners' dock. He drummed his fingers on his desk, turning to glare at the hapless young prosecutor, then at the public defender, then back at Turbee. It was the beginning of the week, and the court docket was crowded with all manner of felonies and misdemeanors. The judge wasn't happy about already being delayed.

"You there, you slobbering mess. State your name, now. This is a courtroom. This is an order. State your name."

Turbee didn't respond. He continued to make small spitting sounds, and moved his right arm rhythmically back and forth. He was wearing the same clothes he had put on the day of the *Haramosh Star* disaster days earlier; his last day in the TTIC office. His last day in a world that had made sense. Both his eyes were encircled with angry purple bruises, and his nose was swollen and disfigured, the result of the vicious blows dealt by the Zigster and his supporting cast. He appeared shocked and bewildered, and was in obvious need of medical attention. Not that anyone was going to offer.

MacDonnell was in no mood for charity. Thirty years on the bench had jaded him. Most of his time was spent in remand court, fixing trial dates, taking pleas, setting bail, and imposing sentences. The drudge of humanity came through his courtroom — the DUI cases, petty larceny, theft and mischief cases, family violence, and the rest of the misery that is the underside of any city. At this stage of his career, approaching retirement, he was more concerned about the state of his prostate than the health needs of a prisoner.

"What are the charges?" he growled, looking at the prosecutor.

"Creating public mischief, resisting arrest, and assaulting a police officer," came the response.

"By the look of him, he's probably a crystal meth addict," said Judge MacDonnell, noting Turbee's skinny frame, his pale complexion, and his unusual mannerisms.

"I would think so, your honor," replied the prosecutor. "I think he's probably still high."

The public defender shrugged his shoulders, not seeing any reason to disagree. He never stopped to wonder how it was that the petty prejudices of the street could find their way into an American courtroom, although that was obviously what was happening.

"What do you think, gentlemen? Do we send him away for a few more days on a psychiatric assessment, until he sobers up, or gets straight, or whatever? What do you think, John Doe?" MacDonnell asked sarcastically, turning his piercing judge-eyes back to Turbee. "Maybe a week or two there will loosen your tongue, young man. I will give you one last chance to state your name. Now what the hell is it?"

Turbee's mind was struggling to understand what was going on around him. He was off his medications and had suffered, in the past days, crippling physical and psychological blows. His system was still reeling from the concussion that the gangsters' kicks and punches had caused. He didn't understand where he was, or how he'd come to be there. His only thought was how to get away from this nightmare and get home. Not to his apartment, but to his home, his father's home, where he grew up, where he still spent most holidays, and where he went when he needed to rest. He turned around and saw someone coming through the rear doorway of the courtroom. With a supreme effort, he gathered his thoughts and began to study his surroundings. He saw the business of the place — lawyers with briefcases, taking last-minute instructions, having quick, whispered conversations with other prosecutors. He saw the social workers, court workers, and other people moving back and forth, fretting over their business. He gulped, then saw through the doors the huge central foyer of the large and busy building, and the blue sky beyond. Home was out there. His concentration narrowed, and he began to see his path.

He flexed his hands slowly; he hadn't been handcuffed or placed in shackles or restraints for his court appearance. The security officers didn't consider him much of a threat, given his size and apparent condition. He glanced around surreptitiously; everyone had already forgotten he was there. Suddenly, in a move that astounded everyone, Turbee catapulted himself out of the dock and made a beeline for the foyer. He slipped and twisted through the bodies in the aisle, and bolted out the door. The security officers attempted to race after him, but were less efficient in moving their burly bodies through the crowded Monday morning remand court.

Turbee made it through the front doors of the building, and was half a block down Indiana Street, before his painful rib injuries and the inability to breathe brought him to a careening halt. The security detail gang tackled him as he stood gasping, and he went down under a heap of uniforms in the center of the street. He rolled and squirmed and twisted with all his might to escape and, in the melee, struck the officers several more times. One of the men responded by falling full force on Turbee's chest, causing one of the previously fractured ribs to puncture a lung. Pain carved through him like a searing knife.

"Stand back, boys," said another officer. "I've got a taser. That'll slow him down." He took his taser in hand and zapped Turbee with a 200,000-volt shock, paralyzing him, and causing his legs and arms to twitch uncontrollably.

"We'd better whack him with a couple more of those," said another, and, with the consent of all except Turbee, tasered the youth three more times.

"Aw, dammit George," said the first man. "You've made him shit himself. Now look at the mess."

"Screw it. Someone at the detention center will sort him out. Let's drag this sorry meth addict back to Room 107."

Before the day was out, three more charges of assault, two more counts of resisting arrest, and one count of escaping lawful custody were added to the docket sheet on someone who was beginning to look like a dangerous criminal. Judge MacDonnell insisted that a count of contempt of court also be added. From there on, Turbee was kept shackled and cuffed. At the end of the day, when he was thrown back in a heap on the floor of his dark cold cell at St. Liz's, no one bothered to clean him up. In addition to the fractured ribs, and the now punctured lung, his skin was burned from four taser shots. The control he had found during the escape disappeared, and he tipped completely into full-blown psychosis. More troubling still, at that point the DC criminal court system proceeded to lose track of John Doe #17 completely.

25

YOUSSEFF WAS TUCKED SNUGLY into his cot, in the midst of a deep sleep, as his Gulfstream made the long trip from Karachi to Los Angeles. He was dreaming of turning 21, and remembering what it had been like. It was a wild and exciting time for him and his friends. With Marak's assistance, Yousseff's competitors from the Frontier Province had started disappearing. Most went to jail. If one of them was clever enough to avoid the police, he disappeared in the dead of the night, never to be seen again. There were many mountain passes in the Pashtun lands along the Pakistan/Afghanistan border, where bodies could easily disappear. Even with all their success, though, Yousseff realized that he needed his security to expand beyond just the Frontier Province and the Path of Allah. Marak could not assist him on the southern reaches of the Indus; he had no authority in Hyderabad, and certainly none in Karachi. In these areas, there were still problems, still competitors, still chances of being caught.

It all started with a suggestion from Omar. Two patrol boats had just intercepted the *Janeeta II.* Omar had seen them coming, and ten kilos of pure heroin had quickly been flushed into the muddy brown waters of the Indus. The officers had searched the ship from stem to stern, but had found nothing. Omar had complained bitterly the whole time. "We are just a simple river ferry, good sirs. We have customers. We have merchandise to ship and deadlines to meet."

The police had ignored him and, if anything, became more aggressive in their hunt. Eventually they left, leaving the *Janeeta II* in a state of disarray. There were many thinly veiled threats about the ship's fate if drugs were ever found onboard. And from a business standpoint, the loss of ten kilos so close to their ocean delivery point was considerable. Omar and his crew continued on to their rendezvous point, for the sole purpose of telling their contact that they had no product and that they would be back in approximately a month's time. Yousseff, who was onboard at the time, then ordered Omar to turn the boat around and head back to Rawalpindi. The two stayed up well into the night discussing the problem.

It was Omar, with his mechanical skills, who came up with idea first. "We could manufacture a second hull for the front of the *Janeeta II.* It would create a hidden space that was waterproof and only accessible if you knew where the hidden switches were. If it were done properly, no one would ever find it, unless they already knew it was there. They wouldn't tap the hull under the water to look for hidden compartments. Search dogs wouldn't find it."

"Can you do it, Omar? Can you create a waterproof outer compartment that they wouldn't find?" asked Yousseff, immediately seeing the utility of such a creation.

"I think so, but we would need to drydock someplace for a few days to do the work."

"Where?" pushed Yousseff.

"At the remnants of KSEW, I think," replied Omar. "There is unused space along the inner harbor of Karachi. We might be able to pick up some harbor land and shop space cheap."

He was referring to the Karachi Shipbuilding and Engineering Works, a company that had been enormous but was now starting to feel the operational difficulties of a multi-union workforce, internal inefficiencies, and government corruption. The corporation had been shrinking for years, selling off small pieces, one at a time. Many of its dock properties, which covered almost two miles of harborside property, had fallen into disuse and disrepair. Some smaller, family-run operations had sprung up in the areas vacated by the large corporation.

"Next trip down here, we'll check it out. We'll take the *Janeeta II* around the corner, and head to Karachi. Might even be fun. In the meantime, let's start drawing up some plans for this," said Yousseff.

A month later they were back, with a load of 20 kilos crammed into a new compartment in the V-berth of the ship. Omar had done the best he could, with the limited facilities they had, and had managed a partially hidden room for the transport of drugs. It wasn't anywhere close to what they had discussed, but was the most they could construct in such a short period of time, without access to a drydock facility. Yousseff was not satisfied with the addition, and spent the entire trip keeping his eye out for the authorities. Happily, rain fell during the entire trip, which Yousseff saw as a good thing. The river police were less likely to patrol in the middle of the monsoon downpours. They preferred the sun, just like everyone else.

They delivered their load to their usual contact — a Captain Bartholomew, who owned a rusting freighter that changed her name and paint colors often. This month, the ship had the name "Marcy B" painted on the sides. They picked up their payment — several suitcases that held more than a quarter of a million American dollars in cash. Then the *Marcy B* headed south, and the *Janeeta II* went north.

Yousseff had never cared for Karachi. You could see the brown hemisphere of pollution covering the massive city even on a dreary, overcast, and wet day like this. The pervading odor was the smell of diesel and exhaust. The city's population was growing so rapidly that the infrastructure had not kept up with the needs of her millions of citizens. The streets were incredibly noisy, and were packed with motor vehicles of every conceivable make and condition. There was also a lot of poverty. It was not uncommon to see a small Peugeot or Toyota held together with duct tape. There were huge areas that were made up entirely of shantytowns — homes patched up with cardboard and bits of lumber, and held together by sections of corrugated pipe.

The huge, protected harbor was as busy as the city, with many cargo and container ships always docked, waiting to be loaded or unloaded. Hundreds of smaller craft whizzed about, with no apparent pattern or logic to their movements. Yousseff watched the action with distaste, as Omar piloted the *Janeeta II* through the outer breakwater and into the harbor itself. Omar motioned to the distant, southeastern area of the harbor. Squinting in the rain, Yousseff could see acre after acre of cranes, gantries, industrial shops, and docks.

"That's KSEW," Omar said. "We go there."

"Doesn't look like much," Yousseff responded. At that moment, he was missing the lazy Indus and his distant mountain home, and wasn't in the mood for new adventures.

Omar directed the ship toward the southeastern shore. As they approached the KSEW land, he changed course and paralleled the shore about 200 feet out.

"Look at the mess, Omar," Yousseff said. "You'd have to take a bulldozer to it and start over."

"No wonder they're going broke," Omar responded. "Nobody seems to be working at anything productive. Look at the cranes. They are almost all sitting idle."

"Take us to where the smaller outfits are. I don't feel good about KSEW doing any type of work on the *Janeeta,"* Yousseff said.

"OK, boss," joked Omar. More than a mile of dilapidated docks, cranes, and warehouses went by. Eventually Omar brought the ship into a smaller, private drydock facility. They tied her up and hopped onto the dock. The only person around was a young teenager, maybe 15 years of age, if that. He was perched high up, repairing a crossbeam on what appeared to be an extension of the main shop building. Youssef motioned to him.

"Yo, boy, come down here. We have work for you." The young welder slid down the main beam in a jiffy, practically falling at their feet. He still had his welder's helmet on, with the face piece lifted up.

"What would you like?" he asked, eyeing them, sizing them both up, and looking at the somewhat aging *Janeeta II.*

"We need some work done on the *Janeeta's* hull. On the bottom. Needs a drydock, and lifts, which it looks like you have here," said Omar.

"What kind of work?" asked the boy.

"We need an exterior, watertight compartment, that can be easily opened from the interior of the boat. It must blend in with the existing hull."

"Ah. Drug smugglers, yes?" the young man responded.

Now Youssef stepped in. "Can you do the work or not?" he asked.

The young lad had bright, inquisitive eyes and a quick sense of humor. Youssef instantly liked him, and felt he could trust him. Of all of Youssef's many gifts, his ability to see the strengths and weaknesses in people was one of the most useful. He saw much strength in the young welder standing before him.

"Yes, I can do the work."

"Can you do it now?" asked Youssef.

"As in right now? As in *now* now?"

"Yes. Now now."

"Cost you more," said the teenager.

"No problem. We'll pay," Youssef answered quickly.

"Cash?" asked the welder.

"Cash," said Youssef.

"Then it'll cost you even more."

The bartering and dealing went on for another 15 minutes. Before long, Youssef had learned the young man's name. "Kumar," he had said. "Kumar Hanaman."

Over the course of the next two days, Kumar's skills amazed both Youssef and Omar. No place to hook the cables in order to pull the boat into drydock? No problem. We'll weld some on. The *Janeeta's* too small for a drydock built for ocean-going ships? No problem, we'll create a smaller lift carriage. Parts of the hull are too corroded to work on (a problem that Youssef and Omar did not know until that very moment)? No problem. We can replace them.

And then there was the masterful solution devised by the youthful Kumar, on the fly, to create an outer envelope, partially accessible through an internal, hidden lever. It was beyond what Yousseff, or the more mechanically gifted Omar, had imagined. Kumar did all of it on his own, without any assistance, and at an amazing speed, chattering all the while, laughing, making jokes, and generally having a ball. Nevermind the rain and chill of the monsoon period.

The work took two days, with both Yousseff and Omar chipping in, assisting where they could. During those two days, Yousseff spent almost all his time talking with Kumar. He was pathetically inept at anything to do with mechanical work, but he stayed by Kumar's side, passing along tools or moving or holding bits of iron and steel, while Kumar and Omar did most of the welding and cutting. To Omar it was almost comical to see Yousseff running to keep up with the chattering, skittering Kumar, passing him tools, and trading stories.

One of the first tales Kumar told Yousseff was the history of the little drydock company. Its name was Karachi Drydock and Engineering Company, which he shortened to KDEC. His father had purchased the dock, crane, and shop building from KSEW 18 months ago. He had planned to handle specialty jobs, involving the repair and manufacture of propellers and rudders for ocean-going vessels. He had been a highly skilled employee at KSEW and had specialized in this very area. He saw many of the inefficiencies of KSEW and felt he could provide a better product at a lower cost. He paid a premium price for the decrepit building and drydock system, which had been overgrown with weeds, and in considerable disrepair. KSEW had not actively used the site for more than 20 years. The vice president for KSEW, Salim Nooshkatoor, a brash young executive seeking to ingratiate himself with the board, had promised Mr. Hanaman that his company would not compete against Hanaman's new venture, and would instead send all their rudder and propeller work his way. In that way, Nooshkatoor proposed, he would be able to pay off his investment quickly and easily.

The elder Hanaman, feeling that this was a no-lose situation, had put his life savings into the venture, and that of a number of his brothers. The opportunity appeared to be too good to pass up; guaranteed employment for all of them in a lucrative specialty area in the ship maintenance business. Hanaman had prepared many scenarios and projections and decided that he definitely couldn't lose. If just a fraction of the propeller and rudder work came his way, he would have a thriving, profitable business in no time. All he needed was a small fortune to invest — a fortune that came from family members. He would be able to repay them entirely, at a substantial interest rate, plus a bonus for their troubles, within a year.

Alas, though, it was not too be. Nooshkatoor had been told by his Board of Directors to liquidate, at the best possible price, much of the unused property of KSEW, in an attempt to make the once-mighty company profitable again. The senior Hanaman had not been able to pay the entire property price, of course, so the balance was made up by a mortgage back to the company at very reasonable terms. "And," said Nooshkatoor, "do not worry if you miss a payment, if business is slow. We will not foreclose. You will definitely have all our propeller work, and that, by itself, guarantees your venture to be profitable."

Of course, Nooshkatoor had every intention of foreclosing, and competing, and none whatsoever of sending any business to Hanaman. After one year of business hell, during which power was repeatedly cut off, and only tiny low-value jobs were sent to the new Karachi Drydock and Engineering Company, the venture was near death. The pressure on Mr. Hanaman became immense. His brothers first berated him, then ignored him, and finally sued him. KSEW had just initiated foreclosure proceedings, and there was only one month left in the redemption period. His wife could not handle the stress and humiliation and ended up leaving him. His health failed, he took to drinking, became ulcerous, and had developed cancer two months before Yousseff came into the picture.

Hanaman had turned to the courts for relief, and countersued KSEW during the foreclosure proceedings. He told the judge, "Look, here was the deal. They said they would send specialty work to me if I bought this property from them. They have not done that. They lied. They should give me the property back, and millions of rupees too, for the hell they have made of my life."

But KSEW was a Karachi establishment, and Nooshkatoor was one of its darlings. In his mid-30s, trained as a lawyer, and on his way up, he could do no wrong. A number of KSEW's directors knew the judge personally and attended the same social club — an organization that a worker like Hanaman did not even know existed. Nooshkatoor, sitting in the gallery of the courtroom, sniggered openly. The judge peered over his horn-rimmed glasses at Hanaman and said, "Look, sir. It's not in writing, is it?" To which Hanaman had replied that they had shaken hands on the deal. The old man got nowhere. He didn't even get a chance to ask Nooshkatoor any questions about it. Now, alone, bankrupt, destitute, his spirit broken, without any wife or family aside from Kumar, he was dying of alcohol and cancer.

"And here you are, laughing and talking as though nothing has happened?" asked Youssеff in amazement.

"But what good is crying going to do, Yousseff?" came the response. "What good are the courts, or judges, or family, or God, or shrieking and wailing for that matter? My father is dying, my mother has left. These things are not going to change. So I may as well enjoy the day, and your companionship. You have given me enough money to buy some food and pay some of my father's medical bills. In another month KSEW will regain possession of this property, and I will be somewhere else, I guess."

Yousseff looked at Kumar long and hard. Catching the look, the lad slowed from his constant movement.

"What is it, Yousseff? You look at me like I'm the devil."

Yousseff spoke at length. "I have a proposition for you. I will pay off the mortgage. I will pay off the uncles and creditors. I will look after your father and take care of his medical bills. I will find work for this drydock company."

"Yes, good. Of course. And you will give me a Ferrari and a partridge in a pear tree. Deal, Yousseff. Deal." Kumar went back to his work.

Yousseff grabbed him by the shoulder and pulled him away from the welding equipment. "Do not ever, ever discount me. I mean what I say."

Kumar was silent for a minute, meeting Yousseff's gaze. "And you want what with me? Why would you do this?"

Yousseff paused for a moment, and continued to look Kumar in the eye. "You know my business. If you join me, you are in that business. You will become a captain in my business. You will get your father to sign this drydock business over to you, so that you are the sole shareholder of Karachi Drydock and Engineering. But you'll hold it in trust for me. No one is to know about it. No one. In return, I will cut you in on the profits, and together, we will build this company."

Kumar was quick. "Well, seeing as how it's Christmas and all, there is something else I want."

Yousseff looked at him with an upraised eyebrow. "Yes?"

"I want to go to school. To the Karachi School of Engineering. I was very good in school, until last year, when I stopped going to help here. I want to go back. I want to get a degree in engineering. I want room to do this. One way or another, I can make this place work, even though I am only 15. My father has taught me every part of this business. I can make it go, if you get me the work. But I want to go to school first."

Yousseff could hardly believe his ears. His investment had just become infinitely richer. All by itself. "Deal," he said firmly.

"Deal," said Kumar. They shook hands. Omar was the only witness.

The question Yousseff now faced was how to pay off KDEC's debt of over half a million rupees. He couldn't just walk into KSEW's posh head office and deposit his suitcases of American dollars on the table. He could not just pay the money to the court. He thought about it for awhile and finally telephoned a business he owned in Peshawar. He talked to his commander there.

"Go into the mountains. Get Ba'al now. Get him to call me at this number." He gave the telephone number of what was now Kumar's domain.

The head man at the office knew that when Yousseff gave an order like that, he meant for it to be done immediately. Forthwith. Yesterday, in fact. Ba'al knew this as well. When he saw a Jeep racing up the narrow mountain road toward his house, he knew what it would mean. He also knew that whatever Yousseff needed done would be taken care of immediately. It was common for Ba'al to leave his home to do business for Yousseff, and did not represent any administrative or production problems. Ba'al's refining plant had come a long way since the early, unsteady steps he and Yousseff had taken almost ten years earlier. Gone were the 45-gallon drum, the bonfire, the burlap sack filtration system, and the slow stirring over a pot like two of the witches in *Macbeth*. Over the years, he and Yousseff had built a neat organization, well stocked in supplies, with appropriate air cover. At the height of the season, as many as 30 local people worked on Ba'al's property alone. Yousseff always paid them substantially more than the going rate, and he always paid in cash. In this way, part of his laundry problem was solved, and he ensured the great loyalty of his fellow tribesmen.

It was also a highly efficient operation. Yousseff had probed, questioned, experimented with, and refined the process. Everything was neat as a pin, and he was planning to build a much larger facility like it underground near Jalalabad. He also looked after the well being of his workers. If one became ill, he would get medical help. Once one of his workers suffered a calamity — his house burned down, and all its contents were destroyed. Yousseff replaced everything before he was even asked. He organized the labor to rebuild the home, and had it re-outfitted. The knowledge that Yousseff would do this dovetailed nicely with the threat of Marak, and his dangerous machete. There were, after all, a number of beggars in Rawalpindi devoid of hands. The two made the classic duo of good and evil.

In Jalalabad and its environs, Yousseff had become untouchable. If he required something, his employees would make the earth stop in its rotation until his request was satisfied, and had done so time and again. Thus, when the Jeep approached Ba'al's headquarters, and relayed Yousseff's command, that was enough. Ba'al gave an order to his second in command, which, loosely translated, meant "take over and don't fuck up." He immediately headed down the steep mountain ridge toward the safe house, where he arrived some five hours later.

LESS THAN TEN HOURS after Yousseff had placed the call, it was returned. He had already bragged to Kumar, "Watch this. Ten hours, and he will call back."

When the phone rang, Yousseff skipped the pleasantries. He felt that they were a waste of time, and could wait to be discussed over a fire in the Sefid Koh. He did not like telephones and had a constant paranoia about wiretaps, even though no taps could be placed without Marak's knowledge. There was also no logical reason for there to be a wiretap on the phone of a struggling little drydock company at the Karachi end. Still, he remained fanatically careful, and always kept his conversations short.

"Mortgage some of our properties. I need $500,000 now, deposited in a foreign bank account. I want you to call Rika at this number. She will give you the account and banking particulars."

Ba'al grunted in assent. "Consider it done, Yousseff. I will call you as soon as it happens. Same telephone number?"

"Yes."

"Give me two days."

Yousseff got Rika on the phone and gave her the same instructions. "Rika, I am going to buy a drydock company. Our business needs it. Ba'al is going to mortgage some of our properties up north. I want the money to be clean. I want you to run it through as many foreign accounts as you need to in order to make it completely untraceable. Can you do that?"

"For you, Youssi, I can do anything. Consider it done." The wonderful thing about Rika was that she accomplished these things quickly, without song, without dance.

A DAY LATER the weather had cleared, and Omar, Rika, Kumar, and Yousseff sat on the dock, enjoying the afternoon sun. Rika had come alone. No one bothered to ask what had become of her husband; he was no longer in the picture. That was enough. It freed her to spend time with her friends, where she was needed.

"Where can we find a good restaurant, and a good time, in this smelly city?" asked Youssefff.

Omar, always bright, became even brighter. He gave the name of a night-club not far away. The four smiled and headed off to sample the iniquities available in Karachi. Youssefff had to do some fast talking for the youthful Kumar, but thanks to their combined skills, virtually every door opened, and they spent a day enjoying themselves in the clubs, restaurants, and opium clubs of the city. Omar watched it all in amazement.

The next day, Ba'al called to say that he had arranged the mortgages. This time the telephone call was even shorter. "It's done," was all he said.

Youssefff did not even reply. He simply gave the telephone to Rika. "Get the mortgage information from Ba'al, Rik. Work from there."

Kumar, for his part, spent the better part of the day with his father, who wanted to meet with Youssefff. Normally, Youssefff would not have agreed to this, but in this case, the man's life expectancy was measured in weeks, possibly days. He introduced himself as the son of a wealthy trading and transportation businessman from the mountain highlands of the Frontier provinces. He told Hanaman of his friendship with Kumar and how impressed he was with Kumar's talents. Another visit, and the payment of all the medical bills, creditors, and miserable uncles, gave Hanaman the necessary motivation to sign the company over to his precocious young son.

"He is gifted, Youssefff. He's the smartest kid I've ever known," he said as he signed the papers.

Youssefff kissed the old man on the cheek and bid him farewell. "I know this, sir. I have spent the past few weeks with him, and yes, he is gifted. You have raised a remarkable boy."

One of the grandest days in Kumar's young life was when he walked into the executive offices of KSEW a day later. He presented himself at the posh ninth-floor office and requested an audience with Salim Nooshkatoor.

"Your name, please?" the sophisticated-looking receptionist asked the longhaired teenager standing in front of her.

"Kumar Hanaman," came the confident reply.

The elegant young woman rolled her eyes and picked up the telephone. "There is a Mr. Kumar Hanaman her to see you, Mr. Nooshkatoor," she said. She nodded as Nooshkatoor replied.

"Mr. Nooshkatoor is extremely busy at the moment. It will be at least an hour before he can see you," she told Kumar.

"Then I will wait," he replied.

One hour became two, and then three. Kumar asked to use a washroom, but otherwise continued to wait quietly. He saw other people come in, ask for Mr. Nooshkatoor, and be ushered down a wood paneled and dimly lit corridor. The receptionist never called him in. At 5 she advised Kumar that the office would be closing for the day, and that unfortunately, the very busy, very important Salim Nooshkatoor was not able to make time for the young Mr. Hanaman.

The following day, at 8:30 in the morning, Kumar once again strolled up to the receptionist on the ninth floor. He received another eye roll. Another telephone call. Another answer of "Mr. Nooshkatoor is oh-so-important don't you know." But Kumar continued to wait.

At 11, Salim Nooshkatoor caved in and asked the receptionist to usher the young man in. As he walked in, Kumar surveyed the teak-paneled corner office, the breathtaking view of downtown Karachi and the harbor, with the buildings, docks, cranes, and gantries of KSEW in the distance. He shook his head at the obvious show of wealth. Nooshkatoor simply smiled at the young man's wide-eyed expression. He knew who Kumar was, and fully expected him to grovel and beg for a further extension in the redemption period; he thought the meeting would be good sport, if nothing else. The foreclosure would be finalized within a few days, and the property would revert back to KSEW. Nooshkatoor already had another buyer lined up for the property. He had used these same strategies to sell and re-sell various properties along the harborside over and over again. The Board loved it.

"So what brings you to my door?" asked the unctuous and overweight executive, surveying Kumar like a cobra eying its prey. "How can I help you?"

"Well, sir, it is about the foreclosure proceedings against my father's property on the harborside," began Kumar.

"I am very sorry about it," said Nooshkatoor, with great compassion in his voice. "But a deal is a deal. I have a Board of Directors to report to."

"But didn't you promise my father that you would send a lot of work his way?"

"Well, we did speak of it, and I said I would do my best, which I did. But that was the extent of the deal. Anyway, a judge has ruled on it, and there is nothing I can do. The only way that the foreclosure can be stopped now is by payment of the interest, and the arrears, and the principal, and, of course, the court costs."

"But this has destroyed my father's health, and he is dying. You made a promise."

"Again, my condolences. But my hands are tied. Now go away, little beggar. I have work to do."

Kumar stood to leave. Before he turned, he looked the smirking executive directly in the eye and smiled. "One more thing, you fat pig. One more thing. Here's the check. For everything. Certified. Now go fuck yourself. The property is mine." He placed the check on the astounded man's desk, turned, and strolled back out.

26

SOME UNEXPECTED TURBULENCE woke Yousseff from his dream. The Gulfstream was approaching Iceland and descending for refueling at Reykjavik. He glanced at the clock; things were still going according to schedule. He thought about the whitecaps of the frigid North Atlantic, no doubt cascading endlessly below him — they would be large enough to destroy anything that came into their path, he knew. Yousseff shuddered at the power of the body of water below him, remembering his experiences with the vast ocean.

What had he been dreaming about? Of course. That delicious tale that Kumar loved to tell, embellished a bit with the passing of years — telling the high and mighty Nooshkatoor to go fuck himself. Yes, it was a good tale, to be sure, but the miserable and arrogant bastard had continued to create his share of mayhem for the young company over the years…

YOUSSEFF, at that time, had wondered if he had taken on more than he could handle. He had just mortgaged a lot of property and spent a lot of money, to buy an aging, dilapidated drydock company that had no employees, no customers, no organizational structure, no credit, and a lot of rusting iron. The only person who knew anything about the business was a teenager who would be away at school most of the time and the founder of the business, who was now dead. But Yousseff didn't believe in entering new ventures to lose money. He wondered — had he acted on emotion, rather than reason? Was it anger at Mr. Hanaman's situation that had led him to his purchase? No, he finally decided. Not at all. He bought the company to buy Kumar. And, as with Omar, and Marak, and the others, he was doing it to build his organization.

Omar also voiced concern over the purchase, at the start. He looked in doubt at the rusting iron, dilapidation, and ruin. "What is it about this dump we just bought?" he asked, motioning to the corroding wharf and gantries of the KDEC. "You just mortgaged a good chunk of your properties to buy this. What on earth are you going to do with it?" For once he thought that Yousseff had committed a serious mistake.

"Is it any worse than your father's boat when I acquired it? I didn't really want the boat, Omar. I wanted you. I wanted your father's connections," replied Youssеff.

"But look at it, Yousseff. It's a pile of crap, and there is no ongoing business at all," said Omar.

"We're going to have to make it work. That kid, Kumar, he's good. And now he's part of my organization. You watch and see what he does."

"But Yousseff, for God's sake, the kid is only 15. Fifteen! And he's not even going to be here. He's off to school for the next five or six years. What about workers, even if we do get the work?"

Yousseff was getting irritated. "Look, Omar, you're a pretty good mechanic and welder yourself. You kept the Janeeta running and watched after the *Janeeta II.* You know every good boat mechanic, welder, hydraulics man, engine overhauler, and metalworker on the river. You can pay them all cash. You can pay them all more than the going rate. It's not going to be a problem. We are going to do this."

And sure enough, it did work. Slowly, in bits and pieces, the work started to come in. Omar and Kumar, when he was not in school or studying, did a lot of the work. Omar started to complain that, for someone involved in the transportation of drugs, he had to work much too hard; it was a thought that struck Yousseff as profoundly funny. Yousseff himself never seemed to stop working or moving, chasing down opportunity after opportunity. He told Omar to be quiet and behave himself. After six months, they hired one employee; after three more months they hired another two. By the time a year had passed, there were a full 20 employees working at KDEC. After two years, the small boat yard, though fully overhauled, was too small to handle all the business coming in.

Omar and Yousseff also began to expand the river ferry business. They bought aging vessels and took them to Karachi, where KDEC repaired and refurbished them. Each was then returned to the ferrying business. Most had double hulls and secret compartments built into their frames. This generated additional work for KDEC and meant that more cash could be placed in legitimate enterprises. Within a year, Omar's business owned three handsome and efficient riverboats, with half a dozen more in the drydock at KDEC, scheduled for repairs and improvements.

TOWARD THE END of the second, hectic year of his ownership of KDEC, a familiar mood captured Yousseff. He became restless, and even irritable. He was feeling constrained. Pakistan was becoming cramped and small. He started traveling constantly from Jalalabad to Islamabad, to Hyderabad, and then back to Karachi. He bought his first plane, a fast twin-engine Cessna Piper Aztec, and found a pilot, Abu bin Mustafa, to fly it for him. Before long he was spending more time in the air than on the ground. He was in his early 20s, and already extremely wealthy. But he was restless. It was the same mood that had taken control of him when he started taking trips through the Path of Allah.

Kumar and Omar saw him one morning, sitting on the edge of the dock, gazing over the Karachi inner harbor. He spent all day sitting by himself, thinking. By the time he had figured things out, the sun was low on the horizon. He joined Kumar and Omar for tea on the rear deck of the *Janeeta II.* "I'm going to leave for a while," he said to his friends.

"How long?" they asked, in unison.

"A year. Maybe two."

"What? What did he say, Omar?" asked Kumar. "Did he say what I think he said?"

"Year or two, he says. Obviously too much sun and opium. He's lost it, I think," responded Omar. "What on earth are you going to do, Yousseff?" he asked his friend.

"I'm going to learn the shipping business," Yousseff answered.

"But Yousseff, you already know it. We've been up and down the Indus hundreds of times in the *Janeeta,* and then in the *Janeeta II.* Now we have half a dozen water ferries skirting around the Indus and sailing to Karachi. What more do you need to learn?"

"No, no, Omar. I am not talking about boats on the river. I'm not talking about ferries. I'm talking about ships. Vessels. Big iron. I'm going with that old pirate, Bartholomew. He's asked me before. He knows I can learn things, and I'm good with people, even though I'm not so good with tools. He's ready to retire. He wants a nice little estate on the coast where he can enjoy his grandchildren."

"You want to buy that rusty old boat of his so you can bring it here to fix it up and have us all go broke?" asked Kumar.

"Not his boat, Kumar," Yousseff replied. "His business. His connections. His boat — take it out to the middle of the Arabian Sea and sink it for all I care. But his business…"

"His business?" repeated Kumar.

"Yes," said Yousseff. "Like I bought this business, KDEC. Like I purchased Omar's father's business, and expanded it, with Omar running it. We can do that again. You can all cut in on the profits. I have no problem with that at all." Indeed, both Kumar and Omar, like Marak, Ba'al, Izzy, and Rika, were becoming wealthy through their association with Yousseff.

"Look at what Bartholomew pays for our product," Yousseff continued. "Compare that to what he charges for it on the other side of the ocean. We can do this. Do you know how much the price of heroin changes between Karachi and Los Angeles? It increases more than fivefold. A huge profit, just for transporting it. If a moron like Bartholomew can do it, we certainly can."

"What do the rest of us do, Yousseff? We have all the farmers in eastern Afghanistan, the refiners in Pakistan, the safe houses, the river ferry company, this thing here," Omar said, motioning to the KDEC yard behind him. "The various laundering operations, all of that. What are you going to do with it if you leave?"

"You can run it without me for awhile. I'll drop in every now and then. Things are running nicely. I may be gone for two months and back for a week or two, then gone again. But this enterprise is running almost by itself. If things become problematic I'll come back and fix it. But I need to travel."

Omar sighed. Yousseff was right; the efficiency of the little company was obvious. Things were running on their own. It was a testament to Yousseff's organizational abilities that a company of this complexity was able to spin along without much guidance from its master. But it was never enough, for Yousseff, to sit back and be happy with what he had done. He was restless. He constantly needed more.

WHILE YOUSSEFF WAS AWAY, learning the smuggling business and the various points of entry into North America, KDEC did manage to take care of itself. Before long it was running too efficiently, and making too much money on its own. Added to the large cash flow that needed laundering, the company's large income began to draw attention. The best way to deal with that was through ongoing capital acquisitions. KDEC started to purchase properties in Karachi, and elsewhere in Pakistan. The concern was that if the business grew too quickly, it would look even more suspicious, so no purchase was overly large. Omar made sure that they were carefully spaced, making only one or two purchases every few months. Some other minor problems arose in the growing, refining, and transportation of opium and heroin, but minor tinkering usually resolved the issues. Sometimes Marak needed to be called upon, but those occasions were few and far between. There was one episode, however, that required more than just a casual visit.

The much older, much larger KSEW had become rife with labor unrest. Seven unions were represented at the venerable old company, constantly making threats and demands. Then Kumar presented them with a check for the full amount of the mortgage redemption. The management of KSEW was astounded. They would not be able to repossess and resell the property as they had expected to do. It threw their budget into a tailspin.

"How the hell did he do that?" Nooshkatoor was flummoxed. Others asked the same question, and when they saw that business was starting to tick for the tiny competitor on the far end of the harbor, they decided that something needed to be done. KSEW wanted to be the only show in town; they could not afford to have successful competitors. This Karachi Drydock and Engineering Company nonsense had to stop. Nooshkatoor, who had recently been promoted to president, was given the assignment of dealing with KDEC; an assignment that he accepted with relish. Like Marak at the Four Cedars many years earlier, Nooshkatoor felt that the battle was already won.

Large corporations have many sly tricks that they use to dismantle competitors. One of them is to stuff unions down their throats. One day, the business agent for the PASWEU, which stood for the Pakistani Allied Shipbuilding Workers and Engineering Union, knocked on Kumar's office door.

"Sahota," the man said. "Just call me Sahota."

Kumar, by then 17 years old and trying desperately to grow a beard, told him to get lost. Sahota informed the young owner that the law gave him the right to be there, and that he was going to talk to the employees. He treated Kumar with as much arrogance as he could sum up. "Go back to your mommy, kid. Where's the boss?" Eventually Kumar gave in and asked the man what it was he wanted.

For two days Sahota spoke to the workers about the benefits of unionism and how the PASWEU was there to bring them great prosperity and happiness. The workers were by and large satisfied with their lot, and their wages, but the union representative did not relent. He continued to shadow the drydock and warehouses, pestering the workers and pushing them to join the union.

Two days after the man's first visit, Yousseff returned from Manzanillo, Mexico, where he had been with Bartholomew. After considering the situation, he asked Marak to have an investigator do a background check on Sahota. When Marak, in his usual expeditious manner, handed Yousseff the report, Yousseff called the union representative into the small Karachi Drydock and Engineering office. "Just for a little chat," he told the man.

Yousseff introduced himself as "Joseph," which was the Anglicized version of his name. He said he was general counsel for the Hanaman family. Then he went straight to the point. No pleasantries. No talk about the weather.

"So, tell me, sir," Yousseff said to the oily little man sitting across the desk from him. They were the only two in the office. Omar had headed back up the Indus, and Kumar was in school. "Tell me… exactly how much money do you want?"

Mr. Just-call-me-Sahota looked at Yousseff in astonishment. He found himself completely at a loss. No one started a negotiation like that. Not in Karachi. Not in Afghanistan. Not even in America, where it was common knowledge that no one had manners, and where it would appear that this man had been spending much of his time. Sahota thought that this Joseph must be some sort of barbarian, completely devoid of manners and culture.

"What do you take me for, sir?" Sahota asked in shock. "I have integrity! I have ethics! I have morals! I am an honest man, and I am just doing my job. Are you saying that you think you can bribe me?" With each question, Sahota worked himself further into a self-righteous rage.

"Yes, of course, Mr. Sahota," Yousseff responded calmly. "That is exactly what I am doing. I know what your salary is. I know how much your house costs you. I even know how much you pay for your whores on Old English Street. Of course I am bribing you. Was I being too subtle? Are you not understanding some part of this?"

In all his life, which had been full of cagey little deals, backroom payments, and money for greasing the wheels, Sahota had never encountered a conversation quite this basic. He started to protest again, but Yousseff quickly interrupted him.

"Mr. Sahota, what part of 'how much' are you not understanding?"

Sahota started to protest again, but broke off, and sat silent and staring. Yousseff just stared back, unblinking. A full minute went by in silence. Yousseff knew about this part of making a deal — the first one to break the silence loses. Yousseff had learned well the art of knowing when to talk and when to stay silent.

"Fine," Sahota broke under the pressure. "I want $1,000 American a month. And it must be cash," he said quickly.

Yousseff couldn't believe his ears. The "and it must be cash" almost made him blink. Obviously this dolt did not know that he had suitcases full, safe houses full, and barns full of cash. Nor did he know that Yousseff's greatest intellectual exercises consisted of finding ways to make the cash morph into other things, such as land, houses, ships, and loyalty. Of course he did not know these things — how could he? And yet it caught Youssef by surprise to be so misjudged.

He paused for a moment and then decided to go double or nothing. "I will make it double. I will pay you $2,000 American a month, in cash, if you keep the union away from my client, and if you make the life of the KSEW Board of Directors a living hell. And I will do this for as long as you honor your part of the deal. If that's for 50 years, it's payment for 50 years."

Now it was Sahota who could not believe his ears. He was 37 years old. The average wage in Karachi was a tenth of what he was being offered. The circus had come to town. Bring out the dancing girls and the beer, he thought. Good beer, in fact. The German stuff.

They rose to shake hands on the deal. Before the handshake, Youssef hesitated and looked Sahota directly in the eye again. "If you forget this contract, Mr. Sahota, you will die. You will die slowly and painfully, as will your children, your wife, and your mistresses." At this point, Youssef named Sahota's four children, from oldest to youngest, his wife, and three of his mistresses. He did this in a slow and deliberate matter, staring directly at Sahota. Mr. Just-call-me-Sahota was chilled to the bone. He found himself shaking terribly. Had he just leapt into bed with a dozen cobras?

"Do you understand me, Mr. Sahota?" asked Youssef.

"Yes, Mr. Joseph. Yes sir, I do. I am your loyal and obedient servant always. Yes, yes." Why worry? he thought. Why mess this up? This circus could be in town to stay, as long as he kept his part of the deal.

Youssef, for his part, had no intention of wiping out the entire Sahota clan, including mistresses. He felt no need to tell Sahota that, however. The threat was all that was necessary.

From that point on, the fortune of Karachi Drydock and Engineering seemed only to increase. There were more sales, more jobs, more employees, and more of everything else. KSEW, on the other hand, became more and more mired in union strife, and had particular problems with the PASWEU.

"What the hell is the matter with you?" an angered Nooshkatoor cried during one dinner with Sahota. "What on earth are we paying you for? One thousand dollars a month, and it has to be American dollars, and cash to boot! That is an enormous sum of money. And still you can't control your damned members. What the hell kind of business agent are you anyway?"

To this Sahota could only wring his hands and say what a difficult outfit the PASWEU had become. A few small labor relations victories would ensue, only to be met by yet another round of wildcat walkouts and ridiculous demands.

Yousseff only smiled when he heard the news. Nooshkatoor now ran the company with an iron fist, just managing to keep the huge corporation solvent. But try as he might, he could not find a way to snuff out KDEC, and that miserable little bastard child, Kumar Hanaman.

While Yousseff's deal with Sahota kept Nooshkatoor from making trouble and provided for some entertaining moments, his arrangement with Kumar was paying rich dividends. Karachi Drydock and Engineering had strengthened his empire profoundly. A thousand tricks had been created by Yousseff, Omar, and Kumar to ease the transportation of product from dock to boat, boat to boat, and boat to dock. Ingenious devices were employed to create false hulls; many of Yousseff's craft measured 30 feet in length from the outside, but only 28 feet from the inside. Kumar delighted in the construction of these invisible storage areas, and before long, they were being used not only in Yousseff's ships but in his automobiles and airplanes as well. Yousseff and Kumar, working together, standardized the size of a pallet of heroin and designed all the transportation machinery to be the same size, so that transfers from craft to craft could be accomplished with even greater speed and efficiency.

Kumar obtained his engineering degree in a record three years and returned to KDEC as its full-time president when he was only 18 years old. He built his first submersible before he was 21.

In the case of PASWEU, the day inevitably came when Sahota approached Kumar and told him he needed more money. It would have to be $3,000 per month, or the agreement would be brought to the attention of Nooshkatoor, and perhaps even the police.

Kumar nodded slowly and said, "Yes, I see your point. Give me a day."

Kumar called Yousseff. Yousseff called Marak. Just-call-me-Sahota disappeared. His body was found washed up on a nearby beach a few weeks later. His hands and feet had been cut off by some sharp instrument, while he was still alive. An autopsy determined that he had been shot once in the head with what might have been a Glock 9 mm. Ballistics analysis was inconclusive.

27

YOUSSEFF WAS 24 when he went to work as a deck hand on the *Arabian Queen II,* the tramp freighter owned and operated by Bartholomew. It was the same old ship that the smuggler had acquired more than a decade earlier; it had already been ancient when Yousseff first started bringing him heroin, and hadn't been kept up. The only improvement, thought Yousseff, was that a few hundred coats of paint had been applied since then. The last few coats had been with the compliments of KDEC. The crew joked that the paint was the only thing holding the ship together.

Bartholomew himself didn't exactly run what would be called "a tight ship." He cursed constantly. He alternately bullied, then commiserated with, his crew. He was profoundly overweight, smoked heavily, and drank more than he smoked; as a result, most of his crew also drank and smoked. He was long overdue for a major cardiac event. His ship was in much the same shape. The engines were constantly failing, and every voyage was plagued by episodes of drifting aimlessly in the shipping lanes while some further makeshift repair was done. His seamen seldom lasted more than one voyage, and the crew was undisciplined and usually intoxicated to the point of insolence, fighting, and uselessness. The ship took on water constantly, and the two functional bilge pumps were badly overworked.

Yousseff had always been astonished that someone as lazy and undisciplined as Bartholomew could possess the skills and wit necessary to smuggle large quantities of narcotics. Perhaps it was all because of his ruthlessness and the way he treated other men, including his crew. Although he allowed them undisciplined run of the ship, he was prone to random bouts of bad temper; he had shot and killed a fair number of his crew over the years. It was rumored that he had even pitched a few overboard into the waters of the Pacific in the middle of their voyages. The only reason he was able to maintain a crew at all was that he paid them well. Even with the money, though, talk of mutiny was never far from the lips of the men. Luckily, they were usually too drunk to follow through.

The truth was that Bartholomew's only true assets were his connections on the other side of the Pacific, on the west coasts of Mexico, America, and Canada. Those associations were what Yousseff was after. It was for them that he made himself as valuable as possible on the newest incarnation of Bartholomew's ship. He did anything and everything, from cleaning the decks and toilets, to preparing food, to assisting in the engine room. As with everything else, he learned rapidly, and had a voracious appetite for absorbing more. He acquired an understanding of the fundamentals of navigation, and learned how to read the stars and navigational charts, the radar (when it worked), and the sonar equipment. He worked from dawn till dusk. The rest of the crew thought that he was completely mad. If he could earn his keep working five or six hours a day, why work 18? Why clean a deck when no one had asked him to? Why stand knee deep in tepid water, with poor lighting, in a steamy, stinking hot hull to fix a pump, when there was no order to do so, especially when he was so mechanically challenged? Why work in the kitchen to help the chef? Why clean the kitchen from top to bottom when the chef told him not to bother? Before long, Yousseff's hard work and diligence were earning him enemies rather than friends.

IT WAS ON THE DECKS of Bartholomew's ship that Yousseff first met Vince Ramballa. Vince was the first mate, and split his time between the engine room and the bridge, struggling to keep the aging engines going and the ship on course. He was the medium between Bartholomew and his crew, and through good people skills and clever negotiation, he had on several occasions prevented the crew from leaving en masse. Vince was the only man on the ship, aside from Bartholomew, who saw Yousseff's value.

The rest of the crew took offense to Yousseff and his keen attitude and began to sullenly grumble about it. Late one night, things came to a head. Yousseff was on the bridge, with his proverbial bucket and mop, cleaning the floor. Most of the crew had been in a common room below deck, gambling and drinking heavily. They were on the third week of what should have been a two-week journey and were still a week away from Manzanillo. The voyage had been beset by breakdowns, storms, and misadventures. On the night in question, the seas were not calm, and moods were surly. Talk turned to Yousseff and his attitude.

"Trying to show us all up, him and that idiotic mop of his," grumbled one man, reaching for the whiskey bottle.

"Trying to help out in the engine room when he obviously doesn't have a clue how to hold a wrench or wield a hammer," said another. "Just doesn't belong on a ship."

"Where is that skinny Pashtun bastard anyway?" chimed in a third. "Let's teach him a lesson."

"I think he's on the bridge," said the first. "Let's have some fun."

The six sailors, liquor in hand, proceeded to the bridge where, sure enough, Yousseff was cleaning the floor and the insides of the windows and doors.

"Hey, shit boy," said one, "clean this." He picked up Yousseff's bucket, which was full of dirty water, and threw it at Yousseff, drenching him from head to foot with the grimy liquid. Yousseff did not look up, nor did he speak. He continued with his task as though the sailors weren't there.

For a few seconds the sailors were perplexed. But the ringleader refused to be put off. He walked up to Yousseff, who was a mere 5′6″. The sailor was at least 6′1″. He gave the smaller man a mighty shove, throwing him hard into the rear bulkhead. Yousseff's head cracked into the hard steel, and a trickle of blood ran from the wound, staining the floor on which he'd fallen. Still he did not utter a word. He simply got up, reached for the mop, and attempted to resume his mopping. While he did this with slow deliberation, his mind was racing. The situation was turning ugly. The sailors were in a foul mood, and there was no telling where things would go.

"Yo, the outside hull is filthy," said the first sailor to one of his comrades. "Grab a rope. Let's give this little bastard a real job to do."

Within seconds, Yousseff was on his back on the deck, his feet tied together with a section of nautical rope. Three of the sailors picked him up and unceremoniously tossed him over the rail. He found himself hanging dangerously just over the side, suspended head first by a thin stretch of rope.

"Clean it, you little bastard!" roared one of the sailors. "Clean the damn hull! Never been done yet. It's got to be filthy."

A stiff wind was blowing, and there were 20-foot swells, cresting in whitecaps, raging below Yousseff. From what he could see, there were only two sailors hanging on to the rope. Two men keeping him from falling into the sea that raged below him. He glanced at the ocean and gulped; he'd never learned to swim.

"Hang on, you Pashtun peasant, you're going for a nice little ride," said the ringleader, as the sailors let the rope slide through their hands.

Yousseff, heart pounding, was buffeted by the wind, and crashed against the hull of the ship as the sailors played out more and more rope. He was starting to have visions of his own death. The tops of the waves began to catch his body, knocking him back and forth some 40 feet below the level of the deck. He was unable to brace himself and became totally disoriented, upside down, first in, then just out of the of the black, raging water. As the sailors let out even more rope, he heard the distant shouts of the drunken men above him. "Clean it, you little desert runt. Clean the hull!"

Youssef's head and torso were caught in the waves, which smashed him ever more violently against the hull. The salt water stung his eyes and burned his throat. It was one of the few times in his life that Youssef felt the gnawing teeth of fear. Was this to be his end? Was this how he would die? The salt water was rushing into his mouth and nose and filling his throat. He gasped every time his head broke the water, desperate for the life-saving oxygen.

Just when he was certain that his death was near, Youssef felt the rope being pulled, and his body being lifted upward, away from the black water and toward safety. He felt strong hands reach for him and pull his body back over the railing and to the security of the deck. He was completely disoriented, and had several gashes and bruises on his head and forearms. He couldn't feel his feet or hands. It was several moments before he could breathe properly again. When his vision finally cleared, he saw Vince, pointing a revolver at the sailors and ordering them to untie the rope and get some towels.

Somehow, over the noise of the wind and waves, Vince had heard the commotion and had come to Youssef's rescue. And not a second too soon.

"Come down to my quarters, Youss," he said. "I've got some first aid supplies there. I can fix you up."

"You saved my life, Vince. Those pigs would have dropped me into the Pacific."

"I know. They've done it before. When we get back to Karachi, we'll get a new crew. Just stay close to me until then," the first mate answered. "We don't want a repeat performance here."

Youssef followed Vince to his quarters, and they stayed up until dawn, discussing life. On that night, Vince became one of Youssef's closest friends; he was given access to Youssef's inner circle, and became a party to many of the less-than-legal operations devised by Youssef. The way of *badal* and *nunwatel* applied here too. For saving his life, Youssef became Vince's servant, and gave him full entry to his multifaceted operations.

OVER THE COURSE of the next two years, Youssef ingratiated himself with Captain Bartholomew. The ship had never run or looked better. Before long Bartholomew was allowing Youssef to take the wheel on their expeditions. Within a year Youssef was plotting his own courses and navigating the small ship through busy sea lanes. Vince remained first mate, but was content to relinquish the captain's duties to Youssef. While Youssef was not mechanically gifted, he had great skill in dealing with people, and the crew was becoming more professional. Within 18 months, Youssef successfully completed his first docking maneuver, at the busy port in Manzanillo, Mexico.

Back home, Omar, Ba'al, Izzy, and Kumar were maintaining their shares of Youssef's empire, and there were few events that required his intervention. Youssef's directions regarding the police were simply to steer clear of them. Nooshkatoor was a thornier problem, as he seemed intent on putting the upstart Karachi Drydock and Engineering Company out of business. But with the property paid for and an abundance of work, mostly in retrofitting old freighters and river craft, KDEC was established, and there was not much that Nooshkatoor could do. Still, he remained a problem, sending union agents to Kumar's door, reporting the business to the port authorities for fictitious infractions, and implying to anti-narcotics agents in Karachi that KDEC was a cesspool of drugs. It was obvious to everyone that Youssef would have to find a way to deal with him at some point.

More importantly to Youssef's immediate plans, however, was that he had started accompanying Bartholomew on the all-important drug transfers. In Vancouver, Manzanillo, and Panama — places where security was low, where boarding a ship was easy, or where dropping a small boat in the water and running a mile or two to a more isolated area was not a big deal — Youssef was Bartholomew's shadow. These moments were always nerve-wracking, even for the normally calm Youssef. They dealt with rough characters, for whom killing, murder, mayhem, and death were normal job hazards. Bartholomew, Youssef, and a couple of crew members, all armed to the teeth, would make their way to some prearranged rendezvous for the exchange of drugs and suitcase. There they'd go through the rituals of sampling, inspection, and counting, always under a cloud of fear, the men alert for ambush or theft. These exchanges took place many times each year, and every time a substantial quantity of drugs was sold.

Youssef had already been traveling with Bartholomew for two years, learning the business. His many hours as Bartholomew's confidant, advisor, and organizer were starting to pay off. Soon, he knew, he would possess not only the ship but also Bartholomew's legitimate and illegitimate businesses. He could see that the pirate was tiring of the trade, and was looking to cash out. When Youssef was 26, Bartholomew came to him with a proposal.

"I am getting on in years," he said. "All this time at sea is beginning to wear on me. I want to spend more time at home. I want to retire. Perhaps I can interest you in buying this ship."

Yousseff pretended to think about it for a while. He had known that this was coming, and he knew that he would buy the ship. But not too hastily.

"Well, Bartholomew," he said. "She is old and rusting. The motors need to be replaced, and I would need proper navigational equipment. She might not survive a hard storm. Even in a 50-knot wind she might buckle and sink. You yourself have not bought proper insurance for years because the old lady just isn't insurable. And I am just a sailor. Where would I get the money for something like this?"

Captain Bartholomew had never been told how wealthy Yousseff actually was. At this point, the young man owned many properties in Afghanistan and Pakistan. He owned Karachi Drydock and Engineering, which was making spectacular profits, given that most of its expenses, including labor, were paid for in cash supplied by Yousseff. Any company profits were invested in high-quality equipment and additional harborside and downtown property in Karachi. Yousseff also owned an extremely profitable river ferry company, which now had a dozen 40 and 50-foot ferries shipping cargos of various sorts up and down the Indus. Bartholomew had never been told about any of the companies. He didn't know that Yousseff owned a string of safe houses on both sides of the Khyber Pass, or that this diminutive man was becoming the largest cultivator of opium poppies in Afghanistan. As far as the captain knew, Yousseff was just another sailor in his mid-20s, sailing because he enjoyed being on the water, and in different ports, coupled with the thrill and profits of dealing with illicit contraband. Unlike the other sailors, though, Yousseff had shown intelligence and interest in the venture; two things that had led Bartholomew to think that this particular young man might be interested in something more than just sailing. It was what had led to the offer.

"I'll make you a good deal," Bartholomew said, stroking his chin in thought. "You can pay me over time from the profits you make. You don't even have to make a down payment. Just pay me over two or three years. But not in cash. I want real money. Clean money. In foreign banks."

"Well," said Yousseff thoughtfully, "I will need to be able to connect with the purchasers in North America. I need to be properly introduced to those people in the US and Mexico and Canada. I need to be more than just another sailor standing around holding an AK-47. I need to know how you contact those people, and how arrangements are made. If you do that for me, I might consider it."

Bartholomew knew that Youssef would ask this. It was a fair question. Youssef knew as well as Bartholomew that the ship didn't make a nickel of profit in bringing its scant 80 or 90 containers across the ocean; that was just for cover, in case they were boarded by authorities. The only profits he made were through the transportation of drugs. Bartholomew looked Youssef up and down, considering. He saw Youssef's hard gaze. He realized that there was a great deal more to this young man than he had originally thought. He also sensed that Youssef would keep his side of the bargain.

"That's a reasonable request," he said at length. "Pay me over two years. Let's talk price."

Youssef drove a hard bargain, regardless of the fact that he could have paid the price, in laundered dollars, many times over, on the spot. They finally agreed on a sum, and a scheme for monthly payments. Captain Bartholomew would introduce him, over the next four or five months, to his contacts in America, Mexico, and Canada.

THE NEXT TRIP to Vancouver's harbor was the last that Bartholomew was to take. The ship waited for a few days in the outer harbor before docking at the container terminal on the other side of Stanley Park. Bartholomew, for all his lack of industry and discipline, had developed an ingenious method for off-loading his illicit wares. On the port side of his ship, a few feet above the waterline when the ship was fully loaded, he had, through a hidden recess in the ship's hull, created a slot in which he stored a small 18-foot runabout, with two very powerful outboard engines. The recess was designed so that it was invisible to anyone conducting either an interior or exterior inspection. A crude winch and pulley system raised and lowered the runabout to and from the water. This craftily designed interior space was the primary reason for Bartholomew having stayed in business for so long. Between that, the constant repainting and renaming of his ship, and the care that he took when transferring product, his operation was more successful than it should have been. These were the reasons that he could retire, with wheelbarrows full of money, with an estate on the coast, a home in downtown London, another in Paris, still another in Karachi, and a lovely 50-foot yacht, on which he spent most of his time, plying the west India and Pakistan coastlines.

The Vancouver introduction was uneventful. No names were used. All Bartholomew told his contacts was that Youssef was his successor, that he could be trusted, and that they would be doing business with him from now on. The apparent leader of the Canadians was a young man, about Youssef's age, with a long ponytail and hard, pale blue eyes. He had three men with him, all openly displaying firearms. There were no handshakes. No pleasant conversation. Two hundred kilos of heroin was traded for 20 suitcases of American currency. The whole exchange lasted less than two minutes. Bartholomew and Youssef were back in the runabout the instant the exchange was made, headed straight for the ship. The captain told Youssef that this was the most dangerous part of any transfer. It was not safe to trust the purchasers — you could never tell if they were going to pull their guns on you at the last second. And the harbor police were always around, hiding in the shadows. He pointed out a number of the taller Vancouver buildings and told Youssef that police with powerful binoculars were almost always scanning the harbor for suspicious activity from any available building. For these reasons, the meetings were always a gamble.

Youssef nodded. He had been watching the whole process intently for two years. And he had discovered another quality that had made Bartholomew so successful. Luck. Sheer, blind luck. He could think of dozens of improvements, especially with the engineering now available to him through Kumar's thriving company. Improvements to make the transfers more efficient, faster, and safer. Improvements that would make every trip more profitable.

To conclude that night, Youssef had been given a telephone number — in four weeks he was to call the number and be given the particulars of the next drop, which would take place eight weeks later.

When he had docked the ship upon his return, Youssef found that KDEC did not have enough time to replace the engines, as he had hoped; they had too much work to do as it was. New engines would have to wait until the next trip home. But Kumar was able to make some of his usual modifications. His men also put a false bottom in the runabout, to create an invisible storage area, where Youssef stashed 400 kilograms of heroin.

Eight weeks later Youssef returned to Vancouver for his first deal. He had hired a whole new crew of his own men for the ship. They were virtually all from the Pashtun mountain villages. They all knew Youssef, and trusted him. Most importantly, they were all absolutely dedicated to him. None of them knew a great deal about the sea, but Youssef knew from experience that it was easier to teach a loyal crew any trade than it was to teach an experienced crew loyalty. And Vince had no difficulty with training new sailors.

The meeting was at an abandoned dock near Port Moody, at the east end of Burrard Inlet. Youssef himself took part, with three of his crew as his personal bodyguards. They all packed AK-47's, and were very comfortable showing them off, so they painted an intimidating picture. But none of them had ever experienced a deal of this nature. Yousseff was decidedly nervous, and his men were downright terrified. Yousseff was also dealing with a personal conflict. He had never considered himself a criminal; he thought of himself as a businessman, and one who kept hundreds of farmers and workers in Afghanistan and Pakistan happily employed. He did not like dealing with the criminal element, and the Vancouver drug dealers were clearly practicing members. The same youthful man with the hard blue eyes appeared, at the appointed place and hour. Yousseff, who had scouted the area out a few hours earlier, was ready and waiting.

"What've ya got?" asked Hard-eyes.

"Four hundred kilos," Yousseff answered.

"Where?"

"In the runabout."

"Get it."

"Show me the money," Yousseff answered.

Hard-eyes motioned to the old pickup truck parked about 50 feet away. Yousseff's eyes did not leave the young Canadian.

"Show it to me," Yousseff repeated.

"You get the horse. I'll get the money. Then we trade," said Hard-eyes.

Yousseff motioned to Vince, who was in the runabout. Vince activated a hidden switch, and a hidden panel silently slid back, revealing a small scissors lift. The scissors lift rose up from the hidden chamber, bringing the drugs into view over the edge of the small boat. The heroin had been placed on a small wheeled pallet, so that the sailor could simply push it forward onto the dock. It was a simplified system that made Yousseff cringe, but was the best that Kumar had been able to do in the two weeks between trips. As the drugs were rolled out, 20 Samsonite suitcases appeared from the truck. Yousseff had a lot of experience with packing money into medium-sized Samsonite suitcases and estimated that the 20 suitcases contained approximately $10 million. He also remembered that Bartholomew had been given 20 suitcases as payment for 200 kilos of heroin. The Canadian was trying to cut the price in half.

"No," said Yousseff. "Four hundred kilos. Forty cases. That's the deal. No bullshit."

Hard-eyes look directly at Yousseff. "You're in no position to bargain, towel-head."

"I'm not bargaining," Youssef answered. "You know the price. No discounts here."

The Canadian motioned to one of his men. Shots were fired, and two of Youssef's men fell to the dock, dead. Youssef now stood alone with Vince, who stood in the runabout.

Youssef had grown up when the Soviets invaded his land. He was familiar with the tribal wars in the Frontier Provinces. He had personally done battle with his rivals in Pakistan and Afghanistan on several occasions. He was no stranger to death. But those had been situations where there was no alternative; it was kill or be killed. This was nothing like that. The drug-runner's action was senseless. The deaths of his men had been completely unnecessary, and it enraged him. He dug his nails into the palms of his hands and bit his tongue, telling himself not to show the anger boiling beneath the surface. But his voice dropped, and his stare became dangerously intense.

"You have made your point, sir." He calmly walked over to the cases, which he and Vince then loaded into the runabout. Youssef picked up one of their fallen comrades.

"Vince, help me carry these two. We will not leave them here on the docks. We'll bury them at sea." Youssef's voice was soft and even.

Vince was terrified, but followed Youssef's lead. He stepped out of the runabout and half carried, half dragged the second dead crewman back into the small boat.

"Wait," said Hard-eyes. "Here are the numbers for the next shipment." He walked to the boat and gave Youssef a sheet of paper. Youssef took it without a word, turned to the wheel, and left. He knew that the man would not harm him; he would not want to jeopardize his supply line. The Canadian had a good deal going. Youssef also realized, though, that he needed to make a stand, to start off this new business relationship.

EIGHT WEEKS LATER, Youssef stood once again on the Vancouver docks, this time with just one crewmember and Vince. The situation played out in much the same way. Four hundred kilos of heroin were produced. Twenty cases of money were unloaded from the old pickup truck.

"My price is, and was, $50,000 per kilo. Not $25,000," said Youssef.

Hard-eyes sniggered. "You said the same thing last time. You know what happened. Don't fuck with me again, you little brown bastard, or you'll all be blown to hell," he said. "And I don't give a rat's fuck if your buddy over there is bigger than the last guys you brought with you. Just makes him an easier target. Right boys?" he said to the three heavily armed thugs behind him.

"Right, boss," one of them replied.

"Actually," Yousseff said, "you owe me 20 cases of money from our last transaction. You want these 400 kilos, you bring out 40 more suitcases. I'm not going to negotiate on that." Yousseff calmly picked up three of the cases and walked toward the runabout, conspicuously turning his back on Hard-eyes and his crew.

The Canadian swelled with anger. "Listen, you two-bit Paki prick. Don't fuck me over. I'll blow you away."

"No you won't," Yousseff said, absolutely confident. "I'm your supplier. You shoot my men, or me, and you lose your supply line. You'll have to sniff and hunt to get someone else, and their product won't be nearly as good as what you've been getting. You shoot me, you're out of business. You know it, I know it." He calmly dropped the cases into the boat and hopped in. He flicked a lever and the heroin descended back into the double hull of the renovated runabout.

Hard-eyes was speechless. Nothing like this had ever happened before. He pointed at his men, all of whom had their guns out and ready. "Shoot that big bastard," he ordered.

Before the thugs could raise their guns, Yousseff's guard pulled his Glock from his shoulder holster. Three shots, three men down. Although Yousseff had heard it often and was expecting the shock, he was still startled by the explosive sound of the specially manufactured gun. He had seen it used many times but was still astounded by the sizes of the wounds it left. Truly an amazing weapon, he thought. And a terrifying one.

Marak turned the Glock and pointed it directly at Hard-eyes. "Don't make me do it, you arrogant asshole," he growled.

"Vince," ordered Yousseff, "grab the rest of the cases and toss them in the boat. I need to have a chat with Mr. Blue Eyes here. Rasta, stay with me, and don't take your eyes off this asshole." He spoke in Urdu, walking toward the blue-eyed Canadian bandit.

He stopped ten feet from the man. "You need to understand this, my friend. You try something like last time ever again, and you will die, slowly and painfully. This time I will let you live, but only because we need each other." Still staring at the man, he backed away toward the runabout, and climbed in. "I trust we have an understanding," he shouted as they pulled away from the shoreline. "I will see you here eight weeks from now — same place, same time."

When they were several hundred feet out, Yousseff turned to Marak. "I hope that straightens everything out."

"We'll find out in eight weeks," replied Marak. "What are we going to do with all that?" He pointed to the floor, and the hidden compartment that still held 400 kilos of heroin.

"I have other plans for it," Yousseff answered. "KDEC installed some monster engines in Bartholomew's old ship. I want to open her up a little, test them out. Want to go to Manzanillo?"

"Sure, boss, whatever you say."

"You know, as long as she's going to be a major part of our operation, we should give Bartholomew's ship a decent name," said Yousseff slowly. "Something fitting for a new shipping venture."

They discussed the possibilities for a while. After some brainstorming, Marak said, "You know, Yousseff, there is that beautiful mountain in the Hindu Kush. I've always thought it was a strong symbol of our country. You and I went there once as children. You know, Mount, Mount…"

"Mount Haramosh," said Yousseff.

"But you can't name a ship after a mountain," Vince pointed out. "That's just bad news."

"No, you're right. It wouldn't make any sense. How about the *Haramosh Star?* That's a good name for a ship," Yousseff mused.

"Yes, Yousseff, I think that's a good name. The *Haramosh Star* it is."

"And we need a name for the shipping line, now that we have become international. A line that Omar is going to run. What about the Karachi Star Line?" Yousseff continued.

"Sounds good," said Vince, as he directed the little boat through Vancouver's inner harbor. "Karachi Star Line it shall be."

Finally, the runabout approached the old container carrier. The crew had seen them coming and had the hoist assembly ready. *"Haramosh Star* it is," said Yousseff, almost to himself, as they climbed out of the runabout. *Haramosh Star.* Haramosh. Haramosh…

WAKE UP, YOUSS," said Mustafa, shaking him. "Wake up, we're in California. We'll be landing in 20 minutes. Put on a seat belt."

Yousseff tried to wipe the remnants of the dream out of his brain. He blinked and looked at Mustafa. "Here already?" he asked.

"Yes Yousseff. You slept the entire flight. I spoke to Kumar. He will be at the hangar to greet you in person," Mustafa answered.

The landing was almost perfect, with the wheels of the Gulfstream coming down gently on the runway. The plane came to a roaring stop at a dull gray-colored hangar. Customs clearance had, of course, been prearranged.

The door of the plane opened, and Yousseff found a beaming Kumar on the runway to greet him. "Yousseff!" he said. "It's so good to see you again. It has been too long."

"It's good to see you too, my friend. How is our mission coming along?"

Kumar sighed. He knew that Yousseff was referring not only to the engineering plans he had sent but also to the two teenagers Kumar had been instructed to collect. The boys had been living in Los Angeles for some time, sent there by the Emir to carry out his *jihad*. Kumar had received orders to pick them up and take them under his wing, teaching them what they needed to know about the equipment they would be operating and the mission for which they'd been chosen. In the process, he'd come to know them well, and was growing more and more unhappy about his involvement in the scheme.

"They've got it sorted out, Yousseff. They are ready. But I'm bothered by it. They're good kids."

"Yes," replied Yousseff, turning his face away. "But they are here of their own volition. What about the submersible? Have you made all the modifications we discussed?"

"Yes, we're done. Everything is in working order."

"What about the device? Has it been built?" continued Yousseff.

"Yes, it's done," said Kumar.

"Good," said Yousseff, grimly. "Then it is time to put the final pieces together."

28

INDY WAS STANDING ONCE AGAIN in the small clearing adjacent to Leon Lestage's trailer. It had been six days since Leon Lestage had held a gun to his head at this very spot. Catherine Gray had confirmed that RCMP members had identified Leon passing through Fernie a few days earlier, westward bound, heading toward Vancouver. He hadn't come back, which meant that the coast was clear for Indy's plan. The night before, he had contacted Catherine from his small highway hotel room in Fernie. They'd had dinner, and arranged to meet at 7AM the next morning to head toward the Akamina-Kishinina.

This time, Indy and Catherine had made sure that no one was home. They'd left the Chevy near the park gates and walked a mile to the Lestage trailer, then watched the small home for 15 minutes before venturing onto the property. They had come fully equipped. Their backpacks contained climbing equipment, should that become necessary, flashlights, extra batteries, cigarette lighters, GPS units, and compasses. They had their RCMP utility belts and service revolvers, and Indy even had 20 feet of rope hooked over one shoulder. They might not need everything they'd brought, but there was no telling what would happen once they entered the mine. In addition to the equipment, Indy had a set of the engineering and development plans from the Ministry of Mines. Before they'd left their respective stations, they'd both made sure that at least one of their coworkers knew where they were going.

"Come on, Cath," Indy said, excited to finally be moving. "Time to fish or cut bait."

"Yeah, it's time. We've already been on the dock too long," she responded.

They stole past Leon's trailer and headed south, past the faded Devil's Anvil sign. The trail curved a bit and widened, heading toward the rocky rampart of Sawtooth Ridge several hundred feet ahead. While the trail was overgrown, it showed evidence of recent usage. The tire tracks that Catherine and Indy passed were fresh.

"According to the plans, the mine starts with a horizontal shaft carved directly into that bluff up ahead," Indy said.

"Well the trail is leading directly to it. Must be something there," Catherine responded.

The trail rounded a bend, and directly before them was a low wooden structure with a peaked roof, built directly into the mountainside. There were two large, barn-like doors at the front of the structure. These were locked with a large metal padlock.

"No problem," said Indy. With the new information produced by the other accounts, he'd had no difficulty obtaining a warrant to search the property and premises of Leon Lestage. This particular structure was, according to his maps, on Leon's property. That meant it was fair game. Without further ado, he produced a set of tools from his backpack and started to pick the padlock. Eventually the lock sprang open.

"Bastard," cursed Indy as he removed the opened lock from the door. Both he and Catherine peered into the gloom ahead of them. There were overhead lights, and Indy found a switch, but nothing happened when he flicked it.

"They must have generator power," Indy said. "We'll have to use our flashlights from here on in. Good thing we brought lots of batteries, Cath."

They squinted into the darkness, trying to see what lay ahead of them. There were two tracks of standard railway gauge, receding into the blackness. The air had a musty, coal-like smell to it. Cobwebs hung from the tunnel ceiling, and large wooden posts and beams appeared at regular intervals. A small rail car was sitting on the tracks just inside the barn doors. Indy felt his heart rate start to rise as he stepped inside the doors. He hated enclosed spaces.

"I'll bet this rail car is used for transporting narcotics. Especially the bulky stuff, like marijuana. They could just load it up and push it down the tracks. With how close we are to the American border, this must be how they ship their contraband across," said Catherine.

"Yes. This has got to be the hole. The leak in the dyke, so to speak. The Yankees will go nuts over this," responded Indy.

"So will Ottawa," said Catherine. "This could be huge."

They stood for a moment, gazing at the dim, narrow tunnel. "Shall we?" Indy asked finally.

"After you," motioned Catherine. "Let's see what James Leon Hallett built for himself."

"Let's take the bus," said Indy, pointing to the rail car. "Hop on. Turn on your flashlight. I'll get us started."

Catherine stepped into the rail car, and Indy started pushing. Initially the progress was slow, but he was able to push the car forward at a slow jog. Then he hopped on, and slowly started to push the large upright lever back and forth, keeping up the pace. They proceeded forward for about 15 minutes before the tunnel ended in a large central space, about 30 feet across. The coal smell was much stronger here; Grandpa Hallett had indeed found a rich vein. Both Indy and Catherine shone their flashlights around the room; in the flickering shadows they could see four other tunnels splitting off from the central excavation. There was a vertical shaft with what appeared to be a simple elevator system descending down the wall. Unlike the posts and beams supporting the tunnel, the elevator assembly seemed to be new and fairly modern.

"Hang on a sec, Cath," said Indy, as he fumbled through his backpack. "Here it is." He pulled out a copy of the original development plan, and they both shone their flashlights on the large sheet of paper. Indy's flashlight shook a bit — the walls and ceiling were starting to weigh heavier and heavier on him. He could feel the panic gradually taking hold of his mind. He gritted his teeth and attempted to regain his self-discipline.

"According to this, there's a lower level. One of the tunnels in that level appears to head due south. It looks like there's a maze of interconnected rooms and walkways in that direction. I say we take the elevator down. It looks new to me."

"After you, Indy," said Catherine again, quietly noting Indy's increasingly obvious anxiety. She could see little beads of sweat on his forehead, and noted his fidgeting fingers. From the signs, she thought he must be claustrophobic, though he hadn't mentioned it. Privately she was surprised that he'd suggested they go down any farther, and wondered how much longer he'd be able to handle the strain.

The rail line they were already riding led them along a narrow path adjacent to the wall, and then connected with two sections of rail on the lift platform itself. Indy gently nosed the cart onto the platform. He found an electrical panel on a vertical wooden post beside the elevator shaft.

"Let's see what happens," he said, pressing a green button. Nothing. He pressed it again, and then pressed all the other buttons on the panel. Still nothing.

"Dumbo," said Catherine. "We don't have electrical power. The lift is obviously operated electrically, and the generator, wherever it is, is off."

"Well let's go back and find the generator and turn it on. It must be outside," said Indy. "I'll go see if I can find it."

Abruptly, and without warning, the lift began to slowly descend on its own. Indy paused mid-step.

"What's it doing?" asked Catherine nervously.

"It's descending," said Indy, attempting to ignore the claustrophobic fears that were rising within him. He was starting to feel as though his throat was closing up, and trying desperately to pretend it wasn't. Suddenly a switch in his brain turned on, and he started to panic. He knew he couldn't ignore it any longer. "Let's get off while we can," he said suddenly, moving to step off the rail car and lift.

"No," Catherine said, grabbing his hand. "We need to follow this through. It can't possibly be a deep tunnel. Let's see where it goes. If we need to, we can use these cables to climb back up." She pointed to what were probably the brake and electrical cables, strung along the wall.

"Yeah, sure," he said, trying to calm himself. "You're the local authority, I guess. I'm just an inspector out of Vancouver. But I want danger pay for this job."

Catherine shone her flashlight upward and saw the shaft opening recede in the pale light. "How come it suddenly went down?" she asked.

"This elevator is probably hydraulically operated, and calibrated to a certain weight. Once that weight is exceeded, down we go. It's actually pretty clever."

As they were talking, the elevator descended into another large chamber and then jerked to a stop. As suddenly as the ride had started, it ended. "See that?" said Catherine, trying to reassure Indy. "We're only 20 or 30 feet down." They played their flashlights around the chamber, which was slightly smaller than the upper room, and had three tunnel openings connecting to it. All three of the openings had rail tracks leading to them.

"Which one?" asked Catherine.

Indy fumbled around in his packsack, and found a compass. "That one," he said, pointing to his right. "That one heads due south. If I'm calculating right, we're probably directly underneath the American border already. In fact, we could be in the States now. Hope you brought a passport."

"Why don't you use your GPS locator?" asked Catherine.

"Can't. We're in a mine. Underground, now. Signals can't get through," responded Indy.

Catherine pulled her GPS transmitter out of her pocket and looked at it accusingly. "So then why'd we bring them, genius?"

"To figure out where we are when we get to the other side," he said, irritation and anxiety creeping into his voice.

He hopped off the platform and rotated it so that the cart was oriented with the southbound set of rails. Then he reached for Catherine's hand and helped her off the platform assembly. Together they pushed the rail car into the southern tunnel. They were a few feet into the southbound tunnel, and getting ready to jump back into the car, when they heard a purring noise behind them. The lift was slowly starting to rise again.

"Oh God. We need to get back on," said Indy, his fear increasing. He darted back toward the lift. "We can't get trapped down here. Let's go back and get reinforcements. Let's come back with a dozen men."

Catherine grabbed Indy's hand again. "Relax. Your office knows we're here. So does the Fernie detachment. If we're trapped it won't be for more than a day. We're hot on the track of this, Indy. Let's keep going."

"Yes. OK. Let's." But Indy's heart clearly wasn't in it anymore.

"Look at the fancy hydraulics," she continued, not fully appreciating his increasing anxiety, but thinking that anything to keep his mind off of it would help. "The Hallett and Lestage boys have certainly spent some money on this system. That platform definitely doesn't date back to the '20s. Those hydraulics are new. Someone very clever engineered this."

"OK," Indy responded, watching the lift disappear into the vertical shaft above the lower opening. He wasn't even listening to his partner anymore.

"Indy, stop being a wuss. This is the biggest case I've ever seen. We can't turn back now." Catherine grabbed the lever of the small rail car and started pumping it back and forth, building up to a speed of about five miles an hour.

Another five minutes went by. Indy had started helping with the lever, and was sweating profusely. His claustrophobia wasn't making the situation any easier. He did his best to hide the fear from Catherine, though; he wasn't proud of this weakness.

"Let me handle the lever, Indy," said Catherine, pushing him gently away. "I may be a woman, but I'm 20 years younger."

"And in shape," said Indy, noting her slender, athletic frame. She had a reputation in the Force for running five or six marathons a year. He also knew that she'd worn out the instructors at basic training in Regina. He gladly turned the lever over to her, and she worked it for a few minutes. The tunnel widened out, and they reached another large opening, with four large metal doors set into its silent, stony walls.

"Let's have a look, Cath," said Indy. "I think we're near the mother lode." He stepped off the rail car and walked to each door. They were all secured with heavy padlocks.

"No worries," Indy said, fingering the first of the locks. "You don't get to be a cop with a quarter century of experience without learning how to bust or pick a lock. Of course you've already seen me do it." He started to rummage through the many flaps and pockets of his packsack, trying to relocate his lock-picking equipment.

"Good thing you have a warrant," Catherine quipped. Then she paused. "Actually, are you sure you've got one?"

"Yes, Catherine, I told you that. Got it early yesterday morning from one of the old goats at 222 Main." He was referring to the address of the provincial court in Vancouver.

She snorted. "No way it's valid."

"Why do you say that?"

"Well," responded Catherine. "If your calculations are correct, we've now entered the United States of America. And if you think those old goats in your provincial courts have jurisdiction in the US of A, you're nuttier than I thought you were."

"Them old goats probably think they have jurisdiction in Beijing," Indy answered, doing his best impression of the strong redneck accent that tended to dominate such courts. "You know how wacky some of their judgments are. In fact, most of the guys I work with believe that 20 percent of all judges are just flat out crazy," he added. "And even if they don't have jurisdiction, I'll just call my buddy, Stan Hagen, with the FBI's Seattle field office. He can get a warrant based on what I tell him, and he can nail the bastards. American courts are one hell of a lot tougher on these dope dealers than BC courts are. It would probably be better all around if the FBI did the bust. We can get one or two of them on the Canadian side of the border anyway."

He started fidgeting with the padlock on one of the doors. Soon he was muttering to himself in a foreign language; Catherine thought it must be Punjabi. Just when she thought the lock was going to snap from his aggression, she heard the tumblers click.

"There," said Indy, as the door swung open. "Got it."

They shone their flashlights into the room. "Oh my God!" exclaimed Catherine. "Oh my God! Look at that."

Indy was likewise impressed. The room was full of American money. "There's got to be millions and millions of dollars here. This is incredible," he breathed.

Before them was a mass of money, most of it clipped together in even stacks. Each clip appeared to have been sorted by bill denomination, and separated into piles of twenties, fifties, and hundreds. The effort to stack the bundles up neatly, one on top of the other, had obviously been abandoned long ago. Now the money lay in massive piles, taking up most of a room that measured at least 20 feet square. Along one wall, some 40 Samsonite briefcases were stacked up, side by side.

"Looks like the smurfs are going to be busy for a while," chuckled Catherine. "In fact, for a very long while. I'd say they're starting to get behind."

"Let's check out the other rooms," said Indy, noticeably excited. He moved to another door and started to work away on the padlock. More fidgeting, more grumbling, and finally more Punjabi, at a higher frequency than before. Catherine had to restrain a giggle. Eventually the lock opened, and she and Indy looked eagerly into the second room.

"Canadian money," exclaimed Indy. Again clipped in bundles, again mostly in twenties, fifties, and hundreds, this time in the more colorful Canadian currency.

"I see it, Indy. They probably have parallel smurfing operations on the American and Canadian sides of the border. They don't need to worry about passports and border crossings. If they need smurfs in the States, they just send clan members through this tunnel to take care of things in Montana. Heck, once they're across the line, they can smurf in California if they want to. There has to be an American accumulation account parallel in its operation to the Canadian accounts. Ultimately, the money gets transferred into offshore accounts, and they can legitimately use it from there."

"We're talking millions and millions of dollars here. This is way bigger than we thought, Cath. We're going to do the bust of the century. We're in the big leagues now," said Indy. "Let's check the other doors." It was becoming a bit like a game show. Door number one, door number two, door number three...

He was starting to get the hang of picking locks, and opened the padlock on the third door more quickly than he had the other two.

"You're pretty good at that Indy," said Catherine. "If the Force dumps you, you've got a ready-made second career."

"Not funny, Cath," he said, as the third door swung open.

This room held a pungent but familiar odor. Catherine and Indy sniffed, paused, and then turned their flashlights into the room's interior. Catherine gasped softly. There were stacks and stacks of plastic-wrapped bricks. On the witness stand, the police described it as "a green, plant-like substance." Marijuana. Mountains of it.

"Holy shit, Cath, there must be at least a ton of it in here," exclaimed Indy. "Maybe two tons. The street value in this room alone has got to be in the millions. Maybe tens of millions."

"Three guesses as to where it came from, and where it's going," Catherine muttered darkly.

"I'm sure it's BC Bud," said Indy. It was the region's second-largest export. The basement marijuana grow-ops must have been kept busy for years to produce this much of the stuff.

"BC's number two product, and quite a stack of it," Catherine said, reading his thoughts. She turned her flashlight to the corners of the room, noting that the marijuana was packed close to all four walls.

"You know, Cath, it may be BC's number one export by now," replied Indy, duly impressed. "No one knows for sure anymore. Most of this, I'm sure, has been lovingly cultivated in high-tech grow-ops in Vancouver."

"Maybe the Ministry of Forests should get involved with regulating and distributing this stuff. Then it would be guaranteed to lose money, and the whole hydroponic industry would cease to function," joked Catherine.

"Good point," replied Indy. "Remind me to bring it up at the next executive meeting." They both laughed.

"Given Leon Lestage's role in all of this, it was probably acquired, wholesale, by motorcycle gangs, and transported here that way," said Catherine, sobering. "Maybe that tour bus is being used to transport some of it."

"And it's all headed stateside, probably mostly to Washington, Oregon, and California. You know, the Yankee West Coast is not all that different from British Columbia. Must be the influence of the Pacific," said Indy. He turned away from the pile of BC Bud. "Shall we see what else we have?"

"I've got a pretty good idea about what's behind door number four," Catherine said.

"Me too," answered Indy. He started to fuss with the last padlock, muttering loudly and nonstop in Punjabi. This was more exciting than any other investigation he'd ever been part of, and that included his undercover days in the '80s. In the excitement of the discoveries, he had completely forgotten his claustrophobia, and now worked with focus and intensity.

The lock gave, and the door swung open. A different smell, one that Catherine did not recognize, greeted them. Indy knew exactly what it was. Heroin, in uniform brick-sized packets, neatly wrapped in plastic, and stacked against one wall of the room.

"Holy shit. These guys have it all, Cath. They're running all the drugs.

That heroin is probably from Southeast Asia or Afghanistan. It reaches BC, probably though Vancouver harbor. They somehow get it past the police there and bring most of it here, for later export." Indy was pacing the room, his accent getting stronger and stronger as he worked the theory out in his head. "They must get rid of some of it in Vancouver, given the big colony of heroin addicts there, but most of it comes here. To the Akamina-Kishinina, of all places. And then they take it through an abandoned coal mine, under the border, to hit the lucrative US market. Whoever put this together is fiendishly clever. Incredible." He stopped pacing and looked around the room in awe. Despite the lawlessness of it, he had to admit a grudging respect for the intelligence that had come up with such a scheme.

"Holy doodle," murmured Catherine, awed by the sheer magnitude of what was sitting in front of them. "Back at the detachment, a pound of marijuana is considered a big deal. And that's just a pound of marijuana. This is absolutely incredible."

"And over there," he said, pointing to the other wall, where they could see more bricks in the shadows. "Those must be wholesale packages of cocaine."

"Sure," said Catherine, working the timeline out. "And that's why there's a whole room full of Canadian dollars. Any drugs sold in Canada would be paid for with Canadian cash. That's got to be cocaine, probably from Colombia, or Mexico, coming into Canada. And the American dollars come from the marijuana, cocaine, and heroin they're selling in the States."

"There's got to be more than $30 million in cash and drugs here," said Indy.

"Welcome to drug central," added Catherine. "James Leon Hallett never hit the mother load, but holy cow, his grandkids sure did."

Indy was about to reply when there was a distant rumbling noise, a click, and a buzz as the overhead lights came on. At the same time, they heard an overhead door open a few hundred feet to the north of the money and drug rooms.

"Shit, Cath, we're trapped," Indy said, his voice falling. "Someone's coming in on the Canadian end, and that's our only way out. Since we took the rail car, they probably already know we're down here. We're trapped."

"Hooped," she agreed. "Totally hooped. What do we do?"

"Let's get back to the central excavation and hide in one of the other tunnels. We can make it if we move fast," said Indy, reaching for Catherine, and turning to run northward at top speed.

But Indy and Catherine didn't make it. They ran toward the central excavation, and had almost reached it, when the lift descended completely, with Dennis, heavily armed, standing on it. Indy recognized the bus driver that he'd yelled at on his earlier trip to the area. He had an AK-47 with him now, and it was pointed directly at them.

29

EARL LEONARD LESTAGE, JR., aka Leon Lestage, was rich, but not nearly as rich as he wanted to be. He was sitting in his fabulous 12,000-square-foot home on an acre of prime British Properties real estate, overlooking the twinkling lights of Vancouver on the far side of Burrard Inlet. On one of the clear days that they did sometimes get in Vancouver, he thought it was probably the most breathtaking view on the planet. During the day, Mount Baker was visible, often appearing to float on a cushion of clouds.

Vancouver, over the past two decades, had acquired a truly big-city skyline. He could see, far below him, the multiple sails of the Canada Place Convention Center, sitting like twinkling gems on the waterfront. He could make out the distinctive soaring shapes of the Wall Tower, the Shaw Tower, and the circular peaks of the Harbor Center. The orange dots of the streetlights traced a path into the distance, disappearing in the working district of Surrey, where he had spent his 20s. To the west were the lights of the University of British Columbia.

He could make out the hangars and modern architecture of "YVR," as the locals called Vancouver International Airport. He loved watching planes taking off and landing; in fact it was part of his frustration. Yes he owned his own jet — didn't everybody? But it was a cheap little Lear, and he was the third or fourth-generation owner. He felt a little embarrassed when he went to the private South Terminal. There were several larger Gulfstreams, a few "fours," and one "five." There were a couple of Bombardiers — beautiful jets made by an eastern Canadian company. One software hotshot stored his private 737 there. And besides all that, he felt like a gunny bagger when he walked into the South Terminal. Maybe he should just chuck the old jet and fly first class everywhere he went, he thought. At least he would be made to feel special and important that way.

Same thing with the yacht. He didn't even know if it rated as a real yacht. A mere 52 feet in length. A pathetic stateroom, and an aft deck so small that he would never have a helicopter landing on it, nevermind being able to afford a helicopter at all. Plus the primitive technology inside. The first radar ever built, it seemed. And then there were the people he had to hire. They cost too damn much money. They all wanted more, all the time. He had a maid/

housekeeper/mistress on staff here at the house. But that was as far as it went. He really couldn't afford his own pilots, or mechanics, or boat captains, or chauffeurs. To be properly equipped, he needed a staff of 12 or 13, and then he would need servants' quarters and the house would be too small.

Dammit, he needed a bigger place on Maui, and he wanted something in Los Angeles, and a place in Europe, and… on and on it went. He was a poor boy and it pissed him off. The more he thought about it, the more he wanted a really big kill. A $4 or $5 million house, $4 or $5 million worth of toys, a few million in the bank, and a whopping big pile of money in Devil's Anvil just didn't do it for him anymore. He was sorely dissatisfied with his life. He was 52 years old and still hopelessly displeased with himself, his meager possessions, and life in general. It was the same attitude that had been pushing him on ever since he could remember. His thin blond hair was now flecked with gray, his middle was starting to go soft, and he needed medication to do things that he'd taken for granted in his 20s. He reached over to the humidor beside him and rolled a large, fat joint, made of the best high-grade BC Bud money could buy.

"Yo, Val, gimme a beer! A cold one!" he yelled in the general direction of the kitchen. He took a long drag on his monster joint and resumed his viewing of greater Vancouver. There, dead ahead of him, were the enormous orange container cranes, on the Vancouver side of Burrard Inlet. They reminded him of where he'd started. Those were the days, he thought. Those were the days. When he was in his 20s, working the docks in a pointless job but getting laid every night. It had been a non-stop party. Endless beer, endless smoke, and endless women.

"Yo, Val! Beer. Get. Me. A. Goddamn. Beer." Jesus. That was the problem, he thought. Cheap help. Cheap service. You get what you pay for.

There was a scurrying behind him, and Val, who was also starting to look a little long in the tooth at the age of 23, came scurrying out with his beer — an ice-cold Corona, with lime, of course.

"Next time don't make me wait, woman," he growled at the stunningly beautiful girl, who managed a quick apology before scampering away, terrified of bringing on Leon's fearsome temper.

He returned to his thoughts. Where was he? Yes, of course. The salad days. The '70s. He poured the Corona into a frosted glass, chucked in the lime, and took a long, soothing draft. Then a long toke. He let his thoughts drift back to the good times. The orange container cranes continued to dance in the humid Indian summer air as his thoughts roamed.

LEON WAS 17 when he left Fernie. "Never coming back to this shit hole," he said to the few friends and many relatives he had there. "Dead-end town with dead-end people." He had jumped on his motorcycle — a small Honda, or "Jap bike" — and, in his words, "just fucked off." He ended up in Vancouver, like so many other young people in the province. Tall, young, strong, and handsome, with a gift for making conversation, he fell into the Vancouver bar scene, and then the easy sex and drugs of a pre-HIV world. He went from drug user to drug supplier, and then to supplier's supplier, within a year. Marijuana use led to cocaine, LSD, and, on occasion, heroin, although he never became an addict in the full sense of the word. He used and sold, and never restricted his business to one specific drug.

Soon he was making copious amounts of money, and Fernie was the farthest thing from his mind. By his nineteenth birthday, Leon was supplying drugs to most of the bars and clubs in downtown Vancouver. His "Jap bike" days were behind him forever. Now he had the money and was in Harley-land to stay. One night he was sitting with two friends, listening to a bar band play, and enjoying the smoky, noisy scene of a downtown bar. The two Harley-riding buddies sitting next to him were both longshoremen, working at the small container terminal on the East Vancouver harborside.

"Can you believe it? You can buy in for $50 grand. Pay the money to the shop steward, and you're in the union, and on the docks. Just like that," one said.

"Price's sure gone up. Just five years ago it was $10 grand," said the other.

"What are you guys talking about?" asked Leon. "You can buy your way into being a longshoreman?"

"Yeah. Pay the money. Show up for work. You're in. And it's the most powerful union in Canada," said the first. "More balls than the teamsters, even."

"Who do I pay the $50 grand to?" asked Leon.

Both men looked at him. "You're kidding, Leon. You got that kinda dough?"

"Yeah," said Leon. "Maybe I do. Who do I talk to?"

One of the men gave him a number. "Tell 'em Barry sent you."

Leon took down the number, and the following day went searching, first for the docks, then for the container terminal, and then for the shop steward. When he found him, he told him that he'd been sent by Barry. And that he had $50,000, and how would the steward like it — in cash or check? And when would he be starting work? The answer was easy… work started immediately. Leon was in the Union. Welcome aboard. The steward guessed that Leon probably had an ulterior motive, but didn't care. After all, $50 grand was $50 grand.

That's how Leon Lestage, a small-time Fernie boy, joined the powerful Vancouver longshoreman's union. The shop steward introduced him to the company and recommended that he be the guy to fill an open position. Leon slipped the company comptroller $10,000, to grease the wheels. Four months later, it was apparent to everyone that Leon only showed up every second or third day, was almost never on time, and mostly slept on the job. The comptroller started expressing some concern. Leon just slipped the shop steward another $20,000, $5,000 of which found its way to the comptroller, to smooth things over again. This system worked for the better part of a decade. So long as there was money to whack around, no one complained, other than the container terminal Board of Directors, who couldn't understand why there appeared to be intractable inefficiencies in the company's operations.

The reality was that Vancouver's port, from a customs and policing standpoint, had more holes than a colander. Inspections were almost nonexistent. Bales of marijuana could be unloaded in broad daylight, and no one seemed to notice. Every now and then there was a high profile bust of some sort, but these events were few and far between, and didn't usually occur at the container terminal. Leon noticed this and, never satisfied, had decided that he was going to use this job and the unsupervised port to move to the next level. He wanted to be the supplier to the supplier to the supplier of the pushers in the bars and clubs. Wholesale wasn't good enough anymore. Importing was the new game. To import, one needed to own the docks, and Leon decided that he was going to set about doing just that.

Vancouver was a much younger city than New York or Boston, and no established mafia or crime family had laid claim to it. The container port itself was very new, as the worldwide trend toward the containerization of ship cargos was just beginning to take root in the early '70s. This meant that there were no other organizations taking advantage of the situation. Leon was unencumbered by conscience, had plenty of smarts and huge amounts of available cash, and possessed more than a few restricted or prohibited weapons. Mastery of the container terminal was not difficult. He didn't even have to kill that many people to accomplish it. Before long he had succeeded in raising his game to a whole new level. Leon Lestage, importer.

A few more years saw Leon's fortunes soaring. He owned dozens of

Harleys, and even some rare antique models. He'd become successful very quickly simply because he was crafty enough to evade detection. And he was very intimidating. While many of his customers were busted, none of them dared to rat on Leon. He was wealthy enough that he could have been set for life, but his restless, moody nature forbade it. He could have stepped back and simply managed his empire, letting other people do the hard work for him, but he couldn't separate himself from the dark turbulence and thrill of his work. He even began to grow bored with how easy it had all become. Eventually, his boredom was alleviated by the fact that he bumped into another ceiling. He developed a supply and demand problem — basic Economics 101. He had access to more heroin than he could sell. For all the media it received, there were relatively few heroin users in Vancouver. He needed a larger market.

One night, in that heightened, euphoric stage produced by combining the right drugs in just the right way, it came to him. He didn't quite say "Eureka," but he may as well have. The revelation was so profound that he actually lurched about his home, searching for a pencil and paper, so that he could write it down, lest the very chemical compounds that had brought on this stroke of brilliance lead to its complete destruction before the light of day. He had experienced that before — waking up in the morning, knowing that deep and profound revelations had danced through his mind during the night, but not being able to remember them. Someone had written, somewhere, that the act of genius lay in connecting two things that had been hitherto unconnected. If that were so, then Leon thought that his stroke of genius was in the same league as Galileo, in concluding that the world was round, or Newton, or Einstein, in discovering whatever it was that they had discovered.

Several days after his revelation, Leon found himself saddling up one of his Harleys and making his way back to the very hometown he'd sworn never to re-enter. He was returning to his ancestral home with a brand new plan, profound and audacious. He, Leon, lord of all he surveyed, was heading back to his roots.

He had telephoned his brother Donald the night before. He had to go through the headache of getting his number from Directory Assistance, which had made his mood even worse than usual. His other brother, Dennis, didn't have a phone, or cell service. He lived too far out in the wilderness.

"Donald, I'm coming home. I'm going to move in with Dennis, in Grandpa's old trailer, by the park. Tell him I'm coming over. Don't tell anyone else. Make sure there's someone there tomorrow evening. Make sure they have cold beer," he had told an astounded brother. There was no "Hello, how are you?" or "Good to talk to you." He didn't even bother to wait for a response — at this point he was used to people dancing to his music. It never occurred to him that he'd ignored his brother, and the rest of the family, for a good four years. They had all assumed the worst and thought that he had died in the basement of some whorehouse or in some gangland brawl years before.

It wouldn't be long before they were wishing that he had done just that.

It was midnight before a thoroughly pissed off Leon finally arrived at his brother's home. He had miscalculated the journey. He'd forgotten about the extra distance from Fernie south to the Akamina-Kishinina, which, though short, was mostly unpaved gravel road. Not exactly the best surface for a Harley, especially not a modified low-rider like Leon's. It hadn't been a pleasant trip.

WHAT LEON HAD RECALLED, on that fateful drug-infested night, was a conversation from almost 15 years earlier, when he was eight or nine. At the time, he'd been visiting his grandfather's somewhat rundown trailer, south of Fernie, almost on top of the gateway to the Akamina-Kishinina. It was the very same trailer that Dennis now occupied. Their grandfather had been an embittered old man, having found a rich coal deposit that was too far from the railway to be viably developed. He had developed the mine himself on the strength of promises from government officials that a railway would be built eventually. After decades of work, with a fortune in sight, and another fortune spent in developing the mine, the government suddenly reversed its position. James Leon Hallett spent the next 50 years fighting for his development. Entreaties to government ministries were to no avail. Petitions to various levels of the Canadian National Railway were ignored. False hopes were raised, then dashed. It was not until the twilight of his life that Grandfather James had finally accepted that his dream of founding a vast industrial enterprise in the southeast corner of the province wouldn't be realized — at least not in his lifetime. He had turned to drink before Leon was even born, and didn't make sense half the time.

Leon's mother, oblivious to her father's treacherous physical and mental state, sometimes left her young boys in their grandfather's custody, especially during the summers. Leon didn't mind. He was more than happy to get away from his mother's home in Fernie. It was crowded with more than ten children, most of the time. James didn't mind much either. "You're the most like me, Leon," he would say. "The only one worth the effort."

The high point of any visit was when they entered Devil's Anvil, James' half-century-old mine. The mine lay directly below Sawtooth Ridge, a high mountain that was a part of the Flathead-Boundary range. Leon had never forgotten the magic of the tunnels and the rails.

The last weekend that he had spent with his grandfather was especially memorable. Leon had begged the old man to take him into the mine again, and Grandpa James had bowed to the young boy's pressure. Together they walked the short distance from the trailer to the mine's opening. Leon had not noticed his grandfather's unsteady gate, or the effort that every step seemed to be taking. Into the mine they went, down the central excavation on an unsteady ladder, and down further tunnels, to the mine's southern-most point.

There James had sat down for a minute, sweat pouring off his face, seemingly oblivious to the youngster's excited prattle.

"Is this where it ends? Does the mine stop here?" asked an enthusiastic Leon.

"Yes. This… this is the southern reach of the mine. Right here." James was gasping for breath. Leon didn't notice. "Do you want to hear a secret, boy?"

"Yes," said Leon. "I do."

"Every mine in the province has something called a 'development plan.' It says where the tunnels can go and how they can be built. Well…" James' voice trailed off, and his breathing became more labored.

"Tell me, tell me," Leon urged him on.

"This here tunnel went further than it was supposed to. I drilled almost a mile beyond where I was supposed to stop. A whole goddamn mile. There was a particularly rich vein that I wanted to follow. Do you know what's directly above us?"

"No," said Leon, his sharp eyes watching his grandfather. All his boyish exuberance had vanished, and his tone was now deadly serious.

"Why, the US of A, boy. The United States." James emphasized the "U," and slowed down the syllables for dramatic effect.

"You mean we're across the border?" asked Leon.

"Yes, son, we are. In fact, almost half a mile beyond it. If we drilled another 200 or 300 feet straight that-a-way, we'd come out on the other side of the mountain that's behind the house." James pointed toward the end of the tunnel. "We'd have drilled straight through. I gave it some thought during the prohibition days, you know. That kinda thing. Good money. But the laws in the States had changed by the time I'd drilled far enough, and it wouldn't've been so profitable. So I went back to trying to convince the politicians and railway guys to build a track to my mine. They screwed me over good, you know. They were in league with the mines in the Kootenays. Tried to hire lawyers, but after a few years and more than $10,000, I realized they were screwing me too."

They turned around and walked back toward the central excavation. James started puffing again after they'd been walking for only a few minutes. He was sweating profusely. "Hold on a sec, boy. Need to rest for a bit." He sat down where he was, not even looking for a chair or raised edge. For 15 minutes he sat on the tunnel floor, while Leon entertained himself by throwing rocks at the central excavation. Finally, James rose with a grunt, and said, "OK, boy, let's go."

When they arrived back at the trailer, they found Leon's mother waiting. "Back to Fernie, Leon. School will be starting in a few days."

So they bid their goodbyes. That was the last time that Leon saw his grandfather. He died of a massive heart attack later that same night. He'd been dead for two days when one of his numerous children finally found him. The funeral was in Fernie, but Leon didn't go. It never occurred to the boy that he was, in fact, the last person to speak to the old man. It still hadn't, even a decade and a half later. What he did recall was the substance of that conversation, word for word.

LEON OPENED THE DOOR of the ancient trailer without knocking. Dennis jumped up, wanting to hug him, shake his hand, or greet him in some way. Leon, however, made a beeline for the refrigerator and found himself a beer.

"So here's what we're going to do, Dennis. And either you're with me or it's your ass," he said. "You with me?"

"Do I have a choice?"

"No. I can get you big money, Denny, really big money. But you do exactly as I say and you keep your fuckin' mouth shut. Got it?"

"OK, Leon," Dennis answered. "What do you want me to do?"

"First thing," said Leon, taking a long swig of cold beer, "get me some food and turn off the goddamn TV."

"OK, Leon," responded Dennis. "I'll grab some food, you turn off the TV. Then we can talk."

"Denny, didn't you hear me? You do as I say. Now gimme food and shut off the fucking TV. It's pissing me off."

Dennis walked into the kitchen and returned with a loaf of bread, butter, and cheese. "My hands are full here, Leon. You turn off the TV."

"One last chance," said Leon. "Turn off the fucking TV. Now." His voice had gone soft which, as Dennis recalled from their childhood days, was not a good sign. But Dennis decided to push his point. This was his house now.

"My house. You turn off the TV."

"OK, Denny. Your call." Leon pulled out his custom-made Sig-Sauer 9 mm, and put six shots into the TV. When the racket subsided and the smoke cleared, the TV speaker was still emitting some garbled sound, and there were still some sparks inside the shattered TV screen. Leon reloaded. He heard Dennis scream no, but Leon didn't usually give a fuck what other people thought. Another nine shots were fired at the catastrophically damaged TV. When the smoke settled again, the TV had stopped giving out any sound or visual images. On further inspection, both the dog and the cat had mindlessly fled the house. The dog had crapped on the floor before it left.

"Clean that shit up," ordered Leon. "And if I get any more static from you, I'll bury you in the deepest parts of the mine. Not even the fuckin' rats'll find you. Now do we have an understanding here?"

Dennis did understand, although he forgot from time to time. Over the years of their association, more bullet holes appeared in the walls, floor, and ceiling of the dilapidated trailer. If Dennis forgot to turn off a light, Leon shot it out. If the doors were not opened, they were generally shot open. Dennis obtained prescriptions for Paxil, and then Prozac. The dog and cat seldom, if ever, came into the house anymore; they scurried into the woods whenever they saw Leon.

AFTER HE WAS SET UP in Dennis' house, Leon went to a Kamloops merchant who dealt in used mining parts. He told him what he needed and found out that the drilling machines would cost him $50,000, freight extra. When the merchant said that he would take cash, Leon went to his saddlebags and counted out the bills. Transportation was arranged, and within days the equipment was sitting beside the tunnel opening behind James Leon Hallett's old trailer. It wasn't hard to get a crew of Halletts and Lestages together to go to work. Leon made the terms of their employment plain. One hundred dollars a day, but if anyone breathed a word to an outsider, Leon would shoot his balls off, and then drop him down one of the mine shafts to die a slow and painful death with only rats and bats for companions.

The work was relatively simple, and the payment even easier. The rail system had to be repaired. A few stacks of hundreds solved that. They needed a functional lift system, which was easily built. More hundreds paid out. The drilling itself was underway within two weeks. At a rate of 30 or 40 feet a day, the project would take five or six months tops. Leon planned to drill a good mile beyond where Grandpa James had stopped. He had done a lot of calculation and measuring on both sides of the border. He had gone to Montana, to Kalispell, and north along State Highway 486, to follow the northern roads that seemed to mark the border. He knew when he was looking at the deserted southern slopes of Sawtooth Ridge that the plan was virtually foolproof.

Leon didn't intend to have the workers punch the tunnel all the way through to the American surface of the mountain. He kept them on until there was about 100 feet to go. It was important that none of his idiot cousins know exactly what he was doing. He thanked them all, paid them in cash, and took five days to punch through the last 100 feet on his own. He resisted the temptation to shout his success at the top of his lungs when he got to the other side of the mountain. Caution was now the order of the day. Instead, he took a few moments to quietly survey the landscape.

It was a pleasant view. Behind him rose the soaring vertical lines of Sawtooth Ridge. Ahead of him, the rugged Flathead River Valley opened up to his gaze. He could see a road in the distance, leading to a solitary farmhouse. He realized that he'd have to pay that family a visit and give them an irresistible offer. But first he would explore a little, get some maps, talk to some locals in that easy way of his, just so long as they didn't get him mad enough to pull the Sig-Sauer on them. He wanted to make sure that this was a very pleasant exercise. Give it a month or two, he thought, and the house on the southern side of the Ridge would be his.

It didn't take him long. Two hundred thousand American dollars bought the farm in northern Montana. Mr. and Mrs. Peterson, the owners, were very taken with the charming, polite Mr. Lestage, and his old-model pick up truck. "Such a nice young man," they said. "So considerate, and charming, and kind." He thought of everything, even hiring and paying for the moving company to deliver their goods to an old folks' home. It hadn't taken long for them to confide in him that they had been thinking of selling for a long time now. They were way too far north for their age. They wanted to be closer to clinics, and pharmacies, and hospitals. It was time to leave remote, northern Montana and get back to civilization. Within a month, Daniel Hallett had moved into the Peterson ancestral home. Both the northern and southern ramparts of Devil's Anvil were now secured by offspring of James Leon Hallett.

Once he'd moved in and made himself comfortable, Daniel, on Leon's orders, purchased a number of Honda four-wheel-drive ATV's, and put in a very rough trail between the farmhouse and the tunnel. He had disguised the entrance to the tunnel as best as he could, with boulders and brush. It looked like just another part of the rugged mountain range. Not that anyone ever came this far north.

Leon installed a large generator and a series of lights in the tunnels. He improved the lift system and installed rails in the lower tunnel. He created a series of storage tunnels and rooms where equipment and product could easily be hidden. Within another two months he was ready to go. He bought ten kilos of heroin from his connection, Bartholomew, a smuggler from Pakistan with whom he had been dealing for the past year. It was time to give the new and improved Devil's Anvil a test run. The whole process took four days, from pickup at the Vancouver docks, to delivery in Los Angeles. Before he left Fernie, he cut the heroin and was able to resell it in Los Angeles for $100,000 a kilo. He'd paid Bartholomew a scant $50,000 for that much. His profit from that first trip, after supplies, travel costs, and payment to his workers, was $500,000. Leon had definitely reached the next level. As an added bonus, he purchased a couple kilos of cocaine while in Los Angeles, and took that back through Devil's Anvil to sell to the surrogate biker gangs in Vancouver. His path was very clear — at this rate it would take only months for Leon Lestage to become one of the heavy hitters in the drug-smuggling game.

A few more runs left a few hundred thousand dollars sitting in his mine. By the spring, there was, by his estimation, close to $1 million stashed away in Devil's Anvil. However, he had a growing problem. How to get rid of it? How to launder it? He already had all the Halletts and Lestages of Fernie and the surrounding area smurfing for him full time. Of course, too much money is never that large a problem. He gradually purchased all the houses and properties along the Corbie-Flathead Forest service road, and even bought the bicycle tour company that ran through the area, to ensure that any contact between the public and the mine would be minimized. In this way he controlled virtually all activities along the road.

There was only one really big wrench in the works. The little Paki asshole who had bought Bartholomew's smuggling outfit. He had come with one sailor and put 200 keys of horse on the docks. Leon gave him $25,000 per kilo, and the little bastard told him that he wanted more. Even told him that he owed him the money from the last time they traded. Then he took off with the money and the drugs, in his piece of shit Pakistani boat. When Leon had tried to take action, the Paki's psycho-eyed sidekick had killed three of his guys. The nerve of the little fucker. These days they had a grudging understanding. Leon had vowed to himself that one day he would make the Paki die a slow and horrible death. Until that day, he might as well make money off of the foreigner.

DROP YOUR UTILITY BELTS and packs right now. Guns on the ground." Dennis Lestage barked. Catherine and Indy did as they were told.

"Now turn around and walk forward, slowly. One false move and I'll kill you where you stand. No one will ever even find your bodies." They turned and headed south, back toward the four rooms, Dennis following them. He noticed that the four doors were open.

"A little break-in, I see," said Dennis, grimacing. "Get in there, now." He shoved them roughly into the American money room. The door slammed shut. They heard a padlock slide into place; even if it was broken, a padlock could keep someone inside a room from getting out. A solitary light bulb hanging from the ceiling provided the only illumination in the room. A minute or two later they heard Dennis return to insert and lock a new padlock.

Catherine looked around her. She started to laugh.

"What on earth could be funny about this?" asked Indy.

"Look around you," Catherine replied. "Look at this. We're locked in a room with millions and millions of dollars. Look at this." She grabbed a stack of hundreds and threw them in the air. "I feel like Scrooge McDuck in his money room."

"At least he didn't lock us up in the marijuana room," replied Indy. "The fumes from that much weed, in close confines, would get to us after a while."

"What's wrong with that, Indy? If we died, at least we'd giggle to death."

Suddenly the distant throb of the generator ceased. The single overhead light abruptly went out. The room became as black as the coal in the walls. The silence was oppressive. Instinctively Indy reached for Catherine's hand. "Oh, God, Catherine. I feel like I'm inside a tomb. Or a coffin." He realized that after having held it at bay for so long, this was the final straw; his claustrophobia was finally going to overwhelm everything else. He was fighting back the panic.

"We'll get through this, Indy," said Catherine. "We'll get out of this somehow." Her mind was racing. She didn't have a clue how they were going to spin this one.

"I have a tough time in enclosed spaces, Cath," said Indy. "I had a near death experience when I was a young undercover officer. I've been to some therapy, but it didn't do a whole lot of good. We've got to get out of here. We've got to find a way out. I can't deal with this."

THE PHONE in Leon's palatial home rang, cutting sharply into his warm drug-laden thoughts. He was still deliciously stoned, gazing at the very container dock where, so many years ago, the party had really started. But when he heard the voice on the phone, he snapped to attention. It was Dennis, and he was beside himself. Cops. RCMP. In Devil's Anvil. They had gone through the storage rooms. Dennis had them locked up for now, but was desperate for guidance.

"Describe the people for me, Dennis," said Leon at length.

"A lady, not bad looking, about 30-ish. A Hindu, maybe 50. Short."

"Keep them locked up. I'm comin' over. How'd they get in to start with, you fucking moron?" snarled Leon, in his usual style.

"They broke in," Dennis responded.

Leon hung up the phone without answering and got ready to saddle up and head out. Didn't matter that he was stoned — the wind would clear that up soon enough. The Hindu might be the same character he saw there a week ago. They were cops. If they were cops, they would have a warrant. No cop in Canada in this day and age would break in without a warrant. Bad news in court. But a warrant meant affidavits and information upon which the affidavits had been sworn. It meant that they had been looking into his affairs, possibly for some time. It usually meant a major investigation. This could be serious. How had they found him? Leon moaned aloud. Not now. Not goddamn now. He would net $10 million, in laundered money, real money, American money, from the deal he had going this month. Not to mention the money and drugs he had stashed away in the mine. Jesus Christ, not fucking now.

Val came to him with another ice-cold beer, which he proceeded to throw down in two gulps. "Where are you going, honey?" she asked, seeing him in his riding leathers.

"None of your fucking business, bitch," came the toxic reply. He stormed out before she could protest. He was seething with rage. The only reason he had acquired that idiot bicycle tour company was to control precisely where tourists could go, and to ensure that no one would accidentally stumble across the mine so close to the park gates. He had left Dennis in charge of that company when he left — it was a simple enough task, one that even an idiot should have been able to handle. Sometimes Leon wondered whether he'd been put in the wrong crib at the hospital. No way could he actually be related to the brainless wonders he was forced to call family.

30

KHASHA WAS WORRIED. More than worried, actually. Turbee had vanished. Yes, Dan had fired him, but no one had actually accepted the fact that Turbee was, in fact, finished at TTIC. Dan had not appointed Turbee to his position. A Senate subcommittee had. Turbee's brilliance had been demonstrated repeatedly. He just needed a good crew around him to tell him what to look for. The success of Madrid had demonstrated that. Even the pointlessness of establishing a connection to the Janjawiid, in the search for the missing Semtex, had demonstrated his usefulness and skill. Khasha was inclined to believe Turbee when he offered the opinion that the stolen Semtex was on the *Haramosh Star.* When he nailed something, he did so with devastating accuracy. Maybe the SEAL teams had missed it. After all, even a small freighter had a few nooks and crannies. Whoever these drug runners were, they had already been devilishly clever in smuggling drugs. Why would that have changed?

Khasha had seen the expression on Turbee's face as he slunk out the door of the TTIC control room. It was a look of shock and utter despair. About an hour after he left, she had started thinking about the many prescription drugs she knew he was taking. What if he forgot to take them? Would he slide into a subterranean world of schizophrenic despair? What if he tried to kill himself? What would her reaction have been if an error on her part, perceived or real, had caused a Presidency to come unglued?

She'd already avoided work for three full days, sickened at the manner in which Dan had treated Turbee. Instead of going to work, she'd dropped by the offices of the Urdu dictionary group at the NSA and commiserated with them. She realized that she was probably breaching all manner of security protocols but didn't particularly care. She'd taken one sick day, then another, then another, barely bothering to call in. Three days after the firing affair she'd finally dropped by the TTIC control room. She had been shocked at how muted it was. At least half the workstations were idle. Rahlson had told Dan to go fuck himself and hadn't been seen since. Rhodes had done much the same, and was rumored to have gone directly to friends in high places to file an official report. Most of the rest of the absentees were engaged elsewhere. Many of them, like George, were not wanting for jobs or money. Dan was on the Hill, subpoenaed by a multitude of committees, who were investigating the *Haramosh Star* affair. No one had seen or heard from Turbee.

When the weekend came along, Khasha had extended a three-day leave to five, spending a portion of it with an old university friend in Philadelphia, letting the pain of the *Haramosh Star* situation dissipate with dry red wine and pasta. Now, as she boarded the early Monday morning Amtrak Acela Express to head back to the capital, her anxiety increased. What would the day bring? Would she too be out of a job? Would TTIC still be there? Would Dan? And, most importantly, what had become of Turbee?

It was this train of thought that eventually led to her self-appointed mission of finding the wunderkind. First she checked in at TTIC and stayed for an hour or so. Turbee was still missing, and no one knew where he was. She had traveled to Turbee's address, talked her way into his very generic apartment building, and threaded her way past some garbage cans to a basement suite. Typical, she thought. Lights bothered Turbee almost as much as loud or abrupt noises. A cellar dweller. The building was typical — part stone, part wood, old and mostly run down. She knocked on the door of Suite 3, but there was no answer. A second knock, and still no answer. She turned the handle and found the apartment unlocked. She opened the door a crack.

"Hamilton?" she asked. "Hamilton Turbee? Are you here?"

There was no response. She opened the door wider and stepped inside. She repeated herself, a little more loudly, "Turbee, are you in here?"

She was met with dead silence. Something was very wrong. Six days since Dan had fired Turbee. Turbee wasn't at TTIC. Khasha knew his fear of social situations, and knew he wouldn't be in any place he didn't know or feel comfortable. But he wasn't in his apartment, and it had been left unlocked. Turbee was a high-strung, antisocial creature at the best of times, and now he had been brutally humiliated in front of his coworkers. He was personally taking responsibility for a growing scandal that reached all the way up to the President's office. Even a reasonable, solidly anchored individual would be in danger of losing his moorings in that kind of situation. Turbee had never been reasonable or even a little bit anchored — he was always riding the edge of disaster. God only knew where he was now.

Khasha raced through each room in the tiny basement suite, stumbling over the archipelago of computers, routers, servers, and screens that littered every available surface. She called out his name repeatedly and, when he didn't appear, began knocking on the doors of the neighboring units, asking if they'd seen him. They all responded the same way… that they knew who he was, but never talked to him, and hadn't seen him in days. She wondered what their reaction would be if they knew that he basically owned the largest computer the government had, that he had solved the Madrid bombings within hours of being given the assignment, and that he was the unfortunate soul now being blamed for the latest international American misadventure.

She tried the university mathematics department where he had worked just prior to joining TTIC. Turbee? No. They hadn't seen him for months. She was given an old address and some old phone numbers but had no luck there either. In desperation, she telephoned Turbee's father's law firm, and asked to speak to Mr. James Turbee, but was told that he was en route back from the firm's Hong Kong office at the moment.

She felt the panic rising in her stomach and swallowed heavily — her mouth had become as dry as sand. That bastard Dan Alexander, out of jealousy or simple derision at someone who thought differently than he, had publicly destroyed this gentle soul. Damn him. Damn the President, for that matter, for not having done his homework; damn the SEALs for screwing up a search, damn the damn drug runners who had started this whole thing, damn them all. Turbee was out there somewhere, probably off his meds, and probably in a suicidal frame of mind. The look in his eyes when he'd left TTIC the previous week had reminded her of the gaze of a wounded puppy. What had happened since then?

She got into her car and began plotting a course in an ever-widening circle around Turbee's apartment. She stopped at the nearest 7/11 and asked at the counter.

"What's his name? Hamilton? Hamilton Turbee? Thin white kid, mid-20s? Don't have a clue. Never heard of him. Seen him? Nope. Sounds like a crystal meth addict to me. They're all over the place," the man behind the counter answered.

She telephoned the office twice, getting through each time to Johnson, who had for some reason stayed on in Dan's absence.

"No, he's not here, Khash," he had said quietly. "After all, why would he be? Dan fired him. I wouldn't come back after a scene like that either."

"Who are his friends? Who are his relatives, Johnson?" she asked. "Everyone has those. Even Turbee. We must have a file on him or something, with next of kin, people to contact…"

"Don't think so, Khash. He was too odd to have friends. I think his father is some high-rolling lawyer from around here, but I would need to check the file."

"Will you please check for anything else, Johnson? I've already talked to his dad's office, but see if there's someone else I could call. He could be hurt. He's probably in trouble. I'm worried sick about him."

"I'll run it past Dan," he said. "But you know we have to follow protocols here."

"Johnson, why don't you stuff those protocols up your ass? Someone is in trouble, and you seem to think it's no big deal. Fuck you!" she shouted, slamming her phone shut in frustration.

She knew she was getting nowhere. She worked for one of the nation's most important Intelligence Agencies, and she couldn't even find a missing friend. There was only one place to go. Turbee was missing. If a person is missing, where does the hunter turn? It would mean formalizing the search to some extent, but there didn't seem to be any alternative.

Dialing 911, she quickly got through to a clerk at the Henry J. Daly building, just off Pennsylvania Avenue. The building housed, among other things, the administrative and executive structure of the DC Metropolitan Police.

"What did you say his name was, ma'am?" came the sterile voice on the other end of the line.

"Turbee. Hamilton Turbee."

"Birth date?"

"Don't know."

"Age?"

"Not sure. Mid-20s," stuttered Khasha, still fighting panic.

"Address?"

"Not sure. Umm, I was just there. It's umm…" In her panic, she started encountering mental blanks everywhere.

"How do you know he's missing, ma'am?"

"He… he hasn't shown up for work in six days."

"We'll, ma'am, lots of people don't show up for work from time to time. That doesn't mean they're missing," came the dry reply.

"You don't understand. He's suffered a major emotional blow. He's autistic. He might be off his medication."

"What kind of blow, ma'am?"

"He was fired," said Khasha, feeling the increasing skepticism coming from the clerk and realizing how crazy she probably sounded. "Fired in a brutal and very public way."

There was a brief pause at the other end of the line. "Well, that could explain, maybe, why he hasn't been at work," the clerk replied sarcastically.

"Look, this guy is in trouble. I've been to his house and he's not there. He's missing. He's autistic. Can you at least check to see if anyone in the Metropolitan Police world has noticed something?" Khasha asked sharply.

"We'll see ma'am. Any distinctive features? Tattoos?"

Khasha tried to imagine Turbee with writhing snakes or naked maidens tattooed on his shoulders. "Not Turbee," she replied. "But he would be exhibiting some odd behaviors. He's got some repetitive right forearm movement. And he's probably not making much sense in what he's saying. He's very, very pale, and probably has dark circles under his eyes."

"Sounds like a meth addict, or heroin maybe?" It was half a question and half an observation.

"Looks like that, but it isn't. Can you check, please?" pleaded Khasha.

"Give me a minute, would you?" the voice on the phone suddenly became a bit softer. This sounded unusual, but the clerk had finally registered how deeply Khasha's concern ran. She checked the new book-ins at the Pre-Trial Detention Center. No Hamilton Turbee there. No one had any record of that name.

SOME TIME PASSED before Zak lost his next body part. Hamani was indeed a master of psychological torment. Every three or four days the guards were sent to bring Zak to Hamani and his laboratory. Each time he was strapped onto one of the tilt-tables. Each time one of the other prisoners was brought in and tied to the other tilt-table. Each time instruments of torture were brought within millimeters of Zak's eyes, ears, limbs, or genitals. Drills were started up, saw engines were started, but nothing was in fact done. On each occasion, though, he witnessed unspeakable tortures performed on the unfortunate other prisoner. Body parts were pierced, torn, and dissected before his eyes. He heard the screams, the sobs, the curses, he smelled the scent of burning flesh, he heard the sounds of limbs being torn.

Zak was a man of great strength, both physically and psychologically, but his mind was taken to the edge of sanity every time he witnessed these deeds. He prayed each time for a return to his cell, and to the relative quiet of the dungeons.

Then one day, the inevitable occurred.

"Well now, sir," began Hamani, in his cheerful voice. "To show you how kind and generous I am, I will give you an opportunity to choose. I will take one of your toes today. You can tell me which one. It is your choice."

Zak remained silent.

"One last time," Hamani prompted. "Tell me which toe you prefer, or I will rip out one of your kidneys here and now and make you eat it. I am in a happy little mood today, and you would do well to keep it that way."

Zak had found, time and again, that stressful situations like this tended to bring on ridiculous behavior. He thought it might be the mind's way of maintaining a sense of humor, even when the worst was about to happen. Instinctive, unconscious self-protection. Suddenly he realized that this time was no different. Out of nowhere, an American nursery rhyme began dancing through his head. He heard his mother's voice across the decades. "This little piggy goes to market, this little piggy stays home. This little piggy has roast beef, this little piggy has none, and this little piggy goes whee whee whee…"

At the memory of his mother, and the sheer inappropriateness of the nursery rhyme at a time like this, Zak felt an uncontrollable urge to laugh. Thinking to himself that laughter didn't fit the reality of his situation, and that it might just make things worse, he used his considerable powers of concentration to remain quiet. Instead, his face became stone.

"Which one, sir? You must pick," Hamani was saying.

Finally Zak relented. If he didn't keep his sense of humor, as his mind was trying to do, he was going to be finished. "You are kind, Hamani. You are a good man, just a little misunderstood. Yes, sir, the small toe, left foot, please."

Hamani was beginning to like this particular prisoner. A good man? Yes, perhaps this man did understand him, and his genius. He smiled happily. "We'll use the same saw," he said, flipping through his notes. "The carpenter's saw, please," he said to one of his assistants.

Hamani slowly brought the saw blade to the skin of the chosen toe, and, with the guards holding Zak's foot to immobilize it, removed it. Zak felt white hot pain, and in spite of himself, screamed in agony. He screamed again when the cauterizer was placed against the wound, burning it, and sealing it off.

As his bonds were loosened and he was released from the table, Zak fell to the ground, moaning. As his head hit the floor he saw, lying an inch from his mouth, a medium-sized screw. It looked like it had fallen out of the mechanism that kept the leather thongs fastened to the tilt-table. In one smooth motion, and in spite of the searing pain in his foot, Zak brought his head closer to the screw and put his lips around it, sucking it into his mouth and stashing it under his tongue. The guards were none the wiser, as he hobbled back to his small cell. He didn't give them any trouble, or require assistance to walk. Even in his state of extreme shock and pain, Zak was busy plotting his next move. This was the chance he'd been waiting for. Days ago he'd noticed that there was a barely perceptible, but omnipresent breeze flowing through his cell. It seemed to be coming from a small iron grate about halfway up the back wall. He wondered where exactly that grate led.

ON THE OTHER SIDE of the globe, in Long Beach, Ethan Byron and two of his engineers were once again reviewing the specifications Kumar had given them almost three weeks earlier. Ethan ran one of the smaller workshops at Pacific Western Submersibles, taking care of design and construction projects that Kumar didn't have the time or inclination to do himself. He and his crew were the best of the best in the company, and had been called on by Kumar to build this particular device, which he said was for studying whales. Already, the structure was almost finished. The base was completed, and the upper saddle portion had been machined. Now came the more difficult chore of putting the different layers of metals along the various surfaces.

It was a head scratcher all right. Why in the world was Kumar insisting that a full 50 percent of the device be made of molybdenum? And why a thin layer of copper? And down the center, did he really want gold? A strip of honest-to-God gold? Like you could just go to Home Depot or Wal-Mart and pick up a brick or two? They'd used 100 pounds of it, more or less, at a value of more than $1 million, before machining. And then tempered steel, and another layer of titanium alloy. It was as though a metallurgist had gone completely mad. The tolerances were incredibly precise, and different metals had to be layered inside one another to within a tenth of a millimeter. And then Kumar wanted an inverse hyperbolic curve to the molybdenum layer, with the gold along the central horizontal axis. The molybdenum was to decrease in thickness, with its greatest mass being along the outer edge, and its least mass where it connected with the central gold strip.

Ethan had reached for the telephone more than once to say sorry, Kumar, so very sorry, but we can't do this one. It's too weird, too complicated for us local guys. But he persisted, partly because he valued their friendship and business relationship, but mostly because he and his men had been promised a very substantial raise and a bonus for taking care of this bit of business.

Ethan and his engineers had started by creating a three-dimensional computer model of the device and then using some of their digital numerical routers to chisel a small model out of hardwood, just so they could physically see, in miniature, the device that they were building.

"What the hell did he say it was going to be used for?" asked the software engineer.

"Kumar said it was some kind of device they were going to use to communicate with whales," answered Ethan.

"My ass. You don't spend two or three million bucks to do that. Nobody does. Nobody," scoffed the shop chief.

"Well, the Federal Government does. I mean they can spend $1 billion for a Navy toilet, or some such BS. They're the Feds. Money has no meaning to them," said a second engineer. "If it costs less than a few hundred billion, no one notices."

"He's got a point," said Ethan. "But it's a damned weird thing, anyhow."

"You know, Ethan, I know where I've seen that type of thing before," said the engineer. "It's like the head of a flashlight, you know, the part where you have the reflector, with the bulb in the center, and a glass cover across it. It's kind of like a lens. Yeah, that's it. Maybe to focus sounds at different frequencies over long distances. Maybe that's what it's designed for. But I'll be damned if I know why they want that ribbon of gold across the central axis. That makes absolutely no sense at all."

31

YOUSSEFF DISEMBARKED from the plane feeling energized and refreshed. The news Kumar brought him was good — the final pieces were ready. Preparation and planning were now over. It was time for the execution.

"Take me to the plant. I want to see the new submersible. Are all of the alterations done?" he asked.

"Yes, Youss," Kumar answered quickly.

"The rails? The supports?"

"Yes, Youss. It is all done." Kumar felt the edge of adrenalin pumping through his system, just as in the old days, when they set out to try a new device. It would be a big moment for him when Yousseff saw the completion of his new design. He rushed Yousseff into his truck and drove him back to the workshop.

Yousseff was impressed every time he walked into the PWS manufacturing facility. It was large enough, he'd always joked, that one could build a 747 in there. The main facility had more than 120,000 square feet under one roof, and an enormous gantry crane that moved along roof rails. Complex metalworking machinery occupied most of the floor space. At the moment, six of the exotic submarines manufactured by PWS were in the lifts, in various stages of construction. Kumar had come a long way since the Karachi days with KDEC.

"A tourist company in Cancun has bought those two," said Kumar, motioning to the two units that were almost completed. "The US Navy wants those two, and National Geographic wants the fifth. No one has bought the last one yet, but the Canadian Armed Forces have expressed an interest."

A seventh, larger craft was sitting at the far end of the line.

"Is the far one ours?" asked Yousseff.

"Yes, that's the PWS-14. You can see the initial stages of the weight platform on its roof."

"On its roof?" Yousseff repeated.

"That's the only way we could think to transport the Semtex," replied Kumar. "Do you see the two large beams on either side?"

"Yes, I see them," said Yousseff.

"They contain a telescoping rail system, similar to the rails that we built into the *Haramosh Star.* Those rails will extend forward 20 feet. That's far enough to transfer the explosives to the exact point the Egyptian engineers asked for. If it doesn't work, it won't be because of us," said Kumar.

Youssef quickly moved on; at this point, failure was no longer an option. "What about the defense systems that we discussed?" he asked sharply.

"We're working night and day on those, to get them just right. You haven't given us much time, Youss," protested Kumar.

"Are you getting old? My God, Kumar, I remember the old days, floating up and down the Indus. I would say build me a small submarine. It's got to be this big, and this long, and be able to stay under water for three hours, and should have a set of arms, and grapples and things on it, to transfer a pallet of product this big, from the hold of one ship into the hold of another, and you would have it done in an hour. Horse shit. Horse and camel shit. Mountains of dung. You're getting old, my man," said Youssef, chuckling over the image.

"Not fair," Kumar protested. "I was 20 back then. I could do all of that at the same time as getting bedded by a river queen. But I have slowed down a bit. For you, Youss, and only for you, I can still do this. You want both systems?"

"Yes. Always a backup. The metal mesh is important. It will slow the torpedoes, if there are any, and confuse their guidance systems. It could get into the propellers. And the second system, to eject a second skin off the rear of the craft. It will confuse anything pursuing the sub still more, and will likely cause torpedoes to explode prematurely. We may not need this, Kumar. But I have been researching the length and breadth of the American Intelligence apparatus. It is a huge, monstrous, multifaceted beast, sucking hundreds of billions of dollars every year out of the American taxpayers. By the time we get this thing to where we want it to be, most of that multibillion-dollar beast will be looking for this very machine. They will find it. We must have these systems in place to protect it when they do."

"For you, I will have it, Youss. But only for you. Consider it done."

"Good, thank you," said Youssef. "Now where are the two operators?"

"You mean Massoud and Javeed? They're in the simulator. You'll like this, you haven't seen it yet."

By this time they were standing on a catwalk above the factory floor. At least 60 men were working on the PWS-13 units still under construction. The sound of drills, riveters, and metal saws filled the plant. The floor was a beehive of activity. Kumar turned and walked off the bridge.

"Come with me," he said. "The simulator is behind my office."

They headed in the direction of the office — Kumar's base of operations, where he planned and oversaw the workings of Pacific Western Submersibles. From there they entered the simulator room. A large metal container, arranged on springs and cantilevered arms, was rocking back and forth as they entered. Kumar pressed a large red "stop" button on the wall, and the unit stilled. Then he opened a door in the compartment. Two young boys were sitting within, one of them holding a rectangular steering mechanism that controlled the direction of the unit in three dimensions on a screen in front of them.

Kumar made the introductions in their native Urdu. These boys were Massoud and Javeed, the two youths handpicked by the Emir to carry out his attack on the United States. They had been with Kumar for three weeks, logging many hours in the simulator, learning exactly how to handle and operate the sub in which they would carry out their mission. Now Youssef did his best to comfort and distract the boys with an account of how things were in their homeland, making up stories about Afghanistan as he went along.

Before long, he sighed and shut the door. "Why must they always be so young?" He turned and looked to Kumar. "Tell me about these children," he said. "What has brought them to this point?"

"Do you really want to know, Youss?" asked Kumar, hesitating. "It is hard enough for me, and I'm not the one pushing the buttons, so to speak."

"No, I do not really wish to know," Youssef sighed. He had been struck by the dull, lifeless eyes of these young *jihadists*. He knew that their stories would be sad, and much like the stories of thousands of other young men from his country. And though he wished it were otherwise, and that he himself didn't have to send these boys to their deaths, he knew that they had decided on their fates many months ago, when they joined the Emir. There would be nothing else for them. "I know that they wish they were dead, Kumar," he said. "I suppose that is all I need to know. If it were not this mission, they would find some other way to reach Paradise. We are not responsible for their deaths."

Kumar gazed long and hard at his mentor. He wondered how much of the speech was meant for him, and how much was meant for Youssef's own conscience. "But how many others will die in this war the Emir is waging, Youssef?" he asked quietly. "How many?"

"Very few," Youssef replied casually, shaking off the gloom that had engulfed him for a moment. "This will be an economic blow. It will fracture the nation's economy, and we will take advantage of that. This is a situation created by the Emir. If we hadn't taken the job, some other group of terrorists would have. This event was cemented when the Semtex was stolen in Libya. We are not responsible for what will unfold, Kumar. None of us are. We just have advance notice. We will take advantage of it. But we are not responsible."

"I am not sure, Youss," Kumar said softly. "Do you really want to be involved in something like this? Is this really who we are? Who you are?"

"Look at it this way. We stand to make billions because of this deal. Because we know what is coming. That money will be used to build schools, homes, and hospitals in Afghanistan. That I will promise you. Thousands in Afghanistan will live, and just a few Americans will die. Weigh the scales, Kumar, and calm your conscience. Have you done as I asked, and liquidated our holdings here?"

Kumar looked a little glum. "It's done. The money is already in escrow accounts. It closes tomorrow."

Youssef knew that selling this business, along with the real estate it covered, was painful to Kumar, even as leaving the Karachi Harbor had been so many years ago. "Kumar," he said, "when we are back home you will have a business many times this size. We will buy the whole inner harbor in Karachi."

"I know, Youss, I know. But I have built an organization here. I have friends, and contacts, who are close to me. None of the employees even know that this is coming. It's difficult to justify."

"Look at the other side of the coin for a second, Kumar," replied Youssef. "You will become fabulously wealthy. Beyond your wildest dreams. You wait. In any event, everything that you know here, all of the knowledge that you gained from this place, you can load onto a bunch of DVD's. You can use it to rebuild what you have here, whenever you want."

Kumar nodded quietly, giving up the fight. He looked again at the man he thought he knew so well, and wondered for the hundredth time where Youssef was leading them, and why. He'd also begun to question why he and his friends followed this man so willingly, when he was taking them places that they did not wish to go.

AT THAT MOMENT, things were taking a decidedly somber turn for Indy and Catherine. Indy was breathing heavily, fighting the overwhelming panic that accompanied his claustrophobia. The lights had been out for more than 12 hours now. The room was becoming stuffy. They had no flashlights

— those had been in the belts and packsacks, which Dennis confiscated when he found them. They had but one cigarette lighter for light, and they were trying to use it sparingly. They had no food or water. The room was getting warmer, and they were both starting to ache with thirst. Catherine, for her part, was exhausting herself with endless mental calculations. Even if Devil's Anvil was a major artery for the Asia-to-America heroin trade, it might be used only once or twice a month. The dealers would have to wait for a large shipment to arrive, in Vancouver or some spot up the coast, load it into a van, drive it to Fernie, and then take it south to the mine. It wouldn't be a daily affair. Maybe not even a weekly one. Catherine thought that they could die of thirst in less than three days. So far she'd kept those calculations to herself. There were more immediate concerns for her to deal with. Indy was silent most of the time, fighting the demons of claustrophobia. Catherine tried to help when she could, but she didn't have much experience with claustrophobia and wasn't entirely sure how it could affect someone so dramatically.

"Would it help if you talked about it?" she asked quietly.

"Yeah, maybe a bit," replied Indy. "Maybe." Her voice had a soothing effect, coming from just a few feet away in the coal-black darkness. They were underground, deep beneath Sawtooth Ridge, so there was no stray daylight to find its way through the cracks. Indy found that anything even remotely soothing was a welcome relief, and thought that it would probably be a good idea to continue talking.

"I wasn't even 25 years old," Indy began. "Just a kid, really. I was hot on the track of a large network of East Indian dealers. It was shaping up to be a major bust, and I was able to use my Toronto experiences with similar gangs to perfect advantage. I knew the lingo and the culture. But I got made."

"How?" asked Catherine.

"A major buy was taking place on a large farming property up the valley. A huge buy. One of the purchasers recognized me. He and I had crossed paths in my Toronto days. Within a second someone had slapped cuffs on me. Someone kicked me in the groin, and once I was on the ground, someone else kicked me in the ribs a couple of times. Hard. I had a couple of hairline fractures. So I was on the ground, in a lot of pain, wondering what would come next."

"I don't even want to ask," came the disembodied voice from a few feet away. "But tell me."

"Things got ugly after that."

"They weren't ugly already?" she interrupted.

"Not in relative terms. Someone pulled out a gun and fired three or four rounds at me. Amazingly, I only got nicked by one bullet. Flesh wound in my leg — not that big a deal, although it hurt like hell and scared me even more. The leader of the gang got pissed with the shooter and told him he'd stuff the gun up his ass if he fired one more shot. Then he said that because I had betrayed the brotherhood, or his brothers, or whatever, my punishment should be a little more dramatic. A warning, he said, to anyone else inclined to undercover work in an East Indian gang."

Indy paused for a second. The total darkness was wearing on him, and the air was getting close. He wondered if talking was using up their small supply of oxygen too quickly. It was hot, and he knew he was perspiring heavily. Catherine reached over until she found him, and put a hand on his knee.

"Go on Indy. I think it'll help you if you tell me."

"I'm not so sure about that. But anyway, we were on a farm up the Fraser Valley — a fruit farm of some sort. A trench had been dug for some culvert work that was in progress. So the gang leader says, 'Drop him in the ditch.' There I was, on the ground, in excruciating pain from the bullet wound and everything else. I was still handcuffed. I was kicked and rolled over to the edge of the trench. Then they gave me a few more hard boots to my head and chest, and I fell over and hit the bottom of the ditch with a nasty crunch. To this day it feels like I must have fallen more than 20 feet. I think I lost consciousness. When I came to, my head was soaked with blood — I could feel it dripping down my face. Then they started to shovel dirt on top of me. Do you have any idea how much that hurts Catherine?"

Catherine slowly shook her head back and forth in the stygian blackness, then remembered that he couldn't see her and answered. "I don't think so. I don't know if I want to know."

"It's pretty extreme. But the worst of it is clawing for air. And when you can't get it, the certain knowledge of death."

Catherine realized that he was having quite a bit of difficulty recounting the experience. She reached for his hand and found it, wondering now about the wisdom of 'talking about it.' She gave his hand a little squeeze and waited.

"Just imagine it, Cath," he continued. "Clogs of dirt and gravel in your throat, as more and more dirt and rocks are shoveled down on top of you. And all the while those hideous bastards were laughing. They wanted to do it slow. I heard them say, 'Give us a better show.' Oh God, Catherine, I get sick just thinking of it."

"Well somehow you must've been rescued. I mean, here you are," she answered.

"Yeah. The neighbors had heard the gunshots. They thought they heard someone screaming. I guess that someone was me, but I don't remember doing it." He squeezed her hand and was silent for a moment.

"Go on," Catherine urged.

"Someone called 911, and even our primitive computers back then were able to cross-reference the location to a place where we had an undercover operation going. Dispatch sent a couple of PC's. There was some gunfire, another officer was slightly wounded, and most of the gang was rounded up. Some of them are still on the rock pile, 20 years later, murderous bastards that they are."

"How'd they find you?" Indy's narrative was beginning to make Catherine nervous. His fear was contagious. She also had a very clear mental picture of what he had gone through. Suddenly the walls seemed to be pressing in on her, too, cutting off her air.

"The police dogs did. I think I was 90 percent gone by the time they found me. I heard the voices, saying, 'Holy shit, there's a guy down here. He looks hurt bad. Holy shit. It's Indy. Call a bus. Get a bus fast.' That's all I remember. I woke up a couple days later at Vancouver General. I had a bad case of pneumonia — a couple of fractured ribs had punctured a lung when I hit the bottom of the trench. I had a badly infected thigh wound and a severe concussion. Physically I was OK in a few weeks. I was out of the hospital in ten days, and back on the job in 12. But psychologically… well, that wasn't so straightforward."

"What happened?"

"I was plagued by nightmares. Had them almost every night. Every single damn night. And in the middle of the day I would drop into this weird state where I was experiencing the whole thing all over again. I thought about it obsessively, and I started getting panic attacks. In the middle of a meeting I would suddenly feel like I was suffocating. It was really awful; I slept without any sheets or blankets for awhile. The weight of them felt painfully heavy, like they were crushing me."

"Did it get any better?" Catherine still held Indy's hand in her own, and gave it another small squeeze.

"A bit. The local shrinks were saying I had Post-Traumatic Stress Disorder. Not a particularly hard diagnosis to make. They put me on meds for awhile, but they didn't do anything, so I stopped taking them. Then I went to counseling for the better part of a year — that may have helped, marginally. The only thing that really helped was the passage of time. Gradually, over the years, things started to settle down."

He paused for a moment, taking a deep breath. "Now with this bullshit, I'm right back there. Catherine, you have no idea how absolutely paralyzing this is. I feel as though I'm in my own tomb, like I'm going to die here, slowly and painfully. It's terrible. The fact that it's drug dealers again…" His voice broke a little.

Catherine didn't say anything. If deliveries only came through the mine once a month, they may very well be locked up in their own tomb. It wasn't a nice thought.

32

BY THE NEXT DAY, Khasha's anxiety over Turbee's disappearance had turned to fear, and by the day after that, to panic. The police weren't interested, and her coworkers weren't nearly as upset as she was. Relax, they told her. He's worth $80 mil, more or less. He's off in Hawaii on vacation. But Khasha knew that Turbee wasn't prone to sudden trips. To get to Hawaii you had to fly. To do that you had to negotiate airports and security, and she couldn't fathom Turbee doing that alone. Something was very, very wrong.

Every few hours she called the police, but there were no developments. The switchboard operators were starting to sound pissed off. Their answers were becoming shorter and more impatient. No. No Hamilton Turbee had shown up. Perhaps that was good, she thought. At least it meant that he wasn't rotting in a cell somewhere. She turned to the hospitals next. There were dozens within the District of Columbia, from Walter Reed to the Children's National Medical Center. Some refused to give her any information over the phone, and these she visited in person throughout an increasingly frustrating and anxiety-laden day. Turbee was a gentle soul with a quirky sense of humor, and tremendous gifts. But he had a history of depression, and after seven days of who-knew-what, with the idiotic standoff over the *Haramosh Star,* and a frothing Dan firing him in front of the entire TTIC staff, thoughts of suicide might not be far off. She was terrified that when she found him, he would be either dead or beyond help.

It was 4PM when she arrived, bone weary and desperate, at the receptionist's desk at Saint Elizabeth's Hospital. It was the twelfth DC hospital she'd visited that day.

"Hamilton Turbee? No, never heard of him." The efficient clerk look up and down a computer screen, then ran a search. "No such person here, miss."

"He's in his mid-20s, blond, and very thin," pressed Khasha. She placed a photograph on the counter.

"Well, a lot of people are. He isn't here, miss. And in any event, this is a psychiatric hospital. We deal primarily with mentally ill individuals who are in trouble with the law. Does your friend fit that description?" Without waiting for an answer, she picked up the picture and inspected it. "Doesn't look familiar to me, but I don't go back in the wards too often. There are safety issues. Can get dangerous, you know. We have some very difficult patients in here." She sternly straightened her glasses and shifted her gaze back to the computer screen.

Khasha pulled a face at the receptionist's self-importance. "Can you show it to a guard? He's been missing for seven days. Maybe he just came here today?"

In response, she received the same question that she'd heard from dozens of other receptionists, clerks, and various law enforcement personnel. "How do you know he's missing?"

At that instant an armed guard came down the hallway. Khasha whisked the picture off the desk and held it in front of his face.

"Has this individual been admitted to this hospital? Hamilton Turbee?" she asked tremulously.

"Yup. That's the guy who came over from PSA 706 six days ago. Don't know about no Hamilton Turbee. That's our John Doe #17. He's curled up in a ball in the corner of his cell." The guard sniggered. "The way he's curled up makes him look like a small bag of flour. This guy's really over the top."

"Oh my God," breathed Khasha. "Can I see him?"

"Nope. Against hospital policy. You can't tell with guys like this. One minute they're curled up like a puppy, the next instant they've killed somebody. He assaulted a police officer. In fact, several police officers. He's listed as dangerous. He has eight or ten criminal charges against him already. Sorry, you can't see him other than during visiting hours, which ended a couple of minutes ago."

"He did what? He assaulted…?"

"Yeah. Police officers, multiple times. This guy is a criminal. He's criminally insane. That's why he's here."

"No way," said an astounded Khasha. She couldn't imagine Turbee assaulting any creature, let alone a police officer. "Please, please let me see him."

"Nope."

"Please."

"No. Rules are rules."

"OK," said Khasha. "Can you give me a moment?" The guard shrugged his shoulders, unconcerned, and Khasha pulled out her cell phone, scrolling through the numbers she'd dialed in the past few days. Finally she found what she was looking for and pressed the call button.

"Henessey van Rijn," came the professional response at the other end of the line. "How may I direct your call?"

"Mr. Turbee's office, please," said Khasha. She waited a moment as the call was connected.

"Mr. Turbee's office," came the second, efficient but friendly reply from James Turbee's receptionist. "How can I help you?"

Khasha gave a brief description of who she was and what had happened, and how it appeared to have caused Turbee's present situation.

"Ah, yes, you're the young lady that called a few days ago. Please hold for a moment. Mr. Turbee is here, but in a meeting. I'll interrupt. This is something he would want to know about."

The phone was switched over to pleasant hold music. Vivaldi, thought Khasha with approval. Very classy. She waited for less than a minute.

"James Turbee here," came a man's voice. Powerful, she thought. Again Khasha explained the situation, including the purported firing by Dan, and Turbee's apparent present condition, in a hospital that by and large housed the criminally insane.

"How is he at this moment?" asked the elder Turbee.

"I don't know, sir. The guard tells me that he's in the corner of his cell, drawn up in a fetal position. They won't let me see him."

"Khasha, did you say that he's at Saint Elizabeth's? That institution is for the treatment of psychiatric issues of people who are in trouble with the law. What on earth did he do that was criminal?"

"They said something about him attacking police officers," she replied.

A few seconds ticked by in silence. "Hamilton? Attack a police officer? No way. Look, please stay there, miss. I'm about half an hour away."

Khasha advised the receptionist that John Doe #17's father was coming, and that she was going to wait for him.

"I really don't care if the Pope is coming. It's after hours. Period," the receptionist said perfunctorily.

TWENTY-FIVE MINUTES LATER, James Turbee stepped through the door. His appearance differed profoundly from that of his son. He wore a Savile Row suit, perfectly cut, with a silk shirt and tie to match, was tanned and polished, and had elegant graying hair; in short, he turned heads wherever he went. The man exuded power and class. He was the managing partner of Henessey van Rijn LLP, a legal conglomerate that had offices in many of the world's capitals. The firm had more than 500 partners, 1,000 associates, and a total payroll for almost 3,000 individuals. James was one of the men in charge of keeping them all in line. He was 65, and had made his career as a litigator, but drifted into firm management in his mid-50s. He had a penchant for it. By the time he was 60, he ruled the legal behemoth with a will of iron. He traveled continually, visiting the many branches of the firm, cutting deals, acquiring more law firms, and fighting competitors for clients. Few saw him the way he was at this moment — a concerned and protective father.

After briefly introducing himself to Khasha and getting the details of the situation, he approached the front counter. "My name is James Turbee. I hear you have my son in here. I want to see him." He caught the receptionist directly in his steely gaze.

"I'm sorry, sir, but it's past visiting hours. You can come back tomorrow, if you wish," replied the receptionist. She turned back to her computer screen, which displayed the latest Microsoft product designed to reduce efficiency to zero, Spider Solitaire. As she busied herself moving the cards around the screen, the elder Turbee pulled out his cell phone and called his office. After being given a telephone number, he made a second call. He stepped briefly outside to make this one. Within a few minutes, he stepped back inside and approached a confused Khasha.

"Watch this," he said quietly. "It could be entertaining."

No sooner had James finished making this remark than the telephone beside the receptionist began to ring. She took her hand off the cursor, frustrated that her strategy for the next card play had been interrupted.

"Saint Elizabeth's Hospital, how may I help you?" she asked. There was a sudden change in her body language. Her posture straitened and the tone of her voice became infinitely respectful. "Yes sir. Yes sir. Immediately sir. Yes. Yes." She put down the telephone, white faced, and said to James, "Come with me, sir."

Khasha followed them into the wards. A guard joined them as they walked through the doors. "How did you do that?" she asked.

"The chain that owns this place is a client of the firm. I know the President of the chain reasonably well. So well that I have his personal cell number at my office. That's who just called. Knowing him, that last conversation was probably spiced with profanity and vigor. She may be out of a job as we speak." James straightened his tie proudly, and stood a bit taller. Khasha just smiled at his posturing.

The receptionist led them through a series of hallways and a large common room. Khasha had never been exposed to severe mental illness or psychoses. To see men mumbling to themselves in corners, demonstrating severely obsessive-compulsive behaviors, talking to nonexistent people, playing imaginary golf, and painting imaginary paintings was chilling. She moved a little closer to the older man and the guard as they passed through the room, down two floors, and through more doors and hallways. Finally they arrived at Turbee's cell. He was still curled up in a little ball on the floor, his knees clutched tightly to his chest.

Khasha looked at the young man lying on the floor. An IQ that was off the Richter scale, but he'd never ridden a bike. No driver's license. No friends. No girlfriend. "Poor little guy," she murmured.

James was likewise moved by his son. He approached the boy, who appeared oblivious to his presence, and shook him. "Hambee, Hambee, it's me. It's Dad. How are you doing?" He lifted his son up to a sitting position. "Say something, Hambee. How are you?"

Turbee winced and moaned with pain, turning his face into his father's chest, but said nothing.

"Hambee," James repeated, reaching down and hugging his son. "Hamilton, how are you doing? Talk to me. I need to know what you need."

After some more gentle shakes, Turbee finally managed to look at his father through glazed and bloodshot eyes. He moaned but said nothing.

"Hamilton. It's me. It's your dad. Speak to me, son. Please."

After a few more attempts, Turbee finally spoke. "I'm bad, Dad. Bad. I've messed up TTIC, the Armed Forces, the President, and just about everyone else. I deserved what I got."

"Don't think so, kiddo. Here, I have some meds for you." James reached into his pocket and took out a handful of pills. He had carried extra medication for Turbee ever since the boy had been diagnosed. He never knew when it would be necessary, and James liked to be prepared when it came to his only son. He looked up and motioned to the receptionist. "Water. Now please." It was not a request, but an order from a man used to giving many orders, and expecting to be obeyed. She went scurrying down the hallway, looking for a washroom.

"You're hurt, aren't you, son?" he asked gently. "Tell me where. What have they done to you?"

Turbee was glassy eyed and disoriented. But his father's voice was a form of medication in itself, and his brain was finally starting to kick in. "Ribs, I think. Bunch of them are broken. My face hurts. Arms, here," he said, pointing to enormous black, red, and blue marks on his forearms and sides. There was still caked blood in his hair, and he had an enormous black eye from one of Ziggy's punches. "Burns," he added, point to the marks from the taser.

The receptionist came running back with a dirty cup filled with water. Turbee gulped down the pills. His father turned to the receptionist.

"You threw him in this cell in this condition?" he almost snarled.

"I'm just the receptionist, sir," she replied, quavering.

"We're leaving now. The three of us. Turbee, can you walk? Here, lean on me. It's a long trip to the parking lot — let me help you."

James Turbee led his injured son out of the maze that was Saint Elizabeth's Hospital. The guard started to protest, saying that Turbee had assaulted a police officer, and was due in court. James gave the guard his card, and a cold hard stare. The guard backed off. It was decidedly unusual, but the President of the hospital had called, and whoever this character was, he was obviously not someone to be trifled with. And all things considered, the guard told himself, the kid really didn't look all that dangerous or menacing. James signed some forms at the front desk, and then he and Khasha gently put Turbee, wrapped in a blanket, in the back of his dad's SUV.

During the ride, Turbee pulled himself together just long enough to insist that they stop by his apartment to pick up some of his computers. When the hardware was safely ensconced behind the seat, he lapsed once again into his semi-comatose condition, sleeping for the rest of the drive south to the family home.

33

BRAMBLETON NARROWS was the huge cliffside manor that served as James Turbee's home away from the boardrooms and airports. With its beautiful oak-paneled rooms and stunning views of Chesapeake Bay, it was the perfect place for Turbee's rehabilitation. And it was amazing how much they accomplished in one day. Doctors of all specialties were called in for him — orthopedic surgeons, neurologists, psychiatrists, and psychologists, to start. He was taken to a posh local clinic, where he was x-rayed, MRI'ed, and CAT scanned. The verdict was six broken ribs, a pneumothorax, severe contusions to his forearms, concussion, a fractured nose, a large laceration in his right eyebrow, and a total of eight taser burns. Fortunately, there was no brain damage, at least not that any of the neurologists could see. Kathy, Turbee's teaching assistant, was called out of retirement and brought to the manor to take care of him. An attempt was even made to bring his mother back to Brambleton Narrows, but she was drunk and busy spending the spoils of her 25-year relationship with Turbee's father.

At the end of the busy day, Kingston came to visit. In Turbee's absence, he had revisited the issue of the *Mankial Star/Haramosh Star* transfer. He too felt that the SEAL team had, somehow, missed the Semtex. He too was disquieted by what had happened to Turbee. And, after days of searching, Kingston had found a gem. A second set of satellite photographs.

"How're you doing, bud?" asked Kingston. Word of Turbee's scene with Dan, and the following assault, incarceration, and sojourn at Saint Elizabeth's, had spread rapidly through the Intelligence Community, egged on by Khasha calling almost everyone she knew. Even the President had heard about it. No one liked it.

"I'm feeling better already," Turbee answered, glad to see his friend. "My chest is still real sore. They told me I have six broken ribs. I'm not allowed to laugh. Can't watch the Simpsons. And my nose is sore. It's broken too. The headache's starting to go away, and I can get around a bit by myself now that I have support. My dad's got a bunch of people here looking after me. Khash is here too. All in all," he added, "it's not so bad."

"When are you getting back to TTIC?" asked Kingston.

"I'm not sure I'm going back," Turbee answered. "Dan Alexander fired me, you know."

"I know," responded Kingston. "Actually, we've all been talking about that." By 'talking' Kingston meant the nonstop multi-party multi-mode electronic buzzing that had been going on within the Intelligence Community since the firing incident. Khasha had single-handedly made sure that everyone she talked to knew exactly what Dan had done, and how. "You were appointed to TTIC by a Senate subcommittee," Kingston continued. "Only they can fire you. Not that politically ambitious and useless blowhard they made the boss over there. This isn't done yet. And don't worry, we've got some people working on it. Anyway, I've got something for you."

"What?"

"A second set of images."

"Images?" repeated Turbee.

"Yeah. Satellite images. A second set of images, taken by a KH-12. On one edge of the images you can vaguely see the *Mankial Star* and *Haramosh Star* linked together. Nowhere near the clarity of the ORION images, but still, a second set."

Turbee grasped the significance of the statement immediately. A second set, from a different angle. If the two sets could be combined, theoretically, they should result in more clarity. He started babbling questions and answers about the possibilities, almost before Kingston had finished speaking. The conversation kicked up to a higher speed, and Turbee's voice rose in his excitement.

"How many images?"

"Another four, but two of them are so distorted as to be almost completely useless," responded Kingston.

"It's still additional information." Turbee's mind was quickly cataloguing all the different ways they could use this new find. "We should be able to sharpen the images we have. Maybe we'll get a clearer overall image of what was going on there," he said.

"I agree. Here they are," said Kingston, handing a CD over to the young man.

"Thanks. Great," replied Turbee. "Do you have the canned programs that you use for image sharpening?"

"Yup," said Kingston, handing Turbee a second CD.

"Thanks."

"Some of that stuff is pretty sophisticated. You may need help using some of the programs," warned Kingston.

"Yeah, I probably will. But I spent a lot of time with these types of programs when I was doing work for Google, updating their maps. I even found new ways to clarify images. I should be okay."

"Good. Let me know how you make out, Turb, and if you need any help. Hope you get better soon."

Kingston left, and Turbee went to work.

He spent the next day playing with the pixels of the seven images he already had — the three old ones from the ORION's, combined with the four new ones from the KH-12's. The programs turned out to be much trickier than he'd expected, and he telephoned Kingston at least half a dozen times. Their conversations spiraled into wild technical discussions of Fourier and Langrangian Transforms, multi-dimensional surfaces and structures, and other things that only mathematicians talk about or understand. And gradually, keystroke by keystroke, mouseclick by mouseclick, the images became clearer. It never occurred to Turbee that, in threading through this exercise, he and Kingston devised new techniques for image manipulation that, if marketed appropriately, could gain them fabulous wealth. His mind simply didn't work that way. He did what needed to be done to solve the problem at hand, and had very little use for anything beyond that.

Two nurses, the doctor, the psychologist, and Kathy, all of whom had been tasked by James with overseeing Turbee's recovery, were dismayed at his persistence in solving the image problem. He needed rest, they said. He needed to talk about his experience, share, open himself to healing... he needed physiotherapy, psychotherapy, and hot chicken soup. Turbee ignored them all. Sailing a boat in uncharted mathematical seas was all the therapy he needed. Against the advice of his various medical advisors, and to their immediate chagrin, Turbee got his teeth into the mathematical problem and found it impossible to rest or sleep until he had solved it.

At 3AM, almost 36 hours after he started, and going on almost no sleep, Turbee found what he was looking for. Kingston had helped a lot, but Turbee had an instinctive grasp of the algorithms used for clarifying obscure images, and had worked on his own to improve the old techniques to make them more efficient. Now he realized that his initial presentation, convincing though it had been, had lacked image clarity. His audience had squinted to see the cantilevered arms connecting the *Mankial Star* and *Haramosh Star.* They were there, but to the untrained eye, detail had been lacking.

What Turbee was able to do, using the second set of images and various pixel manipulation programs, was create a new set of images that showed better perspective. He placed these new images on the largest screen he had, a 61-inch flat panel. He ran them through a series of form-sharpening algorithms, and then again through a series of multi-dimensional pixel-smoothing algorithms. He mapped the images into a color program that assigned colors on the basis of temperature. Ultimately he was able to combine aspects of all seven satellite images into three super-composite pictures.

What the revised images showed was remarkable. There were definitely two ships — one 75 or 80 feet in length, and the second maybe three times as long. The satellite positioning showed that they were resting side by side near the Maldives, off the southwestern coast of India. The new pictures showed two slender arms connecting the two ships and, between them, third and fourth rails running from one ship to the other. In these new images, some of the large bolts in the connecting structures were actually visible, as were many of the fire extinguishers, smaller winches, and anchor chains on the ship decks.

The clarity he had achieved was astonishing. In the first frame, the center rail mechanisms were clearly visible, as were the three men pushing what appeared to be a large load of some kind from one ship to the other. The second frame showed the bundle almost on board the larger ship. In the third frame the center rail mechanisms were absent, and the two outer arms no longer connected the two ships. The frames revealed a sequence that left little to the imagination. The two ships had been temporarily connected to one another, and at least one package of considerable bulk had been transferred from the smaller ship to the larger.

These details provided a nice backdrop for Turbee's most spectacular find thus far. Careful inspection revealed that the bulky package in the first and second frames was in fact a pallet, upon which there appeared to be regularly shaped brick-like objects. Across the top of each label was the word "SEMTEX." Across the bottom, "PARDUBICE CZECHOSLOVAKIA."

IT WAS A SOMNOLENT September afternoon at TTIC. Everything had come to a standstill after Turbee left. A sullen resentment toward Dan Alexander had been building in the office, especially when word got out about the attack on Turbee and his subsequent incarceration. On Dan's order and in Turbee's absence, most of the brainpower of the center was devoted to chasing shadow nukes, exploring tip after tip that led nowhere. First it was nukes in San Diego, then in New York. Then there was a rumor about a dirty bomb in downtown Los Angeles, or perhaps in Norfolk. Attendance was dwindling as those seconded to TTIC started to gravitate back to the agencies from which they had come. There was hushed conversation here and there, and only an occasional clicking of a keyboard or ring of a cell phone punctuated the heavy atmosphere of the room.

Then the telephone in front of George rang, breaking the silence. It was Khasha.

"How've you been, Khash? We're missing you around here," said George.

"Yeah, I miss you guys too. But I'll be coming back in with Turbee in a few minutes. This is your heads up. Turbee has refined those photographs of the *Mankial Star*-to-*Haramosh Star* transfer. Kingston found some KH-12 photos, and Turbee and he have been using the new data to sharpen up the photos that we had. Their new images are incredibly clear."

"Thanks, Khash," said George. "See you when you get here." He hung up and leaned over toward Rahlson. "Turb's back. This is going to be interesting."

George didn't have long to wait. A few moments later, a series of trumpet blasts echoed through the control room.

"What the hell?" exclaimed Dan, rising and glaring around the room. He looked up at the 101's. There stood Elmer Fudd, at attention, blowing into a trumpet. Smaller versions of Elmer appeared on the outer screens.

"L-l-la-ladies and gent-gent-gentlemen," Elmer stuttered. "We present th-three im-im-images, created by Turbee and Kingston!"

"Aw Jesus Christ," cursed Dan, more to himself than anyone else. He was still smarting from the dressing down he'd taken from the Senate subcommittee for firing Turbee, and wasn't in the mood for any foolishness.

Before he could react, however, the three revised images that Turbee had been working on appeared on the screens. There were some smiles, and even a few cheers. It took a few seconds for the content and implications of the revised images to sink in.

Rhodes leaned over to George. "Hey, George, look at these," he said, pointing to his computer screen, where he'd enlarged Turbee's images. "Look at the labels."

"Holy shit," said George quietly. "You can actually read them."

Rahlson had immediately noticed the same thing. "Dan," he said, "you might want to have a closer look at the 101's behind you."

Dan turned around and saw the three frames Turbee had found. "So what?" he asked. "Wait a minute, how the hell did Turbee get into the system?" He was furious, his face slowly turning a dark red. TTIC was supposed to be unhackable.

Rhodes spoke up. "Dan, Turbee pulled those off one of the ORION's and a KH-12 that's floating above the Middle East. He somehow combined the two and enhanced the image. Look at the labels."

"How'd he do that? He hasn't had access to the system for more than a week," said Dan.

George grinned. "Dan, you must have realized by now that Turbee can hack his way into anything, and he did refine most of the programming for this," he said, motioning to the room around him. "He could probably start a nuclear war by himself if he wanted to."

"If he hacked his way into the ORION's, he needs to be called to task on it," Dan said, defensively.

"For God's sake, Dan, please focus on the issue," Rhodes snapped. He was close to the end of his rope with the so-called director of TTIC. "Take a close look at the pictures behind you. Think, man!"

Dan did. "So?" he said. "A couple of boats hooked together. So what? We saw these two weeks ago. And it came to nothing."

Now George started to lose his patience as well. "The labels, idiot. Look at the labels."

"It's not just a couple of boats hooked together, Dan," said Rahlson. "One of those boats is clearly the *Haramosh Star.* The other is the *Mankial Star.* These are the same images we saw before, but Turbee's sharpened them up considerably. Kingston found some additional images from the same time frame, shot by one of the KH-12's. Turbee's used them to get clearer pictures. Look at the center frame. It seems to me that a bundle of something is being transferred from the small ship to the large one. It's obvious what's going on here, Dan. Turbee's found a way to make the evidence that much more clear. He had figured it out long before the rest of us could see it."

"Again," said George.

"Well that is just dandy for him," said Dan in his usual aloof manner. "But the SEALs went through the ship from top to bottom. They went through every single container. Every deck level. The engine room. The bridge. Not only that, but they did it with some of the most sensitive plastic explosive detection equipment that exists today. And THEY DIDN'T FIND ANYTHING."

"Danno," snapped Rahlson, who was close to shouting at this point. "You've got to accept the fact that the SEALs COULD have missed it. Yes, they're highly trained. Yes they're the best of the best. But there is a chance that they missed it. Either that or the *Haramosh Star* ditched the load before the SEALs got on board."

As the angry dialogue continued, Turbee quietly entered the room and sat down at his old workstation, between George and Rahlson. "Welcome back, kid," said Rahlson, pausing long enough to notice the youth sitting quietly next to him. Turbee's face was still swollen, and one of his eyes was blackened. He moved with obvious discomfort, but sat at his computer and began his work with absolute confidence. Dan lost the argument with Rahlson, George, and Rhodes, and stalked out the door. The other members of the team spotted Turbee, and the sound of desk slapping and applause began to fill the room. Almost everyone rose and gathered around Turbee's desk to welcome him back to the family.

With that, Turbee had officially returned to TTIC. Word spread rapidly through the Intelligence Community about the coup. Turbee was back, and he'd established that the Semtex had been transferred to the *Haramosh Star.* The SEALs had missed it.

IT WAS MIDNIGHT, Pacific Standard Time, when Vince led Jimmy Stalmach to the lowest deck on the *Haramosh Star,* and directed him to the hidden compartment. It was accessible only through a tiny trap door beneath one of the two gigantic MAN B&W engines. The inspection by the SEALs almost three weeks earlier had not, and could not have, found it. They would have had to take extremely precise measurements of both the outer and inner hulls of the ship to realize that the hull contained extra space. Even then, finding the way into the additional hold would have been close to impossible. The slender space between the two hulls at the aft of the ship, and its hidden entrance, was the pinnacle of KDEC's engineering achievements. Because of it, the Semtex had remained safely hidden throughout the aggressive and intrusive search.

Vince pressed a hidden lever in the wall, then another under the engines, and the well-oiled trap door slid open. Directly below the trap door was the open cockpit of the submersible, a PWS-12, manufactured by Kumar's facility in Long Beach. Normally the submersible was used for heroin runs; it had seen many stealthy trips through the coastal waters of western North America, navigating toward a predetermined nocturnal rendezvous. Due to the growing sophistication of coast guards, sonar, aerial, and even satellite surveillance, these moves were growing increasingly difficult. With the help of his engineers and the PWS-12 series, Yousseff had nimbly managed to stay one step ahead of both the law and his competition. The theme here was the same as it had been in the Indus River days, but more highly engineered.

This trip, however, was different. The load was much heavier than usual, and the trip much longer. There was also the small matter of the international manhunt that was under way to find the cargo that the submersible would be carrying. Both Vince and Jimmy were being paid spectacularly well for their efforts, but the money failed to lighten the mood of their mission. They both realized that the gates of hell would open at the final destination of the Semtex. Neither knew where that end would be. Neither knew if this would be the last time they saw each other; after years of working together, this particular mission seemed to be the end of the line for their partnership. Both men had known Yousseff for many years, and neither liked the darker turn that Yousseff's smuggling operation had taken. Both had strong reservations.

"How long will this trip take, Jimmy?" asked Vince, as the other was carefully lowering himself into the submersible's cockpit.

"Even at the speeds this thing can do, it will be a good five to six hours. Most will be underwater, and guided by GPS," responded Jimmy. "I'll be happy as a clam when this one's behind me."

Vince continued to peer down at the submersible, the years with Yousseff weighing heavily upon him. After he rescued him from the scene with Bartholomew's drunken and mutinous crew, Vince had taken the young Yousseff under his wing. He had been astounded at Yousseff's intelligence, and the rapidity with which he learned the ways of the sea. He had watched the young man grow and stretch, trying new and different schemes, technologies, and industries throughout the years. Thanks to that association, Vince was now far richer than Bartholomew would ever have made him, and had spoken to Yousseff many times of retirement. Each time, Yousseff had talked him out of it. Now, with a paycheck of more than $1 million, laundered and legitimate, he could retire and afford everything he'd ever wanted. Maybe this would be his last mission. He found himself hoping that it was.

"Everything in order down there?" Vince asked.

"It all checks, Vince. Time to close the cockpit and open the outer hull. I'll see you when I see you," Jimmy said, with his customary devil-may-care smile. Vince shook his head. He couldn't understand how the man could sit in that cockpit for so long, and with the addition of so much explosive packed in around him. He waved as the submersible's cockpit noiselessly slid forward and locked into place with a soft click.

Vince then activated a further series of hidden levers. The trap door in the floor of the *Haramosh Star* slid shut. As it did, four large sections of the outer hull of the ship began to slide open, creating an opening some 30 feet long and 15 wide, just ahead of the rudder of the ship. The compartment had been designed to take in water without affecting the ship's flotation or route, enabling the sub to start its journey in its natural medium. Slowly the submersible slid out of the large ship and dropped down below the hull. It rotated 180 degrees, hovering just below the *Haramosh Star* for a few seconds. Then it headed off in a north-by-northeast direction, making a good 15 knots.

Vince climbed back up to the bridge and ordered the first mate to head south through the Hecate Straight, toward Vancouver. He activated the pumps that would drain the water from the hidden chamber and breathed a sigh of relief. The Semtex was finally, after several weeks, out of his custody.

At this point the *Haramosh Star* was some ten miles northwest of the BC coastal city of Prince Rupert, which, in its turn, was nearly 500 miles north of Vancouver. The coastal geography north of Vancouver was rugged and mountainous, punctuated by long fjords and impassable mountains. The only way to get to Prince Rupert from Vancouver by motor vehicle was through an inland route — north to Prince George, and then 400 miles farther to the west.

Prince Rupert was the terminus of the Grand Trunk Pacific Railway, a northern trans-Canada line, now doing business as the Canadian National Railway, or "CNR." There was also a large coal terminal located there, which served as the storage area for the massive inland mines that delivered coal to the world. With China's ever-growing appetite for raw materials, the port had become a bustling place — very different from the sleepy days of the late Twentieth Century. It wasn't, however, Vince's destination. It was nowhere close.

The *Haramosh Star* headed south instead, toward the container terminal at Vancouver, where she was expected. Jimmy and the submersible headed northeast, about 50 feet below the water surface. His speed was 25 knots. The PWS people had done a lot of tweaking to develop a submersible that was able to reach that kind of speed. It would take him roughly six hours to reach his destination. By that time the *Haramosh Star* would be well on her way, and it would be almost impossible to connect her to the transfer that would take place. Should anyone be looking.

Had the submersible surfaced during the trip, she would have been in some of the most magnificent scenery in the world. She was headed up a long fjord known as the Portland Canal, which served as the border between British Columbia and Alaska. To the northwest lay an amazing view of the Misty Fjords National Monument, one of America's least-visited National Parks. No roads ran through it, and no towns or villages existed within its borders. Blue ice glaciers extended almost to sea level around the sub, and lofty waterfalls cascaded from thousand-foot cliff walls. The sub would travel more than 100 miles through such scenery — the entire length of the Portland Canal. Situated at the head of the Canal was the BC village of Stewart.

Stewart itself was more or less a friendly ghost town. Prior to World War I, it had boasted a population of over 10,000. At the time, several mines had been in production or development in the area, and word was spreading that Stewart was another Klondike in the making, with rich veins of ore just beneath the surface. But gradually the optimism had faded, the mines had closed down, and the development had petered out. Now the town was deserted. The current population of Stewart was less than 700, most of it devoted to tourism and fishing. It had become an important spoke in Youssef's operations, for just this reason.

When he estimated that he was about 50 miles up the canal, Jimmy brought the submersible to the surface. It was 2AM. There was a bright moon, and he could see the silhouetted shadows of the Bear Glacier peaks rising behind Stewart. He was only ten miles from Stewart when the sun finally rose. At that point being so visible made him nervous, and he decided to take the submersible back down. Early morning fishermen often traversed the canal, emptying crab traps and setting lines. There was no point in risking discovery.

A long series of wharves and pilings ran alongside the dirt road that left Stewart — hundred-year-old reminders of the boomtown days of yore. At a prearranged spot, at a prearranged time, measured almost to the second, Jimmy surfaced among them. His sub was three feet away from an ancient, but still sturdy, wharf. The glass cockpit of the submersible slid back, and two ropes were immediately tossed his way. Jimmy caught them and began to secure his sub to the wharf.

"Yo, Ba'al! Ba'al Baki! Good to see you. You too, Izzy," he said, smiling up at the two property barons. This mission's importance was obvious. Youssef had sent two men from his most intimate circle to attend to the reload.

"You too, Jimmy. Wish we could talk, but this one's too serious," said Izzy. "Let's get the reload done, eh?"

Izzy wore blue jeans, an old T-shirt, and a cap that had the words "John

Deere" written across the front. Ba'al wore blue sweat pants, an old plaid shirt, and a windbreaker. They had both been totally Canadianized, right down to their speech.

THE SLEEK *HMS JOHN A. MACDONALD* pulled up beside the *Haramosh Star.* Captain LeMaitre requested permission to board, which Vince immediately granted, given that the *Haramosh Star* was now in Canadian waters.

"Good morning, Captain," said Vince, without the slightest trace of anxiety. "What can we do for you today?"

"Aren't you a little off course?" asked Captain LeMaitre. "What's your destination? You're in the middle of nowhere."

"We are headed to Vancouver, sir," replied Vince.

"That being the case, what on earth are you doing next to Prince Rupert, north of Dundas Island?" asked LeMaitre suspiciously.

"I do realize we're in the wrong spot. But it's like this," said Vince, sweeping an arm over the containers sitting on the deck below him. "You have probably heard of my ship. She is the *Haramosh Star,* remember, the vessel that the American SEAL team intercepted off the coast of Sri Lanka."

"Yes, of course," answered LeMaitre. "We know what happened to your ship. That caused a hell of a political furor. But that doesn't explain what you're doing in the wrong spot."

Vince hung his head in mock embarrassment. "There was a lot of stress as a result of the SEAL incursion. I made a mistake. We were destined for Vancouver, but I became confused after the Americans boarded my ship. I thought we were destined for the new container port in Prince Rupert. We just figured out an hour ago that we weren't, and that what's left of my cargo has to go to Vancouver."

"OK," said LeMaitre. "Vancouver is that way. Around Dundas Island and then straight south through the Hecate Straits. Pull out your charts and I'll show you."

Vince dutifully pulled out a detailed map of the west coast of British Columbia. "You're here," said LeMaitre, pointing to the map. "Here's your bearing. This should be your route around the island. Have a good day." He walked past the damaged and opened containers, looked inside a few, shook his head, and then headed toward the stairs that connected the *HMS John A. McDonald* to the larger *Haramosh Star.* He prepared a brief report, and emailed it to the Vancouver office.

34

MAHARI WAS BESIDE HIMSELF. A fourth message. Four. He was officially a millionaire, more or less — there were now four Samsonite cases, each containing a quarter million big American dollars in cash. Along with that, his prestige and fame were escalating rapidly. Each news segment began with the statement, "This is Mahari Dosanj, reporting for Al Jazeera, Islamabad," and closed in the same manner. He was doing longer summaries as well, and was beginning work on an hour-long documentary about the experience. He had arrived, and was planning to take full advantage. Sure, it was a bad situation, and he wasn't interested in terrorism or *jihad*, but as long as there was money to be made…

For the rest of the world, the new message meant that the time frame had accelerated, and that the area in which the attack would take place had been narrowed.

> *...praise be to Allah and His foot soldiers. Give thanks to His prophet, Mohammed, and His soldiers of the jihad. Mighty are His works, and blessed be His name. After a perilous but courageous voyage, the soldiers are in place, even in the lair of the Great Satan, within the very walls of her house. The weapons of Allah are positioned, and the means of delivery has been secured, praise be His name. Within days the great terror will strike within the serpent's house. Within days, one of her great cities, a city full of abomination and wickedness, will be destroyed. The great and holy jihad will be taken to the underbelly of the Great Satan. A great and holy day for Islam is at hand. All warriors on the path of Mohammed — peace be upon you. Reach for the sword, and strike down the Great Satan in her moment of weakness...*

For everyone watching, there was one unanswered question. There were now four messages. Would there be a fifth? The only one who was truly hoping for another was Mahari. He was already a millionaire. A fifth message, and the accompanying fifth case of cash, would make him fabulously wealthy. He hoped there would be a hundred more.

YOUSSEFF LOVED to tell the tale of how Ba'al and Izzy became Canadian citizens. Legal Canadian citizens. Perfectly, legally, legitimately Canadian. There were, in fact, many Afghani and Pakistani people on Youssef's payroll who were either already legal immigrants or in the process of becoming so. This had happened because of a problem that started the way most of Youssef's problems started. He had too much unlaundered money lying around.

The issue had developed for Youssef in the early '80s. Leon, his Canadian contact, insisted on paying with an occasional suitcase of Canadian cash. While the money was definitely more colorful, it was also more difficult to launder or use. Canadian dollars went nowhere in Afghanistan and Pakistan. The money could be taken every now and then to the Caribbean, to some bank or other in the Caymans, but that was risky, and the banking charges were inordinately high. At that time, the Canadian and American governments had been catching on to what was happening with the banks in the Caymans, and had started pressuring the Caribbean governments to provide the names and sources of the cash that was deposited in their banks. For that reason, it was an option that Youssef had avoided unless he had no other choice.

Over the years, the Canadian money had started to accumulate. Youssef kept it stashed in a mini-warehouse rental establishment in an industrial suburb of Vancouver, but all that ever happened with it was that he required more space to keep the growing collection of suitcases. He rented first one unit, then two. At three he bought his own warehouse, for which he was able to pay a small down payment in cash. All the monthly mortgage payments were paid in cash. But it was getting awkward. He desperately needed a way to launder his Canadian dollars.

By this time in his life, Youssef had learned the three fundamentals of laundering drug money. First came placement — namely, moving the funds away from any direct association with the drug enterprise. Then came layering, or disguising the trail to foil any pursuit. The final phase was integration — making the money available again, with its occupational and geographic origins hidden from view.

It was the first and third steps, the placement, and then the integration, that were most difficult. He had solved the problem brilliantly in Afghanistan, Pakistan, and the USA. The Karachi Drydock and Engineering Company, the Karachi Star Line, the real estate and commercial ventures, and the submersible firm in California were all running so well that he hardly needed to intervene in their operation. Dollars were introduced into these companies in a thousand clever ways, always leading to apparently legitimate deposits. When the submersible business became too successful for comfort, Kumar had opened a corner store and service station business. Now Yousseff owned, through Kumar's companies, 50 different gas station/corner stores in southern California. It was easy to introduce illicit cash into the daily deposits of such a company. The key employees were recent immigrants from either Afghanistan or northern Pakistan, and business was well under control.

Youssef's problem in British Columbia was that he knew no one other than Leon, who was far too unreliable and unpredictable for a serious business relationship. He needed Pashtun tribesmen, loyal to him, involved in businesses in British Columbia. One fateful day in the early '80s, Youssef walked into the Canadian Embassy in Islamabad with a simple question.

"How does one become a Canadian citizen?" he had asked. In the course of discussing that particular question, Youssef found out about the "Investor Exception" that was part of the Canadian immigration policy. To his astonishment, if you could demonstrate a net worth of greater than $800,000 Canadian, and were prepared to put $400,000 in Canadian banking institutions for five years, you were basically in. All you had to do was put the money into an investment account and forego the interest. It was an absolute Godsend, and meshed perfectly with Youssef's business strategy. In no time at all, he had convinced the Embassy that two individuals, Ba'al and Izzy, were indeed wealthy people, sophisticated real estate investors, and entrepreneurs, and yes, of course they would put up the money. Of course they would establish businesses in British Columbia that would employ many Canadians and pay many, many taxes. It took less than two years. Now Ba'al and Izzy were Canadian citizens, and the placement problem of the laundering cycle had been solved.

Taking a page from Kumar's playbook, Ba'al and Izzy promptly started purchasing corner store/gas stations across the province and merging them to create a new company. These stores, especially those located at busy intersections, typically had high revenue and low profit margins. A typical stop at such a station might put $60 or $70 of revenue into company coffers. People would pay $50 or $60 for gas, then a little more for a drink, or a burger, or a carwash, or just a basic candy bar. Cigarettes? Even better, since most customers paid for those in cash. Many of their corner shops had a revenue in excess of $1 million a month. Much of the business was cash based.

Their mission became a relatively easy matter of folding illicit dollars in with regular business revenues, and making enriched daily deposits. They decided on a new name for the small but rapidly growing chain — instead of 7/11, they called the chain 24/7. The business grew rapidly, and branches sprung up outside of Vancouver, and in Kamloops, Prince George, Kelowna, and even Nelson. At the turn of the millennium they moved into Alberta, putting corner store/gas stations in Calgary, Edmonton, Lethbridge, and Red Deer. A store had just been purchased in Saskatchewan. Each store was managed by a Pashtun businessman in the process of becoming a "Canadian investor," pursuant to Canadian immigration policy.

Youssef watched it all grow with delight, and was entertaining the vision of drawing Kumar's stores northward, and Ba'al and Izzy's southward, to meet somewhere in central Oregon. Maybe they could even put the stores in Mexico, so that they were selling merchandise through a chain of stores along the entire western edge of the continent. He had created the perfect laundry machine. And it was making him even more money, with absolutely no effort on his part.

"WHAT THE HELL IS IT?" Ethan and his colleagues were asking themselves, as they stood around the finished product. The new device was sitting on a lift in the center of their shop floor. Halfway through its construction, someone had started to call it "the Ark" because of the way it was shaped, and the name had stuck. It had a base containing multiple layers of stainless steel, titanium, and molybdenum alloys. The base was elliptical, measuring 20 feet along the "x" axis and five along the "y." The same layered alloys made up the "walls" of the Ark, which were approximately six feet in height at each end, decreasing to two feet in height at the center. The base and walls were uniform in their thickness. Kumar had said that there must be no deviation from the blueprints. With the multiple layers of metals, the base thickness was approximately a quarter of an inch. It looked like an incredibly large saddle, made entirely of metal. The interior of the container was even more complex.

Protruding upward from the center of the base, into the open compartment inside the Ark, were five copper spokes, fanned up and outward. The requirements for the length of these spokes had been very precise. They originated from the bottom of the base, and were visible only if one was looking inside the device.

The "lid" of the container was detachable, but had to be handled very carefully, as any dents or scratches would throw off the design and make the Ark useless. The gradient downward from the edges to the central axis was a complex hyperbolic curve. The lid was made primarily of molybdenum, used at a variable thickness. The material was approximately one sixteenth of an inch along the edges, becoming uniformly thicker toward the depressed center, where its thickness was approximately half an inch. The molybdenum was covered with a thin layer of gold, which was only a few atoms thick along the edges and increased to a golden ridge more than an inch thick at the centerline of the lid. Underneath the molybdenum was a thin, uniform layer of copper. There were further layers of titanium, copper, nickel, and silver alloys. The whole thing had taxed the abilities of the best complex metal forming machinery that Cincinnati Milacron had ever made.

"What the hell is it, really?" asked Ethan, more to himself than to the engineers and technicians who stood around. "They said they were making some fancy machinery to try and communicate with whales, or dolphins." He looked at his chief engineer, his eyebrows raised in doubt.

"Dolphins, my ass," said the engineer. "That's just totally stupid."

"What did it end up costing?" asked one of the metalworking technicians.

"Almost $3 million," responded Ethan. "But Kumar said it was a cost-plus job. He made big bucks on this thing. And you know how much we're getting paid for it."

"To talk to bloody whales? And how the devil is this thing going to do that?" asked the chief engineer.

"I guess they plan to put some electronics inside of it," said Ethan. "I guess that probably explains the five copper rods. I just don't see it, myself." He straightened up and shook his head. "Whatever, we all made good money on the job. I really don't care what they do with it. Let's go to the lunchroom and have a beer to celebrate," he added. Kumar had pledged a bonus to the whole staff for working through the weekend to get the job finished, and Ethan wanted to take advantage of the extra money to reward his crew.

"I don't care if they waste it on a new type of marine toilet. Three million bucks is three million bucks. It's just crazy to have used it this way. There's got to be something more to it," said one of the men, as they filed out of the warehouse. They all nodded in agreement, then dismissed the matter, heading for the promised beer and food.

IN THE NORTHERN British Columbia village of Stewart, Jimmy was helping Ba'al and Izzy with the reload. He needed to stretch his legs, and enjoyed conversing with the friends he seldom saw. The Semtex slid out of the submersible easily, in what was a reversal of the *Mankial Star*-to-*Haramosh Star* transfer that had taken place two weeks earlier. Jimmy slid 150-pound lots of the Semtex onto the frontal scissors lift, and raised the lift so that it was level with the powered tail lift of Ba'al and Izzy's five-ton cube van. Each section of 150 pounds had been placed on mini-pallets that were fitted with wheels on the bottom, for ease of movement. Fifteen minutes, and the Semtex was sitting in the back of the van. They pulled some tarps over the load, threw a few tires over the tarps, and slid the van's door closed. The three of them rested for a few seconds, looking at the little submarine.

"What are you going to do with it?" asked Ba'al.

"Every sub that we use can now be controlled electronically. With GPS technology we can send it pretty much anywhere we want," replied Jimmy. "I have just enough fuel left to send her ten miles or so back down this channel. At that point, the hatches will open, and she'll sink to the bottom. It's plenty deep out there. No one will ever find her."

"But it cost a fortune to make it," Izzy protested. "Seems like a waste to me."

"We have dozens like her, Iz. In fact, this is an older model, a PWS-12. Kumar is working on a PWS-14 at the plant down there in Long Beach. This one is expendable. She's served us well. It's time to scuttle her." He hopped back into the sub and turned it around. He fiddled with some of the controls and jumped out of the sub as it began to chug its way westward down the long fjord.

"Give me a lift to Smithers, gentlemen. I can catch a plane to Vancouver from there," he said, watching the sub disappear. "My job is done."

Ba'al and Izzy were happy to oblige. The three of them had known each other for more than 20 years, but because of the far-flung nature of Youssef's activities, seldom saw one another.

Ba'al got behind the wheel of the van. They had already decided that they would take turns driving. Youssef had been clear. They were to stop for nothing. One way or another, the authorities would be right behind them. The distractions that Youssef had planned would throw them off track a few times, but they would come again. The van couldn't make any long stops. Their orders were to fill up the gas tank, grab some food, and move. Take turns driving. Watch out when they stopped at weight scales. No stopping for a second longer than they needed to.

UNBEKNOWNST to the three, the entire scene had been witnessed by an old, worn-out alcoholic who made his home in one of the deserted Stewart houses next to the docks. Wharfdog Charlie, as he was known, had seen it all a few times before. A strange looking submarine would appear, material would be loaded with great haste onto a waiting truck, the submarine would disappear, and the truck would take the highway back to Meziadin Junction, and civilization. Wharfdog had mentioned it once or twice to the cops, but he had very little credibility, and the story usually fell into the pink floating elephant category.

"ARE YOU KIDDING ME?" Richard nearly shouted into the telephone. "You want to send me back on assignment? Now?"

He and Michael Buckingham were on speakerphone in the Embassy in Islamabad. Baxter and Admiral Jackson were on the other end of the line, calling from Langley. The head of the Middle East and Africa Bureau of the CIA and the DDCI, in the same office at the same time. Richard was definitely feeling uncomfortable.

"Why me?" Richard continued, astounded. "I just got back here. I was in Libya. I nearly got my ass shot off in the Sudan. I just found out that my closest friend was tortured to death. I'm tired, and dammit, I need a break."

"You're all we've got, Richard," said Baxter. "We've been complaining about this for years. We don't have nearly enough manpower in the Middle East. And besides, you grew up in Islamabad. You know the language, the land, and the customs. All the signs on this Semtex thing are pointing to narcotics connections, and it seems to be coming out of Afghanistan, and probably also Pakistan."

"You guys are the most powerful Intelligence Agency on the planet and I, little old depleted me, I'm all you've got? No way," responded Richard, cynically.

"Richard, there is no one else right now," Buckingham said, turning to him. "There's enormous concern that the Emir may have a nuclear weapon at his disposal, and all of our available agents are working on that, pretty much around the clock."

"We need you, Richard," Baxter broke in. "We need to know the origin of those damned messages on Al Jazeera. We know that they arrive at their station in Islamabad, pretty much prepackaged and ready to air. We know that they come care of the reporter who's airing them, but we need to know where he gets them. Other sources, and even the NSA, are suggesting that there's a massive strike in the offing. We don't know if it's nuclear or if it's connected to the stolen Semtex. It's definitely one or the other. Either way, everyone's feeling very uncomfortable about this. The Emir's messages are taunting. His confidence is unnerving. The President is damn worried about it. We need you to do this."

"Are you telling me that with a defense budget of I don't know how many billions of dollars, and with the avalanche of money the CIA gets each year, I'm the only person who knows the lay of the land in and around Islamabad?" Richard was shaking his head in disbelief at his superiors. "I'm it?"

"Yes, Richard. Your retention level is better than I thought. We have other assets, but they're all committed at the moment. You are the only available agent we have with the language and cultural knowledge." The Admiral's tone became more insistent. "You're going to the market area in Peshawar. That's where we think the messages are coming from. And you're going to follow the trail from there. No one has been able to do it yet, but we're counting on you to come through."

"We'll have your back, Richard," Buckingham told him. "You won't be operating solo. But when it comes to finding a lead guy for this particular role, you're it."

"Robert, you want me to squeeze the reporter of a high-profile outfit like Al Jazeera?" asked Richard. "Are you nuts? The media on that would be worse than when our SEALs half destroyed the *Haramosh Star!* We rough up a reporter and the entire planet will hear about it."

"We know, Richard. We know," said Baxter. "Of course you need to be discreet, and of course you can't go beating up reporters. But we know that that there's a big strike coming. There's a high probability that it will involve that stolen Semtex or be nuclear. Most of us think they're putting together a dirty bomb, either at a harbor or in a downtown core in one of our major cities. It may be another attack on some major buildings, with thousands of lives lost. We can't just sit on our asses here. We need to know who's behind this, so that we can try to stop it. The orders for this are coming from the top. We'll be deploying other resources, and there will be backup. But you need to do this, forthwith. And Richard, it's not a suggestion, anyway. It's an order."

Richard shook his head. "Come on, guys. This over-the-hill Navy fighter is all you've got? Shit, no wonder the world is going to hell. It's an order, and I'll do it, but you guys have got to get your asses in gear."

"Yes, it's a big problem," responded the Admiral. "We have a serious lack of resources in HUMINT. We have billions of dollars in toys and satellites and drones and such, but almost nothing on the ground. That's why Iraq went to hell after we arrived. That's the problem in Iran and, I might add, in most of the trouble spots in the Middle East. We're training people like crazy, but to get someone in deep cover takes years. That's why Goldberg was such a huge loss. That was a four-year mission. There's only one guy who can do this now, Richard, and it's you. Don't blame me that you grew up in Islamabad. Besides, you won't be on your own. The Embassy is behind you. Your new partner, Jennifer Coe, has a pretty good grasp of what's going on as well. And basically, all we're asking you to do is some detective work. Just find out who's delivering the messages to that reporter."

"Jennifer, huh," responded Richard. "Me and blondie against al-Qaeda. Sure, no problem. We'll just get right at it. Nevermind that neither one of us has any field training." He got up and left the room.

After he left, Buckingham, Admiral Jackson, and Baxter discussed the situation further.

"How sure are you guys about this?" asked Jackson. "He doesn't sound very dependable. And the way he left. You just don't do that. Is he on something? What kind of meds is he taking?"

"Don't know for sure," replied Baxter. "Ever since he splashed that Tomcat, apparently because of his vision problems, he's been on a downhill slide. And this thing with Zak is pretty awful. Those two grew up together. When Richard lost his parents he went to live with Zak and his parents in California. They were like brothers, and there's a rumor going around that Zak was Richard's main support system. When Zak went undercover, Richard's problems became a lot more obvious. He already had a problem with authority, but now he's become a bit of a loose cannon. He may be on drugs of some kind. We're not sure. But he's got a good heart. And dammit, we don't have anybody else."

"I think he's pretty messed up," said Buckingham. "Unfortunately he saw what was left of Zak's body at the airport, before Trufit took it to Tel Aviv. He totally broke down. And then, a couple of days ago, when the President read the coroner's report in his press conference, he got even more upset."

"Michael, is there really no one else?" asked Baxter.

"We have other people," Buckingham replied. "But they're all working on the nuclear threat. For obvious reasons, and on the advice of the director at TTIC, the President has given that priority. Pakistan has nuclear weapons. The nuclear threat seems to be originating from there. Everyone else is chasing various aspects of the same thing. All we need Richard to do is to find out how the DVD's are getting into the Peshawar marketplace. He knows that area better than any other agent we have. He doesn't need to do anything beyond that. He'll be solid when he needs to be. And Jennifer Coe is pretty good. She'll keep him in line."

"OK," said Jackson. "I guess he'll have to do. But after this, we should ship him off to a psychiatrist. I want to get him some help. It really sounds like this guy is coming apart."

"At the seams," said Baxter.

"At the seams," Buckingham agreed.

ONE HUNDRED FIFTY MILES to the west of the Islamabad Embassy, Zak had begun to feverishly scrape away at the decades-old mortar surrounding the iron grate, using the long screw he'd found. His fingers were bleeding as a result of the effort, but it didn't stop him. His left foot, now missing two toes, was sending waves of pain through his body. Zak had decided that Hamani's cauterization efforts were more for the additional pain they caused than for sealing wounds; his foot was bleeding heavily, and he was concerned that an infection was developing in the stub of the baby toe.

He'd been given a new roommate a couple days earlier — a fact that might have interfered with his plans for escape, under different circumstances. But the man was already missing one entire foot and one hand, and spent most of his time babbling nonsensically to himself in a corner of the small cell. He never caused any trouble, and Zak wondered if the man even recognized the presence of another human being in the room. In any case, he hadn't taken long to consider the danger of a roommate seeing his digging. Despite his robust psyche, Zak was concerned that he too would soon be talking to imaginary friends. The mental and emotional strain was almost more difficult than the physical pain, and combining the three made survival a chancy proposition at best. Through the haze of pain, Zak fought to maintain his self-discipline, and stubbornly continued to scrape away at the mortar, stopping every few minutes to brush the gravel under the straw that littered the floor.

35

"I SMELL POT."

"What, Cath? What'd you say?"

Indy had been dozing. The sound of Catherine's voice brought him back to the claustrophobic present.

The two of them were still imprisoned deep below Sawtooth Ridge, in one of the storerooms in Devil's Anvil. They had been there for more than 20 hours now. The air was stuffy. Both Catherine and Indy were severely dehydrated.

"Pot, Indy. Marijuana. It's faint, but I can definitely smell it."

"Well the marijuana room was just down the way," replied Indy. "There are probably a few molecules coming in underneath the door."

"I don't think so, Indy. This is more than a few molecules. This is pretty strong. I wonder if there's a passage that connects this room and the marijuana room. Maybe we should move some of this money around and see."

"I can smell it too, now that you mention it," replied Indy. "Why don't we see if we can hunt down the source. It's better than sitting here, waiting to die."

Catherine nodded, then caught herself. She flicked the BIC lighter on to look around. "Let's start with the far wall," she said. "We can move the money to the center of the room, to see what's back there."

The room was larger than it appeared initially, and the mountain of bills was impressive, but they set to work. The physical exertion relaxed Indy a bit, and Catherine was relieved to hear that he was grunting and mumbling to himself in Punjabi again, making the occasional joke. The smell of marijuana became stronger as they worked, and it wasn't coming from the doorway. Both thought that it must be coming from a shaft or tunnel entering the room from somewhere else, and worked together to move the masses of money back and forth, checking the walls and floor areas to test their hypothesis. Occasionally Catherine flicked on the lighter to give them bearings on the room.

"Yo, Indy, do I look as black as you? You're covered in coal dust," she giggled at one point, holding the lighter up to his face. His skin was darker than usual, streaked with sweat, and smeared where he'd rubbed his hands across his face.

"Yes, Cath, you're as black as midnight. But this ain't a makeup contest. Now let's keep moving this stuff around. I'm feeling an air current here, and it's got to be coming from somewhere."

They labored on for another 15 minutes before they found it. A small black opening, at floor level, measuring perhaps 30 inches high by 30 inches wide, in the very back corner of the chamber. They had moved a mountain of bills to find it.

"There's your passageway," said Catherine. "I think it probably goes to the marijuana room, given that smell."

"Yeah, I think you're right. And if we're lucky, that dumbo Dennis may not have realized that we opened all the locks. He may not have relocked the other rooms. If the tunnel goes there, you might be able to get out that way."

"Me?" gasped Catherine. "You want ME to crawl through that little hole to God knows where? Me?" She was holding the cigarette lighter at the entrance to the small ventilation hole, attempting to gauge its dimensions.

"Think about it, Cath. You're smaller, you're more athletic. You don't have an ounce of fat on you. You're not paralyzed with claustrophobia. You have a better chance at it than I do," replied Indy.

Catherine began to panic. "Indy, I don't know if I can do it. Not even a dog could crawl through there. You drag me on this God-forsaken mission, and we've been trapped down here, no light, no air, for God knows how long. Now you want me to crawl through a little hole at the bottom of a room at the bottom of an abandoned coal mine to go to some damn room full of weed. Indy, I — I don't know–"

"Catherine, I've had years of counseling to get over that incident with the Indian gangs up the valley. I'm having trouble enough in this room, so don't even get me started on what a tunnel like that would do to me. I can't do it. But one of us has to. You're the only other choice."

"Indy, I don't know–" she repeated, but he interrupted again.

"You can do it, Cath. Go back to basic training. Focus on the task at hand. Force everything else from your mind. I don't think I could fit through that hole anyhow. I know you can."

"Jesus, why did I ever become a cop?" she asked herself. "OK, but you need to be able to pull me back if I get in trouble. You've got rope. Tie it around my ankle. If I get jammed and call out, you have to pull me back. Promise?"

"Yes, Cath, I promise. And when we get out of this mess I'll make sure you get the promotion you deserve. This is above and beyond the call of duty."

Catherine sighed. "No it's not. Any member of the Force would do what you and I are doing. This is what the job is all about, I guess. Now tie the rope."

Indy reached for the 20-foot rope that Dennis had either not seen or not bothered to take when he forced them into the storage room. He secured the rope around Catherine's left ankle. She bent down and held the lighter at the entrance to the small tunnel again. Then she knelt down further, and stuck her head into the tunnel to peer ahead. Her heart was racing, and the walls of the tunnel were so close that she barely fit. She had to control her breathing.

"Dammit Indy, I hate this shit."

She plunged into the tunnel and began wriggling down its length. Five feet. Ten. Fifteen. At 20 feet the rope ran out.

"Indy, I don't see anything yet," she shouted back down the tunnel.

Indy thought of the configuration of the rooms. "Keep going, Cath. You've got to be getting close. But we're out of rope."

Catherine panicked. "Indy, I can't do this. Pull me back. Please."

"Cath, just try a few more feet. Please."

Catherine gulped. The walls were closing in. She couldn't breathe. Sweat was pouring off her. Then, just when she thought she really couldn't take it any longer, the tunnel widened. It entered the marijuana room at about two feet above floor level.

"Indy, I'm there. I'm in the marijuana room." She crawled out of the tunnel and walked gingerly toward the door. It opened when she pushed it. "And the door's unlocked. I'm out."

TOMORROW would be the day, thought Kumar. A day too awful to contemplate. A day that would end the lives of the two lads sitting with him, watching television. They were in a private suite of rooms adjacent to the Long Beach PWS manufacturing facilities. The two had spent the last three weeks of their lives moving from this suite to the simulator and back again. Kumar had driven them around some, and showed them the hot spots in Los Angeles — Hollywood, Disneyland, and various movie studios. Neither one had shown much interest in these things, other than stating that America was indeed the home of Satan. When not in the simulator or taking lessons from Kumar himself, they spent their time in prayer, and reading the Koran. They prayed five times daily, and the direction of Mecca was depicted by arrows on the floors in both the simulation room and the suite.

He had ordered pizza for them, on the assumption that teenagers on opposite sides of the globe were, in reality, not all that different. Wisely, he had chosen the vegetarian variety, supplemented by ample amounts of Pepsi. Before long Kumar, who had never married and had no children of his own, found himself becoming protective of Javeed and Massoud, physically and psychologically scarred as they were.

He knew that letting himself care was the worst thing he could possibly do. But Kumar found himself starting to like these wounded children. Did he really have to do this, leading the boys to their deaths? Eventually, though, he shook his head and gave himself a stern lecture. It wasn't his place to worry about things like that. Yousseff was right — there was nothing he could do to help these boys. They had already chosen their path. It broke Kumar's heart to see it. But Massoud and Javeed had their own demons, and the Emir and Yousseff had their master plan. Even if he tried to change things, Kumar knew that he had no chance against men like that.

JIMMY, BA'AL, AND IZZY had reached the Meziadin Junction and were headed south toward Kitwanga, in northwestern BC. They were still driving the old five-ton cube van. The Semtex was buried beneath several layers of tarps in the back. Four old tires lay on top of the tarps, and fishing and camping gear was scattered on top of that. "Fishing in the Charlottes" was the official cover story. There were coolers with ice and gutted fish in the back to cover their tracks, should they need to use the story. They even had fishing licenses. Took the company truck.

Ba'al had taken the first leg of what would be an 18-hour trip, driving from the northwest pole of the province to the southeast corner. After two hours of talking without pausing for breath, Jimmy had fallen asleep in the back of the van, exhausted from his long and stressful journey in the sub. Ba'al and Izzy were talking quietly, hoping to make the time go faster.

"You know what's amazing about this place, Izzy?" asked Ba'al.

"Tell me, oh wise one," moaned Izzy. "Is it something other than the women?"

"No. But compare this to the trip from Peshawar to Jalalabad. There are no guns in BC, or very few anyway. We don't fear for our safety here. We can live here for 50 years without anyone taking any shots at us. You have the same beauty as northern Pakistan, but no guns. No violence. If one person gets shot it makes provincial headlines. If a policeman gets shot it makes national headlines. Compare that to back home, with land mines, bandits, the Soviets, the Taliban, and the endless warring between tribal bosses. The crooked cops… ”

Izzy had to laugh at that. “Marak is totally honest. You just need to know who he actually works for.”

“I know,” Ba’al answered. “Here, though, Marak blows away three guys on the Vancouver docks and it’s still a story, almost 30 years later.”

They reached the Highway 16 junction at Kitwanga, and turned east. The highway, called the “Yellowhead” by the locals, extended to the Alberta border, although Izzy and Ba’al wouldn’t be following it that far. The scenery was once again spectacular, the road winding on an easterly course through the Hazelton Mountain range. Ba’al kept his speed just a few miles above the speed limit, going with the flow of traffic. “Don’t stand out,” Yousseff had told them sternly. “Not in any way.”

“Do you ever get lonely for home, Ba’al?” Izzy asked at length.

“Yes, of course I do. These mountains are beautiful to be sure, but nothing like the Hindu Kush. The river here is nice,” he said, motioning to the white water of the Skeena. “But you can’t drift down it, like the lazy Indus. And the weather is too damn cold. Inland here, 30 below zero in the wintertime. It’s madness. Yeah, lots of the time I pine for home. So does my wife. But a few weeks in Jalalabad is enough. I miss home, but when I am there, I want to be somewhere else.”

“Me too,” said Izzy. “Vancouver is fine for me most of the time. And we do live like kings. I don’t think I’d want to move back home, given a choice.”

It was 7AM when they reached the mountain town of Smithers, their first stop. They did everything they could to keep it short. “Pretend that the police are right on your heels,” Yousseff had said. “They are clever. They are looking for the Semtex. They will be unrelenting.” They filled up on gas, then went through a fast food drive-through. At the Smithers airport, Jimmy gave Izzy and Ba’al bear hugs. None of them knew when, or even if, they would see each other again. It was something they were trying not to think about too much.

GENTLEMEN, which areas face the highest probability of attack?” The President was in the Situation Room, now almost as famous as the Oval Office. He looked around the room at the people who’d been called to meet with him. Thirteen men were debating the problem. All men. Maybe that was the problem, he thought. No women. He wondered if a woman would have a different perspective. Maybe the answer.

As usual, Admiral Jackson was in the thick of it. “The NSA is picking up a lot of chatter from Egypt, Saudi Arabia, and Pakistan. Most of it from the Internet. Most of it highly encrypted. The bastards don't know we can read it. There are ongoing references to a nuclear or dirty bomb threat to one of the coastal cities. It all started with Goldberg's message. The stolen Semtex seems to be related, but no one can figure out how. I suspect a combination of the Semtex and a nuke. A radiological dirty bomb. They may bring the Semtex in one way, and the radioactive material via another route, and then combine them at the last moment."

"How bad would it be?" asked the President.

"Bad," replied the Secretary of Defense. "It could poison an inner city harbor and the surrounding buildings for hundreds of years. Depends on what they use. It could do what nothing else has done so far. If it came down in the business district of New York it would make Wall Street and every building for a dozen blocks around it uninhabitable."

"So which cities do we need to protect, Admiral?" asked the President. "Where are we looking?"

"You can go up and down both coasts guessing," Jackson answered, shaking his head. "I think the West Coast is more likely than the East, given that the *Haramosh Star* is due in Vancouver. Seattle, San Francisco, Sacramento, or maybe Los Angeles. If the stuff is coming north from Mexico, I'd say Phoenix, Tucson, Vegas, and maybe even San Diego would be the prime targets. Las Vegas would be an attractive candidate for any Islamic radical. Maybe some of the southern Texas cities, like El Paso, San Antonio, Houston, or even Dallas Fort Worth. Hard to say at this point. If they bring it through British Columbia somehow, maybe one of the cities in Idaho or Montana. Definitely hard to say."

"God dammit, we spend billions and billions of dollars on Intelligence and you guys can't tell us more precisely than saying this thing is probably going to land somewhere on the West Coast or in the Southwest?" demanded the Secretary of Defense.

"We can, in time. Right now we're half a step behind this thing, and we're having trouble getting ahead of it. We need to take protective measures. We need to go to Threat Level Orange for those areas. We need more eyes and ears than we have. And we need to alert the public about it as well. The Intelligence Community would welcome another hundred million pairs of eyes, quite frankly," responded the Admiral, somewhat defensively.

"Do you have any idea what it will cost to go from Yellow to Orange?" the President demanded.

"I have a fair idea," responded Jackson. "But I don't think you have much leeway here, sir. If this thing went sideways on us, and an inner harbor was polluted for a century, or a nuke went off in the middle of an NFL game, the cost would be infinitely greater."

The discussion raged for over an hour. The executive director of the NSA was called, as was Dan Alexander at TTIC, and the director of the FBI. Information was drawn, sampled, and analyzed, costs were debated, and solutions considered. At the end of the meeting word went out, by telephone, e-mail, television, instant messaging, and whatever else was on hand. The West Coast and the Southwest states were officially going to Threat Level Orange.

36

STONER? A VILLAGE CALLED STONER?" Izzy howled with laughter. They had been keeping track of the strange hamlet and village names along their northern BC route as they drove. They had just passed Prince George — not Prince George County, in Maryland, but Prince George — a flat little bush town that smelled heavily of sulfides and other pulp manufacturing by-products.

Ba'al smiled to himself. He loved his friend's humor and zest for life. Izzy had been like that ever since they were teenagers, acquiring properties for Yousseff on both the Afghanistan and Pakistan sides of the border. The two shared many memories. There was one grand trip that the seven of them — Yousseff, recognized by all as the leader, Marak, Omar, Kumar, Rika, Ba'al, and Izzy — had made together down the Indus. It had been a trip full of opium pipes and many many women. In a predominantly Muslim country, they got away with much more than they should have. Izzy always seemed to enjoy it more, and laugh louder, than anyone else. Sometimes Ba'al pined for those days so strongly that his throat constricted and his heart ached. He loved Yousseff. They all did. And this Canadian citizenship thing was nice. It was good to live in a palace in Vancouver and not worry about someone blowing you away with a gun at any time, around any corner. The Canadians had no idea how good they had it… but the old days on the Indus — there was no life quite like that. Before any of them had ever heard of Semtex or the Emir.

"Iz, as the Canadians would say, shut the fuck up, eh?" he said through his smile.

He was met with more gales of laughter from Izzy. "Yeah, dude, eh? You bet, eh?" There was more laughter. On a trip that was going to end like this one was, they needed that.

They did not stop along the way for anything other than gas and to use the bathroom, and at compulsory commercial weight scales. So far all they had eaten was Egg McMuffins — little cholesterol bombs, Izzy had said, but damned tasty anyway.

It was 2 in the afternoon when they reached Cache Creek, a small desert town with no apparent purpose other than to house fast food joints and gas stations, although Izzy had read that Vancouver's garbage was deposited somewhere in the immediate vicinity. They turned left and headed east through the Thompson River Valley to Kamloops, cruising past some of the most beautiful northern desert country on the continent. Izzy had taken over the driving and, as usual, had started to pick up speed. Seventy miles per hour. Eighty. Eighty-five. He was too much like Yousseff in that regard, thought Ba'al. Everything with him had to go faster and faster. They passed Kamloops in a blur and were heading due east, toward the Rockies.

"Izzy, what the hell are you doing?" asked Ba'al, suddenly noticing that their speed had crept up over 90 miles an hour. But it was too late. The red and blue lights and the siren of an RCMP cruiser appeared right behind them. "You idiot," said Ba'al in Urdu. "We're driving down the road with more than four tons of fucking Semtex and you go 90? Marak would blow your ass off with that gun of his."

"Relax, little buddy," said the unflappable Izzy. "No different from the river police back home. Just stay cool. Let me do the talking."

The RCMP constable walked toward them. Izzy already had the window rolled down and his driver's license and insurance papers at hand.

"D'you know how fast you were going, sir?" asked the police officer rhetorically.

"Yes, constable, I do. I think I was going around 140," Izzy answered. "The speed got away from me. I'm sorry."

The constable was not used to this level of candor, and paused a moment before answering. "Yup, you were, and I'm going to have to ticket you. License and registration please."

Izzy handed the paperwork over. The officer went back to his vehicle, and punched the numbers into his computer. In a few minutes he came back, ticket in hand. "That's three points and a fine. You've got 30 days to pay."

"Thank you constable," said Izzy.

"What d'you boys got in the back?" the officer asked, glancing at the back of the truck.

"Mostly camping and fishing gear. We were out at Rupert, doing a little saltwater fishing," said Izzy. "Wanna have a look?"

The officer nodded. "Open'er up."

Izzy could see the "oh shit" expression and deepening worry lines on Ba'al's face. He rolled his eyes at his friend's cowardice. "No problem officer." He hopped out of the truck, unlocked the back, and rolled up the rear door. The constable peered inside and noted the coolers, tents, food, tarps, tires, and junk.

"Did you guys get lucky out there?" he asked.

"Yeah we did. We got a few nice steelhead, but we have licenses for that," Izzy answered.

"Wow, that's a pretty good haul. All right guys, off you go. But watch your speed. We've got lots of radar out east of here."

"Thanks, officer," said Izzy, taking the ticket. "Have a nice day." Izzy and Ba'al watched the officer enter some information on his in-dash computer and pull back out onto the highway.

"See how easy that was?" said Izzy. "No problem at all."

"It was an unnecessary risk," said Ba'al. "And he has a record of the plates. He knows the owner of this truck. It's on his computer."

"So what? It's a holding company, and the shares are owned by another holding company, which is owned by an employee of the 24/7 chain. You know how it works, Ba'al. It can't be traced. He doesn't know anything that will lead him anywhere."

"Yes, but the chain of stores is mentioned. If they dig hard enough they could find it. I'm not sure how Yousseff plans to pull this off, but it's got to be a big deal, if so much money and manpower is being devoted to it."

Izzy held his hands up in mock surrender, giving in to his friend's lecture. "OK, Ba'al, eh? OK. I drive slower. You just relax."

They cruised by Salmon Arm, a beautiful little lakeside city, and continued east toward the Rockies. On and on they went, at a steady 60 miles an hour. The sun set, and by 9 they had reached the Revelstoke Junction and turned south, into the Kootenay Valley.

THE ARGUMENT had been firing for half an hour in the TTIC control room. Dan, standing against most of the TTIC staff, was definitely on the losing end. He wasn't taking it very well, and gracefully deferring to others had never been his style. The tension level was quickly rising to a boiling point. Turbee's initial welcome back had been joyous, but it had been difficult for the youth. He'd never been good in a crowd, and was even worse at being the center of attention. He was also embarrassed over his black eye, and found the rolling IV stand to be a bit of an annoyance. Standing up to Dan in this condition wasn't something he'd planned on.

"No way. Absolutely no way," Turbee had said, with as much emphasis as his tiny frame would allow. "There is absolutely no way that the Semtex was anywhere other than the *Haramosh Star.* It has to be there. You need to search it again!"

"Turbee, how can you be sure? The last time we had this discussion, the President was almost impeached," said Dan, arms folded, showing no sign of giving in. The new images had done nothing to convince him.

"I'm sure," said Turbee. "Look at the composite images Kingston and I developed. It's open and shut."

"OK, Turbee," said Dan, making no attempt to contain his temper or the biting humor he was inclined to use. "So where the hell is it? And why didn't we find it before? Are all those SEALs just that damn stupid? Is that why they're out there representing our country?"

To his credit, Turbee stood his ground against the cynicism. "Only two possibilities," he answered quietly. "The first is that it's stored in another container on the *Haramosh Star*. There may be a second hull, or a container completely independent of the ship. It would be impossible to find unless you knew to look for it."

"And that's why the SEALs missed it," interrupted Rahlson, coming down firmly on Turbee's side.

"Second possibility," continued Turbee, ignoring Rahlson's interruption, "is that it was transferred to another ship or perhaps a submarine, somewhere in the middle of the Pacific, where we couldn't see it."

"Doubt it. That's an unnecessary complication," said Dan. "Do you have anything other than a hunch to support that?"

"Look, Dan," said Turbee. "They — and as far as I know, we're still not sure who 'they' are — but they did it once, off the south coast of India. These guys are good. Incredibly good. If they did it once, why couldn't they do it again? It wouldn't be a complication; a transfer of a few tons of Semtex probably isn't a big deal to anyone who can design and manufacture the lifts and arms we saw in the transfer from the *Mankial Star* to the *Haramosh Star.*"

"OK," Rhodes stepped in. "Let's be constructive. Let's work this out. Suppose that happened, and they got or are on the verge of getting the stuff into British Columbia. It wouldn't have come through Vancouver. I already spent a few hours on the phone with senior guys from the RCMP, the Vancouver City Police, and the Coast Guard. You'd have to be nuts to try and smuggle stuff like that in through that port. It's under constant surveillance. They have thousands of cameras and hundreds of eyes. It would have to be somewhere else. I suggested Prince Rupert. It's another option, but the cops there doubt it. Even the port of Prince Rupert is under incredibly tight surveillance right now. But suppose they found a way in? I think I know what they would do." He paused, gathering his thoughts.

There was a short spell of silence. "We're waiting with bated breath, Rhodes," said Dan through his teeth. It didn't sit well with him when anyone took Turbee's side over his own. Right now, everyone was taking Turbee's side over his.

"The people who are transporting the Semtex are drug smugglers," continued Rhodes. "They're from Afghanistan or Pakistan. They've been moving heroin around the globe for years. They're a natural fit for transporting bricks of Semtex. It's no different, really, from a large shipment of heroin."

"So, where does that get you?" Dan interrupted again. "You're wasting time, and we're still no further ahead."

Rhodes gave Dan a scathing glare. He bit his tongue to keep from pointing out that Dan had wasted days and hundreds of hours searching for non-existent nukes. "Yes, we are," he continued evenly. "There are apparently a couple of choice BC entry points into the US. If it's the same crew, then they've obviously already developed their route across the border. They would also have a prearranged coastal location in BC, for getting things onto the continent in the first place."

"Yes, but we don't have a clue where or how, or even IF, the Semtex entered BC," said Dan. "And there are a lot of 'if's' embedded in that theory."

Turbee interrupted the conversation. He had been searching Canadian and American Coast Guard communications and had stumbled across a gem of information. "Liam," he said, completely ignoring Dan, "we've just received information from the Canadian Coast Guard that the *Haramosh Star* has been spotted near the British Columbia port city of Prince Rupert, just south of the Alaskan Panhandle. The ship was apparently a bit off course. They didn't know whether they were going to Prince Rupert or Vancouver. George," he said turning to his friend, "can you put this point on the Atlas Screen?"

George looked at Turbee in surprise; the young mathematician seemed to have very suddenly come into his own. His orders were sharp and precise, and even the tone of his voice had changed. Standing up to Dan had been good for the boy, he noted with approval. Smiling at the thought, he brought the Atlas Screen online.

"Take a look," Turbee continued, once the screen lit up. He pointed to the pulsing red dot that appeared just west of Prince Rupert.

"So what's the point of that?" asked Dan scornfully. "We already knew that the *Haramosh Star* was heading for Vancouver. So now they're a day away. They seem to be on schedule, and headed the right way."

"Not exactly, Dan," replied George. "Not quite. Take a look at this," he added, changing the view of the Atlas Screen so that it depicted the Pacific Ocean, showing the Aleutians and Kamchatka Peninsula to the north, the west coast of North America along one edge, and Japan, the Philippines and the Indonesian archipelago along the opposite edge.

"Ocean-going ships, when traversing large bodies of water, obey the same rules airplanes do. They follow great circular routes. The closest distance between two points on a sphere is not a straight line, but a curve."

"Yes, George. Thanks for that trip back to Math 101," replied Dan, with his usual edge of disdain. "What's your point?" Even though TTIC opinion, en masse, was beginning to lean toward Turbee, Dan saw no reason to be polite.

"Well, Danno," replied George with equal sarcasm. "I've plotted the shortest route from the Philippines, where the *Haramosh Star* would have entered the Pacific Ocean, to Vancouver. And here it is."

A red dot, pulling an ever-lengthening red line behind it, traveled from the Philippines northward, toward Alaska, and curved gradually south toward Vancouver.

"Nice animation, George," said Dan. "But I still don't see your point."

"Just look over here, Dan," snapped George as he enlarged the map west of the Alaskan Panhandle and Prince Rupert. "Can't you see that, according to the path she must have taken, the *Haramosh Star* was more than 100 miles closer to Prince Rupert that she should have been? She should have been at least 150 miles west of Prince Rupert but was actually 10 miles northwest, well inside the Dixon Entrance between the Queen Charlotte Islands and Alaska. The Canadian Coast Guard had been following her closely, even when she was a good thousand miles out, because of what happened off the coast of India. She was so off course that the Coast Guard finally boarded the ship and talked to her captain, asking what the hell he was doing. The captain apparently said that the search by the SEALs had confused him, and somehow he thought they were going to Prince Rupert. They corrected their course and began heading directly south, to get to Vancouver, where she's due in less than 12 hours."

"Logically, then," said Turbee, "the question becomes what was the closest port when the *Haramosh Star* was the most off course, which I guess would be the location of the red dot that George first put on the map. Can you put a circle around that point, George, and magnify that portion of the map a little more?"

"Sure can, little buddy," smiled George, pleased that Turbee had figured out the issue he'd been driving at. He punched a few buttons, and the section around the glowing red dot was enlarged on the Atlas Screen. "The closest port is, of course, Prince Rupert, with its new container port and its deep-water coal port. Maybe the Semtex was off-loaded there, assuming that it was still on the *Haramosh Star,* somehow," he suggested tentatively.

"Doubt it, George," said Rahlson. "The Canadians are watching their ports as closely as we are. The new container port has literally hundreds of cameras on it. It's probably being patrolled and monitored as extensively as our own deep-water ports. And the *Haramosh Star* was being watched. She couldn't have gone into the port without someone seeing. And there's no way that a speedboat could have approached her, taken on a four-ton cargo, and brought it ashore, without anyone noticing. No way."

"What about a submarine?" asked Turbee, going back to one of his original ideas.

Dan interrupted. "Listen Turb. Now you've become completely ridiculous. What next? A transporter beam, maybe? Alien conspiracy?" he asked sarcastically.

"Nevermind those things," interrupted Rhodes. "From everything that we now know, we need to keep watching that ship. We've seen a lot of engineering excellence so far. A sub might not be out of the question, Dan. And when the ship arrives in Vancouver, she should be searched from end to end. Again."

"Again?" asked Dan.

"Yes, again," said Rhodes. "If our Canadian friends would consent to such a process, given the twisted history of this ship."

The room was silent for a few seconds as everyone studied the three photographs that Turbee, with Kingston's assistance, had developed. There was no mistaking it. No fuzziness lending itself to argument or contrary point of view. It was Semtex. A pallet full, being moved from the *Mankial Star* to the *Haramosh Star.*

"There are only two possibilities," said Turbee. "Only two. Either the Semtex is still on the *Haramosh Star,* or it's been off-loaded at some point."

"Looks like the SEALs missed it after all," said Rhodes.

"Well assuming that Turbee's right — which I'm not admitting, yet, but assuming maybe he is — it could have been off-loaded before the SEALs got to the ship, in which case they didn't miss it," argued Dan.

"No way could it have been off-loaded between the Maldives and the east coast of Ceylon, where the intercept took place. We have satellites focused on that area and would have photos of it happening," Rahlson answered. "It was still on the ship. The SEALs missed it."

"Damn right they did," said George. "And in the process, made us an international laughing stock, almost got the President impeached, got the Secretary of Defense fired, and the Chairman of the Joint Chiefs too, and double dammit, almost got Turbee here killed." He chucked a thumb toward the still wounded and bandaged Turbee.

"We need to find the *Haramosh Star* again," sighed Rhodes.

Dan swelled defensively. "If you think I'm going to be party to a move like that you're nuts. No way. And I'm the guy running the show. No way," he snapped. He was no longer trying to get along with his crew.

"Aw fuck, Alexander will you–" started Rahlson.

"I already know where she is," Turbee interrupted.

"Who?" retorted Dan.

"The *Haramosh Star.* She's sailing along the Hecate Straights, between the Queen Charlotte Islands and the British Columbia mainland. She'll be in the port of Vancouver in 17 hours and 30 minutes."

"You see, Dan, that's why we need this kid," said Rahlson, with an edge in his voice.

"How'd you do that, Turb?" asked Khasha in amazement.

"Well, I read somewhere that the Canadian Coast Guard tracks all Pacific ships destined for either Prince Rupert or Vancouver. I got into their web site. Didn't even need to hack into it or do anything illegal because Canada is on board with TTIC. They have a continually updated database that shows the present location of all inbound ships. The *Haramosh Star* is in the database, and…" His voice trailed off for a few seconds.

"What is it, Turbee?" asked Khasha.

"There's a note here about the course deviation. It doesn't say where, or how, or why. It just says there was a deviation," said Turbee, slowly. "It also indicates that the *Haramosh Star* was boarded by a Captain LaMaitre. We should probably talk to him."

"Yes, I guess so," muttered Dan. "Johnson, god dammit, get me someone in the Canadian Coast Guard who knows more about this. And make it fast."

"THIS IS CAPTAIN JEAN LAMAITRE from the bridge of the *HMS John A. MacDonald.* To whom am I speaking?"

"This is Daniel Alexander, Director of the Terrorist Threat Integration Center in Washington, DC. You are on the speakerphone in our central control room. There are some two dozen TTIC members listening to this conversation."

"Very nice. Good morning, TTIC. I gather you need some information from us."

"Yes, Captain, we do," replied Dan. "We certainly do. We need to know about the course deviation of the *Haramosh Star.* What can you tell us about that?"

"An ill-fated vessel, to be sure," said LaMaitre. "First that delightful incident off the coast of Ceylon, and now this. Yes, the *Haramosh Star* was plenty off course all right. So far off that I boarded the vessel with a small group of my men and had a look around. Those SEALs made quite a mess of things, by the way."

"OK," said George. "This is George Lexia, with TTIC. I'm the map keeper here. Can you tell me where she should have been, and where she actually was?"

"Sure. She should have taken a great circular route, the same as jet planes would, going north from the Philippines, turning to cut just south of the Aleutians, and then straight on, to approach British Columbia from the northwest. Let me give you a few coordinates."

As the points of latitude and longitude were given, George plotted them on the Atlas Screen, and created a red curve connecting them. He sent an "I told you so" smirk in Dan's direction. "OK," he said, sitting back. "I've got it plotted. Now where did you board her?"

"Just outside of Prince Rupert. North of Dundas Island." The Captain gave George those coordinates as well.

"I see what you mean," said George. "She's 200 miles east of where she should have been. What did her Captain say about that?" At this point George actually mouthed the phrase "I told you so" at a red-faced Dan.

"I knew the Captain of that ship from other encounters. Vince Ramballa. Decent guy. Very experienced sea hand. He said that he'd become confused about their point of destination. He thought it was Prince Rupert, and not Vancouver. When I looked at the papers, they stated very clearly that Vancouver was the destination. He said that the SEAL episode two weeks ago had created havoc on his ship, and that was where the confusion stemmed from. So I told him it was fine, and ordered him to hightail it to Vancouver, which he's currently doing. Funny thing, though."

"What's that?" asked Rhodes.

"Even if she was going to Prince Rupert, she would still have been off course. They were about ten miles northeast of Dundas Island, near the mouth of the Portland Canal, whereas they should have been about 12 miles south of Dundas, to approach Prince Rupert. An experienced sailor would never make a mistake like that."

"Did he say why he was off course for an intended destination of Prince Rupert?" Rhodes responded.

"I never pointed that part out. Didn't occur to me until I was back in my own quarters."

"What's at the end of the Portland Canal?" George asked slowly, tapping his pencil on the desk as he stared at the map.

"A mostly abandoned mining and fishing village called Stewart," came the reply.

"Are there docking facilities there?"

"Yes, in fact there are. It used to be quite a mining hub, so they have infrastructure left over. Hundreds of feet of abandoned docks. Just the odd fishing boat hooked up to them now, though."

"OK, thanks," said George. He and Turbee glanced at each other. As far as they were concerned, that answered the question of where the Semtex was.

Dan asked a few more questions, and the conversation ended.

37

NICE PLACE, RIK," said Yousseff, glancing at his childhood friend. "A long way from the school yard in Jalalabad."

He was standing in Rika's thirty-seventh-floor office, looking toward downtown Los Angeles. The name on the door read "Rika Mahafi Financial Corporation." She had a staff of 15 workers; all were Pashtun, and most were women. Each had been chosen for two qualities — first, loyalty, and second, an adeptness with numbers. The financial controls for all of Yousseff's North American operations were headquartered here. It was here that the company moved money from one numbered account to another, from a Liechtenstein Trust to a Nigerian Bank, through mazes of numbered companies and accounts spread throughout the world. It was here that the profits from the Canadian stores and gas stations, Pacific Western Submersibles, and hundreds of real estate properties were tabulated. It was here that the shares for Ba'al, Izzy, and Kumar, among others, were assessed and weighed.

A sister company existed in Karachi, where Rika was also in charge. The Pakistani company was called the Karachi Mahafika Accounting Corporation, and had about 30 employees. That was where Rika handled the accounts of Karachi Drydock and Engineering and Karachi Star Line. The Karachi branch also managed and tracked thousands of real estate investments held by a host of shell companies, in both Afghanistan and Pakistan. And it managed the jewel in Yousseff's crown — more than $100 million in prime downtown Karachi real estate. It also kept accounts on the drug sale operations, though these accounts were heavily disguised.

If one were searching for the nerve center of Yousseff's operations, the Karachi and Los Angeles accounting offices would be a prime place to start. If a paralyzing strike were to be made against his criminal enterprise, it would have to be focused here, in Rika Mahafika's offices. Yousseff realized this, and it was for this reason that he and Rika had hand picked each and every employee. The currency of loyalty held sway, and everyone in the company knew it. A betrayal here would destroy the entire organization. Before it did that, however, it would bring on Ghullam or Marak, with their guns. This fact alone had kept the employees in line for the last 20 years.

Rika had picked Yousseff up at the PWS Long Beach factory and driven him to Century City to show him around her offices. The door leading from the reception area to the main office of her building was equipped with locks and deadbolts. The office contained workstations, but no separated areas, and her own corner office. When Rika wasn't there, a state-of-the-art security system was activated.

Rika's personal office had more than 400 square feet of floor space, and was equipped with a massive black granite desk, facing outward toward the window that overlooked Los Angeles. Half a dozen computer screens were sitting on the desk, all displaying the ever-changing colors and shapes of Microsoft screen savers. Youssef and Rika were sitting in two comfortable chairs at a low coffee table in a corner of the office.

"Say you want me to go to Jalalabad, Youssi. It's still home. Always will be. I could go back there today and be comfortable and happy." She was two years younger than Yousseff, and even in her 40s still possessed the striking beauty of her youth. She had an ex-husband in Karachi, an ex-husband in Los Angeles, and an on-and-off-again relationship with a lawyer working in another building in the Century City complex. Neither ex-husband nor lover had ever been allowed into Rika's office, and neither was privy to the nature of the commerce that flowed through its doors and Internet connections.

"Four children, Rika, and you still look great," Yousseff said affectionately.

"Go on, Youssi. You're going blind in your old age," she replied. "And probably desperate too."

He smiled and bowed. "Yes. To both." They both knew that, despite their sporadic connections, and visits that numbered only three or four a year, she still loved him. It had been true at the great battle of the Four Cedars. It was still true today. They both knew that his feelings toward her were almost as strong.

"What brings you here to me, Youssi? Surely not just to make love?" Rika joked.

"Well, maybe that, and an exit strategy," he replied.

"Exit strategy? We talk of making love and all you think of is an exit strategy. Men are pigs," snorted Rika.

Yousseff smiled. "For business. Not for love, dummy."

"What are you up to, Youssi? I feel something big afoot." They had both switched to their native Urdu at this point.

"Yes. There's going to be a large event. Soon. It will create a financial earthquake that I want to take advantage of. It will also create an intense manhunt."

"Youssi, you had better not be thinking of sending airplanes into buildings. If you're ever a part of anything like that, I will never work for you or see you again. What are you planning?"

"I can't tell you, Rika. But I can say that there will not be a large loss of life. Not even 100 people will die… less, I think, than the number killed every hour when that madness with the Soviets was at its height in Afghanistan. Less than the number that die every day in Iraq. But it will be truly spectacular. I can promise you that."

Ever since the battle of the Four Cedars, Rika had believed anything Yousseff told her. If he said something would come to pass, and would be spectacular, then it was undoubtedly so. She grew more serious.

"What do you need me to do, Yousseff?"

"A couple of things. We are going to have some fun in the stock and commodities markets. Here is a list of stocks to short. On margin. I want you to use that Liechtenstein Trust, together with one of the Russian or Nigerian offshore banks. This has got to be hidden so deep that Allah Himself couldn't find it. Can you do that?"

"Youssi, what do you think I've been doing for you ever since we started Karachi Drydock and Engineering? I've been burying things that deeply for more than 20 years now. Yes, I think I can do that."

"Good, my love. Very good. Here is a list of companies whose shares I want you to buy, also on margin. Hide this the same way, but use a totally different connection of banks and trust companies. If, perchance, someone finds out about the first series of transactions, I don't want them to automatically find the second."

"I think I can probably do that too, Youssi." She looked at the list. One entry stood out. "You want to short KSEW?" she asked, looking at the name of their old nemesis.

"You noticed," replied Yousseff.

"You're going to whack Nooshkatoor?"

"Kind of," said Yousseff. "He made things very miserable for Kumar and me for many years. In several ways, actually."

"You know he lives in England now, in some fancy district in London? You know he's become very important and powerful and all that, right?"

"I know, Rik. It will make things all the more delightful," Yousseff replied.

"Anything else?" asked Rika.

"Oh yes. Don't do all the purchases, sales, or stock positions at once. Use multiple transactions, spread out over the next two days, starting now. Try to vary the banks, trusts, offshore banks, and Third World banks. Can you do that too?"

"Of course, Youssi, anything for you. Nothing is impossible. I'll probably have to work a little harder, but I can do it. Sure. My staff is capable. We can handle it."

"Good," he continued. "We need to go short in some commodities and long in others. Do you know your way around the Chicago Mercantile Exchange, the London Metal Exchange, the Beijing Commodity Exchange, the Hong Kong Futures Exchange, the Tokyo International Financial Futures Exchange, the International Petroleum Exchange, you know, places like that?"

"I've been doing it for many years. You know I know," she said, starting to become frustrated with the way he was questioning her knowledge and ability.

"Here is a third list of commodities on which I want you to go short, and a fourth list for long. Can you do that too, starting now? Again, everything on margin."

With each request, her response became a little less eager, her smile a little smaller. "Yes, Youssef. Yes, I can do that too. I will get some more coffee, and will sleep less. I can also do this for you," she said, sighing.

"And Rika, I know I am asking much. But you must use different banks and offshore institutions than with the other transactions. And it can't be done all at once. There must be different paths. You realize that, right?"

"Yes, Youssef, but can we talk about something else now? This is much that you ask. Yes, I can do it, but I'm tired of talking about it."

"There is one last thing," added Youssef.

"There is more?"

"Only a little thing. We need an exit strategy."

"There you go again," she pouted.

"Business, Rika. Business. The Americans are very clever. They will throw great resources at the perpetrators of my plan. There have to be a few sacrificial lambs. You know how they are. There always has to be a 'bad guy,' like in the movies. We need to create one. I need money deposited in these bank accounts, in these amounts, via the following banking trail. Can you do that too?"

"What, you are giving money to Nooshkatoor?" Rika asked, glancing at this newest list. "Are you crazy? After what he did to Kumar's family? Why give the bastard any money?" Rika couldn't see the sense in it.

"Rik, use your head. What do you think is happening here, exactly?" asked Youssef.

For a moment she looked perplexed, and then a smile started to play about her face. "Ah. I see it. I see."

Youssef gave her a few more instructions. She took his sheets of transfers, purchases, and sales. She whistled to herself. This was nothing short of a multi-billion dollar bet. She smiled to herself at Youssef's audacity, to be planning such a thing. But then she saw how much work it would be. She would need to be at it for most of the next 48 hours. Forty-eight hours without sleep.

Suddenly the smile was gone. There was weariness in her features, and wrinkles appeared around the down-turned corners of her mouth. "Yes, Youss. Yes. Why don't you just ask me to refinance General Motors while I'm at it?"

"Rika, there will be time for pleasure in a week or two. When this is all done, you can take $100 million for yourself, if you like. There should be money to spare."

"It's not the money, Youssi. It never is, for me. We need more time to talk. To catch up on old times, and what is going on today. To be real people, with real lives and real relationships. That's what I need. That's what I want, Youssi."

"I know. I know. I will see you in a few days. Please do this for me."

He kissed her on the forehead, and then was gone, vanishing like smoke. "No different than 30 years ago," she whispered to herself as she saw the outer door swing shut. "Always with an exit strategy, and leaving the rest of us in the dust."

THEY CAME BY SEPARATE FLIGHTS, though both came through Heathrow. Both came with superbly forged passports. Vijay arrived as Donovan Smith, computer systems specialist. Ghullam had adopted the identity of David Priestley, security specialist.

Ghullam was of Pashtun heritage, from the Northwest Frontier Province. He'd been assisting Marak for years, doing whatever it took to ensure that Youssef's heroin shipments were the only ones that made it down the Indus to Hyderabad or Karachi. He possessed a multitude of skills, many of which had been honed to perfection by his mentor. He was a gifted marksman, able to use almost every firearm imaginable. He was physically imposing at 6′1″, and was in peak physical condition. He was the master of many forms of martial arts, and possessed the same reptilian gaze as his master. He could pick any lock, break any bone, and kill in a thousand different ways. Some of the deaths on his list of accomplishments included government officials, rival drug lords, and rivals in Youssef's vast commercial affairs. He found killing up close to be especially satisfying. To feel the fear, and to see the look of death, to touch it… that was almost sexual for him. He was Marak's star pupil. He was the one that was sent when there was killing to be done.

Ghullam met Youssef at his small suite in the Long Beach hangar. Youssef had just traveled from Los Angeles and was already exhausted. Much had happened since they had last met, in an almost identical apartment, in Islamabad, Pakistan. But this was just the beginning, and there were still many details to be discussed and attended to. Youssef skipped the pleasantries and started giving orders the moment Ghullam entered the room.

"Here are three telephone numbers," he said, handing Ghullam a sheet of paper with the names and numbers of the Emir's LA-based sleeper group. "The leader's name is Ray. He'll be at one of these three numbers. Identify yourself as the Emir's messenger. Then give him the following numeric sequence." He read the numbers and made Ghullam repeat them back to him. "I will call you in exactly 24 hours, with your instructions. These men must begin their journey the moment I call."

YO. RAY HERE," came the thoroughly American trucker's voice, with a hint of southern twang. The man who answered the phone had shoulder-length black hair, peppered with gray, and combed back into a ponytail. He wore faded jeans and a black T-shirt with the moniker of the Orange County Choppers emblazoned across its shoulders. His hat had the insignia of the White Sox stitched across the front. He listened to the other voice on the phone for a moment, and the smile disappeared from his face. The day and the hour had come. He had known that it would. He had been following the newscasts, and had seen the image of his master many times of late. He'd heard the Emir's messages, along with billions of others. He'd been wondering if he had a role to play in the great attack the Emir had so publicly promised.

For the first five years after coming to America, Ray had read the Koran daily, and kept up with his prayers in the privacy of his apartment. He'd eaten only appropriate foods, avoided women, and had no alcohol. He met with his three comrades as often as he could, to share memories of their homeland. It had been a painful, lonely journey, and each evening had been a disappointment when the call still hadn't come. Each dawn had brought the hope of a call to arms.

Slowly, however, the task of fitting into the mosaic of a new country began to erode the hard enamel of his beliefs. Ray came to know the joy of a cold Budweiser and a rare steak on the balcony on a Saturday evening. The serene rhythms and spiritual cadences of the music of the high Afghan deserts were slowly replaced by the decidedly more lively rhythms of Jamaica and Nashville. Then there were the women. A nibble here and a bite there had turned into an orgy of feasting. He knew the Emir would not approve, but, as the Americans would say, "Fuck him."

This lusty embrace of what he assumed to be the American lifestyle was brought to a screeching halt by this one telephone call.

"Come to the Day's Inn in Glendale, Room 237," the man said.

"When?" Ray asked in Urdu.

"Now."

The telephone clicked, and there was silence. The Emir's messenger. The assigned sequence of numbers, which he'd memorized years ago. This was not a joke. Ray knew too well what the call implied. He remembered the day that he had looked into the one living eye of the Emir as if it was yesterday. The eye was dark, black even, and immensely powerful. At that time the Emir had been the lord of a princely realm in Kabul, as opposed to what Ray assumed was now a home somewhere in the caves of the Sefid Koh. Even then, Ray had known that the earthly trappings had meant nothing to the holy man. Kabul had been a convenience, with its wider streets, its airport, and its communications. The Emir was every bit as powerful in some cave or desert hovel as he had been when he was at the center of civilization. To do something to endanger the mission of the Emir would mean certain death and, most likely, a slow and painful one. He had very little choice about responding. The call to arms had finally come, after ten long years, and its announcement after all this time was definitely unwelcome.

38

AS A RESULT OF THE CONVERSATION with Captain LeMaitre, Dan was able to involve the RCMP, who had Constable Klassen from the Hazelton detachment make the 130-mile journey to Stewart and "poke along the docks a bit," as Lance put it.

Constable Klassen made occasional trips to Stewart to keep an eye on things there and already knew the denizens of the small town well. He had run into Wharfdog Charlie on a number of prior occasions. He had a respect for all people, until they gave him reason to believe otherwise. The worst offence Wharfdog had ever committed was that of public drunkenness, which was, unfortunately, an offense he committed more or less continuously. This time, Wharfdog told an amazing, unbelievable story, but with such detail and consistency upon retelling that Klassen figured there must have been some kernel of truth to it. He had been given TTIC's number before he started his investigation, and now asked Wharfdog how he felt about telling this story to some other people.

"Sure, no problem," Wharfdog Charlie replied. "Just so long as they don't piss me off. Sure."

The call was put through TTIC's exotic speakerphone system, so that Klassen and Wharfdog came through with crystalline clarity for the whole group.

"You're on our speaker system, Constable Klassen," said Dan. "Maybe give the mike to, uh, what's his name, Charlie?"

"Fine by me, sir," said Constable Klassen in distant Stewart, BC. "Here he is."

"How many'ov you fuckin' assholes are in on this telephone conversation anyway, eh?" asked a truculent Wharfdog, when he got on the phone.

"Oh, just a couple of us, Mr. Charlie," said Dan. "Just a couple."

If he had been honest, he would have said that there were about 25 people in the main control room, and that every word of the fully duplexed conversation was being broadcast through the large control room speakers. Given the importance of the call, it had been piped to Langley as well and, for all he knew, from there to the Pentagon and the White House Situation Room. Because the call originated from the microphone inside a police cruiser, and was transmitted via satellite to a ground station in Vancouver, and from there to the Heather Street complex, it was also being relayed through a crowded RCMP conference room, in which 15 or 16 people were listening. A more forthright answer would probably have been that there were maybe 100 in on the call.

Wharfdog processed Dan's answer with suspicion. "What do you want to know, then?" he asked.

"Can you describe what you saw?" asked Dan.

"It was the strangest looking boat I've ever seen," said Wharfdog. "It came in very low in the water. But I've seen it before, the same one. It might be a little submarine. Tiny little fucker, eh." He paused for a second.

The voice of Klassen came on the line. "Hang on guys, he's just taking a slurp here." He sounded embarrassed.

Admiral Jackson was one of the many higher-ups in on the call. "Oh Jesus Christ," he muttered to himself.

"The hatch slid back," continued Wharfdog. "And dammit, some guy hopped out and hugged two guys by this truck. This box truck. On the wharf. And then these mechanical arms come out of this boat thing, and there was another platform on rollers and shit, eh. It kind'ov loaded itself into the back of the truck and like holy shit, these pallets came along and–"

"Charlie," interrupted Dan. "What kind of material was–"

"Don't interrupt me, asshole. And it's Wharfdog to you. In fact, it's Mr. Wharfdog."

Wharfdog and Dan continued to interrupt one another, drawing the spiral of Wharfdog's elliptical descriptions out farther and farther. Eventually, amidst a chorus of fuck you's, and asshole this and that, the tortured recitation of the Stewart reload from submarine to truck was provided to a raptly attentive audience. In the middle of it, Wharfdog was even able to give three of the letters on the license of the truck — DGO.

"I remember because it's a funny spelling of my name, you know, D-O-G," he said.

"Well, thank you, Mr.Wharfdog," Dan was able to say at the conclusion. "You've been a great help and we all appreciate it."

"I thought it was just a couple of you, you said. Now it's 'we all'," said Wharfdog.

"OK, there are a few more than a couple. But thanks."

"Fuck you too, asshole," came the tart reply. "Fuck all of you."

At that point, the call was abruptly ended. An uncomfortable silence filled the TTIC control room, interrupted by a short burst of laughter from Turbee.

"Turbee, will you please shut up," Dan said impatiently.

"I just can't believe this," said Turbee. "Here we are, the cream of the Intelligence Community, some of the smartest people on the planet, some of the most connected people on the planet, sitting on top of a multi-billion dollar computer, in the center of a trillion-dollar Intelligence Agency, with the ability to pulverize entire countries into powder if we wanted, and we're listening to a guy with a name like Wharfdog, who lives inside a pickle jar, he's so hammered, calling us from the middle of nowhere. And we sit here in stunned amazement, listening to every syllable. I'm rolling on the floor with laughter here."

He giggled again, and was actually close to rolling on the floor to demonstrate, until he saw the sober and worried look on the faces of many of his colleagues. No one else was laughing.

"Shit, I've done it again, haven't I," he said, when he realized that the only person seeing humor was him. "Dammit. Sorry people. Shouldn't have laughed. Sorry. Very sorry."

It was one of the most critical aspects of Turbee's disorder; he had almost no understanding of traditional humor. He laughed when he shouldn't, and didn't laugh when he should. He couldn't read the facial expressions or the fine shadings in tones that were at the soul of comedy. In his attempts to compensate for this lack of understanding, he often forced himself to laugh in situations that he thought would be seen as comical. As it did now, this often resulted in highly inappropriate behavior. Although few knew it, this was the reason he compulsively watched and re-watched TV series such as the Simpsons, Bugs Bunny, and all the rest. He studied humor like most people would have to study the mathematics, engineering, and programming that came so naturally to him.

Looking around, he quickly realized that no one in the room was willing to listen to explanations like that at the moment. Grabbing his rolling IV stand, he retreated to his desk and began aimlessly tapping on the keys of his computer. The rest of the group ignored him and began to discuss what they would do with the new information from Wharfdog Charlie.

THE TRIP FROM STEWART to the American border had been long, and, as Yousseff had insisted, there had been no breaks. Ba'al and Izzy had taken turns driving and sleeping, but they were both exhausted. Their trip had started more than 48 hours earlier. They had flown from Vancouver to Prince

George, rented the van, and driven from there to Stewart. Then, after a wait of some six hours, they had connected with Jimmy, loaded the explosives, and started their lengthy southward journey. At Fernie they had turned off the highway and headed toward the Akamina-Kishinina. The last two hours had been spent bouncing over the bumpy, rutted, potholed road from Fernie to the park.

"Here at last," said Izzy as he pulled onto the old trail that led to Leon's trailer and Devil's Anvil. They had both been there before, and knew what to expect. They slowly drove down the narrow trail toward the mobile home, past it, and toward the mine entrance itself. Dennis Lestage was already there, sitting in a lawn chair, smoking a cigarette.

"About time, boys," said the ever slothful Dennis, not getting up. "Been here waiting for you for hours now. I'm gonna get overtime for this."

"How about we do you a favor, Dennis?" replied Izzy. "We won't tell Leon that you actually said what you just said."

"And another favor, Dennis," added Ba'al. "Butt the cigarette."

Dennis was not one to take orders from anyone other than Leon, least of all these two Paki types who thought they were so much better than everyone else. He tapped another smoke out of his Export A package, and lit it with the butt of the last cigarette. He threw the old cigarette, unextinguished, on the ground. Without moving any further, he flicked the generator button and pushed open the doorway to the mine with the heel of his boot. Then he motioned grandly for them to get started with their business.

"Listen, blockhead. Butt the cigarette," Ba'al repeated. He was in no mood for jokes. He had just traveled 1,000 miles, and had almost 1,000 more to go.

"Why?" Dennis asked, spoiling for an argument.

"Because we'll blow your ass to hell if you don't," said Izzy. He was as tired and cranky as Ba'al. He dearly wanted to say that they had more than four tons of Semtex in the back of the truck, but there was no point in adding it. Instead he pulled out his Beretta 9 mm and pointed it at Dennis. "Butt the smoke, asshole," he said, with sufficient malevolence in his voice to convince Dennis that this was not the time to draw a line in the sand. Grimacing, he tossed the partially smoked cigarette on the ground and extinguished it with his boot.

Ba'al continued to glare at the Canadian. He didn't like that someone so stupid and lazy was involved in such an important project. If this were his plan… "Let's get to work," he sighed, rolling up his sleeves.

The three of them started unloading the Semtex onto the railway trolley, which was parked just outside the mine. When it had been piled as high as was safe, they started the cart toward the entrance. Ba'al halted the cart just before they entered the doors.

"This is going to be a four tripper, gentlemen. Izzy, stay with the truck. Dennis and I are going to the other end to unload. We'll be back in an hour or so, tops." Ba'al didn't trust the chain-smoking, curious, and monumentally stupid Dennis alone, in such close proximity to such a large volume of high explosives.

"What the hell is this shit anyway?" asked Dennis, pointing to the cellophane-wrapped bricks.

"Same stuff as always, Dennis. Just a new way of wrapping it, eh. Now shut up."

CATHERINE pushed the door a little wider, glancing out into the tunnel, and looking first one way, then the other. The space was pitch black, and there was nothing to be seen. She listened carefully, then snuck one foot out the door, wondering what she was going to do once she got out of the marijuana room.

At that moment, she heard the distant sound of a generator starting up. There was a click, and the lights came on again, blinding her.

IT TOOK ONLY 30 MINUTES to get from the north end of the mine to the south end, even though the total distance was more than three miles, and there was an elevator ride in the middle of it. The trip was made in silence, the only noise coming from the iron wheels on the rails. Even with the artificial lighting, the darkness of the mine had always made Ba'al nervous. The coal black walls and low ceilings were a marked contrast to the spacious caves back home, in the Sefid Koh. The whole place had a closed, dangerous quality to it. He'd never dealt with it very well, and looked forward to finishing this part of the trip and being on his way.

They passed through the hexagonal space that served as one of the hubs of the lower tunnels. Ba'al saw Dennis' nervous stare toward one of the doors and almost asked him about it, but decided not to. Hell with it, he thought. No telling what was going on in the dolt's brain. On with the task at hand.

At the far end of the tunnel they reached another doorway. Opening it revealed the back end of a five-ton van, similar to the one that they had left parked on the Canadian side of Devil's Anvil. This new van had been supplied by the Hell's Angels of the Billings, Montana chapter, as arranged by

Leon Lestage.

This van also had a powered tailgate. The usual rail system had been built into the trolley, under a false floor, and the two were able to roll their wheeled pallet easily into the truck. It took less than ten minutes to unload the cargo into the back of the truck and turn around for the next load. The sun was rising as they returned to the Canadian end of the mine, to greet a silent Izzy.

LOAD TWO," said Ba'al at the north entrance of Devil's Anvil. "Let's hustle here." Without further ado the three of them began loading the trolley with a second load of Semtex, which they managed to do in ten minutes. Ba'al pushed the trolley immediately into the mine, motioning for Dennis to accompany him. Not a second was wasted. Ba'al remembered Yousseff's theory that the reloading at any point, whether from truck to boat, boat to boat, truck to plane, or anything else, was the danger point, and had to be done with maximum speed and efficiency. Many of the transfer systems built by Karachi Drydock had been designed with this mantra in mind. Speed was paramount.

"Put a little effort into it there, Dennis. With this much money and risk, we're not going to dawdle. For the next few hours or so, it's time to actually work," groused an annoyed Ba'al.

Dennis tried to hide his anger. Here he was, the present custodian of Devil's Anvil, and this foreigner was lecturing him. "Whatever," was the only reply he could muster.

They traveled back to the southern end of the mine again, without a second to sit and relax. Dennis' bones ached, and he longed to rest, but Ba'al's direct, unblinking stare was unnerving and accepted no excuses.

CORPORAL CATHERINE GRAY panicked. She had spent the last ten minutes crawling through a ventilation tunnel that was barely big enough to accommodate her body. For 24 hours before that she'd been locked in a room, choking with money. She was dehydrated, stressed, and pig-filthy. And now the lights went on. One of two possibilities. Either someone was coming in the north entrance, in which case she had 15 minutes to hide, or someone was coming in the south entrance, a few hundred feet away, in which case she had a second or two to hide. No point taking unnecessary risks, not with people the likes of Leon and his clan. She darted back into the marijuana room, hoping to God that she wouldn't be too stoned in 20 minutes to figure out what the next step in this elaborate dance was going to be.

She crawled back into the ventilation tunnel for additional cover. “Indy,” she whispered. “Indy, someone’s coming in.”

“Sounds like it,” came Indy’s hoarse reply. “Stay back. Maybe we can learn something here.”

“Yeah, maybe, but maybe that dolt Dennis has told Leon about us and we’re about to be toasted.”

“If that’s what’s going on, we’ll just have to deal with it. Let’s see what happens,” said Indy. “If I hear them putting a key into the lock, maybe I can scurry through the ventilation tunnel at the last moment. But it’s a last moment thing, Cath. I can’t go in there unless I have to. Just can’t.”

“Shush,” said Catherine sharply. “I hear the elevator.” She felt her blood pressure rising as she listened to the squeaking wheels of the rail car approaching. The blood was pounding in her temples as the squeaking passed within three feet of her. No pause, no change in speech. She was imagining the shapes of the thoughts in Dennis’ brain. “Do I tell Leon? Do I deal with it later? Shoot them now? Shoot them later? Kill them slowly? Shoot him, rape her and…?” She tried to stop the free-flowing anxiety, with little success.

But nothing happened. No doors were wrenched open. No execution squad appeared. Instead, she heard outer doors squeaking open at the American end of the mine. There were grunts and the noises of a reloading taking place. There was not much doubt in Catherine’s mind about what was going on. A load of BC Bud, or Afghan heroin, was making its way into the American homeland, within their hearing.

Catherine crawled through the ventilation tunnel and into the small underground money room, where Indy sat against one wall. She sat with him, listening to the sounds of what they agreed was an unloading at the south end of the tunnel. Then they heard the sound of the trolley heading north again, back toward the Canadian end of the mine. Once they heard the elevator, and felt sure that they were alone again, Catherine and Indy began discussing the situation in hushed tones. Soon they began to argue, in whispers.

“I’m going to check it out, Indy,” Catherine was saying.

“Like hell you are. Do you have any idea how dangerous these people are?” responded Indy.

“Well, yes I do, Indy. I’m in the business too, remember?”

“I know, Cath. But we’re dealing with a high-level importing scheme here. This is the border hole, and that means that millions of dollars worth of product goes through here every month. These guys will kill to protect it. The fact that you’re with the Force means nothing to them.”

"But all I'm going to do is go out there, maybe check out the plates, get descriptions, you know, the usual stuff. We may find out who these guys are. At the very least, we'll know what they're driving. The FBI will be able to nail them before they're out of Montana. And I'll stay hidden. I'm not going to strike up a conversation about the weather with these guys."

"Fine," responded Indy. "Go ahead. But please watch yourself. And please, when you come back, find some bolt cutters to get me out of this tomb."

Catherine wondered suddenly if Indy's real concern was over her safety, or due to his fear of being left alone in a bedroom-sized space, in the dark, deep within Devil's Anvil. Trapped, really by his own fears and his memory of his near-death experience in the Fraser Valley, almost 20 years earlier. She sensed his struggle with the phobia, and heard the barely restrained panic in his voice.

"Don't worry, Indy. If it's the last thing I do, I will come back for you." She tried to make her voice as soothing as possible. "I will."

"Can't do it if you're dead, Cath," he responded.

"I'm a big girl, Indy. I can look after myself."

They sat silently, side by side, for a few minutes. Catherine held Indy's hand and put her arm around him. The minutes stretched on and on. In what seemed like hours but was in fact less than 40 minutes, they heard the distant sounds of the elevator. Then the squeaking of the trolley's wheels become louder, passed by them, and ultimately stopped at what was the Montana side of the mine. They heard the door open, and the sounds of what had to be a second off-loading. After a few minutes, the rail car came by again, heading toward the central elevator and the Canadian entrance. She heard Dennis' voice.

"Two more loads, buddy, and we can call it a day."

The other individual, whoever he was, did not respond. She heard the trolley squeak its way by, this time from south to north, presumably going for load three of four. She heard the elevator in the distance.

"Indy, I'm just going out there to reconnoiter," she said. "I'll be back in a few minutes."

Over his objections, she wriggled back through the tiny, but now familiar, shaft, into the marijuana room, and darted out the door. She gingerly stepped into the main passageway, looking both north and south. Then she walked to the door of the money room.

"Indy, the coast is clear," she said. "I can't pick this lock. I have no equipment, and I'm not nearly as good at it as you are. You have to come through the ventilation shaft to get out. You need to do it now, while they're busy."

Indy was no coward. He had been undercover in extremely dangerous situations. He'd been shot at, beaten up, and nearly killed twice, the first time in the Fraser Valley incident, the second, in a high-speed chase. But crawling into a tiny ventilation tunnel deep underground in an abandoned coal mine? No, he would not, could not, do that.

"You go on Cath. You can get out of this mine. Just come back and get me, OK?"

"I'll be back, Indy. Hang on. If you start dying of thirst, you can make it through the ventilation shaft. Hang on."

Catherine ran toward the barn-like doors on the southern end of the tunnel. She swung one of them open and stepped into the sunlight of an American dawn. The majestic Flathead River Valley unfolded in the distance. The view was breathtaking. She closed her eyes and raised her face to the sunrise for a moment, ecstatic to be in the open air and out of the tomb-like environment of the mine.

When she opened her eyes again, she saw that backed up to the mine entrance was a five-ton box van with a power tailgate. It was a dirty white color, and the rear doors were open. Row upon row of cellophane bricks, obviously heroin, were stacked there. "Curious," she said aloud to herself. "They're wrapping the stuff in red cellophane now. Probably a marketing ploy. Afghan red, they'll call it."

The bricks weren't the truck's only contents. A couple of large tarps were piled up in a corner. Two large coolers were sitting along one side. She wondered if she had time. Thirty minutes from north to south, by her estimation. Ten minutes or so to load the rail car at the north end, then 30 before they got back here. Sure. She thought she must have a good 15 minutes, still. She hopped up onto the rear bumper of the truck, and from there into the interior. She pushed open the lid on one of the coolers. It took her only seconds to reach for a bottle of water and gulp its contents down. It was only after she had done so that she realized her foolishness, given the nature of the investigation, but her thirst had been overpowering.

She hopped out and ran to the cab, reaching into the glove compartment. The registration was Californian. A numbered company. No Visa or charge card receipts. She flipped open the central console. No surprise there. It was loaded with American bills — tens, twenties, fifties, and hundreds. Made sense, she thought. Just grab a briefcase full from the American money room. There was easily $1,000 in the console. Considering the millions and millions they had stashed in the mine, this was pocket change. Gas money. Fast food money. Play money.

She had no pen with her, and couldn't see one in the cab, so she took the registration and insurance papers and pocketed them. Then she closed the doors, retreated to a hiding place behind a nearby rocky outcropping, and waited.

Twenty minutes later the mine doors opened, and a man whom she recognized as Dennis Lestage came out, accompanied by another man — smaller in stature, but quicker in movement. She tried to use her training to do a cursory ID of the second man: Mediterranean, perhaps, or East Indian? She watched the two men load the contents of the rail car onto the powered tailgate. It took them ten minutes at most to complete the task, and to stack the cellophane-wrapped drugs in the back of the truck. "One more load," she heard Dennis say, as the two men retreated back into the mine. As they disappeared from view, she formulated a plan. She thought she had an hour or so before they were back. She waited five minutes, grabbed four bottles of water, and ran back into the mine, toward the central storage area. She opened the door of the marijuana room and scooted back into the room in which Indy was imprisoned. It was easier, psychologically, now that she knew how long the narrow, claustrophobic tunnel was.

"Indy," she called out as she wriggled her way back into the marijuana room, "here's four bottles of water. Drink half of it now. Conserve the rest. They have one more load to bring through the mine, they said."

"Whatcha doing, Cath?" he asked.

"Those guys are loading up a truly massive shipment of heroin. Several tons, Indy. Tons. And it's weirdly wrapped. In bricks, in red cellophane. Least I think that's what it is. I'm going to check it out."

"Are you nuts?" said Indy. "This is a heroin crowd. I've been undercover with their sort for years. They'll put a bullet in your head just because they don't like your hairdo. Stay here. We can get out the Canadian end of the mine, get to a phone, and get that truck pulled over before it reaches Whitefish, Montana. Stay here. That's an order."

"Indy, think about it. We don't know where that truck is going. The FBI might miss it, even if we give a perfect description. But we know who these traffickers are. If I can find out enough, we can put the entire Lestage/Hallett gang in the big house within 48 hours. We might be able to nail whoever's at the other end of the pipeline. A shipment of drugs this big is probably headed to California, and there must be some heavy-duty guys at that end. I didn't get to be corporal with the Force by sitting still. I'm going back out there. I can hide behind some trees. I may get lucky and pick up some more scraps of information. I'll be OK."

With that she was gone, this time crawling her way through the narrow ventilation shaft as though it were a school hallway. Back in the main tunnel, she ran toward the southern entrance and clambered into the back of the truck. She had not mentioned this part of the plan to Indy. He would have forcibly restrained her had he known what she was thinking. It occurred to her that she might regret it later, but for now she was set on tagging along. She buried herself underneath one of the tarps and crouched down behind the drugs, as close to the wall of the truck box as possible. Then she reassembled, as best she could, a stack of the red bricks in front of her. There was the odd crack in the pile, which she hoped the smugglers wouldn't notice.

She didn't have long to wait. Soon the mine doors opened again, and Dennis reappeared, this time with not one, but two other men. Both men were of the same slight build, and moved quickly. Both expressed supreme frustration with Dennis in their body language. Both seemed to be saying, "Let's go, let's hustle, don't dawdle." Catherine curled into the smallest ball she could manage, thanking God for her small frame. At one point she could swear that one of the men had touched her, but thankfully, with the poor light inside, and the now bright light outside, she was not seen.

After the reloading, the three of them stood talking for a moment, and then Dennis headed back into the coal mine. One of the strangers hopped into the back of the truck, pulled several of the tarps over the load, and placed the coolers on the edge of the tarps to hold them down. The second man walked a short distance into the woods on the other side of the truck and stopped to relieve himself. Thirty seconds later, she heard the rear door of the truck slide down, and the lock click shut. Then the truck engine started up, and they began a lurching, bumpy ride away from the mine.

Catherine reached into her pocket for the cell phone, which Dennis had, in his sloppy manner, neglected to take from her. Had he seen it, he probably wouldn't have cared anyway. They were many miles from the nearest cell tower, and had been deep underground. She flipped the cell phone open. A large red icon was blinking, signaling a low battery. Dammit, she thought. Hooped. Oh well, at least she had the… desperately, she searched one pocket after another. No GPS locator. She couldn't believe it. No GPS. It must have fallen out of her pocket at some point while she was running toward the truck. What rotten luck. Double hooped. No telephone. No GPS. She fiddled through her pockets again, more carefully this time. The only thing of any use was the cigarette lighter that she and Indy had used for light in the subterranean room at Devil's Anvil.

IT WAS 7:30 in the morning when Izzy and Ba'al finished the loading and drove away from the southern end of Devil's Anvil. The day was gorgeous, the sky a bright metallic blue, with the occasional puffy cloud floating by. They were at the headwaters of the Flathead Valley, with the razor sharp peaks of Glacier National Park to the east, and the ruggedness of the Flathead National Forest to the west. The tiny hamlet of Polebridge was only 16 miles ahead of them, but they were 16 rough miles, along the winding and unpaved road that ran parallel to the Flathead River. The first two miles toward the old Peterson homestead were particularly difficult, in that there was no road at all, just a rugged trail, almost completely hidden by the fir and pine trees that covered the lower mountainside. "It's those damned satellites the Yanks have," Leon had complained when he first showed them the trail. "They look at every inch of the border, and if they see a trail that shouldn't be there, presto, instant trouble." South of the Peterson ranch, the road, though still unpaved, was at least well graveled and easier to travel on. From there it would be a straight shot to Polebridge, where they'd connect with real roads.

The first hour was particularly rough on Catherine, as the truck lurched from one pothole to the next, and in and out of various ruts, sideswiping the odd fir tree. She was able to relax and stop bracing herself against the wall when they finally connected with old skid trails, and relaxed even more a few miles later when they got to the logging road that ultimately led to Polebridge. At Polebridge, a town that consisted of a few houses, a gas station, a store, and a saloon, the road crossed the Flathead River and became Highway 486.

Both Izzy and Ba'al sighed with relief as they pulled onto the highway. They were through another step of their plan and finally on their way. They were also totally oblivious to the extra passenger they were carrying, under the tarps, in the back of the truck. It was 8AM, Pacific Standard Time, September 1, when Izzy pulled out the satellite phone and dialed a prearranged number. In distant Islamabad, a telephone rang three times and stopped. Then four rings, then five. It was a signal that had been arranged months earlier. The explosive was going to be delivered on schedule. Time to initiate the next step in the plan.

At 8AM in Los Angeles, the sky was a smoky brown. While the pollutants were a constant source of irritation, they did produce beautiful sunrises and sunsets. Massoud and Javeed were facing southeast, toward Mecca. They were, on this penultimate morning of their lives, in a state of intense and focused prayer. They'd been told that there would be no pain. Only a blinding flash of light, and then they would enter Paradise. They would have struck a blow for the *jihad* that would eclipse any other terrorist strike ever made. Maybe Yousseff, Kumar, and the others had a collateral purpose, but not these two. In their minds, this was a mission for Mohammed, peace be upon Him. It would make their lives the most important of the day, in the service of their religion and country.

39

BUCKINGHAM SIGHED IN FRUSTRATION. There was no way the Al Jazeera reporter was going to talk. He had personally spoken to Mahari after both the third and the fourth messages had been delivered. He'd tried everything he knew — begged and pleaded, threatened and yelled. But nothing had worked. "Reporter's privilege," was Mahari's only reply. "Have to protect my sources. Don't you do that in America?"

The Islamabad Al Jazeera station was being watched around the clock. Various Embassy personnel were taking turns recording car plate numbers and taking photographs of the visitors coming to and from the station. For the better part of three weeks now, various agents had also been trailing the increasingly joyous reporter, and it was during the course of this exercise that they found out about the second apartment, and the growing collection of Samsonite cases. This was reported back to Buckingham, who let the Intelligence Community back home know. That little bit of information left no doubt that Mahari's contacts were drug dealers. A major drug exporter would have rooms full of unlaundered American currency, to fund Mahari's growing collection; a religious leader, such as the Emir, would not. Turbee's connection between the terrorists and the drug lords was once again reinforced. Not that it helped them much.

Mahari was careful when he went to pick up the DVD's and the payments. He never used the same route twice. Over three weeks of following him, though, Buckingham had become convinced that the supplier of the messages was located somewhere within the busy Peshawar marketplace. That was the reason that he had suggested Richard's involvement. Richard had practically grown up in the Peshawar marketplace, and knew every one of its twists and alleys. Twice in the week before, Mahari had made the trip from Islamabad to Peshawar, and each time he could be seen entering an area full of tiny shops. That was where he shook the tailing agent. Every time. He was always seen leaving the market area an hour or two later, with a happy expression on his face and a Samsonite case in his hand. It was obvious what was happening.

After this most recent message, Buckingham and his superiors had decided that, on the next trip to Peshawar, Richard, with Jennifer in tow, would follow Mahari. Buckingham reminded them both about the President's orders. A light touch was required. No knocking reporters over the head, or mindlessly destroying a shopkeeper's home and business. Al Jazeera was a station that was acquiring an enormous viewing audience, not just in the world of Islam, but throughout the world. They would delight in showing the world anything the Americans did wrong. More bad publicity was the last thing the American military needed.

Richard's orders were to stand by, and be ready for a call from Embassy staff. As soon as it became apparent to the agents that Mahari was making another trip to Peshawar, Richard was to be contacted, and then report to the Embassy forthwith. An Embassy helicopter would whisk him off to Peshawar within minutes, since a motor vehicle would take a good two hours to traverse the clogged and overused highway. Richard would follow the reporter into the market area, and hopefully find out where Mahari was giving them the slip.

While Ba'al and Izzy were proceeding southward through the Flathead Valley in Montana, Richard, at his home in distant Islamabad, was receiving the call from Embassy staff. Mahari was on the move. He looked like he was heading toward Peshawar. It was time to put Buckingham's plan into motion.

First, however, Richard had some requirements to see to. He opened his medicine cabinet. It had been an incredibly difficult week. He didn't feel up to another mission, and especially not one where he would be responsible for another agent's life. But he hadn't been given a choice, and his conscience wouldn't allow him to offer anything less than his best. In his current state, his "best" would require reinforcements. The Vicodin was necessary, of course. He had three bottles, from various Internet drugstores. Maybe 100 pills. He also found a small amount of Ativan. Before he left the house, he took three Vicodin and one Ativan, downing the pills with a tumbler of scotch. He pocketed the rest and headed for the door, ready to take on the bad guys.

PESHAWAR. The city of flowers. It was only a short journey from Islamabad, and the scenery was beautiful. After returning to the Islamabad Embassy and moving back into his childhood home the week before, Richard had made several visits to this very marketplace. He had practically grown up among these shops, and was naturally drawn back. Sometimes nostalgia brought him here, to walk the streets and reminisce about safer times, when his father and Zak had been at his side and his mother had been waiting for them at home.

Sometimes it was just an attempt to escape the house and neighborhood in which he'd experienced the death of his parents. Now, dressed in a Pashtun *dishdash*, with a beard tacked on, and with his dark complexion, he came here on a mission for his country. He had learned the languages spoken here as a boy and knew that his speech would mark him as a local, if his complexion didn't. The only possible problem was his blue eyes, but he solved that with a pair of dark sunglasses.

The mission was almost ridiculously easy. Jennifer was waiting for Richard in the chopper, and when they got to Peshawar they had almost an hour to wait for Mahari. They had been briefed on where he would park his vehicle. Once the reporter arrived, they picked up the tail easily, and since Richard was as familiar with the marketplace as Mahari, it was like tailing someone through a basic shopping mall — and not even a large or busy one. The path meandered a bit, and Mahari even tried the "in the front, out the back" trick a few times, but Richard was able to follow without being detected. Eventually Mahari entered a small shop, located in the older section of the marketplace. The shop seemed to sell pipes of various kinds, along with the different substances one would use for those pipes. Richard and Jennifer stalled in the street behind him, doing their best to look like casual locals.

IT WAS 4PM on the late and rainy September 1 afternoon. Ray was sitting in room 237 at the Day's Inn in Glendale, with his friends Sam, Hank, and Ted. These were the other men the Emir had sent to Los Angeles as part of his cell. They'd been little more than boys when they made the trip over, and had spent months huddled up together in a single house, trying to regain the feel and comfort of home. Now they were older and had all started living like real Americans. They'd long since lost the religious fervor that had driven them into the Emir's service as children. None were happy about being called into action. They sat across the room from Massoud and Javeed, who had been personally delivered by Kumar. In keeping with the central rule of cutout cell organization, no one in the ever more crowded motel room had even noticed Kumar when he came in. Ray had given the two boys a short, cynical stare. He didn't need to say what he thought of their involvement.

The air within the room, now filled with seven people, three of whom smoked, was sullen and heavy. Ghullam was giving instructions in short, staccato Urdu monotones. Each participant was given specific and detailed direction as to his role. Both Ray and Sam were truckers, and had spent most of the past ten years hauling eight-axles across the vast USA. Both loved the open road, and neither wanted to be in this tense, cramped motel room. However, they both had a healthy fear of the Emir. They warily took note of Ghullam's steely gray eyes, his size, and his movements. They'd seen his type before, and knew what his role was.

They were each given maps and diagrams. For three hours they went over the plan again and again, tackling each possibility. Ray was secretly relieved. Even after all the talk of details, his only responsibility was to drive a truck from point A to point B, and back again. No crashing into fuel dumps or refineries, no blowing things up in the middle of Los Angeles. Just drive the truck to the middle of nowhere and assist with some minor details. That was it. He'd be working with Ted as his wingman. Hank and Sam would be working together, and were taught how to use the television camera and the satellite uplink that came with it. They were told that it was absolutely necessary to have a video broadcast of what was about to happen. Hour after hour, day after day, the American networks would replay it. The coming events needed to be embedded in the American psyche, in the way that previous attacks had been. It was part of the terror.

In the middle of what seemed like their tenth time through the plan, Ghullam's cell phone rang, and he answered. Yes, he would be there he said. He would get a taxi. He turned to the six. "You must stay here. Do not talk. Do not leave. Wait for me."

VIJAY MET GHULLAM at one of the many airport hotels in the vicinity of LAX. He had already checked out and was waiting by the hotel's front doors. They didn't delay, but went first to Ray's apartment, then to Hank's, and then to Sam's. Ghullam had equipment for picking the locks and gaining access to each apartment. Vijay marveled at Ghullam's almost magical skills when it came to entering almost any apartment. In a way, Vijay thought, those skills were similar to his own abilities to break into computers and networks of any sort. He and Ghullam plied the same trade, albeit in different domains. Ghullam's role was to gain entry to the apartments of Hank, Ray, Sam, and Ted. Vijay's was to gain access to their computers. His job was to rework the computer hard drives of each of the four men. Ray and Hank's apartments had posed no problems. The break-ins were quick and easy, and the computers they found had off-the-shelf set-ups. Nothing quirky. All he did was slip a CD into the appropriate bay and let the programs load. It took less than ten minutes to sabotage Ray's computer, a 20-minute taxi drive, and a similar process at Hank's small home. A brief reference to Nooshkatoor in one email, to various members of the Karachi government and police force in others. Occasionally, mention of one or two Afghani drug lords — rivals of Yousseff's. Messages that were encrypted, but not too highly.

He was in the middle of repeating the same steps at Sam's house when the front door opened and Sam's girlfriend, a vivacious, high-striding beauty named Julie, appeared. She was carrying a bag of groceries, which she dropped in shock when she saw them.

Ghullam pulled out his gun, a small copy of the Silenced Mag Ruger, modified by the gunsmiths of Darra Adam Khel. He looked at the girl sternly, and placed a finger across his lips, motioning for her to be silent. He smiled when she nodded in compliance, as she stood, rooted to the ground. Then he approached her and, unencumbered by conscience, and a broadening smile, shot her twice in the head and once in the heart.

He turned to Vijay as though what had occurred was as inconsequential as swatting a fly. "Reconfigure the computer," he ordered. "Then we go to Ted's home. Quickly."

"Yes, Ghullam. Let me work here," replied Vijay, feeling a little faint at what had just occurred. He had witnessed Ghullam in the act of murder. What was particularly chilling was the calm, almost serene manner in which the assassin had done it, and the smile that appeared to be playing around his lips afterward. Vijay shuddered and continued with his work, hoping never to be on the wrong side of Ghullam's gun.

He quickly gained access to the operating system and loaded the contents of his CD onto the computer. Ghullam busied himself with wiping the door handle clean of all fingerprints. He left the body where it was. It would confound the investigation that was to come.

Within minutes, the job was done, and they were off to the last apartment. Ghullam had the lock open in under a minute, and they entered. Another 15 minutes passed, and the fourth computer was reconfigured. Ghullam had Vijay call a cab.

"Day's Inn, Glendale," was all Ghullam told the taxi driver. "Hurry."

The driver eyed them nervously in the rearview mirror. Ghullam was weighing the pros and cons of killing him too, just for being nosy, but he thought it best to leave the matter alone. The driver dropped Ghullam off at the Day's Inn, and was instructed to take Vijay on to LAX. He would be taking a transatlantic flight to Schiphol later that day. From there, he would catch a connecting flight home to Karachi. His work was done.

It was 9PM before Ghullam returned to room 237 at the motel. Ray, Sam,

Hank, Ted, and the two teenage *jihadists* were waiting anxiously. Ghullam extended a gloved hand toward Ted, giving him the Mag Ruger. "You may need this. Hang on to it," he said.

"Sure, Ghullam. Not a problem."

"Watch it. Keep the safety on. It's loaded," added Ghullam, watching Ted place his fingerprints all over the weapon.

The plan was for the six of them to head out in two vehicles. Ray was to drive one, Sam the other. They took cabs from the motel, and by 11PM they had reached a series of warehouses just off the I-15. Two vehicles were parked in one of the warehouses — a five-ton van and a large semi. A number of unusual modifications had been made to the vehicles while they had been in storage at the PWS facility at Long Beach. The van had, stashed inside, a satellite uplink station, set to an NBC carrier frequency, compliments of Kumar and his technicians. The van also carried the Ark, while the semi carried the modified submersible. The men were not told what the equipment was for, or who had provided it; it was not their place to worry about such details. Sam slid behind the steering wheel of the smaller vehicle, while Ray stepped into the cab of the semi, still thankful that his role was only that of transporter. Ghullam stayed behind in the warehouse. His job was to sanitize.

40

AT TTIC, the members of the team were working 24 hours a day. It was 2AM, and most of them were still at their desks, tracking down whatever information they could find. Before long, Turbee made the next break in the case. He was happy to let Dan continue to fret and foam about the apparent impending nuclear attack on an American port city. For his part, Turbee was hot on the Semtex chase. While Wharfdog Charlie was clearly lacking in presentation, and likely intelligence, he had been very clear about some of the technical aspects of what he had seen of the submarine-to-truck reload. The curious scissors lift systems and the self-loading pallets he had described sounded similar to those they'd seen in the pictures of the ship-to-ship transfer near the Maldives. It had the same feel. For Turbee, that was enough. He hacked his way into the RCMP internal communication system and began searching.

Before long he found the electronic residue of Izzy's speeding ticket. A dirty white box van. Two occupants, apparently of central Asian descent. And a license plate that began with the letters DGO. It was a hit.

"Look at that, George," said Turbee to his neighbor. "Same truck. Has to be. Heading east from Kamloops, moving toward the Rockies on Highway 1. Put the whole track, from Stewart to the speeding ticket, on the Atlas Screen. Let's see where they're going."

Turbee lowered the lights a bit (Johnson was still trying to figure out how he did that) and pointed to the map, where George had plotted the coordinates he'd asked for. "A few hundred miles from the border, Dan," he said. "That's where it was at four this afternoon. I doubt very much that they'd go through all this trouble to hit a Canadian target. Nothing truly valuable or important up there in any event. They're coming to the States. They have a route. They have a plan. We just haven't figured it out yet."

Dan grumbled and telephoned Admiral Jackson.

AT ROUGHLY THE SAME TIME, on the other side of the world, Richard and Jennifer were walking across a narrow cobblestone street toward the small pipe store that Mahari had entered. The Peshawar marketplace was rich in memories for Richard. Every fragrance, every image and sound, released another swarm of childhood experiences. Memories of parents. Memories of Zak. Memories that were bittersweet. He was trying to keep the memories of their deaths at bay. Now wasn't the time for an emotional breakdown. But the longer they stayed in the atmosphere, the more difficult it became. The gnawing pain in his forehead was reaching a crescendo, and that wasn't helping matters. He was slipping, mentally, and the pressure in his head was building. He didn't think it would be long before the emotional problem became physical as well. The sooner they completed this mission, the better.

They stopped momentarily outside the little shop, and then stepped inside. Richard took off his sunglasses and blinked his eyes, trying to accustom them to the dim room. Jennifer picked up some of the ornately carved hardwood and bronze pipes, using the action to disguise her eyes, which were feverishly scanning the small shop. Richard cautiously stepped further into the dusky interior, every bit as alert as Jennifer. There was a faint smell of opium and hashish in the air.

When no one came to the counter, Jennifer put the pipes down and stepped behind it, parting the hanging bead curtain that separated the main shop area from a smaller back room. In the back room, a young man looked up from a computer keyboard, startled at their sudden appearance. Both Jennifer and Richard recognized him immediately.

"What do you want?" Mahari asked.

"We would like to buy some pipes," Jennifer replied. "Nice carved wooden pipes. What do they cost?"

Mahari got up from his small workstation. "Yes, my name is Mahari. Let me help you. Let me show you our best." He had already identified both as foreigners, regardless of the skillful attempt at disguise. Mahari had grown up in Peshawar, and the pipe shop they were in was owned by his uncle, an old and faithful acquaintance of Yousseff. He knew what kind of people came into the shop, and this man and woman didn't fit.

As the reporter got up and entered the display area, Richard, in one smooth motion, slipped by him and sat down at the keyboard. It was a new computer, equipped with Windows. In an instant he had opened the "Files" menu, and before Mahari could protest, had clicked on the "Open" option.

Mahari, hearing the clicking of the keyboard, darted toward Richard, his hands outstretched. "Excuse me sir. You cannot do that. Get off the computer now or I will call the police."

Jennifer pulled out her gun. "Actually, we are the police. The real police. The police who want to prevent another terrorist attack. Sit down or I'll blow your balls off."

Mahari suddenly grew unsure of himself. He seemed ready to fight, but hesitant over whether he really wanted to.

"Don't even think about it, camel shit," said Richard, as he pulled out his gun. "Sit down on the floor right there, and we may let you live." Richard motioned to the corner of the back room with his gun.

As Mahari seated himself, Richard looked over the file list that he had activated. It was an amazingly long list. One entry seemed interesting. It contained the single word, "Messages." Richard clicked on it. Six sub-files appeared. "Message One," then "Message Two," running all the way down to "Message Six."

"Well, what do we have here, Mahari? These wouldn't be the Emir messages that Al Jazeera has been broadcasting, and is going to broadcast in the next few days, would they?" asked Richard.

Mahari said nothing, but Jennifer could swear that he was smirking at them both. "Richard, just go to the last message. Let's see where this nonsense ends."

Mahari was in fact gloating to himself. In his eagerness, Richard had not seen the knee switch that Mahari had activated. He didn't realize that virtually the entire bazaar was controlled by Pashtun drug smugglers. Mahari played a key role in a complex mission, and was closely protected and watched as he delivered the messages, one by one, to Al Jazeera. If it weren't for Richard's deteriorating condition, he would have immediately grasped the complexity of the situation.

Instead, Richard casually clicked on the final message, ignoring the reporter. The media file loaded itself and began to play. It took all of three minutes. Richard and Jennifer watched and listened to it in rapt fascination and horror, silent for a few seconds after the last word had been uttered.

Finally Richard roused himself into action. "Holy shit, Jen. Call the Embassy right now. We know where this thing is going, and we may still be in time to stop it. This is worse, much worse, that we thought. Call them now."

Jennifer touched the speed dial on her cell phone with shaking fingers, ringing through to the American Embassy. She reached Buckingham's personal secretary. "Lauralee, get me Michael now," she said, her voice shaking. She heard Buckingham's rough voice in the background. "Give me a minute," she heard him say.

Precious seconds ticked by. Finally she heard Buckingham shuffle toward the phone. "Buckingham," he said.

"Mike," breathed Jennifer. "We've seen the last message. The sixth message. We know the target."

That was as far as she got before an enormous hand pulled the flip phone from her hands. In a second it was twisted into two pieces. The remnants were thrown onto the floor of the shop. Richard, who was still staring at the computer, heard Jennifer gasp, and half rose from the computer table, turning and receiving a vicious kick to the head for his trouble. Pain spidered through his skull, and he sank to his knees. Four other people came in, through both the back door and the beaded curtain.

Richard was thrown to the floor and brutally handcuffed, with his hands in front of him. The attackers kicked him a few more times, in both his head and ribs. He gasped in pain, feeling reality begin to fade away in a pink and frothy haze. He heard the click of another set of handcuffs, then felt a constriction around his hands as he and Jennifer were imprisoned in a connected set of manacles.

"I'd kill you both now, but I need a little bit of information from you. I hope you don't mind," one of the men said in heavily accented English. "It'll only take an hour or two, I can assure you. I hope you will enjoy it as much as I will." He motioned to his men. "Take them both back to the van. Go to the Inzar Ghar fortress. Put them in one of the basement cells. I'll let you play with them after I'm done."

Having grown up in Islamabad, Richard had heard the stories about Inzar Ghar, and felt his blood run cold. He looked groggily over at Jennifer. Her face was white as a sheet, and blood ran freely from her nose and one ear. He was on the verge of saying something when he received another blow to the head and, in a shattering of pain and black spots, lost consciousness.

"WHAT TO DO, what to do…" Baxter was now talking to himself. He played the call back several times. There was some significant information there. "The sixth message…" They had only received four so far. What did the other two say?

He copied the sound file to his computer and then sent an email to Big Jack, the executive directors of most other Intelligence Agencies, the SECDEF (new at his job, since his predecessor hadn't survived the *Haramosh Star* affair), and Dan Alexander and his crew at TTIC.

Attached find a phone call that the Islamabad Embassy received at 18:30 today, Karachi time. Richard Lawrence and Jennifer Coe have been either captured or killed. Note that there are six messages, according to Jennifer. The most significant message is apparently the last. Jennifer was captured before she could give full details. There is some background chatter in the phone conversation; I suggest that the NSA or the FBI analyze that for more information. We need to organize a rescue mission now or we'll lose them like we lost Goldberg.

There was a general chorus of exclamations up and down the Intelligence Community chain, as the email bounced from office to office. This couldn't be good.

"Any more of this bullshit," the President had said, "and we'll be declaring war."

41

INDY COULD BARELY KEEP HIS RIOTING NERVES under control. He had tried deep breathing exercises, meditation, and prayer. Nothing worked. His anxiety was coming over him in waves. He wanted to scream with fear and anger. He was imprisoned, but the escape route was right in front of him. A little ventilation tunnel, which, within 20 feet, would take him to freedom. He had gone as far as sticking his arms and head into the tunnel, but that was the extent of it. At that point the terror had rolled over him and he'd had to scramble back into the money room. Imprisoned in the dungeon of his own making, he had been handed the key to his freedom but didn't have the strength to use it. Even Catherine had been fearful, and she didn't have the psychological obstructions that he did. He could see the route. Any person could. But he had to actually take it. Walking the walk or, in this case, crawling the crawl, was required. Talking the talk, as usual, accomplished little. Though he realized the true nature of his imprisonment, he was in the dark when it came to what was going on outside the mine. Had he known what was going on in the rest of the world, and how the information he held could arrest the development of the situation, he might have been able to do it.

He reached for the water Catherine had brought him and took a long, satisfying gulp. He tried again to enter the ventilation shaft, and got as far as his hips before the fear became too great. He swore silently to himself. Surely someone of his training and intelligence could gather the mental strength to overcome a little thing like fear of enclosed spaces. Then another wave of anxiety rushed over him, so intense that he became nauseated, and his resolution vanished. He was never going to get out of here. Never. Where was Catherine? Had they found her? Killed her? What if no one other than he and Catherine knew the true location of Devil's Anvil? What if the Fernie RCMP didn't know? What if, by the time any massive manhunt found him, he had died of dehydration? What if the thugs dynamited the tunnel? Time and again his mind drifted back to that incident, 20 years earlier in the Fraser Valley… the gunshots, the trench, the grave, the searing pain and panic, his lungs bursting for air. Not again. Please, God, not again.

INSPECTOR BLACKMAN and Corporal McCloud, from the Heather Street complex, had arrived in Fernie via the RCMP chopper. They were very concerned about the disappearance of Indy and Catherine. "Not like either of them to do that," they said. Both Blackman and McCloud had worked with Indy for years. Both knew that Indy and Catherine had planned to go to some kind of mine near the Akamina. Both were concerned when neither had called in. The Fernie detachment had been called and told to wait for Blackman and McCloud, as the RCMP heli-service would be bringing them to the Kootenays. Constables Brink and Koopman, both local officers who worked on a daily basis with Catherine, were waiting for them. They were equally concerned about their friend's disappearance, and were happy to be doing something about it.

As soon as the helicopter landed, the four of them headed south toward the Akamina-Kishinina and Dennis Lestage's trailer. The Lestages and the Halletts were trouble, to be sure. Brink and Koopman knew the ill-fated story of Benny Hallett, his destroyed truck, and the shattered knee. They were suspicious of what might have happened. All were aware of the contents of Indy's affidavits, sworn the week before. Inspector Inderjit Singh was a legend within the Force — they all felt flattered at an opportunity to help him.

They arrived at the trailer by 8PM, and kicked an already-sleeping Dennis out of bed.

"Wake up, my friend. We have two missing cops, and I think you know something about it," barked Koopman as they entered the bedroom. The trailer had been unlocked, and they knew that Indy had a warrant, so they figured they were probably OK. Even if they weren't, their concern was for the fate of two members of the Force, not for fine details about the admissibility of evidence in a courtroom.

"Don't know what you're talkin' about," mumbled Dennis, more fearful of Leon than of cops or any sentence a judge could pronounce.

"Older cop, maybe 50, and a lady, maybe 30. You haven't seen them?" asked Constable Brink.

"Nope. Haven't seen them. No sir. Not here. Definitely no."

"Corporal Gray was telling us that there's a mine out here. Devil's Anvil, she said. Ever heard of that?" asked Koopman.

"Mine? Devil's Asshole? Nope. Never heard of it. No sir," replied Dennis.

"He's lying," said Blackman. He had seen his share of police questioning and could spot the signs. Not that it was hard. Dennis looked to have the

IQ of a rock. Not exactly the sharpest tool in the shed, and no good at lying, either.

"Aw, come on, Blackman. Maybe he's just got naturally shifty eyes," responded McCloud.

"Which way is south?" asked Blackman.

"That way," said Koopman, leading them out of the trailer and pointing toward a large granite bluff directly behind the home. There was a small, overgrown trail that headed in that direction.

"I think that's where we're heading," said Brink. "Cuff him, Koopman," he told his partner.

"Cuff me? What the hell for? I ain't done nothing!" protested Dennis.

"Oh, relax," said Koopman. "We'll think of something."

Blackman had to smile. He admired the style of his colleagues. These boys were doing it right.

"Where's the trail go, Dennis?" asked Koopman.

"Don't know," replied the disconsolate Dennis. Leon was going to kill him, for sure. This was very bad. They would find the two cops, and the millions of dollars in drugs and money. Leon would kill him slowly, brother or not, just for the pleasure of doing it. He started sweating just thinking about it.

"Yeah, right," said Brink. "You live here and you don't know where the trail goes. Come on guys," he said, motioning to the other three. "Let's go exploring."

Koopman pulled Dennis stumbling along behind them. It didn't take them long to find the mine. A white five-ton box van was parked by the entrance.

"Whose truck, Dennis?" asked Koopman.

"Truck?"

"Yes, dumb nuts. Whose truck?"

"Never seen it before, sir. Never. Don't know how it got here," responded Dennis.

"Koop," said Constable Brink, "why don't you run the plates through the Sat-phone. Let's see what pops up." The RCMP had recently implemented a system whereby information could be transmitted and retrieved via a secured satellite link. The research only took a few seconds.

"Rental vehicle, Brink," said Koopman. "Rented in Prince George. Driver had a speeding ticket last night east of Kamloops. Some guy by the name of Izzy al Din. D'ya know who that might be, Dennis?"

"Not a clue. Never heard of him."

"I see. Well this looks like a mine entrance to me, Dennis," said Koopman, turning to look at the opening in the mountain. "Where does it go?"

"I have no clue. Never seen it before. Nope, not me. No clue," whined an ever more despondent Dennis Lestage.

"Can you turn on the lights, Dennis?" asked Koopman.

Reluctantly, and with great lethargy, Dennis stumbled over and turned on the generator. Benny's blown out knee would be nothing compared to what would happen to him. Not even jails would be safe. Leon was a Hell's Angel, and they practically ran the jails. He was doomed. Doomed.

He never stopped to think that by turning on the generator, he'd directly contradicted his claim of ignorance. The officers found this extremely amusing. Laughing to themselves, they entered the mine, dragging Dennis.

BEHIND THEM, hidden around a bend in the trail, a man with piercing blue eyes watched. Leon had seen the cop cars in the driveway when he arrived, and had waited until the officers dragged Dennis out of the trailer and down the path before sneaking onto his property. He'd already been into the trailer, to check for anything that might lead them to his Vancouver address. He didn't mind letting Dennis take the fall for what they found here, but he didn't want to be connected in any way. Now he watched them enter the mine, his thoughts racing. They would probably find the cops Dennis had imprisoned there, along with the drugs and the money. This operation was obviously finished. All that time and money, down the drain. Along with the mine itself. He grimaced. He was losing more than he cared to count. But Joseph's shipment should have already come through, and that meant he would have $10 million waiting for him in the bank in the Caymans. Maybe after the cops left, as they inevitably would, he could sneak into the mine and get some of the cash out. Added to the funds he'd already deposited, it should be enough to see him through until he could come up with something else.

He turned and hurried away, leaving Dennis to his fate with the RCMP.

IT TOOK AN HOUR, as they received no assistance from the ever-uncooperative Dennis, but the men from the Force eventually made it to the central area, and the hydraulic elevator. Dennis required a little more coaxing before he showed them how to use the elevator. Koopman was happy to supply the motivation. It took another half hour to find the storeroom area, with its four separate doors.

"Shush, guys, I hear something," said McCloud. They all stopped, feeling hot and compressed in the narrow tunnel. "There it is again," he said, walking toward one of the doors. "That door."

Koopman yelled loudly. "Catherine! Indy! Is that you?"

To everyone's surprise, Indy's voice came echoing back from inside the room. "Yes! Let me out of this damn dungeon!"

Koopman reached for the door and saw the large lock on it. "Got a key, Dennis?" he asked.

"I know nothing," said Dennis. "Didn't know any of this was here. Honest, eh?"

"Stand back Indy!" Koopman shouted. "I'm going to shoot out the lock. Everybody, get back. In this kind of situation things could ricochet all over the place."

The explosive noise from Koopman's firearm was amplified in the small space. A few small rocks fell out of the low dirt ceiling. Koopman wondered nervously, and belatedly, if the intensity of the sound could cause a cave-in. A few more chunks of rock were dislodged, but nothing else happened. The bullet shattered the lock, and a black and disheveled looking Indy almost fell out of the room.

"Am I ever glad you people came by! It's about time! Need air. I've got to get air." He almost ran down the tunnel toward the American entrance. He threw open the mine doors and breathed deeply of the pure Flathead Mountain air. He wasn't sure he could go back into the tunnel, even to get to the Canadian side.

Brink and Koopman watched Indy go. "Guess he's been there for a while," said Brink smartly.

Blackman, meanwhile, was peeking around the door into the room that had been Indy's prison. "Holy smokes, guys, look at this."

The others looked around the door at the mountains of cash stacked up against the walls of the room. "Oh my God. There's got to be a couple million dollars here," said McCloud.

Koopman was already opening the other doors. "You all had better come and look at what else we have," he said.

They took turns looking behind the other doors. Drugs. American money. Canadian money. More drugs. Marijuana. Cocaine. Heroin.

"Jesus, I guess Indy was right. He and Catherine found the mother lode, all right," said Koopman. "This has got to be one of the biggest drug busts in Canadian history. It's incredible."

"Knew nothing about this, eh Dennis?" asked Brink.

"Nope. Nothing at all. Didn't know this was back here," he said. "I just live in the trailer. I don't know nothing." Blackman rolled his eyes and smirked at McCloud. They all said that.

"Koop, you should go and get Indy," said Brink. "We've got to figure out what to do here. This completely blows me away."

Koopman and Blackman walked toward the American entrance. They tried hard not to laugh at the sight of the 50-year-old Inspector Inderjit Singh, face blackened by coal dust, lying flat on his back, arms and legs spread-eagled, staring at the sky, watching the stars come out.

"How long were you locked up, Indy?" asked Koopman.

"More than 36 hours by my count. And I'm claustrophobic. I almost went nuts in there," he replied.

"Nutser," corrected Koopman. "Where's Catherine?"

Indy sat up abruptly, looking around. "Oh damn. I was in such a hurry to get out of there that I forgot about her," he said. "We've got a bigger problem than just drugs, guys."

"What could be bigger than drugs? This is a major Canada/US drug corridor. I'm sure huge amounts of heroin, cocaine, marijuana, and money have been flowing back and forth through this hole for years. And God knows what else. This is going to make international headlines," said Koopman.

"But Catherine's disappeared," Indy said. "I don't see her around here. I'm sure she followed the drug smugglers out this end of Devil's Anvil. Maybe she hooked a ride with them, somehow."

Brink hadn't been listening to what Indy said. "How big a load came through here, Indy?" he asked.

"Huge. Absolutely huge. It took a total of four trips with that trolley they have in there. Catherine went out between the second and third loads, to have a look around. She came back and told me that it was a large van, or small truck, or something. She said she was going to get the plates and details, but she didn't come back after that. God, I hope those guys didn't find her."

"How big is huge, Indy?" Brink pressed.

"A couple of tons, at least," Indy responded. "At least. Millions of dollars, street value. Tens of millions. There was something unusual about it, guys. And I'm not only talking about the size of the shipment."

"What was that, Indy?"

"The way it was wrapped. Catherine said that it was divided into individual bricks, and that each brick was wrapped in red cellophane. I've spent my share of time working narcotics, and I've never heard of that before."

"Me either," responded Blackman.

"Indy, how is it that she got out and you didn't?" asked Koopman, scratching his head.

"There's a tiny little ventilation tunnel between rooms," Indy replied, trying to wipe the coal dust from his face with his wrinkled and torn shirt. "She was able to get out through that. I just… uhh… I just couldn't get through it. But she came back and told me about what was going on outside. She was pretty excited by it all. She went back out again, and didn't come back after that. If she's not here now, she must have somehow hitched a ride. She told me that there were tarps and coolers in the back of the truck with the drugs, and gave me this water. She may have got in behind the tarps somehow. At least I'm hoping that's what happened."

Koopman was scratching his head. "Red cellophane. Red cellophane. Why does that ring a bell?" He shook his head, then turned back to Indy. "How long ago did Catherine leave, Indy?"

Indy paused, and looked at his watch. "The last load was maybe 11 or 12 hours ago. It would have been early this morning."

Suddenly Koopman slapped his hand to his forehead. "Indy, you're right," he gasped. "This is way bigger than drugs. Red cellophane, my God!" He turned to the other officers, and was faced with blank stares. "Jesus, don't you guys watch the news or listen to your scanners? Mysterious loads transported in the middle of the night? Bricks wrapped in red cellophane? That Semtex that was stolen in Libya. It's in bricks, wrapped in red cellophane. Rumored to be heading for an American target."

With Koopman's announcement, the atmosphere became electric, and the men turned on Dennis with renewed purpose.

"OK, Dennis, I think you probably know more than you've been telling us," said Brink. "Who was it that came through here?"

Dennis only shrugged. Thinking again of Leon's psychopathic rages, he said woefully, "I don't know. I saw nothing. Not me. Nothing."

"Can you describe what they were transporting?" pushed Koopman.

"Describe? Me? No sir. I didn't see anything."

Blackman interrupted. "Listen, you jackass, there's a very good chance that what came through here was not drugs, but explosives. Semtex, headed toward the States, on the way to some massive terrorist attack. Haven't you been listening to the news? The Emir promising the destruction of an entire city?"

"Oh, maybe. Yeah, I guess I heard something about that. But I didn't think he would blow up Fernie."

"Good, Dennis. Then you know that we may be dealing with international terrorism here. That means this is a real crime, not like getting caught with a joint. We've got you on the scene of that crime. You won't be going to some nice, peaceful, happy Canadian jail. You'll go to Guantanamo Bay and stay there until scorpions are crawling out of your asshole. If you talk now, we'll take you back to the Canadian side of the border, where Canadian law governs. Otherwise we'll leave you here until the FBI shows up, which, by the way, is not going to be very long. Do you want to talk now?"

Dennis reflected on that for a second or two. He knit his brow and fixed his gaze on the ground in front of him. Leon or Guantanamo? Shivs or scorpions?

"OK," he said. "I'll talk. But I go to the Canadian side."

"Smart boy, this one," said Koopman. "Sharp as a tack. So tell us, Dennis, what came through here, and when, and in what amounts?"

TURBEE had been monitoring activity north of the border. He had been able to track the Semtex from Stewart, BC to Highway 1, east of Kamloops. With the assistance of the NSA, he was monitoring any satellite communications coming out of the southeast corner of BC. This yielded rich dividends when he picked up the Sat-phone license check by the Canadian cop.

As was his custom, Turbee raised his hand and waved it in the air, seeking someone's attention.

"Now what?" snapped Dan.

"We just intercepted an RCMP Sat-phone transmission. It came from a location less than half a mile north of the Montana border. It was a vehicle plate check. The first three letters of the plate were DGO."

When Dan didn't respond, Rhodes decided to take over. He quickly glanced at the time the license plate check had taken place and did the math in his head.

"It's arrived, people," he said calmly. "There is now more than four tons of high explosive in the hands of terrorists, somewhere in the United States."

"Assume that they're going a steady 70 miles an hour on our freeways. Assume that they've been in the country for 12 hours. Here's the area where they could be at the present time," George added. He drew a large arc on the Atlas Screen, with Devil's Anvil at the northernmost point. The arc included Kansas City, Cheyenne, Oklahoma City, Las Vegas, most of California, all of

Oregon, Washington, Idaho, Nebraska, and on and on. George looked at Dan expectantly. "So what do we do, captain?"

CORPORAL CATHERINE GRAY had been in the truck for several hours. The first hour had been almost unbearable, with a good amount of crashing and banging, as the truck navigated old skid trails and overgrown logging roads. But eventually the trip became smoother, and within two hours, she thought that they were riding on asphalt. There was a heavy stuffiness in the air, and the heat in the back of the truck increased as the day wore on. Then she remembered that there were a number of coolers sitting in the back of the truck with her. She flicked on her cigarette lighter and found them. She opened one and, to her delight, saw several cans of soda sitting in the bottom. She reached for one and had a long, pleasant swig of the pop. It was even cold.

Her thirst quenched, she sat back and used the flickering flame of the lighter to inspect the red bricks more closely. The drugs were definitely wrapped in red cellophane. She wondered again what that was all about. Maybe marketing, she thought. Even the criminals were getting MBA's now. She had a closer look and found that there were labels on the cellophane. Printed on the center of the each label, apparent in the light of the flickering lighter flame, was the word "SEMTEX." Semtex, Semtex, she mused to herself. Where had she heard that? Sometime in the past week… Then the penny dropped. The Libya explosion. The Presidential embarrassments. There had been missing Semtex. Was this it? Had she found the Semtex, here in the state of Montana, and heading south? What could that mean? Where was it heading? And damn the fact that her cell phone was dead!

Suddenly she realized that she was holding a cigarette lighter, and its little loop of flame, an inch or two from the brick's label. She dropped it, and was happy to make the rest of the journey in darkness. "Oh shit," she kept repeating quietly to herself. "Oh shit."

42

SOMEWHERE IN PAKISTAN, Richard and Jennifer found themselves in a similarly dangerous situation. They were blindfolded, and then tossed unceremoniously into the back of a van. Richard was fading in and out of consciousness. He was alert enough to notice that the van turned and stopped many times as it made its way to the outskirts of Peshawar. They reached a highway, but he was unable to tell in which direction they were headed. The van appeared to be climbing, and that would mean either north or northwest. Not a good sign. They were probably entering the lawless tribal lands, where Pashtun warlords reigned. He reflected on what had happened to Zak. Would parts of their bodies also end up being autopsied in some forensic lab in Tel Aviv? He put that aside as unhelpful, and tried to think about things they could do to get out of the situation instead.

"The cavalry's on its way, Jen," said Richard. "They got enough of the phone call to know we're in trouble." He wasn't sure if he was trying to offer comfort to her or to himself.

"Yes, of course. I forgot. The several million Marines that we have stationed in the Frontier Province are going to descend on us at any moment and take us back to the Embassy just in time for a late night snack," said Jennifer sarcastically.

"Warm milk and cookies," Richard tried to joke.

"Don't joke, Richard. I think we're headed into the mountains. Listen to the sound of the engine. He's down shifting a lot, and we're switching back and forth," said Jennifer.

There were a few final steep switchbacks, and then the van came to a halt. The back doors were opened, and they were both dragged roughly out of the van and thrown to the ground. Richard, unable to brace himself, felt a blinding stab of pain to his right temple as his head hit the ground again. He saw lights, then nothing. Knocked out for the third time in less than three hours. It was 6:30PM, September 1, Pakistan time.

THE HOURS PASSED SLOWLY. Richard vaguely recalled lurching to a halt, and his body being thrown out of the truck and then dragged down a dark stairway into a subterranean prison cell. His left hand had been cuffed to a large, heavy iron ring that protruded from the side of a cold, dark cell wall. He could only assume that they were in the basement of the Inzar Ghar safe house, located, from what he could remember, on the Pakistan side of the Sefid Koh.

The pounding pain in his temples quickly became unbearable. Richard had experienced chronic and debilitating headaches ever since he'd suffered an upper back injury in basic training. The intensity of the headaches was multiplied tenfold by the back spasms that came along with them. This particular problem had led him from aspirin, to Tylenol, to ibuprofen, and ultimately, when his life started to fall apart, to narcotics. Vicodin was his current drug of choice, only because it was readily available over the Internet. Some part of his brain realized that the various opiates, real and synthetic, led to ever-greater dysfunction. Another part of his brain justified and enabled the addiction. After all, he was taking medicine, not street drugs. Medicine that had initially been prescribed by doctors. He suffered chronic pain and was entitled to relieve it. He wasn't an addict, and he didn't use needles. He had a condition, like diabetes, that required medication to alleviate the symptoms. He had a job that carried with it great responsibility. He was functional, and the USA had a crying need for his services. In fact, had he not been told by Baxter that he was the one, the *only* one, who had the qualifications to do this?

On a more immediate and rational level, Richard knew that he'd never be able to perform those services, or take care of Jennifer, if his hands were tied by debilitating pain and the inevitable withdrawal that would come from a lack of medication. He knew how bad it would get, and how useless it would make him. The back spasms alone would have him paralyzed and completely helpless. He was able to reach, with his free hand, into his inside jacket pocket, where he'd hidden the bottle of Vicodin. He fumbled with it, sweating and cursing, trying to undo the tamperproof lid with one hand and his teeth. In his agitation, he dropped the open bottle on the ground, where it rolled, spilling about five of the pills. He was able to bring the bottle back toward him with his foot, and then started doing the same with the small white pills. Anchored to the wall by the handcuffs and the iron ring, he scraped the little pile of pills to within half an inch of his reach, less maybe. He pulled harder against the cuffs and ring, getting closer and closer, and was finally able to reach one, which he picked up and brought hungrily to his mouth. He was able to do the same with a second, and a third, and…

"Richard, what the hell are those?" asked Jennifer, who was similarly manacled on the opposite wall. "What are those little pills?"

"Oh, nothing. Nothing really. Just some stuff for my head. I have an upper back injury, and–"

"Richard, I'm with the CIA, OK? I know the signs. I know a little bit about your history. What are they? Oxycontin? Percodan?"

"I have chronic pain, Jen. Maybe you can't understand that. But I need those pills. I won't be functional without them. They're Vicodin."

"Oh Jesus Christ," she snorted. "Now Langley is sending drug addicts along to do high stakes missions. Why on earth did they send you, anyway?"

"Look, I'm not all that burned out. I've had some problems. Most people know that. I had a couple of marriages turn on me. My eyes went and I couldn't fly the Tomcats anymore. I had a nasty injury in basic training. Fractured a couple of vertebrae in my back. Set me back six months. Then I had to redo basic with an injury like that. I basically had to ignore the pain all the way through, just to qualify."

"So?" said Jennifer.

"What do you mean, 'so'?" he retorted. "Try walking that road for a mile or two. And I'm telling you, Jen, without those pills the pain will make me totally useless. We'll be worse off than we already are."

Jennifer bit her lip. "Sorry, Richard. This is the last place we should be arguing. The whole world knows what happened to Zak Goldberg. These are probably the guys who did that. We don't want to go there. We should be working together, to figure out how to get out of this."

"So nice of you to mention Zak," responded a straining Richard. "When my parents died, Zak's family took me in. I grew up with him. I heard the President read the coroner's report. I saw his body at the airport when Trufit brought me in. Dismembered him, skinned him, while he was still alive…" His voice trailed away, but he continued to reach for the pills on the ground.

Jennifer didn't respond, but watched him quietly. How extraordinary, she thought. He was actually expending more effort to get his drugs than he was to get out of this cell. Richard was pulling as hard against the handcuffs as he could, striving with all his might to reach the last three Vicodin, which were lying just outside his reach. He put one foot against the wall and pushed against it as hard as he could, reaching with his only free arm. The handcuffs dug brutally into the wrist of his manacled hand, and Jennifer worried that he might actually wrench a ligament or pull a joint from its socket. But the last pills remained just out of reach, no matter what he did.

Richard continued to reach, determined to either get the pills or dislocate a wrist, elbow, or shoulder in trying. He didn't care about the pain from the handcuffs. That was temporary. The pain in his back would be much, much worse.

All of a sudden he lurched forward, smashing his head against the hard stone flooring of the cell. More blinding pain, more stars, more wretched borderline consciousness. Why the hell had he ever joined the military, let alone the CIA? Then he realized where he was. On the floor. With the Vicodin. He turned around, scooped up the last three pills, and popped them into his mouth, dry swallowing them.

"Um, Richard? I know you're busy just now, but there's something you should notice here," Jennifer said, as politely as she could manage.

"What's that?"

"You're free. Well, more or less. At least, you're no longer manacled to the wall. I think that's more important right now than the drugs."

Richard, in his desperate struggle to get to the Vicodin, had missed the fact that the iron ring had come clean out of the wall. It had been anchored into the concrete by a metal prong, some ten inches in length, for God knew how many decades. The moisture, and likely overuse of the cell, had caused the prong to rot, and the pressure Richard had put on it had worked it loose. Richard looked around in amazement, flexing his hands. His increasingly drug-addled mind was struggling to come to terms with this change in position when he noticed that when he'd fallen forward, he'd landed right on a chunk of bone. In his unbalanced state, his focus rapidly changed from his freedom to the bone.

"What the hell is this, Jen?" he asked, holding the bone up to the light.

"It's a piece of bone. I think it's a tibia. Look, it's shattered on one end, but intact at the other. See, there are a few pieces of ligaments still hanging from it," said Jennifer.

"What a bunch of evil, vicious bastards these guys are," said Richard in disgust. "Probably tortured some guy to death right here."

Then it hit him. The moment of epiphany. The shocking horror of death. "Jen, it was Zak. This came out of Zak," whispered Richard hoarsely.

"You don't know that, Richard. It's a stretch," she said quietly, hoping he was wrong.

"Oh my God, it must have. Remember the President at that press conference? He said that one tibia had been torn from Zak's body, and hadn't been found. This is where they did it. Right here, in this cell. This is the torture chamber. Oh my God," breathed Richard.

They were both silent for a good five minutes. Richard clung to the tibia, the last piece of his best friend, and felt his defenses begin to crumble. The weeks of tension and years of pain, the people trying to kill him, Zak's terrible death, and now the responsibility of another mission, and Jennifer's life, all added up to more than he could take. A tidal wave of grief reached up to overwhelm him, and his delicate psyche began to break down. He started sobbing quietly. Jennifer tried to kick him out of it.

"You need to keep it together, Richard. You have to reach inside yourself and focus with whatever strength you have left. You're no longer chained, and that piece of bone probably belonged to a total stranger. Get over here and help me get loose."

Richard tried to gather himself. "I'm okay, Jen. I'd have figured it out eventually. I'm not totally addled… not yet anyway," he grunted, wiping a small trickle of blood from his forehead. "You know, if my ring came out, maybe yours will too. They were probably constructed at the same time. And this place hasn't exactly seen any upkeep. Let's see what we can do."

Richard walked over to her side of the cell, and reached for the iron peg to which her handcuffs were chained. He tried to jiggle it back and forth, but it didn't budge. He whacked it a couple of times with the iron ring assembly still handcuffed to his own wrist, but there was still no movement. He hit it a few more times before Jennifer asked him to stop.

"They'll hear that clanging, Richard. Try and pry it loose with that metal rod attached to your ring. Maybe you can lever it out," she said.

Richard, momentarily forgetting his own pain, stuck the short iron prong attached to his own ring through the ring that secured Jennifer's handcuffs to the wall. He put one foot against the wall, high up next to the ring, and pulled on the free ring and prong with all his might. His grip slipped loose, and he was sent hurtling across the cell once again, smashing the back of his head against the wall on which he had been chained. He cried out at the impact. More blinding pain. More stars. Seemed to be a pattern today, he thought wryly. He felt like he'd gone a few rounds with Mike Tyson. The back and top of his head, and both temples, were cut open and bleeding extensively. He clutched his jacket and found the second bottle of Vicodin. He took two at once.

"Richard, don't," pleaded Jennifer. "If we get out of here — and that's a big if — you'll need to have your wits about you."

"My wits are just fine," said Richard. "My head hurts, for reasons that I trust are obvious. I'm holding a chunk of tibia that came out of my best friend's body. I'm locked in some sort of torture chamber with no immediate chances of getting out, waiting for those bastards to come back for me. And I've been tasked with taking care of you and keeping those guys from destroying my country. Under the circumstances, I'd say I was doing pretty good. Now let me try again."

He walked back to Jennifer, slid the rod through her metal ring, found a firm fulcrum point in the damp stone wall, and pulled again. Jennifer marveled at the sudden change in his mood. He was babbling, barely coherent, and pitiful one minute, and the next he was rational and focused, planning for the next move. In truth, it was pretty amazing that he was lucid, nevermind being able to think or communicate logically. She couldn't even imagine the physical and emotional pain he was feeling. She was distracted from her thoughts by the movement of her ring.

"I think it's coming loose, Richard. Try again."

"Think so. Hold steady."

Three more yanks, and Jennifer's iron ring was definitely starting to come free. Richard pried it back and forth a few more times, and after one last gigantic effort, it sprang free from the wall. Richard fell backward yet again, but this time was able to break the fall with his shoulder.

He moaned loudly, then looked up at his partner. She was free. Now all they had to do was find a way out of the room.

ZAK STOPPED HIS DIGGING. This time he was sure about it. He'd heard the racket when the guards brought new prisoners into the dungeon. They sounded like they were in a cell in the chamber that connected to his. Not long after they'd been brought in, Zak had heard them speaking to each other. One man, and one woman. There had been a lot of crashing in the cell, as though they were trying to get out. He'd heard the screech of metal, and what sounded like a body hitting the floor, or maybe the walls, repeatedly.

There had also been a cry or two, and quite a bit of cussing. The first time he heard the voice of the man, he thought he was delusional. He was in enough pain, and had been through so much psychological torture, that he was actually starting to hear things.

The second time, he'd become more curious, and started listening a little harder.

At the third cry, and the next string of profanity, muffled by the intervening wall, he'd been sure. He knew the voice. He knew that tonality. He knew who was on the other side of the wall.

"Richard?" he mouthed silently.

JENNIFER stared at the ring assembly attached to her wrist in shock. "I'd love to say 'free at last,'" she said, "but we're a long way from that, I'm afraid. We've got to get out of this place, wherever this place is, and get back to friendly territory. I have a feeling friendly territory is a long way away."

"I think you're right. We're somewhere within the boundaries of the Northwest Frontier Province, which is Pakistan's version of the Wild West," Richard responded. "There's no government here. Different people have been trying to gain dominion over these lands for thousands of years, but it's a non-starter. This is Pashtun country."

"Nevermind that," replied Jennifer. "Even if we get back into Pakistan, we're not out of danger. The Pakistani police are probably corrupt. Like as not, we're now being advertised as dangerous murderers, to be shot on sight. I'm sure that somewhere in the upper echelons of their law enforcement there's a link to either the terrorists or the drug smugglers, or both. We won't be out of danger until we're back in the Islamabad Embassy, and maybe not even then."

"I agree. These people have billions of dollars at stake here. All they need is to find someone soft, someone who can be bought," said Richard.

"So what do we do? We have to get out. We have to find a way to get in touch with the Embassy, to let them know what the target is. Sitting here discussing the problems isn't going to get us anywhere."

"I have a plan. It's a little crazy, but we have to try something. We're going to have one chance, Jen. One shot. Only one. If we make it, we're out of this cell, but no guarantees beyond that. If we don't, we're gonna be finished. We're going to be running a gauntlet, Jen, and it's a big, scary one. Here's what we do."

During Richard's moments of lucidity, they planned it, critiqued it, improved it, revised it, and planned some more. Richard clung to Zak's tibia throughout. Jennifer was certain that, with the shock, the drugs, and the head injuries, Richard's stability had long since flown the coop. At one point she was even sure she saw him stroking the piece of bone. But he hadn't stopped trying yet, and he certainly hadn't given up. At least that was something.

As it turned out, they didn't have to wait much longer to try their plan. A door above them clanged open, then shut, and they heard the ominous march of heavy footsteps approaching the cell. It was 3AM local time, September 2.

43

IZZY AND BA'AL had reached I-15, and were headed south at a steady 70 miles an hour. They were now approaching the Idaho/Utah border, and were talking about anything that came to mind, trying to keep each other awake.

"Just like east Afghanistan, isn't it?" said Ba'al, looking at the fabulous panorama of ochre, brown, and green in the mountains and valleys sliding by them.

"Yes. It's truly beautiful here," his companion responded.

"You know," continued Ba'al, "this system of interstate highways spreads throughout all of the USA. Pretty incredible when you think about it. Put it on cruise control and float from Seattle to Miami."

"What's more amazing, though, is that you can travel from one end to the other without any fear of someone trying to bomb the hell out of you, or worrying that you might drive over a landmine, or thinking that you run the chance of getting some warlord and his band of soldiers on your tail," Izzy replied.

"So true," said Ba'al. "So true. The only thing you have to worry about is some nutcase in Alabama, or some crystal meth addict in LA, picking up a gun. That's nothing. And in Canada there's even less worry. No guns up there."

"Plus there's a restaurant every few miles. Food is dirt cheap. Hamburgers, steaks, Mexican, Italian, Greek, Pakistani even — you name it," added Izzy. "No fear that you're eating horsemeat, or a dog. No gruel. No *borange*."

"And look at the price of gas here," Ba'al said. "Dirt cheap. That's probably why the Americans are fuck sticking in Iraq, or even Afghanistan. They get Mid-East oil dirt cheap there."

Izzy thought about that for a while. Afghanistan was a beautiful country, with many striking vistas, especially when one neared the Hindu Kush. It was not the endless desert portrayed so often on CNN. And it would always be his homeland, the place where it all started. But it was an unruly country, with many warlords along its borders, and now the American occupiers in the cities. It was a land full of violence, bombs, and guns. He didn't want to go back there. Western civilization had opened its arms to him, and Vancouver had become home.

"These Americans, they don't have a clue how good they have it. A highway like this will never be built in Afghanistan, and if it was, you could never drive it, other than in an armored vehicle, with armed escorts. I don't miss that bullshit from the Frontier lands, Ba'al. I'm not even homesick anymore. This is home now."

THE NEWLY DESIGNED and modified PWS-14 was sitting in a large, 40-foot enclosed trailer, heading northeast on the 15. Ray was driving the modern Mac tractor unit, Ted was in the passenger seat, and Javeed was in the sleeper. There was very little conversation, and even if they'd had anything to talk about, the mission didn't exactly inspire friendly banter. The instructions from Ghullam had been very straightforward. Get the trucks and head north on the 15 until they reached their destination. Once there, they were to drop off the submersible and help with any manual labor needs, then return to the warehouse, drop off the truck, and go home. Not a big deal. No gun play. No blowing up buildings or airports. And most importantly, no mindlessly going to their own death. Just transporting a load from Point A to Point B. When that was done, he could return to his grand American lifestyle.

Sam was following him in the five-ton van. Neither of them knew what their cargo was. Massoud and Javeed presumably knew, but didn't speak of it. For his part, Ray didn't want to know. It was 1AM, PST, on September 2.

IT WAS EVENING when Kumar arrived. Yousseff and Rika were waiting at the Long Beach hangar. Another plane — a small, older Lear — was parked outside, fueled, ready, and waiting. The Gulfstream was still dormant, waiting inside the hangar. Yousseff discussed the situation with Kumar for a moment, then turned to Rika.

"It's time for Kumar and me to go, Rika. We'll be back here within 12 hours. Use my suite. Stay here and make yourself comfortable," he said.

Rika watched the two of them climb up the small ladder and into the Lear. "Goodbye, Youss," she whispered, waving. She didn't know the plan, didn't even know the extent of the mission, but found herself deeply troubled. She'd spent the last two days working nonstop on the assignments he'd given her. But now she wondered; what had Yousseff become? What was he planning to do that would have him toss his entire fortune, close to $1 billion, on the table in one grand bet? Would only a few people really die? And even if there was just one death, wouldn't that be murder? When had Yousseff changed so drastically that he would even consider doing something like this? And if he already had $1 billion, why did he need more?

UPON REACHING HIGHWAY 9, and then 89, the two large trucks slowed their pace. Eventually they turned onto unpaved roads, and there the progress slowed even further, to less than 20 miles an hour. Ray and Sam drove north, as they had been instructed, following the shore of the reservoir. They proceeded some 20 miles past the campsites and RV hookups that marked the public areas of the park. The entire road was unpaved, pockmarked with potholes, and marred with ruts. It took them more than an hour to travel along this last leg of their journey.

The facility itself was very small. The building was only 3,000 square feet, steel beamed, and metal clad, with a concrete floor and an overhead gantry system. Two large Gensets in a smaller, separate building supplied the power. PWS had worked with a consortium of universities and the Federal Department of Environment to construct underwater maps of the reservoir, and had built this facility as their base during the study. At the same time, they had used it to test various aspects of their subs' instrumentation in freshwater, and in this case murky freshwater, conditions. The contracts with the universities and government had expired years ago, but Kumar had maintained the test facility. He had personally visited the scene a few weeks earlier, just after he'd picked up Massoud and Javeed. He'd wanted to ensure that there was enough fuel for the Gensets and that everything, including the all-important central gantry crane, was in perfect operating condition. This was their meeting place, the jumping off point for the climax of Yousseff's plans.

The day had flown by, and it had been dark for an hour by the time the trucks, and their dangerous cargo, arrived from LA. Yousseff and Kumar were already waiting for Ray and the others at the facility. They had used the small rented Lear to fly from Long Beach to Page, Arizona, since Yousseff didn't want to arrive in his own plane. Should they be discovered or tracked, painstaking diligence would reveal only that the company leasing the plane was a numbered company out of the Caymans, which was in turn owned by a company in Nigeria. Beyond that, little else would be discernable. At the airport they'd rented a Ford crew-cab, again covering their tracks by renting it with a numbered company. It would be untraceable. Ray and Sam passed this truck on their way in, and headed toward the facility. Izzy and Ba'al were still on the road up north, but were due to arrive at any time.

Ray had some difficulty backing the tractor-trailer rig up, as the cleared space between the facility and the road was cramped and narrow. Eventually it was done, and Sam backed the smaller, five-ton van up next to it. Once the two rigs were sitting parallel to one another, the tricky unloading process began. Youssef smiled at Kumar. They had worked together many a late evening at Karachi Drydock and Engineering, creating, dimensioning, and drafting exotic assemblies that would facilitate the transfer of product from truck to truck, truck to plane, truck to ship, ship to ship, and, in the last decade or so, from ship to submarine. This had been one of the strengths of Youssef's vast enterprise. All his people had the ability to reload precious merchandise under dangerous circumstances, in hostile environments, with astonishing speed and efficiency.

The same engineering, coming out of KDEC and PWS, had eventually led to the magical machines Kumar now created. The PWS-14 represented the culmination of his achievements in this area. He couldn't wait for Youssef to see it. Youssef, for his part, was on pins and needles with the anticipation. He'd seen the PWS-14 during its construction, but hadn't seen it since its completion. His smile was that of a young child waiting to open a birthday present.

"Watch this, Youss," said Kumar. He opened the rear doors of the long trailer like a magician pulling the rabbit out of the hat.

BA'AL AND IZZY entered the fabulous Mormon land of Utah in the late afternoon of September 2. The endless blue expanse of the Great Salt Lake was to their right, and the sun was playing its dying rays across the complex peaks of the Wasatch Mountains to the east. Izzy kept the needle rock steady at 73 miles an hour. As the spires of the Temple and Tabernacle of Salt Lake City came into view, Izzy pulled into a truck stop, just long enough for a bathroom break, some cold pizza, and old coffee.

In the back, Catherine Gray was sitting against one wall, knees by her ears, head down, elbows up. The thirst problem had been solved many hours ago. There was plenty of ice water in the coolers, and a few cans of pop and beer were still waiting, unopened. She was no longer worried about dying of thirst, a fear that she had been developing while she was stuck in the money room with Indy. She felt a twinge of guilt. His claustrophobia had been palpable. Imprisoned in the dark and airless room, even she had become anxious and fearful. But Indy, with the emotional baggage that he carried, must have been going through hell. She shouldn't have left him, and she hoped he'd found a way out by now.

Her focus returned quickly to her own situation. Her problem now had nothing to do with thirst. She had to pee. And her upbringing simply wouldn't let her do that in someone else's vehicle. It didn't matter that the vehicle belonged to drug pirates who would as soon kill her as say good morning. It didn't matter that they would probably never know. She simply couldn't do it. But as the hours drifted by, and the pressure reached intolerable levels, she compromised as best as she could. Taking the drinks from one cooler and moving them into the second, as there was no telling how many more hours or days she'd be here, and pouring the ice water from the first into the second cooler as well, she squatted over the empty cooler. She didn't dare flick on the lighter, given that she was surrounded by several tons of high explosives. She felt her way around, apologized to her deceased mother, and to the owners of the truck, and let her bladder go. "Mom, I'm sorry," she breathed, feeling a grateful release of pressure. She put the lid back into place, and resumed her cramped posture against the van's front wall.

She would need to bolt in relatively short order once the unloading process got started. Even if someone took a short glance into the back of the truck, they would quickly notice the smell of urine in the air, and even an oaf would be able to figure out that there was an occupant somewhere in the back of the van. Catherine was surprised that the smugglers hadn't been into the back of the van already, for the drinks they'd left here. She thanked whatever lucky star was guiding her that they had been pulling over so often; they must be buying drinks rather than coming back for the coolers. She was under no illusions about what she would need to do once the rear door of the van was finally opened. She would have to run like hell. Fortunately, she had lots of experience at that. She also had the advantage of surprise. Depending on location, she might even be able to scoot out of sight before the two drivers of the truck figured out what was going on. If she sprinted the first few hundred feet, she might be able to escape, find a phone, or a police officer, or a friendly face. Anything. But if the truck stopped within a closed space in a compound, she was probably doomed. She started to regret not taking Indy's advice, and staying at Devil's Anvil.

44

BACK AT THE INZAR GHAR FORTRESS, Jennifer and Richard were listening to heavy feet tromping down the narrow stone stairs leading to the basement dungeon. Two men, thought Richard, struggling to process information through a veil of Vicodin and pain. Only two.

There was a jangle of keys in the door, and a few words were spoken in Urdu. The best translation that Richard could put to them was "a jolly good time." Oh, well then, let's just get a few pints of Guinness going, an irritating voice in his brain answered. The voice shut up when the cell door swung open with a loud metallic creak, and two men entered the small subterranean prison. Both were dark and swarthy, and the smaller man had dull and lifeless eyes.

The two entered the small cell. There were now four of them, Richard realized. Enough people to square dance, the Vicodin added. Guinness and square dancing. Maybe they should switch to spiked lemonade. Fun, fun, fun. Richard tried desperately to bring his imagination to heel. This was no time for jokes, he told himself sternly.

As they walked in, the smaller man let loose with another stream of Urdu, addressing the larger man by name — Marak. Richard tried desperately to remember if he'd ever heard the name before, and who it might have been connected to. Before he could make any progress in that direction, Marak walked right up to him and snarled in his face.

"Are you ready to die slowly, you American Jew pig?"

"Doh-see-doh your partner," was all Richard could think to say. The words slipped out before the more rational portion of his brain could voice an objection.

In spite of the precarious state of things and the horrendous fate that was awaiting them, or maybe because of them, Jennifer burst into a giggle. The smaller, younger man, with the dead-looking eyes, slapped her hard across the face. "Quiet, bitch," he hissed in English.

Richard decided to let his giddiness take over just a bit more. Not that he actually had much choice in the matter. "Doh-see-doh, little man," he babbled, nodding in the other man's direction.

"What?" Marak hissed.

"And allemande right," continued Richard, wondering what part of his brain knew the language of square dancing.

Marak put his face inches from Richard. "First I break your bones. Then I rape your bitch right here, in front of you. Then you will die, very, very slowly."

Just then, the voice of sanity decided to make another appearance from the ever diminishing drug-free portion of Richard's brain. He had one chance, he remembered. One shot. One move. And only one. He needed to focus all his power and concentration on that one move, and make it count. If he miscalculated, it would be over, and they'd both pay a severe price. He wasn't going to let that happen. Richard knew exactly what his move was. He had practiced it over and over in his mind, but could he actually do it? How badly had the drugs affected his reflexes, his judgment? If he were 20 again… dammit all to hell, Richard, he told himself. You're Navy. Or at least you used to be. Not just Navy, but super elite Navy. Tomcats on aircraft carriers, at night, remember?

He recalled the iron concentration he had felt every time the distant aircraft carrier lights came into view. One landing in particular jumped into his mind. It was night. Worse yet, an Indian Ocean storm front had come in, and there were strong cross winds. His concentration locked him unwaveringly on the tiny row of lights in the distance. He was flying by instinct, his hands feeling the engines, his eyes watching the carrier lights approach while simultaneously reading the information on the HUD. Only a few people in the world could do this, and he was one of them. By instinct. By feel.

Marak was bringing his face close to Richard's as he started explaining, in greater detail, the promises of pain and mutilation to follow. Richard had stopped listening, but was snapped back to the present by the man's close proximity. He almost smiled as he realized that this Marak had made two mistakes. The first was his failure to observe that Richard's ring and pin assembly were no longer fastened to the wall. Richard had reinserted the pin when they'd heard the footsteps, but it was loose in the socket. The second was to mention that they'd had another American in that very room recently.

"This is where we cut him. Right here. While he was still alive. The American Jew pig. It was great fun," Marak snarled, grinning hideously.

Without telegraphing the move, Richard's left hand, gripping the steel ring, flew forward with amazing speed. The iron ring smashed into Marak's temple, not quite hard enough to knock him out, but hard enough to send him staggering backward. Marak clutched his bleeding head, howling in pain and rage. Richard seized the moment and kicked the staggering man in the groin with all his might. Marak bent forward in pain, and Richard followed up with a knee to his face, cracking teeth and breaking his nose. As Marak staggered back Richard hit him with the heavy iron ring once again, this time on the back of the head. Marak fell to the ground and moaned once. Richard hit him a few more times until he was still.

"Doh-see-doh, you fucking son of a bitch. Doh-see-doh," he muttered, breathing heavily.

ZAK HEARD THE GUARDS come down the stairway, and enter the room where the new prisoners were being held. He heard the man called Marak taunting the prisoners. And he heard Richard's caustic responses. There was the sound of a struggle, of metal hitting bone, and then the thump of a heavy body hitting the ground. Zak continued to dig feverishly. Richard had managed to get one of the guards down. If Zak could finish digging his way out before Richard made his own escape, he might be able to find him and join him. They would be on the run, and in one of the most dangerous situations possible, with little hope of success. But they would be together. He wouldn't be alone anymore.

He pulled his left arm up and began to use the raw wrist joint to supplement the digging, ignoring the searing pain of mortar in the open wound. His only thought was to get out and find Richard.

JENNIFER HAD BEEN WAITING, and took advantage of Richard's attack on Marak. The other man had been contemplating her in an overtly salacious manner and, in so doing, had for a brief moment lost concentration. He turned around when he heard the sound of Richard pulling the iron ring out of the wall. Jennifer immediately pulled her own ring out of the wall behind her, and smashed the man in front of her hard across the back of his head. A few more satisfying cracks, and the man with the dead eyes might as well have been truly dead.

Richard didn't stop to survey their handiwork. He stripped Marak of his gun — a huge, ungainly thing that looked a bit like a Glock. Then he flipped open the man's jacket and grabbed his cell phone.

"He's got a gun, too," said Richard, pointing to Jennifer's downed guard. "Grab it and let's run." With some concern, Jennifer noticed that Richard had also grabbed the piece of bone that he presumed was Zak's tibia. More weird behavior, she thought. Richard had truly gone over the top.

Richard and Jennifer were racing up the stairs when she turned around and ran back down. "Dammit, Richard, we forgot to lock the cell door. Could give us a couple more minutes," she called over her shoulder.

She ran back to the basement cell door, taking the steps four at a time. Reaching the bottom, she saw that Marak had pulled himself up and was now stumbling toward the door, his eyes bright with a murderous rage. She was able to shut and lock the door mere seconds before the furious and bloodied man reached it. He pounded on the wall in frustration, raging to her about the dismemberments, tortures, and decapitations that would befall her once he got his hands on her. She ignored his words and ran back to the top of the stairs, where Richard was waiting.

As Jennifer passed him and raced for the door, she noticed that Richard had paused on the stairs, and was looking back down toward the dungeons.

"What the hell are you doing?" she hissed, running back down and grabbing his arm.

"Jen, I just heard someone call my name," he said slowly.

"You're crazy! You've taken too many of those drugs," she whispered, tugging at him.

"No Jen, I'm serious. I heard it. And I knew the voice." Richard was turning, attempting to go back down the stairs. "Jen, I recognized the voice. It was Zak."

Jennifer almost hit him. She couldn't believe that he was that delusional. They were in the middle of trying to escape a torture chamber alive, and he was hearing the voice of a friend who had died weeks ago. She pulled him around to face her, putting her face in his so that he had no choice but to look at her.

"Richard, listen to me," she hissed through her teeth. "I know this is hard for you. I know you've lost a very good friend. I know things are going badly. But you have GOT to keep it together. If we're going to get out of this alive, you have got to keep your wits about you. There is no way that Zak could be down in that dungeon, calling you. You've seen his body. You know he's dead." She saw the look of utter pain flash across his face, and felt terrible for saying these things to him. But her life, and his, depended on it.

"We've got to go," she continued. "If we're going to make it out of here alive, if we're going to save the USA, we have got to go. Now let's get out of here."

She turned to climb the last steps again, and was relieved to feel him right behind her. He must have made another of his transitions from crazy to sane, because he now began moving at top speed, pushing her from behind. They came out of the staircase at a dead run, rounded a corner, and found themselves outside, where it was now night. There were three US Army-style Jeeps sitting in a large driveway, beyond which stood the large stone-walled and heavily fortified Inzar Ghar safe house. It had slits for windows, and armed guards could be seen on the roof.

"No problem. Just your standard Pashtun safe house. Heavily guarded. They probably process heroin here. There are probably rooms full of heroin, precursor chemicals, and stacks of cash inside," whispered Richard. "God, it would be nice to come back here sometime with one of those fancy new Longbows. A lot of misery could be eliminated by blowing up this one building."

"That's just naive, Richard. You burn one down, and two go up in its place. Or the price of smack goes up in San Francisco. It would make no difference at all. Anyway, the keys are probably in those vehicles, right? Only mad or desperate people would try to rip off a drug lord."

"I think that describes us perfectly," he replied. "Let's find out."

"If we get out of the driveway, which way do we turn?" she asked.

"All mountain people know only two directions, Jen."

"And what are those?"

"Up and down, my girl. Up and down."

"Looks like down is to the left," she replied.

"Hope you're right. We definitely do not need up," replied Richard, eyeing the Jeeps. "Let's try and sneak to the closest Jeep. If we're spotted, run like crazy. I'll drive," he said.

"Like hell you will," Jennifer snorted. "You're juiced to the gills and your eyeballs are almost twice as old as mine. You actually think I'm going to let you drive down an unknown country road in a strange vehicle in the dead of night? No damn way. I'll drive."

"You do have a point," Richard conceded. "Let's go." He grabbed her hand and they made a dash for the nearest Jeep. They were almost there when one of the rooftop guards started shouting.

"We've been spotted! Hurry!" yelled Jennifer. She shot into the driver's seat, found the key already in the ignition, and turned it. The metallic wa-wa-wah of a weak battery and ailing starter motor greeted her.

"Come on, you bastard!" she screamed. She was fumbling with the vehicle controls, struggling with the handcuffs and the iron ring assembly still attached to her wrist. Richard jumped into the passenger seat, then turned around and pulled out Marak's gun. He pointed it at the Jeep parked directly behind theirs. Jennifer was too busy trying to start the Jeep to ask him what he thought he was doing.

"Wa-wa-wa-wah," went the stalling motor. A beam of light started to play across the driveway, and within a second would come across the Jeep. The engine started up just as the first gunshot was fired from the roof. Richard fired twice, then a third time, and then a fourth. A hail of bullets rained down on them as the Jeep spun gravel and whirled out of the driveway, taking what they both hoped to be the downward direction.

"What the hell were you shooting at behind us? Those assholes were on the roof, not in the driveway!" Jennifer fumed as they went racing down the road.

"I was shooting at the other Jeeps."

"What the hell for? You'll never disable a Jeep with a handgun," she shouted.

"Only too true. But those Jeeps don't have headlights anymore. And Jen, put yours on bright, please."

"Oh for God's sake, Richard, it's almost dawn. We won't need headlights in a few more minutes."

They drove for a few minutes. Then she giggled.

"What's funny?" Richard asked. "We're one hell of a long way from being out of the woods here."

"Doh-see-doh, Richard? Doh-see-doh? What the hell was that?"

"Square dance moves, partner," he said. "For some reason it was the only thing I could think of to say."

"That's actually 'dosado,' but I'm not sure those assholes care much about that distinction right now."

They both laughed, sharing the momentary relief of being out of the cell and in motion. Jennifer shot an almost affectionate glance in Richard's direction, then did a double take.

"Richard, you look like hell," she observed cynically. "There's blood in your hair, on your face, and all over your clothes. Are you sure you're okay?"

"No, I'm not, actually," said Richard, still clutching Zak's tibia. "I've taken about 50 shots to the head. I've been knocked out three or four times. I've got major head wounds. I just had the snot beat out of me. I heard my best friend's voice in that dungeon. And I'm in a lot of pain," he said, popping a few more Vicodin out of the container. "But I'm still up and kicking. Just get us the hell away from this place. That guy has got to be totally pissed by now. If they catch up with us, whatever they did to Zak will seem like a walk in the park." He paused for a minute and held the chunk of bone in front of him. "Right, Zak?"

Jennifer shuddered. It was 4AM, Pakistan time.

BACK IN HIS CELL at Inzar Ghar, Zak had listened in shock to the sound of footsteps running up the stairs. He couldn't believe they'd escaped already, and with so little trouble. When one of them turned and headed down again, he decided to take his chances. There was a world of possibility, if it worked. And what was there to lose, really?

"Richard!" he called, trying to make his voice carry as far as he could, while still keeping the pitch low.

He stood stock still, praying. There was dead silence on the stairs, and then the sound of a fierce argument. He knew that Richard had heard him. But of course the woman wouldn't have, and wouldn't believe Richard when he told her what he'd heard. He could hear the two of them shouting at each other in whispers, each trying to convince the other. Then the woman won. Zak smiled wryly. He wasn't surprised — Richard's heart was usually in the right place, but his will had never been as strong as it should have been. The two of them raced up out of the stairway, and Zak listened nervously to the sound of yelling, gunshots, and a dead motor trying to turn over. Finally, whatever vehicle they had found started up, and they sped away from the fortress, unknowingly leaving Zak behind to fend for himself.

Zak sighed deeply, and started digging again. He was glad that Richard had escaped so easily, but knew that he couldn't brood on the close call for long; he had far more important things to think about. Things like his own escape. The grate in his cell had indeed connected to a tunnel, which he was now widening. He put renewed force into his digging, determined to make it out before the sun rose. Dig, dig, rest. Dig, dig, rest…

45

AT THAT MOMENT, in the American southwest, Kumar was getting ready to demonstrate his latest toy for Youssef. Beaming, he pulled down a lever on the inside of the trailer.

Two elongated steel beams slid out of the rear of the trailer, and then further beams, on metal wheels, and then a whole array of smaller metal rails and parts. The wizards at KDEC had created a beautifully designed and engineered ramp. It had been constructed in Karachi and delivered to Long Beach by one of the ships from the Karachi Star Line. When the device had stopped feeding itself out of the truck, Kumar pulled back on a second large lever.

There was a whirr of electrical motors, and the PWS-14, which Kumar had nicknamed the "Pequod" after Ahab's ill-fated vessel in *Moby Dick*, rolled itself silently out of the rear of the large trailer. It came to rest at the top of another ramp and roller system built into the facility floor. From the top of this ramp it would, with a small push, roll into the passage of water that divided the center and front portions of the facility.

"She's gorgeous, Kumar," said Youssef, surveying the strange but exquisite craft. The modified PWS-14 was one of a kind — this was the working prototype of Pacific Western Submersible's newest model. It had been two years in the making, and Kumar was looking at mass producing it. It was larger, longer, and more powerful than all the preceding models, and came equipped with two multi-jointed arms, complete with complex pincer claws that were capable of holding and manipulating a wide variety of power tools. Kumar had been impressed with Gallo's work in exploring the Titanic, and was determined to outdo him. It was something that he was fully capable of accomplishing. His company had acquired an international reputation. None of Kumar's competitors could match his research and development budget, or the incredible things that came out of his workshop. But then, his competitors were not saddled with the burden of laundering drug money.

"I will hate to lose her," Kumar replied. "But all the information we need to reproduce her is in our computers. She's served well as a prototype, and we're going to manufacture these on a larger scale in a couple of months." He looked at Youssef's frown and added, "In Karachi, of course."

Youssef nodded, surveying Kumar's latest creation with fascination. He thought back to the old smuggling days on the Indus, and what the first underwater creation had looked like. A small, leaky, one-person submarine, no more than ten feet in length, without any navigation equipment, with a maximum depth of five feet. They'd come a long way.

"What I have in the smaller trailer is even more interesting," said Kumar, walking to the van. "Watch this. Ethan Byron's engineers started to call this thing the Ark. No one has ever seen anything like it before. This is what those Egyptian engineers and mathematicians designed, based on the technology that they stole from Livermore National Laboratories. On a much larger scale."

"They guaranteed it would work," said Youssef. "But then, lots of people guarantee lots of things. If it doesn't, we'll just lick our wounds and carry on."

"Hopefully not to rot in some American jail," said Kumar.

"That will never happen, Kumar. They'll never put this together. And the cover-up plan is almost complete already."

"I don't have a clue if this is going to work," replied Kumar. "It's one bizarre looking contraption, though. For all I know, it could be some twisted cosmic joke. I told the crew that it's a device for communicating with whales, so they wouldn't ask questions."

Youssef laughed. Only in America would engineers create a multimillion-dollar device so that the government could communicate with whales. Only in America. The two of them waited in suspense for the Ark to unload itself from the back of the smaller truck. Kumar activated a lever and a similar, smaller ramp fed itself out of the van and onto the facility floor. He pulled on a second lever, and with a whir of electrical motors, the Ark slowly rolled out of the van and came to rest beside the Pequod.

"It's amazing," said Youssef. "Absolutely stunning." And indeed it was, until its purpose was considered. It was the shape of a gigantic saddle, 20 feet long, five feet wide, six feet high at each end, and about two feet in height in the middle. More remarkable were its many colors, all polished and machined to an obviously high degree of precision. The ridge of gold running down the center of the saddle was especially prominent, becoming wider and deeper toward the middle of the structure.

Youssef walked slowly around the Ark, touching its glassy smooth surface at various places, noting his reflection in some of the many metallic alloys that constituted its roof and walls. "She is beautiful, Kumar. Absolutely stunningly beautiful."

"Well, sure, Youss," replied Kumar. "A lovely $3 million conversation piece. A housing for a whale communication apparatus." They both laughed.

"Help me position the gantry over her, Yousseff," said Kumar. He also motioned to Ted, Sam, Ray, and Hank to help out. "We need to place the lid on its side, so we can fill up the body with the Semtex," he explained.

Yousseff and the other men moved over to help position the gantry crane. "Assuming the Semtex arrives here soon," Kumar added darkly.

"It's Ba'al and Izzy. They will make it, guaranteed. Those two will not let us down, Kumar. There should be no worry there."

"Let me stretch out some blankets on the floor here," said Kumar, as the highly machined lid lifted away from the body of the Ark. "If this gets dented or deformed in any way, the device loses its effectiveness."

It took a few more minutes, but ultimately the lid came to rest beside the base, attached to it by three large, thin titanium hinges. Yousseff ordered the four truckers to return to their vehicles to wait. Kumar and Yousseff headed into the small office of the facility, where Kumar made some coffee in the small Pyrex pot. Massoud and Javeed were already sitting in a small machine shop at the other end of the building, reading the Koran and deeply immersed in prayer. The central working area was left to the gleaming Ark and the flat, space age Pequod sitting next to it. Nothing else could be done until the Semtex arrived. Minutes turned to hours, and the anxious seconds ticked by.

THE LAST LEG of the journey, from Cedar City south, along State Highways 14 and 289, was the most difficult. Both Izzy and Ba'al were fatigued to the point of seeing double. They switched from driver to passenger every half hour. Their bodies were swimming with caffeine and sugar, and they were heavy with the junk food they had consumed. The satellite radio was on constantly, tuned to CNN. As they reached the gravel and then the rough dirt roads, the first reports were coming out about the possibility of an imminent terrorist attack on the American homeland. Roadblocks had been set up along the freeways, and specifically on I-15.

Ba'al looked at Izzy and smiled. "Just under the wire," he said.

Izzy nodded. "Yousseff was right, again."

It was past midnight local time, on September 3, when they finally reached the PWS testing facility. The two large trucks that Ray, Sam, and their passengers had brought from Los Angeles were pulled over to the side of the parking area. Izzy backed his five-ton truck up to the building, parking it beside the Ford F-350 that had been rented at the Page airport. Ba'al opened the door and almost tripped in his rush to greet Yousseff. They did see each other from time to time, but it was rare for Yousseff, Ba'al, Izzy, and Kumar to find themselves in the same place at the same time. There was the usual exchange of hugs and pleasantries, but all four knew that time was short.

"It was on the radio, Yousseff," said Ba'al. "The American government knows all about the missing Semtex. They may already suspect that we took it through Devil's Anvil. There are roadblocks along I-15."

"Then we must get on with it. I told you they would be right on our tails. America's billion-dollar security apparatus is, as we speak, trying to sniff us out. We need to move quickly. This stuff," he said, motioning to the van, "has traveled halfway across the world. Let's not make a mess of it in the last few miles. Let's get to work." He opened the sliding rear door.

"This should make that old bastard in the Sefid Koh smile," said Izzy. "From the Libyan desert to the heart of America."

"I wouldn't be so sure," said Yousseff. "You know the Emir. The goat is incapable of laughter. It's rumored that he smiled after the last terrorist attack, but then got pissed off because he hadn't thought of it himself. He's wanted to outdo bin Laden ever since. Like it's a contest of some kind."

"Black and twisted prick, I would say," said Izzy. "But this has definitely been an interesting scheme."

"Indeed," Yousseff answered. "But let's worry about our side of the deal. There is no telling what's going on in the Sefid Koh, and it is not our concern."

DEEP IN THE SEFID KOH, Jennifer pulled over and cut the engine.

"Now what the hell are you doing?" slurred Richard.

"I'm listening for the sounds of their engines," said Jennifer. They both sat for a moment, listening intently.

"They're gaining," said Richard.

"Of course they're gaining. They know the road. I don't," snapped Jennifer. "But at least they don't have any lights."

"And whose idea was that? Jen, we have more to think about than just the guys behind us. These guys have immense power. I'm certain that they're in league with the police. They'll have specialized communications. There will be some sort of roadblock at the other end of this road. Likely a Jeep or two, at the very least, coming the other way. We're probably boxed in, here."

"So what do you want me to do about it, Richard? If we're boxed in, we're toast. Those two guys from the cell were mean sons of bitches, and then we whacked them on the head and booted them in the balls. They're going to be in a truly black mood now. Help me out."

Richard clutched at the pockets of his jacket, looking for the pill bottle, and found it with a prayer of thanks. He flipped the lid, shook out two pills, and knocked them back. He had mastered the art of taking pills without liquids many years ago.

"Oh Jesus Christ," swore Jennifer. "If I ever get out of this I'm going to talk to Big Jack personally about getting you into rehab. You're too valuable to be wasted on drugs."

Richard ignored the remark. His brain had switched back to rational thought, and he was considering their current situation. "Here's what we do, and we've got maybe five minutes to sort it out. Keep the lights on and go slower," he said.

"Slower?"

"Yes. Slower. There must be some kind of path, goat trail, farm trail, whatever. It may only be a driveway, or it may take us to the next valley over. Whatever it is, it'll buy us half an hour, maybe more. We've got a Jeep, so we can do some cross-country traveling. We've got weapons, and I've got American money, which may also buy us some time. All we need is a telephone. Or to get into cell range, I guess, since I grabbed that guy's phone. We need to communicate, one way or another, the contents of the last message to the Embassy. They'll handle the rest. And maybe they can come pick us up afterward."

Jennifer looked over at Richard. For a messed up addict, he did sometimes show flashes of brilliance. Maybe that was the Richard of old, before his eyes went, before he tanked a plane, before divorce one and divorce two, and before the drugs. There was certainly a lot of sadness in his eyes.

"Will do, Richard. Keep your eyes peeled."

"Yes, but we should turn right, not left. Downhill is to the right. Our chances are better if we turn right," said Richard, slurring his words again.

A nerve-racking five minutes followed. Once they thought they saw a trail to the right and backed up, but it had been a trick of shadows. They saw a couple of trails to the left, but ignored those. Their anxiety sharpened, and they stopped talking completely. This had become a life and death exercise, and death would likely be short on palliative care.

"There," barked Richard. "Right there. Sharp right, Jen. Now."

Jennifer almost flipped the Jeep turning, but she managed to right it, and they found themselves on a narrow, heavily rutted trail. They pulled ahead 20 feet.

"Cut the lights, Jen. We go forward in the dark. Give your eyes a minute to adjust. Then keep going ahead, slowly."

They edged along in the darkness. Five minutes later, they heard the roar of the other Jeeps as they raced downhill, chasing a gopher that had just bolted into a different hole.

Jennifer continued to creep along the mountain trail, drawing farther and farther away from the main road. Occasionally the trail widened enough that two vehicles would be able to pass each other, only to narrow again to a trail so closed off that cedar and pine trees slapped against the windshield and sides of the Jeep as they drove. The trail would climb, then descend, and appeared to move through the valley opposite a fast-flowing mountain creek, on the other side of what appeared to be the main road.

An hour went by, then two. The Jeep continued on its slow journey, heading toward what they hoped to be the valley floor. Tiny twinkling lights could be seen in the distance. Little hamlets in the Frontier Province, perhaps friendly, perhaps not. All they needed was a telephone, or a cell signal. All they needed was 30 seconds of conversation, and the looming catastrophe could be averted.

Richard was not doing well. His head was throbbing, and the pain had moved on to a full-blown migraine. He stretched every once in a while, to ease the spasms in his back. He'd long since realized that the medication wasn't helping, but continued to take more pills from time to time. The pain had almost completely taken over, and he was starting to have more complex conversations with Zak's tibia. Jennifer had to stop the Jeep twice, as Richard retched and vomited violently. Then more moaning. More Vicodin. She was astounded at the sheer volume of medication the man was consuming.

"Richard, you've got a problem there. You need to detox and get in a program somewhere," she said at one point.

"Bullshit, Jennifer. There's nothing wrong with me other than the blinding pain in my head, thanks to a couple of shots from that bastard and smashing my own head into a stone wall back in that dungeon, oh, I'd say five or six times. I've had migraines all my life, and I've got one now. Don't lecture me unless you've walked a mile or two in my shoes." He shouted out the last words in a whisper, managing somehow to remember that they were trying to hide.

"Yes, that may be true. But it's still one hell of a pile of meds, and powerful stuff to boot. Vicodin is addictive. I think you need some help," she continued. "Your road's going to lead straight to a heroin addiction if you're not careful."

"Go fuck yourself, Jen. We may be dead here. Look at the lights on the other side of that canyon. They're looking for us. Those guys will have us for breakfast. I don't know about you, but when that moment comes, I would like to be very, very stoned."

"Richard, you cannot give up like that. You used to be the best of the best. I need you to get back to that. I need you alert and helping me, if we're going to get out of this mess," Jennifer snapped.

Richard knew she was right. He knew that he needed to stay sharp if he was going to come through this. If he was going to bring his partner through safely. But the pain and stress were overwhelming. He was squinting his eyes constantly now because it hurt too much to open them all the way. He could count his heartbeats by the surge of the blood pounding through his temples.

"Jen, I will come through when you need me," he mumbled. "I can promise you that. I just can't stay sharp every second. Give me a break, here."

"Whatever," she retorted, and continued to focus on the goat trail ahead of her.

Another hour passed, and the night sky started surrendering to a pink pre-dawn glow on their right. They kept driving — there was no time to rest or contemplate the beauty of the early morning. Jennifer was about to make a comment about the dawn when the Jeep's engine missed a few beats, restarted, missed a few more strokes, and died. Richard, who appeared to be fading in and out of consciousness, roused himself enough to note the change.

"What's up?" Richard asked. "Restart it."

"Out of gas. It was inevitable. And dawn is just over the horizon. By now those drug guys will have searched every inch of that road. They'll know we turned off. They may be on this trail as we speak. We've got to keep moving, Richard."

"Which way?"

She looked up at a draw leading between two high hills. According to the sunrise, that would be east.

"That way," she said, pointing up.

"No Jen, there's very little vegetation up there. No cover that way."

"It's our only choice. When they find the Jeep they'll send a team downstream, along this trail, right away. That would be the logical way for us to go," she replied. "So logically, we can't take it."

"Maybe you're right," he admitted. "But before we start our trek, let's hide the Jeep. See that little ravine, there?" he said, pointing. "Let's push the Jeep down that way, and cover it up some. They'll find it eventually, but it may save us an hour or two."

"Good idea," said Jennifer. Together they put their shoulders to the Jeep, and pushed it into the ravine. Jennifer hopped down after it, and arranged grass and brush to cover it. As she climbed out of the ravine, she was nearly knocked over by Richard, rushing down after the vehicle.

"Wait!" he shouted. "I left Zak in the Jeep. I can't leave him. I can't leave Zak."

Before Jennifer could stop him, he had jumped back into the ravine where they'd hidden the Jeep. "Richard, you idiot! It's just a bone. It might not even be Zak's. We don't have time for this. Please!"

He ignored her, and disappeared from view. She could hear him rustling and cursing at the bottom of the ravine. Ten minutes passed before he finally returned with his grisly memento.

Jennifer was jogging in place when he got back, itching to be gone. "Richard, I've been thinking. I got in a few words to Buckingham just before we were nailed. He knows that we're in trouble. The cavalry's coming. We just need to stay alive a few more hours. Let's go. Please, PLEASE don't waste any more time." She grabbed his hand and, half pulling him, half supporting him, clambered up the hillside.

THE PATH had started as a gentle draw, but after about 15 minutes of walking it became steeper, and grew into low cliffs that had been invisible from the roadside. In the increasing daylight, Jennifer could see Richard's decline more clearly. His shirt was covered in dirt and blood. He was sweating heavily and gasping for breath. Dried blood caked his temples. He suddenly looked 75, and she thought his hair had more gray in it now than it had 12 hours earlier.

He seemed to read her thoughts. "Jen, I need to rest. Just for a second. Please, I can't go another step. Please." Richard was sounding more pathetic by the minute.

"Richard, they're behind us, somewhere. They're coming. Every second you delay is a second closer to death. We need to keep moving."

"Every second I climb this cliff face is a second closer to death," he gasped, wiping the sweat out of his eyes.

"OK, Richard. Go back to when you were 20. Go back to basic training.

Your original training wasn't to fly Tomcats, or do housekeeping assignments for the CIA. Your training was for this moment. For right now. Take a deep breath. Reach inside you. The strength is there. It must be there. Tap it. Reach for it. Take another breath. Now let's go."

Richard did just that. He reached. And just like in the movies, he went. For another five minutes.

"That's it, Jen. I'm done. I'm going to sit right here, in this spot. I'll sit here, and for five minutes, Zak and I will enjoy the view. Or I will follow you, and be dead from a heart attack five minutes from now. Go on if you want to. I'm not moving. Zak and I are now sitting," he proclaimed to the world, as he sat down on a rocky ledge, holding Zak's tibia tightly to his chest.

Jennifer sighed. "Alright, Richard. We'll sit for a second." She could see that there was no point in trying to push him any farther. He was well beyond the point of rational discourse, and had descended once again into a state of babbling, drugged psychosis. It was noon, local time. Midnight, in Arizona.

46

I CAN'T BELIEVE THIS," said the President. "The arrogant bastards have actually announced which city they're going to destroy? Before destroying it?"

His new Secretary of Defense nodded. "Yes. That's what the fifth message says. They've named the city. Las Vegas."

The Chairman of the Joint Chiefs was also with the President and his chief advisors in the Situation Room. "We need to put major assets on the ground and in the air, sir. We can do that. We can create a 50-square-mile no-fly zone around the city. We can mobilize battalions of Marines in there. Say the word, sir, and we'll move immediately."

The President looked around the long boardroom at his many advisors. They seemed to be of one mind about this, and the President finally agreed. "Yes. Create the no-fly zone. Put our assets on the ground."

The Chairman reached for his cell phone and gave some cryptic instructions. He put the phone away and nodded at the President in affirmation.

"I guess we need to consider one other issue," said the President slowly. "Do we go to Threat Level Red and evacuate the city?"

At this point, Admiral Jackson weighed in. "We need to look at what we have here, starting from the beginning. Our best agent in Afghanistan, Goldberg, told us that a huge terrorist strike was in the making. He got killed before he could tell us anything more specific. We have this Emir character delivering messages, which have been broadcast around the world. He would never make those threats if he couldn't deliver, we all know that. The loss of face would be too great. But if he promises to attack a specific target, and then does so, that's big-time power for him. Then we have the aborted telephone call from Jennifer Coe, on Richard Lawrence's mission. They found the sixth message, and the impact is obviously huge. But they were captured or killed before they could relay its contents. Put together, these things are of huge concern, and certainly justify going to Threat Level Red, at least in the Southwest."

"I think you're right," answered the President. "What do you make of this Semtex thing?"

The Chair of the Joint Chiefs answered. "Maybe this is the Semtex, maybe it's something else. At this point, I don't think it matters anymore. Some kind of weapon is apparently now aimed at Las Vegas. Given what the NSA and TTIC are uncovering, I think it's likely to be nuclear."

"My opinion is that it's a dirty bomb," said the Secretary of Defense. "Somehow, a large volume of radioactive material is going to be combined with the Semtex, and it's going to be detonated, somehow, somewhere, close to the strip. Could make the city uninhabitable forever."

"I agree," said the President. "Four and a half tons of Semtex could topple a building, even a couple of buildings. It can create a lot of mayhem all right, but from what I've been told, it can't destroy an entire city on its own. There is only one way that I know of to do that, and that's through the use of a nuke or a dirty bomb."

"A dirty bomb will create a large radioactive area well beyond the range of the blast itself. It would certainly destroy the entire area," agreed the Chairman.

"What about specific targets?" pushed the President. "Things like nuclear facilities, large chemical plants, that sort of thing. Do we have anything like that in the area, that could be a more specialized target for the attack?"

"Anything like that could create a lot of damage," said Admiral Jackson. "But to destroy an entire city, he'd almost need a nuke of some kind, wouldn't he?"

"That's what I was thinking," said the President. "But our Intelligence Agencies are getting nowhere with that. We do appear to be piling up an incredible amount of material from Internet sources, but nothing concrete."

The debate went back and forth. The Vice President suggested playing the fifth message once more. One of the technicians present obliged them by doing so. A screen descended from the ceiling, to display the powerful aura of the Emir, giving his message of hate and destruction.

Praise be to Allah and His foot soldiers. Give thanks to the prophet, Mohammed, and His soldiers of the jihad. Mighty are His works, and blessed be His name. After a perilous but courageous voyage, the soldiers are in place, even in the lair of the Great Satan, within the very walls of her house. The weapons of Allah are positioned, and the means of delivery have been secured, praise be His name. Within a day the great terror will strike within the serpent's house. One of her great cities, a city of vile iniquity, will be destroyed. That city is Las Vegas, an abomination in the eyes of Mohammed, peace be upon Him. This city's existence is a stain upon the earth, and Las Vegas has to die. All those who remain will perish with it...

"Joe, what's the state of things on the ground in Vegas right now?" the President asked his FEMA director.

"Not good, sir. I have concerns that riots or looting might break out soon. The TV channels are playing the fifth message nonstop. There's definitely panic. Look at some of the television feeds we're getting," he said, motioning to the plasma screens located on most walls of the Situation Room.

The FEMA director wasn't exaggerating. Incidents of road rage were breaking out throughout the city, as people rushed to get out. Traffic gridlock had set in. The airport terminal was jammed, as were the bus stations and freeways. Mass chaos and fear reigned, and the social structure of the city seemed to be falling apart.

"Well, that's that," said the President, shaking his head. "Impose martial law on the city. Bring in the troops. We need to evacuate. We need to do it now. Get on it, gentlemen," he said. "Get on it now."

MASSOUD AND JAVEED were still immersed in their meditations. They had remained in the facility, reading the Koran, and in focused and passionate prayer, preparing for their voyage to Paradise. The other eight men were working at moving the pallets of Semtex from the rear of the cube van to the floor beside the Ark. The first pallet had already been moved onto the powered tailgate, and to the floor, and the men were in the process of unwrapping the individual bricks and packing the plastic explosive into the Ark. Yousseff occasionally saw one or another of the men stop to look more closely at the polished surface of the Ark. It appeared to be a multi-colored mirror, reflecting random objects back into the interior of the building. It was a beautiful creation, and could indeed have passed as art in many communities. He knew that the men were probably also thinking about the damage the device would wreak.

"How do we connect it to the PWS-14?" asked Yousseff. "After all, we have more than four tons of explosives, plus the weight of all that metal. Together there's got to be about five or six tons." He looked at Kumar expectantly, raising one brow.

"It won't weigh that much in the water, Youss. We've counterbalanced the Pequod. Its tail extends to account for the extra weight. The sub has to be in the water before we set the Ark on top of it. The only moment of concern is when the Ark is actually put on top of the roof assembly you see there. The Pequod will need to be sinking at that moment. If the timing is exactly perfect, everything will be fine. I've oiled and lubricated the gantry crane. Did that shortly after the Semtex was hijacked."

"And if the timing is not perfect?" asked Yousseff.

"I'd rather not talk about that," said Kumar, nonchalantly.

"And I guess that's where the two lads come in," said Yousseff softly in English, motioning toward Massoud and Javeed.

"Yes. They still believe in that Paradise shit. It's one of the most tragic things I've ever seen. The Emir has to find boys to do his dirty work. Traumatized, orphaned children. Because no one over the age of 20, or with any family, would put stock in his bullshit. It's an ugly business," said Kumar.

Kumar was right, of course. It troubled Yousseff that these two would die. Usually he was able to remain detached from such issues. He had worked hard to build a wall in his mind, to make sure that emotion was never involved in any of his endeavors. But with these two boys…

He cleared his mind and brought himself back under control. He should know better than to let himself become emotional over such things. He had taken great pains, over the years, to ensure that his world operated in a purely utilitarian manner, and didn't take moral absolutes into account. In the end, these two children would die, whether he was involved in the equation or not. If not here, and in this manner, it would be in Iraq or Afghanistan, in a suicide bombing or in some mischief on Jerusalem's West Bank. Although he hated that it was so, the boys' deaths were a certainty, and just a matter of time. This was all that mattered, in the end.

Hence, Yousseff, with his elegant risk and cost calculus, felt justified in doing what he did. It was his own personal life formula. He often went to great pains to explain to others the difference between him and Marak. Yousseff said that he had a conscience, of sorts. Marak didn't. He tried not to think about why his path still ran parallel with the other man's.

While Yousseff reflected on the mission, Kumar was mumbling something under his breath and beginning to pack Semtex farther into the base of the Ark, taking a long time to ensure that the five upwardly angled copper prongs were evenly encased by the explosive. He too was attempting to keep the image of the two teenagers out of his brain.

"Why be so careful with that area?" asked Yousseff.

"These copper spikes will act as detonators. The plans were very strict with respect to the angle, length, and diameter of these rods. If things are not perfectly accurate, the blast may deflect sideways. It could lose its focus very easily. The blast needs to cut, Yousseff, and this object will act like a magnifying lens, narrowing the blast until it is almost completely flat. Anything less than perfection on the angles won't give us that."

"I presume that a powerful electrical charge will be flowing through those at the critical moment," said Yousseff.

"Exactly. The charge will come from the Pequod itself. The underside of the Ark contains a series of indentations that will be connected to copper and gold connectors on the roof of the Pequod. You can see the connectors there," he said, motioning to the Pequod. "I've already checked. They are perfect mirror images of one another. It will be a perfect fit."

THEY HAD BEEN UNPACKING the Semtex for some time already. Yousseff's mind was already moving on to the next stage of the plan. "So we will pack this stuff into the Ark, and head back to the airport as rapidly as possible," he said. "We must move as quickly as we can. Get those two to stop reading the damn Koran and help with this," he barked at Ba'al. "Time is critical now."

Ba'al did as he was ordered, and went to Massoud and Javeed to ask them to assist in what would be the final reload. He also had Izzy back the truck up a little further, to minimize the distance between the Ark and the truck, so that the reload would be more efficient.

Izzy hopped into the back of the van again, to bring a second pallet of Semtex down to the unwrapping and packing crew. He looked at Ba'al, who was standing idle, and asked in Urdu, "Did you piss yourself there, old friend? Was the load so heavy that you let your bladder go?"

"Screw off Iz. I did nothing of the sort." In fact, Ba'al was becoming progressively more troubled by what was occurring. He felt as though he was watching the end of their world, being stacked and organized in the strange metal contraption of Kumar's. After seeing even this much of the mission, he knew that they would be flying back to Afghanistan, hoping to stay under the wire of the American pursuit. He would never return to the lifestyle he had grown to love in Canada. His wife and children would be forced to find their own way home, for Ba'al would be far away and unable to help them. With this one action, everything in his life would change for good, and against his wishes. Realizing that, he had very suddenly lost his motivation for working toward this mission.

Izzy grabbed Ba'al's arm, shaking him from his thoughts. Both men jumped to the ground and began to assist the others in unwrapping the bricks and stuffing them into the Ark. Even though the explosive would have to be ignited to cause damage, and was relatively harmless until that happened, no one was inclined to run with it, or be overly hurried or reckless with their movements. Everyone could see that the job would still take a good hour or two, even with ten men working. Youssеff was concerned when Ba'al reported to him that the Semtex story was still dominating the news channels and that the media, and specifically radio stations, were reporting that there was still a danger. The Americans were right on their heels, and one way or another, they would have this sniffed out by morning. Youssеff pushed them on, by example and by chastising them if they were too slow. "You are working slower than a Pashtun great grandmother," he said to Ba'al at one point. "Move along. Faster."

The men were intently focused on their work, and none saw the almost imperceptible movement of the canvas tarpaulin. Catherine was peeking through its oily folds, surveying the scene. What she saw frightened her. Ten men, or rather, eight men and two teenagers, were unwrapping the bricks of Semtex, and putting the putty-like substance into a large and peculiar container that was sitting below a sliding gantry crane. Beside the peculiarly shaped container was an even stranger craft — a boat of some kind, with fins and stubby wings, looking like some gigantic mechanized shark.

Catherine couldn't understand how the men could be totally oblivious to her presence. Apparently they were old friends becoming reacquainted. They were chattering on as they worked, and every so often one of the men clapped another on the back in apparent affection. But their preoccupation with each other didn't make her feel safe. The tarps barely covered her figure, and she was sure that one of her sneakers was poking out beneath them. Sooner or later someone would smell urine, and thereby smell a rat. She didn't know that Izzy and Ba'al already had, but had failed to realize the implications.

It was 2AM, local time, on September 3. Catherine continued to peak through the tarp, watching the rapid reloading of the Semtex from the pallets into a strange, glassy smooth container, and planning her next move.

47

IT WAS 4AM IN WASHINGTON, DC. During more tranquil days, the TTIC control room would have been empty, save possibly for Turbee's workstation. Not now. There were at least a dozen people at work, scrolling through data on computer screens, holding meetings on telephones, and working with their Blackberries. All had seen the chilling fifth message, and saw the impact it was having on the city of Las Vegas. Johnson had the major news channels running on the 101 screens, so that they could see the repeating images of violence and panic. Looting had indeed broken out in one section of the city, and with the enactment of martial law, one looter had already been shot. A major event was developing. The terrorist attack was officially underway, although no bomb had been detonated. One of the Emir's goals had been to create chaos and terror. His mission had already been successful.

Turbee wasn't watching the screens. He didn't need to know what was going on in Las Vegas right now. There were more pressing things to think about. How was the Emir going to destroy the city? That was the important issue. He didn't believe that there would be a nuclear attack, or even a dirty bomb. He couldn't accept the validity of the decrypted messages that the NSA was pulling off the Internet. Turbee was of the view that the whole nuclear issue was a ruse, to deflect attention away from the true threat, which was the Semtex.

He tried to follow the logic. Assume the Semtex was now in the States, assume even that it was in Nevada or Arizona. Maybe in Las Vegas itself. How could 4.5 tons of plastic explosive destroy a city? He had become something of an explosives expert in the course of the past four weeks. His original equations to calculate the Libyan crater size had been taken from the standard equations used to calculate blast forces at certain distances from the center of the explosion. If those equations were correct, then there was no way that this amount of Semtex could destroy an entire city. If the entire Libyan stockpile had been detonated on Hotel Row, yes, most of the hotels would be obliterated and an enormous blast force would result. But not with only 4.5 tons. He was missing something.

Turbee put the city of Las Vegas up on the Atlas Screen, placing it in the center of a 50-mile circle. The database's library was rich enough to plot every chemical factory, refinery, and critical site within that radius. Turbee spent a long time looking at the map, first zooming in on one feature, then another, but nothing clicked. There was just no way to blow up Vegas with the amount of Semtex the terrorists had at hand.

Then he pulled the text of the fifth message up on the screen in front of him. The message did not say that the Emir would blow up Las Vegas. He said that the city would die, and all who remained within it would perish. How did you do that with only 4.5 tons of explosive? He became obsessed with the issue. Those who knew him well knew that he wouldn't be able to rest until he had it figured out.

One of the strengths of TTIC, on paper, was that each branch of the Intelligence Community was represented by at least two, and with some of the larger agencies, three, individuals. Theoretically, if critical information was developed by one branch, it would be immediately available to all branches. Khasha, for instance, would send information obtained by Turbee on the Internet to the various NSA Dictionaries and other groups. DEA information developed by Lance could be used by TTIC, the CIA, or the FBI, almost the instant that the information became known. Each individual in the control room acted as a node within an incredibly complex neural computer. In theory. The problem, in part, was that it was a very young agency, and there was a considerable degree of ambiguity in its mandate. Matters weren't helped by Dan's arrogance. But occasionally, it worked. It was the reason that they were heading this investigation. The government believed that they had the best chance of finding the bad guys. The nation was waiting with bated breath, counting on TTIC to figure it out.

Knowing this was making Turbee work twice as hard. He sighed, turned to another screen, and opened up a new search program.

KHASHA threw down her pencil in frustration. "Turb, I'm just completely fed up with this. I feel like I'm chasing ghosts. Not one scintilla of hard evidence."

"What's up, Khash?"

"Dan is obsessed with the hypothesis that the Emir's threats involve a nuclear attack," she said.

"Well, I guess it's reasonable," Turbee replied. "There's a lot of chatter on the web about it. Goldberg's message is consistent with the theory. Personally, though, I don't believe it. It is going to be the Semtex, I just can't figure out how it's going to happen."

"Fine. Fine and fine. But it's now 5AM, and Dan's nowhere in sight. I'm sure we'll have the Semtex cornered within the next 24 hours. Why don't you help me out on this? Maybe you can figure something out."

"What's the issue?" asked Turbee.

"Simple. Help me find out where all this stuff is coming from. All we seem to be getting is Internet chatter, for want of a better word. Highly encrypted, obscure dialect chatter, tons of it, from servers in Russia and Nigeria. Full of weird proxy stuff that we can't nail down. There's no hard evidence at all," she said, rubbing her temples with her fingers. "Not one stick."

"This sounds like a job for Lord Shatterer," said Turbee with a sly grin.

"Lord what?"

"Umm, an, um… Internet gaming proxy that I use every now and then," said Turbee, smiling a bit. "Lord Shatterer of Deathrot. I use him in multiplayer Doom-type games. He's actually very famous."

"I don't see how that can help, but can you have a go at it?"

"Sure, Khash. I'm stumped on the 'Death of Vegas' message. I can't figure out how it's going to happen. Might as well give this a whirl. Point me to a few of the websites," said Turbee. "Let me see what I can do."

"Actually, Turbee, there are thousands of them."

"Thousands? Of websites?"

"Yes," responded Khasha. "Thousands of websites dealing with the coming nuclear strike against America."

Turbee puffed his cheeks out in a silent whistle. "OK. Give me the list," he said. "I'll see what I can do."

THE SUN WAS COMING UP. It was 7AM in Washington, DC, and 4AM in Nevada. It had taken Turbee less than two hours to ascertain that all of the chatter, and all of the websites, had been created by two highly skilled, very imaginative, and very clever computer programmers — one in Cairo, the other in Karachi. It was all obviously a hoax. They had used a dizzying array of techniques to disguise their identities. Everything had been accomplished through a nested series of proxies, using servers from one end of the planet to the other. They were brilliant, thought Turbee. Absolutely brilliant.

When Turbee shared his news, it was Rahlson who stated the obvious. "So we apply Occam's Razor reasoning to this. There were two likely candidates for the vehicle of the Emir's terror. One was the nuclear threat, the other the stolen Semtex. Now that we know that the nuclear threat was a hoax, it gets knocked out of the picture. Only one possibility remains."

"Wonderful," replied Turbee. "Now all we need to figure out is where the Semtex is, and how it can possibly be used to destroy a major American city."

"You're the one who gets to tell Alexander when he shows up," Khasha told Rahlson. "He's used 95% of TTIC's work force to chase smoke for the last week."

Turbee laughed loudly at the irony. "Now we're the ones waiting for him to show. And we're the ones who get to tell him how he screwed up."

"Yeah," said George, who had just arrived. "Maybe he'll get to spend a night or two at St. Liz's."

48

IN THE SEFID KOH, Jennifer and Richard were moving east, in a desperate attempt to get within cell phone range. They ran for 15 minutes, then rested for five, as Richard tried to orient himself and recover. Jennifer urged him onward, but it was a losing battle. He was in terrible shape, his hair caked and matted with dry blood, and his clothes soaked in perspiration. He had become totally unfocused as a result of the pain, fatigue, and drugs. He was carrying on long and emotional conversations with the bone he had found in Inzar Ghar. It was late afternoon when Jennifer detected a distant but ominous sound. The dull whapping noise of rotors.

"Richard, that's a helicopter," she breathed. "Of course. The drug lords would have alerted the local police force. All they had to say to get a helicopter or two in the air would be that two dangerous cop-killing psychopaths were on the loose in the Frontier Province. That would be enough to get helicopters going back in the US. Why not here?"

"So it would." Richard had perked up a bit when he heard the sound — the lucid side of his brain seemed to kick into action if the danger became more immediate, a fact for which Jennifer was supremely grateful. He grabbed her arm and pulled. "Let's go, we don't have a lot of time left."

They continued on their upward journey. Occasionally a helicopter would come within a half mile or so, and they would duck down under whatever cover was available. The ascent was steep in parts, gentle in others, but ever upward. It was well into the afternoon when they reached subalpine grassland, dotted with small yellow cedars, poplars, and wormwood. There was nothing but sky at the far end of the pasture.

"Could be a drop off there," said Jennifer. "Watch yourself."

Richard was making grumbling noises, which sounded a bit like "yes." He continued to moan in pain, and was mumbling incoherently about plane crashes and car accidents. He had obviously slipped back into his psychotic realm.

They covered the next 100 feet slowly, with Jennifer looking toward the sky anxiously, watching for helicopters or search planes. When they reached the pasture's edge, Jennifer instinctively stopped, and pulled a reeling Richard back from the cliff. She leaned over the side and realized that she was looking at least 2,000 feet straight down. The precipice at the bottom of the drop snaked on for what appeared to be miles in both directions. There was no apparent path or negotiable trail visible. They had reached a dead end. The drug runners and their helicopters were looking for them, and would be broadening their search upward from the valley floor. They could not go back. Their only option was to follow the cliff edge, either to the left or to the right.

"Holy shit," breathed Richard, still hanging on to the chunk of bone. "That's half a mile straight down." He was reeling, fighting vertigo and nausea, and backing slowly away from the cliff edge. Jennifer grabbed his shoulder, concerned that in his drugged and delusional state he would simply lurch over the edge, either from lack of balance or just because he believed that he possessed the power of flight.

"That way," said Richard, pointing left, in one of his flashes of lucidity. "As the crow flies, that will take us further away from that fortress. They'll be searching in concentric circles from there. Let's put as many miles between them and us as possible."

"Brilliant strategy. What do you think we've been trying to do for the past 12 hours?" came the acid reply.

Richard muttered under his breath and fumbled through his jacket pocket in search of more medication. Jennifer rolled her eyes again and grabbed him, dragging him along before he had a chance to pop any more pills. Soon they found themselves on a long plateau, with grassy fields between them and the cliff's edge. Had their circumstances been less desperate, Jennifer would have taken time to survey the stunningly beautiful panorama beyond the ridge. Snow-capped mountains loomed in the distance, with small villages interspersed along the valley. At the edge of the horizon, obscured by haze, meandered the mighty Indus River.

"We need to go in that direction," slurred Richard, pointing east.

"I agree," said Jennifer. "But we'll need to stay away from unprotected ground. We follow the edge from back there," she said, pointing to the thicker tree cover that ran along the meadow about 50 feet back from the cliff. "Every once in a while I'll go to the edge and see if there's anything navigable along that face."

"Shut up. I was talking to Zak," responded Richard. "And besides, I can go check the cliff just as easily as you can."

"Yeah. Right. You'd stumble and fall in a parking lot. As if I'm going to agree to you getting near a cliff," Jennifer snapped. "As for taking you down that cliff without a path… I'd have to take a bunch of those pills to be crazy enough to do that."

Richard mumbled incoherently in response.

Jennifer threw her hands in the air, finally losing patience with the situation. She wasn't trained for the field. She'd never had to deal with people chasing her, trying to kill her. And the fucking CIA had partnered her with a drug addict! She didn't know if she could count on him to help the situation, and now it turned out that she had to watch his every step, just to make sure he didn't fall over the edge of a cliff while they were trying to escape. Now that the adrenalin of actually running was leaving her system, she was starting to feel like it was hopeless.

"Screw it, Navy boy," she almost shouted. "I don't know what the hell to do. Maybe just staying alive for the next 12 hours is all it'll take. By then Buckingham may have got things moving on finding us. It's all I can really think of."

Richard began mumbling again, directing his comments primarily to Zak, who was silent as they retreated to the cover of the trees. The pounding pain in his head had not subsided, and he was desperately thirsty. He was down to his last few Vicodin. He would run out soon, and at the moment he feared that more than he feared the possibility of capture.

FOR THE NEXT HALF HOUR, as they walked through the trees, Jennifer made several short trips to the cliff edge, and each time coming back to Richard shaking her head. No trail, no easing of the precipice. Several times they shrank under the cover of the cedar and poplar trees, fearful of detection from the air. There appeared to be several helicopters now involved in the chase, and they were flying ever closer to their location. At one point they found a small stream that cascaded over the cliff edge. The water seemed to invigorate Richard, but in truth, it only helped him in swallowing another three Vicodin. The gnawing fear was increasing. He knew that he was slipping over the edge, but had lost the ability to care. It was all too much.

When he started feeling too dizzy and weak, he simply announced to Jennifer that he was going to sit down and await his fate.

"You go on," he told her. "Now I'm really done. Leave me be."

"No, Richard, that is not going to happen. You are a soul in trouble, in many different ways. But you're also a fellow soldier, in distress. I'm not going to leave you. If we're captured, it's going to be together."

"Jen, listen to me. You can go much faster alone. You'll be better off without me," he argued, in a bizarre version of chivalry. "I'll just take the last of my drugs and wait. Maybe I'll just heave myself off the cliff. With enough drugs in my system, it won't be all that bad an end. In fact, I feel like I'm floating off a cliff right now."

"I'm not leaving you, as much as I would like to," Jennifer muttered.

The two of them viewed that day in completely different ways. From Richard's point of view, the day consisted of standing, sitting, or lying down, ingesting more medication and experiencing sheer panic when he thought he might be running out. In his clear moments, it consisted of the immense guilt he was feeling about letting his country down, and leaving Jennifer to deal with the situation alone. For Jennifer the day was a pattern of prodding Richard along, getting him back on his feet, or pulling him bodily off the ground, and ducking for cover from low flying planes or helicopters.

It was just after 5PM, and growing darker, when they heard the dogs.

49

AT THE PWS TESTING FACILITY, Youssef had ordered the two teenagers, Javeed and Massoud, to pick up their pace. He didn't care about their religious sensibilities or what they were there to do. All he cared about was having the unwrapping and packing process finished, so that he could get out of the way.

"It must be evenly packaged," said Kumar. "There can be no spaces or holes. The slightest deviation will affect the cutting power."

They had been at it for another half hour, taking the red cellophane wrapping off each brick, and squeezing the putty-like substance into the interior of the Ark, when a rustle in the rear of the cube truck caught Youssef's attention.

"What the devil–" he started to say. Before he could finish, a woman, in shorts and a T-shirt, and black from head to toe, appeared in the rear of the truck, jumped down, did a U-turn, and ran, at a very quick rate of speed, down the gravel road that led from the facility. It was Corporal Catherine Gray, making her bolt for freedom.

Youssef was so shocked that it took him a moment to recover. Then he started barking instructions. "Ba'al, take my truck. Get her back now. If she gets away she'll ruin the plan. Go now!" Youssef tossed Ba'al the keys. "There is a small Beretta in the central console. Get her back, or kill her."

He looked around at the rest of the crew, standing with mouths agape. "The rest of you keep working. We can't deviate from the plan. Ba'al will get her back."

"How on earth did she get in there?" asked Kumar.

"Good question. Izzy, would you mind telling me why a woman was hiding in the back of your van?" asked Youssef, his tone edgy.

"Must've been at Devil's Anvil," responded Izzy. "She was covered in what looked like coal dust, which means she was probably wriggling through one passage or another at that mine. When we were loading the truck, she must have stolen her way onboard. Ba'al and Dennis brought the explosives through Devil's Anvil in four loads while I stayed with the truck. Each load took about an hour, from beginning to end. I guess she got onboard, underneath the tarps, probably between loads three and four. We were almost done, and they probably weren't paying attention like they should've been."

"Why didn't you check the load, and the tarps, before you left?" asked Yousseff, angrily.

"We should have, Youss. We didn't. Didn't expect this. We were in the middle of nowhere — who knew that there'd be some woman wandering around? Anyway, we're almost 30 miles from civilization, and far from cell phone range. She can't get far. Ba'al has a truck and a gun. I mean, how far can you run?" asked Izzy, not familiar with Catherine's athletic history.

"Keep working, and fast, all of you," ordered Yousseff. "If she gets to a telephone before the sub is in the water, this mission, after incredible risk and cost, is doomed."

Izzy had known Yousseff for almost 40 years. There had been many, many tricky situations, where they were foiled by the river police, or attacked by pirates, or dealt with a crew mutiny, or even had a problem on the Vancouver or Manzanillo docks. He had never seen Yousseff angry or losing his composure. Yousseff was able to talk himself out of almost anything. He seemed to delight in using his prescient intelligence to wiggle out of distressing circumstances. But when Yousseff saw the woman jump out of the truck, he was as close to furious as Izzy had ever seen him. Izzy wondered again exactly what they were involved in.

AS YOUSSEFF and his Pashtun crew continued unwrapping brick after brick of Semtex, Ba'al drove south, looking for the strangely clad American woman. There she was. Five minutes had passed and she was already more than half a mile down the road.

He hit the accelerator. The truck shot forward, and in moments he was directly behind her.

"Stop now, or I'll shoot," he barked.

He saw her slow, looking as though she was going to stop. He got out of the truck and started walking toward her. He was 30 feet from her when, rather than stopping, she sprinted away at what Ba'al considered to be an astounding speed. Little did he know that the woman ahead of him was a Canadian, with an extraordinary level of physical fitness; a woman who could run the 100-meter in under 12 seconds, and who could and did run half a dozen marathons a year, invariably in less than three hours. After being cooped up for almost 24 hours, the sensation of physical movement was giving her feet wings, and increasing her speed even more.

"Damned bitch," cursed Ba'al. He fired a shot in her general direction, and then hurried back to the truck to continue the chase. "Should've driven right over her."

Catherine's thoughts were racing. She was not panicked, and was feeling exhilarated in the open air after spending so long in the back of a cube truck with more than four tons of Semtex, no light, and some coolers containing a few cans of pop and beer. But she knew that she couldn't outrun the truck. The driver's next tactic would be to simply run her down, but she was already 100 feet farther down the road when Ba'al clambered back into the truck. She darted off the traveled portion of the roadway and threw herself into a shallow ditch, praying that the driver would not see her.

She smiled as the Ford crew-cab went roaring by. Yes, he'd be back, but for now she had some time to think.

The early morning sky was still inky black. There was no moon, and the sky was overcast. Without the background glow of city lighting, visibility was almost nonexistent. In pulling herself out of the ditch into the dead black night, Catherine was struck by a flash of inspiration. Yes, she knew how she could even up the odds.

She saw the truck turn around and start back when it was more than a mile away. Ba'al had obviously concluded that his quarry had successfully eluded him, and was slowly coming back, looking at the ditches and woods on both sides of the road. His bright lights illuminated the entire road, extending outward for several feet into the brush. Catherine held the large chunk of rock that she had found in the ditch at the ready, unsure of exactly how this was going to play out.

"Come on, big boy," she said as the lights from the Ford slowly approached. "Come to mama."

Ba'al was driving very slowly, taking time to survey both sides of the graveled roadway. One hundred feet. Sixty. Forty. Twenty. Ten…

In one quick and athletic move, Catherine launched herself out of the ditch, rock in hand, and smashed in the driver's side headlight. Jumping backward and rotating, she managed to damage the passenger side headlight as well. It made a fizzling noise, and then went out. Before Ba'al could reach for the gun lying on the passenger seat beside him, Catherine was running by the passenger side and sprinting, again at top speed, up the road in the opposite direction.

Ba'al cursed when he realized what had happened. He still had his parking lights, and one signal light, but, for the rest, he might as well have been driving blind. It was still only 4:30AM, and the dawn would not be upon them for another hour and a half.

"Shit," he cursed emphatically. "Shit, shit shit."

Ba'al turned the large pickup truck around on the narrow gravel road, mowing down bushes and small trees in his way, and then proceeded up the road at a speed of 15 miles an hour. He drove for a few minutes, looking both ways, before he realized that she had again given him the slip. He cursed more violently, this time in Urdu, and then in several other Pakistani languages, before turning around and heading back toward the test facility. Before he realized what was going on, the same thing happened again. The woman flew past him at a dead run, streaking back up the road in the opposite direction.

Catherine, for her part, was beginning to enjoy this game of cat and mouse. She could hear the Ford coming, and its four-way flashers and orange parking lights were still on and extremely visible. When it was within 100 feet or so, she ran for the ditch, or some other formation of rock or trees, to take cover. She would stay there until the truck turned around, and when it passed by, would get back on the road and sprint for all she was worth, running anywhere between a quarter and a half mile up the road. When she heard the truck turning around again, she would head for cover. He couldn't spot her without his lights. There was no way he'd catch her, if this kept up.

Four-thirty became five, and by 5:30AM Catherine knew that this particular phase of the battle would soon be over. A thin ribbon of pink was appearing over the eastern horizon, and by six headlights would no longer be required. As Catherine was deliberating her options, and looking for another roadside stream with which to quench her thirst, she felt the "whomp" of a distant explosion. She saw smoke in the northeastern sky, presumably the location of the building from which she had run. A few minutes later she saw a small convoy of trucks go by, heading toward the Ford on the road ahead of her. In the lead was the cube van that had been her home for the past twenty-some hours, followed in turn by two larger trucks. The vehicles were not going slowly, given the nature of the roadway. They were obviously in a hurry to get away. Fifty miles an hour or more, she estimated. After they passed, she climbed back onto the road and started running at an easy and relaxed pace toward what she hoped would be civilization, wary of any approaching traffic.

BY FIVE IN THE MORNING they had been ready for the final phase. The Semtex had almost all been packed into the Ark. Kumar went to the outbuilding and started the second, larger Genset to supply additional power to the overhead crane. He returned and positioned himself behind the controls of the gantry system. He then used it to "close the lid." It was an extremely tricky operation, with all the men positioned along the base of the Ark, trying to ensure that there was no slippage. Once this had been accomplished, a series of lever latches were used to clamp the lid to the base.

Next Kumar, with the assistance of Izzy and Yousseff, threaded the two large slings from the gantry underneath the Ark. When the Ark appeared to be appropriately balanced, it was slowly pulled aloft, and maneuvered so that it was directly above the Pequod. The steel in the gantry crane system groaned under the weight of the heavy and fully loaded Ark. For a moment Kumar wondered if he had underestimated the carrying capacity of the system, but the crane held. He gradually lowered it so that the bottom of the Ark was parallel with, and directly above, the Pequod. The Pequod itself had been pushed across a ramp and roller system, and was floating in the water that ran along the front and center portion of the facility. The structure of the Pequod was not robust enough to carry the weight of the Ark and its contents, unless it was in the water, where buoyancy would make the chore feasible. But before the Ark could be so positioned, the passenger cockpit of the vessel would need to be closed, and before that, Massoud and Javeed would need to be inside. It was time.

50

Youssef motioned to Massoud and Javeed. The moment of denouement was at hand. Youssef had seen a lot of death over the past forty-some years. His childhood and teenage years had been marred by the war, death, and destruction brought on by Soviet aircraft, through civil wars, and through the reign of murderous warlords in the Northwest Frontier Province. He had seen thousands of people die in battles in and around Kabul and Khandahar. But the certain death of these two boys troubled him more than anything else ever had. Perhaps it was the ugly set of circumstances that had brought these two individuals to this place. Even though they were both set on their suicide mission, Youssef could see that there was a deeply subdued, but as yet unextinguished, ember of life in their eyes. Or perhaps Youssef had overestimated himself. While he was a capable and even brutal drug smuggler and businessman, this situation had put him in the business of terrorism. He wondered if those were shoes he could actually fill.

He tried to shake these thoughts. It was too late to turn back now. And this mission would happen, eventually, with or without his involvement.

"It's time, boys," he said. "It's time. You must now focus on the mission that the Emir, peace be upon him, has given you. Allah has brought you to this hour, and this place." Youssef was speaking in the Pashtun tribesman's version of Urdu that the two boys had grown up with. It wasn't to give the boys comfort, since he didn't feel it was his place. It was to make sure that they understood every word of their mission. He quickly outlined their directions, making sure that his words were precise and detailed. Any mistake on their part would mean a failure in the mission; because of the gamble he had taken, a failure would destroy what he had been working toward for his entire life. This made his words even sharper than he meant them to be.

The two boys nodded, but did not reply to his brisk tone. Massoud, and then Javeed, stepped into the narrow two-person cockpit of the high-tech vessel. They had never been in it before, but the simulator in Long Beach had duplicated the conditions and the instrumentation in its cockpit precisely. Kumar and his team had equipped the Pequod with an exotic GPS-linked sonar system that reproduced, in three dimensions, the contours of the reservoir floor. The craft also had powerful running lights and TV cameras, linked to a series of displays similar to the HUD's carried by all modern fighter aircraft. Between the HUD, the forward-contour modeling, and the view available to the occupants of the vessel, navigating the Pequod was pretty much a walk in the park. The simulator had reproduced these conditions perfectly, and the two teenagers were as comfortable here as they would have been walking along an alley in Jalalabad. They settled in, and nodded their readiness to the men around them.

The cockpit of the Pequod slid shut noiselessly. Youssef motioned to Kumar to begin lowering the Ark onto the roof of the Pequod. A series of hydraulically operated clamps were positioned along its roofline, with a further series of recessed sockets in the steel base of the Ark to match. A perfect fit was required to ensure good connectivity for the power supplied by the Pequod, at the appropriate moment, to the copper firing rods of the Ark.

Kumar held his breath. His engineers had told him that this was the most dangerous aspect of the mission. If the Ark were lowered too quickly, it would create too great a downward force on the Pequod, which could be crushed. Would it be such a bad thing if it were? he wondered. His reservations about the mission were becoming stronger and stronger, and for a moment he paused, thinking about how his actions right now could change the events to follow. But he maintained his composure, and kept the Ark's descent slow and steady. The sub sank as the weight of the Ark was lowered onto her roof. There were audible creaks and groans of metal bulkheads becoming stressed. Kumar winced at the sound and nervously bit his lip. At the instant that the roof of the Pequod was level with the waterline, the hydraulic clamps clicked into place. The match was perfect, and the now-united combination of Ark and Pequod dropped slowly from view. Kumar's hands eased a bit on the controls of the crane; it had worked. Youssef motioned to Izzy to open the outer doors of the facility, which were at water level.

For a few seconds, they could see the outline of the Pequod in the early dawn light. But as it pulled away, and descended, it disappeared from view. It was 6AM, local time.

Youssef and Izzy quickly walked to one of the walls of the facility and picked up the containers of gasoline that had been lined up there. Youssef directed Izzy to splash gasoline about the facility. He himself opened four barrels of the diesel used for the Gensets, and poured the contents out onto the floor. He then poured a trail of gasoline from the interior of the test facility to Izzy and Ba'al's cube van. He ordered Izzy to pull the van ahead a few hundred feet, then told Ray and Jimmy to do the same with their vehicles. He walked behind the two trucks and the van, spilling gasoline on the ground as he did so. Kumar climbed out of the crane and joined him.

"Kumar, get in. Iz, you're driving. Hustle now. Time to move, here," Yousseff shouted. He ordered the two larger trucks to follow the cube van.

As Yousseff reached the van, he flipped open a matchbox, struck a match, and tossed it into the gas trail. They watched the flame jump forward to enter the facility, then sped out of the driveway. The building exploded just as the three trucks pulled out of sight.

IT WAS 7AM. The Pequod had been in the water for an hour. Massoud and Javeed talked little. Occasionally they spoke of their boyhood in Khandahar, of their dreams, and sometimes even of their dead parents, brothers, or sisters. Navigation was easy. The underwater route had been mapped years earlier by a joint venture between PWS, the Federal government, and a number of universities. The undersurface contours had been fed into the Pequod's HUD, and following those contours was easy. The same contours had been programmed into the simulator back at the Long Beach PWS manufacturing center.

With the heavy weight of the Ark riding on the sub's shoulders, their maximum speed was ten knots. Most of the engine's power was diverted to two vertical propellers mounted beneath the Pequod, to prevent the craft from sinking into the reservoir's floor. Occasionally a solitary fish, or a small school of them, darted across their field of vision. The Pequod was following a course along the reservoir bottom, and was as deep as she could be without actually scraping the lakebed itself. "Stay low, boys. Stay low," Yousseff had said. The minutes slid by in the silent subsurface wonderland.

FIVE MILES SOUTH of the facility, Yousseff, Kumar, and Izzy came across Ba'al and his lightless truck. He was still looking for the woman.

"Where is she, Ba'al?" asked Yousseff, leaning out of the passenger side window of the cube van.

Ba'al looked harried and tired. "She is out there someplace," he said, pointing toward the woods. "She took out my lights, and we've been playing cat and mouse ever since."

Yousseff thought for a moment. He shook his head, dismissing her as unimportant. "We need to get rid of the van here. It can be traced. We'll push it off the edge, into the river. It's important that it be discovered by the American police forces. It's important for the cover-up."

Youssef got out of the van and walked toward Ray's large truck. "We're going to drop the van into the water here. My associates and I are going directly to the airport. You and your assistant here need to get yourselves back onto the 15, and get back to the Los Angeles warehouse immediately. You drop the truck off there, and get back to your normal lives."

"That's it?" asked Ray.

"That is all the Emir requires. Stay here until we dump the van." Youssef walked back toward the second truck, operated by Sam.

"As soon as we're done here, I want you to follow the Ford and stay at the directed spot near the main access road, understood?"

"Yes sir," said Sam.

"Sam," Youssef continued, "remember the timing. It has to be 8:45AM exactly. After the explosion, you must stay for at least ten minutes, to ensure that the images are being transmitted. Is the equipment in order? Is the video working? And the satellite uplink?"

"Yes, it's all in order. We spent the past half hour checking and testing everything one last time. Everything is perfect." The smaller of the two trucks, which had carried the Ark, also carried with it state-of-the-art television and satellite uplink equipment.

"Good," said Youssef. "When it's set up, come to the airport. We'll be waiting for you there. Make sure that the camera catches the explosion. The destruction must be captured on camera."

"Yes sir," said Sam, giving Youssef a nod.

Youssef did not tell him that he had no intention of waiting. He didn't say that within 15 minutes the Lear would be winging its way back to California, where the faster Gulfstream was now ready and waiting in the Long Beach hangar. Nor did he tell Sam or his swamper that by 9:05AM they would both be dead. That might have complicated things.

Youssef walked back toward the crew-cab and Ba'al.

"What about the woman?" asked Ba'al.

"Can she identify you?" responded Youssef.

"Possibly," responded Ba'al. "She was probably watching us reload the explosives at Devil's Anvil. If she's with the RCMP, or the FBI, or the American police, she will have been trained in making ID's. Yes, she may well be able to ID both Izzy and myself. Maybe you too, and Kumar and the rest of the crew, depending on how much she saw back there." He motioned back to the burning facility they had just come from.

"We don't have time to chase her down," responded Youssef. "Besides, you'll be back in Jalalabad before the Americans know what hit them. We're more than 30 miles from the airport. By the time she gets to a phone, we'll be long gone. And with the false trails we've planted, they'll never sort it out. We'll just have to leave her."

They turned to walk back to the cube van, where Izzy and Kumar were waiting for further instructions. Yousseff handed Ba'al the large chunk of rock he'd just picked up. "Put the vehicle in drive, and toss this rock on the gas pedal. Get ready to jump back, Ba'al, or you may lose a set of toes, or worse."

Ba'al peered over the cliff edge, and, in the gathering daylight, saw the black waters 100 feet below him. No, he didn't want to go in that direction.

"Hold on for one minute," said Yousseff. He opened a small briefcase that he had brought with him. Within the case was a sealed plastic bag. He put on a pair of gloves, also hidden in the briefcase, and opened the bag. Inside was a copy of the Koran and a poorly forged passport in the name of Raymond Hillel, listing the man's Los Angeles address. He flipped open the van's glove compartment and dropped the book and passport in.

"On the count of three," Yousseff said. Izzy and Kumar had been looking down at the water, but now joined him behind the van. They all put their shoulders against the back of the vehicle.

Yousseff started the count, and Ba'al put the gear into drive as the van drifted slowly forward. On three, Ba'al placed the rock on the accelerator and sprang back in one motion. The van surged forward, smashed through a low metal guardrail, and plummeted down toward the waters, landing with a gigantic splash and disappearing beneath the surface.

"Ba'al, Izzy, take that section of guardrail hanging over the edge, and make it a little more obvious. We want the American authorities to find this as soon as possible. We need the false trail to stand out," Yousseff directed.

Ba'al and Izzy did as they were ordered, but gingerly, keeping wary eyes on the cliff edge and the water raging below. After placing the briefcase in the Ford, Yousseff and Kumar moved to help, and between the four of them they were able to bend and pull a second section of damaged guardrail so that it was swaying in the wind, high above the waters of the reservoir. The damage was obvious, and the authorities would find it within hours.

The four of them regarded their handiwork for a second and then, as one, turned and headed toward the idling crew-cab. With Kumar driving, they continued on their speedy southward course, leading the other two trucks. Within 20 minutes they reached the highway. Yousseff was pleased to see that Ray turned left and headed in the direction of the Interstate, going back to LA. He also saw Sam stop by the side of the road. The plan was unfolding just as it was meant to. It was 7:30AM.

51

AT THAT MOMENT, on the other side of the globe, Jennifer and Richard were in a far more dangerous race — one that held their lives in the balance. The sun was beginning to set. Chemicals were washing like tidal waves through Richard's overtaxed body, and were nothing like the euphoric, pain-alleviating endorphins Catherine was currently enjoying. Jennifer was trying to make as much headway as possible, which was difficult, given Richard's profoundly damaged state. The knowledge of the Emir's attack against the USA, and the thought that she and Richard might be able to stop it, only served to add more stress to the situation.

A few moments earlier, the dogs had picked up their trail. The barking and howling was getting closer. Richard's vision was increasingly impaired by dots of light, and he felt as though his heart was going to stop at any moment. He was terribly thirsty, and the pounding in his head would not go away, no matter how many pills he took. He clung steadfastly to the tibia, and rifled through his inner pockets as he ran, looking for more drugs. Jennifer swore at him, pushed him, cajoled him, and half carried him along the strip of pasture that ran parallel to the cliff edge. Occasionally she thought she heard helicopters in the distance, and sometimes almost overhead. The dogs were coming closer, and the helicopters were right on top of them. They were cornered, and they both knew it.

Jennifer put her arm around Richard. They came to a stop on a small knoll about 20 feet from the cliff edge. The sun was setting, and the mottled colors in the distant valley were gorgeous.

"Stunning view, isn't it," said Jennifer.

"As good as gets," Richard replied.

"The dogs, maybe 200 or 300 feet away, I think."

"Helicopters, down in the valley. I can't see them, but I know the sound. I know the type," Richard added. "Sound like Super Stallions to me. The Marines have those." Despite the drugs coursing through his system, the rational side of his mind was still trying to keep track of what was going on.

"You know," he continued, "I didn't know that Pakistan had Super Stallions. Must have just bought some." He was just starting to ramble. He knew it, but couldn't stop himself once he'd started.

"A stunning view," repeated Jennifer, trying to ignore the fact that Richard had drifted once again into a dazed silence. Instinctively she edged closer to him. Despite his presence, she'd never felt more alone, or more frightened. Was this where it would all end? With a drug-addicted burned-out Navy star who was clutching the perceived tibia of a dead friend, 10,000 miles from home? All her training, all her ambition, working so hard to become the number two at a bureau like Islamabad, before she was 30, and it was all coming down to this. Sitting on the edge of some grand canyon, in the lawless Federally Administered Tribal Areas in northwest Pakistan. Suddenly the dogs popped into view. They were maybe 300 feet away, and coming fast. Dobermans? Rottweilers? Didn't matter much at this point, she realized. She tried to stop thinking at all.

THE AMERICAN MILITARY MACHINE had a large array of surveillance technology in place over the Sefid Koh. When it became apparent that Afghan and Pakistani heroin merchants were involved in the missing Semtex case, the number of electronic eyeballs there tripled. The Pentagon knew it was getting warm. If those were the men involved, then the Emir's lair was almost certainly in the Sefid Koh, south of Jalalabad.

A total of ten Global Hawks were in the air, at the 30,000 to 40,000-foot sector. They had been equipped with surveillance cameras in the visual and infrared spectrums. Each Global Hawk was controlled by a crew of three pilots at Edwards Air Force Base in California. They were connected directly to the War Room in the Pentagon.

In addition to these assets, two Keyhole Satellites had directed their observational equipment toward the area. Flying above it all, in an orbit more than 30,000 miles outside the atmosphere, was ORION-3, with its massive telescoping cameras now pointed directly at the region as well. In total, there were more than ten flying video recorders trained on the Sefid Koh. If so much as a grasshopper moved, someone at the NSA or Pentagon would capture the event. Admiral Jackson noted to himself, walking through the Pentagon, that it took several rooms to display all the images. They'd need to create a new War Room. Then he realized that the Pentagon wouldn't be large enough for such a central video display room. Maybe it was time they considered doing something new.

Kingston and his crew of blobologists at the NSA were in a war room of their own. While they focused their efforts on the three satellite returns, a smaller series of displays along one wall of their workroom showed the feeds from the Global Hawks.

The video feeds were also relayed to TTIC. Turbee and George had devised a way to display the feeds from the Global Hawks and satellites on the 101's, when they weren't being used for other data. They had also programmed the Atlas Screen to alternate between a detailed map of the Sefid Koh and the American Southwest, seeing as how those were the spheres of operation toward which the Semtex/terrorist threat was gravitating.

Of course, there were many other issues and events drifting through TTIC that day. Dan's authority and capability as a leader had been compromised, and it was becoming obvious that if he wasn't fired, the majority of his staff would leave. The nuclear issue had completely fizzled, and there was increasing anger that only a handful of people — Lance, Turbee, and at times Khasha — had been assigned to tracing the missing Semtex. Rhodes, Rahlson, and George had mutinied and were working on the Semtex problem when they could, despite Dan's insistence that they concentrate on other things. The search for the Emir continued unabated, and information was pouring into the TTIC boardroom with respect to that. The search for Richard Lawrence and Jennifer Coe was also well under way, as Jennifer's aborted call suggested that they knew the ultimate target of the looming terrorist attack.

Thirty minutes earlier, there had been a lucky break. It had been picked up first by Kingston and his staff at the NSA as they were monitoring the ORION-3 feed.

"Cranston, can you increase the magnification in the southwest quadrant? What is that?" Kingston asked.

"Looks to be two people moving along a ridge. No big deal. We see that a lot in there."

"Good," said Kingston. "Let's zoom back out." The magnification decreased by ten. "Hold it there, guys. I want to watch this for a while. This is Grand Central Station for the Afghan/Pakistani drug lords. We're looking for drug smugglers. Maybe, just maybe, those are the guys we're looking for."

Kingston bided his time, and kept the live feed on his 42-inch plasma. He was slowly unwrapping a ham and cheese sandwich that his wife had prepared for him more than 24 hours earlier. He smiled to himself. She was long suffering, and he was lucky to have her.

More movement. It would have gone undetected by anyone lacking Kingston's training and experience. One or two flashing pixels, at most. But there it was again. Just a flicker. "Cranston, zoom back in on the southwest quadrant. Just a factor of four, please."

Cranston was happy to oblige. "Hey, you guys, look at this. What do you think is going on here?" Kingston asked his team.

"A search?" volunteered one.

"A chase, maybe?"

"How about a search and chase," replied Kingston. "Look at these figures over here. People on foot? No… zoom in, Cranston. Aren't those dogs?"

Cranston increased the magnification to the maximum possible. "You're right, chief," he said as the small workgroup clustered around the plasma screen.

"Zoom out a bit, fourfold, maybe," ordered Kingston. The map zoomed back outward. The dogs became a small moving collection of dots. "Now look here. I would say that over here we have the handlers of those dogs. Behind them, more personnel. There seems to be a separate group over here. And there seems to be some vehicular activity in the area as well."

He watched the screen for a few seconds, getting the big picture. "Zoom out a bit more. There. Do you know what we have here, gentlemen?"

There were no takers. Everyone waited breathlessly. "It's a chase. These two people here are on the run. And it would appear that a good 100 people are after them, with dogs and off-road vehicles." He sat back, seeking a different angle of the screen.

"Lawrence and Coe were tracking the source of the Emir's messages," he continued, after a moment. "They were going to see how Al Jazeera got those videos. They've disappeared. And here, we have two people being chased by dogs, men, Jeeps, and Lord knows what else. I think we've found them. This has got to go to the top right now." He picked up his telephone to call the office of the Deputy Director of the NSA, was put through almost immediately to the Pentagon, and found himself speaking to Admiral Leonard Jackson.

Big Jack talked to the President directly. "It's like this, sir. We think we've spotted Richard Lawrence and Jennifer Coe. They're on the run somewhere in the Frontier Lands of western Pakistan. They probably have critical information about the Emir and those damned messages of his. They're being pursued, as we speak, and may well die in the next ten minutes. We need the State Department to talk to the ambassadors for both Afghanistan and Pakistan. We need permission to scramble the choppers we have sitting at the Islamabad Airport. We need to do this now or there will be no point."

Big Jack was lucky with the timing. Agreement was reached speedily, and the Marine helicopters were dispatched.

THE SOUNDS of the Super Stallions came closer, rising up from the valley floor. The dogs were 200 feet away. Then 100. They burst through the brush at the edge of the clearing. Four bloodhounds — no, six — charging at them at high speed. Richard heard the sound of the helicopters increasing rapidly, coming up from somewhere below the cliff edge. He closed his eyes and saw his parents again. He saw his two children, as infants, growing up, before everything went to hell. He saw the carrier crash — the dangerous crosswinds, the pitching sea, and the heaving deck of the *Super Sara.* The beautifully executed approach bedeviled by stormy seas. He almost had it. In conditions like that you went more on instinct than on what the HUD was telling you. He almost had it. A titch more left aileron, a touch of right elevator, a tiny bit of rudder, more thrust, no, less, no…

At the critical moment, the deck had drifted out of focus, just by a hair, just for an instant, but in those most dangerous of conditions, that had been enough. He overshot by a foot and landed long. The tail hook didn't grab, and he crashed into a parked Tomcat. Richard, along with a good $20 million worth of fighter jets, had hit the black and roiling waters of the Indian Ocean. He was able to free himself from the cockpit as his Tomcat sunk below the surface. He felt the cold fingers of death surround his throat as he struggled for breath in the huge ocean swells. He was rescued, but then came the endless interviews, investigations, and hearings. The loss of flight privileges, the embarrassment, the anxiety, depression, and fatigue. He'd gone through a peer review, in which he was found wanting. The shame, psychological and physical anguish, and escalating drug use had come hard upon the heels of that decision. Soon after, there had been the divorce, the anger and rejection of his children, the bankruptcy, and ultimately the loss of all hope. Then there was a second marriage, a second divorce, and utter desolation. It was all too much.

"Fuck 'em all, Jen," he said suddenly. "I'm done. I want the last 15 seconds of my life to be pleasurable. I'm done." Holding tightly to his piece of bone, Richard took a few faltering steps toward the cliff edge, and jumped. He fell flat on his face.

"Fucked up my own suicide attempt," he mumbled, curling into a fetal position in the dirt as the dogs closed in.

At that point the helicopters appeared, rising up from the valley floor before them. Jennifer turned to them, her hands raised in surrender. Then she saw the markings on the choppers. Americans. The Marines. They weren't being captured, they were being rescued. She could scarcely believe the good luck, and stood mute for a moment. Then her training took over, and she broke into action, waving her arms, and pointing to the dogs rapidly closing in on them.

"Don't worry, ma'am, we've got 'em," said the Master Sergeant over the loudspeaker. He pointed to one of his men, who sprayed an ark of bullets from the mounted M240G machine gun, bolted to the helicopter floor, into the dogs. One was killed instantly, and the rest, either wounded or terrorized, turned tail and ran yelping back toward their masters. The M240G kept the pursuers at bay as the lead Super Stallion came to rest beside Richard's limp body.

"It's the Hoover Dam!" yelled Jennifer, struggling to be heard over the roar of the helicopters. "The Hoover Dam! The terrorists are going to destroy the Hoover Dam! That's the sixth message!"

The officer was on the radio immediately, hooked by satellite to the Embassy at Islamabad. "Terrorists are going to blow the Hoover Dam," he said, once he had a connection. "Let the Pentagon know."

52

ONCE THIS INFORMATION WAS OUT, it didn't take long for it to be passed down the line. Islamabad called someone at the Pentagon, who called the Joint Chiefs of Staff, Langley, and the White House. From there the message went through offices like a row of stacked dominoes. It bounced down the chain of command of each arm of the military with lighting speed. The Intelligence Community knew almost immediately, as the message was beamed along at the speed of light, by fiber optic cable, laser, satellite, and telephone, by email, voicemail, and Blackberry and Treo message, from one department to the next. Within five minutes of Jennifer telling the Master Sergeant, most of the military higher-ups knew. The contingent of troops already patrolling the Hoover Dam was profoundly reinforced. Additional armaments, men, and material were moved from nearby Nellis, and the various bases in California. The President met with his National Security Advisor. The Southwestern states were brought under martial law within ten minutes of Jennifer's announcement.

It was immediately apparent to Turbee that he had missed the obvious. This was how 4.5 tons of Semtex could destroy a city. They would blow up the Hoover Dam, not Las Vegas. With the dam gone, Las Vegas would be deprived of power and water. Without power to run the air conditioners, and without water, Las Vegas would return to the desert that it was. The city would die slowly. The buildings would remain, but they would be uninhabitable.

IS HE OUT OF HIS FUCKING MIND?" shouted the President, addressing his National Security Advisor. "We have battalions of troops, helicopters, Marines, Army Reserve, boats, and fighter jets swarming all over the Hoover. How in the hell can he blow it up? And why haven't we figured it out yet?"

All those assembled in the Situation Room were likewise perplexed. Within 20 minutes of Jennifer Coe's news that the Hoover Dam was the target of the terrorist strike, the sixth message had hit the airwaves. All of the American networks were interrupting regular programming to run commentary on the Emir's threat. Within hours? The Hoover Dam? After Message Five, the Hoover had become heavily fortified. After Jennifer's warning, it had a greater level of protection assigned to it than the White House itself.

The Secretary of Defense was likewise perplexed. Perhaps a missile strike on the dam? The Chairman of the Joint Chiefs nixed that. It would have to be a huge missile, and there was no Intel of any sort about that. And in any event, the hit would need to be very precise, which meant highly sophisticated missile guidance systems, and there had been no indication of such a possibility. Perhaps it had been inserted into the dam itself, someone suggested. After all, with all of its complex diversion tunnels, intake and outtake works, and the powerhouse, the Hoover was a monstrous structure, much larger than it appeared to be in photographs.

"No way," said Admiral Jackson, who was linked to the meeting by fiber optic line from the Pentagon. "We've had hundreds of people combing through every inch of that structure, and nothing has shown up."

"Make them search again," growled the President.

Admiral Jackson nodded in agreement, not saying that, with the fifth message, the search crews within the dam structure had doubled in number, and had now doubled again. "We will, sir, but there is no evidence of any Semtex in, on, or under that dam."

"We're missing something," said the President. "God dammit, we're missing something. The Emir must believe that he is actually going to do this. This bastard wants to boot the US in the balls, and become the next living legend for doing it. How the hell can we stop him?"

"What do you want us to do?" asked the Secretary of Defense. They were all looking at the President intently, waiting for their orders. They were ready to do anything to stop the tragedy, but they needed guidance. Ultimately, the burden rested with the President.

"Go to maximum mobilization, gentlemen. Martial law in the Southwest. Everything we can mobilize in that region should be mobilized. And, regrettably," he added to his Chief of Staff, "regrettably, get the head of FEMA on the line. This is starting to look very, very ugly."

THE PANDEMONIUM that always reigned in Las Vegas, which had multiplied since the fifth and then sixth messages, intensified with the President's orders. What had been a bad situation became even worse. The outbound lanes of the freeways were clogged with traffic, and the Nevada Department of Transportation decided to flip all six lanes of the 15 and 95 freeways to outbound. The city's emergency planners called such a reversal of traffic a "contra flow." The military guys called it a clusterfuck. Not all exits and onramps were monitored and patrolled, and there were invariably those individuals, drunk, doped, or just plain inattentive, for whom a routine drive to work was mindless and automatic, who failed to notice the change in traffic flow. The resulting accidents just added to the chaos. Ambulances and fire trucks began using the shoulders and even grass medians, trying to get through to those who needed their help. Trucks scattered into the desert surrounding the freeway, taking advantage of four-wheel drive to avoid the congestion.

Adding to the commotion were the low-flying squadrons of F-117's and other jets coming from nearby Nellis Air Force Base. Military helicopters of every description were hovering in and about the strip. McCarron International Airport was jammed with passengers, all outgoing. Despite the usual American practice of grounding planes in times of crisis, the President had ordered that every form of transportation be utilized during the evacuation. The results were mixed. As the planes were filled and then packed almost to bursting, the airport stewards were forced to turn would-be passengers away more and more often, resulting in riots and violence. Airport rage, freeway rage, hotel rage, and bus rage were the order of the day. Tempers flared and moods were desperate.

The few vehicles entering Vegas were routinely stopped and searched. Crank calls multiplied, and overworked law enforcement agencies were stretched to the limit, some units working without any breaks, in heat that reached 110 degrees in the daytime. Search crews patrolled the sewers, the streets, the stores, and the casinos. Parked vehicles were towed. Towed vehicles were searched. There were many strokes and cardiac events, and the Lake Mead HMC, Sunrise, and other major medical centers began to feel the strain. For the first time in the city's history, the slot machines were silent, and the card tables empty. The first stages of a terrorist attack were already underway. Terror ruled the city.

During the chaos of the evacuation, almost no one in Las Vegas had actually seen the airing of the sixth message. But they knew about it, and everyone had seen the fifth message. Public theories ran rampant as the stream of humanity leaving the city about how it would be destroyed. What would it be? A nuclear strike? An airliner plummeting into a casino? Buildings blown up? The Hoover destroyed? Anthrax or bubonic plague? Were they already infected? Were they already the walking dead? The public speculation was endless and, at the end of the day, pointless.

THE EMIR was well aware of these events, as he had an extensive network of informants. While he could not, for obvious security reasons, upload information in his tunnel computers, he could download. DVD's of western newscasts were brought to him as they happened. He chuckled to himself. A twenty-minute videotaping, split into six equal parts, had brought an entire American city to her knees. Power. He had it. Maybe he should send out a DVD advising the world that he would take out New York as well, and then stand back and watch the fun. Of course, the whole world would go crazy, but only if he had credibility, if he had the power to deliver. That was why the messages were so vital. To advertise in advance that he was going to take out a city, and then in fact do it, and much more, would give him god-like status. In his visions, Mohammed had told him this — that he, the Emir, would be seated beside Mohammed in Paradise. He, the Emir, was the new Mohammed, the new sword of Islam, the next Saladin. This had been foretold, and it would come to pass.

I DON'T GET IT, George," said Turbee.

"What, little buddy?" asked George, staring avidly at his computer screens, in the workstation next to Turbee.

"We've got more than four tons of high explosives loose, in the hands of terrorists, in the American heartland," Turbee responded. "The Emir has said that he's going to take out the Hoover Dam, presumably using the Semtex. But it won't work."

"Why not?"

"There's not enough of the stuff. Not enough punch," said Turbee slowly, still trying to do the math.

"Come on, Turb. There are more than four tons of it. Look what a few ounces of it did on the Lockerbie 747 disaster. This stuff is powerful."

"Yes, but I don't think it's powerful enough," Turbee responded. "The Hoover is an absolutely massive structure. That Semtex will cause substantial damage, but I don't see how it could possibly cause a catastrophic failure. Maybe some dams, but not the Hoover. And the Lockerbie thing, that was just placing the explosive in exactly the right spot. An ounce could do it if it were to take out the computers controlling the plane. But not this dam."

"Are you sure, Turb?" asked George.

"Well, do you remember when all of this started, there was a betting pool in Vegas about how large the crater would be when the original 660 tons was detonated in the middle of the Libyan Sahara? I don't normally bet, but I did in that case."

"Yes, Turb, as I recall you came in second. Some housewife beat you by quite a bit."

"That's beside the point," Turbee responded. "The blast was way bigger than anyone expected, because of the way they stacked the Semtex and put in the fuses. And don't even get me started on the fact that they were 4.5 tons short. What I'm saying is that losing that bet pissed me off. I wanted to know why I'd lost, so I started doing some research about Semtex and what it could do. Read everything I could find about the damage it can cause. I think I've become a pretty good authority on the depths and diameters of craters created by bomb blasts. And there is absolutely no way that 4.5 tons of Semtex can take out that dam. No way."

"Care to explain?"

"Well, George, for starters that dam is ridiculously over-engineered. It's unbelievably massive, because when it was built it was a project to kick start things during the Great Depression. At its base it's more than 600 feet thick. That's 600 feet of solid concrete and steel."

"Yes. And?"

"According to the site dedicated to the dam, it has a unique design feature. It's built out of gigantic concrete and steel blocks."

"How do you mean, Turb?" This came from Rahlson. He'd been following the conversation from the next workstation over, and decided to get involved.

"The dam was built in blocks or vertical columns, varying in size from about 60 feet square at the upstream face of the dam to about 25 feet square at the downstream face. Adjacent columns were locked together by a system of vertical keys on the radial joints and horizontal keys on the circumferential joints."

"Go on," urged Rahlson.

"Sure. So the Hoover dam is constructed with interconnected concrete blocks. Then cement grout was forced into the spaces created between the blocks. The contraction of the cooled concrete between the blocks formed a very strong monolithic structure."

"How would it compare to other large dams built around the world?" asked George.

"I'm not an expert, but I've been checking on the Internet. Many dams have central cores that are filled with earth or stone. The Hoover doesn't. It's solid reinforced concrete through and through. Four and a half tons of Semtex might put a hole 20 feet deep and 50 or 60 feet across, but that's it."

"You're saying that the stolen Semtex cannot in and of itself cause the catastrophic failure of the Hoover?" Rahlson asked slowly.

"That's exactly what I'm saying. Unless the Semtex were somehow taken inside the dam, through one of its internal piping structures, and even then, it's doubtful," Turbee added. "There is no way that Semtex can do what the Emir says."

"The Emir's people can't take anything inside Black and Boulder Canyons," said Rahlson, referring to the two canyons that separated the dam from Lake Mead. "There are dozens of patrol boats and submarines in the water there. The canyons, and the dam intake towers, are protected like Fort Knox. He cannot take that volume of Semtex into the inner workings of the dam."

Rahlson called Dan over, and explained the essence of the conversation to him.

"You're saying, kid, that there's not enough Semtex blow the dam?" Dan asked.

"Yes, sir, I'm saying that."

"Well there you go, it's just as I said. It must be a nuclear attack after all," said Dan smugly.

"I don't think so, Dan," responded Turbee. "There has been zero real Intel about that. It was all a ruse."

"Then what the hell are we missing?" Dan shouted.

"I don't know, sir, I just don't know." Turbee looked at the close-up of the Hoover that George had displayed on the Atlas Screen. "Pull it back a bit, George," he said. "I want an overview. I want to look at it from a distance for awhile. We're missing something." He got up on top of his workstation, stood up, crossed his arms in front of him, and gazed, as if in a trance, at the Hoover Dam and the areas surrounding it.

It had been a miniature submarine that brought the Semtex to the wharf in Stewart, BC. The Hoover Dam was now the Emir's target. Again, the presence of water. Mulling these things over, his mind returned to the first message that Goldberg had delivered. The attack would be "by water," Goldberg had said. The Karachi Star Line was involved, somehow. Drug smugglers were involved, and their preferred method of transporting drugs was by water. There had to be something else. What was he missing?

53

MASSOUD AND JAVEED were approaching the dam from the north. At the dam site, they were more than 300 feet beneath the surface. They could hear the metal skin of the small craft creaking and groaning under the pressure. Despite the noise, they both trusted that Kumar had readied the sub for this mission. He knew the depths to which the Pequod could travel, and had reinforced the skin and increased the size of the small bulkheads, to keep them safe no matter how deep they went. They were deep enough now that the only illumination came from the craft's forward lights. The HUD told them that they were within a few hundred feet of the dam itself, but they still couldn't see it. The tricky part of the trip was still to come. Penstock Three, Four, or Five, Yousseff had told them. Any of these three would do. But the penstock needed to be closed. If they chose an open penstock, they would be sucked into the dam, and the Pequod and its precious cargo would be destroyed.

A sophisticated program designed by Kumar's software engineers showed relative water flow, and indicated whether a penstock was open or closed, displaying the information on the HUD. Critical exterior features of the dam had been programmed into the HUD's hard drives. Amazingly, even after the recent attacks on American soil, it was possible to obtain this kind of critical design information on much of the nation's infrastructure over the Internet. The complete plans of a number of dams spanning the Colorado River had been available to the brilliant Egyptian and Saudi engineers who had conceived the mission. They had studied these plans very carefully, again and again, over the past months.

Javeed played with the keyboard in front of him, and the outlines of the dam appeared, complete with the eight penstocks. They were color-coded to show whether they were open or closed. Penstocks One and Eight were orange, Two, Six, and Seven were red, and Three, Four, and Five were green.

"Take the middle one," he said, pointing at Penstock Four. "Safest bet."

Massoud operated the controls, and deftly brought the Pequod to within 50 feet of the monolithic structure. The water of the Colorado River was extremely murky around them, and in the darkness they still couldn't see the dam ahead of them. They had to rely on the graphics of the HUD to provide them with accurate information for navigating.

At 8:05AM, the gigantic outline of Penstock Four suddenly appeared out of the gloom, directly in front of them. The three vertical steel mullions that transected the penstock opening would need to be cut before the mission could continue. The steel beams looked larger than they had on paper, but this eventuality had been planned for. One of the sub's two cantilevered arms had a powerful, high-speed, carbide-tipped circular saw blade attached to it. In trial runs, it had been determined that each beam could be completely severed in under ten minutes — five minutes for the upper cuts, and five minutes more for the lower cuts. Javeed assumed the controls and was able, without difficulty, to perform this task. He had done the same dozens of times in the simulator. Massoud kept the Pequod stationary and perpendicular to the dam face. Each set about his task with confidence and precision.

SAM AND HANK were waiting near Wawheap, in the smaller five-ton truck. It was 8:15AM, local time. The military air traffic was steadily increasing as they waited. A wing of F-15 Eagles. Helicopters. Then some Tomcats. Things were definitely heating up.

They had spent the last hour waiting in a nearly deserted campsite. The satellite uplink station that had been sitting in the rear of the truck had been checked and checked again. The video camera was tested, and then the sliding side door and retracting roof — last-minute improvisations designed by Kumar.

They packed up and left the campground, taking the winding Lakeshore Drive toward Highway 89. By 8:35 they had reached the highway. Sam made a left-hand turn onto the highway and, without saying a word, headed south toward Page. Looking toward the massive dam, they saw three large helicopters, stationary, almost at the water's surface. A flight of five F-117's flew low and slow, no more than 1,000 feet above the land. The two looked at each other. With the combined capability of the American Intelligence Community now searching for them, the plan, and its participants, would not remain secret for long. The issue was really whether or not the strike could get off the ground before it was stopped.

At 8:30AM, they crossed the bridge just east of the dam, turned around at the dam access road, and crossed the bridge a second time. Sam brought the truck to a halt in the center of the bridge, getting as close to the northern railing as he could. Thus positioned, he retracted the roof door and opened the sliding doors on the passenger side of the van. Wordlessly, Hank reached for the door handle. The passenger door could only open a foot before it hit the bridge railing with a sharp clunk. Hank squeezed through the opening, trying not to look down. The Colorado River, reformed through the dam's penstocks, was more than 600 feet below him. In his younger life he had known the grandeur of the Hindu Kush, and had once even accompanied some friends from Jalalabad through the Path of Allah, in the Sefid Koh. The soaring heights there were much greater than what was now below his feet, but the drop still made him nervous. It was 8:45AM. Sam and Hank stood looking at the Glen Canyon Dam.

Suddenly Sam heard the sound of helicopters. Half a dozen, maybe more, were approaching the bridge from the north. At the same time, police vehicles could be seen racing from Page toward the dam access road, sirens blaring, lights flashing.

A small contingent of Marines were on patrol on the dam itself. Sam counted about 20 men, and armed Jeeps parked on both ends of the dam. Las Vegas was, as usual, hogging most of the attention, and while the Hoover Dam was looking like a staging point for a fresh Iraq war, the Glen Canyon Dam, northeast of its larger cousin, certainly wasn't without its share of protection. The level of military protection in Nevada alone had increased dramatically. Most of the airspace now had increased restrictions. With the word from Canada being that the Semtex had come through Devil's Anvil and into Montana, there were belated roadblocks being thrown up throughout the western states. The I-15 had become, much to the inconvenience of local residents, subject to tight restrictions. Izzy and Ba'al had left the Interstate just under the proverbial wire. Security in the American Southwest was now stepped up to its highest point. They'd barely made it.

Sam flipped the hood latch for the truck. Hank opened the hood from the outside and placed a slow-acting smoke generator in the recesses of the engine compartment. He then set up four orange triangles behind the truck. Sam activated the four-way flashers, and, by 8:47AM, they had created the appearance of a thoroughly disabled truck.

Sam activated two more switches underneath the dash of the truck. The scissors lift, much favored since Yousseff's early days on the Indus River, began to rise from the floor of the truck's cargo area. The uplink, using GPS technology, was quickly able to find the correct satellite — in this case, one from the Iridium system. Kumar's technicians at PWS had been able to hack into this system without too much difficulty. Through the miracle of communications technology, the signal from the camera was directed from one

Iridium geostationary satellite to the next, and to the next, until it reached the head offices of NBC, in New York. There had already been a number of "tips" coming from various sources, telling the station to be ready for an interesting satellite feed coming in at 11AM Eastern that day. It was said that it just might gain the dowdy old lady from Rockefeller Center a few more viewers.

Hank had finished setting up the triangles, and came back alongside the truck, pulling himself into the van through the side door. He checked the viewing angle of the DVD recorder, which was aimed directly at the center of the massive concrete structure just to the north of the bridge. He checked his Casio. It was 8:50AM.

Suddenly they both heard jet engines whining at an unusual frequency. Two military jets came roaring up Marble Canyon toward the dam. They were less than 500 feet above the bridge.

"Hey, Sam, they sound like flying vacuum cleaners," joked Hank.

"Yes, they do. This could get very interesting," replied Sam.

TURBEE, after programming further searches for his web-bot, finally dozed off. He awoke as he usually did, sluggishly, with a headache, and his brain slightly unfocused. He knew the sensation well. His medications were out of balance. In younger years he would have screamed and thrown things, or curled up inside an oversized T-shirt in an effort to stem the painful barrage of unfiltered sensations. Now he just took a deep breath and looked around at an agitated and noisy control room. The big 101 screens were displaying the main news feeds, most of them live from Las Vegas. The Atlas Screen displayed a map of the western USA. A red circle surrounded Las Vegas. A red trail crossed the border in Montana and proceeded down I-15. Phones were ringing incessantly, Blackberries and computers were in overdrive, and a cacophonous commotion prevailed.

He reached toward the series of bottles that sat on his desk and took double doses of most everything he needed. He knew that he'd still be on a sharp edge, close to losing control, for at least the next hour. He resolved to do everything he could to keep himself under control, and looked long and hard at the cluster of computer screens in front of him.

From there his behavior became progressively more eccentric and bizarre. He got up and stood on top of his desk, looking down at the massive Atlas Screen, which was still centered on Las Vegas, with a 100-mile radius around it.

"George," he said finally, "can you create a circular map, putting Las

Vegas on the western edge and the east end of the Glen Canyon Dam on the other?"

"Can do, Turbee," came the reply, and with a few keystrokes a map was created with Las Vegas and the Hoover Dam to the west, and Page, the Glen Canyon Dam, and Lake Powell to the east. The Grand Canyon bisected the map from southwest to northeast. Turbee gazed at the map for a good five minutes, entranced. Dan saw him — he was hard to miss — but sighed and ignored the unusual display. Turbee squatted down, peering at one of his computer displays, then stood up again.

"George," he said in a sharp tone of voice. "Put a red dot at the following coordinates, please." He read out the latitude and longitude coordinates, and a red dot appeared on the northern tip of one of the many arms and bays of the gigantic Lake Powell reservoir.

"OK," Turbee continued. "Now put a red line showing the shortest route that can be taken by water from that point to the Glen Canyon Dam." George complied. Turbee looked at the Atlas Screen for another minute, then at one of his monitors, then at the Atlas Screen again. He suddenly became extremely agitated, jumping up and beginning to yell.

"It's wrong, it's wrong, it's wrong! Wrong, wrong, wrong! Wrong dam!" he babbled.

George looked over at him. "Keep it down, Turb. You're pissing people off at the wrong time. We have major shit coming down the pipe."

But Turbee was already waving frantically at Dan. "Wrong dam, Dan!" he yelled, when Dan wouldn't come to him. "Wrong damn dam!"

"Turbee, shut up. We're in the middle of a terrorist attack right now. Half of the world is calling, wanting to talk to us," said an irritated Dan, nervously fidgeting with the keyboard before him.

"No, no. Dam, Dan, dammit! Wrong, Dan! Wrong Dam! Damn. Damn!"

Dan looked around the large control room. "Can somebody stuff a pill into the little bastard, or do I have to get him tasered again? Someone do something."

Rahlson marched into the melee. "Dan, you almost got him killed ten days ago with the way you handled things. I think you owe him at least five minutes. I don't give a rat's ass what's going on in Vegas or at the Hoover Dam. Shut the fuck up and listen to the kid. And if I hear you say anything else about tasering him I'm going to drop you down the elevator shaft. Got it, you pompous ass?"

When it looked as though Dan might continue to argue, Rahlson took a step closer, leaning in. "Have you got it asshole?"

Dan looked around the noisy control center, and could see that the tide was going with Rahlson. "OK, Turbee, five minutes. That's all you've got."

Turbee began slowly, halting and stuttering a bit. "It's like this company in Pakistan. We've seen it before, like, we think it's involved in drug trafficking, you know, Karachi Star Line. We've seen it lots of times before. There's another company I found out about. It's called KDEC, Karachi Drydock and Engineering. They build shipping parts. Looks like they're owned by the same people as the shipping line. And a third company. A Californian company. It's called Pacific Western Submersibles. These companies are all part of them."

"Part of who?" Dan's words were sharp and choppy.

"Them. The heroin smugglers. They're related to them. They're another arm. They are them."

"Who the fuck is who?" Dan spat out the words.

"Nevermind the grammar, there, Dan," said Rahlson. "Kid, you're going to have to give the ass chapter and verse. Lives are at stake. How do you know that this Long Beach company is in league with this KDEC and the Karachi shipping line?"

"OK, yeah. OK. It's like this." Turbee felt his lips and tongue turn into sandpaper. He desperately looked around, and grabbed a cold cup of coffee from George's desk.

"The banks. All three use financial institutions in the same three jurisdictions — Nigeria, Russia, and Lichtenstein."

"That's not–" began Dan, but one glance from Rahlson quashed the sentence before it was formed.

"Second point. Many of the parts and fittings used by PWS have been manufactured or machined by KDEC. I found that out be checking the RFID tags of containers of parts manufactured by KDEC and sent to the container facility at Long Beach."

"So they buy parts from–" began Dan, but, at this stage, just the upward lift of one of Rahlson's eyebrows stopped him.

"Third point. PWS makes small submarines. They're used by the military, for scientific research, and for expensive tourist amusement toys at places like Cancun. Here's a picture of their 'Model 12.' If you look closely at it, and remember what Wharfdog Charlie had to say, you will see that–"

Dan interrupted. "Oh, so now Wharfdog Charlie is going to dictate tactics in–"

"Shut the fuck up and listen to him!" Rahlson roared.

"That they're quite similar," Turbee finished, glaring at Dan. "Fourth point. All of the KDEC shipments to PWS were done aboard container ships from the Karachi Star Line. All of them. And, more significantly, while there seem to be more than 30 ocean-going vessels flying Karachi Star colors, the ship that travels most often, according to the information that I've been able to get, is the *Haramosh Star.* You've heard of her before, I'm sure, Dan." Turbee had to curtail a smile when he saw Dan's reddening complexion.

"Fifth point." Turbee could see that he had everyone's attention. "PWS grew in the same way KDEC did — very rapidly, coming out of nowhere. Its competitors can't match its research and development funding. Looking at it, there's no way that the sale of a few subs can pay for an army of engineers and scientists like this."

"Look, Turbee," Dan broke in again, with a wary eye on Rahlson. "All of that is hopelessly circumstantial. None of it proves anything."

"Yes, sir, that's right. But it raises the index of suspicion over PWS, so a few hours ago I programmed a series of web-bots that scoured every particle of information on the net with respect to the company. And I found some real interesting stuff. Besides, you're always saying you want ALL the facts before we make any moves."

There was a moment or two of silence, punctuated by the odd snicker. "What?" asked Dan finally. "What what what?"

"PWS controls a very large number of holding companies, trusts, and various offshore entities. Lots of them. And tracking it the best I could, these entities seem to own or control, believe it or not, service stations and convenience stores. Like, there's just piles of them. Dozens. All over California and north into Oregon and a couple in Washington."

"What is the significance of that?" asked Dan, a little more cautiously.

"Couple of things. Most of the proprietors of those stores and service stations seem to be refugees from Afghanistan, mostly from northeastern Afghanistan. Pashtun country. But that's not the clinker."

"Clinker?" muttered George.

"Yeah. A number of these establishments have been under investigation by the DEA. Nothing obvious, it's pretty covert. But they seem to be spinning off a very large amount of cash."

"I know about that one," said Lance, who was the DEA voice at TTIC. "It's been going on for awhile. The investigation isn't going anywhere, but there was, and is, a high degree of suspicion there. Are you saying that, one way or the other, PWS controls these stores and stations?"

"Yes," responded Turbee. "It looks that way to me, though I can't be 100 percent certain."

"Fine," said Dan. "PWS may be in the laundry business. How does this help us in dealing with the current terrorist threat?"

"You see the red dot on the Atlas Screen, on the Lake Powell reservoir? That's a piece of property owned by one of those numbered companies. Turns out that PWS used that as a base when it took part in an underwater mapping project, along with a number of universities and government agencies."

"Uh-oh," said Rahlson as he realized what Turbee was saying. "You don't think that…"

"Well, yes I do. I couldn't figure out how 4.5 tons of Semtex could take out the Hoover Dam. It's just too well built, and you can't really get inside of it, which is what you need to do, especially with the level of protection that exists around it right now. But if you took out the Glen Canyon Dam…"

"Turbee, that's where your logic breaks down," said Dan triumphantly. "If you can't figure out how the Semtex could destroy the Hoover Dam, how can you say that the same amount could, in fact, destroy the Glen Canyon Dam? That makes no sense."

"I'm not sure, Dan. It's a different dam. It's not as well built. I'm not sure, but maybe you should look at it."

"Fine, I'll pass it along," Dan muttered, and began dithering with communications links that he didn't fully understand. Other emails and telephone calls were made, but with Turbee's equivocal answer and Dan's hesitation, the new evidence of the involvement of PWS did not gain prominence until much later.

54

IT WAS A RUNNER'S DREAM. The early morning temperature on September 3 was in the high 60s. The sun was warm but not hot. The scenery was gorgeous. A different view of the huge reservoir appeared every couple hundred feet. Traffic and other pedestrians were nonexistent. Catherine Gray had what she called her "forever legs" on, clocking an easy, rhythmic 6.8 miles to the hour. After the first hour she was in the zone, and if it weren't for the intrusive thought of an unfolding national catastrophe, the endorphin-laden cadence of her strides would have been perfect.

The sun was rising higher as she approached the cliff edge where Yousseff had ordered Ba'al to ditch the truck in the murky waters of Lake Powell. The guardrail was conspicuously swinging in the breeze, drawing attention to the mischief that had gone on there an hour earlier. Catherine paused for a few moments, looking down into the muddy water. The unmistakable outlines of a box van could be seen in the lake, far below. She would be telling the local police force or FBI about that at the earliest opportunity. With modern forensic science, a great deal of information would likely be found there. She carried on with her run. One hour became two, and two was pushing three by the time the first residence appeared: a mobile home just north of the Wawheap Marina and Campsite Complex. She pounded on the door, then looked at her watch, which had automatically reset itself to the local time zone. It was 8:45AM.

DUANE BECKER and his wife of forty-some years had been happily retired for ten years. They were enjoying their peace and quiet when the staccato knock, sharp and professional, came from the side door of their still-new-looking double-wide mobile home.

They had decided to retire here. They had spent most of their working lives in Las Vegas, he a janitor, she a waitress. Through all the dazzle and bling of that city, they remained true to each other, and both swore that they loved each other more now than they had when they first married. Three children had come, been raised, and left. Two stayed in Vegas, the third was in Los Angeles somewhere. They had spent many a weekend on Lake Mead, north of the Hoover Dam, but found that it was becoming too noisy for their taste. They had migrated north then, and had spent their share of holidays in the Wawheap area, where greater tranquility and more restful trips had become more and more welcome as they both passed 60. They finally decided to pull up stakes in Vegas. To their glee, they discovered that their small home, purchased for $50,000 so many years ago, was now worth $450,000. The couple took a small amount of what they considered to be a fortune, and purchased the isolated double-wide trailer, formerly owned by one of the Wawheap Camp caretakers. The balance of their money was carefully invested and, along with the combined cash flows from two small pensions, they now considered themselves to be fabulously wealthy and blessed.

They'd already finished breakfast, but the delicious smell of coffee and fried bacon still permeated the air. They seldom had company, other than their children and grandchildren, which was just fine by them. A knock at 8:45AM was unusual, especially after the tourist season had finished. Duane became more attentive as his wife reached for the door.

He lunged for the side cupboard the instant he heard her shocked gasp. He kept a loaded Mossberg 590 sawed-off shotgun, just for this kind of situation. At close quarters, the Mossberg would be a potent and lethal weapon. He hadn't needed to use it yet, but now he thanked God he'd had the foresight to keep it ready.

"I'm there, hon, I'm there," he yelled as he moved with a quickness that belied his age.

When he got to the door, Sandra Becker was standing absolutely still, staring in shock at the person standing on their front step.

"You'd best explain yourself, ma'am," said Duane, pointing the Mossberg directly at the intruder's midsection. "And no sudden moves. This gun'll shoot you clean in half."

Sandra backed up, and moved behind her husband's ample frame.

"I'm Corporal Gray, of the RCMP," Catherine said, breathing heavily.

"The who?"

"The Royal Canadian Mounted Police, that's who," replied Catherine sharply between breaths.

"Yes, of course you are. On an early morning patrol no doubt. Lose your way in Toronto?" Duane did not lower the Mossberg. "Lady, if you're with the RC whatever, then I'm the tooth fairy. Show some ID, and slowly," he said, his steady eyes not leaving hers.

It was then that Catherine came to terms with the true nature of the problem. In the past 48 hours, she had been locked in an underground room in a deserted coal mine, crawled through a filthy coal-black tunnel, multiple times, spent hours squatting behind more than four tons of plastic explosive, peed in a cooler, played cat and mouse in the pitch black with a furious terrorist/drug smuggler, and to top it all off, had just run a distance in excess of a marathon.

"I must look like hell," she said, fishing around in her pockets for ID. Of course, at critical moments like these, passports, badges, and other forms of ID were completely lacking.

"Yes ma'am, you do. Now who the hell are you?" repeated Duane, lowering the gun ever so slightly.

"I'm a corporal with the RCMP. I've been following a stolen shipment of high-powered plastic explosive from Canada to here, and I'm not even sure where 'here' is," Catherine replied.

"We're just north of Page, Arizona," he replied. "We're adjacent to Lake Powell, just over yonder." He motioned with his head, still keeping his eyes firmly locked with hers.

"OK," said Catherine. "Is there anything in the immediate vicinity that terrorists might want to destroy? Something big, something of significant national interest?"

"I can't really think of anything," said Duane. "No huge buildings, no airports, no nuclear power stations. Unless," he added, "unless maybe it's the dam itself."

"Dam?" asked Catherine. "What dam?"

"Well Lake Powell is a reservoir, created by the Glen Canyon Dam, which is next to Page. The town was built when the dam was built." The Mossberg was lowered again, but only slightly.

Catherine's face grew still in horror. "I need to use a phone, right now," she said quietly. "I think terrorists are going to blow the dam. I think it's going to happen in the next hour or so. Please, I must use a phone."

Duane stared at her in amazement. She did indeed look awful. She still had a residue of coal dust in her hair and streaked across her face. There were twigs and bits of bush in her hair and clothing from her cat and mouse game with Ba'al. Both her hands were still pitch black. She was now sweating profusely and, to her horror, realized that she did not smell all that good.

"Hon," Duane said to his wife, "grab the portable phone for this person. I'm not letting you in just yet," he said, half to his wife, half to Catherine.

The phone arrived, born by a tremulous Sandra Becker. She handed it to Catherine, who immediately dialed Indy's cell phone. Two rings and he answered.

"Indy here," came his terse greeting.

"Indy, it's Catherine. I know–"

He cut her off. "Catherine, where the hell are you? Are you OK?"

"Indy, be quiet and listen very carefully. I'm near Page, Arizona, in the US. There's a huge dam nearby, and they're going to blow it. This information needs to get to the American Intelligence and military people. Can you connect me?"

"Stay on the line, Cath. I'm at the Heather Street complex. The officers here just talked to an American Intelligence outfit called TTIC a few hours ago. They're the people who are tracking this. Do not hang up."

At the moment, Indy was indeed in his crowded little cubicle of an office. Blackman was sitting across from him. They'd just been on the phone for what seemed like hours, connected to various Intelligence Agencies, and to TTIC in particular. Indy was ecstatic to finally be hearing from his partner again.

"It's Catherine," he said to Blackman. "She's in northern Arizona someplace. She knows where it's going down. What's the number of that TTIC outfit?"

He punched a series of numbers, and got Johnson at TTIC on the first ring. "This is Indy. We know where the Semtex is. We know the target."

"Have your guy call this number," Johnson answered.

Indy relayed the information to a sweating, filthy Catherine Gray. "I've got to call this number. It's the TTIC control room," she told the Beckers as she started dialing.

"What? The who?" asked an astounded Duane Becker, putting the Mossberg down completely.

"Honey, let me get you a cup of coffee," exclaimed Sandra, darting back to the kitchen. "Cream? Sugar?" She suddenly became the perfect hostess.

And so it was that an RCMP corporal, covered in sweat, twigs, leaves, and coal dust, sat down at the kitchen table of the Beckers, and explained what had occurred to a rapt TTIC audience.

DAN DID MOST OF THE TALKING. He pressed her again and again. Describe the sub. What was that other device? Where was she exactly? How much Semtex, and again, where did you say you are? Had they known what was occurring 300 feet under the surface of the nearby lake, neither would have fiddled for so long with the nonessentials. Rhodes and Rahlson were both reaching for their individual telephones. This was taking too much time already.

Frustrated, Catherine finally handed the telephone to Duane. "Tell this dumbo where we are," she said.

Duane gave the details. "You know where Page is? Guess not. Well look at the map. You guys got a map?"

In distant Washington, George smiled. "A map, you say? Have we got a map?" Within seconds, he had a map centered on Page, Arizona, some 30 feet in size, displayed on the Atlas Screen. The dam was clearly labeled, as was the huge Lake Powell reservoir and the Grand Canyon. For added measure, he displayed a large photograph of the Glen Canyon Dam on the central 101.

"OK," said Dan. "We're looking at a map. We have Page. Where are you in relation?"

"It's not complicated," said Duane. "You take Lakeshore Drive north to Wawheap Marina. Go past that. There's an old mining road winding north along Lake Powell. We're about ten miles beyond that. Technically we're over the line, in Utah."

"Are there any residences or structures beyond that?" asked Dan.

"Yes," replied Duane. "Go another 20 miles up and there's a couple of buildings. It's a testing facility of some kind, owned by some Californian company."

"Thanks. Can you put the Corporal back on the line?"

Catherine accepted the phone, and the coffee that Sandra had poured. Duane glanced at his wife, impressed that she was still holding up. This was more excitement than the Beckers had seen in years. Yet Sandra was calmly pulling the little bits of twigs, moss, and leaves from Catherine's hair, the picture of warm maternal concern.

"Corporal Gray," said Dan, firmly in charge, "we've got General Odlum from Army Intelligence sitting here. Can you describe the other piece of equipment that you saw? Not the submarine, but the container that they were packing the Semtex into."

"It was a very strange device. It looked highly machined, highly polished. Very precise. It was made of different metals. Maybe steel or nickel alloys, maybe molybdenum. It had a very odd shape, almost like an ancient ship. High in front, and in the rear, but very short in the center."

"Was there a ribbon of different metal running along its crest, perhaps even gold?" asked the general sharply.

"Yes, I think so. They were taking their time packing the Semtex into it too," said Catherine.

"Shit," was all General Odlum said.

"Corporal Gray, please stay by the phone. We'll probably have more to ask you in a minute or two." That was all Dan said. The line went dead.

Catherine and the Beckers looked at each other. "They're going to take out the Glen Canyon Dam," said Catherine, as she continued to pick coal dust out of her ears, and twigs and dirt from her clothing. "Enjoy your waterfront view. You may not have it for too much longer."

"Would you like some bacon and eggs?" asked Sandra. "You must be hungry. And let me get you some damp towels. Honey, you are a mess."

Duane smiled. His wife had always thought that a cup of tea would solve even the most dire of problems. She always managed to take the edge out of a tricky moment. But they'd never been in a situation quite like this one, and Duane was quicker to realize the possible danger here. He was also more to the point. "This is the Semtex that was stolen out of Libya, isn't it?"

"Yes, sir. Yes, I think so," Catherine answered.

"And terrorists really have commenced an attack on the dam, haven't they?"

"Yes, I think so," Catherine responded quietly. "I'm pretty sure. The attack is probably under way right now. It's taking place many hundreds of feet below the surface."

THE AGITATION in the TTIC control room had quickened after Turbee's announcement, and heightened still further once Corporal Gray divulged her story. General Odlum, from Army Intelligence, wanted the floor.

"What is it, General? What are you thinking?" asked Dan.

"The description the Corporal gave," said the aging General. "It's a shaped charge explosive. If they do it right–"

Dan interrupted him. "Who knows more about these types of explosive devices than anyone on the planet?" he said. "We need to talk to this person. We also need to get more information."

"If it's what I think it is, then it's like a bunker buster," said the General. "If that's what it is… Johnson, can you get me Livermore Labs on the line? There's a guy there, name is Sandilands. Dr. William Sandilands. He knows more about this stuff than anyone on the planet."

"Johnson, get him on the line," barked Dan to his sidekick. "Now!"

"Why do we need to talk to this guy?" asked Lance, nervously tapping his desktop. "We've been just behind whoever is orchestrating this every step of the way. The seconds are precious. We need to call the cavalry now. Let's just assume that it's powerful enough to blow the dam. We can worry about the fine details later."

"No, Lance. I'm the one in charge here," Dan snapped. "We need to get the facts straight first. We can't just be pulling assets from the Hoover Dam and Las Vegas. Johnson, get Sandilands on the line, NOW." The word "now" was emphasized with his fist striking his desk. He did not see that most of the TTIC personnel were feverishly talking on cell phones already.

Getting in touch with the right person took a few minutes. Sandilands was not at work, or at home. Johnson got him on his cell, but the call was dropped and he had to redial. Another two or three minutes were lost in the fiddling. In the many hearings that would ultimately follow, much focus was placed on this time frame.

Turbee was back in mumble mode. His medication had kicked in, but the extra dosage he'd taken had had an adverse effect; instead of functioning more normally, he had slipped into a quiet, disconnected state. Looking at the floor and speaking to no one in particular, he said, "Why don't you just open all the penstocks?"

Rahlson and George, both sitting next to Turbee, heard it. "What did you say, Turb?" asked George. Before he could respond, Johnson yelled to Dan.

"I've got Sandilands on the phone, Dan! Can I put him on the speakers?"

"Yes. Now please."

"Hello Bill, been a long time since you and I have talked. How are things?" General Odlum opened up, once the call was connected.

"Jesus Christ," Rahlson exclaimed. "Get on with it! There's a sub in the water carrying a massive amount of plastic explosive. Dan. Call. The. Fucking. CAVALRY!" Dan, the General, and Sandilands all ignored him.

"Not bad. What can I do for you, Odlum?" responded Dr. Sandilands, his voice crackling and breaking up a bit over the control room speakers.

"We're at TTIC, in Washington. The Terrorist Threat Integration Center. We've been following the trail of the stolen Semtex. We think that it's now in a submarine in Lake Powell, heading toward the Glen Canyon Dam. We also think they might have a shaped charge explosive. Could a properly shaped explosive device destroy the dam, if you had, say, 4.5 tons of Semtex?" the General asked.

"Holy doodle," responded Sandilands. "You guys have got a problem. The device would need to be properly shaped, and have the proper metals along its upper and lower walls. It would have to be machined with great precision. The construction would need to be perfect. And the device would need to be placed inside the dam. But if it were…"

"Suppose the device was in the interior of the dam. Like inside one of the penstocks, for instance. Could it destroy the dam then?" asked Odlum.

"Possibly. We've been developing some incredibly powerful shaped charge explosives. It's amazing what you can do with these things. About three months ago we tested a device like that, and with less than 2,000 pounds of high explosive, we were able to blow through 25 feet of solid steel." He paused for emphasis. "Twenty-five feet."

"Of steel?" responded Dan, incredulously.

"Yes. Of steel," affirmed Sandilands. "It's highly classified. Up until now, I guess," he continued. "A couple of our guys invented a new type of shaped charge. We call it a Tiani/Melvin Lens. It was developed by a team of highly skilled mathematicians and engineers. Down the center we used depleted uranium, a heavy metal, to increase the power of the device. We've got a couple of them sitting in inventory, actually. No guy off the street would be able to create or manufacture something like that." He was silent for a second or two. The clock ticked to 10:39AM. "Umm. There is something you guys need to know."

"What's that?" asked Dan.

"We believe that a set of plans for the design of a T/M Lens may have been stolen. I'm not sure where they ended up. The FBI was involved in the case."

"I can help with that," said the FBI representative at TTIC, who had been quietly sitting at his workstation, taking notes the old fashioned way.

"You're right when you say the FBI was involved," he said. "We traced the theft to an Egyptian guy. Nasser somebody or other. He got them from someone at the Livermore Labs. It might have been the coinventor of the device, Mr. Tiani. We've been looking at some unusual spending habits of his in the past six months or so. We think that he gave someone else a computer key, allowing them entry to the server that contained the plans. We think the culprit emailed them to someone in Egypt, but we lost the trail there. With this computer-based theft, once someone has the information on a hard drive, it's game over. You can't control it or track it after that."

The clock ticked to 10:40AM. Rahlson was drumming his fingers on his desk in disbelief and agitation. "Dan, God dammit, sound the alarm!"

"Quiet, Rahlson," rebuked Dan. "We need the facts first. I'm in charge. We don't want another *Haramosh Star* misadventure. The President was almost impeached over that." Dan was now standing, ramrod straight, looking at the Atlas Screen. "George, get us in closer to the dam. Go ahead, General."

Turbee's mind was struggling to overcome the fog of too many drugs. He was still mumbling, this time a little louder. "Just open all the penstocks. No submarine of that size could withstand the turbulence that would create."

"What, Turbee?" George asked again. Before Turbee could answer, General Odlum interrupted.

"OK," said Odlum. "Bill, the question still stands. If someone made a device precisely in accordance with the plans you've developed, could 4.5 tons of Semtex destroy a dam?"

"Yes, I think it could," said Sandilands. "What the device does is to focus the blast in a very narrow way. Almost like a knife-edge. All that power would be funneled along one plane. If you were to stand 100 feet behind it, you probably wouldn't be hurt. But if you were 100 feet in front of it, it would cut you in two."

"There's 500 or 600 feet of concrete and steel above the penstocks. This device would cut the dam in two?" the General confirmed.

"Yes, I think so. It would be a very narrow blast. But the dam would be cut in two. Water pressure would do the rest," Sandilands said slowly.

The room had become deathly silent. Everyone had stopped what they were doing and was listening to the conversation. The dam cut in two? And it might be only minutes away?

It was Rahlson who broke the silence. "I think Sandilands is right. The Glen Canyon Dam is done for unless the submarine is intercepted. But it's much worse than that. If this happens, the dam will have a catastrophic failure. It will all go at once. Lake Powell will thunder down the Marble Canyon, and into the Grand Canyon. A massive amount of silt and mud will go with it, along with the remnants of the dam itself," he said, wiping the sweat from his forehead.

"The water will hit Lake Mead maybe an hour or two later," he continued. "God alone knows what will happen there. Maybe the Hoover won't be able to withstand the increase in water. Maybe it'll go too, and then every dam on the Colorado below that. If that happens, there will be no power or water for years to come. Vegas will become a ghost town. Without water or air conditioners, it will be uninhabitable. The Emir was right. He will destroy Vegas. The city will slowly cook to death. He'll destroy the Hoover Dam, and a lot more besides. And all of this may be minutes away. I don't see how that can be prevented. That submarine is 300 or 400 feet below the water surface.

We can't send divers down that far. I think it's game over, people. I think we're done for."

Turbee continued to fight an internal fight against the sleepy, drugged state that was threatening to engulf him. "Just open all the penstocks at once," he mumbled as the clock ticked over to 10:42AM. Again no one heard him.

The control room had gone dead silent with Rahlson's words. No one looked up. If Rahlson was correct, TTIC would be a failure, and worse yet, untold economic damage would visit the USA. Maybe fewer people would die than in past terrorist strikes, but the cost would be far, far greater. Through the past month, they had been continually one step behind the Emir, or whoever it was that had engineered this attack. The technique was classic. They were always looking at spot A, only to find that the Semtex was already in spot B. Right up to the present moment, when the military forces of the country were protecting the Hoover Dam instead of being where they were needed, at the Glen Canyon Dam.

"For fuck's sake, will someone please call the goddamn cavalry!?" shouted a highly agitated Lance. He was standing now. "If some terrorist bastard is down there in Lake Powell with a sub and this shaped charge thing, will someone please blow it the hell up now? Please?!"

"We'll see about that," said General Odlum. "We've got a couple of Hoovers flying over Lake Mead. They've already been directed to the Glen Canyon Dam. And we have other firepower up that way from Edwards. Yes, the cavalry is definitely coming."

"Hoovers?" asked George.

"Hoovers. Otherwise known as Vikings. Lockheed S-3B Vikings," said Odlum. "They're used specifically for the detection and attack of submarines. We had two of them patrolling the Lake Mead area already, to make sure that there was nothing illicit in the waters. Nobody really thought of patrolling Lake Powell."

The S-3B Viking was an exotic, high-tech aircraft, if there ever was one. It carried a crew of four, including the pilot, copilot, tactical coordinator, and sensor operator. It had highly efficient engines, which sounded like vacuum cleaners when in operation — hence the nickname "Hoover." The Viking's powerful computer system processed information generated by acoustic and nonacoustic target sensor systems. The plane also possessed an impressive array of airborne weaponry and antisubmarine ordnance. One of these weapons was the AGM-84 Harpoon, a self-guiding missile that gave the Viking below-surface capability. This weapon turned on its seeker, located its target, and struck it, without further guidance from its launch platform. Once it was in the water, any target would have considerable difficulty avoiding the missile. General Odlum, who knew all these details, noticed his hands shaking as he dialed the numbers on the phone. The entire American Southwest would be depending on those very missiles for its future.

THE GENERAL UPROAR in the control room increased with every passing minute. Sandiland's call was dropped at some point. No one but George and Rahlson heard Turbee, still mumbling to himself.

"Turb," George finally asked, "why open the penstocks?"

"Because it's a small submarine," said Turbee, rousing himself enough to answer. "It will head toward a closed penstock. If it goes toward an open penstock, turbulence in the water will pull it in and destroy it. To be successful, it will have to go toward a closed penstock. If these guys are half as smart as they seem to be, the pilots of the sub will have received these as their most important instructions. It's really basic, you guys. It's our best bet. And I think it might be the only way to stop them, at this point."

George and Rahlson, almost as one, yelled from their stations. "Open the penstocks! The turbulence will destroy the submarine!"

"What?" asked Dan, typically slow to react.

"Get the dam to open the penstocks! It's your best bet," urged George. He had exploded from his seat and sprinted toward Dan. Now he grabbed his arm and shook him.

Dan slowly extracted his arm from George's grip and looked at Dennis Daley, who had come over from FEMA. "Can you get them to do that too?"

"I think so. Let me call FEMA headquarters." He did so, but was then transferred from one station to another, put on hold, and then disconnected. Ten minutes later, he was still lost in the endless maze of Washington bureaucracy. When he was asked, at the hearings that took place in the months after, why he hadn't simply called directory assistance, or Google'd the dam for the number, all he could do was shrug. It wasn't policy to go around the other agencies like that. They had a protocol.

55

MUSTAFA WAS WAITING FOR THEM at the Page airport. The Ford screeched to a halt, and Yousseff, Kumar, Izzy, and Ba'al ran toward the idling Lear. The plane roared down the airstrip. When the rental agency clerk came running out of the terminal, he found the truck still idling on the runway, with no one else in sight. "You haven't signed the paperwork…" he said quietly to himself.

It was 8:50AM, Mountain Standard Time, and 7:50AM in California. Yousseff's second pilot, Badr al-Sobeii, already had the Gulfstream running when they arrived in Long Beach. Rika was by his side. Both were worried and stressed almost beyond endurance by the time the rented Lear finally taxied to a halt in front of the PWS hangar. Ba'al, Izzy, Kumar, and Yousseff disembarked. They wasted no time. The five of them, friends since childhood, boarded the jet. Mustafa cut the engines on the Lear, then ran to join them. Badr taxied out the second the door was closed.

THE VIKINGS arrived at the east end of the canyon within 15 minutes. It took a few more to reach their destination. There, just ahead, was the awesome structure of the Glen Canyon Dam — every bit as large and impressive as the Hoover. At 9:02AM, the two planes dropped four AGM-84 Harpoon missiles into Lake Powell, just upstream from the dam.

SAM AND HANK watched the two jets fly overhead, pull a steep turn, and come directly back toward the dam at a low elevation. They saw puffs of smoke from each wing, and then watched four missiles enter the water and disappear from view.

DEEP BENEATH the surface, Massoud and Javeed had cut though the last of the steel vertical mullions protecting the penstock. It was time to start the final transfer. This was the trickiest part of the mission. The payload was extremely heavy. The Ark itself weighed more than a ton, and the Semtex within it weighed 4.5 tons. It had been set on the roof of the Pequod as the little submarine was starting to descend, so that the buoyancy of the water lessened the pressure and weight of the load. According to physics and the engineers, this had been the only way to saddle the small sub with such weight. Moving it to its final destination would be just as complicated. The Ark was sitting on the small platform, equipped with small rubber wheels, that made up the Pequod's roof. Javeed pressed a button, and the latches that attached the transfer platform to the sub were automatically loosened. The platform lifted up, away from the body of the sub.

Massoud positioned the Pequod so that the submarine was below the penstock entrance and the Ark itself level with it. The platform assembly on which the Ark was mounted had, built underneath it, two telescoping rails that extended a little more than 50 feet forward. Javeed flipped a series of switches on the console before him, and flawlessly, noiselessly, the two rails extended through the penstock cavity deep into the interior of the dam. As a final piece of wizardry, Kumar had created further extending tracks, along which the Ark's platform would glide, traveling even deeper into the structure of the dam. The technology that had connected the *Mankial Star* to the *Haramosh Star* looked archaic compared to this, the final transfer. Power was provided to the platform for this process by a mini power cable, which connected directly to the powerful engines of the Pequod.

Now came the final hurdle. The ballast tanks of the Pequod were large and, at this point, full of air. Normally that would not be the case at this depth, but the weight of the Ark had required it. This had been the only way to keep the sub from sinking into the mud and silt at the bottom of the lake, trapped by the weight of its cargo. If the Ark slid off the sub willy nilly, the sudden change in weight and buoyancy would be so great that the Pequod would be wrenched upward in a wild and unpredictable course. The Ark would derail, and the mission would fail. Instead, as the Ark was slowly pushed forward into the penstock, controlled by Massoud, the ballast tanks were slowly discharged and filled with water by pumps controlled by Javeed. It was a slow and dangerous process, with the Pequod's tail sometimes lurching upward, sometimes down. There were many times when one or the other of the *jihadists* jumped, sure that they had lost the precarious balance and failed at the mission. Gradually, however, the platform, with its deadly cargo, moved from the Pequod onto the rails that had been deployed within the penstock tunnel.

They had almost finished when a buzzer sounded, and a red light started to flash on the HUD.

"Countermeasures, Javeed," said Massoud. "There are torpedoes in the water, coming toward us from the rear. They've found us."

"Damn. There are four of them. We can handle two, maybe three, but four?" said Javeed.

"Peace," responded Massoud. "We are in the hands of Allah. We are at the gates of Paradise."

"Yes, brother, we are, but we have to deal with this before we go in."

Almost three weeks earlier, in Kumar's manufacturing facility in Long Beach, Yousseff had ordered Kumar to install two defense systems in the small sub. Kumar had tried to protest, but Yousseff would have none of it. "Two defense systems," Yousseff had said. "At least two. Always a backup for the backup."

And two they had. Javeed flipped a number of switches on the complex console. A large box that had been installed near the tail of the Pequod opened. The box had looked odd and out of place, and many people had questioned it, but the craft was not designed for appearances. The sides and roof of the box fell away, and four large mesh wings unfolded. In the center sat a small torpedo, which, with the flick of another switch, slowly began to rise. Each mesh wing unfolded until it was approximately ten feet by ten feet. The overall size of the structure was 20 feet by 20 feet. About the same size as the sub itself.

The design of the weapon worked. Once it was launched, three of the harpoons changed course and headed directly toward it. The onboard computer systems of the missiles were unable to differentiate between the dish system and the Pequod.

The fourth harpoon, though, continued on its steady course toward the Pequod.

"Watch out Massoud. The fourth missile still comes toward us."

"Javeed, in our position we cannot be afraid to die. That is what we are here to do. Now let us wait until the fourth missile is 100 feet away, and we will use the second skin Kumar installed."

Their HUD was registering in diminishing numbers the distance of the fourth torpedo. Javeed grew nervous, and soon found that he was unable to wait any longer.

"Now, Massoud. Now."

Massoud flipped another switch, and the metal second skin on the rear of the Pequod was launched, meeting the fourth harpoon approximately 50 feet from the Pequod. Backups to backups.

All four of the harpoons exploded almost simultaneously. Three when they hit the mesh, and the fourth when it hit the second skin. The shock waves from the blast nearly destroyed the Pequod. The little submarine swayed violently back and fourth, and the Ark was nearly pulled from its platform. There were wrenching sounds as the bulkheads and rails were twisted by the force of the blasts. Some damage was done to the Pequod, and water came rushing in. A number of red lights started flashing, and for a second or two it appeared that they might lose power, but everything held precariously together.

"Keep going, Javeed. Remember the mission. Get the Ark into the tunnel."

"I'm trying, dammit," said Javeed. "But it's hard to do it when you've almost been blown to Hell."

"Blown to the gates of Paradise, you mean. That's where we're going."

Water was pouring into the small cabin now, but they were able to continue their mission. Ultimately, Javeed was able to get the Ark completely into the tunnel.

"We are there, Massoud. Now let's push her in."

Massoud was able to detach the Ark and its platform completely from the Pequod, aside from the connecting electrical cable, which was now played out of the Pequod to give them more maneuvering room. Massoud raised the Pequod up eight feet and moved her forward. Once again, Kumar's elegant and simple solutions to problems made the mission. The wounded Pequod began to slowly push the Ark's platform forward, ever deeper into the penstock tunnel. Another ten seconds passed and they were completely inside.

AT THAT MOMENT, Daley, the FEMA representative at TTIC, was finally put in contact with the foreman of the small crew looking after the Glen Canyon Dam's operations that day. "Open all the penstocks. Open them now. You are under attack," he shouted.

THE CLOCK ticked forward. From 9:03AM, to 9:04, to 9:05. Nothing happened. No one moved.

YOUSSEFF'S PLANE was over the Pacific at that moment, having taken the longer route to get back home to Pakistan. Yousseff had ordered Mustafa to get them out of American air space as rapidly as possible. Regardless of whose airspace they were in, he would be able to monitor international news feeds in this plane — a technological luxury that had cost him a few million dollars. And it was better for them, at this point, to be over international waters.

Youssefff was cool under pressure. He had demonstrated that to Marak 40 years ago, and countless times thereafter. But now he was starting to fidget. Nothing. No regular program interruptions. No CNN, NBC, CBS, or even Al Jazeera breaking news banners drifting across the bottom of the screens. Nothing.

"Dammit Izzy. Did we mess it up?" he asked his lifelong friend.

There was no response from the group; everyone was silent.

"Ease up Youss," said Kumar, at length. "Give it a minute or two. And if we've screwed up, big deal. We keep going."

"I'm not sure, Kumar," said Youssefff. "Can you go back to the States? Can Izzy and Ba'al go back to Canada? And me? Most of the money is gone if the market doesn't do what I've bet it to do, which it won't unless Massoud and Javeed come through. Hell, we'd be lucky if we all ended up working for Marak, if this doesn't work."

Again there was no response. No one wanted to state the obvious — that it had been Youssefff's decision, and ultimately his actions, that had put them all in this position.

"Be patient, Youss," said Rika, who was also watching the less-than-perfect images of the world news feeds. Even with $10 million thrown at the technology of watching TV in a fast-moving jet, the results were hit or miss.

They all continued to watch the TV's... 9:04... 9:05...

THREE PAST 9AM. Catherine had accepted Sandra Becker's invitation to clean herself up a little. She was horrified when she looked in the small medicine cabinet mirror. No wonder the Beckers were freaked out. The mystery was that Duane Becker hadn't actually shot her. If she had seen a stranger coming to the door in her condition, covered in twigs, dirt, and a sweaty layer of coal dust, she might well have shot first and asked questions later. Finally exiting the bathroom in a somewhat cleaner state, she agreed to a second cup of coffee. It was 9:04.

IT WAS 11:04AM in Washington, DC. The TTIC control room had gone quiet, as had innumerable board rooms in Langley, the Pentagon, and of course, the Situation Room in the White House. Dennis Daley, the FEMA representative, had been able to get through to those in charge at the Glen Canyon Dam, but had been told that opening the penstocks was not a quick process. There was a collective holding of breath.

AT THE New York Mercantile Exchange, a few futures traders were looking at what would obviously be a substantial profit that day. Who was the idiot who had sold short these contracts? At so high a margin? The same observation was being made at the Chicago Commodities Exchange, the London Metal Exchange, and in other of the world's buy and sell arenas. Someone out there was clearly a few bricks short.

IT WAS 9:04PM in Pakistan. Marak was sitting in his living room in Islamabad, watching a bank of TV's. It was also 9:04PM in the mountains of the Sefid Koh. The Emir, looking to be in a black mood, and getting blacker by the moment, was watching his Internet connection, delivered by the servants of Satan themselves.

SAM AND HANK had been waiting on the Glen Canyon Bridge with rapidly growing concern. A squadron of F-15's had flown overhead, and appeared to be circling. Two Navy planes had dropped bombs of some sort into the reservoir. The helicopters were stationary, hovering directly behind the dam. The police had noticed their presence, and their apparently disabled truck, and were headed their way. The television camera was trained on the Glen Canyon Dam, and their uplink system was transmitting. It was now four minutes past the appointed time of detonation. Still nothing. But their orders, from Yousseff himself, had been very clear. Stay with the truck. Keep transmitting the images. They were soldiers in a much broader war, and they were not to abandon their post.

IT WAS 11:04AM in New York City, where concerned engineers, working at the Rockefeller Center, were clustered around one of the hundreds of monitors in the central NBC newsroom.

"Johnny," said Floyd, the associate producer, to the chief engineer on the floor that morning. "Are you saying that we don't know who is transmitting that particular image to us? Seriously?"

"Yes, Floyd. Mind like a steel trap. You've got it. Someone has hogged one of our frequencies and is sending this to us," answered John, gesturing to the screens in front of them. "How, I don't know. The 'why' is for you news guys to figure out."

"We've got an uplink on location at the Hoover Dam right now. What we're seeing on the screen, Johnny, is a dam. Is there some way that the uplink at the Hoover is sending this?"

"Floyd, you're not an engineer, I know," said an exasperated John. "But if you look at those couple of dozen monitors over there," he said, chucking a thumb behind him, "you will notice that the images are profoundly different. It's not the same dam."

The alliteration that had had Turbee stumbling a short time earlier was starting to spread across the nation. First at TTIC, then through the Intelligence Community, then the military, and now at the nation's news desks.

"It's a different damn dam," breathed Floyd. "What on earth for? Who's transmitting this?"

"We don't know who's doing it," repeated John. "We don't know why. I'm pretty sure I already told you that. But there could be a huge story here. I'm going to get some more engineers in on this to try and sort it out. But you guys need to be recording every second of this, and your news guys shouldn't stray too far."

AT 9:04AM, Javeed pushed the Ark to the very center of the Glen Canyon Dam. The darkness and silence around them were unworldly. Perhaps they had failed and were already dead, he thought. This was Hell. Cold, deathly silent, dark, and full of fear. He searched his heart, but couldn't find any regret at the thought of failing in the mission.

Massoud checked the dials and the now only partially functional HUD. "We're there, Javeed. It is time," he said.

Javeed nodded and reached for the large button just below the HUD. He had started to doubt the mission, and his part in it, and was anxious to finish things before he thought any further. He pressed the button. Nothing. Pressed it again. Still nothing. He pounded it with his fist, desperate to have this done. Nothing.

Massoud gently pushed Javeed's hand away. "You must push it gently. Like this."

It was 9:06. Massoud reached for the button, and gently pressed it. Everything disappeared in a radiance of light.

56

THE MOMENT OF TRUTH came at 9:06AM, Mountain Standard Time, when Massoud pressed the red button on the console before him. This sent an electric impulse to an extremely accurate digital distributor, which sent simultaneous signals to five equidistant capacitors. Those, in turn, sent more powerful pulses to five detonators, set along an elliptical path within the Ark. Kumar had made sure that all of these electronic components functioned perfectly.

The five detonators each simultaneously developed small pressure waves. As these pressure waves traveled through the Semtex, the material was compressed and heated, causing complex nitrogen, oxygen, hydrogen, and carbon bonds to rupture, creating enormous amounts of energy. This created even greater pressure waves as the chain reaction ripped upward through the Semtex, moving at a high rate of speed. Almost instantaneously, the detonation wave hit the first of the many elements precisely crafted into the lining of the Ark. Once it reached the cone liner, the detonation wave created a planar plasma jet, moving at over six miles per second. Because of the complex internal geometries of the Ark, the jet was flat, and almost laser straight. As the other elements of the Ark were caught up in the blast, they too were converted to plasma and ejected upward, but at a slower rate. This resulted in a jet of energy that stretched up for hundreds of feet. The jet was followed by steel, molybdenum, and gold, all traveling in its path at slightly slower speeds. When the leading end of the jet struck the soft concrete of the dam, pressures of tens of thousands of atmospheres were produced. Pressures of this magnitude far exceeded the yield strength of the concrete, which flowed like water out of the jet's path. This process, called hydrodynamic penetration, lay at the center of the destructive power of the Ark. The factors governing the process were linked together by the complex equations that had been developed by Tiani and Melvin. If the two scientists had been correct, the destructive power of the Ark would be enough to slice through the dam like a knife through butter.

At that moment, Sam and Hank were on the verge of being arrested. The cavalry was coming, all right, and it was coming for them. Three police cruisers, sirens blazing and lights flashing, had just raced onto the bridge. For a brief second, Sam thought of throwing himself off the edge. But he'd never been trained in the craft of the suicide bomber. In fact, he'd never meant to *be* a suicide bomber. Why had he become involved with the Emir in the first place? he suddenly wondered. What misguided boyhood mistake had led him on this path? This ugly introspection was cut short by a blinding flash of light, followed almost immediately by the ear-splitting roar of an enormous explosion. The percussive wave was so powerful that it knocked both men backward. Sam saw what appeared to be a gigantic pillar of fire rising from the dam's crest to the heavens. The two helicopters closest to the blast were knocked violently backward, and fell into the waters of Lake Powell.

"Allah be praised," breathed Hank.

"Holy shit," said Sam, who had become better versed in the American tongue than his friend.

"They did it," said Hank, overjoyed that two of their countrymen, whom they had sat with just five hours earlier, were now dead. "They are heroes. They did it."

"Yeah, and now they're dead. But the dam, Hank, the dam is still standing. Look at it," Sam said, pointing.

Sure enough, the Glen Canyon Dam still stood. There was a tendril of smoke curling irregularly from the center of the dam crest, but that was all.

"Maybe not," replied Hank. "Look along the center. From the midline, about a third of the way up. Isn't that a thin line of water? Look closer, Sam. Do you see it?"

"Yes, I see it. But it's tiny. That won't amount to anything, will it?" asked Sam. The two were yelling at one another, their ears still ringing from the percussion wave and the roar of the blast.

"Maybe it's a trick of perspective and distance," Hank answered. "The dam is so huge that the water doesn't look like much, but maybe, maybe it's bigger than it appears. Give it a minute or two."

They sat on the bridge, still stunned from the blast, watching the dam.

WHAT THE HELL was that?" asked Floyd, looking intently at the video signal that had somehow been transmitted via satellite to the NBC New York offices, in the Rockefeller Center. A flash of light appeared to spring vertically from the center of the dam. Then the picture shook, until, within a few seconds, the camera was once again steady on the gigantic dam. There was, for whatever reason, no sound coming from the transmission.

"Floyd, you'd better run and get the boss," said John, slowly. "I think someone's just attempted to blow up one of America's major dams."

"But it's still there, John."

John, being an engineer, immediately saw what other people continued to miss. "See that dark gash across the centerline over here?" he said, pointing to a thin, dark line on the dam face. "I think the dam's been cut by an explosion. A shaped charge explosion, if I'm remembering my engineering correctly. See this distortion over here? Probably caused by water squeezed through the breach under high pressure. A slightly different camera angle would show it for sure. If I'm right, the structure of this dam has been profoundly compromised, and the thing is probably a sitting duck. The news brass'll want to know about this. Quick."

THE FEROCITY of the blast carved a gash, eight feet wide, that led from Penstock Four all the way up to the crest of the dam, cleaving the structure in two, from the upstream face to the downstream face.

The line that Hank and Sam had noticed was the water rushing through this breach, under immense pressure, and being ejected several hundred feet beyond the dam face. While it was just one relatively narrow gash, the integrity of the dam had been fatally compromised. The engineering principle was akin to a double door system. If the doors were connected together, through an interlocking system, it took a lot of energy to force them open. The interlocking mechanism was strong enough to hold it all together. But if the system was disconnected, or the locks were unhooked, a slight breeze would cause the doors to swing apart. And this was exactly what was happening to the dam. The west and the east halves of the structure were no longer connected. Enormous force was being applied to the upriver face, and the dam's strength was now greatly diminished. Thousands and then millions of gallons of water were rushing through the breach with every passing second. Chunks of concrete were being ripped out of the dam and smashed against the rapidly fraying dam walls, hastening the erosion.

After 30 seconds, the dam catastrophically failed. The 1500-foot long structure blew apart in one horrifying action. Millions of tons of concrete and rebar blasted high into the air as the full fury of the Colorado River, dammed for too many years, found release.

57

AT ROCKEFELLER CENTER, the pressure was rapidly notching higher. "Holy holy," was all Floyd could say, watching the explosion of concrete and water on the screen in front of him. "I don't care if we haven't found the producer. I don't care if he's taking a crap someplace. We are going live with this right now. We are going to break into the normal feed. Right now. RIGHT NOW!" he yelled. The technicians shrugged and broke into the regular programming.

The anchormen and women were still on the set, and didn't quite know what to make of Floyd's ranting. But none of them had reached the upper echelons of the mighty corporation's news group by being slow on the uptake. The lead anchorwoman immediately noticed the astounding images being played on many of the huge plasma screens that littered the main newsroom floor.

"Good morning America," she began. "We interrupt regular programming to bring you extraordinary images currently being transmitted to us. We are not yet sure of the locale, but we believe this to be the Glen Canyon Dam, on the Colorado River. What you are witnessing appears to be the catastrophic collapse of this dam, probably occasioned by an incendiary device of some sort. We repeat that this is probably the Glen Canyon Dam, and definitely, definitely not the Hoover Dam farther downstream on the same river." She looked directly into the camera and went for gold. "While we are awaiting further verification, we do not believe that these images are a hoax. They are real, and they show the catastrophic collapse of the Glen Canyon Dam." She knew that if that statement proved to be false, she would end up doing the weather on some northern Canadian channel. If it was the truth, she would be promoted above anyone else for her quick thinking.

As the anchor was ad-libbing on live TV, Floyd was on the phone with the producer of the helicopter crew currently in the air above Boulder City. "Get your asses up to Lake Mead and to the Glen Canyon Dam, now!" he all but shouted. "We think the dam has collapsed as a result of a terrorist attack. You guys are at the wrong damn dam. Go, go, go!"

THE GLEN CANYON BRIDGE was itself a marvel of engineering. It was one of the highest single-arch bridges in North America. It was completely constructed and assembled in California, then disassembled, trucked to the Glen Canyon, and reassembled. Completed in 1959, its construction enabled transport of concrete and steel across the canyon, which permitted construction of the dam to proceed. The bridge was superbly engineered, and was able to withstand huge loads and earthquakes. It was not, however, engineered to withstand the enormous assault that was now heading toward it.

Sam and Hank had been ordered by Youssef to stand by their post, no matter what, for at least ten minutes after the explosion. The images must be transmitted, he had said. The world must witness this. It was the Emir's wish. The two men were still following their orders, but with growing apprehension. The breach in the dam, from thin knife wound to total collapse, had occurred in under a minute. They were stunned by the explosive force of the collapse, and were now beginning to wonder about the fate of the bridge itself. While the explosion of water was taking place well beneath the bridge's supporting arch, the canyon walls had never endured forces of that magnitude before.

"Bridge is shaking a lot, Sam," said Hank. "I'm not sure it'll hold together."

Sam was attempting to mentally assimilate what had just happened. He was experiencing what the survivors and neighbors of terrorist attacks across the world had dealt with millions of times over the past years. The scope of the collapse of the Glen Canyon Dam was so enormous, so loud, so breathtakingly huge, that it was beyond comprehension, even though he had been forewarned of the event.

"Holy shit, Hank. Were we just involved in doing this?" he asked. "I can't believe what we're seeing."

"Believe it. We will be heroes back home."

"I'm not sure we're going to get home," replied Sam, finally looking away from the dam. "Feel the bridge."

The shaking of the bridge was intensifying. Sam could see that the canyon walls between the bridge and the remnants of the dam were starting to disintegrate. Huge boulders were being knocked loose from both the east and west cliff walls, and mudslides were beginning to take out the soil.

"Look there," Sam shouted above the roar of the water, pointing to the east canyon wall. "It's starting to crumble. This bridge is going to go, Hank. We have to get off!"

"Yousseff said to stay by our post," said Hank. "We're here because everyone followed the battle plan. He said stay here."

"Yeah, but this thing is going down. Look there. The cops realize it. We're the only ones stupid enough to be up here. We've got to get out of here or we're toast. I didn't sign on to die," shouted Sam.

With those words, there was a terrible scraping sound of metal on metal, and the eastern portion of the bridge suddenly lost its foundation, dropping almost 50 feet straight down toward the now raging water. It left the bridge moored and grounded only at its western end.

"I'm done here," yelled Sam, starting to run, now about ten degrees uphill, toward the western end. "If you don't come with me, Hank, you're dead."

The truck had already started to slide down the bridge, toward the destruction and mayhem below. Hank had been working to keep the camera trained on the dam, holding it by hand. Looking around him, he thought about it for a second, and then deserted their post, running after Sam. The moment he left the camera, it rocked back and forth violently, and within seconds, flipped over on its tripod.

BACK IN THE CBS STUDIOS in New York, John saw the camera view rock, slant, and go vertical. For a second or two the images it transmitted were sideways. Suddenly the signal was snuffed out altogether. John fiddled with some controllers and dials but could not bring the signal back.

The on-set anchor did a splendid job of tying the story together with what they were getting from the helicopter, now heading at maximum speed, cameras on, over Lake Mead and eastward toward the Glen Canyon. The NBC technical assistants were able to splice and remix the feed in record time, and the network began to show the dam explosion, and the devastating collapse that followed over and over, in greater detail, with close-ups and, of course, in slow motion. NBC had just lucked into the story of the year.

SAM AND HANK did not make it. The bridge, attached to solid land only on one end and buffeted by the always-present canyon wind, began to sway back and forth, and up and down. More and more of the steel I-beams that kept the structure intact were starting to buckle and bend under the unnatural forces being placed upon them. The east end of the bridge dropped down further, another 100 feet or so, leaving Sam and Hank with a climb upward of 30 degrees to reach the western bank of the canyon. As the canyon walls continued to wash away, the eastern end of the bridge dipped closer and closer to the uncaged waters of Lake Powell, now rushing and seething through the canyon below.

They were within 50 feet of the western bank when the unfettered eastern end of the bridge finally came into contact with the water. When it did, an entire section of the bridge was lurched powerfully downstream, wrenching loose the steel beams still embedded within the western canyon wall. With a terrible screaming of metal on metal, the eastern end of the bridge was pulled downstream, ripping the western end out of the canyon wall.

"We are martyrs, Sam," yelled Hank, desperately hanging on to a girder, swaying back and forth hundreds of feet above the raging waters. "I will see you in Paradise."

"I was kind of hoping for a cold beer and a good woman at the end of a hard day," Sam yelled back, knowing that this would not be so.

Sam's last memory was of hanging on to the bridge railing, just before the entire structure was ripped loose. Then the entire bridge was sent tumbling, scraping, and tearing its way down toward Marble Canyon. Sam's body was smashed by metal beams and chunks of concrete long before his mind could grasp the fact that he was going to die. Hank met a similar fate.

DUANE, SANDRA, AND CATHERINE rose as one when they saw the blinding flash, and heard the sharp crack, followed by booming, rolling echoes of thunder, coming from the south.

"Oh my God, Duane. Is it really happening?" Sandra gasped.

"I think it is," said Catherine, crushed that she had not been in time. "I could have stopped it if, if…" Her voice trailed away. She had run 6.8 miles an hour. She could just as easily have logged sevens. She hadn't pushed. She had stayed in the five-ton truck too long. She had started to enjoy the cat and mouse game with the drug runner, she had let the cell phone die, she had dropped the GPS unit, she had…

"Honey, honey," said Sandra, circling her arm around Catherine's shaking shoulder. "You're beating yourself up over this. From what you've been telling us, you have gone miles above and beyond the call of duty. If you had gone by your job description, you would be sitting in a donut shop in Fernie right now, rather than here trying to save a country that's not even yours."

She was interrupted by more booming explosive sounds, echoing again and again over the expanse of Wawheap Arm. The sounds were so powerful that the windows rattled, and the dishes danced in the kitchen cupboards.

“Oh my God,” exclaimed Duane. “I’ve never heard anything like this. Never.”

The booming and shaking took many minutes to subside. The three were hanging on to one another, looking out toward the reservoir, when the earth finally stilled beneath their feet.

“Thank God that’s stopped,” breathed Catherine, who had grasped Sandra Becker’s hand in hers, and was leaning up against Duane for support.

“I’m not so sure it has,” said Duane.

“What do you mean?”

Duane silently pointed at a half-finished cup of coffee resting on the kitchen counter. At first Catherine didn’t understand the gesture, but a closer examination revealed tiny concentric wavelets dancing within the cup. The shaking had not stopped at all.

“And look at that,” he said, pointing to the reservoir on the other side of the road. “Look at those leaves.”

Again Catherine had to squint to catch what Duane Becker’s eagle eyes took in. Then she saw it. A few leaves in the reservoir itself were lazily starting to drift toward the south.

“Things haven’t stopped at all,” he said, holding on to his wife’s other hand, thinking of a huge wall of water rushing toward the Grand Canyon. “In fact, I do believe they’re just beginning.”

58

THE WALL OF WATER was over 400 feet in height, and moving with incredible speed. Steel and concrete, now from both the dam and the bridge, were traveling with the torrent of water, acting as scouring agents against the banks, dislodging huge chunks of dirt and sandstone, and hastening the multiple collapses that accompanied it. Everything in the flood's path was demolished. The canyon walls were in the process of being instantly and destructively changed. This was no slow millennium-by-millennium erosion by wind and gentle water. This was a geologically catastrophic change, a 9.0 earthquake, a violent eruption, a tsunami beating against one of the most geologically spectacular sites in the world.

There were a number of beautiful camping spots, and some motels and lodges at Lee's Ferry, farther downstream. This also marked the starting place for most Colorado rafting tours. Many people were camped there, and some were already making their way down to the docking sites, to begin water tours of the canyon. While some of these groups had a minute or two of warning, the wall of rushing water made clambering up the steep canyon walls to safety impossible. Everyone within Marble Canyon died. The death toll was well over 200 before the floodwaters even reached the head of the Grand Canyon.

There, the ground shook with the oncoming flood, and the canyon came alive like a great writhing, convulsing snake. The canyon walls, already harrowing and steep, had become deadly, raining ever larger stones down into the depths. The rushing apocalypse of water was yet to be seen, but the magnitude of the tremors was increasing rapidly, and the canyon was becoming unstable.

To the north, in the areas already being blasted by the flood, gigantic slabs of sandstone were tumbling into the raging torrent, dislodged by both the water and the shaking that preceded it. The water would be momentarily blocked by these impediments, but would then flood over them and continue on its unstoppable course. The volume was increasing as more and more of the Glen Canyon Dam deteriorated and collapsed from the force of the pent-up water in Lake Powell. The flood gained the power and unstoppable forward motion of a runaway freight train, as it rushed toward the Grand Canyon proper.

PANDEMONIUM REIGNED in the TTIC central control room. The Atlas Screen displayed Lake Mead, the Grand Canyon, and the Lake Powell area. George had quickly obtained estimates of the speed of the rushing flood from the military helicopter pilots who were ordered to follow the front. He entered the speed, which was estimated to be 50 miles an hour, and programmed an advancing red line through the canyon to simulate the water's progress. Two of the 101's were displaying the television footage, taken by the two helicopters that were following the flood, beamed over the satellite system to the Pentagon, Langley, and TTIC. The other 101's showed news services, most prominently NBC, which had, through pure happenstance, captured the video of the Glen Canyon Dam actually being destroyed.

So far, no one had come up with a plan.

MORE THAN AN HOUR had passed since the destruction of the Glen Canyon Dam. Two military helicopters were following the leading edge of the floodwater as it catapulted from canyon wall to canyon wall, moving ever closer to Lake Mead. Evacuations had been put under way immediately, but were not all successful. Not everyone could get out of the way of the oncoming flood. The President and his key staff had all witnessed in graphic and repeated slow motion the horror that had occurred at Lee's Ferry, where 100 people had been swept from their campsites by the rushing water. Canyon Village, along with about 500 tourists, had fallen into the canyon gorge soon after. Dozens of small settlements and camping spots had disappeared into the developing catastrophe. More and more water poured through the Glen Canyon Dam, and Lake Powell was quickly emptying itself. The same question was repeated over and over again. What would happen to the Hoover Dam? Could it hold? Could the floodwaters be contained there? If the penstocks at that dam were opened to the fullest, could a collapse, or a flooding of the Hoover, be prevented?

UPON THE PRESIDENT'S ORDER, the technicians in the communications department had contacted Jordan McKay, head of the Bureau of Reclamation of the Lower Colorado Dam, setting him up on a video link to the White House Situation Room. The question the President asked him was simple. Would the Hoover Dam hold?

The video link was transmitted to other offices. Staff at Langley, the FBI, the Pentagon, and TTIC were seeing the same video that the President was receiving. The security, Intelligence, and military agencies watching this had, between them, the power and intelligence to assess and address the national disaster that was now unfolding. If they were given the chance. The Emir was at the forefront of their thoughts. He had planned it. He had told the world that he would take out Las Vegas. He would not have said that if he hadn't had a specific plan; one that had been designed by someone who knew what they were talking about. Someone with considerable analytical and engineering skills, who was aware of the weaknesses of the dam. What had this person known that they were missing?

Jordan McKay was speaking. As the head of his office, he knew more about the Hoover Dam than anyone. He had spent the last 30 years of his life working at, and in, the enormous structure. An engineer by training, he knew every inch, every nook and cranny of the dam, its penstocks, internal flows, intake towers, and power plants.

"This dam is probably one of the most solidly constructed dams in the US," he began. There was some trembling in his voice. He knew that there was a large audience listening to him and, as part of that audience, the President himself, the Chairman of the Joint Chiefs, and some of the most learned and powerful individuals in the Intelligence Community. So he made his summary of the dam's internal workings almost absurdly short, going for a quick, hard impact.

"What does that mean?" asked the President when McKay was finished. "Can you put it in layman's terms, without all the technical stuff?"

"Yes, Mr. President, sir, I can," replied Jordan. "Think of it as a gigantic Lego set. These enormous blocks of concrete that I've described are like the individual Lego blocks. They're hooked together not only top to bottom, but also end-to-end and face-to-face. It makes for a very robust structure."

"Can the dam hold if the reservoir fills to the very top of the dam itself? Can it do that?" asked the President.

"Are you asking if we can increase the water elevation in Lake Mead to the point that it reaches the crest of the dam, and have the dam survive? If that is the question, Mr. President," continued Jordan, "then the answer is definitely yes. This dam is very complex. For cost reasons, I don't think we'd build a dam like that today. And we have had times in the past, during wet years when there was a lot of mountain runoff from Utah, Wyoming, and Colorado, where the reservoir was very high. The dam has shown that it can hold its own in that situation. The fortunate thing here is that the water level in Lake Mead is already very low because of predominantly dry weather over the last five or so years. The same can be said for every lake along the

Colorado — that river is not currently at its maximum capacity. In fact, it's rather dry. The Hoover won't be dealing with as much water as it's seen in the past."

"Good," replied the President. "Now if we keep the dam's flow rate consistent with what it is now, how long will it take for the water to reach the dam crest?"

"Our engineers are looking at that, Mr. President," Jordan answered. "We have some very preliminary information now, and are computer modeling this as we speak. We'll be able to refine this information shortly, once we get a better idea of flow rates through what is left of the Glen Canyon Dam. However, overall, the information we're developing is positive."

"What could possibly be positive about this situation?" asked the President.

"It's positive in the sense that we know what's coming. We can control flow rates through the Hoover Dam. We can store water downstream in Lake Mojave. It's positive in the sense that the Hoover Dam will hold, and the loss of life in the past hour is probably the last that you will see in this situation. Yes, the floodwaters through the Grand Canyon are uncontrolled, but we can control the flow in various lake systems and reservoirs from there down. We can open all the diversionary tunnels and all the penstocks. We can manage the flow. It makes this a disaster of limited proportion."

"Well then get those goddamn pipes and penstocks and tunnels open, right now! Now, sir. Understood?" The President was forceful.

"Yes, Mr. President," said Jordan.

The President turned to face the men around him. "How sure are we that these terrorist bastards don't have the mechanisms in place to take out the Hoover Dam?" asked the President. "Jennifer Coe specifically referred to the Hoover, and the Emir said he would destroy it in that last message. He hasn't made a strike against it yet. Is there any possibility that that strike will come through some further bombing or focused charge application?"

The Chairman of the Joint Chiefs responded. "Sir, we have had agents over, under, above, and through the dam. We have two mini-subs of our own patrolling the mouth of Boulder Canyon. There is a no-fly zone in effect, and if any plane infringes upon it, the rules of engagement are to shoot it down."

"Good," the President replied. "And Mr. McKay, assume Lake Mead is being filled at a record rate from the breach of the Glen Canyon Dam. How rapidly are you able to drain water from Lake Mead when you open the spigots to the maximum?"

"The internal ductwork of the dam, once you consider the penstocks, the diversionary tunnels, and so on, is very complex. The outer diversionary tunnels were used to control the river when the dam was being built. They're 50 feet in diameter, and there are four of them. When they were used during the construction, two of them could carry the entire flow of the Colorado River. The flow was much greater then, since the Glen Canyon Dam hadn't been built yet. The tunnels remain. The inner diversionary tunnels now contain the 30-foot diameter steel pipes that connect the towers to the power plant. They can also be used. I hope I'm not rambling, sir," Jordan added.

"No. Please go on," came the command from the Situation Room.

"The four tunnels I'm talking about each have cylindrical gates, 32 feet in diameter and 11 feet high," said a still nervous Jordan. "These can be completely opened, which I presume is what you meant by turning on the spigots. These tunnels are plugged, and it would be a bit complicated to unplug them; we would have to do it one tunnel at a time, and it would be time consuming. But it can be done. And it would increase our chances of success."

"How long will it take to drill or blast through these concrete plugs in the tunnels?" asked the President.

"Surely it wouldn't take that long," Dan interrupted from the TTIC control room, looking for a moment in the sun. "We have all kinds of armament on or around the Hoover, and there should be enough explosive to drill into and blow up the concrete plugs."

"Actually, that would be a problem," said Jordan. "I mean, it would be a tricky bit of work, as you could cave in the tunnels themselves. Especially if you were using explosives. It's almost like you need one of those gigantic tunnel boring machines that the Swiss and Japanese use for their train tunnels. Remember that the tunnels are also very long, almost three miles all told."

"Is everybody just plain daft?" snapped Rahlson, not caring that the President was in on the call. "Just a few minutes ago we had Dr. Sandilands from Livermore Labs on the line. Did he not say that he had a few of these focused explosive devices just lying around?"

"I think he said he had a few in storage," said Rhodes.

"Why couldn't we use them to vaporize the concrete plugs?" Rahlson asked excitedly. "Don't you see? If they work like the Glen Canyon Dam device worked, we should be able to knock out the plugs instantly, hopefully without too much damage to the tunnel, given the tight focus of the plasma."

One of the military advisers present agreed. "You're right," he said. "Call Sandilands back. I need to know the size and weight of those devices. We may be able to fit them in the bomb bay of an F-22. If everyone cooperates, we could have those devices mounted and ready to go within an hour. It will take three hours for the water to reach Lake Mead. We have the time to do this."

"Then get it done. Do it, and I mean do it NOW!" said the President. The edge to his voice was sharp and strident. The man who had volunteered immediately pulled a cell phone from his shirt pocket and began to make a series of calls.

HERE'S THE QUESTION. With the present intake system set to the maximum, how long do you think we have before the water crests the dam? Regardless of whether the Hoover holds, we need to think about what will happen when the water gets past it."

After sending several men on their missions in regard to the tunnels, the President had kept Jordan McKay, TTIC, and some of his security advisers on the line to continue their discussion. They needed to be prepared for every possibility.

"I don't know, Mr. President. But my gut says at least a month before we have to deal with the water cresting the dam, and probably longer," said Jordan. "I feel confident about that number, as I've been looking after the Hoover for many, many years. I've directed my people to start mathematically modeling the system. I'm sure that before this is done, we'll have propeller heads from Harvard to Oxford working on this problem. We'll be getting the best help possible.

"The important thing," he continued, "is that this will not happen overnight, or in the next four or five hours. It will take a good month before the Lake Mead water level reaches the top of the dam, and by then I'm sure we'll have fancy dyking systems in place to protect our downstream users. If we can successfully use all four of the outer tunnels, they should theoretically be able to handle twice the volume of the Colorado River. If we have the penstocks open to their maximum, and all four of the diversionary tunnels, we can probably take three times the flow of the original river. As we speak, engineers are working to figure out how high the dykes downriver should be, and how strong. I'm more concerned, quite frankly, about having reservoirs in place so that the extra water can be impounded, rather than wasted. It's a dry area, and it would be a shame to send so much freshwater straight to nowhere."

"Thank you, Mr. McKay. Thank you very much," the President said. He turned to the men in the room. "Gentlemen, you heard the man. Yes, a major dam has been catastrophically attacked, but we can and will rebuild it. We can avoid any further catastrophe in this situation. There has been significant loss of life, but our country has seen worse. We will recover."

TURBEE watched the footage of the Lake Powell floodwaters propelling themselves through the Grand Canyon over and over again. First a torrent of water, then a cave-in or collapse of some geographical feature, then the temporary damming effect, and then another torrent of water. He had listened to the White House Situation Room interaction between the President and various members of his team. They had a problem. They were assuming a uniform and continuous flow of water. But the video evidence now displayed on all the 101's showed a very different process at work.

"Here's what I think is going to happen," he said, not talking to anyone in particular, but speaking loudly enough to be heard by all. He did not notice that the floor was becoming quiet. They knew Turbee was cooking something up. "People along the shores of Lake Mead," he continued, "need to get a long distance from that shoreline. If you look at the west end, where all the marinas and people are, this is where the waves will be the most dangerous. We'll have classic cresting and undertow conditions, like what you saw during the Boxing Day Quake." Turbee cleared his throat, glad that the meds were now working properly. "We could have waves 200 feet high crashing along the western shore. People have maybe two and a half hours before this starts, but when it starts, if you can see it, you're probably in trouble." He was pointing to the western shore of Lake Mead on the Atlas Screen.

"What was that, Turbee? How high will the waves be?" asked Dan.

"He said 200 feet, Dan, maybe more. Pay attention," George barked sharply.

Turbee carried on as though Dan didn't exist. He tapped a couple of keys on his keyboard. The map on the Atlas Screen altered slightly. "This is a simulation of what will happen. I've put in the shore features, roadways, and so on. We're in a hurry, so I don't have all the hotels and motels. But you can see what's happening. We do have the land's topography programmed in here, so the area on the map will show how far we expect the waves to go inland. It could easily be a mile. It could be two. I think even people in Boulder City should be thinking about moving to higher ground."

"Turbee, what makes you think that the waves will be so high?" asked George. "No one connected to the White House Situation Room conference said that."

"Well, look at the videos on the 101's," said Turbee. "You can see that the motion of the water is sporadic. It's discontinuous. It is literally lurching from cave-in to cave-in. You get a 300-foot-high cascade, then a landslide, a temporary dam, then another 300-foot-high cascade. It's an effect that started at the Glen Canyon Dam and is continuing throughout the entire Grand Canyon. When the huge cave-in at Canyon Village occurred, the waters were dammed for a full 30 seconds. With the flow rate, the water piled up to a height of, I think, close to 500 feet. Then the water literally exploded through that, and the effect continued, further downstream."

"So how does that affect what will happen at the Hoover Dam?" asked George.

"Just look at it. It is a discontinuous process. Those bolts of water shooting through the canyon right now could be 400 or even 500 feet high. There is nothing to compare this to."

"What happens, Turbee, when those waves hit Lake Mead?" interrupted Rhodes.

"Just imagine it," Turbee replied. "A 400-foot wall of water and sand and rocks and whatever hits Lake Mead at a good 25 miles an hour, judging from the progress that it's making through the Grand Canyon. It's elementary Newtonian mechanics. That force doesn't just disappear. It has to go somewhere. It hits the lake and creates a tsunami. Then there's a period of lesser flow, and then another one of these huge waves, which creates another tsunami, and so on."

"So? What does that have to do with the Hoover?" Dan interrupted.

"So that's the point, sir. It won't be just one wave. It will repeat, over and over again, until the flow of water from Lake Powell is finished. The erosion of the Grand Canyon will continue, so long as that flow is maintained. That could be years, but that's not important. What is important is that the waves will start to interfere with each other. They'll create super waves of unimaginable height, especially in the relatively enclosed spaces of the Boulder and Black Canyons, immediately adjacent to the Hoover. What those guys in the Situation Room are missing is that it's not going to be a smooth flow. It is not like turning on a tap. It's going to be very violent, sir. Very, very violent. George, can you put the Black and Boulder Canyons on the Atlas Screen?"

"Glad to oblige, little buddy," George said.

"I think the Hoover will come apart at the seams, and I think that will be very soon after the first wave hits," continued Turbee. "You'll see that the Hoover Dam channel commences here, at an angle from the direction of the lake, and veers toward the south. Initially, it will only catch the edges of the waves that are going to be generated. These waves may only be 50 to 100 feet high."

"Only. Only 100 feet high. Like only as high as a ten-story building," interrupted Rahlson. "Only my ass."

Turbee carried on. "The dam structure is probably sufficient to withstanding that. Now here's where we get into a problem. The Hoover Dam is, more or less, a planar surface on its upstream facade. The waves will rebound from it nicely, and head back toward the main lake area. It took a good 17 years to fill Lake Powell, and it will take a while to empty it. You can expect the wave crests to be coming for a long, long time. That's what makes this different from the Boxing Day Quake."

Turbee paused for a second to take a sip of cold coffee. His thoughts were moving so quickly that he was having trouble getting the words out fast enough, and his voice was quitting on him. "The Indonesia quake produced only one series of tsunami, broken up into a set of 11 or 12 separate waves. With the configuration that we have here, these waves will come, for all intents and purposes, forever. Throughout the lake, but especially in the Hoover Dam channel, which is long and narrow, with high side walls. There is going to be a lot of destructive and constructive interference. Where a crest from one wave hits a trough from another, they cancel each other out," he continued, "and in theory we have no wave. But where a crest of one wave meets the crest of another, we get a doubly high wave. A super wave. It's called constructive interference. Theoretically, there is a very real possibility that a super wave crest will hit another super wave crest, and I don't have a clue what will happen after that."

59

IT TOOK LESS THAN AN HOUR for the four Tiani/Melvin focused charges to be transported from the Livermore Laboratories to the downstream entrances of the four diversion tunnels. Four Raptors landed at an airfield less than a mile from the many buildings that constituted the Labs. The shaped charge devices had already been taken out of storage, and were immediately hauled to the runway. The Raptors had been chosen because they had internal bomb bays and, in this situation, bomb bays just large enough to contain the Tiani/Melvin devices; one in each. It took 20 minutes for the exotic planes to traverse the 400-mile distance between the Livermore Labs runway and Nellis Air Force Base in Nevada, just north of Las Vegas. By the time the bombs reached Nellis, the raging waters released from what had once been the Glen Canyon Dam had passed the midpoint of the Grand Canyon.

It took a few minutes to transfer the four bombs to two HH-60J Jayhawk helicopters, and another ten minutes, at 200 miles per hour, for the Jayhawks to land beside four M3 Bradley Fighting Vehicles, each weighing more than 30 tons. The weight of these vehicles would be used to wedge the Tiani/Melvins into the concrete plugs within the original bypass tunnels. The Bradleys for the east (Arizona) side of the Colorado would also require a military transport vehicle, to ferry them across the river along the top of the dam. Each Bradley had a crew of four. The four separate crews were quickly named Team Arizona One and Two, and Team Nevada One and Two, for clarity during any radio communication.

The concrete plugs were located just north of the dam itself, and the trip down each tunnel was nearly three miles. Following the Bradleys were four Jeeps, each carrying another two men. When the four parties entered their respective tunnels, intent on their mission, the first blast of water was still an hour from the east end of Lake Mead.

The wall of mud and water was more than 300 feet in height, and would be traveling at an astonishing rate of speed when it reached South Cove, Lake Mead. According to the workup Turbee was doing in the TTIC control room, that wave would create an enormous impact when it hit the lake's calm waters. It would be carrying with it millions of tons of silt and debris. The flow of water would not be even but would mimic the ebb and flow of the ocean tide. The size of the waves created by this action would be dictated by simple geometry. As the lake widened, the energy created in the waves would be dispersed over an ever greater area. At the widest part of the lake, the waves might be only 40 or 50 feet in height, with no crest. They would simply be large swells, moving at a high speed toward the southwestern end of the lake. But as the lake narrowed again, and became shallower, the power of the waves would, according to Turbee, be reconstituted. A portion of the waves would enter the narrow channel containing the marinas and homes that formed Lake Mead's western shore. Another portion would enter Boulder Canyon and, from there, Black Canyon, which was blocked at its distal end by the Hoover Dam. According to Turbee's calculations, the entire lake would become a chaotic environment of super wave after super wave. Also according to Turbee's calculations, the marinas and homes that formed Lake Mead's western shore would disappear. And that was only a start to the destruction. Once the waves from the flood entered Boulder Canyon and Black Canyon, they would reach the Hoover Dam. According to Turbee, the dam would not withstand the impact.

It was a possibility that left Turbee and those around him breathless with horror.

According to the calculations of the mathematicians, engineers, and technicians at the Hoover Dam, however, if the plan to open the diversionary tunnels worked, and the next hour was spent in draining Lake Mead, any waves that formed would be minimal. The volume of water in Lake Mead would be significantly reduced, and the possibility of super waves would be infinitely smaller. The Hoover would be able to weather the test of the water coming toward it. If the diversionary tunnels could be opened quickly enough. If the water was drained from Lake Mead at the rate they calculated. It was what the men in, around, and on the dam were hoping for.

THE TTIC CONTROL ROOM was quiet. One of the helicopters had a video camera focused on the Hoover Dam. At Turbee's request, the helicopter increased altitude, so that the entire channel leading to the Hoover Dam was shown. The signal was delivered over one of the Milsat satellite's many channels. Other cameras were trained on the flood waters, from various elevations and angles. As they watched, wave after wave formed in the narrow chute that was the Grand Canyon. Behind each wave there were still more, lining up for miles, as the uncaged Colorado River smashed its way through cave-in after cave-in along the canyon, rushing toward Lake Mead.

THE TWO DIVERSIONARY TUNNELS within the dam itself were already fully opened, and a massive volume of water was roaring through them. The four teams had traveled from the south ends of the outer diversionary tunnels to the concrete plugs that had been placed there more than 70 years earlier.

Each team proceeded to jackhammer notches into their respective concrete plug, so that the Tiani/Melvin devices could be neatly inserted. When the holes were large enough, the T/M devices were wedged in place by the 30-ton Bradleys. No one had time to worry about whether the devices would be damaged by such action, or whether they would even work in such tight quarters. Once the placement was accomplished, timers were set, and the crews raced out of the tunnels to the relative safety of the tunnel outlets, where hovering helicopters were waiting to pick them up.

Seconds later, a booming sound was heard, deep within the tunnels. An explosion of water and stone burst out of the downstream outlets of all four outer tunnels. As with the initial, but much larger, T/M charge that had cut the Glen Canyon Dam in two, each device had sent a super-heated blast of plasma directly into the concrete plugs, vaporizing them. With the plugs out of the way, the water had quickly found and entered the tunnels, pushing the debris out of its path in a quick and powerful surge.

From above, it was a spectacular sight, with all four diversionary tunnels now open, along with the penstocks and tunnels of the dam itself. All told, a volume three times greater than the original volume of the Colorado was now flowing through, under, and around the Hoover Dam. Massive plumes of water were being ejected hundreds of feet into the air. Rainbows could be seen playing in the mist that now partially hid the great structure. The engineers calculated that at this rate, Lake Mead would be dropping close to a foot an hour. They thought that it just might be enough.

"You see, Mr. President," Jordan McKay was saying over the phone. "It is not as bad as it could have been. The Glen Canyon Dam failed catastrophically, but the Hoover is strong enough to withstand the extra volume. With all the diversionary tunnels now open, the level of Lake Mead will not rise nearly as quickly. Our engineers are calculating the net rate of increase of water volume in Lake Mead. It is starting to appear that for a few weeks water will flow over the top of the Hoover, but the dam itself will not be compromised by this."

"What about downstream from the dam? Lake Mojave, Lake Havasu, and so on?" asked the President.

"Those lakes are large enough to hold the overflow volumes. Obviously there will need to be emergency dyking. The Army Corps of Engineers will be working overtime on it, along with many other companies, but it is a manageable problem. The Hoover will stand, sir," replied Jordan. "The Hoover will stand."

"A manageable problem…" These were the words that were being echoed up and down the chain in the Intelligence Community. This was the phrase picked up by the media. Yes, a major dam had been destroyed, but the question of controlling the huge flows was a manageable problem. All of the media corporations had helicopters above the Hoover Dam. The fantastic picture showing the enormous geysers of water ejected through the four diversionary tunnels and, in addition, the massive flow of water through the dam, via the penstocks, was comforting. The rainbows were beautiful. People began to breathe a little easier.

60

THEY'RE CRAZY about this diversionary tunnel stuff, George," said Turbee. "No way that's ever going to work. The extra drainage may even make the situation worse."

"How so, Turb?" George asked.

"That drainage of water is from the bottom of the reservoir. If one wave in a series suddenly disappears because it has been sucked into the diversion tunnels, the subsequent wave has a greater distance to fall, and the kinetic energy from that will be even greater. Maybe half the waves will disappear, but the remaining waves will skyrocket in energy. We're going to get constructive interference, on a truly massive scale. I don't think the Hoover is going to be flooded to death. I think it will be pounded into obliteration. Everyone should get off that dam."

"But what about the draining of Lake Mead?" asked Khasha. "Shouldn't less water mean less danger?"

"I don't know, but I doubt it," replied Turbee. "I think the dam is toast."

"How long, Turbee?" asked Rhodes. "Best guess."

"It's not going to hold. The velocity of those giant waves will become over 50 miles an hour. Some of those waves will be more than 300 feet high. Once they get to that point, it won't take long at all," Turbee replied.

"How long?" repeated Rhodes.

"Four or five of those suckers a minute," said Turbee. "I have no idea. Pounding and running water are going to take it down, no question. It won't go in the same way that Glen Canyon did, but then again, we now have Lake Powell and Lake Mead both knocking on the Hoover's door. From there on, it will blow over everything else until it gets to the Sea of Cortez. And no one seems to have a clue."

They continued to watch the footage of the rampaging water. Dan was once again nowhere to be seen.

CATHERINE had been watching the pandemonium on TV. "I could have stopped it," she moaned. "I had a chance. But I didn't. I did nothing. Nothing."

"Now stop this, girl. I doubt that you could have," replied Sandra Becker.

"If you are going to hold yourself personally responsible for all of this, you will never be able to think straight again."

They had been going back and forth on this theme for ten minutes when the telephone rang. Sandra picked up the phone and answered immediately. It was Big Jack.

"This is Admiral Leonard Jackson. Is Corporal Catherine Gray of the RCMP there with you?" he asked.

"Why yes, she is. Hold on one second." She handed Catherine the phone and whispered, "Sounds like someone important."

"Corporal Gray here," Catherine answered.

"Very good, Admiral Jackson on this end. I will be sending a helicopter to pick you up in a few moments. We will land in the RV parking lot."

For a moment Catherine couldn't speak. When she finally found her voice, she asked, "Where are we headed?"

"Washington, DC," came the reply.

"That's lovely, Admiral, but I have my job to attend to back in the Kootenays. I need to get back to work."

"I have spoken to your superiors about this, and specifically with your friend Indy. They all think it's a fine idea for you to come to DC, young lady," Big Jack boomed.

"But I need stuff," Catherine stuttered. "I stink. I need a shower and a change of clothes."

"Don't worry, miss," the Admiral replied. "All these things will be provided for you. This has been fully approved by the RCMP in Vancouver. We need both you and Indy at TTIC. Drug traffickers are involved in this plot. You two have already been tracking them, so you know more than anyone about it. Both of you can help us a lot. Technically, you have been seconded to TTIC for a few months. It's all to the good, Corporal. The whirly is two minutes away. I suggest you say your goodbyes."

Catherine hung up the phone slowly, shocked at the turn of events. "I guess that this is goodbye, Duane, Sandra. You have been truly wonderful, and I will never forget you."

"Come and visit us sometime, missy," said Sandra. "There's always coffee here for the likes of you. You are a courageous young woman, and you've done amazing things today. You'll be in our prayers, dear." The older woman reached out to wrap Catherine in a maternal hug, worrying for a young person who'd gone through so much and was about to go through much more.

Duane, not prone to such emotional displays, contented himself with patting Catherine roughly on the shoulder. She looked up at him, her eyes brimming with tears.

At that moment the distinct sound of a slowing army helicopter was heard from outside, and Catherine left the couple to jog lightly out to the central parking facility. The chopper came down in one corner of the lot, and Catherine ran, head down, toward the rear doors and climbed in. She was immediately given a set of headphones.

"Next stop, Washington, lady," said the pilot. "Specifically TTIC. They apparently require your services over there." He studied her for a moment. As a pilot at Nellis AFB, he had seen many strange sights, but this was a bit over the top. "You can clean yourself up a bit in the washroom when you get there," he said dryly.

Catherine watched the mountains recede below her. Soon they were flying over the great flat lands that made up eastern Colorado. She'd never seen it from the sky, and thought that it was really too bad that she was too tired to appreciate the rugged beauty before her. She lay back, thinking that she should go over what had happened, to have her story clear and ready for the agents at TTIC. Within an instant, she was fast asleep.

RICHARD was in the air as well, stretched out on a medical pallet, and hooked up to an IV. He was being transported, via a military 747, to a military hospital in Kansas. He'd been taken to Ramstein Air Force base in Germany first, by a Gulfstream flight out of Islamabad. The pilot and crew of the Gulfstream had kept their radio on, listening avidly to the play-by-play report of the happenings in the Grand Canyon. Even in his seriously depleted state, Richard had been shocked and upset by the reports. He and Jennifer should have been able to stop it. True, they hadn't known the way it was going to happen, but they'd known the general area of the attack. If they'd tried harder, gone faster, maybe they'd have been in time…

His train of thought had changed quickly from what might have happened to what had actually happened. The moment they'd arrived back at the Islamabad Embassy, Jennifer had kept her word and gone straight to Buckingham with a full report on Richard's condition. He'd been undeniably heroic throughout their mission, she said, and she thought that he should receive commendation for his actions. It was, after all, his plan that had saved them. More importantly, she'd seen, first-hand, the addiction, stress, and depression with which he was living. Things that he had to wake up and deal with, alone, every day of his life. They'd formed a strong bond during their captivity and ensuing escape, and she'd come to care for the old Navy fighter. She wanted to see him taken care of. Buckingham had agreed wholeheartedly, and made a call directly to Big Jack to see it done.

After his arrival in Ramstein, and an hour on the ground, Richard had been loaded into the 747, to be taken to a top-notch government facility that looked after those who had walked the path that he'd found himself walking. The men transporting Richard had seen the mess he was and had their doubts, but these orders came directly from Admiral Leonard Jackson, the DDCI. Orders such as these were to be complied with promptly, and with alacrity. What they saw before them was a washed-up, bruised, broken mess of a human being. The guy didn't look like he was worth saving. But if the Admiral saw some smidgen of hope in him, if he wanted to save this man, then they were not about to interfere. They had all been briefed on what Richard Lawrence had been through in the last 24 hours and had to admit, grudgingly, that it had been one hell of a situation. He and Jennifer Coe had been lucky to get out alive, and it sounded like a lot of the credit for their escape should go to Richard. So in Ramstein the crew watching after him had attended to their duties, placed Richard carefully on an Army 737, and sent him on his way to some destination in central Kansas, where the doctors would do whatever they could to fix him.

Before they allowed the plane to take off, they had recommended heavy tranquilizers for the man. During the hour he'd been on their base, he had been, like Catherine Gray in far off Arizona, rambling on about how the disaster was his fault, and how he should have been able to stop it. The medics at Ramstein agreed that it was unfair for someone in Richard's condition to be awake and blaming himself for that sort of catastrophe. Richard began his journey to recovery, and what the men around him hoped would be a promising future, once again heavily medicated, in a deep sleep brought on by the military's best tranquilizers.

ADMIRAL LEONARD JACKSON strode purposefully into the TTIC control room, four hours after the destruction of the Glen Canyon Dam. He walked to the elevated desk that stood front and center of the Atlas Screen. Dan Alexander sat at that desk, watching with glazed eyes the footage of the Glen Canyon Dam falling apart. The Admiral was 67 years of age, but still stood straight and tall; he was in his military uniform and reached at least 6′. He came to an abrupt stop right in front of the TTIC director.

"Stand up, Danno," commanded Jackson. "Now."

"What are you doing?" growled Dan. "I'm trying to manage a crisis, in case you haven't noticed."

"Yeah, sure. We'll give you the gold star," muttered Big Jack. "Now get up and listen good."

The Admiral looked at Liam Rhodes, who had just entered the control room. "Liam, for the moment, I'm promoting you to acting director of TTIC. Dan Alexander's presence here is under review due to his lack of experience and inability to deal with pressing situations. As demonstrated in the last two weeks."

Dan still hadn't stood up. At Big Jack's words, he looked up at the looming figure in amazement. "You can't do that, Jackson. I was appointed by the Senate subcommittee. Only they can fire me. Same thing as with Turbee. I fired him, the subcommittee made me take him back."

Jackson almost laughed. "The review is on my recommendation, numbskull, and it is my recommendation that you be removed from command. There will be an official meeting on this sometime within the next week. For now, just pack your shit and screw off. This little agency could have stopped this attack." He pointed to the 101's behind the desk, raising his eyebrows and daring Dan to say anything else. "You should have listened to Turbee and his crew, instead of following your own dumbass instincts. Now are you going to go on your own, or do I have call some MP's to ball-hoof you out the door?"

Dan said nothing, but grabbed a few pens, his laptop, and some knickknacks he had, and slunk out the door. Rhodes was wearing a lopsided grin as he watched the scene unfold. He turned to watch the former commander of TTIC exit the room, reveling in every moment. When the door finally closed behind Dan, he turned back to the room.

Seeing that he had Rhodes' attention back, Jackson began listing names. "Turbee, Khasha, George, Rahlson, and Lance. Conference room A, please. Now. You too, Rhodes."

Even Turbee could sense the urgency in the Admiral's voice. He could hardly comprehend that everything was happening so quickly. Dan had been placed on suspension, and Rhodes was now the acting director. They were receiving orders directly from the DDCI. And they were receiving them by name. He took a deep breath and rose from his desk. When he and the others reached the conference room, they found Big Jack already seated, waiting to proceed.

"Here's the situation, people," he began. "We are uncovering, with record speed, traces of the evil bastards who have executed this terrible crime."

"Well, that's good, I guess," said George.

"I'm not so sure," said Big Jack. "A vehicle that carried the Semtex has been found, pushed over a cliff into Lake Powell, just north of the Glen Canyon Dam. In the glove compartment, the GLOVE compartment, we found a passport and a copy of the Koran. Through the passport, we were able to get the LA address of a man. We sent agents to go through his computer. Everything was encrypted at 24 bits."

"No way," said Rhodes. "That's like saying it was coded with a Captain Crunch Decoder Ring. Nobody encrypts at 24 bits. With today's computers, you could crack the code in 14 or 15 minutes. Anyone sophisticated enough to pull off this kind of an operation is going to be encoding at least at 96. And nobody leaves a fucking Koran and passport in a glove compartment."

"I absolutely agree," said Big Jack. "It's all very simplified. Overly so, if you ask me. This trail also led us to some of the other people supposedly involved in this plot, and we were able to retrieve their hard drives as well. They were sent immediately to the NSA. So far we've only conducted a quick search, but what we've found is interesting," he continued. "There are emails that lead to a number of individuals in the Karachi anti-drug police, and from there, to a number of drug lords in Afghanistan."

"The whole thing sounds pretty fishy, if you ask me," said Rhodes. "Way too easy. Way too neat."

"Oh, it gets even better," continued Jackson. "According to the emails, the whole operation was masterminded by a retired billionaire from Karachi. Some guy by the name of Nooshkatoor."

"I remember him," piped up Turbee. "He was the President of Karachi Shipbuilding and Engineering Works. A rival of Karachi Drydock and Engineering. KDEC was definitely involved in this attack. And they're definitely owned and operated by some powerful people. Maybe Nooshkatoor made enemies in the wrong places, with people who were more dangerous than he realized. If it's a fishy trail, and it leads too easily back to Nooshkatoor, maybe it's because someone's trying to frame him."

Rhodes nodded. "That's a good point, Turb. You're getting better with this conspiracy theory stuff. Either way, we should be able to figure out how and why this trail was constructed, and maybe find the real perpetrators from there."

"Get to work on that," said Jackson. "I'm having the hard drives we found brought here. George, Turbee, Rahlson, I want you guys working on them. Dig up everything you can find, and track it. Find out where it leads. The President is going public with the passport in the glove box idea. He is going to say that all the conspirators have been found, and are either dead or incarcerated. It's the easiest way to clean this up for the public. And there are some higher-ups who would rather let it end there. But I think we all know that it's just bullshit. The people who are involved in this are brilliant. They've pulled this off, but they've made a mistake. They got sloppy when they framed someone else. I'm willing to bet that they've been sloppy in other places, and that they might have left a trail somewhere. From what I've seen, you six are the smartest people in this community. You are going to find whatever trail they left. No one is to know what you're doing. Liam, you're in charge. You will report directly to me."

"That's our job, at this point?" asked Lance.

"Yes, that is your assignment. Your mission. And a lady from Canada will be joining you — Corporal Catherine Gray, and also a cop by the name of Indy Singh. They tracked the drug runners in Canada, who own the mine that the Semtex came through. I'm also bringing Richard Lawrence in. After his detox. He's been in the field. He knows the people. I think they will all be invaluable to this little group. You have to work together to find the men responsible for this."

The Admiral paused to look around, meeting the eyes of each member of the team. His voice became even more serious. "We've been put in a very critical position here, people. Someone out there had the nerve to attack the USA. We need to find out who it was. And then we need to design our counterplay."

SITTING IN HIS JET, Yousseff watched the TV coverage of the Glen Canyon Dam and smiled. It was going exactly as he had hoped it would. One dam was down, and the other, he hoped, was on the verge of failing. He had succeeded. Around him, his friends and accomplices turned away, their faces set in a wide range of disgust, disappointment, and horror.

AS SOON as the meeting was over, Turbee slipped by Admiral Jackson and darted back to his workstation. He already knew where to start. Rahlson followed him, curious.

"What're you up to, Turb?" he asked, watching as the young man fell into his chair and began feverishly typing on his computer.

"This man the Admiral thinks is out there. I think I might already know who he is, Rahlson." He grabbed his mouse and started scrolling through a screen full of data. "And I think I know how to find him." Then he looked up at the older man standing over him. "We're going to need a man or two in Afghanistan."

FAR ABOVE the dark stone fortress of Inzar Ghar, on a dangerous, ancient smuggler's trail, two dark blue eyes looked back on the fortress one last time. From his vantage point, Zak had witnessed the commotion of several motor vehicles roaring down the mountain road toward Peshawar, carrying dogs and men. Undoubtedly reinforcements, going after Richard and his partner. But he knew that, at this point, his own absence had also been discovered, and that a massive manhunt would soon be underway to find him. He did not fully understand why the men, vehicles, and dogs had all been directed toward the valley floor, downhill from the fortress. Although it didn't really matter, as long as it left his way open.

He shivered again, and pulled the ragged blanket he'd brought closer around his shoulders. It was bitterly cold, and wisps of snow drifted lazily down around him. The stumps of his missing toes, and his raw wrist joint, were screaming in pain, but Zak persevered, and continued to crawl toward the summit of the Path of Allah. Now that he was under the open sky again, all he could think of was getting to his people, and telling them what he knew.

IN NEVADA, the water continued to rush through and around the Hoover Dam. News and military helicopters still numbered in the dozens in the area, and the Marines and Army were both heavily represented. Because of the waves now hitting the dam, and because the President had officially proclaimed the structure safe, all personnel had been pulled out of the structure. No boats or subs patrolled the raging waters on the south side. No cameras were trained on the base, which was invisible in any case, lost in the haze of mist and rainbows.

For this reason, no one saw the cracks that began to form, small at first, but snaking rapidly up and out, as the dam fought to stand against the increasing rush of water.

ACKNOWLEDGEMENTS

Many thanks to my editor, Carrie White, for the magnificent job she did in helping me take a dung heap of dangling prepositions, non sequiturs, and grammatical hell and make it a publishable work. I also want to thank the people at Glass House Press for their faith, their insights, and even their critiques. I am eternally indebted to Lauralee for her flawless copyediting, and her many constructive suggestions. The three of us made an incredible team, and I look forward to working on many projects together!

I have to thank my publicist, Antoinette Kuritz, and Shel Horowitz, the marketing maniac, for guiding my book on its path. Jacqueline C. Simonds acted as consultant and sometime therapist, and I couldn't have done it without her. A big thank you to Eric Kampmann for having faith in both Carrie's judgment and my writing ability. To my faithful readers, Chuck and Cathie, who supported the book when no one else could see the "diamond in the rough." Without your help and input, Zak would have met a different fate. Thanks to Brie for the spectacular new title. Thanks to Mike Lee and Chris Decatur, the geniuses behind the design of the book — you two gave *Gauntlet* an identity I would never have imagined on my own. I want to thank the authors who helped me along the way: Jim Rollins, Chris Reich, David Morrell, David Hagberg, John Foxjohn, and Dale Brown. Thanks to Trey and Quay Terry, two brothers of the military persuasion, who were kind enough to offer feedback, criticism, and eventually endorsements.

Finally, I want to thank my wife, Foxy Lady, my four children, and the two dogs and two cats that complete my household, all of whom formed the opinion, many months ago, that the lord of the manor has completely lost it. Without your faith, support, and love, *Gauntlet* would have remained nothing more than an idea.

ABOUT THE AUTHOR

RICHARD AARON lives in a cold, northwestern city with his wife, four children, and various dogs and cats. He has a university degree in mathematics and a masters in law. Neither has anything to do with his burgeoning career as a writer. He worked in the real world for two decades before realizing that he was actually meant to be a writer. *Gauntlet* was produced soon thereafter.

If You Enjoyed

GAUNTLET

Don't Miss Richard Aaron's New Novel

COUNTERPLAY

TTIC and the US government are forced once again into a race against time and a faceless enemy. The threat: nuclear arms programs in unfriendly territory, with unknown players. At stake: control of the Middle East, and the safety of the entire world. Will TTIC find a way to stop these untraceable enemies and the danger they bring before it's too late? Or will they find themselves one step behind, at the moment when it matters most?